Acclaim for Ama

'Brilliant new novel ... F_____
writing today explore the m_____
ships with quite such warm_____
Henry Sutton, *Mirror* on *Sist___*

'I savoured every second of this deeply satisfying book. Amanda
Brookfield goes from strength to strength. Her best yet. Treat
yourself'   Patricia Scanlan on *Sisters and Husbands*

'The novel walks a fine line between comedy and wrenching
sadness. It is fluently written and its depiction of domestic chaos
and a man's bewilderment when unexpectedly faced with a
young son's needs is all too recognisable'
Elizabeth Buchan, *The Sunday Times* on *A Family Man*

'Perceptive and very readable'   *The Times* on *Walls of Glass*

'Superb in its minute observation' *Northern Echo* on *The Lover*

'Amanda Brookfield's assurance and intelligence make *Alice
Alone* stand out ... A strong sense of humour, a natural narrative
gift and controlled, understated characterisation signify a promising debut'   *Evening Standard* on *Alice Alone*

Also by Amanda Brookfield

Alice Alone
A Cast of Smiles
Walls of Glass
A Summer Affair
The Godmother
Marriage Games
Single Lives
The Lover
A Family Man
Sisters and Husbands

About the author

Amanda Brookfield gained a First Class Honours Degree from Oxford before working at an advertising agency for several years. She wrote her first novel while living in Buenos Aires with her diplomat husband, and her second while in Washington, D.C. She has two young sons and now lives in London and divides her time between writing fiction and looking after her family.

RELATIVE LOVE

Amanda Brookfield

FLAME
Hodder & Stoughton

First published in Great Britain in 2004 by Hodder and Stoughton
A division of Hodder Headline

1 3 5 7 9 10 8 6 4 2

A CIP catalogue record for this title
is available from the British Library

ISBN 0 340 82620 7

Typeset in Monotype Plantin Light by
Hewer Text Limited, Edinburgh
Printed and bound by
Mackays of Chatham Ltd, Chatham, Kent

Hodder Headline's policy is to use papers that are natural,
renewable and recyclable products and made from wood
grown in sustainable forests. The logging and manufacturing
processes are expected to conform to the environmental
regulations of the country of origin.

Hodder and Stoughton
A division of Hodder Headline
338 Euston Road
London NW1 3BH

'Things fall apart; the centre cannot hold'

W. B. Yeats, *The Second Coming*

For the Hesworth Cousins:
Ceel, Jonny, Kiki, Emma, Kate, Josh, Izzi, Ben and Ali

Thanks for permission to quote from *The Great Gatsby*
by F. Scott Fitzgerald/06.11.03
Published by Penguin

Also, thanks for permission to quote from *The Second Coming*
by W. B. Yeats
kindly given by A. P. Watt on behalf of Michael B. Yeats

I would like to thank the following people for their help in a variety of invaluable ways:

Angela Brookfield, Andrew Charles, Liz Clifford, Sara Menguc, Hazel Orme, Nick Sellick, Sara Westcott

DECEMBER

John Harrison, returning from the lower field with a barrowful of holly, the leaves a polished leathery green, the berries blood-red baubles in the dusky light, paused at the familiar sight of his home. A sudden drop in temperature, coming after the freakish un-seasonal warmth of the day, had created a thin band of waist-high mist, as thick as wool from a distance but dissolving to invisibility as he waded through it. The slate tiles and grey stone chimney-stacks of Ashley House rose out of this trick of nature like some magical and majestic ship on a ghostly sea, its numerous lead-latticed windows – extravagantly illuminated, thanks to the arrival that afternoon of four children, several spouses and seven grand-children – shining like portholes against the darkening sky. John, inclined normally to keep a beady eye on thermostat dials and light switches when Pamela and he were alone, felt a glow of pride at so much evidence of occupation.

Apart from the absence of horses and hay in the outhouses and barns, and the thick twists of ivy and wisteria trunks across the walls, there had been few physical changes to the property since a windfall on the corn-market had allowed John's Victorian grand-father, Edmund Harrison, to commission the building of the family home. It had been called Ashley House after his wife, Violet Ashley, who had died in childbirth. The only significant architectural addition since that time had been undertaken by their son Albert, John's father, who had installed a long, arched porch, running the full length of the back of the house, connected to each of the affected rooms by a series of french windows. Known in family parlance as 'the cloisters', and built in the same soft grey brick as the walls to which it was attached, it was a construction that stole a lot of natural light from the interior, but which was generally forgiven this defect for looking so fine, particularly from the outside, and for providing excellent sitting-out space in the summer. John's own architectural dabblings had been restricted to a conversion of the largest barn into what was, somewhat disparagingly, referred to as the 'granny flat', but which was in fact a spacious two-bedroomed little house, complete with its own kitchen and bathroom and front door, ideal for overflow at busy times of year. On this occasion, Alicia, his widowed and increasingly irascible sister, was housed there; so she could be completely comfortable, Pam had soothed, easing over the crinkle of suspicion in her sister-in-law's eyes that her company was not as eagerly sought after as she would have liked.

John released his grip on the barrow handles and flexed his fingers, which were stiff with cold (and sore, too, from foolishly tackling the holly without the protection of gloves), and continued to stare at the house, squinting as, from time to time, figures moved across the windows, busy in various, easily imagined ways, unpacking suitcases, wrapping gifts, preparing infants for bed or food for the evening meal. There would be salmon, as usual on Christmas Eve, steamed with Pamela's customary light touch to a succulent white-pink so that the flesh fell off the bones and melted on the tongue; and a generous selection of vegetables that always included beetroot – a particular favourite of John's – freshly pulled from Ashley House's own well-stocked vegetable garden. The sprouts served at lunch the following day would also be home-grown, their leaves pale green and tasting faintly of earth and mint. For the younger members of the clan, with palates not yet sufficiently discerning to enjoy such flavours, there would be simpler alternatives: toad-in-the-hole instead of fish, peas instead of beetroot. The sprouts, however, were unavoidable. At least one on each plate at Christmas lunch was one of those small traditions that had somehow become unquestionable over the years, as such things did in established families, where the minutest ways of speaking and doing took on the comforting resonance of ritual.

'Here we are again, old fella,' John murmured, prodding the

mud-clogged tip of one wellington boot against the grizzled belly of the black labrador slumped on the ground next to him. 'Christmas at Ashley House. Won't be too many more of those for you, eh?' The dog, who was twelve years old and painfully arthritic unless in pursuit of rabbits, half raised its head, offered a desultory wag of acknowledgement, then dropped its jaw with an audible thwack back on to its outstretched paws.

John bent to pick up the barrow handles and began to weave a somewhat unsteady route up towards the garden, aware of the heaviness of his boots and the mounting knot of stiffness in his lower back. He chose the nearest of the various gates posted round the garden, and paused to check on a lopsided hinge, making a mental note to return that way soon with a hammer and nails. Boots lumbered after him, ignoring the open gate and burrowing under a loose section in the mesh wiring which John had painstakingly rigged round the garden's substantial boundaries in a bid to deter the rabbit population from socialising on the lawn. A few seconds later the dog trotted back to his side, looking at once triumphant and sheepish, his nose smeared with fresh mud, and an assortment of dead leaves and twigs scattered across his back.

'Daft beast,' growled John fondly, adding the loose meshing to his list of things to see to, a list that never seemed to shorten or end and which, while he liked to groan about it, was, he knew, connected to some vital sense of purpose and well-being. The tending of the garden itself never touched his conscience. He had learnt over the years to leave all such nurturing and forethought to his wife, Pamela, who was as dextrous and skilled with seedlings as she was with the jars of ingredients ranged around the oak shelves in the kitchen. She had a library of books on English country gardens and a visionary talent for applying their lore to the fenced two acres surrounding the house. A local man called Sid helped her, emitting monosyllabic grunts of acquiescence to her every command, whether it involved weeding, mowing or lopping branches off trees. No physical challenge ever seemed too great for his wiry frame, although he puffed at pungent roll-ups all day and had the weathered face of a man well past his seventieth birthday.

Occasionally John teased Pamela about the physical prowess of their employee, professing jealousy not because he felt any (after fifty years together sex and all its exhausting complications – lust, envy, frustration, longing – had slid so far down the agenda they were practically out of sight) but because he liked to see how the echo of a reference to such fierce emotions made her smile. In truth, John was happy to be left to dabble in the fields and woods comprising the remaining twenty acres of the estate, attending to clogged ditches, sagging fences and rebellious outcrops of brambles and nettles. Armed often with just a walking stick (he had several to choose from lined up along the wall of the garden shed, their knobbled handles smooth from use), his beloved multi-purpose penknife and a few bits of wire and string, he would spend up to several hours at a time lost in the Ashley House grounds, humming contentedly at his small, invariably doomed, attempts to keep nature at bay. Sometimes, on chilly or particularly dank mornings, Pamela would slip into his anorak pocket a little Ther-mos of tea, which he would drink sitting on a tree stump, sucking on his pipe, marvelling at familiar things, like the cosy undulating beauty of the Sussex countryside, or that he had somehow arrived at the outrageously advanced age of seventy-nine without serious mishap to himself or any member of his family. All four of his children were in good health, as were their various offspring; his sister Alicia had lost her husband some years before, but was otherwise well, as was her son, Paul, who had married an Australian girl and settled in Sydney.

The only real shadow to fall across the picture had been cast by Eric, his elder brother, who, thanks to a severe stroke in his fifties, had for many years been resident in a nursing-home. But, then, as Pamela was so good at pointing out, Eric had had a marvellous innings, playing soldiers in foreign countries and pursuing all manner of hare-brained adventures before Fate had played its cruel hand. The home he was now in was just a few miles away, allowing them to make regular visits and keep an eye on the quality of nursing care, which had not always been top-notch. These days – since Eric's own savings had dried up – John paid the nursing-home fees, which were substantial. There was nothing more they *could* do, Pamela had assured him that morning, when the combination of a bill from the nursing-home and the prospect of yet another Christmas without the once-stimulating presence of his beloved big brother had made John sigh. They would visit him on Boxing Day as usual, with a string of grandchildren in tow, she said, offering instant and marvellous solace as she always did.

'If it wasn't for him . . .' John began, sliding a piece of toast into the right side of his mouth, because of some twanging among the roots of his teeth on the other side.

'We wouldn't be here,' Pam had finished for him, using the brisk tone she reserved for this inevitable next-step in any Eric conversation, which referred to her brother-in-law's decision five decades earlier to hand over the family home to John and take off round the world instead. Although Eric had never made any show of regretting his decision – on the contrary, he had seemed always to revel in his rootless, bachelor life – a residue of uneasiness about it had pursued John through the years. He had given Eric the lion's share of the money instead. But money wasn't the same as property. Eric's savings were exhausted, but Ashley House was now worth two million at least. More importantly, the house was like an integral part of the family, a character in its own right, whose mossy, weathered walls had protected three generations of Harrisons with the quiet defiance of what felt to John (particularly in a sentimental mood, as he was now, with the house bulging and the scent of Christmas in the air) like some kind of timeless, protective love. Over the years the house had not just contained the family, but grown round them all, as intertwined and insepar- able from their lives as the Victorian roses twisting through the old arched pergola skirting the lawns and the honeysuckle knotted along the stone wall of the kitchen garden.

John pushed the barrow slowly, trying not to hunch his shoulders in accordance with the Chichester chiropractor's advice and stamping his feet in the hope of shedding some of the mud from the soles of his boots. Inside the tunnel of the pergola, his favourite route back to the house, it was dark and silent, save for the gentle scrape of the dog's claws on the paving-stones and the occasional squeak of the barrow wheel. Around him a few brave rosebuds, pearly white bulbs, glimmered from among the tangle of leaves. Through the criss-crossed thicket overhead stars were twinkling between patches of dispersing cloud. John, a little chilled now, hurried on. There was still so much to do. For one thing he would need a bath, if there was any hot water left, which he doubted, with hordes of women washing their hair and the children having the mud scrubbed off their knees. Pam would require help putting up the holly, wine had to be cooled for dinner (Peter had kindly brought several bottles of Saint-Veran, which were still sitting on the sideboard), after which a contingent of the family would bundle into a couple of cars to attend midnight mass at St Margaret's, the little Norman church on the far side of Barham village. And he had still to wrap his gifts, a modest clutch as usual (Pam orchestrated all the serious present-giving within the family), but which would take some time since he was all fingers and thumbs when it came to Sellotape and folding paper corners. It seemed incredible that he had once fitted in so many duties with a full-time job. Not long ago Christmas Eve would have been spent in the office, before a scramble for last-minute shopping in Victoria Street and a sprint for the six-fifteen. The thirteen years since John's retirement had slipped through his fingers with terrifying speed; although, as a Lloyds Member, he continued to take a serious interest in the business, regularly meeting with ex-colleagues in London to discuss old times and the vagaries of the insurance market, still reeling from the Twin Towers atrocity two years before. Talking shop was always a joy, but afterwards John would slump gratefully into his train seat for the journey home, relishing without shame the simple prospect of a pot of tea and the steady hand of his wife to pour it for him.

John was a few yards from the house when the necklaces of lights – arranged by him with much cursing – among its tangle of rampaging ivy sprang to life, triggered by a timer switch, which, no matter how cunningly he tried to outwit it, continued each year to pursue a schedule of its own. Every year John treated Pamela's suggestion that a new device might be a worthy investment with a gruff dismissal. Like the single sprout on the plate of each protesting grandchild, grappling with wilful Christmas lights had somehow become integral to his view of the festive scenery: a challenge when they resisted, a cause for immense satisfaction when they didn't. Besides, he didn't like throwing things away. Even things that didn't work. It felt too much like giving up and he'd never been one for that.

Cassie, at thirty-seven the youngest of John and Pamela Harrison's children, pulled her bedroom curtains shut, kicked off her shoes, which looked fabulous but hurt like hell, and settled herself among the half-unpacked clutter on her bed. She would put them back on to go downstairs, slip them off under the table during dinner, then put them on again for church. A family Christmas had always demanded a certain sartorial elegance, which she enjoyed – being grand did make things feel special – and in a week or two the shoes would be fine. It was her feet that were the problem, small and wide, so that practically everything rubbed in the wrong places to start with even if they got to be as comfy as slippers later on. She had been staring out of the window for some time, thinking that the veil of rolling mist was just as atmospheric as snow and wondering whether to make her own small contribution to it by lighting a cigarette (she was supposed to be on five a day and had already had six) when she spotted her father wheeling his barrow of holly up from the copse at the bottom of the field, Boots waddling at his heels. She raised her knuckles to rap on the window, but stopped at the last minute, overwhelmed by troubled fondness at how decrepit he looked, as lumbering and stiff-limbed as his dear old hound. He wouldn't see her anyway, Cassie told herself, tugging the curtain shut, feeling suddenly that she was spying. These days, his eyesight was poor, a problem compounded by his reluctance to acknowledge it and the family's tacit willingness – led by Pamela – to collude in the process. The hair-raising experience of a car journey in his company was never due to his glasses' prescription being out of date but to the bloody-mindedness of other drivers. They were all protecting him, but from what? He would die anyway, whether he wrapped his car round a tree, lost his footing on the reedy edge of Ashley Lake or had a heart-attack.

Cassie sat down on her bed with a sigh, trying to picture a world without her parents, who annoyed her terribly at times, but to whom she was unequivocally devoted. It was impossible to imagine pain of any kind, she decided, impossible really to *feel* anything in advance of the feeling itself. Especially not on Christmas Eve when everything was poised and perfect, and when all she really wanted to think about was Daniel Lambert, a London GP for whom she felt an altogether different and entirely consuming love; whose very presence on the planet, even miles away in Derbyshire, surrounded by his wife, children and, by all accounts, quite hideous in-laws, made Cassie feel both immortal and blessed. Placing her mobile phone tenderly on the pillow next to her, even though Dan had warned that he probably wouldn't call, she folded her arms and looked round the familiar contours of the room, which had been hers ever since she could remember and which always made her feel a curious combination of comfort and frustration.

She was an established freelance interior designer, Cassie reminded herself, with a string of clients and her own website. Yet sitting now on the old threadbare beige counterpane, she felt as if she had never moved on from being a little girl and never would. Her surroundings were like a kaleidoscopic snapshot of the first two decades of her life: the pinboard of faded rosettes, the framed music and ballet certificates, the collection of soft toys propped against each other like a band of war-weary veterans on top of the bookcase, the beads she no longer wore draped round the mirror on the dressing-table, the trinket boxes containing obsolete coins and single earrings whose partners had gone missing, but which she still hoped, vaguely, to find one day. Peachy silk curtains had replaced the Barbie pink on which she had insisted as a schoolgirl and several layers of creamy paint had long since freshened the once fuchsia walls. The carpet was still the same, however, covered in rugs these days to conceal its age, but fraying visibly at the edges, especially where it met the little cast-iron fireplace set into the wall opposite the bed. Overhead, the heavy roof timbers, which ran the length of the top floor of the house, seemed to sag slightly, as did the stretches of ceiling between, as if the entire structure was preparing to cave inwards. As a child Cassie had devoted many dark hours to worrying about this, especially when she could hear the scrabble of rodent feet behind the plaster, which conjured terrifying images of debris and animals with sharp teeth tumbling out of the night on top of her. A series of Ashley House cats had eventually sorted out the problem, the latest of which, a ginger tom called Samson, was lying now in the furthest corner of the window-seat, curled up tight with his head half buried under his paws, stoutly ignoring both Cassie and the muffled thumps coming from downstairs.

Cassie's was the only bedroom in the house without a basin (a cause, at some hazy adolescent stage of her life, for serious complaint), but it had a wall of oak panelling, which none of the others did, and a dear little rolltop desk full of tiny drawers that had belonged to her grandmother and where she had once spent many hours pretending to be a serious student. Unlike her elder sister Elizabeth, who had been sent away to a fierce school run by nuns, Cassie had been allowed to remain a daygirl until at sixteen she had decided to board, opting for a small co-ed school where everyone had pets (by then she had been through her horsy phase and had taken with her a beautiful lop-eared rabbit called Horace) and where getting a part in the school play was given as much praise as doing well in exams. With a mind that retained interesting but not necessarily useful facts, Cassie had acquired respectable exam results without managing anything spectacular. Even now, as a fully fledged grown-up, she struggled to remember who was in charge of which government department and why joining the euro was probably a good idea, even if the thought of losing all those chubby pound coins made her irrationally sad. That her three elder siblings were all more obviously academic than her was something Cassie had always accommodated with ease, as much a fact of life as the tear-shaped birthmark next to her tummy-button and being the only one to have blonde curly hair. Bobbing along as the baby of the family in the less pressurised slipstream of family life, Cassie had watched the highs and lows of her brothers' and sister's faltering advance through adolescence to adulthood with a combination of compassion and curiosity. Particularly Elizabeth's, for there was no doubt that her sister had suffered most. Through a combination of being unhappy at school, arguing with Pamela (a maddening adversary because she never got cross), opting for disastrous hairstyles in the seventies (pudding-basin page-boys and frizzy unforgiving perms), misguided dalliances with fashion (hot-pants, miniskirts, thick multi-coloured knee-length socks) and even more misguided dalliances with men (Elizabeth's first marriage to an unemployed journalist, called Lucien, had lasted three years), her sister had had a very bumpy ride indeed. Cassie had quietly observed it all, finding her sibling, who was nine years older, easier to love for these struggles but inwardly determining that *she* would never endure such public and catastrophic failures herself.

Trying to behave as if she wasn't waiting for the phone to ring, Cassie began to fish all the presents out of the bottom of her suitcase and line them up across the bed: a blue cashmere scarf and a book on cooking curry for Elizabeth (she and Colin, her second husband of fourteen years, were mad about Indian food); a state-of-the-art chrome corkscrew for her eldest brother Peter; a bland but safe silky grey scarf for his wife, Helen, who made a habit of dressing severely even for country walks; a book of after-dinner speeches and a silly tie for Charlie, her other brother, who at forty-three was the closest in age to her and who, in spite of being a civil servant, was the joker of the family; an arty print of some flowers for his wife, Serena; a set of tapestry wool for her mother and a pair of leather gloves for her father. For Colin there was a bottle of wine, looking worryingly bubbly from its ride in the bottom of her bag, and for all her nephews and nieces there were cheques as usual, fifteen pounds each, apart from Roland, Elizabeth and Colin's nine-year-old, who was her godson and therefore got twenty. The only child for whom she had ventured to buy an actual gift was Tina, Serena and Charlie's sixteen-month-old, the fourth and youngest of their brood. After much agonising, Cassie had settled on a rag doll with yellow woollen hair and freckles stitched across her nose, which reminded her vaguely of a much-loved dolly she had once had. To give a baby money didn't feel right, she had explained to Serena that afternoon, worrying both about appearing fair to all the children and her choice of toy, which in retrospect seemed a bit unimaginative. Serena had laughed, then said it sounded lovely and that Tina would probably enjoy the wrapping-paper just as much as whatever was inside it. Cassie had laughed too, while hoping secretly that this would not prove the case, since the doll was hand-made and had cost rather a lot.

Cassie's phone rang when, absorbed in writing gift-tags, she had at last forgotten about it. 'My darling,' she whispered, her heart leaping as it always did at the sound of her lover's voice. 'My dearest darling, how are you?'

'Missing you.'

'Me too. Is it awful?'

'Fairly.'

'I can hardly hear you, it's a bad line.'

'I'm outside, pretending to put the rubbish out. I just had to call. I miss you so much.'

'And me. I'm in my room. Refuge from children and noise.'

'I wanted to thank you for my present. So sweet.'

'It's only a little thing.'

'A beautiful little thing. Like you. I shall treasure it. And you liked mine, didn't you?'

Cassie's fingers leapt to the gold necklace concealed under the collar of her shirt. 'I love it,' she whispered, 'and I love you.'

'I love you too, but I've got to go. I'll call when I can. Think of me tomorrow – our first Christmas.'

'Of course, my sweetheart, of course.'

Elizabeth tiptoed backwards out of the room, her eyes fixed upon Roland's sleeping figure – he had been suffering all week with a streaming cold. Holding her breath, she pulled the door shut behind her, frowning in the direction of the bathroom at the end of the corridor where the splashing and shrieks were reaching a new frenzy. 'Sorry to interrupt.' She opened the bathroom door just enough to put her head round it. Inside, Serena was kneeling on a sodden bathmat, her long chestnut hair streaming with customary artlessness out of a loose bun, her arms elbow-deep in one of the huge lion-footed, cast-iron baths, which resided in all four of the Ashley House bathrooms. The front of her blue jumper was dark with water and there were pink spots in her cheeks. In front of her, baby Tina, wispy hair plastered to her face, was batting at mountainous suds with both arms, squealing with delight as flecks of foam and water splattered over the sides of the bath and up the tiled walls. 'She likes soap, look,' announced Chloë, Peter and Helen's seven-year-old, who was perched, looking equally drenched and thrilled, on a stool next to the taps. 'Here, Tina, what's this? She even likes licking it, see? She doesn't mind the taste or anything.'

'Goodness, so she does,' murmured Elizabeth, too concerned at the possibility of the rising noise level waking her son to offer anything more enthusiastic, and marvelling as she so often did at her sister-in-law's ability not to fret about soap-eating or any of the other worrying things children got up to. Colin said it was because, after four, she had got used to anything. But Elizabeth, watching as Serena expertly slid the soap from view and began blowing raspberries on her daughter's pink barrel of a tummy, knew that it went rather deeper than that; that if she herself had ever been courageous or insane enough to produce three more offspring she would have collapsed under the strain, even if they weren't fragile and prone to allergies like Roland. 'You couldn't . . . I hate to ask . . . but you couldn't keep the noise down just a tiny bit, could you, Serena? Only Roland's full of cold and I've only just managed to get him to sleep and if he doesn't get a good night he'll be so crabby tomorrow and probably ruin everything for everybody.' She offered an apologetic smile. 'Sorry to be a bore.'

'It's okay. You should have said sooner. We're making a frightful din, aren't we, my dumpling?' Serena returned her attention to her daughter, widening her eyes and raising her index finger to her lips. 'Ssh, bunny, or we'll wake Roland, won't we?' The baby went very silent, transfixed by the suddenly solemn face of her mother.

'Well, Father Christmas might wake him anyway,' put in Chloë, in part wanting to test out a concept about which, thanks to various loose comments made by her big brother Theo and some of the elder cousins, she was having serious doubts, and in part wanting to get revenge on the least favourite of her aunts for ruining the fun. It was Christmas Eve, after all. And Roland was *always* ill. He couldn't even stroke Samson because he said it gave him itchy eyes, though he was always hugging Boots – usually just when Chloë wanted to – which was ridiculous. At least, Theo had said it was ridiculous and although her big brother could be mean he was also frightfully clever. 'When he comes down the chimney,' she continued, her voice reedy with uncertainty, 'Roland might wake then, mightn't he? I did last year – at least, I did just after he'd gone. The reindeer had eaten the carrots and I heard his sleigh bells and everything.' She paused, feeling important as she always did at this point in her story, fresh conviction at the existence of Father Christmas welling inside. 'The sleigh bells might wake Roland too, mightn't they?'

'Yes, they might,' conceded Elizabeth, her expression softening although inside she felt helpless. All of the things that were supposed to be fun, like Christmas and birthdays, were precisely the things her own beloved boy seemed to find so hard. Overexcitement of any kind invariably distressed Roland. When she had taken him as a toddler to visit Father Christmas's grotto in Guildford, he had howled in terror the moment they stepped inside; and when it dawned on him that the same bearded creature was due to tiptoe into his bedroom in the middle of the night he had been inconsolable. They had let him sleep with them that year, squashed hip to hip in the narrow spare bed at Colin's parents' place in Brentwood. After that the annual challenge of getting the stocking to the end of the bed became, not the jokey chore that her brothers' families seemed to find it, but an ordeal involving huge stress all round, with Roland terrified he would wake up, and she and Colin arguing into the small hours over whether it was safe to go in and whose turn it was to make the attempt. Against such a background it had been a positive relief the year before to admit that it was in fact the duty of parents, rather than a team of reindeer driven by a fat man with a bushy beard, to deposit gifts on children's beds. Yet this news – which Roland had seemed to want so badly – had only made him weep in complicated disappointment, triggering one of his headaches and two days off school.

'Don't worry.' Serena had recognised the anxiety in her sister-in-law's face, the jaw set firm and square like her father-in-law's when he was hunched over the business section of the paper, and wanted to be kind. She had learnt long ago that one woman couldn't tell another how to be a mother, especially not a woman like Elizabeth who, in spite of being intelligent, seemed to have an inbuilt mechanism for believing herself in the wrong. 'He'll be fine tomorrow, I'm sure. Ed was hacking like an old man last week and the twins both brought some dreadful bug home on the last day of term, but they all bounced back pretty quickly. They always do.'

'Yes.' Elizabeth wrung her hands, looking doubtful. She was fond of Serena and would have liked to talk to her some more. Like Charlie, to whom she was enviably well suited, her sister-in-law had a fabulous and refreshing ability to bat away life's problems. The pair of them just did not seem to mind things in the way other people did. They lived surrounded by the inevitable clutter and chaos generated by four children in an Edwardian terraced house in Wimbledon. Even with a loft conversion they were very squashed, cupboards visibly bulging and bits of furniture wedged up against each other, like ill-fitting pieces of some vast three-dimensional jigsaw. Maisie and Clem, their fourteen-year-old twins, had adjoining rooms on the top floor, their brother, Ed, who was twelve, had a box of a room on the landing, while Tina's cot was slotted into the spare bedroom, between piles of laundry and old art projects of Serena's, of which there were many. Visiting them, which didn't happen very often, these days, with her and Colin in Guildford, Elizabeth was always torn between admiration and incredulity at how they managed, not just to live happily but to find anything. Keeping track of her own modest family's bits and pieces was hard enough, and they lived in a spacious mock-Tudor semi, with two spare bedrooms, an attic and a garage. 'And he'd been so well, too, right up until this week. Typical.' She tried out a grin, feeling better.

She was on holiday, she reminded herself – no screechy violins to listen to for three whole weeks, no fidgeting choirs, no grubby grade-five theory papers with squashed, unreadable chords, their notes like misshapen beetles crawling up the stave.

In spite of the severe patches of misery she had experienced as a child, and the still somewhat problematic relationship she had with her mother, Elizabeth found herself drawn back to the family home more and more. The memories of her unsatisfactory youth were still vivid, but so now was the recognition of her sheer good fortune in having such easy access to somewhere as large and beautiful as Ashley House. From the start she had loved bringing Roland there, not just for the glory of giving him so much space to run around in but also because playing regularly with his cousins provided some relief from the burden of being an only child. They were an alarmingly robust bunch, her brothers' children – it tore at Elizabeth's heart sometimes to see Roland's efforts to keep up with them – but by and large they were kind.

'Poor Roland, it's too bad.' Serena had dried Tina and was deftly fitting her into a sleepsuit, bending and steering her chubby limbs into the arms and legs. 'Do you want to do the poppers?' she asked Chloë, who had moved off her stool and was standing very close to her lap, breathing hard, her big blue eyes shining with hope.

'Yes, please.' Chloë set about her task with both hands, biting her lips in concentration, wet strands of her thick black hair still glued across her face. 'And then can I carry her to bed?'

'Of course.' Serena, catching Elizabeth's look of concern, smiled. 'And then I think we've all earned a drink, don't you? The men are downstairs opening bottles. Maisie and Theo are laying the table and Pamela is doing a thousand things in the kitchen and refusing help from everybody, as usual. She's a miracle, isn't she, your mother? Charlie always says it's unnatural to like your mother-in-law so much but I can't help it. If I'm half as capable and beautiful at seventy-three I shall be completely thrilled. Fat chance, though,' she continued cheerfully, talking now over the top of Chloë's head, 'on the beauty side of things, anyway. Sixteen months on and I've still got this huge spare tyre. Look.' She let

Chloë take full charge of the baby, turned sideways and gripped what looked to Elizabeth, who'd had curves in all the wrong places long before she'd had Roland, like a modest roll of flesh. 'And with this last pregnancy some more veins exploded on my legs, only small ones but they're quite hideous. She seized the hem of her skirt and hoicked it up round her waist, revealing long socks and shapely white thighs. 'There, see?' She stabbed her index finger into her flesh. 'And there. And there.'

Elizabeth could see only a couple of tiny pink spidery veins. She herself had a fat blue river of a blood vessel on the inside of her own thigh that she wouldn't have pointed out to anyone. But Serena had a way of saying anything and making it sound okay. It was entirely her doing, for instance, that everybody knew Tina had been conceived at Ashley House after a particularly merry New Year's Eve family gathering when – as Serena had cheerfully put it – she and Charlie had been too pissed to bother with precautions. Instead of minding (Elizabeth always shuddered to think how Colin would have reacted to her disclosing anything so personal), Charlie had laughed gustily, saying, and thank God because Tina was a complete darling and they wouldn't be without her for the world. Tina herself was now dangling at a precarious angle in Chloë's arms. Elizabeth knew it wasn't her business to be worried, but it was hard nonetheless, like a reflex one couldn't control. 'She's all right like that, is she?' she blurted, clenching her hands in a bid to restrain herself from reaching for the baby.

'Oh, heavens, yes.' Serena dropped her skirt. 'She gets much more manhandling than that. Chloë's in complete control, aren't you, sweetheart?' Chloë nodded fiercely. 'You lead the way, then. Tina's cot is in the little room at the end next to the big green room where Uncle Charlie and I sleep. So we can hear her if she needs us in the night. I'll see you downstairs in a minute,' she added to Elizabeth, then trotted to catch up with her niece, who was staggering visibly under the weight of her load. 'I'll put her in, shall I?' she said gently, as they approached the cot, 'and you can wind up the musical box. It plays "Twinkle, Twinkle, Little Star" for hours. Tina loves it.'

'Does she?' Chloë sighed dreamily. 'I'm going to have *six* babies when I'm a mummy and not make any of them go to school.'

'Really? That will be hard work.'

'Theo *lives* at school now and it's horrid. And I've got to one day as well, when I'm eleven.'

'Eleven, but that's ages away. Not something to worry about now. Especially not on Christmas Eve.'

'Will Father Christmas come to Tina as well?'

'Of course.'

'Where's her stocking, then?' She eyed her aunt suspiciously.

'I'll put it out later, when Uncle Charlie and I go to bed. Now we must hurry away, before she notices we're gone, while the music is still playing. Look, she's put her thumb in her mouth – that's a good sign.' Serena ushered Chloë out of the room, turning the light off, but leaving the door ajar.

Downstairs the sweet smell of poaching salmon filled the kitchen. Pamela Harrison, her fine silvery tresses coiled into a neat French pleat, her apron fastened loosely round her slim waist, to protect her silk blouse and skirt from the splash of vegetable water and Hollandaise sauce, hummed to herself as she worked. She had listened to the King's College nine lessons and carols and the tunes were still with her, swelling like joy inside her chest. For 'Once in Royal David's City' she had settled herself in front of the telly, wanting to see the face behind the sound, pouring like an invisible thread of gold from the cherry mouth of the chorister. The boy's pale face and tar-brush hair – so adorable against the starched frill of his ruff and red gown – had reminded her of Theo. Although Theo was, in fact, the least musical of her grandchildren and currently afflicted with a speaking voice that squeaked between octaves like notes in search of a tune. Poor Theo. Thirteen was such a difficult age for a boy. Pamela had sipped her tea, remembering vividly Peter and Charlie going through exactly the same adolescent ordeal. She had closed her eyes and must have nodded off for a few minutes, although when the door opened and Theo himself had sidled in, his face flexing in disappointment at the realisation that both the room – and, more importantly, the television – were engaged, she did her best to conceal it, getting briskly to her feet and patting her hair. 'Do you want to watch something else?'

' 'Sokay, Gran,' he had muttered, shoving his hands into his pockets. 'I was just looking for the others.' He looked listless, she noticed, clearly searching for something, although Pamela doubted that it was really his cousins. Charlie's twin girls were already young women, wearing heels and bras and – in Maisie's case – quite a lot of makeup whenever a pretext presented itself. While their younger brother Ed, at twelve only a year behind Theo, was still very much a boy, full of enthusiasm for simpler pleasures like football and pizza. Theo, with his spotty chin, stringy limbs and screechy voice, was stranded somewhere between, a tadpole on the edge of a pond. It didn't help that he wasn't a handsome child, with the Harrison square jaw and one of those over-earnest faces that looked as if it might grow into itself somewhere around the age of thirty-five.

'I expect TV is rationed at boarding-school, isn't it?'

'Rather. Not too bad.'

'Here.' She handed him the remote. 'I've got lots to do anyway.'

'Would you like some help?'

Impressed, Pamela had laughed and told him not at the moment, but she'd ask if she thought of something. She was only truly happy when she was busy, especially in the kitchen. To her it was the heart of the house and she loved it, particularly when all the family were staying and needed providing for. It made her feel like the conductor of a huge orchestra for whom only she knew the score. The entire room glowed with warmth and light. On top of a shining blue Aga, set into the huge arched recess that had once housed its Victorian ancestors, several saucepans bubbled, releasing spirals of steam that spread like a thin mist beneath the strip-lights and timbers overhead. Bunches of dried herbs, strings of onions and garlic hung from hooks scattered between the oak dresser and wall units, their faint scent mingling pleasantly with the aromas of cooking and fresh flowers; a crystal vase of red and white carnations stood in the middle of the kitchen table (a thick oblong of weathered oak almost as old as the house itself), while more slender arrangements of roses, each in scarlet and cream, were slotted into two small stone alcoves on either side of the fireplace. Although the table formed the centrepiece of the room, such was the extravagance of the space available that between the walk-in larder and the back wall there was also room for a hefty mustard-coloured sofa and matching armchair, cast-offs from a previous generation of sitting-room furniture. This cosy corner, lit by a blue ceramic lamp on the windowsill, constituted one of Pamela's favourite refuges. The light from the lamp was gentle, and stacked next to it were all her most-thumbed cookery and garden books, together with an ancient, sagging coil pot Charlie had made at primary school that housed all sorts of vital implements, like scissors, pens and a spare pair of glasses.

It had taken a while to get the kitchen thus, exactly as she wanted it. Stripped of its accoutrements, it was a vast, potentially austere space, with stone walls, quarried floor tiles and big plain windows overlooking the measliest of the lawns and the scrawny bit of privet hedge that ran into the upper wall of the vegetable garden. As an area originally designed for the use of servants it had received little cosseting before her arrival. John's mother, Nancy, a delicate, willowy woman with soulful eyes, had performed marvellously at the end of dinner-party tables but could barely lift a teaspoon to serve herself. She had entered the kitchen only to discuss menus and shopping lists and had not thought to update it, beyond installing taps to replace the old water pump and an ugly fat beige electric cooker to replace the old stove. During Eric's brief (servantless) reign as master of the house the kitchen had suffered yet more neglect. Pamela retained a particularly vivid image of her brother-in-law standing in front of the beige cooker in a tatty tartan dressing-gown, feet bare, cigarette in one hand and frying-pan in the other, blithely spattering fat that he had no intention of wiping away. When she and John had moved in, they had been too strapped for cash to see to much beyond fresh coats of paint and treatments for woodworm and rising damp. It was several years into John's tenure as a Lloyds Member before the Aga saw off the beige cooker and a friend of Sid's built all the handsome oak cupboards to replace the greasy black shelves.

Pamela glided between the sink, the oven and the table, adding to the array of bowls and plates of food. Centre stage was the Christmas cake, which she had iced and decorated that morning with the little figurines she used every year: three fir trees, two reindeer, a squat Father Christmas, a church and two golden angels, who were disproportionately large for the scene but who always looked charming anyway, with the dusting of snow on their tiny songbooks and the icing swirling in drifts round the bottom of their gowns. In a white pudding basin next to it the Christmas pudding glistened. Wrapped in muslin since October, it smelt so strongly and deliciously of brandy and fruit that on peeling off the cover Pamela had felt the saliva burst inside her mouth. The children, she knew, preferred mince pies and only ate the pudding for the money, thrilled, as only children could be, at the notion of stumbling upon buried treasure, even the little five-pence pieces, which everyone – apart from dear little Tina – knew had been eased inside by Granny with a spoon.

But no treasure on John's plate this year, Pamela reminded herself, thinking of her husband's poorly teeth. She turned aside from her cooking and wrote '*DENTIST*' across the opening page of her new diary. He would put off doing anything about it himself. And she had seen how he was struggling with his food, steering each mouthful to one side until his cheek bulged and taking twice as long as usual to clear his plate. She hadn't said anything, of course. The timing was all wrong, with Christmas just a day away. He would have been irritated at having his discomfort observed. But in the peaceful aftermath of January, with Christmas and New Year safely behind them and the house back to themselves, she knew it would be easy to find exactly the blend of compassion and sternness with which to broach the subject. In life timing was everything, Pamela mused, sliding a knife into the belly of the fish and dropping a fresh sprig of mint into the now boiling potatoes. From cooking to marriage, expertise lay in the ability to seize the right moment to do the right thing. She smiled to herself, pleased at the thought, which had occurred to her before but never so lucidly, and which, like many good thoughts, she decided to keep to herself. She retreated to the sofa and picked up her diary again, which was large with embossed leather corners and illustrated with flowing-haired pre-Raphaelite women to mark the beginning of each month. She opened it at random and smoothed her palms across the crisp white pages, infused for a moment with a sense of all the possibilities ahead, as if the skeleton of the year lay under her fingertips. It promised to be a good twelve months. Her children and their families would, as usual, make several visits during half-terms and holidays, Peter was talking of a summer party to celebrate his fiftieth, and her old friend Dorothy was planning a trip from Boston. And then there was the young man who wanted to write about Eric. A book about war heroes, the letter had said. Unsung war heroes. He had wanted to come before Christmas but she had put him off. Timing, Pamela thought again, closing the book as her head did one of its whirls, depositing her suddenly and for no particular reason at the notion of sex, which she had once enjoyed but which she now regarded as one might a dear deceased friend, recalled with fondness rather than loss.

'Can I do anything?'

She looked up to see her eldest daughter-in-law framed in the doorway, her dark hair cropped briskly round her fierce cheek-bones and earnest brown eyes. 'Helen. How kind.' Pamela slipped the diary back into its place on the shelf. 'I don't think so, except to call everybody to the dining room. Maisie and Clem did the table – oh, and I promised Ed he could light the candles. He asked specially.' Moments later the kitchen was filled with people: Charlie looking for Sellotape, Peter tugging corks out of bottles, Cassie with wet hair and a towel round her shoulders asking if anyone had seen her hairbrush, and, Maisie, self-conscious but radiant in towering heels and sparkling purple eye-shadow smeared like bruises across her pale lids.

St Margaret's, half empty most Sundays of the year, was so full that a few latecomers had to stand at the back. Every time the huge oak doors were opened, the flames of the candles fixed into brass sticks at each end of every pew shivered in protest, threatening to cast the packed congregation into darkness. Clem was standing between her twin sister, who was much taller than her in her heels, and her mother, who looked thrown together but somehow splendid, with a black silk shawl across her shoulders and her hair messily tucked up into a wide-brimmed black hat. Clem was aware of her perfume, a musky scent, which had been the same for as long as she could remember. Her father stood on her other side, his usually jovial face slack with solemnity. His hair, still thick and only faintly peppered with grey, hadn't quite grown into a new hair-cut and was sticking up a bit at the crown. There were little flecks of dandruff on the shoulders of his overcoat, Clem noticed, and longed to reach across the back of the pew and brush them off. Her eyes moved along the line to light on the figure of her uncle Peter, lean and imposing in a long dark cashmere coat, his jaw jutting, his bald patch glinting through his thinning mesh of grey hair. Beside him, her aunt Helen, with her short-back-and-sides hairstyle and dark blue trouser suit, might, at a distance, have passed for a miniature man. She was fidgeting, apparently concerned about keeping her hymn and prayer books in a tidy pile, but glancing all the time at Theo, who was slotted into the pew behind, between their grandparents and Aunt Cassie. The poor boy had been made to wear his new school blazer, which was so huge that the sleeves hung to his fingertips, while the shoulders bulged from all the unoccupied space inside.

With such a large group, Elizabeth and Colin had been forced to make do with seats to the far right of the church, where they were half hidden by a stone pillar and a fat woman in a fur coat. The only adult absentee from the service was Aunt Alicia, who had been enticed into remaining at Ashley House in the role of babysitter for the younger ones. Although, having seen her wedged among cushions in the deepest of the TV room armchairs with her sticks propped next to her and the telly on full blast, it had occurred to Clem that the old dear would have trouble hearing an earthquake, let alone anything going on in the bedrooms upstairs. Her aunt

Elizabeth hadn't seemed too happy about it either: at the last minute she had even volunteered to keep Alicia company, but Uncle Colin, whispering fiercely into her ear, had more or less frogmarched her out of the front door. Every time her aunt's face bobbed into view between the pillar and the fat woman's coat Clem could see that she still looked unhappy. During the hymns she hardly opened her mouth and when everyone was supposed to have their heads down in prayer Clem, peeking between her fingers, saw that Aunt Elizabeth's eyes were wide open and staring fixedly ahead, as though her thoughts were a million miles away from the vicar's prayers for the homeless and starving babies.

Clem found it obscurely comforting that one of the grown-ups should appear to be as little in the mood for Christmas as she was. Usually, coming to Ashley House triggered a surge of happy feelings, connected not to the prospect of anything specific so much as a general sense of anticipation. But this time all the familiar things – Granny in her apron, fussing over food, jolly questions about school from aunts and uncles, hanging up her smart clothes for Christmas Day – just made her feel flat. Like she'd done it all before and there was nothing in the world to look forward to ever again. Her cousins – normally great comrades when they were thrown together, regardless of age or sex – had struck her as either impossibly alien (Theo) or impossibly irritating (Chloë and Roland). So lacking in jollity herself, she had found it hard to believe in any show of such emotions in those around her. Before coming out that night she had written in the notebook she kept for her most private thoughts, 'Christmas is for hypocrites', underlining the last word because it was a favourite in her burgeoning arsenal of vocabulary and she was pleased to have found so perfect an opportunity to use it. Maisie, she knew for certain, had only been keen to come to church because she thought it was grown-up to stay out till past midnight and – even more pathetically – because she had believed that the pop star Neil Rosco might be there. It was true that the man had bought the big manor house on the other side of Barham – Clem had read about it in the paper – but unattached millionaire celebrities were, in her view, unlikely to

spend Christmas Eve on their knees in a country church. When she
had said as much to Maisie, prompted by the sight of her dolling
herself up in front of the little mahogany dressing-table in their
bedroom as if she actually had a *date* with the man, her sister had
exploded with righteous indignation, saying just because she liked
to make the best of herself it didn't have to mean it was for the
benefit of the opposite sex. Clem had gone very quiet. Thanks to a
tousled new sixth-former called Jonny Cottrall, she herself had
devoted considerable energy during the course of the previous term
to doing just that, bullying her thick dark hair daily with washing
and conditioning and, on occasions, making furtive use of Maisie's
eyelash curlers. She had even gone through a phase of rolling up the
waistband of her school skirt to reveal more of her legs, which,
unlike the rest of her, had a decent shape. 'Sorry.' She had breathed
the word miserably. She didn't often quarrel with her sister and to
do so on Christmas Eve, when the nameless wretchedness had
taken residence in her heart, was almost more than she could bear.
The pair of them were very different in looks (Maisie was slim with
chestnut hair like their mother, while Clem was thicker set with her
father's darker colouring) and personality, but also fiercely close.
At one stage they had even developed a bit of a secret language,
until Ed got the hang of it and there no longer seemed any point.

'Me too. Friends?'

'Friends.'

'I've got you a gorgeous present, Clem, I just know you'll love it.'

Clem had smiled, thinking of her own gift, a pair of glittering lilac
earrings nested in cotton wool in a box so tiny that she had feared,
dropping it into the ocean of presents already swamping the laden
Norwegian pine downstairs, that it might never be found. 'And
you'll like yours, I promise.'

'Want some of this?' Maisie, in awe of her own generosity, held
out the new and much prized box of sparkling purple eye-shadow.
'I mean it, honestly.'

'No, I won't, but thanks.'

'It is exciting, though, isn't it?' Maisie threw herself on to her
sister's bed, scissoring her legs as she talked. 'I mean of all the places

in the world Neil Rosco could have bought a house and he goes and chooses *Barham*. When I told Monica Simmonds she was so jealous she almost wet herself – she practically cries when she sees a picture of him. I mean, I think he's quite good-looking and everything, but it's his music I'm really into. He's pretty talented, you've got to admit.'

'Oh, sure,' agreed Clem, although the great Rosco's tunes were far too *obvious* for her to get really excited about them. But the sisterly truce was going well and she hadn't wanted to blow it off course. She could write what she really thought later in her secret notebook, she decided now, sneaking a look at her watch to see how long the vicar had been talking and musing on what a simple, perfect receptacle a private sheet of paper was for any honesty, no matter how brutal.

'Are you okay?' Elizabeth touched Colin's sleeve. Since they had arrived at Ashley House that afternoon she had been aware of him retreating into himself, away from her. She wondered if he was still brooding about the promotion fiasco that had overshadowed the end of term. He had got the job of deputy head only to find that he would be sharing the post with Phyllis McGill, the abrasive head of Physics, with whom he had never got on.

'Fine.' He patted her hand, keeping his gaze fixed on the altar where the vicar was now preparing the wafers for holy communion. She could see the vein in his temple pulsing above the dark limb of his glasses, just where his thin grey hair met his face.

'And I'm sure Roland's all right,' she whispered, hoping both for his forgiveness over her earlier anxiety and to remind him that it was Christmas when the happiness of their son should be paramount. 'I've got the stocking all ready. It should be easy.'

'Great.' Colin patted her hand again. He had been thinking not of their son, or of Phyllis McGill, but of a conversation during dinner with his brothers-in-law. About wine. Of course. It was always about something like that. Wine or sport, with Peter making a show of seeking other opinions but only as a pretext for voicing his own. What did Colin think of the Saint-Veran? Colin, his thoughts

lurching to the five bottles of Sainsbury's Own Label that constituted his own wine stocks, had said – what else? – that it struck
him as very pleasant. Whereupon Peter had launched into one of
his diatribes about grapes and soil-types until Charlie had banged
him on the back and said he was being a bore and nothing mattered
except the stuff tasting good and hitting the spot. Colin had been
grateful, but not particularly consoled. When he had first made the
acquaintance of his brothers-in-law some fourteen years before,
their friendliness had caused him to overlook the fact that they
belonged to an invisible club from which he would always be
excluded. A club based on public-school and privilege, and a form
of inner self-belief for which Colin had striven in far more laborious
ways. He tried not to mind. The Harrison family always endeavoured to make him feel welcome – bent over backwards, in fact.
Which sometimes made it worse. Like Charlie bailing him out like
that, telling Peter to shut up because he knew Colin was out of his
depth. Saying what Colin would have given anything to be able to
say himself but which he never could because at the end of the day
he was still an outsider, without the luxury of the confident
insouciance that Charlie had – that they all had, apart from
Elizabeth, who had grasped at him all those years ago, like an
insect clinging to a blade of grass . . .

'Darling? Everyone's standing.'

'Sorry.' Colin gripped the back of the pew in front and hauled
himself to his feet, smiling in fierce defiance at the embarrassment
of having been caught one step behind.

Roland dreamed he was swimming. It was mostly a nice dream;
scary, because the water was dark and cold, but nice, because he
was gliding and weightless and because although he had been
holding his breath for hours it didn't hurt. In the water he was
strong and powerful. Like a fish. Like Theo and Ed who had races
across the lake in the summer, not minding its iciness or the thought
of the creatures underneath; nameless, shapeless slimy things that
brushed against one's shins and toes. In the dream the water
was getting less dark but colder too. He was swimming towards

something, a light, maybe. And he wanted to reach it badly, so badly that it hurt but felt wonderful at the same time, just knowing that he was going to arrive there, if only he could hang on a little longer. And then his lungs started to hurt and his tummy too, and he wanted to cry out but no sound would come because he hadn't reached where he was going. Just as he thought he would explode with aching there was a sense of wonderful release. A moment of relief followed before he was suddenly wide awake, with the tick of the clock on the bedroom mantelpiece and a terrible warm wetness between his legs. His pyjama bottoms, sheets and even part of the pillow case were soaking. For a few minutes Roland lay very still, torn between the urge to cry out for his mother and a gut-wrenching sense of shame. He had wet his bed before and been told, many times, by Elizabeth that it did not matter. That it was something some children did, that sheets could be washed, that it was just something that happened from time to time. But it did matter, Roland knew, because of his father's jokes about putting him back in nappies and because on the rare occasion he had been invited to stay overnight at friends' houses he had refused for fear of committing the same crime in another family. It was a few minutes before he had assembled his thoughts sufficiently to recall that he was at his grandparents' house and it was Christmas Eve.

Trying to ignore the wetness of his pyjamas and bedclothes, now horribly cold and sticking to his skin, he gingerly slid his feet from side to side, searching for the weight and rustle of a full stocking, unsure if he wanted it to be there or not. If it wasn't there his parents had yet to come in. If it was they would be asleep in the next room, beyond consolation or disapprobation until morning. Roland wasn't sure which would be worse. He could feel nothing with his feet so he gripped the edge of the bed and peered over the side. Because of being ill he had been put on his own, instead of sharing one of the lovely big top-floor bedrooms with Ed and Theo. This room was square and very small, having once served as a dressing room to the bedroom next door where his parents were. There was just enough space for the bed, a chair and a small chest of drawers, on top of which sat a large white porcelain bowl with a matching jug. They had been for washing in the olden days, before taps and basins, and he was to be careful not to break them, his mother had explained, as she folded his clothes and tucked him up. Roland, his head thick with his cold and a sense of gross injustice at being herded into bed before even the youngest of his cousins, had said he thought it was dumb that a jug and bowl could be so special. But now, seeing the white glow of the porcelain in the dark, he thought it did look sort of special and, if he screwed his eyes up, like a huge white bird, a ghostly swan, gliding through the pitch black of the room. Below, propped against the chest of drawers, was his small holdall of clothes; and leaning against that, he saw suddenly, his heart clenching, was a bulging version of Uncle Eric's large woollen sock (one of several relics from his days in the army, which traditionally served as Christmas stockings for all the grandchildren), which had been draped across the end of his bed a few hours before. Which meant his parents were indeed asleep on the other side of the connecting door. Roland toyed for one last brief moment with the idea of fetching his mother, then decided finally against it. She would be kind – she always was – but his father would be cross. Coming into their bedroom in the middle of the night, like wetting sheets and crying when he fell over, was something he was supposed to be growing out of. Because he was nine and a quarter and had to learn to be brave, Roland reminded himself, biting his lower lip, which was trembling and threatening to let him down.

He hugged his damp pillow to his chest, crawled to the other end of his bed, tugged all the bedding out from the mattress and wriggled down inside. If he kept his legs to the left with his knees bent up to his chest he couldn't feel the wetness in the sheets. And the pillow wasn't too bad either, turned the other way up and upside down. There was a smell, sort of sweet but not very nice, although it was hard to be sure of anything through the thickness of his cold. In a few minutes he was asleep again, breathing heavily through his mouth, and emitting little squeaky wheezes with the rise and fall of his chest.

At Christmas the dining room came into its own. Of all the rooms in Ashley House, it was by far the grandest. Generally passed over in favour of the kitchen, where the old oak table could easily accommodate huge numbers, it had been sufficiently underused and unassailed by modern furnishings to retain all the elegant formality of earlier times. A long mahogany dining-table, with rounded corners and flamboyant pedestal legs, held centre-stage, with a large crystal chandelier, suspended from an elaborate ceiling rose by a heavy brass chain. Oil paintings, including a couple of stiff portraits of Albert and Nancy Harrison, were ranged round the walls, illuminated by gleaming brass picture lights. Between them, sprouting like flowers, were several delicate pairs of wall lights with tulip-shaped glass shades and curvy brass stems. The curtains were of burgundy velvet, matching the wine red of the carpet and setting off to perfection the sumptuous damask cream wallpaper and the dark polished wood of the furniture. With an antiques shop's worth of silver and crystal adorning the table, the effect was spectacular. Even Tina's high chair had been laid with a crisp folded dove of a napkin and a tiny silver spoon and fork. Helen, entering the room with a dish of bread sauce in one hand and a silver gravy-boat in the other, paused to take in the scene, struck, as she was from time to time, by the effortless magnificence of the family into which she had married. Her own family had money but – as she had realised when she met Peter during her final year at law school – absolutely no equivalent sense of style or history. When her father retired her parents had moved to a bungalow near Plymouth, which was sizeable but soulless and housed their accumulated hotchpotch of possessions without any obvious affection or cohesion. The garden surrounding the bungalow was large and might have been attractive, were it not for the cumbersome presence of the caravan in which they liked to holiday. Family ancestors were rarely mentioned and only in passing. Consequently Helen had little sense of where she came from, other than in purely geographical terms, nor that it mattered particularly.

In contrast, Peter's sense of family was immense, his pride in his pioneering ancestors almost palpable. To be invited to become a part – even an imported part – of such a clan, so reverential of the past and still functioning so well in the present, had given Helen an unprecedented and inspiring sense of self-definition. It was only as the years passed that she had learnt it could be overwhelming too at times, when she wasn't in the mood. Or when, as was occurring with increasing frequency these days, Peter talked in sweeping terms of the time when Ashley House would pass into their own hands. The nearing of this once-distant prospect made Helen, fearless about most things, rather afraid. Pamela would be a hard act to follow. Particularly for a woman like her, with a full-time job as a lawyer and no feel for country life. Sharing such apprehensions with her husband, however, was proving difficult. Just the night before they had argued about it – after midnight mass, too, which somehow made it worse – when Helen, exhausted from a week that had stretched her energies almost to breaking point (work deadlines, Christmas shopping, school carol services, threats of resignation from their irksome Turkish au pair) had been misguided enough to seek reassurance on the subject.

'I don't know how your mother manages. I'd need an army of helpers if I lived down here.'

'Would you? Why?'

'Oh, Peter, you know why.' Helen flopped on to the stool in front of the long cherrywood dressing-table next to their bed, peering warily at her pallid reflection in its gleaming oval mirror. 'Commuting to London and trying to keep the place nice . . . the garden and so on.' She screwed the lid off her night cream and dabbed several blobs on strategic places across her face.

'Sid helps with the garden.'

'Sid won't live for ever.'

'Son of Sid, then.'

'He hasn't got a son, he's got a daughter who lives miles away and who has that dreadful child Jessica who's always coming to stay and pushed Chloë into all those brambles last year.'

'Really, Helen, stop being so literal, would you?' Peter offered his wife an eyeroll of despair, then stepped into the bathroom and switched on his electric toothbrush. The conversation was suspended for a few minutes, the tension it had created visible only in the angry dabbing of Helen's fingertips across her face and the unnatural thoroughness with which her husband steered the vibrating bristles round his teeth.

There was an audible click as he slotted his toothbrush back into its portable holder. 'My parents have always managed without an army of helpers,' he continued, emerging from the bathroom.

'Your mother was at home all day.'

'Without a nanny and twice the number of children to look after.'

'I won't give up my job,' Helen had snapped, prompted by a sudden terrifying image of being buried in the countryside all day with no one to talk to but Labradors and gardeners. Her face was shining slightly from too much cream. A few specks had caught the edges of her hair, lending a greasy sheen to her sideboards. It was a convenient if not especially flattering cut, to which she had resorted after Theo was born, when the time pressures of getting both herself and a baby presentable by seven o'clock in the morning had precluded anything involving a hair-dryer.

'Of course you won't give up your job.' Peter sounded both despairing and exasperated. 'I've never suggested otherwise. Look, Helen, I haven't the foggiest why we're arguing. All I said was that, in the extremely unfortunate event of my mother and father's demise, I would prefer to run Ashley House informally, as they have, without a posse of staff. Instead of getting hot under the collar about it, we should perhaps focus instead on our good fortune. My dear siblings, as you know, will inherit nothing like the equivalent value of this place.'

'I know, I know.' This, too, was a well-worn subject. Peter, as the firstborn, would get Ashley House; the others would divide up their parents' liquid assets, estimated to be around a million, once the tax man had taken his share. No one, therefore, would suffer too badly. 'And of course I'm grateful,' muttered Helen.

'We're agreed on that, then,' he replied briskly, tugging back the bedcovers. 'Besides, in a few years Chloë – with a little cajoling – will also be at boarding-school, which will simplify things all round, won't it?'

'Yes.' Unconsoled, Helen had mouthed the word, watching in the mirror as her husband clambered into bed and reached for his book. These days, boarding-school was a subject on which she felt as confused as the prospect of their inheritance. It hadn't always been so. Indeed, for a long time the plan of sending the children away to be educated had seemed like the answer to her dreams – the answer, indeed, to every career-mother's relentless juggling act. The six years separating the births of Helen's children bore testimony to the constant and supreme effort of managing a job and a family. The decision to allow the conception of Chloë when she was forty years old had been one of the most difficult she had ever taken. The pregnancy was fraught and draining but she had rushed back to the firm of lawyers where she worked six weeks after the birth, desperate to prove herself, openly articulating her longing for the day when boarding-school would take some of her domestic responsibilities off her hands.

As the day approached for Theo to start at St Peter's, however, Helen began to feel rather differently. By the time they had to say goodbye she was a wreck. Even now, recalling the tight desperation in her son's big square face as she finally released him, the crimson tips of his ears, the tug of his lower lip as he turned back towards his dormitory, where several intimidatingly large boys had started a pillow fight, brought tears to her eyes. Back in Barnes the house had felt hollow and somehow *unbalanced*. Instead of getting on better she and Chloë – always the more prickly, emotionally complicated child – seemed to spend most evenings bickering about everything: table manners, homework, music practice, television. Rushing home to relieve the au pair, Helen would often wonder – guiltily – why she had bothered. Sitting alone on the sofa in quiet moments between such wearing confrontations and Peter's return from the office, she would find herself longing for Theo's easy bear-hugs, with such a physical hunger sometimes that she thought she might be going mad. Peter, himself the happy product of a public-school education, was kind but essentially uncomprehending of her anguish. It would pass, he said, as it had for his mother and millions of other women. She should concentrate on Chloë – who needed a lot of concentrating upon – and try not to be sentimental. Almost harder than anything for Helen was that the boy who returned from

St Peter's looked and seemed so different from the one she had sent away. Not just because he was taller and bulkier, with a faint oiliness displacing the fresh apple look of his skin and a rumble in his once sweet treble of a voice but – harder still – because there was a new aura of distancing self-consciousness about him. A distance that Helen could not – and knew she should not – try to cross. On the odd occasion that he did put his arms round her, she wanted to squeeze him till his ribs cracked. She wanted to say, 'This is me, your mother, remember me and the love I have.' It was like the end of a love affair, Helen thought now, gripping the handle of the gravy-boat, tears pricking her eyes as she watched Theo laughing with Maisie about something at the far end of the table. Her son no longer loved her in the way he had and never would. The mother passion of his boyhood was over.

'Thank you, Helen.' Pamela took the dishes from her hands and set them down on the table. 'There's more of both in the kitchen if we need it. Are you all right, dear?'

'Oh, yes, quite all right,' Helen replied, her voice dry, touched yet unnerved that her mother-in-law should have spotted her distraction. 'I'm a little tired but, then, we all are, aren't we?' she continued brightly, smoothing her skirt under her thighs as she slipped into a seat between Charlie and Colin, fielding enquiries about whether their children had enjoyed their stockings and how long they were planning to stay.

After lunch there was a frenzy of present-opening followed by a rather less enthusiastic assault on the washing-up, which eventually resulted in the women shooing the men and children from the kitchen and getting on with it themselves. Happy to be evicted, the group drifted back into the drawing room, the younger members returning to closer examinations of their gifts while the men cradled glasses of port and lolled in armchairs, easing their belt buckles. John turned on the television for the Queen's Speech, but only Aunt Alicia showed any sign of listening to it. Colin, Peter and Charlie, meanwhile, fell into a discussion about terrorism, triggered by the news of another suicide bomber in Palestine and recent claims by the American president that the war on extremist factions was being won.

'I'm only saying they're kidding themselves if they think they can wipe it out. It doesn't matter how many tanks or SAS teams go into these areas there'll always be budding new Osama Bin Ladens to take up the cause. It's like some monstrous hydra – cut off one bit and another grows just as quickly . . .'

'These places – Iraq, Afghanistan and so on – are a topographical nightmare too.' Charlie endeavoured, without success, to suppress a burp. 'I certainly wouldn't fancy trying to find my way around all those caves and mountains on my belly in the dark with a compass and thirty tons of gear in a backpack.'

'The ethics are interesting, though, don't you think?' said Colin. 'It's essentially about a clash of cultures, isn't it? The Taleban and all these extremist religious groups see western civilisation as the enemy. Who's to say we're right and they're wrong?' The question, which had triggered some lively debates in the classroom during the course of the year, proved less effective with his brothers-in-law.

'Of course we're bloody well right,' snorted Peter. 'They're barking mad for one thing, barbarians for another. Two years ago they *murdered* several thousand people in one of the most heinous attacks the world has ever seen.'

'I'm only saying—'

'I knew five people in those towers,' growled John, an observation they had all heard many times before but which prompted a moment of silent respect none the less. 'An insurance syndicate. Good men, all of them. Wives and families. Half the bloody company wiped out. Horrific.'

'Truly horrific,' echoed Colin, fearful of having cast himself accidentally in the role of terrorist sympathiser and wanting to atone for it.

'Well, I thought she was very good this year.'

'Pardon. Sorry, Alicia?' Peter set down his empty port glass and reached between their armchairs to pat his aunt's arm. 'Who was good?'

'The Queen. I thought she was very good this year.'

'Very good indeed,' he agreed heartily, catching the eye of Charlie, who was chuckling.

'Just the right tone. And all that trouble she's had, too. She's a marvel.'

'What trouble is that, Alicia?' said Charlie, raising his voice for the benefit of his aunt, who was very deaf.

'With her family, the poor creature – all their comings and goings – no sense of duty, these days. She's the only one with honour and decency, apart from her dear mother, of course. Now, there was a special lady. I remember her during the war, you know.' Alicia pulled a small folded handkerchief from her sleeve and pressed it to the tiny folds of flesh at the corners of her lips, where a few stray crumbs of Christmas pudding were still lodged. 'Visiting London in the Blitz . . . She was like an angel, bringing hope to the people.'

'And how old would you have been then?' enquired Colin genially, wanting to show that, unlike the poor old lady's nephews who were exchanging schoolboy looks of sufferance, he was truly interested.

'That's not for you to know, young man,' replied Alicia tartly, thereby dashing Colin's hopes of impressing anybody and causing Charlie almost to fall off the sofa he was laughing so much. Alicia, oblivious to this back-row amusement, tucked her handkerchief back under the cuff of her cardigan and reached for her stick. 'What I need is another cup of tea, though I shouldn't. It goes straight through me, you know.'

'Here, let me get it,' exclaimed Charlie, who was actually very good with his aunt and rather fond of her brusqueness. He leapt to his feet and seized her cup and saucer with a gallant flourish. 'Unless you'd like a drop of port instead.'

'Heavens, no.' Clearly delighted, Alicia fluttered her fingers at him. 'Charles, you bad boy – the very idea, after all that wine. I should be high as a kite.'

'High means you're on drugs,' put in Ed, who happened to be passing the armchair on his skateboard. Clutched to his chest was an advanced form of weaponry called a BB gun, which he had been given for Christmas. Having studied the instructions, he was *en route* out of the mayhem of torn wrapping-paper still littering the drawing room in search of a suitable spot for some target practice.

'Lovely, dear,' said Alicia, glad to have been addressed by one of the children, even though she hadn't the faintest idea what the boy had said. She got confused with their names and ages, too, and whether they played trumpets or violins and where they went to school. In her monthly bridge group she was always talking about her brother and his family, feeling genuine delight in the knowledge of their existence (not to mention a faintly competitive urge to stir envy in the hearts of her companions). Yet the reality of them – the reality of anything, in fact – remained somewhat harder to enjoy. *En masse*, such a large group of people was noisy and demanding, full of fast talk that she couldn't follow and references to things she didn't understand. Charlie was sweet and Pamela was kind (sometimes suffocatingly so), but she often wondered whether the monumental effort of the journey from her cottage in Wiltshire (a taxi and two trains) was really worthwhile. The uncomfortable truth, barely acknowledged by her and certainly not admitted to the bridge group, was that, widowed and with her only son Paul living in Australia, she didn't really have any options. 'Isn't he too young to have a gun?' she added, responding to a need to assert herself and addressing the comment to Colin because he was the only one still looking in her direction.

'He certainly is.' Colin spoke tightly, unsettled by both his thwarted attempts at a decent conversation with any member of his wife's family and a mess-up over Roland's present, a metal-detector, which Elizabeth had wrapped without including the necessary batteries. That she could have forgotten something so elementary was maddening. 'But it's not a real gun. It fires plastic pellets. We gave Roland a metal-detector,' he began, seeking some congratulation for the idea of the gift in spite of their failure to get the thing functioning.

But he was interrupted by Charlie returning with a fresh cup of tea, which he carefully set down on the table next to Alicia's chair, announcing as he did so that she was the prettiest aunt he had and if she got whisked off down the aisle again he wanted to be the first to know. Alicia tutted delightedly, then fell asleep, her tea undrunk, her veiny feet, propped on a box of three-dimensional chess which somebody had given somebody else, swelling out of her smart shoes. In an armchair across the room John, too, was asleep, his mouth slack, the biography of Colonel H. Jones that Peter had given him open on his chest.

'I'm going to walk the ancient hound,' declared Peter, getting up from his chair and stretching as he glanced round the room for support. 'Any takers?'

Pamela appeared in the doorway behind him, carrying a tea-towel. 'Don't be too long, dear. Sid's dropping by and I want him to take a photograph of all of us.'

On hearing this news, Ed slipped out of the door leading on to the cloisters, followed by Roland, who knew he wasn't particularly wanted but who was so desperate to be given a turn with the gun that he didn't care. Disappointment still burned in his nine-year-old heart, not just because of the batteries but because he had been defeated by daunting books of instructions to two construction kits and had eaten so much chocolate he felt sick.

'A photo?' Peter clicked his fingers at Boots, who twitched, then heaved himself out from under John's feet, his tail thumping in expectation.

'Yes. A photo. It will be lovely. All three generations of the family together. I'll make him take several to be sure at least one comes out well.' Pamela's voice was no-nonsense, communicating to all those present that it was a matter on which she would not be thwarted. A far grander plan, to have just such a photograph used as the basis for a family portrait, she had decided, for the time being, to keep to herself. It was to be a present for John's eightieth birthday in the autumn and she wanted it to be a complete surprise.

Clem, scowling at the idea of a photograph, crept out of the drawing room and raced upstairs to her bedroom to write with trembling reverence on the first page of the brand new leather-bound five-year diary she had been given by her sister.

I don't know how I could have been sad before because right now I feel so glad. I have had the best year ever for presents. Maisie gave me this diary, which I am going to write in every day for the next five years of my life. It has a key, so I can write ANYTHING. Everyone has been really nice, especially Aunt Cassie, who said she thought my hair looked really pretty, though I can't think why because I'd only washed it, and Theo, who was being sort of all stuck-up at first but is now his normal self again. He got this *amazing* video camera from Uncle Peter and Aunt Helen. (Mum says they are spoilt and I suppose they are, except that spoilt should mean behaving horribly and Theo and Chloë don't really do that. At least, Chloë does sometimes but that's mostly because she's only seven.) Anyway, what I was going to say was Theo got this idea that he was going to do interviews with everyone on his camera – sort of like a documentary, he said – and he chose to do me first. It was a real laugh, though I thought I looked pretty dumb when he played it back to me afterwards. Must stop now as I can hear someone coming. PS Have eaten so much – feel so FAT I never want to eat another thing.

'You're looking so well, Cassie,' remarked Serena, draping her damp tea-towel over the Aga rail and sinking down into the kitchen sofa next to her sister-in-law.

'Yes, isn't she?' agreed Helen, joining them with her cup of tea. Now that the drama of lunch and presents was over she could feel herself beginning at last to relax. Theo had given her a dear little box he had made in carpentry, and Chloë a crayoned self-portrait with the words 'I love Mummy' scrawled underneath. Peter, too, had been very sweet, refusing to admit that the suede jacket she had given him was a little too large and kissing her with a tenderness she knew was designed to communicate that the disagreement of the night before was behind them. Christmas was nothing but a bloody strain, she decided, taking the remaining space on the sofa and blowing across the steam of her tea. 'So work's going well, then, Cassie?'

'Oh, yes, very well indeed,' Cassie gushed, flushing at the

compliments of her sisters-in-law, wishing she could tell them that the radiance beaming out of her had nothing to do with the number of commissions she had to decorate people's houses and everything to do with being in love. Really in love. For the first time in her life. Nothing she had ever felt for another human being came close. It was ten months now since she had met Dan (at his surgery, although he wasn't the doctor she had been seeing so it wasn't unethical) and her heart still galloped at the mere thought of him. It galloped even more when she saw him. And when he touched her, with his cool, expert slim fingers, she was at times so close to ecstasy that she wanted to weep with the joy of it. She kept waiting for the bubble to burst, for him to say or do something that would jolt her back to the sanity of realising she was better off alone (a regular occurrence that had triggered the death-throes of every other relationship she had ever had), but it didn't happen. No wonder people noticed. It was as if ten thousand lightbulbs had been switched on inside her. She felt energised, beautiful, empowered. Given half a chance, she would have gladly shinned up St Margaret's spire with a loudspeaker to proclaim her happiness to the whole world. The moment they were properly – openly – together she might do just that, Cassie decided, pressing the rim of her mug to her lips to hide her smile. In the meantime she had to be the soul of discretion, for Dan's sake. He had wanted to get Christmas out of the way before he told his wife and she respected him for that. There were his children to consider, after all (two girls and a boy, all under ten), and the question of money, about which he was consulting a lawyer friend. 'In fact I'm not very busy,' she confessed, 'but the jobs I'm doing I'm enjoying enormously.' (In truth her meetings with Dan, grabbed at odd hours and often at very short notice, meant the number of clients on her books had fallen considerably.) 'There's one in Battersea that's particularly challenging – a flat at the top of a Victorian mansion block which was gutted by fire so I've been given *carte blanche* to start again.'

'Who caught fire?' asked Elizabeth, returning from a final fruitless quest for the right size batteries in various drawers and cupboards suggested by her mother. Not being able to try out the metal-detector had made Roland cry and she felt all the failure of it. She felt, too, the weight of her husband's displeasure: dense and invisible, like the sort of heaviness in the air before a huge storm. She perched on the edge of the kitchen table, folding her arms and smiling at her little sister, looking so like an angel, with the lamp on the shelf behind the sofa shining through the blonde waves of her hair. How simple life is for her, she thought fondly, with only her own happiness to worry about. Boyfriends had come and gone over the years, but were rarely mentioned and even more rarely introduced. There was certainly something selfish about such an existence, but also something admirably brave. Elizabeth herself had never quite believed in her ability to face the world alone, longing, even as a teenager – even after the souring of her first marriage – for the safe haven of partnership.

'Just one of my clients – or, rather, their flat. A spark from some out-of-date wiring or something. But no one was hurt and I've been given a big budget to redecorate. There's some tea in the pot if you want it.'

'Has Mum had some?'

'No, she's busy worrying about this photograph. She's got a real bee in her bonnet about it. Poor old Sid, getting landed when all he really wants is his Christmas bottle of Scotch. And it's going to take ages to round everybody up. The children have scattered and I saw Aunt Alicia sneaking back to the barn with a box of Turkish Delight under her arm. God, she's a miserable old bag, isn't she? Except with Charlie – she adores him.'

'That's because he flirts with her,' put in Serena. 'Old ladies love to be flirted with, I suppose because it makes them feel young again.'

'What's flirting?' enquired Chloë, popping up next to the sofa.

'Never you mind,' began Helen, but Serena, speaking over her, said that it was trying to get people to notice you and think you were pretty. 'But not in a good way,' added Helen quickly, spotting the sparkle of happy recognition in her daughter's face and wanting to crush it. 'It's a bit like showing off.'

Serena, feeling for Chloë, who was looking both puzzled and

crestfallen, got up from the sofa, saying that if they were all to be on parade for Sid she ought to wake Tina from her afternoon nap. 'And I could do with some help changing her nappy,' she added, eyeing her niece, 'but I warn you, it might be a bit smelly.'

'Oh, yukky,' shrieked Chloë, making no secret of her delight.

'Thank God I'm through all that baby business,' said Helen, with a sigh, after the two had gone. 'Food and drink in one end and out the other – they're just bivalves, really, aren't they? All that mopping-up mothers have to do. I suppose, looking back, it's not actually for that long, though at the time it does seem endless.'

'Doesn't it just?' murmured Elizabeth, toying with and rejecting the idea of mentioning Roland's sodden sheets, at that moment whirling round in the tumble-dryer in the utility room at the end of the passage. It seemed cruel to blurt out his problems to the whole world. Pamela knew and that was bad enough. When she had spotted the stripped bed that morning, her mother had suggested that it might be time to consult a doctor. Which, while sensible and well intended, had stirred ancient resentments in Elizabeth's already troubled heart. She had never been good enough, never getting-it-right enough. Battling to turn the mattress, she had marvelled at how quickly – how violently – the old feelings could sear through her, as if thirty seconds rather than thirty years separated her from the debilitating sense of inadequacy that had underpinned the turbulence of her teens. Of course Roland should have grown out of such habits and, as his mother, she felt all the burden of being the one who should know how to assist him in doing so. According to family legend, she and her siblings were all potty-trained by thirteen months; washing nappies was such a bore, Pamela claimed, that it had been the only thing to do. As if all it had taken was a steely click of the fingers. As if that was all it should take Elizabeth, if only she could click hard enough and in the right way.

'Well, I shall be quite hopeless at absolutely anything to do with babies,' declared Cassie cheerfully, unaware both of her sister's dilemmas and of the fact that, for the first time in her thirty-seven years, she had used the future tense rather than the conditional to address the notion.

As several had predicted, the photograph took a while to set up. Peter took charge of the operation, while Pamela talked Sid through the mechanics of pressing the right button. After some debate – mostly with himself – Peter settled upon the drawing-room sofa as the ideal focal point round which the group should assemble, instructing the tallest members to stand behind (himself, Charlie, Colin and Theo), the oldest to sit on the sofa (Alicia, John and Pamela) and the youngest to assume various poses at their feet on the carpet. The remaining group, who fitted into none of these categories (the twins, Elizabeth, Cassie, Serena and Helen), he directed to the sides of the sofa: Maisie and Clem perched on each arm while the women stood at their shoulders. It made for an impressive group, as Sid said many times, frowning more wrinkles into his creased old face and trying to keep his stout, calloused fingers steady on the button. They posed for several shots, during which baby Tina, resplendent in a new pink towelling Babygro, was passed along the rows like a parcel, landing finally with Cassie, who held her stiffly at first and then more snugly as the child, latching all ten fingers on to her big beaded necklace, relaxed in her arms.

All the children were patient and co-operative apart from Maisie who, worried that her aunt would smell the cigarette smoke on her hair and clothes (Uncle Peter, stamping round the garden with the dog, had almost stumbled right into her), kept tossing her head and saying what a drag it was. When Theo pleaded with them all not to move while he fetched his video camera, she groaned until silenced by a stern look from her father.

'But then *you* won't be in the picture, Theo,' squealed Chloë, who was thoroughly enjoying sprawling on the carpet, shouting, 'Cheese,' every five seconds and keeping a firm grip on Boots's collar. Slumped with exhaustion from his walk at John's feet – right on top of his shoes, to be exact – the dog didn't need holding, but Chloë, feeling proud and powerful, couldn't resist the chance to lay claim to him.

'It doesn't matter that I'm not in it,' Theo assured his sister, when he returned a few moments later with the lens of his camera glued to his right eye. Behind him Sid was shrinking back into the room, dreading a request either to pose with the family or to handle this infinitely more complicated piece of equipment. 'Any decent documentary-maker has to remain outside his subject, be objective and so on.' There was a ripple of exchanged looks: some, among the grown-ups, of admiration, and some, among his cousins, of baffled toleration.

'Just get on with it,' hissed Maisie, breaking off to yelp with pain as her tiny sister, bored with Cassie's necklace, seized a clump of her hair. 'Ow, Jesus, bloody hell, Tina.'

'Maisie,' growled Charlie, who had a post-lunch headache, 'that's quite enough.'

'It jolly well hurt. And my leg's gone to sleep.'

'Well done, Theo, I think that will do,' purred Pamela, rising from her seat to restore calm. 'Thank you, all of you. And to you, dear Sid. So kind.' She floated across the room and looped her arm through his to steer him from the room, knowing that without such assistance her employee, especially when he was full of mulled wine and good cheer, sometimes found it hard to make his own way to the front door. 'Love to Vera. Is Jessica coming to stay this holidays? Oh, good. Well, do send her round whenever you want, won't you? The more the merrier, as far as the children are concerned. Isn't that right, children?'

'Yes,' they chorused, not catching each other's eyes because they all hated Sid's granddaughter, even though they were supposed to feel sorry for her because her father had run off with a barmaid and her mother, as Pamela frequently put it, 'couldn't cope'. 'Of course, Granny.' They kept their laughter in until Pamela had left the room and their parents had drifted out of earshot, drawn by someone's suggestion of more tea. Then they all exploded, united properly for the first time that holiday by the invisible bond of antipathy against a common enemy. 'You're a stinking rude boy,' shrieked Theo, imitating Jessica's whining falsetto and all six children collapsed on the floor, holding their bellies and rolling with laughter, Ed seeing suddenly that Theo hadn't transformed into a pompous git after all, Chloë feeling for once blissfully old and included, Roland truly forgetting the ignominy of his wet bed, Clem thinking that *this* was what she had needed to get finally and thoroughly into the Christmas mood, and Maisie deciding that, as a form of recreation, smoking cigarettes alone by the manure heap had its limitations.

JANUARY

Pamela had packed carefully for her visit to Eric. As always, she used her big black leather handbag, of which she was not particularly fond but which had enough wide compartments to accommodate all the normal essentials together with a book, glasses, needlework and two bumper bags of sherbet lemons. Although he was unable to speak, Eric still took great pleasure in food, particularly sweets, and most particularly sherbet lemons. His appetite was probably why he had lived so long, the nurses said, but his once-broad, muscled frame, confined for so many years to beds and wheelchairs, was sagging and shrunken, as if caving in on what was left of the body inside. As fragile as a birdcage, thought Pamela now, hugging him gently and feeling the spokes of his ribs press against her chest. She released him and stroked his hair, which was white and thick, thinking as she always did how incongruous – how cruel – it was to have so much healthy growth on top of a face that was already more skull than skin. He had excellent teeth, too, for his age, in spite of the sweets, although the huge smiles with which he had once shown them off were a thing of the past. He looked, if anything, more alert than he had at Christmas, when perhaps he had been overwhelmed by the number of visitors (as well as John and herself, Elizabeth, Charlie and Peter had come with an assortment of grandchildren, including little Tina, who had toddled round the room lunging for ornaments and medicine bottles); his eyelids had hung so heavily and still throughout the visit that he might have been asleep.

'John sends his love. He's at the dentist today. Root-canal treatment, poor love.' Pamela settled herself in the armchair next to the window, manoeuvred his wheelchair so that he was facing her and pulled out her needlework. She was stitching a new cover for the piano stool, a complicated trellis of entwined flowers that was testing her skill to the limit. 'He put off going, of course, you know what he's like. Turned out to be some horrible abscess – he's on antibiotics and everything.' She fed the needle through one of the tiny holes in the hessian and gave it a sharp tug, checking before she continued that the back of her handiwork looked as tidy as the front. Her mother had always said that the sign of a truly good needle-woman was when the hidden stitches stood up to as much critical scrutiny as those on display, without knots or loops or loose ends. She would often add, in a tone so menacing that Pamela still quailed to recollect it, that it was the same with people; that truly good characters could be turned inside out without fear of what might be revealed.

'I'll read to you in a little while – I've brought a John Buchan, *Greenmantle*. I expect you've read it, but it's nice to re-read things, isn't it? Like visiting old friends. Talking of visiting, did I tell you that the young man who wants to write about you is coming next week? So exciting. He's called Stephen Smith and the book has been commissioned by some publishers in London. I hadn't heard of them, but John had. He's going to look out some of your bits and pieces from the attic. He said he might want to come and see you, though I said I'd check with you first. I don't want to put you under any strain, so we'll see how you are, shall we? You never were one for chatting to strangers very much, were you?' she murmured, and paused in her stitching to sigh, then reached with a tissue to dab away a tiny overspill from the rheumy half-closed eyes.

John kept his mouth open as wide as he could, trying to ignore the ache in his jaw and the unpleasant sensation in his gums. Not pain exactly, but acute discomfort. As if pain was just round the corner and might explode into being at any time. The antibiotics hadn't entirely cleared up the infection, the dentist said. He would need another, stronger course, together with a couple more sessions of cleaning out the roots. Seventy-nine was wretchedly old, reflected John miserably, wishing he could close his jaw and run his tongue round his lips, which felt stretched and ready to split with dryness.

'Okay down there?' The dentist offered a grin of encouragement over the top of his white mask. 'Not much fun, I know, but we'll get there in the end, Mr Harrison.' John widened his eyes in an attempt at a response, thinking as he did so of Eric, and the appalling tragedy of being trapped inside one's body without resource to communication of any kind. Who knew what his brother really thought and felt about anything? Pamela, like the dentist, was quite happy to pursue one-sided conversations, finding enough response in her imagination to continue for hours at a time; but even after twenty years the sight of his stricken sibling still reduced John to a state of tongue-tied compassion coupled – if he was honest – with a sort of terror that he might one day end up the same way, sliding towards death with a dribble on his lips. It was one of the harshest tricks of life, he mused, that one could choose neither the manner nor the moment by which one left it. Just that morning over breakfast he had read about a woman embarking on a legal battle to have herself killed. There had been a picture of her bent almost double in a wheelchair, her body all warped and witchy from some dreadful disintegrating disease, her stoic husband at her side, huge sleep-deprived pouches puckering his eyes, his lips thin with suffering and determination.

John let his eyelids close, blocking out the glare of the dentist's angle-poised light. A small but persistent tickle had started at the edge of his left nostril. Would he take eternal life if it were offered to him? No, he wouldn't, John decided fiercely. Life only derived meaning through its transience. And yet he longed for the re-assurance that he would leave some imprint on the world after his death, some echo of immortality. Like Eric having an entire chapter devoted to his exploits in the war. For a brief moment an absurd envy flickered inside John's heart. His own few months of active service – all spent in England – had been singularly inglorious and a career in insurance would never warrant a biographer's interest. Access to anything equivalent would arise simply through the continuation of the family line, through his strapping sons and daughters, and Ashley House, of course, the jewel in the proverbial crown, nestling at the heart of the Harrison name. Cheered immensely by these thoughts, John opened his eyes to find the dentist pulling down his mask.

'There we are. You can close now, Mr Harrison. Not too bad, I hope? I'd like to see you again in five days' time. The nurse will write out a new prescription. One more course should do it.'

During the process of paying for his treatment, John remembered that he hadn't yet sent his four children their annual cash gifts of seven hundred and fifty pounds, three thousand being the annual tax-free total that the Inland Revenue allowed. It wasn't much, and lately, with the recognition of his own advancing years, he had been considering ways of handing over more. While this was alarming in that the inevitable approach of death did not make pondering its implications any easier, he had discovered that being organised about such things was also rather consoling.

On the way out of the surgery John checked his appearance in the mirror, thoughtfully hung in the entrance hall, to see if his face looked as lopsided as it felt. It didn't, which was reassuring, although when he tried a smile only half of his lips moved, which was less good. It would be a couple of hours at least before he could decently manage even a cup of tea. As he got into his car he checked his watch. There was still time to join Pamela at the nursing-home, but he didn't really feel up to it. Instead he would go back and rummage in the attic on Eric's behalf, he decided, a chore he had been putting off for days, deterred by both the physical effort of sifting through dusty boxes and the fact that he had no clear notion of what he was supposed to be looking for. Any memorabilia to do with Eric, Pamela had said, to help the biographer flesh out the facts. It would kill an hour or so anyway, John reasoned, give his face a chance to thaw to the point where he could manage some lunch. A few minutes later he was lurching out of his parking space into what turned out to be a dangerously narrow break in the traffic. An approaching white van braked within a couple of feet of his rear bumper and hooted vigorously.

'And the same to you, mate,' John muttered, unnerved in spite of himself, and accelerated so hard that it was several hundred yards before he remembered to change gear.

Cassie lathered the shampoo into her scalp with extra care. It was a matter of some pride that the white-blonde waves of her hair had never required the boost of chemicals. They had the advantage, too, of camouflaging the few grey strands now sprouting along her parting, which she never dared pluck out for fear of the old adage about two twice as wiry growing in their place. Staring at her reflection in the bathroom mirror as she towelled herself dry, she tried to imagine her features as they appeared to her lover, wishing she could be as sure of her own beauty as he seemed to be. She would have given anything to have met Dan earlier – ideally before he had married, but also before the hint of old-lady wobble in her thighs and the permanent indentation of laugh-lines at the corners of her eyes and mouth.

His wife, Sally, was a couple of years younger than her but, Dan gallantly assured her, far less attractive. They had met as medical students and got married because, after a few years of going out, it seemed the obvious thing to do. They had both gone on to qualify, she as an anaesthetist, he as a GP, but she had given up working after the birth of their first child. Dan said that it was with the arrival of babies that things had started to go wrong; that as well as picking fights about everything Sally had got sucked into the vortex of domesticity and let herself go. In subsequent years things had deteriorated badly, sex in particular becoming a reflex action, a release of steam rather than an act of love.

Cassie adored hearing such things, although when Dan showed her photos of his family (at her own request: she had wanted to know everything about him and had felt a sort of love for his children because they were his), the sight of his wife triggered neither the sense of triumph nor the half-baked pity she had been expecting. In none of the pictures did Sally look as if she had let herself go. Casually dressed in jeans and T-shirts, her hair long and dark with a firm fringe, she had looked not only attractive but also entirely *normal*, so wholly integrated into the family scenes (buckets and lumpen sandcastles on beaches, barbecues with friends, toddlers clinging to her in fields and in front of famous monuments) that Cassie had experienced a surge of murderous resentment. How dare she, this attractive woman, so unappreciative, so selfish, so unloving, so nagging towards her dearest darling, hog the privilege of remaining at his side? It made her sick with anger. Dan was forty, his life was ticking by, he deserved some happiness. With her. Cassie gave her wet hair one last, vigorous rub and hung the towel in a tidy rectangle back on the rail. She was not, by nature, a tidy person, but these days made a special effort for Dan. His own house was, by all accounts, a tip, overflowing with piles of laundry and toys. Cassie wanted him to feel that her spacious two-bedroomed flat in Pimlico was a haven of comfort and orderliness.

Having emptied the bins, pummelled the sofa cushions and switched on the table lamps, she set to work in the kitchen, unpacking the thick, bloodied slabs of fillet steak she had bought from the butcher and re-reading the recipe for the *béarnaise* sauce she planned to serve alongside it. It was new to want to cook for a man. Normally she would have been pressing to go out to restaurants, interested in enjoying courtship over appetising plates of food without the bother of having to prepare them. Left to her own devices, she was quite happy with Polystyrene boxes and a microwave. But Dan had triggered in her an unprecedented desire to nurture: she wanted to rub his temples when he had a headache, to fold the clothes he left lying by her bed. If he had asked her to she would gladly have washed his socks and clipped his toenails (he had beautiful feet, unlike those of any other man she had met, with slender, perfectly aligned toes and soft uncalloused heels).

He arrived a little late, looking becomingly tousled and cheerful, clutching a small bunch of daffodils. 'My darling.' He crushed half of the flowers in his eagerness to hug her, burying his face in her hair. 'At last I've got you to myself.'

'You can have me whenever you want me,' Cassie murmured, loving the smell of his skin and the warm expression in his big brown eyes. They had been the first thing she had noticed about him all those months ago at the Ryle Street surgery, when she had been red-nosed with flu and he had burst out into the street after her, his sandy hair flopping across his forehead, waving the prescription she had left on the reception desk. Having rescued the flowers, she clipped their stems and began to arrange them in a vase, inwardly warning herself not to rush into difficult questions, to give him the chance to speak. With the flowers and the food and the pair of them standing so snugly in her little kitchen, it felt for a few glorious moments as if he was her husband, not someone else's, returned from a regular day at work for a quiet night in. Going with the flow of these thoughts, she asked, 'How's your day been, my darling?'

Dan pushed his sandy fringe off his eyebrows, his expression darkening. 'Fairly hellish. Roger called in sick so the rest of us had to cover his patient-list—' He broke off, not wanting to sour the evening with trivial complaints about the realities of his everyday life. Cassie was his oasis, his promise of sweeter, better things, and he wanted to make the most of every treasured second in her company. 'I'm here now, that's all that matters. You're all that matters to me, Cassie, I hope you know that. I hope you know that without you there would be no point to my life.' He came to stand behind her, slipping his arms under hers and pulling her to him. 'I've been so excited all day,' he whispered, 'just at the thought of seeing you . . . I could hardly concentrate. You don't know what you do to me, my sweetheart, you don't know what you do . . .'

Cassie dropped the daffodils and leant back against him, closing her eyes. I want this to go on for ever, she thought, this moment in all its perfection. He slid his hands up under her shirt and began stroking her stomach. 'Whatever you're cooking smells wonderful, but could it wait, do you think . . . for a little bit?' He nuzzled her ear with his nose. 'Or maybe for not such a little bit . . . maybe for quite a long time . . .'

'Oh, Dan, I've missed you so.' She turned to face him, finding herself almost nose to nose in her high heels. 'You – make – me – happy,' she added, planting kisses on his mouth between words.

He smiled. 'Well, that's a relief.' He peered over her shoulder at the array of half-prepared food. 'Fillet steak, eh?'

'And some really expensive wine – I got a cheque from my father this morning, seven hundred and fifty pounds . . . I thought I'd celebrate with you.' Her voice was dry and dazed. She didn't care a hoot about money or meals or wine. She wanted only to be held by him, to lose herself in him, to feel possessed by him. 'Dan, I love you. In a way I wish I didn't, but I do.'

'Hush.' He spoke fiercely, pressing his index finger to her lips. 'Never say that. Never say you wish you didn't love me. It breaks my heart.' He began kissing her again with new urgency, at the same time steering her out of the kitchen. Half walking, half staggering, clumsily like two animals locked together, they made their way into her bedroom, which she had Hoovered and dusted in preparation for his visit. The sheets on the bed, changed that morning, were as crisp as an envelope. On the bedside table, between her book and the radio alarm, she had lit a perfumed candle, which cast a warm soft light across the furnishings. The room was full of its sweet scent, of honey and roses.

'Don't move. I'm going to undress you.'

Cassie lay down on her back and watched as his fingers released the buttons of her shirt and his mouth brushed her stomach with kisses. He stared intently at her skin while he caressed it, as if seeing it for the first time. She closed her eyes, feeling the love flow like electricity from his lips and fingertips. 'Dan?'

'Yes?'

'Will you always love me?'

'Always.' He shifted his position so that he was lying on top of her, resting on his elbows so as not to crush her chest. 'And now I'm going to show you how much.' He began to kiss her again and Cassie responded feverishly, wishing she could feel as certain of the future as she did of the reassuring solidity of his body sliding over hers.

It wasn't until after they had made love that she felt one of the old familiar twists of desperation. With sex over, there was just the meal to eat and then he would be gone, back to his other life. The evening, which an hour before had stretched ahead as a prospect of endless joy, was disappearing, seeping through her fingers like water. 'When will you tell her, do you think?' she ventured, knowing he knew whom she meant, hating herself for pressing the question that hung between them as it always did.

Dan turned to her, his face tensing. 'I know it's hard for you, my darling, all this waiting. But it will come to an end soon, I promise. Her sister is coming to stay – we've got to get through that.' He placed his palms on either side of Cassie's head, steering her gaze to meet his. 'Please understand how it is . . . We're barely talking at the moment. I think she knows what's coming. I think, in fact, that she's reaching a point where she wants a way out as much as I do. It will be a relief for both of us. The time to tell her will come soon, I promise. I can't live without you, Cassie, you know that, don't you?'

'Yes.' She sighed, rolling away, loathing her own neediness and the pressure it placed upon him. It was always harder to disguise after they had made love, when her confidence ebbed out of her, when she could already feeling him pulling away from her, mentally preparing himself to leave. 'Shall we eat?'

'Yes, but I must shower first.'

'Okay.' She spoke brightly, even though she hated this part of the proceedings, the way he rushed to wash every trace of her away. Of course he had to. He was supposed to be out to dinner with a colleague from the practice. In a couple of hours he would be slipping into bed beside his wife. It was different for her, being alone. After his evening visits she never washed herself until the next morning, not even her face, so that she could curl up blanketed by the faint mingling smells of his aftershave and their lovemaking.

Before getting out of bed he ran one finger down her cheek, studying her with a tenderness that she knew meant he sensed her sadness and wanted to make up for it. He always knew what she was feeling. It was one of the many astonishing things about him. 'One day,' he whispered, 'one day, very, very soon now, you'll be mine. If your cooking's up to scratch, that is,' he teased, switching moods in an instant and giving her a gentle poke in the ribs. 'Which means there could be a lot at stake tonight, ha-ha.'

It wasn't a good joke, but Cassie laughed, and hurled a pillow at his retreating bare behind. He caught it deftly and tossed it back at her, then disappeared into her bathroom.

The ball bounced high off the front wall, just below the red line, then soared towards the back left-hand corner of the squash court. Peter, ready for this eventuality, turned and sprinted towards it, his trainers squeaking on the wooden floor. It was a difficult shot and one that, as he was so far in the lead already, he could have afforded to concede. Charlie, he could see out of the corner of his eye, was making no preparation to move, already half relaxing under the conviction that this one small triumph would be his.

Peter ran so fast that he careered into the back wall. He turned at the last minute, so that his left shoulder took most of the impact, and swiped at the ball, flicking his wrist to ensure that it travelled back in an almost straight line. Both men watched, only their heavy breathing breaking the silence as the ball kissed the corner of the main wall, then dropped like a stone to the floor.

'Shot!' exclaimed Charlie. He pulled up the hem of his shirt to wipe away the perspiration that was pouring off his face. 'Game, set and match, I believe. You bastard. Six years older and still fitter. I'll buy the first round.' He offered his brother his hand, which Peter took, feeling as he always did that Charlie's genuine good-humour about losing rather took the edge off the pleasure of winning. 'Are you playing a lot, these days?'

'Once every couple of weeks,' replied Peter, then added, with some pride, 'And I'm going regularly to a gym now, one of a chain of places near chambers.' He poked the bulge of his brother's stomach, protruding over the waist of his shorts, with the end of his squash racket. 'Looks like you do could with a bit more exercise, though.'

Charlie laughed, sufficiently used to and comfortable with his rotund frame to be unriled by the remark. 'You're just having a mid-life panic because you're almost fifty and bald as a coot,' he quipped, giving his brother's shining crown a fond pat as they left the court and headed back down the corridor to the changing rooms. They were at Peter's club, where they met every so often for a game of squash and a drink. 'Anyway,' he continued, a few minutes later, struggling with his socks because his feet were still damp from the shower, 'I get loads of exercise charging round the park after a football with Ed. He's bloody good for a twelve-year-old, you know,' he added, unashamed as always of the fatherly pride he took in all his children. 'He practises for hours. If he applied half as much commitment to his schoolwork we'd have a child genius on our hands. He's got entry exams to St George's in a few weeks and he's doing bugger-all. God, it's a pain being a parent sometimes, isn't it, all the nagging one has to do?'

'Yes, I suppose it is,' murmured Peter, thinking not of his own parenting, which had never involved nagging – least of all at Theo, who tackled any academic task with alacrity – but of Helen's recent bout of complaints about Chloë. She missed her son but spent every evening shouting at her daughter. It was baffling. 'Tell me, Charlie, would you send your lot away if you could afford it? I mean, looking down the track, you know, you probably *will* be able to afford it when . . . that is, when Mum and Dad kick the bucket.' There was a faint look of apology in his eyes, both for mentioning the unhappy inevitability of their parents' death and the undercurrent of a reference to the essentially unequal terms of their inheritance. In the same instant he recalled Helen's increasingly jittery attitude towards this prospect, and flushed with irritation. Even without Ashley House he was far wealthier than any of his siblings. To be so fortunate made it seem almost criminal to entertain doubts of any kind.

Charlie, however, whose genial nature had long since accommodated the inherent unfairness of the application of this primogeniture ruling for the long-term protection of their beloved family home, showed no corresponding flicker of concern. 'Send our lot to boarding-school? Christ, no. Serena would lynch me if I ever suggested it. Not having a proper job and so on like Helen she'd go mad without the children. She likes to pretend Tina was a mistake but between you and me I'm not at all sure that's true.'

Peter, now threading cufflinks into his shirt, looked up sharply, appalled at the notion of any wife, especially one as sweet-natured as his sister-in-law, being so devious. But Charlie was chuckling. 'Serena would have babies till the cows came home, given half a chance. She was just *made* for it. Now, what about that beer? We're celebrating, by the way, not just your usual mashing of me on the squash court, but the fact that I have somehow managed to get moved at work. No more bloody railways.'

'A new posting? That's great – you should have said. What have you got this time?'

'The Shipping Directorate – bit of a sideways move, but much more out of the public eye, thank God, and the new minister is decent too.' Charlie rubbed his hands, beaming. 'Now, what's it to be? A pint?'

'Of orange squash, please.'

'Have a beer, Peter, you arse.'

'Maybe later.'

'I've been very lucky, really,' Charlie went on, happy to talk of a matter that had, in fact, given him much private anguish. 'I mean, let's face it, I'm not always the most motivated creature, which one could get away with in the early days, but I tell you, being in the civil service now is quite a different show – management systems, downsizing, corporate plans, targets, public accountability. It's become a minefield. Putting myself forward for the job I half expected to be shown the door – join the long list of poor sods being assigned to "voluntary" redundancy.' He raised his fingers to indicate quotation marks and then took a long, slow swig of beer, gasping with exaggerrated satisfaction afterwards. 'So, all in all, I'm rather pleased.'

'I should think you are. Congratulations.' Peter raised his glass, delighted at this latest evidence of his unashamedly unambitious brother's knack for landing on his feet.

'So, how are your lot anyway? Christmas seems an age away.'

'Doesn't it just? My lot are good, thanks,' Peter continued quickly, never having been one for outpourings – to siblings or anyone else – on the ripples in his domestic life. 'And yours?'

'Great. Tina's really started to talk in the last couple of weeks, which is keeping us all very entertained. She pointed at our neighbour the other day apparently and shouted, "Fart." Serena said she nearly died of embarrassment. Ed's not working, as I mentioned, except on his football and computer games – he's bloody good at those, leaves me standing. And the girls, well . . . no doubt you saw how they were at Christmas. Both right little madams. Just you wait till Chloë gets to that age. Christ, they grow up quickly, though Maisie's streets ahead of Clem – which is funny, I suppose, given that they're twins, but I think siblings take on different roles, don't they? Like us lot. You and Cassie were the good ones, while Lizzy and I battled away in a rather more unorthodox fashion. Poor old Lizzy, she seems so miserable all the time and I don't know what any of us can do about it.'

'Is Elizabeth miserable?' Peter was genuinely surprised.

'Well, Serena reckons she is and Serena's usually right about these things. And Colin is a dull old stick, isn't he? And they're both bloody hopeless with Roland, treating the poor kid like some kind of breakable ornament.'

'I've always thought Colin is just what Lizzy needs,' said Peter stoutly, prompted by a dim sense that he, too, was something of a dry old stick and that the breed in general should be defended. 'Someone solid and dependable after . . .' he hesitated, struggling to recall the Christian name of his sister's first husband '. . . Lucien.' They groaned in unison. 'There was an idle sod, if ever I saw one.'

'Oh, I don't know . . .' Charlie caught the eye of the barman and pointed at his empty pint glass. 'I think he was genuinely mad about Lizzy, but just so hopeless at organising himself – all that puff about being a freelance journalist and never writing any articles. It was really quite sad if you think about it. Mind you, I saw his name at the bottom of something in a magazine a couple of years ago, so I suppose he did go on to get some work in the end. Another pint . . . of *orange squash*?'

'No, I've got to go. Sorry, Charlie, I really have. I promised Helen I'd be back by nine.'

'Well, call her, for God's sake. Or I will.' Charlie patted his pockets in search of his mobile phone. 'Christ, it's not often we get together. She's probably pleased to have a night on her tod. I know Serena is. She told me so, several times. She's sprawled on the sofa watching some tear-jerker with a girlfriend and a bottle of wine. Come on, Peter, relax for once. Have a half of something decent and tell me what you're working on.'

'Quite an interesting case, actually,' Peter admitted, tempted suddenly at the thought of forgetting the demands of his waistline and his wife for a little longer. He loved talking about his work and Charlie was a good listener. 'Eighteen-year-old rape victim. No witnesses of course. Strange girl too – very mature, very . . . *in control*, which, of course, cuts both ways with a jury. Far easier to sympathise with a *victim* than someone holding their own. My opposite number is very able too, quite capable of putting her through it.'

'Poor girl. Mind you, do you think she's telling the truth?'

Peter's eyes twinkled for the first time. 'Ah, the million-dollar question. Which, as you well know, Charles, is irrelevant. My job is to present the best case for my client that I can. Having said that, the great thing about the British adversarial system, for all its faults, is that it is a very good way of exposing flaws in the truth. No advocate, however good, can win – or lose – a case that is full of holes. Cross-examining does not mean examining crossly . . .' And he was off, fuelled by promptings from his sibling, whose questions were both intelligent and based on genuine interest. The second beer disappeared fast, as did the third and the one after that, which they consumed together with two rounds of beef and horseradish sandwiches and several packets of cheese and onion crisps.

'Maisie? Maisie . . . are you awake?'

'Uh . . . uh . . .'

'It's me.'

'Oh, Clemmy, I'm so tired.'

Clem stood by the bed watching helplessly as her sister rolled over towards the wall, hugging a bulging portion of her duvet to her chest.

'Mum's awake,' Maisie muttered, 'I heard her with Tina . . . you could go and speak to her.' She made a few small sucking sounds with her lips, as if tasting something very delicious. Clem waited for a few more moments, shivering with cold (the heating tank, which – for some unfathomable and infuriating reason – lived behind the disguise of a cupboard in her bedroom, had clicked off with its usual burps and hiccups a good hour before), then padded back to bed and groped for her torch and diary. Once upon a time when she had shared a room with her sister, they had spent half the night on each other's beds, talking about nothing in particular, plaiting each other's hair and – during one particularly dangerous phase – playing with matches and candlewax. Their father had caught them one night, with three lit candles balanced across the bed and the pile of waxen figures they had moulded spread around them on the counterpane. It was one of the few occasions Clem had seen him truly cross. He had shouted so loudly that both Ed and her mother had come running up the stairs. The candles were snuffed out and hurled into the wastebin, along with all the waxen figures, which had made Clem sad because there had been one of a giraffe of which she had been particularly proud.

Now, alone in her bed with only the feeble beam of the torch and her own handwriting for company, it occurred to Clem that life at ten years old had been blissfully simple. There had been Right and Wrong, Happiness and Misery, all connected to obvious things, like being told off or not getting her own way. Now her moods swung at her from nowhere, invisible hammer blows, bludgeoning her without warning into unmanageable and complicated states of mind. Like Christmas, when she had been so not in the mood and then suddenly so happy. Or like Jonny Cottrall, whom she had barely thought about during the entire Christmas holidays, but whose lanky frame, spotted from any distance, still made her knees buckle and her blood pound.

And then there was food. Once hunger had been an easy thing. Now if she ate too much she felt bloated and guilty. Clem sighed, resting her open diary on the mound of her stomach, seeking consolation from the words she had written earlier that evening. Regular writing definitely cleared the mind, she had discovered, even if one put two conflicting statements down side by side, as she had about Jonny Cottrall: 'The thought of him putting his tongue in my mouth makes me feel sick. *But* the thought of him doing it to someone else makes me feel even worse.' Clem read these two sentences several times before starting to write again, frowning because the torch was very small and now seriously low on battery power:

> He thinks he's so cool it's PATHETIC. But I don't want him to think I'm a complete minger either. Have decided to lose weight – *properly* this time. Ate salad and four fruit pastilles (Penny gave them to me – she's being REALLY nice at the moment) for lunch, one biscuit after school and only a tiny bit of mash with sausages at tea. Ed and Maisie had three biscuits each and seconds of everything. It makes me sick how they can eat anything they like and stay like stick insects. Dad says I'm like him and not to worry, which is very sweet but also sad as Dad is FAT!! Mum says I'll lose weight when I grow, but I haven't grown for ages. My boobs are already a 34B whereas Maisie has got practically nothing at all. She only wears a bra because she thinks it's womany. Or something. I don't understand Maisie any more, she's always off with Monica and that gang, making it quite clear they don't want me. I've got Penny at the moment so I don't care, but it's still not nice KNOWING you're not wanted. Got all worried about it tonight and tried to talk to Maisie but she pretended to be asleep. At least, I think she was pretending. Though I guess it is nearly midnight and she's always whacked after a netball match . . . I'm beginning to write boring pointless stuff so I'll sign off. French vocab test tomorrow and I haven't looked at it. Oh, F—
> PS (**** = Period. Came today. How I hate it!)

Checking on his sleeping children, Charlie, primed with beer and sentimentality, hovered over each one, stroking wisps of hair from their faces and, in his son's case, tugging a heavy football annual out from under his arm. A few minutes later feeling sentiment of a rather different kind, he rolled over in bed and slipped his arms round his wife.

'You smell of beer and . . .' Serena sniffed the air over her shoulder where he was resting his head '. . . something else . . . Onions, I think. Yuk. Did you have a lovely time?'

'Hmm, lovely, but not so lovely as now.'

'You can put any wicked thoughts from your mind right now, Charles Harrison. I've told you, you smell like a pub and I've had so much wine I can feel a headache coming already.'

She had spoken sternly, but did not remove Charlie's arms from round her waist, so he knew there was hope. 'You smell yummy.' He nestled his head more deeply into the warm cosy space between her head and shoulder.

'No, I don't. Tina puked up on me half an hour ago. Some of it got stuck in my hair and I don't think I got it all out. I think she's going down with something . . . or teething . . . It was hours before she stopped crying. How was Peter?'

'Peter-like.' He turned his head and licked her ear, very gently, just along the lobe where he knew the balance between tickling and pleasure was most finely poised. 'We put the world to rights.'

'Well done you. Are you going to let me go to sleep now?'

'I don't think so.' He rolled her over and raised himself on one elbow to look at her, even though it was dark and all he could make out was the pale outline of her face. 'I got the transfer. Instead of railways I'm going to look after ships.'

'Oh, Charlie – oh, darling! You bastard not telling me sooner! Oh, I knew you'd get it, I just knew. All that stuff about being made redundant . . .' She snorted. 'Of course those ship people can't do without you – I certainly can't.' She was prevented from continuing by her husband's mouth pressing firmly against hers. 'Show me, then,' he whispered, pulling back, his breath all beer and onions, 'show me that you can't do without me, oh wife of mine, whom I love more than I can say. Whose beauty shines like a rich jewel in an Ethiop's ear.'

'Shakespeare, eh? Now I know you're pissed.' Serena laughed softly, pulling him on top of her. 'Love is . . . not minding a drunken sot for a husband,' she teased.

'Love is . . . what Charles Ashley Harrison feels for Serena,' he whispered, pressing himself more firmly against the soft curves of her body. They made love slowly, moving with a grace born of intimate familiarity, with each sensation as shared and known as the steps of a private dance.

It was only as she turned over to go to sleep, gently removing Charlie's arm, which was heavy, from across her chest that Serena remembered she had some other news. 'Charlie, darling . . .' He was lying on his side with one arm curled round his head, as if to ward off any unexpected assaults during the course of the night. He had been snoring faintly, which he always did after drinking. He stopped the moment Serena tapped him but did not wake up. Serena raised her arm to shake him more forcefully, then didn't have the heart. The news, which was that his aunt Alicia had fallen and broken a hip, could wait until morning. Pamela had said that her sister-in-law was shaken but being well looked after in a local cottage hospital. There was nothing any of them could do and her poor darling deserved a good night's sleep, Serena concluded, tracing one fingertip very gently down the little furrows next to his ear. Although he'd hidden his worry from her – and from the rest of the world – she knew he had been fretting badly about the job move. As had she. That her husband was so unambitious – that he worked purely to earn a living – was one of the many things Serena loved about him. He was never happier than when he'd managed to wangle a morning off or skip home early to help with homework and bathtime. But at the same time she had the sense to recognise that this attitude would hardly receive comparable appreciation from his employers. He had been miserable in the stressful environment of the Railway Directorate and made little secret of it. That such a visible lack of enthusiasm might result in unemployment was a possibility that Charlie himself had entertained so volubly that Serena, a profound and natural optimist, had begun to believe it herself. She had seen the spouses of several friends going through the redundancy mill and knew it was something to fear at any age, not just for the obvious havoc of financial worries but for the beating it gave even the sturdiest self-esteem. After six months of fruitless job-hunting one father at Ed's school had tried to kill himself. 'So, thank you, God,' Serena murmured now, though her religious convictions were hazy at the best of times, 'thank you indeed.' She planted a last tender kiss on Charlie's forehead and then turned over to go to sleep, sliding back to her side of the bed where the sheets were fresh and cool.

Helen was sitting up in bed, holding her book – like a shield, Peter could not help thinking. Her glasses, which had small brown rectangular frames, had slipped to the end of her nose, emphasising both its pointiness and all the other sharp angles of her face. She couldn't have looked more angry if she had had huge stickers saying ANGRY plastered all over her.

'Sorry, darling, I know I'm late.'

'It doesn't matter.' She turned a page, briskly, as if seeking something specific among the paragraphs.

'I did call.'

'Yes, you did. You said you'd be another hour. That was . . .' Helen lifted her wrist, peering at the dial of her watch over the rim of her spectacles '. . . by my reckoning, well over two hours ago. Two hours and forty minutes to be precise.'

'Charlie sends his love,' Peter ventured, in a bid to steer the conversation back into warmer waters.

'Does he?' She turned another page, although she couldn't possibly have read enough to warrant it.

'He's come through a redundancy scare – got a new post in shipping.'

'Jolly good.'

'Look, Helen, is this really necessary?' Peter, sobered by her hostility, could not keep the edge out of his voice. He had apologised, hadn't he? If she'd had a bad day it was hardly his fault.

'Is what necessary, Peter?'

'This? You. How you're being.'

Helen closed her book and folded her arms. 'It might interest you to know that your aunt had a serious fall today. She has fractured her hip and is in hospital.' There was a tinge of triumph in her tone. She had been saving this information, waiting, like a warrior poised with a missile, for the right – the most effective – moment to deliver it. 'Your mother phoned to tell me. She sounded upset.' In fact, Pamela had been matter-of-fact, relaying the news in the same just-to-keep-all-members-of-the-family-informed tone with which she had mentioned, at greater length, the impending visit of Eric's biographer.

'Well, I'm sorry to hear that, obviously.' Peter lifted the lid of the laundry basket and dropped in his socks and underpants. 'Poor old Alicia, that's too bad. I'll call Mum about it tomorrow.' He looked round the bedroom, a part of him dimly seeking inspiration from its chic furnishings and handsome proportions. They had decorated their home, a large detached Georgian house in one of Barnes's quietest and most salubrious roads, with the help of Cassie. Designers Guild fabrics, silk weave carpets, mahogany furniture, fine prints on the walls – thanks to two successful careers and clever investments, no expense had been spared. Even five years on from seeing the project through, Peter still experienced a swell of satisfaction every time he put the key into the door and felt the polished parquet beneath his feet. Their bedroom, which had four sets of double windows overlooking the garden, was particularly lovely, with shimmering green velvet curtains, Wedgwood wall-paper and a marbled *en-suite* bathroom big enough to host a small party.

It was in there now that Peter sought refuge, running the taps harder than was strictly necessary while he battled with the un-characteristic urge to be unpleasant to his wife. In the twenty years of their marriage there had been little unpleasantness. He had been drawn as much to Helen's fine brain as her fine figure and both had proved constant. She was a respected partner in a firm of corporate lawyers and worked pretty hard. Unlike dear Serena, who openly declared herself both ignorant and uninterested in the intricacies of Charlie's daily toil as a civil servant, Helen was always happy to talk shop or act as a sounding-board if he needed to thrash out his thoughts on a difficult case. She was also a good mother, far more on top of all the school events than he was and much better at getting home in time to relieve Rika, their Turkish au pair. That she was so organised and efficient – so *together* – had always made Peter proud. He returned to the bedroom in his pyjamas, determined to put things right.

'Look, darling, you've obviously had a hateful evening, what with the Alicia business – and Chloë, no doubt up to her usual tricks . . .'

'She hid.'

'What?'

'Chloë. For hours. She hid for hours. She said it was a game, but it wasn't.' Helen put her hands to her face and, much to her husband's amazement (and a little to his horror), was crying.

'Helen, darling, she's seven years old. Of course it was a game.'

Helen shook her head fiercely, tears pouring down her cheeks. 'She meant to hurt me, I could feel it. I called and called and she wouldn't come out. She meant to hurt me.'

'Nonsense, Helen. Stop it this minute, you're getting yourself into a state about nothing.' Peter clambered on to the bed and pulled her a little clumsily into his arms. He wasn't good with tears. They made him feel gormless. 'Come on, Helen, this isn't like you. Stop . . . please stop now. You're being silly.' He chose the word deliberately, wanting to prick the drama from the moment. And it seemed to work, because the crying subsided at once. 'There, that's better. Maybe a sleeping tablet tonight, eh?' He squeezed her shoulders and tapped the point of her nose with his finger. 'Silly Helen.'

'Do you love me, Peter?'

'What is this? Of course I love you.'

'I'm forty-seven. I'm getting all withered and scrawny. You'll fall in love with someone else soon, some lovely young girl with energy and big breasts.'

'Helen, what the hell has got into you? First Chloë and now this – you're being *ridiculous*.'

'I know,' she moaned, sobbing again, 'I know. Ignore me.'

'Here.' He handed her a large clean white handkerchief from his suit pocket and watched as she blew her nose and mopped her face. Then he fetched a sleeping pill and a glass of water and stood over her, like a concerned doctor, as she swallowed it. 'A good night's sleep and you'll feel quite different.'

'She wants a dog.'

'I beg your pardon?'

'Chloë. She says she'll do her piano practice properly if we get her a dog.'

'How you can even listen to such nonsense?' Peter threw up his arms, bringing them down with a hard slap against his pyjamas. 'Look, Helen,' he continued, more gently, doing his best to sound reasonable rather than exasperated, 'for one thing that's blackmail, and I will not be blackmailed by my own daughter. For another, all children go through a phase of wanting a dog – it's like girls and ponies, it passes. Believe me, I know, I had two sisters who went through the lot.'

'I didn't,' muttered Helen. She was feeling sleepy now but fighting it. 'I always wanted a dog but wasn't allowed one.'

'Because your parents were very sensible.' He pulled back the duvet, then tugged at the bottom sheet to make it smooth, as he always did, before getting into bed. 'There are several very cogent reasons why it would be pure insanity to get a dog. First, in terms of commitment it would be like having a third child, and – correct me if I'm wrong – I'd say you have quite enough on your plate as it is. Second, Chloë is behaving like a spoilt brat, and third, having animals only really works in the country. Tell her we'll get one when we live at Ashley House. That might shut her up.' Pleased with this last thought, Peter switched off his bedside light and rolled on to his left side to go to sleep, a feat he usually managed in a matter of seconds, but which took a little longer on this occasion because of the bruising on his shoulder from his careering volley on the squash court. In spite of her tablet Helen, too, lay awake for some time, her head spinning with images of dogs, Ashley House and her daughter's hot, angry face located at last in the corner of the dining-room windowsill behind the curtains.

Stephen Smith walked quickly out of Barham station and turned left down the high street as the man sweeping the empty platform had instructed. On hearing that he was headed for Ashley House the man had added that it was a good two miles and if he looked on the wall in the phone-box he'd find a number for a local taxi service. He liked walking, Stephen explained, which was true, although perhaps less significant than the fact that penurious would-be writers had to think twice before resorting to such luxuries. Barham itself comprised two antiques shops, a tea-house, a post-office-cum-newsagent and pub called the Rising Sun. After that the pavement petered out and Stephen found himself picking his way along a narrow grass verge, trying to avoid the muddiest bits for the sake of his shoes. Whenever the road was clear he skipped on to the Tarmac, pressing his hands into his pockets for warmth. In the rush of leaving his little flat in Hackney and squashing on to the tube to get to Victoria it hadn't occurred to him that he would be cold. His jacket, chosen in preference to his tatty Oxfam trench-coat, felt thin and inadequate against the cut of the wind. It had seemed important to look smart. Of all his potential interviewees the Harrisons sounded by far the grandest (Pamela's reply had come on parchment-like writing-paper, with the address embossed in thick lettering across the top, while her voice on the telephone had positively purred with confident refinement), so he was more than usually anxious to create a good impression. Most of all, he hoped, via a decent black wool jacket and a silk tie (blue and green specks), to appear like someone who knew what he was doing, instead of someone stumbling to realise a project for which he was fast running out of money (his princely advance of ten thousand pounds was dissolving at terrifying speed) and the confidence to see it through.

After the bustle of a Friday morning in London the quiet of the countryside was a shock. The sun, though still wintry and distant, had burned through a bank of heavy grey cloud and was bestowing a sumptuous sheen across the muted January browns and greens of the landscape. Even the cows, casting lazy glances as he passed by, looked glossy and well groomed, as if they knew they were in the five-star luxury version of the global options on offer to their kind. As he blinked the wind-blur from his eyes, Stephen felt at once deeply separate from yet hugely drawn to these surroundings. He had only a passing acquaintance with the Home Counties; the first eighteen years of his life had been spent in a shabby terraced house on the outskirts of Hull, after which he had got a place at Leeds University to study history, then thrown it in to do a TEFL course and escape abroad. A job at a language school in Madrid had been followed by the chance to work in South America, where he supplemented his mediocre teacher's salary by writing articles for travel guides. Largely comprising updates on prices and bus timetables, it had been tedious and only whetted his appetite to write seriously about something quite different. A chance encounter with an editor on a travelling sabbatical (one of those rare, instantly strong connections with a stranger that only ever seem to happen abroad) had led, circuitously, to the commissioning of the book he was now researching. With a private passion for the history of both world wars, Stephen had dared to imagine it would be easy. As he discussed his ideas with his new friend and a cold beer on the stony coast of Chiloé in southern Chile, the chapters had felt as good as written. When the cheque for his advance dropped on to the doormat in Hackney a few months after his return, Stephen had almost wept with joy, sure that, at the ripe old age of thirty-two, his life had taken the turn he had been seeking.

Compared with the rolling horizons and arid scrub of Venezuela and Ecuador – still vivid in Stephen's mind – the English country-side was as cosy and welcoming as a well-stocked garden. Each field, forest and garden, stitched into asymmetric but solid shapes by stout fences, hedges and winding lanes, looked as integral as the squares on a counterpane, part of some civilised, thoughtfully ordered pattern. Next to the station there had been a row of stocky stone cottages with tidy front gardens and brightly painted front doors. Beyond them, scattered between the shops and the pub, were several larger houses with thatched roofs and fenced lawns. As Stephen progressed along the road out of the village, though, the homes he glimpsed behind yew hedges and five-barred gates, grew fewer and further between, until he hit a forested stretch where there were no houses and the trees arched at such a height that the sky was almost obscured from view. Deprived of the sun, the chill in the air struck with fresh force, needling its way up his cuffs and behind his collar. A bird bursting out of a mesh of grey trunks on his left made him jump. He fumbled for the solid edge of the notebook in his pocket, gripped it hard, and willed away the sense – always vaguely present – of alienation. He would write the book, he told himself, he would make it happen, make it real. The editor who had organised the commission had faith in him. It was a question of self-belief, of having the courage, perhaps for the first time in his life, to see something through to the end.

It was a relief to emerge from under the vaulted roof of the forest and feel the pale sun again on his face. As he passed a small church with a square spire, he peered over its surrounding wall at the rows of tidy gravestones, trying to make out the name 'Harrison' and thinking how reassuring it would be to know that one's final resting-place was among friends and neighbours in such a green and quiet corner of the world.

'Your young man's here and he looks cold.' Pamela's friend Dorothy, over from America where she lived comfortably in a Miami condominium, craned her neck through the hall window for a better view of the drive. She had only just got in, having spent the previous forty minutes striding round the grounds in trainers and tracksuit (at seventy-two she had given up trying to break into a proper jog) in a bid to work off some of her old friend's fabulous cooking. She always ate shamelessly on her visits to Ashley House, her appetite sharpened by the moist country air and a break from the tyranny of cholesterol and calorie-counting. (Her body retained fat easily, her doctor said, and if she wanted a long life she had to look out for it.) 'He looks young, too. How old did you say he was?'

'I didn't,' murmured Pamela, joining her at the hall window. 'Heavens, he must have walked from the station. I should have offered to meet him – I didn't think.'

'He didn't say he wanted meeting, did he?' said John, appearing down the stairs behind them, a large, sagging cardboard box in his arms. 'So there's nothing to feel bad about, is there? Where shall I put this lot?'

'In the drawing room, I should think. Was that all you could find?'

John was tempted to make a sharp retort. Wading through the attic with toothache earlier in the week had not been fun. It had taken some time to gather together his brother's memorabilia and the dust had made his throat sore. And the morning had not gone well: he had cut himself shaving, so badly that he had had to keep two blobs of tissue paper stuck to his chin right through breakfast. Dorothy, with her usual American tact, had kept remarking on it, offering to dab his wounds with TCP, then volunteering the cheery information that during the latter stages of her husband's life (Walter had died of Parkinson's some ten years before) she had had to do all his shaving for him. Then she had commandeered the main section of *The Times* and – between comments on the state of his face – had read aloud whole paragraphs. John always forgot, until the moment she burst across the threshold, how trying he found the visits of his wife's oldest friend. He hated people who read bits of newspapers out loud. He hated people who talked at breakfast. Pamela, sailing round the table with fresh coffee and toast, had appeared oblivious to it all. Although he knew she wasn't: after five decades together it was impossible to be oblivious to such things. Which meant she was ignoring it. Which was even more irksome. 'Well, if you'd like to look for yourself, darling . . .'

'Oh, no, darling, you've done very well, I'm sure.' Pamela flapped her hands at him, dismissing him, just as the doorbell rang.

'Mr Smith, come in, please come in.'

Stephen, his hand still on the wrought-iron handle of the bell-pull, which was half obscured in the ivy next to the door, jumped back in surprise. Having been cold on his walk he now felt the sweat of discomfort breaking out across his back. 'I'm sorry if I'm a little late . . .'

'You're not, you're just right,' Pamela assured him, seeing at once that he was unsure and in need of soothing. 'This is Dorothy, who is staying with us. And this is my husband John, Eric's younger brother, of course.'

John had emerged from the drawing room and reached between the women to shake the young man's hand, thinking as he did so that the chap didn't look capable of writing a comic strip let alone a serious book and that all the attic-rummaging had almost certainly been for nothing.

'Such a wonderful idea . . . We're so thrilled, aren't we, John?'

'How many others are you doing? I mean, how many unsung heroes are there in the world?' John rubbed his palms together as he spoke, relishing the notion of putting the biographer on the spot.

'I'm sure there are millions, but I plan to write about ten. A chapter on each. Though it's still quite early days – a lot of it depends on the research.'

'Of course it does,' interjected Pamela, 'and we'd like to help in every way we can. Now, how about coffee? Or tea, perhaps? Do come this way, Mr Smith. And I apologise in advance for any mess. You take us very much as you find us, I'm afraid.' The comment, as Pamela well knew, was unnecessary. The house, with the help of Dorothy, who liked dusting, and Betty Seymour, who came in from the village three afternoons a week, looked perfectly presentable.

Stephen walked slowly down the main hallway behind his hosts, his eyes wide. He had never been in a house that was at once so large and so comfortable-looking: at every turn there were beautiful pieces of furniture – dark wood bookcases, corner cabinets, chests and elegant chairs – all looking valuable but also much-used. *En route* to the kitchen he peered through the open doorways, glimpsing the vast oak fireplace in the drawing room, the grand piano in the music room, the widescreen TV in the room next door and the impressive line of windows running along the arched veranda outside. The furnishings were all huge – the sofa was twice the size of his bed and each curtain a waterfall of velvet – but the colours were welcoming country greens and rusty reds, sufficiently faded in appearance to indicate that they had been in position for some time.

'Did you say tea or coffee?'

'I . . . Coffee, please . . . I . . . Could I just say this is the most lovely house?'

'Thank you. How sweet of you.' Pamela beamed at him, noting with pleasure that some of his initial stiffness was wearing off. He had an interesting voice, soft and low with a hint of something northern. 'It's been in my husband's family for three generations. We are all very fond of it.'

'I'll say.' Dorothy was torn between taking herself off for a bath and staying downstairs for coffee. That Pamela was clearly flirting with her young visitor made it no easier to decide. Making people feel good about themselves – which was what flirting amounted to at their ripe old age – was one of Pamela's supreme skills and Dorothy knew she hadn't a hope of competing. On the other hand she wasn't going to hang around the kitchen feeling left out. 'I come here every year – best hotel in town.'

'Really? That must be very nice.'

'Oh, believe me, it is. The Harrisons *really* know how to make a girl feel at home. Pamela and I have been friends for – what is it now, Pam? Forty . . . Oh, my God, fifty years. We met on a secretarial course in Kensington. My parents sent me over to Europe to be *finished*, as people did in those days, but then I met my husband and – but, hey, I shouldn't go on like this. You guys have lots you need to talk about and I must freshen up. I'll catch you later.' She took her coffee and left the kitchen, tugging her tracksuit top down over her hips to hide the sag in her backside.

'So, how did you get on to our dear Eric?' asked Pamela a few minutes later, when they were seated on the sofa in the drawing room, the box John had brought down from the attic on the coffee table in front of them. 'We would so love to know, wouldn't we, darling?'

'We would indeed,' agreed John, whose mood had sweetened with the lighting of his pipe and the assumption of a satisfactorily separate yet dominant position in one of the armchairs on the other side of the table. He puffed gently, enjoying now a surge of excitement on his brother's behalf. There was something indisputably timeless and permanent about a book; a chapter on Eric would be a marvellous record for posterity – a toehold on the future for every member of the Harrison clan.

'I've always been fascinated by the world wars,' began Stephen, 'particularly the second – been a bit of a pet hobby for years. First I loved the poetry – Siegfried Sassoon, Wilfrid Owen, Keith Douglas, and so on – and then I got to studying the battles and, well, it just escalated from there.' He talked fast, aware that his hosts were weighing him up, assessing his credentials not just for the literary task he had set himself but as a human being. What he was asking of them was essentially very personal; he realised that now, although he hadn't at the beginning. One little old lady in Slough had wept openly as she showed him sepia photographs of her husband as a young soldier, even though it was fifteen years since he had died and a good fifty since she had kept vigil for his safe return from the front. 'I mean, names get thrown up and so few actually make it into the obituary columns and when they do they are always fascinating . . .'

'Are they all alive, the men you have chosen?'

'No, not all, Mr Harrison. In fact . . .' Stephen frowned, embarrassed by the knowledge that Eric Harrison's hold on life was fragile '. . . just three.'

'You won't get much out of Eric, these days, I'm afraid.' John picked at a loose stitch on the cover of his chair.

'Mr Smith—' began Pamela.

'Call me Stephen, please.'

'Stephen . . . I did explain that, didn't I?'

'Yes, you did. I would be honoured to meet Eric, of course, but it would be for my own gratification rather than the needs of the book.' His shy smile illuminated his pale uncertain face so beautifully that Pam decided he must at all costs be persuaded to stay for lunch.

'So, how can we help?'

Stephen reached into his pocket for his notebook. He knew quite a lot about Eric Harrison already and was happy to show it. 'In terms of his war exploits I'm really just looking for verification . . .' He flicked through several pages of notes. 'Commissioned in 1939,

Fourth Regiment Royal Horse Artillery in the Middle East and Europe, lots of action during the withdrawal through Belgium to Dunkirk, where there was all that dreadful business of the guns being destroyed by our own gunners and where he got his first medal. Then he was in the thick of it in the Western Desert from El Alamein in 1942 till the fall of Tunis the following May. After that he took part in the Salerno landings and that torturous advance with the US Fifth Army to the crossing of the Volturno before the advance along the Italian coast towards Mount Massico. His regiment was then withdrawn to England along with the rest of the Seventh Armoured Division. They fought from the Normandy beachhead, through Belgium and Holland to beyond the Rhine. Eric commanded a battery for the final months of the war and was awarded the George Cross.'

'Well, you've certainly done your homework,' said John, his voice thick with admiration and pride.

'What I'm looking for from you, I suppose,' continued Stephen, his face flushed with enthusiasm and one of those spurts of self-belief that kept him going, 'is help with the flesh on the bones, so to speak, the family angle, what he was like as a man, as a brother.'

'Mad as a hatter.' John laughed.

'Very shy,' said Pamela.

'No, he wasn't,' her husband corrected her, only to falter with the realisation that he had used the past tense. 'He's just bloody-minded. Fought his war and then – well, this is my theory anyway – couldn't quite get the hang of real life again. It was all so daring and glorious that he didn't want to give it up. He handed this place over to me, you know, lock, stock and barrel, didn't take so much as a carriage clock, and went off to become a mercenary instead – fought in all sorts of dreadful places, wouldn't tell us the half of what he was up to. Then in his forties he packed it all in, bought a boat and made it his business to sail round the world. Oh, and mountain climbing. He took that up too. A real daredevil, was my brother, although you wouldn't know it now to look at him.'

'More coffee?' asked Pamela.

'No, thanks.'

'But you will stay to lunch, won't you? It's almost twelve o'clock and we've barely started. It's only a shepherd's pie, but quite big enough. Don't shake your head at me, Mr Smith, I've quite made up my mind. You carry on talking to John now and if you need me I'll be in the kitchen. I think we might have a glass of wine, don't you, dear, seeing as Mr Smith – I mean, Stephen – has come all this way? And I'll look out some more photographs for you later on – we've got some lovely ones in albums that aren't all covered in dust. Do you like sprouts, Stephen? They are fresh from our vegetable garden, but not everybody's favourite thing.'

'I love sprouts.' Which happened to be true, although Stephen would have said it anyway. He could think of nothing pleasanter than prolonging his visit until the afternoon, with these welcoming people, the blaze of the log fire and the grey sheets of rain now streaming on to the garden, which was framed like a sequence of huge snapshots through the stone arches of the veranda outside. He turned to look at an array of silver-framed photographs on a low table behind him: group shots and portraits of smiling faces, all with echoing resemblances of each other.

'That's our lot,' said John proudly. 'Seven grandchildren we've got now.'

'Wonderful,' murmured Stephen, his gaze drawn to one black-and-white photo-portrait in particular, of a girl with fine features and wavy fair hair blowing across her mouth and cheeks.

'That's Cassie, our youngest. Next to her is Elizabeth, and behind that our two sons. The one who looks most like me is Peter – he's a barrister – and the other is Charlie, who's in the civil service. Do you have a big family, Mr Smith?'

Stephen shook his head. 'One sister. She lives in New Zealand. My parents are in Hull. We've rather lost touch.'

'That's a shame.'

'I've lived abroad a lot, you see.'

'Ah, yes. Like Eric. All we ever got over the years was a flying visit now and then. Nice to have a base, though, somewhere to return to.'

Stephen shook his notebook to a clean page, wondering what it would be like to have a base other than a flat in Hackney, or a family home to which one wished to return, even for flying visits. 'What I would really like to know, Mr Harrison, if you can cast your mind back, is what view Eric gave *you* of the war, how he was on home leave, what his letters were like . . .'

Cassie drove fast, relishing the heave in the pit of her stomach as the car flew over the undulations in the road, which was narrow but straight and clear. It was easily her favourite bit of the journey, when the countryside really opened up and began to feel familiar. Flicking at random between radio channels, she had found a string of her favourite songs and had sung along to them. It was that kind of day. A good day. A lucky day. A day of love and hope, as so many were now because of Dan. He had phoned early in the morning to say he was unexpectedly free and had booked a hotel in Brighton. A seedy tryst, he had joked, for their secret love. But it hadn't felt seedy. They had walked along the pier holding hands in full view of the world, sharing a stick of candyfloss, licking round the edges until their tongues met. When the rain came they had raced into the hotel, still holding hands, standing at Reception and going up in the lift, as if they were any ordinary couple celebrating a birthday or anniversary. And it had felt so natural, so beautifully *ordinary* that Cassie had enjoyed it almost more than the ripping off of clothes that had ensued once the door was closed. Although the sex had been unbelievable too.

Slowing now to take a sharp bend in the road, Cassie felt a shudder of recollected pleasure. Dan was the most dedicated and expert of lovers. During the ten months they had been together he had worked almost methodically at getting to know her body, so that he could gauge exactly how far advanced she was along the spectrum of arousal and time his own climax accordingly. And on this occasion, instead of rushing to the shower afterwards, he had kept his arms round her, moaning into her hair that he could not live without her, that he would like them, one day, to have a child. Cassie, recalling the moment, felt again the leap in her heart. Her usual post-coital desperation had vanished in an instant. His child.

Daniel Lambert's child. The idea must have been there, of course,
floating in her subconscious, but it was only when he had said it out
loud – given it the reality of articulation – that the notion had taken
shape as something concrete and desirable. Out of their love they
would make a baby. Of course they would. The future, usually so
ungraspable, seemed suddenly secure. Dan would leave Sally and
start a new, better family with her. All the years of not feeling
remotely maternal, of eyeing Serena, Helen and Elizabeth's
motherly travails with a wary relief, of feeling no horror at the
proverbial tick of her own bodily clock had not been about being a
career girl, Cassie saw now, or fearing the loss of independence, or
emotional responsibility, but had derived purely from not having
found the right person. Dan was that person: he had brought her
life into focus, made all the hitherto neglected parts of her suddenly
vivid and important – made her whole.

Cassie was jolted from this happy reverie by a phone-call from
the client she was supposed to have met that morning. It was not an
easy conversation. The client, who had too much time and money
on her hands and who had acquiesced easily enough to Cassie's
suggestion that their meeting was postponed, had clearly decided
since that she had been badly treated. It took all Cassie's considerable charm to smooth her ruffled feathers; she resorted in the end to
talk of discounts and faster completion times. After that she phoned
her parents to alert them to the imminence of an impromptu visit to
Ashley House. (Brighton was so close and the idea of delaying her
return to piles of work and an empty flat so appealing that once the
idea had taken shape she had acted on it without a moment's
deliberation.) Her mother said, as Cassie had known she would,
that they would be delighted to see her and asked if she would mind
stopping at the butcher's in Farncombe to get two extra chicken
breasts for dinner.

> *Dear Theo,*
>   *I thought I'd write and ask how it's all going. I think school is*
> *boring whether you are a day boy or a boarder. I HATE school*
> *at the moment because all we're doing is test papers and I get*

lousy marks all the time. Not being a boffin like you! Still, the
exams are over by half-term so I can chill out then. Mum and
Dad are going to buy me a CD Walkman if I do okay. I wanted
a mobile but they said I have to wait till I'm fourteen. You're so
lucky having one already. We're going to AH for half-term, what
about you? Apart from that nothing much is happening. Scored
two goals yesterday, should have been three but one was
disallowed because the w— ref said it was offside. Maisie says
she's going to pierce her own ears but I bet she doesn't. There was
that woman who pierced herself so much she died of blood
poisoning, did you read about it?

   See ya,
   Ed

Ed, who had only written the letter to his cousin after a good deal of
cajoling from his mother, sealed it inside the envelope with some
satisfaction. At the last minute he unsealed it again, tearing a bit of
the flap where his saliva had already dried, and stuffed in a couple of
squares of chocolate. 'PS Hope you like the war rations – sorry it's
not more, I got peckish!' Then he put the envelope on top of his
history exercise book, which he had abandoned in favour of a
Championship Manager computer game. Soon he was on the point
of leading his team out to face Brazil in the World Cup Final.

Elizabeth spent the afternoon buying food for the dinner party they
were giving that evening. Their neighbours were coming, but only
as a front. The real purpose of the event was to butter up the other
guests, a headmaster and his wife from a rival school, whom Colin
had met on the golf course the week before. Not because he had any
definite strategy, he had assured her, but simply because the
opportunity to develop the relationship had fallen into his lap
and only a fool would have ignored it. Two weeks into the spring
term, his partnership with Phyllis McGill was already showing
signs of strain.

   Elizabeth offered what counsel she could (Phyllis, from the
glimpses she got in the staff room was, in her view, trying quite

hard) but Colin – within the privacy of their own home at least – remained as glowering and brooding on the subject as a tiger in a cage. The night before he had kept her awake for hours ranting about it all: the job should have been his and his alone. The head clearly had no faith in him. Appointing two such different characters as his deputies showed that the man had no coherent vision of where the school was going or how it should be run. As a part-time music teacher and therefore on the fringes of things, Elizabeth could not possibly understand.

Which wasn't true at all, reflected Elizabeth now, experiencing a sort of delayed effrontery at the remark (by one in the morning she had been too exhausted to feel effrontery or anything else). She dropped six Cellophane-wrapped pork chops into her shopping basket, with a pot of double cream and a packet of fresh sage. She understood ambition. She knew, dimly, that she had some herself, lurking beneath the daily grind of screechy cellos, dinner-party recipes and how to be a decent wife and mother. Going part-time had proved a compromise on all fronts. She felt torn all the time, as if she was doing a lot of things quite well rather than one thing really well: although she was only working twenty-five hours a week, life was a long race against the clock, a non-stop marathon between home, school gates, shops and classrooms. Elizabeth checked her watch. Only half an hour remained before she was due to pick up Roland from his rather fierce all-boys preparatory school on the far side of town, south of the new traffic-calming one-way system that made everyone who came into contact with it seethe with rage.

That afternoon the traffic was worse than usual. Bored and tense with waiting, Elizabeth delved for sustenance in the shopping bags on the seat next to her. First she ate an apple, because it was wise, and then three chocolate wafer biscuits because she was still hungry. She turned on the radio and listened to a woman, who sounded like Serena, talk amusingly about the affliction of being tone-deaf; she thought fondly of her sister-in-law, who had rung the evening before to suggest a girls' day in London, and somewhat anxiously of the child to whom she had given her last lesson of the day. With his grade-two piano just a week away Elizabeth had elected to concentrate on aural tests. 'Think of your voice as an instrument,' she had suggested. 'Make it sing this sound.' She had played just one note – middle C – several times and managed to keep her face expressionless at her pupil's tuneless attempts to reproduce it. She had given up and asked him instead to play his best piece, which he did at top speed, like a horse galloping for a finishing line.

Whenever she told people that she was a music teacher she was aware that it sounded like a lucky sort of job to have, one of those rare occupations where the passion of a hobby and a true vocation could converge. The reality, of course, was infinitely more complicated and far less satisfactory. Labelled early in life as the one fortunate enough to have received the lion's share of Pamela's musicality, Elizabeth had been encouraged to learn two instruments. She had chosen the cello, because it looked interesting, and the piano because Pamela insisted it was invaluable to any would-be musician. While her siblings were permitted to pursue stop-start relationships with half an orchestra's worth of instruments, Elizabeth had been persuaded to stick with these chosen two, passing all the grades and developing a genuine proficiency in both. She wasn't that good, though, and she knew it. Hard work produced technique, but nothing approaching the instinctive flair of true musical genius she had glimpsed occasionally among the clutch of young musicians with whom she had jostled for recognition in youth orchestras and competitions. It had been a relief to give up in her A-level year and concentrate on her academic studies. At university she had hardly played at all. Though afterwards, during the Lucien years, when she was working in PR and hating it, she would sometimes, after a glass of wine or three, sit down at the piano and rattle through some of her old repertoire. Lucien, who played the guitar badly but with great aplomb, would whoop with appreciation for a bit, then persuade her to accompany his strumming. Musically they made a questionable duo, but had had many hours of fun, ploughing through wrong notes and splashing the sheet music with wine.

When the marriage fell apart, Elizabeth, wanting a completely fresh start to her life, had given up the hateful PR (she hadn't been glib or committed enough) and retrained as a teacher. Maths, which she had read at Imperial College, was her primary subject, but in her first post at a shambolic school in Battersea she had soon found herself sucked into the music side of things and enjoying it far more. By the time Colin joined the school she was running both departments practically single-handed and beginning to think that a career in PR might have been an easy option after all. Colin, ten years older and infinitely more confident, had taken her in hand. The maths stressed her so she should give it up, he said. With his backing she renegotiated her position and became head of music instead, which she had enjoyed enormously. A couple of years into their marriage an opportunity for Colin had brought them to Guildford, where Elizabeth – eager to continue working alongside him – had settled for a considerable demotion. With the arrival of Roland she had taken maternity leave, then gone back part-time. The stress had decreased, but so had the satisfaction. She missed being in charge of a department. Teaching singing to some of the more rebellious classes was a bit like managing a crowd of unruly football supporters, but she always forgave them in the end, melting when they belted out the tunes, often half-shouting in their enthusiasm to drown their neighbours. In individual lessons, she did her best to encourage rather than criticise, remembering only too well from her own childhood the chore of practice and the burden of parental expectation.

'I was hoping you'd do your beef thing,' said Colin, when he saw the chops.

And I was hoping you would be nice, Elizabeth thought, but did not say because Roland was within earshot and she was banking on the evening putting her husband in a good mood.

Spotting a key on the window-ledge, Stephen unlocked the french windows in the music room and stepped outside into the arched porch they called the cloisters. A light, positioned to his right in the rafters overhead, flicked on, illuminating a set of worn wickerwork garden furniture and several folded deck-chairs. A hardy black spider was abseiling up the canvas, legs flailing, like a climber searching for a foothold. Stephen, who didn't like spiders, turned to walk the other way, the rubber soles of his shoes squeaking faintly on the stone floor. As he walked, more lights burst into action, making him feel self-conscious, but in a delighted way, and adding to the curious sensation, building inside him all day, that his collision with this charming family and their extraordinary house was somehow *meant* to be. His initial fear that he was out of his depth had quickly dissolved, thanks not just to Pamela's effusive warmth but to the old man, who had opened up considerably during lunch, bombarding him with so many questions about his experiences in South America that Stephen had had to remind himself that he was there to research them rather than the other way round. Even the loud-mouthed American woman, smacking her lips at the food (which had been delicious), and flinging amusing and often irrelevant remarks into the conversation, had seemed endearing. The four of them had drunk a bottle of wine with the shepherd's pie and then, at John's suggestion, had brandy with their coffee. Later, talk of Eric had flowed so easily that Stephen's hand ached from trying to scribble it all down in his notebook. Solitary, fearless, heroic, giving up his inheritance to fight as a mercenary in foreign wars, arriving home unannounced with kitbags only to take off again to sail oceans and tackle mountains (including three assaults on Everest) then to be cruelly felled by a stroke at the age of fifty-five – the copy was fantastic. Listening to it all, with so many verifying documents, letters and photos scattered across the table in front of him, Stephen had felt like a prospector who had struck gold. Before he knew it the afternoon was gone. He was on the point of announcing his departure when Pamela appeared with a tray of tea-things, including a toffee-coloured fruit cake, thick with raisins and cherries, and crustless egg and cress sandwiches, cut into bulging triangles and arranged with mathematical precision on a delicate porcelain plate. 'We'd like you to stay for dinner, Stephen,' she declared, pouring tea into cups that matched the plate.

'Dinner?' Stephen had indicated the tray of food and laughed. 'I won't need any dinner after all this.'

'Food feeds the brain, doesn't it?' Pamela had replied, cutting three generous wedges of cake and a sliver for herself. 'All those notes you've made – I should think you're exhausted. John can't sit in his study for more than ten minutes without needing fuel, can you, darling?'

'That's because I'm invariably responding to demands for money,' John quipped, frowning momentarily at the recollection of his accountant's proposal about cash gifts to which he had yet to reply.

'And you are most welcome to stay the night,' continued Pamela.

'I couldn't possibly.'

'Why ever not? It's the least we can do. Besides, it's far too late to start back now. John could drive you to the station in the morning, couldn't you, darling? We've got a timetable for trains somewhere – I'm sure we could find one that would suit you.'

Stephen, pressing the last cake crumbs off his plate, had protested weakly, then given in.

The cloister lights illuminated little more than the near fringe of the garden. As he stared into the darkness, already dense at five o'clock, Stephen became aware of the layers of sound it contained: a wood pigeon cooing, the rustle of plants, stirring at the touch of the breeze, unseen animals, scuffling round the lawns and flower-beds. He stepped off the veranda on to the lawn and inhaled deeply, savouring the damp, earthy smell of the air. The ground beneath his feet felt soft and heavy. It, too, was making a noise, he realised, listening hard, wanting to attune his senses to every detail; something between a click and a gurgle, triggered by the rainwater that was still seeping through the soil.

'Hello.'

Stephen jumped. 'Hi. I was just . . .'

'It's lovely, isn't it? All fresh and sort of bursting. After London it's like another world. Mind you, it *is* another world down here – bit like a time-warp. I think that's partly why we all come back so much. I'm Cassie, by the way.'

'I thought you were,' murmured Stephen. She was standing on the veranda under one of the lights, her arms folded across her chest. Her hair, falling in curls round her face, looked almost gold. She was wearing a soft blue top and matching cardigan, a long wide-panelled skirt and brown suede boots with high fat heels. The echo of Pamela in her features – round blue eyes, firm cheekbones and a full, wide mouth – was striking, although the photo had prepared him for that. What it hadn't prepared him for was her radiance – her eyes, her teeth, seemed to glow – and her size: she was so slender and small (a good few inches shorter than her mother), like a little bird. At the sight of her, shivering in her thin cardigan, Stephen's initial instinct was to rush forward and press her into the warmth of his chest. 'I'm Stephen Smith.' He stepped back towards the cloisters, holding out his hand.

'The biographer. I know.' Her fingers were only in his for a second. They felt dainty and very cold. 'You're going to write about the dashing life of Uncle Eric, which is great because most of us have only ever known him as he is now, which is basically ga-ga – oh, God, that sounds so mean, doesn't it?' Cassie clapped her hand to her mouth. The exuberance of her day was still bursting out of her, impossible to control or conceal. For one wild moment she was even tempted to tell him all about Dan. It was awful not being able to talk about it, to have to pretend to family and friends that she was still getting over Richard, whom she had gladly discharged from her life and whom she only ever thought of these days with irritation, particularly when she saw the shapeless green anorak he had left hanging on a peg in her flat. Talking to strangers was easier, *safer*. But out of the question, Cassie reminded herself, grinning at Stephen and thinking that he was rather sweet-looking, as her mother had said, but also rather sad. 'I came to tell you that dinner's almost ready and to offer you a drink,' she said. 'We've got most things, I think.' She turned back to the music room and let out a small involuntary shriek. 'Fuck – I mean, Christ, sorry! Can't stand the bloody things.'

'What?'

'Spiders.' Cassie pressed one hand to her chest and pointed with the other at a creature, much bigger than the one Stephen had seen, enthroned in the middle of an intricate webbed metropolis above the door.

'We have something in common, then.' He laughed, unable to hide his pleasure at this small triumph of coincidence. 'I hate them too. My sister used to collect them and put them in my bed.'

'You poor, *poor* thing. How utterly vile.' She looked genuinely appalled.

'Yes, it was.' Stephen followed her back into the music room. She wiped the soles of her boots on the small threadbare mat inside the door, so he did the same. 'Who plays the piano?'

'Oh, God, all of us at some stage, though mostly very badly.' She paused in the doorway to the hall, winding a strand of hair absently round her fingers. 'Mum was quite good once and so was Elizabeth, my elder sister. She's a music teacher, but I don't think she likes it very much. She never *says*, but you can tell things like that, can't you, between siblings? There's this huge invisible thing of knowing each other and not having to say things, don't you find?'

Stephen, recalling his own sister as perpetually surly and disengaged, frowned. There had been invisible things in their family, all right, things to do with survival and pain. 'My family was crap,' he said, surprising himself – and Cassie, who let her hair fall and looked at him with an intensity that made his knees tremble.

'Oh dear, I'm sorry,' she said.

'Some families are – most, I think.' He tried to sound breezy, wanting to avoid her pity. 'What was that you said about a drink?'

'A drink, of course.' He was relieved to see the concern leave her face, but pleased that he had touched her in some way, made her notice him. 'Let's find Dad. He's master of ceremonies in this house,' she added, her voice light and playful now. 'What else are you afraid of besides spiders, Mr Smith?'

'Call me Stephen, please. Heights – I'm not too good up a ladder. And water, but only when it's deep and there's lots of it.' He spoke in a rush, torn between presenting himself as a fool and a powerful urge to be totally honest.

Conflicting impulses remained with him throughout the evening, confirming the terrifying fact that he was falling in love, that he had been from the moment Cassie had appeared under the light in the cloisters. Stephen had been in love before, once with a friend's mother, who, restless and disillusioned with her marriage, had taken it upon herself to seduce him in true Mrs Robinson style over several months. It had taken a while for the scales to fall from his eyes, by which time he could at least boast considerable proficiency as a lover. (She had been a good tutor, although it turned out he had been one in a string of eager students.) In Venezuela he had fallen in love again, with the raven-haired daughter of a local politician, who was far more eligible in terms of age but rather less so when it came to coping with the real world. Eventually Stephen had recognised that she was a spoilt little girl, incapable of forging a life of her own. So he knew about love. How it could strike unexpectedly. How it made the victim blind. How utterly untrustworthy it was. How usually a process of falling out of love ensued, in which all the ridiculous initial idealisations were slowly knocked on the head as the object of one's passion revealed herself to be human and flawed like everyone else. As he watched Cassie across the dinner table, making them all laugh with wicked imitations of her most difficult clients, Stephen endeavoured to remind himself of this, but the light in her blinded him. It was the light, so rarely encountered, of a person with the gift of being happy, of losing themselves in the moment, of laughing at the world, of infecting a room with the sheer positive force of their personality.

After dinner, at Cassie's suggestion, they played Scrabble. While Stephen slaved to prove his intellectual prowess by using as many letters as possible, she mounted a devious and infinitely more effective campaign involving cunningly positioned prepositions. The game ended when Stephen, after one of several lengthy contemplations, managed 'dovetail'. Whereupon Cassie used the last of her letters to form 'love', managing to make the *e* fall on to a square offering a triple word score.

'Got you!' she exclaimed, sitting back in her chair and slapping her thighs in triumph.

'Yes . . . yes, you have,' he murmured. 'You really have.'

Lying in bed afterwards, in an L-shaped room with cornflower walls and dark roof beams the width of trees, Stephen found himself imagining what it would be like to feel the softness of Cassie Harrison's skin against his. He had spent all evening absorbing the details of her body, the soft down on her cheeks near her ears, the blue vein running down the side of her neck, the ridge of her collar-bone, just visible over her top, the slender curve of her thighs pressing through her skirt, and felt as if he knew each part of her. He had absorbed every snippet of other, more practical information too: she was single and lived alone in Pimlico, she designed interiors, liked driving fast and her favourite colour was blue. She often skipped breakfast but couldn't do without lunch. She preferred white wine to red, loved champagne (but only in small doses because it gave her a headache). She played a little tennis, hated football, but enjoyed cricket. She loved animals, especially horses and dogs. All of these facts glistened in Stephen's mind. Nothing was too trivial to treasure. And he wanted to know more, much more. He wanted to climb inside her head and explore, with infinite tenderness, every corner of her mind. And he wanted, with equal ardour, to be inside her body, to push into her and feel her round him, her belly against his, her arms across his back, her legs round his thighs.

Wide awake, heavily aroused, it was impossible to sleep. Having been virtually celibate for almost a year Stephen was used to relieving the discomfort of his own lust. But he knew that tonight he did not want to, that his longing went beyond the simple release of ejaculation. Instead he put the light back on and got up to look out of the window. He drew the curtains, casting a small square of yellow onto the lawn below. Alongside it he could make out the ghostly frame of the pergola and beyond that the dark hunch of the boundary hedge. The land behind was a blur of grey and black, although from a walk with John late that afternoon he knew that it comprised four fields, a wood and a small muddy lake, which swelled and subsided according to some underground water source that nobody had mapped or understood. 'Water finds its own way out,' John had explained, his craggy face flushed with the pride of

showing off the estate. Like feelings, Stephen thought now, remembering his host's words, and wondering how on earth he could
contain what he felt for John's daughter. His gaze returned to the
patch of yellow light on the lawn and his own, lone silhouette
framed in the middle of it, and he was overcome by a sense of acute
isolation and fierce hope. Maybe, he thought wildly, Cassie was
awake too and thinking of him. She had liked him, he was sure of
that. Maybe, if he focused hard enough, he could make her get out
of bed and come to her own window, which he knew was on the
same floor but several rooms away. She would switch on her light,
see the reflection of his on the grass below and know that she was
not alone. Stephen watched, willing this impossibility into being.
He watched and watched, until his body was stiff with cold and the
moon had withdrawn its glories behind a damask wisp of cloud.

Cassie, oblivious to the fire burning in the biographer's heart, slept
soundly. On the pillow beside her lay her mobile phone, which was
both on and charging, the wire strung between the bed and the wall
socket like a lifeline.

FEBRUARY

Alicia greeted the news of her imminent discharge from hospital with mixed feelings. She had missed the little routines of life in her cottage, but in her still-fragile state she feared returning to them. For several weeks yet she would be walking with two sticks, and the thought of it made her feel panicky inside. She saw, more painfully than ever, that getting old was about adjusting to a shrinking world: all the simplest things got steadily harder until even the body's most basic acts – movement, passing waste, breathing – could not function without assistance.

Home help was being arranged on various fronts: Beryl Harper, who cleaned, was also going to do her shopping, and a physiotherapist would visit three times a week to put her through her paces. But Alicia only liked Beryl in small doses and had hated all the physiotherapy to which she had been subjected in hospital. The doctors said exercise was good, not just to prevent stiffness but because it improved the flow of blood, which would help her fracture to heal more quickly. But movement in almost any direction hurt and Alicia was no good at dealing with physical pain. Giving birth five decades earlier to Paul, who had taken thirty-six hours to emerge, remained the most traumatic experience of her life. People said women forgot about the pain of childbirth, but Alicia never had.

In hospital again, with all the white coats and antiseptic smells, she had found herself recalling the relentlessness of the contractions, how the pain had felt like a caged beast, tearing out her innards with its claws. Trevor, pacing impatiently on his own somewhere as men did in those days, had appeared afterwards, smelling of old tweed and nicotine, like some distant, unknowable relative. 'All right, then?' he had said, pecking her cheek and peering at Paul, with his pink scrawny limbs and monster head. When Alicia tried to tell him what she had been through, how endless it had seemed, how afraid she still was of the tenderness where they had stitched her, his eyes had glazed with incomprehension. It was a failure of intimacy from which they had never recovered.

'How are you, dear?'

'Mavis . . . I . . .' From the bubble of the past, Alicia took a few moments to register the appearance of one of her bridge companions.

'We've missed you.' Mavis lowered her sizeable frame on to the chair next to the bed and folded her arms across her handbag.

'Have you? Have you really?'

'Of course, dear.' She leant over and patted Alicia's hand. 'Belinda's been playing with Penelope who, as you know, is quite hopeless – lost *all* her marbles, in my opinion, but there we are.'

Alicia, who might once have encouraged Mavis in an acerbic analysis of the failings of someone on the fringe of their group, found herself changing the subject. God knows what they had been saying about *her* in her absence. And Penelope, though she repeated things and dyed her hair the most ridiculous shade of auburn, always had the best of intentions.

'I've brought these, which I'll leave here.' Mavis fished out a small brown bag of grapes and set them carefully on the bedside table next to the lilies – now somewhat droopy and pungent – which Charlie and Serena had very sweetly sent the week before. 'And your post, which Beryl asked me to bring when I dropped by yesterday. She said you're going home soon, which is nice,' she added, plucking off a grape and popping it into her mouth.

'Yes, very nice,' murmured Alicia, unequal to the task of admitting to her terror, how safe she had come to feel in hospital. She studied the letters instead. There was a gas bill, an offer for cut-rate health insurance and a letter in spidery writing which turned out to be from the biographer Pamela had mentioned during the course of her several kind letters and phone-calls.

Dear Mrs Morrell,

I believe you may have been forewarned of my writing to you by your brother, John, whom I have lately had the pleasure of meeting. I am researching a book, which I hope will include a chapter on your eldest brother, Eric, focusing on his many achievements during the war. The book is to be called Unsung Heroes *and (with any luck!) will be published next autumn by Greaves and Maple. I am writing on the off-chance that there might be anything – any thoughts or memories of that time – that you would like to contribute. I want to build up as detailed a picture as I can, so anything would be of interest. If you would like to call or maybe write to me, my address and telephone number are at the top of this letter. There is, of course, absolutely no obligation on your part to contribute. Your brother and sister-in-law have already been incredibly helpful.*

I hope this letter puts you to no inconvenience.

Yours sincerely,

Stephen Smith

'Anything interesting?'

'The man writing about Eric. He wants to know if I have any thoughts or memories to contribute.'

'Oh, my, how exciting. And do you?'

'Heavens, I don't know. I can't possibly think about it now.' Alicia quickly slipped the letter back inside the envelope. She had memories, all right, but wasn't sure either that they were appropriate or that she would like to hand them over to some strange young man. She had been nineteen when Eric went to France, old enough to know and share the numbing agony of waiting for news. As her elder brother he had been her hero and she had made many private pacts with the Lord for his safe return. Yet after the war he was so obviously restless and keen to take off again that it was as if they'd all lost him anyway.

'Can I have one of those as well?'

'No, Edward, you can not.'

'But I'm starving.'

'Darling, you can't be. You've only just had breakfast and I really think one double chocolate muffin is enough. Besides, they cost about two pounds each. Are you sure you don't want anything, Clem? Okay. And, Maisie, you've got a Danish and you, my little sausage, can share mine, can't you?' Serena bent down to squeeze the nose of her youngest, who was wriggling furiously in her pushchair. 'Stop teasing her, Ed,' she scolded mildly a few moments later, delving into her purse for a crisp twenty-pound note and catching sight of her son making a threatening lunge at his little sister.

Ed, his teeth clogged with chocolate muffin, waited till Serena had returned her attention to the girl at the till, then lunged again at the pushchair. This time he made an ogre face, not one of his funny ones but a Dracula-style grimace, and Tina whimpered in confused dismay. It was Saturday morning of half-term and they were at Victoria station, about to be packed onto a train to Barham so that their mother could have lunch with their aunt Elizabeth, who had already dropped Roland at Ashley House and was on her way up to London. Both women would return to Sussex that evening, with Charlie who was spending the day at Twickenham with a work colleague. The whole thing, in Ed's view, was a thoroughly stupid plan, since it meant being at the mercy of his sisters for two solid hours and with no prospect of anyone decent to play with once they got to Ashley House. Roland didn't count as decent and Chloë and Theo were skiing, which was something his parents had said they weren't going to do again until Tina was old enough for ski-school. Which would be years, reflected Ed bleakly, ramming the hefty remains – a good half – of his muffin into his mouth, then attempting vainly to close his lips round it.

'You are disgusting,' said Maisie.

'I quite agree,' echoed Clem, still light-headed at her own saintly strength in resisting the array of baked goodies in the glass cabinet next to them.

Ed, his mouth spurting soggy chocolate crumbs, mouthed, 'Fuck off,' and strolled back to the table where Serena had instructed them to leave their coats and bags. He got out his Game Boy and began feverishly to work the buttons. He wished he hadn't wolfed his food and he wished his sisters liked him. He had had a deadly week doing the St George's entrance exams. It was a relief the exams were over, of course, but not a nice sort of relief because they had gone so badly. 'Describe and illustrate four types of weather patterns, giving named examples.' Just thinking about his answer, the sketchy drawings, badly copied from over the elbow of the boy at the next desk, made Ed feel quite sick. 'Was Henry VII a good or a fortunate king?' Ed knew things had gone more or less all right for Henry VII, but had no factual recollection as to why. Henry VIII was the only Tudor monarch he had done any revision for: he was reasonably interesting, being fat, a spendthrift and having had so many wives. And he knew a bit about King John, how he was weak and bad and got all the barons to sign the Magna Carta. But there hadn't been any questions on Henry VIII or King John so he might as well have not known anything at all.

Serena got the girls to carry the drinks and food to the table so she could wheel the pushchair. The plan to meet Elizabeth had been hers, but it had been postponed and reorganised so many times that some of her initial enthusiasm had waned. She liked Elizabeth and wanted to be kind because she was Charlie's sister and clearly somewhat unhappy, but there had never been much real affinity between them. On the phone that morning – to finalise the arrangements, which, with all the ferrying of children, had grown unbelievably complicated – Serena had sensed, too, that Elizabeth was wondering why they were bothering. It didn't help matters that two out of Serena's four children (Ed and Tina) had chosen that morning to be impossible, Tina because she had a cold and Ed because . . . Serena looked at her son, who was scowling into the tiny screen of his Game Boy, chocolate smeared across his chin, and felt a gust of tenderness. Because, she decided with a sigh, he was fast becoming a teenager. Because with his exams over he felt that some sort of VIP treatment was called for rather than another half-term flopping at his grandparents. Because – and here she really did pity him – he had three sisters.

'We'll get your friend Garth over, shall we, Ed, when we get back to London? Go and see a movie or something? The new James Bond, perhaps.'

'James Bond sucks.'

'I'd like to see it,' put in Maisie.

'And me,' chimed Clem, both of them playing the easy-to-win game of Outshining the Ungrateful Sibling.

'I want to go to Alton Towers,' snapped Ed, flicking off his Game Boy because he had run out of lives.

'Well, that might not be so easy,' said Serena, working hard now to maintain her patience, 'because it takes a whole day and Tina—'

'Yeah, yeah, yeah, Tina can't cope with it, like she can't cope with anything yet, not even skiing.'

'I'm sorry you find your little sister such a burden, Edward.' Serena spoke very quietly, having learnt from years of practice that it was a far more effective way of shaming a child than a raised voice. 'Now, get your things together, all of you, or you'll miss the train. Maisie, keep your mobile on, won't you? And if Granny isn't at the station when you get there, don't, for heaven's sake, wander off. Ed, could you push Tina, please, while I dump this lot in a bin?' She scooped up the bits of Cellophane and polystyrene and crammed them into an overflowing plastic barrel. Maybe a day off for shopping and lunch with only her youngest to worry about was exactly what she needed after all.

Roland felt self-conscious at Ashley House on his own. When Elizabeth drove away his stomach had tightened and his throat had knotted even though he knew it was stupid because she was coming back that evening. It had made him wonder how Theo could bear to be away for weeks at a time and not be sad every minute of every day. His grandparents were kind but at first rather preoccupied, Pamela with getting things ready in the kitchen and telling Betty which beds to make up, and John with the door from the music room on to the cloisters; it had warped in the rain and wouldn't close properly. Roland, riding round the garden on one of the old bikes that lived in the garage, kept half an eye on his grandfather's progress, veering away in ever-wider circles at the mounting evidence of anger in the way John banged and scraped his tools. At one point he stood up and swore, saying the F-word with such venom that Roland, his cheeks burning with a combination of horror and fascination, felt duty-bound to hide inside the pergola. Grown-ups weren't supposed to behave like that, especially not grown-ups like his grandfather who said 'bathroom' instead of 'toilet' and 'would you be so good' instead of 'please', and who was generally about as ancient and polite as it was possible to be. Peering through the thicket wall of rose briars he saw his grandmother emerge through the doorway and say something about Sid taking a look, which made his grandfather bark even louder, though not a swear-word this time. Grown-ups, it seemed to Roland, wheeling the bicycle back to the garage, were always cross these days. After a dinner party the other night he had heard his parents talking in such loud, fierce voices that he had crept out on to the landing to investigate. He craned his neck to listen, almost getting his head stuck between the banisters. But after a few moments the voices stopped. Almost as if his parents had known he was there. Then the sitting-room door opened and he scampered back to bed, where he lay shivering and worrying that they were cross because of something to do with him.

Back inside the house his grandmother asked for his help in peeling mushrooms, which was boring but then asked him to carry a box upstairs, which was a bit better, even though the dust made him sneeze.

'Somewhere over there will do,' she instructed, pointing across the attic, which was huge and poorly lit, with great slanting ceilings so low that his grandmother had to stoop to protect the grey pincushion of her bun. 'I'd ask Granddad only he's busy with the door and you're so strong now. We got it down for the man who wants to write about Uncle Eric.'

'Is that Great-uncle Eric, the soldier?' Roland picked his way across the room, his eyes widening at the bulging boxes and laden shelves, all thick with dust. The attic at his house contained a couple of broken dining-chairs and some empty suitcases. This was an

Aladdin's cave of a place that made him itch to explore. He would tell Ed about it, he decided, the moment he arrived from London.

'It is.' His grandmother looked pleased. 'And this man's going to put him in a book, which is *very* exciting. Can you manage?'

'Oh, yes. Easy-peasy.' Roland had set the box down for a rest, but picked it up again the moment she spoke, feeling Herculean and important. 'Where did you say I should put it?' He sensed a sneeze coming and stopped, closing his eyes in expectation, but it went away again, which was curiously disappointing. 'Granny?' Pamela had moved deeper into the attic, where the eaves forced her to bend almost double, and was examining a small leather suitcase. 'Granny, where shall I put it?'

'Oh, darling, sorry.' Pamela pushed the suitcase back into its place and manoeuvred herself to a position where she could stand upright, which she did with a sigh, looking suddenly so old and worn out that Roland felt it was just as well he was there. 'In that corner would be lovely. And then it'll be time for me to go and meet your cousins at the station. Would you like to come too? We could stop at the village shop on the way to get an ice-cream, but only if you promise to keep it as our secret and still eat up all your lunch.'

Roland beamed his acquiescence, thinking his grandmother was actually quite cool and wondering why he hadn't noticed it before.

The airport lounge was hot and smelt faintly of bodies and fried food. They had rushed to get there, worrying through traffic jams on the M4 and queues of people at the baggage check-in desks only to find that their plane was delayed. Peter was using the extra time to make a long phone-call to his number two, hopping from one place to another in search of relative silence and a good signal. Theo was plugged into his portable CD and reading a book, absently chewing the skin off his fingers and picking at a large crimson lump on his chin. Chloë was sprawled dramatically across the hand luggage, hugging a huge purple kangaroo called Bindy, which she had insisted on selecting as her companion for the holiday from the array of furred creatures with whom she shared her bed.

Helen tried to read a paper, but found she was too tired to care about ricocheting share prices or hunts for bearded terrorists and closed her eyes. She had been up till very late the night before, first attempting to clear her desk at work, then to create order at home, tidying, packing, emptying the fridge and the bin, dead-heading and watering plants, writing instructions to the milkman, the paper boy, the au pair . . . No matter how many things she did there always seemed to be ten more left to do. And, these days, she kept almost forgetting things too. Important things, like collecting the ski-suits from the dry-cleaner's. And gloves. *Gloves*. Of all things. Not exactly an optional extra and yet it was only at the last minute that she had remembered to get them out of the drawer. The countdown towards any holiday was always stressful, but this year it had definitely been worse than usual. Much worse. And that was for a number of reasons, Helen reminded herself, seeking solace in being rational: because of Theo not being around to pack his own stuff or try on clothes that she knew were almost certainly too small; because of Chloë sulking and Peter looking baffled. Because she, who never cried, felt for some reason like crying all the time.

Stumped by this, Helen opened her eyes. Chloë appeared to have fallen asleep, spreadeagled awkwardly across the bags. Helen folded the newspaper and slipped it back into the side compartment of Peter's briefcase. Skiing was one of the rare leisure activities that still bound her family together, despite their disparate ages and temperaments. And this year they were going to Verbier, to a hotel recommended by one of Peter's fellow silks. It sounded spectacular, within walking distance of the main lifts, with an indoor swimming-pool and a huge outdoor spa where residents could wallow in heated comfort under the stars. The cost was huge, but Peter, usually wary of overpriced resorts, had made a grand speech about starting to spend some of their considerable wealth instead of accumulating it and how a bit of indulgence would do none of them any harm. It was because of her, Helen knew, because of how she was behaving.

'I'm just going to the loo, okay?'

Peter had returned to his seat and was busy with a wodge of

papers, scribbling tiny clusters of notes in the margins. He peered at her over the rim of his spectacles, nodding absently.

In the ladies', Helen washed the newsprint from her hands, then stood at the row of basins, wondering if the light was cruel or whether she really looked as bad as her reflection suggested: violet shadows under her eyes, lifeless, ash-streaked hair, colourless lips, pasty washed-out skin and all of it somehow so *tight*-looking, as if her jaw and cheekbones were trying to push their way out of her face. Most of the women Helen knew considered themselves too fat; several were openly envious of her slim figure. But Helen struggled to derive any satisfaction from her appearance. All of her, she decided, not just her face but her whole body, looked *etiolated*, like a plant that had survived for years without proper sunlight.

'Going anywhere nice?'

A woman had appeared from one of the cubicles and was standing at the basin next to her, spreading a thick line of crimson round her lips.

'Uh . . . skiing. Switzerland.' Helen knew she sounded unwelcoming, as if she resented being talked to. Which she did. 'And you?'

'Lanzarote. A bit of sun.' The woman dropped her lipstick back into her handbag and began to backcomb her hair, which looked dry and brittle from many previous such assaults. 'But, then, you need it at this time of year, don't you? Bloody February. Gets to us all.'

'Oh, doesn't it?' Helen felt tears prick her eyes as the pendulum of her emotions swung the other way. In an instant all the hostility was gone. Instead she experienced a rush of absurd affection, as if this woman could see to the heart of her and knew every vibration of confusion and misery swirling inside. 'I hope you have a nice time.'

'And you, dear.'

Helen returned to her seat feeling much better. Peter was right: a little luxury was just what they needed. A week of exercise, bracing mountain air and five-star food would do her the world of good. She kissed Peter, who looked surprised, and gave the children the packet of sweets which she had been saving for later on. 'I'm going to ski the socks off you lot,' she said. 'I really am.'

Elizabeth and Serena took the tube to Oxford Street. Tina, awed by the rumblings of the trains and the crush of people went wide-eyed and quiet until they emerged on to the street, where she whined and plucked at the straps across her stomach. When Serena gave her a beaker of orange juice, she sucked the spout for a few seconds, then hurled it on to the pavement.

'Oh, God, I'm afraid it's going to be one of those days. Is there anything special you wanted to get, Elizabeth? Don't let Tina put you off. I can buy time with a biscuit – I've got some really chunky ones that keep her quiet for ages. And these work wonders too,' she added, pulling out a bunch of keys from her bag, which her daughter immediately swiped from her hand and attempted to shove into her mouth.

'Oh, I don't know. Tights . . . I think I need tights. And I could do with some new bras, though I hate buying bras – they never fit properly.'

'M&S, then?'

'Fine by me. Don't you want anything?'

'Lunch mainly.' Serena grinned, then added kindly, 'Just a bit of window-shopping will be a treat, honestly. Although if we're going to M&S I might keep an eye out for some pyjamas for Ed. He's in the most phenomenal growing phase at the moment and, of course, can't have hand-me-downs from the girls. Long gone are the days when I could get away with that.'

They set off, Serena manoeuvring the pushchair expertly through the crowds and pausing every so often to point out something in a window to her sister-in-law, who seemed distracted. The day was overcast but mild for February. So much so that both women soon had their coats off, Serena tying hers carelessly round her waist, while Elizabeth slung hers over one arm. Underneath she was wearing a long brown skirt and a beige polo-neck, neither of which flattered her colouring or her shape. 'You should wear brighter colours,' announced Serena, once they were inside the shop, driven to such frankness by the sight of her sister-in-law eyeing up a horrible black sack of a skirt. 'More like this.' She took the black skirt from Elizabeth and replaced it with a shorter, prettier purple one, with wide panels and a small frill round the hem. 'Which would go beautifully with this.' Turning to another rail, she seized a lilac cotton top with a round neck and three-quarter-length sleeves. 'I can just see you in these.'

Elizabeth groaned but looked pleased. 'Well, I can't. My God, and look at the prices. I'm buying underwear, remember?' They soldiered on into the lingerie department, where Elizabeth bought a sturdy bra and a pair of thick black tights.

Over lunch a little later as she studied her sister-in-law's rather heavy features, noting the tall but broad frame, the strong, dark Harrison brows and the brooding look that clouded her handsome blue eyes, it occurred to Serena that having to grow up with all the parent-pleasing accomplishments of Peter and the charm of Charlie and Cassie could not have been easy. Even at her happiest there was a tension in Elizabeth's manner, a profound impression of uncertainty. She seemed to be opening up now, though, since they'd ordered a second glass of wine.

'We're all just acting, don't you feel that sometimes? Playing our parts.'

'I suppose so.' Serena spoke guardedly. She enjoyed all the components of her life far too much to worry about where they came from. 'I know just what you mean,' she added, with rather more encouragement, reminding herself that one of the original intentions behind the expedition had been to cheer Elizabeth up.

'Striving to be things,' continued Elizabeth, 'mothers, wives, workers. I tried to say that to Colin the other night, but he's too stressed to think about anything except not being the only deputy head. This woman he's sharing the post with, he can't stand her. He *cares* so much – he feels it undermines him. I tried to say that it shouldn't matter so much, that it's only a job, one small part of who he is and what he does, but he got so cross. He gets so cross. He says I don't understand, that I'm just not ambitious in the same way. Do you and Charlie ever have conversations like that?'

'Not exactly.' Serena sensed that they were now close to the root of her sister-in-law's gloom and spoke carefully, wanting neither to discourage further confidence nor to appear greedy for it. The women she knew talked frankly to each other all the time, pouring out their feelings in huddles round kitchen tables over mugs of coffee and packets of biscuits. Relationships, children, money – no subjects were barred. A good bellyache about what was getting them down always helped: it made big issues seem small and manageable. It made them all feel less alone. But those sessions were voluntary and about trust, which had to be mutual. Elizabeth, Serena knew, wasn't like that: there was a solitariness in her, something ring-fenced and tightly private. Her life consisted of rushing around after Colin and Roland and doing her job. Even before the arrival of this new, visible unhappiness, Serena had never seen her sister-in-law relax properly, not even at Ashley House. 'But, then, Charlie isn't really ambitious, is he?' Serena pointed out. 'He would be perfectly happy looking after the children all day.'

They both laughed, united by the pleasure of knowing and liking someone so well. 'You are the best thing that ever happened to him, Serena, you really are. It makes me feel . . .' Elizabeth's eyes flooded with tears. At which crucial moment Tina, waking from her nap to find herself both hungry and nose-to-nose with an unfamiliar table-leg, began to sob violently, prompting looks of disapproval from neighbouring diners. Serena jigged the pushchair in a vain attempt to ease her back to sleep, while Elizabeth hastily dabbed a tissue at her eyes.

'I'm going to have to let her out for a bit,' said Serena. 'When she gets like this she just needs to run around. Perhaps we could walk to St James's Park or something. She'll want food soon and then she'll probably sleep again.' She unstrapped her daughter, who clung briefly to her leg, then waddled off to smile radiantly at an unsuspecting businessman. He tried to ignore her, then gave up and smiled back, even offering a quick peep-bo from behind his napkin. The waiters, who were swarthy and Spanish-looking, stroked her tufts of fluffy hair as they dodged round her, their faces creasing with indulgent affection. Tina patted her palms together and tottered on to the next table, delighted to have both her freedom and a receptive audience.

Later, Serena would remember each of these moments with the clarity of slow motion. At the time, she was preoccupied with settling the bill and with her sister-in-law, whom she sensed had been close to saying something of huge emotional import. She would remember, too, the feel of cold air on her back as the door to the restaurant opened and closed behind them, releasing some lunchers into the street outside. And she would wonder a thousand times, a million times, why that cold air on her neck had made no impression at the time; what failure of intuition had prevented her turning round. Even when Elizabeth dropped coins into the saucer as a tip, saying, 'Where's Tina?' she had felt no alarm, but instead wasted several precious seconds looping bags over the handles of the pushchair and pulling on her coat. And when she finally did turn, and saw no sign of her daughter, even then she did not panic. Toddlers toddled. They explored corners and spaces under chairs. She had learnt over fourteen years and with four children that they bobbed out of sight and bobbed back again. But she began to look more earnestly, apologising to diners as the pushchair bumped against the backs of their chairs. A Saturday lunchtime in the West End had ensured that the place was full to bursting, its windows steamy with breath and cigarette smoke.

It was only at the screech of tyre on Tarmac, a long ear-splitting screech, like the cry of an animal in pain, which would ring in her ears for ever afterwards, that Serena awoke to the nightmare unfolding around her. She thrust the pushchair to one side, barged between the tables and ran outside. She looked up and down the street, hearing nothing but the blood pounding in her ears. The pavements on both sides of the road were swarming with people: hateful, uncaring strangers, going about their trivial lives, ignorant of her terror.

Then she heard someone shout, a male voice, high-pitched with shock, 'It's a child.' And she knew, even as she pushed through the crowds, slowing now at the edge of the pavement a few yards away, that it was her child. 'She's mine,' she said, long before she got there. 'She's mine.' It was a relief just to see her, to see the familiar clothes: the green dungarees, bulging round the bulk of her nappy, the bib still flecked with dried biscuit, the tiny corduroy pumps that passed for shoes still firmly on her feet. She was lying on her back at the side of the road, looking as relaxed as she did in her cot sometimes, staring up at the sky, just as she liked to stare, glassy-eyed with exhaustion, at her mobile of coloured elephants.

'Best not to move her.'

'It's the mother.'

'Poor soul.'

'Call an ambulance.'

'One's on its way.'

'The bike just hit her and drove off. I saw the whole thing.'

Elizabeth, elbowing her way through the crowd, the pushchair bashing her ankles, the handles of her shopping-bags cutting into her arms, started towards Serena and stopped. She was on her knees, stroking Tina's face with her palm. There was a halo of crimson blood round Tina's head. 'It's all right, sweetheart, it's Mummy. It's Mummy and I love you very much.' A woman, standing near by, started to sob. Otherwise the crowd was still. A siren sounding in the distance grew louder.

Serena shuffled closer, pressing her knees into the spreading pool of blood. She bent her head and put her mouth close to her daughter's ear, feeling a wisp of the soft baby hair tickle her lips. 'You're going to be all right, my darling. You're going to be all right.' There was terror inside her, but for the moment it was caged in shock. Her voice, she was relieved to hear, sounded calm, quite unlike the gibbering inside her head, the echoing screech of rubber. Or had it been a scream? Had she heard her daughter scream? The thought of Tina suffering even an instant of pain or fear was so unbearable that Serena, losing her guard for a moment, let out a low, involuntary groan. She wanted only to gather her child into her arms but knew she shouldn't, that it would be better to wait for the ambulance team. Instead she smoothed back the baby curls from Tina's small round face and gently cupped both her hands under her head, wanting to protect the pulpy underside of her skull from the dirty road.

Pamela was touring the garden in her Barbour and wellies, making mental notes of what to talk to Sid about when he came on Monday. Lunch had been served and cleared away and the children despatched on an errand to the village shop. She had given them a short list: eggs, frozen peas and corn flakes, none of which she really needed (not for a couple of days anyway), but they had seemed a bit listless and she thought it wise to give them something to do. She found it disheartening that, these days, bored children did nothing but slump in front of screens and always did her best to offer alternatives. Not so long ago just being at Ashley House would have been entertainment enough, with a huge garden to play in and boxes of old toys stored under the beds upstairs. But as they got older it was getting harder. Chloë still loved a lot of the toys, particularly the dolls' house, and the boys (when the weather was fine) still disappeared to play games in the woods, but not nearly as often as they used to. Ed seemed to think his footballing skills were too superior to waste on his cousins, and the bikes remaining in the garage were mostly too small or unrideable. Things changed, Pamela mused, feeling suddenly wistful. Children grew and the present became the past the moment one experienced it.

At the sight of the quince blossom edging the main lawn, her spirits lifted. Its colour, a brilliant pinky crimson that lit up the otherwise drab February landscape like an exploding firework, never failed to amaze her. She would make jelly as usual with the hard green fruit when it came, not too much and only in her smallest jars, because it was an acquired taste and not popular with the children. Alicia loved it, though, Pamela reminded herself, and made a mental note to look out a jar from last year, bubble-wrap and post it to Wiltshire. During their most recent conversation her sister-in-law had sounded poorly still, talking about wanting to get home but without much conviction, as if something more than her hip had been fractured in her fall.

John, Pamela knew, was worried, not so much because they were close (his sister had always been too preoccupied with her own woes to prompt any easy flow of affection between them) but because the frailty of both his elder siblings made his own mortality seem more real. He never said as much – he didn't have to: Pamela could hear it in his voice, the way he gruffly dismissed his anxieties, how he strode more purposefully on his excursions round the estate, rubbing furiously at his back when he thought he was out of sight, as if sheer determination would allow him to keep hold of the energy stuttering so visibly now in his brother and sister. She would put together a hamper, Pamela decided, not just of quince jelly but of all sorts of other treats too: chutney, marmalade, honey, fruit, sugared almonds and maybe even a little bottle of cherry brandy. She would have it delivered on the day Alicia was discharged from hospital as a welcome-home present and to help ease her back into the real world. Pleased with the thought, she returned her attention to the quince blossom: she clipped off several sprigs and slid them carefully into the large pockets of her coat.

She had reached the rhododendrons when the phone rang. There were scores of them, thick, towering bushes that took up half of the sky if you were standing beneath them. Every branch was already laden with tight green buds and had been for some time. Pamela reached out and stroked one, enjoying the thought of all the violent colour inside, enjoying above all the *indulgence* of so many months of preparation for a display that lasted only a few weeks. The sound of the telephone, connected to a special Tannoy system, echoed round the garden. One, two, three, four, five. She counted with mounting impatience, willing John to get from wherever he was to take the call. He knew she was in the garden and he knew the children were in the village. Half-way through the sixth ring it stopped, which meant he had got there. Pamela stood stock still in the silence that followed, all her senses alert to the possibility of being summoned, the vibrations of the phone still ringing in her ears.

'Well, I'm going and you lot can bugger off.'

'Thanks. That means we've got to carry the shopping.'

'Diddums.'

'Oh, let's all go, for God's sake. There's nothing else to do, anyway, is there?'

'There's the attic,' said Roland, in a small voice. So far he had kept out of the argument, certain that Maisie's plan of trying to catch a glimpse of the pop star Neil Rosco was unwise but fearful of saying so. Maisie was a scary proposition, tossing her long shiny hair and flashing her eyes, full of fire and certainty and defiance; a far cry from the girl who, he could remember dimly, had liked to dress him in funny clothes and push him round the garden in a wheelbarrow. It was disappointing that Ed, magnificently unafraid of her, appeared to be caving in too. Clem, clutching the small bag of shopping, was looking equally uncertain. 'Granny won't like us being late.'

'Well, we'd better get a move on, then, hadn't we? I saw his car in the drive on the way back from the station, so I know he's there. All we're going to do is look through the gates. What harm is there in that?' Maisie turned on her heel and began to march through the village, so sure of her victory that she didn't even look over her shoulder to check that the other three were following. One glimpse through the gates was all she wanted, partly for the sheer knee-weakening thrill of getting near to a real celebrity, and partly to bring reality a little more in line with the version of it she had been peddling at school. Not that she had lied outright, but Monica sort of presumed that when she was at her grandparents' she bumped into Rosco all the time and so far she hadn't had the heart to disillusion her. Monica wanted it to be true as much as Maisie did. It was like sharing a dream, but a special magical dream that had a toehold in reality.

Clem walked between her cousin and her brother, watching the swing of defiance in her sister's hips and hating it. Before they had left for the walk Maisie had changed into her new denim skirt, ankle boots and black jacket, which meant she had planned the whole thing. Just like when she'd got all tarted up to go to church at Christmas. It was pathetic. Clem slowed her pace, torn between making a stand and the unattractive prospect of fuelling her sister's hostility. Their easy alliance against Ed during the journey down from London that morning was over. Maisie cared about no one but herself, Clem decided bitterly, and she was fed up with it.

'What's all this about the attic, then?'

Ed shrugged, while Roland tugged a leaf off the hedge running along the pavement next to them and scrunched it to pieces in his hand. Up ahead the heavy iron gates protecting the drive to the great Rosco's country retreat were in sight. 'I went up there with Granny. There's lot of stuff in it – and it'd be good for playing with guns.' He cast a sideways glance at Ed, who ignored him.

'Well, I think it sounds a much better idea than this silly walk.' Clem stopped, compelling Ed and Roland to do the same. 'Don't you?'

'I guess.' Ed kicked a stone, too caught up in his own wretchedness to care what they did. He had been in the Ashley House attic before and didn't think much of it.

'Maisie?' She had to call twice to get her sister's attention. 'We're going back. This is pointless. It's obvious no one's there and Granny will be worried.'

'Okay, Miss Goody Goody. I'll see you later.'

'Maisie?' But she was already walking on, her nose in the air and her shoulders back. 'See you later, then,' Clem called, trying to sound strong because of the two younger ones but also hoping that her twin would turn to offer some sign of conciliation. 'I'll tell Granny you'll be back soon, that you're just—'

'Oh, bollocks to her,' muttered Ed, nudging a new stone with the toe of his trainer and setting himself the private challenge of kicking it all the way back to Ashley House.

'Okay, Roland?' Clem patted his shoulder. 'You can go on with Maisie or come back with us. Whatever you like.'

'With you,' Roland muttered, aware that what had started as a lovely day was somehow in shreds and that he was powerless to set it right.

That Saturday afternoon Cassie was in a gloomy maisonette in Fulham looking at carpet samples.

'I know you suggested green, but I was wondering about gold. There's gold in the curtains, isn't there?' The client, a woman in her fifties with crisp bleached hair, knelt down beside the swatches Cassie had laid out on the floor and began rearranging them like a pack of cards.

'Gold would work too,' said Cassie smoothly, 'but it's much less forgiving. I mean, when it comes to wear and tear, a tiny stain will show up terribly, whereas with the green – especially this lovely bottle green one here – you'd get away with far more. And I think, on balance, it goes just a little bit better with the curtains you've chosen. The overall effect will be stunning – sort of sumptuous but practical too . . .' She tailed off, hoping she had said enough. The gold sample, which her client had produced, was perfectly horrible. And although she had every right to make the wrong choice – it was after all her money – Cassie had learnt through bitter experience that if the client was allowed to go ahead it was very often the designer who was left with the blame. A bully of a man in Ealing had once refused to pay the final instalment of her fee on the grounds that the paint on the walls – chosen with huge obstinacy by his wife – looked hideous.

'Oh, God, I don't know, I really don't.' The woman, who was the worrying type, as capable of agonising over the colour of toilet roll as twenty feet of curtain fabric, wrung her hands. 'It's so jolly hard, isn't it? Whatever one does, it's bound to be wrong.'

'Not at all. With colours there simply isn't a right and a wrong. It's entirely up to individual taste. And, of course, I'm here to help you.' Cassie sneaked a glance at her watch. It was already half past two, well after the time she had hoped to leave.

'And you are *such* a help.' She picked up the square of muddy gold and put it down again. 'Another coffee I think, don't you?'

'Not for me, thanks,' Cassie replied briskly, her mind scrambling for a polite way to bring the meeting to a close. 'Perhaps it would help if I left you to think about it for a bit longer, Mrs Shorrold. There's no hurry, is there?'

'Oh, but there is. I've got hordes of visitors coming in a couple of months and I *so* want the house to be right by then.' She got to her feet and straightened her skirt. 'I simply must have another coffee. Are you quite sure you won't join me?'

Cassie declined again, thinking how insufferable people were and how selfish. She had agreed to come on a Saturday as a favour, wanting to make up for cancelling a previous appointment in favour of a last-minute rendezvous with Dan. That this pampered middle-aged woman thought she had nothing better to do than twiddle her thumbs on a weekend afternoon was deeply insulting. She would add five per cent to her usual commission, she decided, wreak revenge in the only way she could. 'Let's have another proper look, shall we?' She picked up all the samples and spread them out on the table, placing the gold and green bits of carpet on either side of the swatch for the curtains.

'Do you know?' said the woman, her voice tremulous with inspiration, her hands clasped round her fresh mug of coffee. 'I think it's the curtains that might be wrong. Maybe the gold carpet should be my starting point. What do you think?'

Cassie, whose view was too insulting to express, was searching for a suitable reply when the muffled trill of her mobile sounded from inside her handbag. 'Excuse me.' She made a show of rolling her eyes in exasperation, although inside she felt jubilant. It would be Dan, telling her that Sally had decided to go to her mother's and he was free to see her after all. 'Hello? Cassie Harrison speaking.' She did her best to sound businesslike, hoping he'd understand it was because she was working.

'Cassie, it's me, Elizabeth.'

'Elizabeth?' Cassie was so surprised that she forgot about putting on a show for Mrs Shorrold. 'I can't really talk right now, Elizabeth, I'm . . . in a meeting.' She cast an apologetic look at her client, who had begun to make sharp tapping noises on her saccharine dispenser with the pearly tips of her nails.

'Cassie, something terrible has happened.'

'What sort of terrible?' Cassie, aware now of Mrs Shorrold stirring vigorously – meaningfully – at her coffee, was still only half concentrating. Part of her was still thinking of Dan, wondering if he was trying to make contact at that very moment and getting annoyed that her mobile was busy.

'Tina. Charlie and Serena's Tina. She's – she's been killed.'

'Killed?' The stirring teaspoon stopped abruptly. 'What do you mean, killed?'

There was a long silence.

It was Elizabeth's third such phone-call and she was running out of the steam, courage, or whatever it was, that had empowered her thus far. Her father, to whom she had spoken first, had responded so inadequately, with such a hotchpotch of platitudes and gruff monosyllables that she almost cried out in frustration. This won't do, she wanted to say, what has happened is too huge. It requires a bigger response. Since the first numbing shock of the accident had worn off Elizabeth's own emotions had been spilling out of her unchecked; the images of Tina, innocent and impish in her green dungarees, then so pale and still on the hospital bed, were too vivid, as was the sight of Serena, her eyes wild and swollen, on her knees before the doctor, beyond dignity or reason, begging for some intervention that would bring her child back to life. Pamela was in the garden, her father had said. He would tell her and call back. The conversation had ended with a laboured exchange about where to call and what her mobile number was, when Elizabeth knew it was written perfectly clearly in the leather address book next to the telephone. Hearing the slow scratch of his pen on the pad, it had dawned on her that her father was as devastated as she was, clutching at the act of writing the numbers only as a refuge from shock. Between bouts of crying she had been doing similar things all afternoon. Would Serena like one spoon of sugar in her tea or two? Were they allowed to use mobiles in the hospital? When was the rugby due to end and what had Charlie been planning to do afterwards? Offering to phone the family had been part of the same pattern: something to do, something necessary and useful within the vacuum of helplessness in which she found herself.

After speaking to John Elizabeth had called Colin. When she heard her husband's familiar voice she had broken into sobs, feeling a sudden rush of belief in what had recently seemed precarious.

The petty quarrels, his obsession with the problems at school, anxieties over his strictness with Roland paled into insignificance. They had so much that was good and should be grateful for it. Life was precious and fragile and to be treasured. The creak of emotion in Colin's responses, his concern and simple offers of support, made Elizabeth wonder how she could have lost touch with such things. He was the old Colin, the one whose strong shoulder she needed to lean on, her anchor. He would come to London that instant, he said, or drive to Ashley House, or wherever she thought he could be of most use. Elizabeth, as yet unsure of where and how Serena and Charlie would end the day, suggested he drive to Sussex. 'And hug Roland for me,' she added hoarsely, seeing again the image of her little niece lying in the road and experiencing a sudden aching need to press her son to her chest.

The trauma of phoning Charlie was something Elizabeth had left to Serena. Their suffering she knew, even at this terrible early stage, was private territory, a path they had to tread alone. Serena had gone into a corner to make the call, curling up on a hard chair with her mobile as if she wanted to hide herself for ever from the world. Elizabeth, holding Serena's styrofoam cup of lukewarm tea, had retreated to the hospital corridor, overcome by the realisation that her darling brother and his lovely wife were at the beginning of something not only endless and terrible but also isolating. Serena, bending protectively over Tina at the roadside, had already looked so alone in her suffering that it had taken all of Elizabeth's courage to push her way through the crowd and crouch next to her. While ambulancemen, heroically gentle and kind in their plastic yellow livery, had gone about their business she had groped feebly for words to offer comfort, all the while knowing that no such words existed. As an aunt this was the greatest tragedy yet to befall her. As a mother she could hardly begin to glimpse the pain.

Slowly Cassie returned her phone to her handbag.

Mrs Shorrold laid down her teaspoon. 'I'm so sorry, my dear, has something happened?'

'Yes . . . I . . . My niece . . . just a baby . . . has been run over. I'm afraid I have to go.'

'Of course, of course. I'm so sorry. *So* sorry. I'll fetch your coat, unless . . . Are you sure you wouldn't like a cup of tea – or maybe a brandy?' she added, alarmed by the pallor of Cassie's face. 'Something like this . . . such a shock for all of you . . . Does she . . . Are there other children?'

'Yes, three,' Cassie murmured, reluctant to admit the fact for fear that it in some way diminished the magnitude of the tragedy; as if people with several children could afford to lose one. 'But Tina was so . . . such a . . .' She stopped, biting her lip as she plunged her arms into the sleeves of her coat, not wanting to break down in front of a woman she barely knew and for whom she felt neither affection nor empathy. 'I'll call you.'

'Oh, heavens, don't worry about that.'

Once outside, Cassie ran to her car, the tears now pouring down her cheeks, so thickly that it took her several minutes to locate her keys. She knew she should call her family – her parents and, of course, poor, poor Charlie and Serena – but first she wanted, needed, Dan, more fiercely than she had ever needed anything in her life before. Not just because she loved him but because he was a doctor and would understand better than most what they were all going through. They had talked of death several times and how he dealt with it. He had once moved her to tears describing the final minutes of a young man with cancer. The sense of the spirit leaving the body was almost palpable, he had said, as if the invisible human component had got up and walked away, leaving the shell behind. Cassie found it hard to think of Tina as a shell, impossible to imagine her chubby limbs and dimpled smile without the energy that animated them.

She closed her palm round her phone and willed Dan, through some telepathic power, to sense her need and call. It was impossible for her to call him because it was Saturday and he would be with his family. They hadn't spoken since the previous afternoon when he had offered the tenuous thread of a hope that Sally might visit her mother. Silence meant that she hadn't. All Cassie could do was sit and wait until Monday. The thought was suddenly so appalling – so unmanageable – that Cassie, abandoning all their rules, punched in his mobile number anyway. It rang ten times before he answered.

'Darling, it's me.'

'Cassie? Jesus . . . hang on.' There followed a series of muffled footsteps and the sound of a slamming door. 'What the hell are you doing? Jesus, Cassie, I've told you *never* to call me at home, it's just too dangerous.'

'Sorry, Dan, sorry . . . It's just – Oh, Dan, Tina, my baby niece, has been killed, knocked down by a motorbike, and I just – I feel so – I'm sorry, I know I shouldn't call you, but I just had to. I feel so wretched and alone and so bloody helpless and I knew you would be the only person in the world to understand.'

'How terrible. Cassie, I'm so sorry.'

'Oh, Dan, I want to see you.'

'And I want to see you,' he whispered fiercely, 'but I can't. You know I can't. Sally's decided to stay in London because two of the kids have got birthday parties to go to. I'm sorry, darling, but there's no way round it. Your niece,' he added, more gently, 'how old was she?'

'Seventeen months, something like that.'

'Where did it happen?'

'Off Oxford Street somewhere – a motorbike, it didn't stop.'

'Which hospital was she taken to?'

'I'm not sure . . . I . . . Dan, I need you.'

'And I need you, Cass.'

'No, Dan, I need you with me now.'

'Cassie, I can't, I just can't. Look, I can hear one of the children coming, I've got to go. I'm so sorry, my love, I'll call you when I can.'

Cassie looked bleakly through the windscreen. A small fly was crawling across the inside, hopping occasionally and making small buzzing sounds with its wings. She picked up a used tissue from the seat next to her and reached out to kill it, then froze, her hand poised, while her heart pounded with a doubt that had nothing to do with the fly. From nowhere a quotation popped into her head: 'As flies to wanton boys are we to the Gods, they kill us for their sport.'

During her A levels she had been able to recite whole passages of *King Lear* by heart but only a few remained, filed on some indestructible hard disk in her brain. Dan's love usually made her feel indestructible, but at that moment, more than ever before in her life, she felt crushed and powerless. She killed the fly with a twist of her wrist, then wept, unaware that Mrs Shorrold was peering anxiously at her through the window of her front room.

In the taxi Serena held Charlie's hand. If she gripped his fingers hard she could, momentarily, halt the shaking that had started at some dim point in this dark, endless, timeless day. It might have been when they left the room where Tina lay. Or maybe as they went in. It was hard to know, hard to be sure of anything. But now every joint in her body ached from having been in so prolonged a state of perpetual motion; even her teeth were clacking together, as if resisting Arctic temperatures, when in fact the taxi's heating vents were blasting at them, cocooning them in stale heat, drying the life from the air. There was no consolation in Charlie's hand. Neither did Serena expect any. There was none for him in hers either. For there was none to be had, anywhere, ever again. He was a crumpled stranger next to her, stricken and unreachable. They held hands as two drowning people might grasp at a twig in an ocean; because, although it couldn't save them, it was something to reach for. They had left their daughter, their *dead* (Serena stopped at the word, holding it up in her mind as someone might examine an alien object, feeling no connection to it) daughter at the hospital and were going home. Not that that seemed possible either. To be going home without Tina. Leaving her behind, never to hold her, never to feel her solid warmth again . . .

'Oh, God, I can't – I'm going to—' Serena groped for the handle to wind down the window. 'I can't breathe – I can't—' She stuck her head out into the dreary London night, throwing her sobs, which were dry and stomach-wrenching, more like being sick than crying, into the mêlée of car engines and hurrying figures. It was the end of the day and people were scurrying into buses and tube stations like rabbits into their burrows. Somewhere a siren wailed and Serena, remembering the other siren, opened her mouth wider, wanting to scream. But the sobbing had stopped and no sound came out, almost as if it had locked on to the unutterable pain inside. The shaking stopped too, quite suddenly. She brought her head back inside the taxi, but left the window open, letting the rush of night air dry the tears on her cheeks. She felt rigid and bruised and wide awake, so wide awake that it seemed possible she might never sleep again, even if she took the pills the doctor had given her. She had wanted to leave the hospital, but also not to. The still, waxy-faced child lying under the hospital sheet was not her daughter. Yet to leave felt like abandonment. Next to her Charlie groaned. He prised his hand from the grip of her fingers, put his arm across her back and leant his head on her shoulder. She could feel his tremors and his tears dampening the collar of her shirt.

'Oh, God, the pushchair! We left the pushchair!' Serena sat forward, knocking Charlie's head off her shoulder, and tapped the glass divide.

Charlie stroked her back. 'It doesn't matter.'

'It does, of course it does, it's Tina's pushchair. The hospital, please.' Her voice was querulous but commanding. 'We need to go back to the hospital.' The cabby nodded and swung the taxi across the road to wait for a break in the oncoming traffic.

'For God's sake, Serena, we can call them, we don't have to go back – I mean, it hardly fucking matters, does it, the fucking pushchair?'

'It's got her – Dolly's in the pushchair, tied to the side.'

'Oh, Jesus.' Dolly was the rag doll with flaxen hair and pink sequined clothes that Cassie had given Tina for Christmas, so instantly and madly loved that Tina had refused to be parted from it. Charlie dropped his head into his hands. 'All the same, it hardly matters, does it? After what's happened, it hardly fucking matters.'

Serena, still sitting forward in the seat, turned to face him. 'You might as well say it, Charlie, just say it. You think it's my fault, don't you? What happened, you think it's my fault.'

'Shut up.' He groaned. 'Of course I don't – how could I blame you? How could I? Don't say that ever again, do you hear me? I never want to hear you say that again, Serena, do you understand?'

The cabby was speeding back towards the hospital. The dim strains of his radio came through the sealed partition, headlines about the rugby, which England had lost, reports of traffic congestion on the M25.

Serena continued to stare at her husband, his mouth opening, the pain etched like knife cuts round his eyes and mouth. His words meant nothing to her. Nothing meant anything to her. 'But it was my fault. I was there and I couldn't stop it. It was – *preventable* and I didn't prevent it.'

'It – wasn't – your – fault.' Charlie forced each word out, saying what he knew to be true, but without the energy to give it conviction. 'We must be strong. For Ed and Clem and Maisie. We must be strong.'

Serena sat back in the seat and began to cry again, silently this time, too exhausted either to fight the tears or to speak. When they got back to the hospital the cabby waited, his engine running, while they went inside. The pushchair, Dolly dangling at its side, had been parked behind the desk at Reception. Charlie explained who they were while Serena, with trembling fingers, undid the knot of string that she had – only a few hours and a lifetime before – tied round Dolly's arm. It was tight and still faintly damp from having spent much of the day in Tina's mouth, so it took a long time. Charlie and the receptionist watched in silence. When Serena had at last untied the string she pressed the doll to her face, absorbing the faint sweet traces of her daughter. Then she held it against her chest, cupping the flopping head in the palm of her hand as she would a newborn baby.

Charlie began to wheel the pushchair, but then, unable to bear the poignancy of the empty seat, folded it up and carried it instead. When they got outside the cabby jumped out and opened the door for them, making a big to-do of helping to stow the pushchair. 'I turned the meter off,' he said, looking desolate.

'That was kind, thank you.' Charlie let Serena get in first, then slid into the seat next to her. On the dashboard, stuck down with a tatty bit of Sellotape, was a picture he hadn't noticed before, a blurred family snap of a smiling woman and two children, with freckled snub noses and gaps in their teeth. Staring at it, Charlie experienced a fresh heave of shock, just as strong as the one that had sucked the air from his lungs that afternoon, when Serena, her voice ghostly, had phoned him at the rugby. He reached again for his wife's hand, unable to breathe, seeing only the abyss before them. They would never be happy in the same way again. Not with each other, not with their children.

The house was so empty and terrible that Charlie said they should leave for Ashley House at once. Echoes of Tina were everywhere: a tiny blue sock on the hall radiator, a sticky beaker in the sink, a half-done wooden jigsaw of Goldilocks and the three bears. Serena moved as if in a trance, picking these objects up, stroking them and putting them down again. She had tucked Dolly inside the front of her shirt, so that only the top of the head was visible, its yellow stringy hair dangling over her shirt buttons. 'I can't go yet,' she murmured. 'Not yet.'

'But the kids . . . they need to see us. It's terrible for them too.' She nodded, but Charlie could tell she wasn't really listening.

'I wish I knew there was a God,' she murmured. 'Then I'd know she'd see Mum.'

'What?' Serena's mother had died of pancreatic cancer shortly after Ed was born. Deserted early in her marriage by her husband, she had brought up Serena and her elder sister, who now lived in Canada, on her own.

'In heaven or whatever.'

'Right.' Charlie didn't want to pursue the thought. The notion of heaven or any other religious construct seemed an unlikely prospect at the best of times. A God who steered small children under motorbikes wasn't worth contemplating. 'I'm going to have a drink. Do you want one?'

Serena shook her head absently. 'I'm going to look for . . . They'll want to dress her for . . . I must choose something nice.' She started up the stairs, tugging roughly at the strands of hair falling out of her big combs. Charlie watched until she had turned the corner on the landing and was out of sight. He went into the kitchen, poured two inches of whisky and drank it in one go. Then he reached for the kettle and a tea-bag, dropped his head into his hands and wept.

In the evening light the mountains were towering white pyramids streaked with black and purple where outcrops of rock and forest scarred their sides. Several snowploughs were zigzagging their way across the slopes, moving like ants across a vast landscape, their flashing lights tiny fireflies pricking the darkness. Helen, standing on the balcony of their hotel room, shivered inside her fleece and tugged its collar round her ears. From the dining room several storeys below faint strains of jollity broke the silence. Their rooms, two doubles side by side, were positioned on the quietest, most expensive wing of the hotel, facing towards the mountains and away from the bubbling outdoor pool where Chloë, Ed and Peter had spent a good hour splashing off the grime of the journey before dinner. Helen had been prevented from joining them by a monumental ache in her abdomen, an ache that had quickly translated itself into a rush of menstrual blood. In one way she was relieved – it went some way towards explaining her recent emotional turbulence. The arrival of a period, no matter how painful and unpleasant, always contained an element of catharsis, a sense of purging, not only of blood but of invisible tension. Less reassuring was that it had happened, on this occasion, and a couple of previous ones, so unexpectedly and with such vehemence. Helen had never been one of those women enslaved by her cycle; her periods had always been regular and easily managed. It was both alarming and disorientating to feel now that her body was losing touch with such patterns. Where once tampons and an occasional aspirin had put the matter from her mind, she had lately taken to using heavy-duty analgesics and wodges of sanitary towels to get through the ordeal of the first couple of days. The idea of joining her family for swimming had been both impossible and faintly abhorrent. The prospect of managing a day up the mountain, stuffing tampons and pads into the small zipped pockets of her ski-suit, then racing between the various lavatory facilities stationed round the slopes was equally unappealing. And there was the pain to contend with: muffled unsatisfactorily by pain-killers, it was a constant pulse – like the regular stabbing of a knife – that ran not only through her womb but into the deepest reaches of her lower back. She couldn't imagine staying upright for more than thirty minutes, let alone leapfrogging down a mountain after her husband, who ski'd hard and well.

Helen moved forward to rest her elbows on the balcony. Even through three layers of clothes she could feel the icy metal of the railing. She clasped her mug, which was empty but still warm. Unable to face dinner, she had made herself hot chocolate, using one of the sachets and the kettle provided in the room. She had eaten a packet of shortbread, and a bag of peanuts from the minibar, which had made her so thirsty she had used the last sachet of chocolate to make a second cup. Her tummy, straining against the usually loose waistband of her jeans, felt bloated yet curiously hollow, as if a firm puncture from a sharp pin could reduce it to its normal size.

Only one snowplough remained on the mountain. Helen followed its progress, torn between the notion that man had an impressive capacity to imprint his influence on the natural world and a more compelling sense of how ultimately futile it was to try. The mountains, ancient and imperious, glowed with energy and presence; one rumble of their power could flatten not just a snowplough but an entire community. Just the week before there had been an avalanche in Austria: five killed, three missing and scores trapped in chalets in the valley. Theo and Chloë, seeing it reported on the news, had thought it exciting, Theo because being marooned in a chalet would introduce the possibility of not having to return to school and Chloë because it made for a thrilling story and she was still at the age where she felt immortal.

Frozen, Helen had already turned back towards the room when the telephone rang. Her first thought was that Peter was calling from Reception to see how she was and to report on the progress of the meal. She knew he had been put out at the prospect of eating alone with children and a little disappointed – suspicious, even – of her suddenly fragile state. 'Well, if you're really feeling that bad . . .'

'Yes, Peter, I am. I'm sorry, but I am.' She had been lying on the bed, one hand across the swell of her stomach. 'And I'm not sure about tomorrow either, whether I'll be able to cope—'

'But, Helen,' he interrupted, looking not so much compassionate as exasperated, 'at the airport you said you were going to ski the socks off us.'

'That was before—'

'Okay, okay.' He had held up his hands, not wanting to be subjected to any more details of her condition than were necessary. 'I'm sorry, obviously, and hope you feel better soon. And Chloë is fine with anything so long as it's got chips, right?'

'Right. And ketchup helps.'

She got to the phone on the third ring and lay on the bed to take the call.

'Hello, Helen, is that you?'

'Yes.'

'Is Peter there?'

'Peter?' Their voices were so similar that it took Helen a few seconds to register that she was talking to her father-in-law and not her husband. 'No, John, he's downstairs having dinner with the children – I'm feeling slightly under par.'

'It's taken a while to track you down – had to get hold of Peter's secretary in the end. Look here, Helen, the fact is there's some bad news on the home front, some very bad news. We thought the pair of you ought to know.'

'Oh, no, John,' Helen murmured, thinking immediately of Alicia.

'It's Tina.' He spoke brusquely, almost coldly. 'Charlie and Serena's Tina. She's been killed in a hit-and-run, Helen. It happened this afternoon and we're all at our wits' end. Thought you ought to know.'

'Oh, no.' Helen was bolt upright now and clutching the phone. 'Oh, the poor, poor things – oh, how unspeakable. We'll come home at once.'

'Oh, no, don't do that, I'm sure they wouldn't want you to do that.'

'How . . . I mean . . . how are they?'

'Too soon to tell. They're coming down here tomorrow. Charlie wanted to tonight but Serena won't leave the house. The doctor's given her some tablets. We've got the girls and Ed. They're pretty cut up, as you can imagine, but not saying much . . . all in shock, of course.'

'Of course, of course. Oh, John, how utterly terrible. I'll tell Peter at once. And we will come home, I really think we should, at such a time. Is there a date for the . . . funeral?' Saying the word brought Helen, for the first time, in touch with the full reality of what they were discussing and she began to cry.

'Easy does it,' John muttered, his own voice choked with emotion. 'As to the funeral, it's not yet been decided. Charlie said something about early next week. We'll keep you posted. Go and find Peter. Let us know what you decide.'

> During the course of the last century not only did the nature of war change, but also the nature of the heroism at the heart of it. Nowadays, with the action live on our television sets, there is a sense of outrage for every soldier's life lost, often accompanied by public questioning as to the manner in which he or she died and the merits of the commands they were following. Media access to battlefields has brought accountability on a scale that would have left First and Second World War generals quaking in their boots . . .

Stephen lifted his hands from his laptop and folded his arms. The week before he had had lunch with his editor and talked convincingly of his manuscript, as if it actually existed instead of floating, as it still did, in some garbled form in his mind. They had agreed that good writing required passion and conviction, that even the simplest sentences shone with authenticity if they came from the heart. The editor had paid, and Stephen had splashed out on a taxi home, full of pasta, wine and self-belief. He had spent the rest of the afternoon vigorously arranging his notes, which had somehow extended into an energetic overhaul of the flat. As it comprised only four small rooms, this would not have been a huge undertaking, were it not for the scores of half-unpacked boxes, piles of books and unhung pictures stacked along the skirting-boards, with several unassembled self-assembly units in which much of it was destined to be stowed. It wasn't just laziness that had caused this lamentable state of affairs. On receiving the packing cases several weeks after his return to England, the eclectic collection of belongings they contained – dog-eared Spanish manuals, carved wooden figures, rainbow-coloured wall-hangings, a leather saddle – had looked so incongruous in his cramped urban surroundings that Stephen had not been able to muster either the heart or the inspiration to grapple with them. But on that Monday afternoon, when all his notes were tidily filed, he found himself erecting bookshelves and pinning up his Ecuadorean tapestries with precisely the sort of passion he had been discussing with his editor. It was an arduous task that took several days and which he was frequently tempted to abandon. There was something comforting about untidiness, something, perhaps, to do with its possibility of improvement. As a child, the chaotic state of his bedroom was one of the many misdemeanours that had prompted his father to slide his belt out from the waistband of his trousers. Stephen thought of this many times as he laboured, marvelling at the ineffectuality of punishment as an incentive for anything. If his father were to walk in the door Stephen would probably have turned the place upside-down again just to rile him. As a child, resistance and disobedience had been his only weapons. And not crying. He had got good at that, too, even when the edge of the belt buckle swung into the spaces between his ribs.

It was only as he had been putting the last things in place that Sunday morning, hanging a Brillo-scrubbed pan on a new hook above the stove next to a hand-painted tile depicting a Spanish bull-fighter, that it had dawned on Stephen that all this sudden rush of domestic fervour stemmed from one source: Cassie Harrison. He wanted her to see his home, to see him and all the odd little pieces of his history. He wanted to point at the bull-fighter and describe the day on which he had bought it, a steamy day in Paloma when he had gorged himself on tapas and chilled sherry, then almost brought it up at the sight of the bull, lumbering blindly at the matador, blood and spikes trailing from its hide. He wanted to show her the polished pink stone he had found on the shores of Lake Titicaca, the little silver horse given to him by a grateful student. He wanted to point at his shelves of dog-eared novels, tell her when he had read them and what each had meant to him. He wanted, in short, to spill himself open to her so that she could love him, all of him, as he loved her.

> Heroes are a strange breed. They are people who are brave when there is no hope, people who rise above all the normal human preoccupations with fear and self-preservation in the interests of a greater good . . .

Stephen stopped, reread all that he had written, then pressed the delete button. He didn't want to think about heroes, unsung or otherwise, he wanted to think about Cassie Harrison. The silky waves of her hair, her startled blue eyes, the faint outline of her bra pressing through the fine blue wool of her top. He imagined reaching out and tracing one finger from her hairline through the centre of her face, across the tiny shallow lines etched along her forehead and down the smooth slope of her nose to her wide pink mouth. He longed to press his face against her neck and breathe the scent of her skin, to run his tongue along the ridge of her collar-bone, to taste her . . . God, how he wanted to taste her, all of her, every crevice, every dimple, every downy blonde hair.

'For Christ's sake,' Stephen shouted, slapping the keyboard and causing a nonsensical string of letters to burst on to the screen in front of him. It was intolerable, this obsession. Mad, insupportable. Unlike anything he had ever known. It sapped all his energies, ate away at his concentration (dubious at the best of times). He had to see her again, he simply had to. Either to push the thing forward or to stop it in its tracks. He had to make something happen. He grabbed his address book and the phone, then dialled Ashley House.

'Is that Pamela Harrison?'

'Speaking.'

'It's Stephen Smith, the, er—'

'Ah, the biographer.'

She sounded distant and unwelcoming, not at all as he remembered. 'I was wondering if I might call again to—'

'We've shown you all that we have, Mr Smith, there's nothing more.'

'And I am so grateful,' he ploughed on, heedless of the evidence that Pamela had little desire to prolong the conversation, 'but I wondered if I could just drop by one more time to clear up a couple of points . . . maybe in a few weeks?'

'A few weeks? I suppose . . .'

'Maybe one weekend, if that's not too inconvenient?' At a weekend there was a small chance of Cassie being there. If she wasn't he would wangle her address or phone number or NHS number or *something* through which he could make contact. Stephen had kicked himself a million times already for letting her go without establishing anything beyond that she lived somewhere in Pimlico. Directory Enquiries, offered this one fact on several occasions, had been consistently unhelpful, making him feel like an axe-murderer in pursuit of a potential victim.

'A weekend . . . I'm not sure.' Her voice was so thin and uncertain that Stephen feared he had pushed her capacity for co-operation too far.

'A Tuesday, then,' he blundered. 'In, say, three weeks. March the nineteenth, in the afternoon.'

'Yes, yes.' She sounded truly impatient now, almost angry. 'Very good, Mr Smith. We'll see you then.'

Stephen put down the phone and punched the air with his fist. It was a tenuous thread of a hope, of course, a desperate strategy devised by a desperate man. And if ever he did get to know Cassie, it probably wouldn't work; socially, they were worlds apart, and emotionally too, damaged as he knew he was by the gritty unhappiness of his youth, while she radiated the self-confidence of one who had been nurtured in all the right ways. What could he offer her that she didn't have? Money, career, security, a solid, happy family, striking looks – she possessed everything already. And even without a ring on her fourth finger (her lovely slim, bare fingers) she almost certainly had a boyfriend. Such women always did. Stephen didn't like thinking about the boyfriend, did his best to avoid it. But even given a boyfriend there was hope, he decided fiercely. Even if she told him to fuck off there was hope, because there always was, if you looked for it hard enough.

Pamela had taken Stephen's call in John's study. After putting the receiver down she remained standing by the desk for a few minutes, resting the fingers of one hand on the worn, smooth leather inlay of its top, edged on all sides by an intricate pattern of faded gold. She knew she had been distant on the phone and hoped that the biographer hadn't thought her rude. With all that had happened she was finding it hard to concentrate.

The room smelt of John – that indefinable smell of human that had nothing to do with laundry powder or aftershave – and of wood and leather. It was a man's room, with heavy furniture, dark green furnishings and the resonant stillness of a library. Three of the four walls were taken up from carpet to ceiling with bookshelves, many of them leatherbound ancient editions that had belonged to his father and grandfather. An equally ancient set of library steps was positioned half-way along the furthest wall; John insisted on using them even though the feet had worn at different rates over the years causing them to wobble whenever they were subjected to the most modest weight. During the Christmas break Tina, mistaking it for a climbing frame, had been discovered very near the top, toothy with glee and triumph. Pamela, in charge while Serena had taken the other children shopping, had whisked her down in trembling arms, breathless with guilt at her own lack of vigilance. Later on she had confessed the episode to her daughter-in-law, profuse with apology, and been greeted with gales of laughter, followed by several other proud tales of Tina's recent flirtations with disaster: falling down the stairs, climbing out of her cot, crawling through a hole in the fence to a neighbour's garden. Remembering the incident now, Pamela caught her breath. Every moment of every life was a hair's breadth away from disaster. She had known that once but, like most people when things were going well, had forgotten it.

'Pam?'

'Oh, John.' She lifted her hand from the desk, without seeing the deep, semi-circular imprints where her nails had cut into the leather.

'Are you all right?'

'Yes . . . I . . . Not really. But, then, none of us is, are we? How are they all doing out there?'

He shrugged, picked up a book, then put it down without looking at it. 'It's quiet. The children are watching a film, Cassie is making tea, Colin is doing some marking, Elizabeth is with Serena and Charlie helping them choose hymns, I think.'

'I wish Peter was here. I understand his decision not to cancel the holiday, but all the same I wish he was here, don't you? He's so . . . *solid* and, of course, it would be a comfort for Charlie to have his brother here.'

'He's got his sisters,' John reminded her gently. 'As for Serena . . .' He faltered, as speechless now about his daughter-in-law's dazed desolation as he was in her company. He had never known anything like it, at least not since . . . 'Pam, I've been thinking . . . wondering if it would help to – to tell them about . . .'

'Miranda?' She said the name for him, her eyes glittering, her jaw clenching round the word as if it needed controlling.

He sighed. 'Yes. Miranda.' He looked at her properly for the first time, his eyes heavy with despair, not so much at the memory of their own distant loss (Miranda, as they had christened her, had been stillborn at six months, when Peter was a toddling two-year-old) but at the recognition that he never had and never could feel the loss as his wife did. He felt closer to Charlie and Serena's pain: every room in the house was thick with it, a tangible presence, as impossible to ignore as a ringing bell, audible through silence and conversation alike. And Tina had been such a bouncy enchanting thing, already, at the grand age of one and a bit, with a vivid, endearing personality, a shining little light in all their lives. He moved towards Pamela, studying her face, seeing not the soft deep lines of old age, glistening faintly with powder, or the thin, lipsticked outline of her mouth, which had shrunk, as mouths were inclined to, over the years, but the fresh beauty with which he had fallen in love fifty years before. 'Not if you don't want to, Pam, it was just a thought . . .'

'And a good thought,' she said firmly, folding her arms and crossing to the window to peer out through the arch of the cloisters at the garden. A storm was threatening: the sky was purple with it, the grass an iridescent green. Somewhere, in the background – her eyes were so poor now without her glasses – she could just make out the pink fuzzy blur of the quince blossom. 'Though, of course, there's a world of difference between a tiny . . . a half-developed six-month-old foetus . . .' she struggled to get the words out, her tongue and teeth seeming, curiously, to get in the way '. . . and Tina . . . Dear, dear little Tina, she was *such* a little person. Wasn't she, John, a dear little person?'

'Yes, Pammy, she was.' He hurried to the window and put his arms round her. She seemed to tolerate rather than welcome the embrace, keeping her own arms folded across her chest, hugging herself. But there was consolation in the physical contact. She didn't let him in easily to her heart. She never had. And he was just the same. But it had never stopped them being happy, never blocked the oxygen of easy companionship on which they thrived.

'I will say something . . . when the moment presents itself,' she murmured. 'You were right to suggest it.'

Outside, impenetrable grey clouds were squeezing the light from the day. A wind was getting up, making the windows hum in their frames and causing the trees, bare-limbed since November, to claw at the sky. The pergola, thinly protected in its skeletal winter gear of pruned laburnum and roses, was swaying visibly. Pamela almost remarked on it, then realised it didn't matter; that nothing mattered as it once had. 'I will say something,' she repeated dully, 'when the time is right . . . Timing is everything.'

Maisie knew she wasn't really feeling anything yet, not properly. It was almost like being outside herself, looking in, like she was *seeing* the tragedy of losing her baby sister rather than experiencing it. When their grandmother had broken the news the afternoon before, with the three of them sitting round the kitchen table, her crinkled blue eyes all watery and her mouth twitching, Clem had cried at once while Ed had gone a sort of puce colour. Maisie, who had been expecting some sort of massive telling-off for abandoning her siblings on the walk to the village and then not getting back until an hour later, had at first been struck by a brief (and utterly despicable) thunderbolt of relief. This faded quickly at the magnitude of what they were being told although, throughout the subsequent turmoil of emotions, she felt a keen and new awareness of how weird life was, with its twists and turns, how just when you were all hyped up about one thing another quite different thing whacked you on the head from behind.

She had walked to the gates of Rosco's country retreat alone, expecting little beyond a glimpse of bricks and mortar. She had been peering through the railings, one hand clasped on either side of her head, feeling sort of excited and let down all at the same time when a man, whom at first she took to be a gardener, appeared from out of the shrubbery to her left and asked if she was looking for anything in particular. He was wearing muddy wellingtons, ripped jeans and a huge shapeless sweater full of holes. His hair, scruffily cut and plainly in need of a wash, screened so much of his facial geography that it was a good minute before she realised she was being addressed by Rosco himself. 'No, I'm just looking,' she had replied, before this moment of enlightenment, wondering as she spoke what, indeed, she had been hoping to find beyond something to ease her conscience about Monica. 'Is he at home?'

'Yes, he is.' The man shifted the curtain of hair from his eyes and shot her a grin, revealing the trademark diamond stud in his front tooth.

'Oh, my God . . .'

'Not a form of address I'm used to, but you can call me that if you like. Come in, if you want.' He was already pulling a bunch of keys from his front pocket. Maisie watched spellbound as he slid one into the padlock and released one half of the gate. It creaked as he pushed it open. 'Come and have a wander.'

'Oh, my God . . .' For a few moments she clung to the side of the gate that he hadn't opened. The metal was rusty and chips of old black paint were sticking to her palms. She longed to accept the invitation. It felt wrong, but also exciting – the most exciting thing that had ever happened to her. 'Well, maybe just for a bit.' She side-stepped through the gap in the gates, rubbing her hands on her skirt to get the bits of paint off, feeling at any moment as if her knees might buckle under her. 'I suppose you get a lot of this – fans and stuff.' The diamond in the tooth was amazing. She couldn't take her eyes off it.

'Some. Not so much down here. I'll give you a quick tour, if you like, round the grounds anyway.' He looked at his watch. 'By which time my breakfast will be getting cold.' He gave her another grin, at the same time – or did she imagine it? – running the tip of his tongue round his lips.

'Breakfast?' Maisie had laughed uncertainly. 'At this time?'

'Oh, yes. I'm a night dude. Breakfast in the afternoons, lunch in the evenings, often don't bother with dinner. Such a waste of time, eating, don't you think?'

'Oh, God, absolutely.' Maisie, who had been hungry – who was always hungry – felt her appetite vanish. He pulled a squashed packet of cigarettes from his back pocket and offered her one, cupping his hands so closely round hers to light it that at one point she felt the tickly contact of his skin against hers. The cigarette was strong, almost choking her, which was embarrassing, but she sorted herself out eventually, at one point even managing to let the smoke stream out of her nostrils, a trick she and Monica had practised for hours. During the course of the tour she smoked a couple more, disclosed that she was on a visit from London to her grandparents, implied that she was studying for A levels rather than GCSEs and asked him where he got his inspiration for his music. 'Nowhere and everywhere,' he had replied. 'And from people like you.' They were back at the gates by this time, so Maisie was able to reach out and grab one for support. 'Will you call again, do you think, Miss Maisie?'

She had blushed, unsure whether the teasing was kind or con-descending. 'Oh, yes . . . At least, I should think so.'

'Good. There's a little bell here, see?' He walked to the wall and pulled back an armful of hedge. 'Ring it twice very quickly and I'll know it's you. You're very pretty, Maisie. Anyone ever told you that before?'

'I . . . well, no, I guess not . . . not really.'

'Boyfriends must have.'

Maisie's brain had whirred through her list of meagre conquests: Peter Masham, whom she had snogged without much enjoyment at three parties; Phil Dormund, who had put his hand inside her bra and kneaded her breast with all the subtlety of a four-year-old attacking a lump of Plasticine; and Jonny Cottrall, who had kissed her rather tenderly a couple of times behind the school gym. 'Sort of . . . I guess.' She shrugged, glad to feel some composure seeping back into her, glad, too, that she had taken the precaution of wearing makeup, heels and a decent jacket.

Now sitting at the kitchen table with her siblings, images of this encounter had flashed across Maisie's brain, making her feel at once consoled and guilty. To be able to think of anything other than the unimaginable horror that had befallen Tina was, she knew, a sin of criminal proportions. Ed, too, was looking stricken with guilt. She could see it imprinted on his face, as if someone had punched him on the nose. Maisie, filled with empathetic compassion at the sight of it and guessing its origin, found herself blurting out clumsy reassurance, telling him not to feel awful about how he'd behaved at the station, that he had just been in a bad mood and it didn't mean anything, especially not to Tina who had loved everyone regardless and Ed especially. Her brother squirmed, then burst into terrible, coughing tears, prompting a hug from their grandmother, which had gone on for ages even though Ed looked like he didn't want it.

With both her siblings crying Maisie, feeling bleak and exposed, had crept upstairs to be on her own. Lying on her bed with her face to the wall, a sense of outrage had crept over her because the best and worst events of her life so far had happened on the same day. It just wasn't fair. She'd got out her phone to text Monica, then hadn't known what to say. Later on in the evening her uncle Colin and aunt Elizabeth arrived. They talked in quiet voices with her grandparents and the rest of them were despatched to the TV room with mugs of hot chocolate and a plate of biscuits. They were allowed to stay up really late, even Roland, who could barely keep his eyes open and who had spent all afternoon gawping at the three of them as if they were exhibits in a zoo.

The worst bit of all had been the arrival of their parents that morning. Hearing the crunch of car wheels on the gravel the three of them had raced outside, each half hoping, as Maisie realised later, that these two loved authorities in their lives would have some sort of miracle solution as to what on earth they were all supposed to do. A tiny desperate part of her had even hoped to see Tina, riding high on their father's shoulders as she had loved to do, gurgling and unrepentant at the terrible scare she had given them all. But there was no Tina and no solution, miraculous or otherwise. Only her mother and father, dishevelled and shell-shocked, their eyes puffy and red, their faces engrained with deep, frightening lines. They had all hugged and wept, her dad crying most of all, so much so that Maisie had felt a sort of rage at his misery, at the sheer uselessness of it. Her mother cried silently, stroking their heads and nodding as if to keep herself in the scene when in fact she was miles away, in some lonely, desolate place where she might never be reached again. Clem and Ed seemed to want to stay near them, but Maisie couldn't bear it. She had retreated upstairs, with this hateful feeling that she was watching herself – watching all of them – in an unfolding drama of other people's lives.

After a few minutes she noticed the diary she had given Clem lying, in a rare moment of unlocked vulnerability, next to the pillow on her bed. Beyond talking when they had finally trooped upstairs the night before, her sister had scribbled furiously in it before she fell asleep. Without any compunction, feeling that the drama of the situation warranted it – warranted anything – Maisie reached for the diary, which fell open at the words: 'Tina has died. I can't believe it. Tina is dead. A motorbike ran into her and drove off. This is a nightmare. I know I must be strong, but I can't. I hate the world more than I have ever hated it before.' Opposite, a page and a universe away, was an entry from the day before: 'I think I love

Jonny Cottrall. I don't want to, but I just do. But, then, that's what love is, isn't it, something that just happens whether you want it to or not, like a DISEASE?' At this point Maisie did cry, explosively, with her face buried in Clem's pillow, feeling as if she was weeping for the sorrows of the entire world.

MARCH

Winter, having bided its time with four months of drizzle and half-hearted frosts, pounced with icy ferocity during the first two weeks of March. Spring flowers, lulled into a false sense of security by the mildness of the preceding weeks, wilted in the frozen ground, clamming up their half-open buds in a vain bid to preserve their future. Temperatures plunged, then rose slightly, releasing truckloads of snow; large crusty crystals that did not melt upon contact with the ground, but held their shape even as a thousand others landed on top of them, building up layer upon layer until, across the country, roads were indistinguishable from fields and entire villages woke to find themselves cut off from the outside world. News reporters filed stories from touring helicopters, describing road collisions and marooned hypothermic pensioners, their voices raised against the roar of wind and machine, their faces clenched with the grim concern of those experiencing a battle at first hand. Behind and below them the white undulations of the landscape shimmered, alien and indifferent.

At Ashley House the lake in the wood froze, and the pergola sagged and swayed under its heavy white coat like a staggering beast. On the surrounding lawns and fields the snow lay as thick as cake, inching inwards during the course of each day, then hardening again at night until the grounds looked as if they had been laid with a patchwork of huge linen tablecloths, each with a pea-green trim where the snow had melted sufficiently to reveal strips of grass. Up by the house a stretch of unlagged piping, which fed the outside tap by the garage, burst and spilled gallons of water that froze overnight, converting a large portion of the drive into a treacherous ice rink. Sid, called out to apply his plumbing skills, slipped and sprained his wrist, which Pamela soothed with some of her witchy homeopathic creams, then bandaged expertly with crisp white gauze and a small gold safety-pin. John, proud yet envious of her tenderness, hovered in the background, thumbing through the *Yellow Pages* in search of alternative assistance. Twenty minutes later, the muffled stillness outside was broken by the sound of the plumber he had summoned negotiating the snow-rutted lane in his van. John, going outside to watch the last few yards of its approach, felt like a castaway witnessing the arrival of a ship.

During the two weeks of inclement weather, access to Barham and the rest of the world had remained possible, thanks to his Range Rover, but because of the hazardous conditions he and Pamela had kept their sorties to the minimum, buying basic supplies and retreating to the house. Compared to many they had managed comfortably enough: the phone had been down for a while, but there was no shortage of dry logs for the open fire and they had enjoyed many meals in front of the TV, sipping wine and tutting at the images of the weather-induced dramas flickering across the screen. Belying such scenes of cosy domesticity, however, the atmosphere between them had been heavy with the ache of isolation, as nagging and constant as the pain at the base of John's spine. It had felt sometimes as if they were the last two old people in an old world. This was partly because they were marooned by the snow, but mostly because of the grief that, weeks after their granddaughter's funeral, still hung round the beams of Ashley House and their own withered necks like an invisible lead weight. Their silences, usually so companionable, were heavy and unrelaxing.

Outside, the blanketing whiteness reduced even the most intricate shapes to lumpen masses, at times appearing to be smothering the earth, pressing inwards as if bent upon crushing the life out of everything in its path. As he dragged Boots round the grounds on their daily walk, the monochrome landscape was so unrelentingly dense that at times John struggled to distinguish the usually solid slope of the South Downs from the snow-laden sky overhead. The glare made his eyes sting too, so badly that he had taken to wearing an old pair of Pamela's sunglasses whenever he ventured outside, not caring that the huge wing-tipped frames made him look camp and comical. As he stepped forward to greet the plumber on that Tuesday morning, he took them off, causing his eyes, with depressing inevitability, to flood with tears. It took several trumpet blows into his handkerchief before he was capable of speech. 'Good of you to come. It's over here. Watch your step, it's devilishly slippery.' He stood to one side while the man fitted and lagged a new shiny section of brass piping along the garage wall, fiddling with the sunglasses, which had a loose arm, and casting meaningful glances at his watch (he knew how these chaps dawdled to boost their fees). Afterwards he paid by cheque, pressing awkwardly on his knee to write it and shaking his pen several times to keep the ink flowing. After the man had gone, John fetched a spade from the garden shed and set about chipping the ice off the driveway, knowing in his heart that it was futile, but driven by some deep conviction that effort on any level was better than surrender.

'Are you still going to go?' Pamela set a cup of tea in front of him and turned back to the sink, running a cloth round the already gleaming stainless steel. She was bursting to reprimand him for chiselling at the ice with his fragile back (she had seen from the kitchen window, her heart wrenching at each hurl of the spade), but instead directed her criticism at his plan of taking the train up to London, an idea against which she had been chiselling, in a rather subtler manner, for days. He was due to meet Peter – and Charlie if he could get away from work – for lunch, before joining a gathering of ex-Lloyds colleagues at his club.

'Yes. I see no reason to cancel. Most of the main roads are fine now. According to that plumber a proper thaw is on the way. I shall catch the eleven-twenty.' John spoke quickly, swinging each sentence like a bat at a ball. He hated her disapproval. He also hated his own guilt at being so keen to get away. 'Life goes on, Pammy,' he added, more gently. Although her back was to him, he saw her shoulders tense. The hand working the cloth round the taps stopped.

'Yes, John, I know it does.' She folded the cloth into a neat rectangle and draped it over the edge of the sink before turning round. 'Well, if you are going, perhaps you could take a jar or two of marmalade. I'm sure Helen and Peter would like some and I did promise Serena . . . that is, if Charlie turns up. It's the new batch. I'll wrap them and put them in your briefcase. It's only a little thing but . . .' Her voice tailed off.

She felt helpless, he knew. So did he. Marmalade wasn't much consolation for a lost child but, then, nothing was. She had been to Wimbledon herself to see Charlie and Serena once since the funeral – before the onslaught of the virulent weather – taking with her all sorts of gifts for the children and several foil-wrapped parcels of food for the deep freeze. Since then all offers of such active intervention – further visits, children for the weekend – had been gently refused. Regular phone contact reported that Charlie was more in the thick of things than ever at work and that Serena was doing well with the support of local friends but thinking of seeing a bereavement counsellor. The three children missed their little sister, but were fine otherwise. 'Marmalade. Of course. No problem.' John, detesting the idea of carrying the jars in his briefcase, however securely wrapped, rose stiffly from the table with his mug of tea. 'I've just time for a bath.'

An hour later he was on the train, speeding through the snowy wastelands of the Home Counties towards Victoria, his heavy briefcase on the seat beside him, his heart shamefully light. The prospect of some male company presented him with much-needed respite from Ashley House. It would be good to see his sons too. Grief-stricken though they all were, John knew that being with them would be easier than being with their mother – or any of the women in the family – around whom the air was so thick with emotion that it was hard at times to breathe. As men they would give each other space, talk round the subject instead of wading through the middle of it. And afterwards he could relax properly with a glass of port and some business chat with his old chums. He might not even mention Tina. Not because he didn't care – Christ, he cared – but because he needed time out, and if he told them what had happened they wouldn't be able to give it to him.

After the Range Rover had disappeared round the bend in the lane Pamela stepped back from the window and put the kettle on. She hadn't wanted John to go, but now that he had it felt okay. Good, even. She made herself some milky coffee, put the radio on and settled to the task of labelling the rest of the marmalade jars and checking that the rubber bands were tightly sealed round their blue gingham lids. When she had finished she arranged them in lines on the largest of her trays and carried them carefully into the larder, managing not to trip on the little step down (where John, in spite of so many decades of familiarity with all the foibles of the house, regularly stumbled) and transferred them one by one to the top shelf, next to the cluster of little jars that contained the quince jelly. Then she fetched the diary from the shelf next to the sofa and slowly turned the pages, checking what had to be prepared for in the weeks ahead. Easter. She would cook a goose, as always, paint funny faces on eggs and hide foil-wrapped chocolate bunnies in the garden for the children. And then there was Peter's fiftieth, scheduled for the end of May, the children's summer half-term. She had promised Helen to look into the cost of marquees and to check out some local caterers. She would phone Marjorie Cavendish who had organised something similar the year before for her and Geoffrey's fortieth wedding anniversary. Or had it been their fiftieth? Not knowing caused Pamela a stirring of unease. It was such a simple fact and therefore unforgivable to forget it. They had given the Cavendishes a cut-glass fruit bowl and been to the party, where they ate lobster (rather chewy) and waltzed, with some trepidation, on a wobbly wooden dance floor.

Forty or fifty? Pamela frowned as she continued to ponder the question, unable to turn another page until she had resolved it. And during those moments, the melancholy, which had been waiting in the wings all morning, saw its chance and swooped, obliterating the hitherto interesting words of the woman on the radio and her own thoughts about anniversaries and jam-jar labels. If John had been around there would have been a chance of deflection, or dilution at least. But Pamela was alone and there was nowhere to hide. As if to verify this, she scurried out of the kitchen, along the hall, into the music room, into the study, into the drawing room, then back into the hall, and stopped in front of the large gilt-framed mirror. Her bun perched with its customary precision on the crown of her head; her eyelids, dusted as always with a fine pale blue powder, hung heavily over the still vibrant blue of her eyes; her lips, virtually without lipstick, thanks to the coffee, looked thin and drawn. Pamela pressed the palm of her right hand to her mouth as the first real tremors of distress took hold, tugging at the corner of her lips. She was sad because of Tina, she reminded herself. Little, chunky-legged Tina, so robust and loud, yet so completely fragile. And because of Serena, glassy-eyed and distant, floating round in a bubble of private misery, which hurt Pamela all the more for being so familiar.

The funeral, which had taken place against Charlie's and the rest of the family's wishes, in the windswept Cheshire parish where Serena's mother had breathed her last, had been surreal in its awfulness. The tiny white coffin with brass handles, carried by Charlie and Peter, one shoulder under each side, toppling slightly because Peter was taller, had looked like a toy, a mockery of the real thing. Behind it, shuffling but dignified, their faces pinched and pale against their black outfits, Serena and the other three children had held hands in a line, gripping each other as if staying upright depended on it. The girls, like their mother, were in hats, their eyes hidden under the brims, making Ed's startled misery all the more exposed and brave. They were a strong family, the vicar said, and would pull through. Theo, in his squeaky vibrato, read a poem: 'You are not gone for ever, You are just ahead, a flower in another world.' Peter, looking ashen but resolute, immaculate in his dark suit, had stepped into the pulpit and spoken about his niece in strong, determined tones, reading words that Serena and Charlie had composed, relating Tina's countless endearing ways, her early capacity to sleep long and soundly, her love of chocolate yoghurt, her stubbornness, her serenity in the still hours of the morning when she woke before the rest of the household and lay whispering baby nothings to her dolly. The poignancy of it had been almost unbearable. Unbearable and unreal – but not unreal, because it hurt so much.

Pamela, in a front pew among the rest of the family, her face behind a dotted black veil, had concentrated hard on dignity and strength. Beside her John had wept, silently but for one blow of the nose, which he timed to coincide with the start of a hymn so as to have the foghorn blast drowned by the swelling chords of the organ: 'When I needed a friend, were you there, were you there?' Many choked at the task of singing, but Pamela had found her voice flowing. Not because she felt the comforting presence of the Lord (she didn't), but because, with so much evidence of desolation in the family, she had been overpowered by the need to hold them together. Everywhere she looked handkerchiefs were pressed to crumpled faces. Cassie, standing on her left, was so overcome that she dropped to her knees, burying her face in her hands. Even in the midst of the trauma of it all, Pamela found a small moment in which to be amazed at this disconsolation of her youngest, usually the least sentimental of all of them and certainly the least engaged by her posse of nephews and nieces. Pamela, keeping her right hand in John's, had reached out to stroke Cassie's head, for a moment almost exhilarated at this physical chain-link of support fusing them all together, with her – the lynch-pin – in the middle. The family. It was everything.

After the service there had been a subdued reception in the soulless modern box of a parish hall next to the church. Pamela, catching Serena in a rare moment alone, had ventured, at last, to tell her about Miranda. 'Of course it's not the same, I know, and it was a very long time ago, but it was a huge . . . bereavement.'

'Poor you, Pam, I'm sorry.' Serena had spoken mechanically, too drowned by her own emotions to feel anything on her mother-in-law's behalf.

'I know it's not the same,' Pamela repeated. 'I mean, it was just a very late miscarriage . . . no funeral or anything – not like there would have been these days, time for proper mourning and so on . . .'

'Well, I've got that at least – a funeral, time for proper mourning.' Serena's voice trembled.

'My dear, I'm sorry, I didn't mean to make you feel worse.'

'Worse?' Serena looked at her in disbelief. 'Worse? You can't do that. No one can. I feel worse than worse. Look, Pam, thank you for telling me – I appreciate it. Really, I do.' Charlie had shuffled up then, looking dishevelled in spite of his smart suit, his eyes darting and anxious, one hand gripping an empty glass, the other clutching a full plate of miniature sausage rolls. 'Mum?' He held out the plate with a look of such pleading that Pamela took one, forcing dry pastry between her lips and chewed clods down her throat. Serena just stared mutely at the plate, shaking her head.

As a child Pamela had sometimes scotched the self-indulgence of tears by watching her face in a mirror as they started to spill out of her, shaming them out of existence by the ugliness, the sheer silliness, of the sight. She tried the same trick now, aged seventy-three, standing before the mirror in the hall of Ashley House, her face powder glistening on her cheeks and in the small purple pockets under her eyes. But the unhappiness was beyond containment. Not seeing well for tears, she turned away from her reflection and made her way towards the music room, groping blindly along the wall, then bumping into the music stool before she managed to sit on it. She didn't play much now. Her fingers were stiff and uncooperative, the tunes, so clear in her head, faltering and amateur when she tried to translate them to the keys. Elizabeth had been the talented one, but she had turned the talent into a labour, stopped loving it. Pamela chose a Beethoven prelude she knew by heart, playing with her eyes closed, missing notes, but moving on, trying to vent her emotions through the tune. She played badly and hated herself for it. The joints in her fingers felt old and unwieldy and all she really wanted to do was claw her thin silky hair from its prim package and hurl herself on to the carpet. She wanted not a tune but an explosion that would release the madness of her misery and shatter the ordered sanity of her life. She wanted, above all, to race upstairs, up all three flights to the top floor, along the landing to the door with the stiff handle that led into the eaves of the attic and the little leather suitcase full of baby clothes. Miranda's clothes. Unworn, unstained, smelling not of talc and milk but of mothballs.

Serena had been robbed, but, by God, so had she. The injustice of it, the pain, buried, *contained*, managed, channelled for so many years, felt as raw as it had five decades before, when they took her miniature silent baby, with its soft pink head, to be disposed of.

Even as this image formed in Pamela's mind, a part of her – the strong sane part – said, *Come on, now, such indulgence, stop this at once. You held the family together, remember? You had no choice but to carry on.* Pamela's fingers jerked over the keys. She was sane, she knew she was, but just for these moments, this peculiar day alone, shipwrecked in the snow, she didn't want to be . . . She wanted – oh, God, she wanted—

The doorbell – was it really the doorbell? Pamela's hands crashed together in discord and then dropped to her sides. She listened, breathing fast. It sounded again. The dreadful Victorian ding-dong John had insisted they restore. Postman? Milkman? Lost rambler? Her mind flew over the possibilities as she willed herself to have the courage to stay where she was, to complete the business of falling apart. But her fingers were already checking her hair and her throat working furiously to swallow the spasms of emotion. Of course she had to answer it. It was like life knocking at the door, real life, the one that needed responses and attention, the one that could be managed and mastered instead of the inner one that raged unseen.

The worst thing about his little sister dying, Ed decided, slapping more snow on to his lopsided and highly unsatisfactory snowman, was that nothing felt *normal.* Having fun of any kind felt wrong – like he didn't care enough or something. And being naughty felt positively evil. Getting back late from kicking a ball in the park with some friends the previous afternoon, his mother had seemed, literally, to erupt, the veins standing out round her eyes, the sinews in her neck straining from the effort of shouting at him. These days, if she wasn't exploding like that she was ignoring him and Ed wasn't sure which was worse. The quiet lack of anger about his failing the St George's exam, for instance, had made the hairs on the back of his neck stand on end. Both his parents had practically dismissed the matter in one sentence. It didn't matter, they said, he could do Common Entrance for Kings Grove later in the year. Like they really didn't care. Or had given up on him completely. He didn't want to go to Kings Grove. It was several bus stops away and it was reputed to have such a low pass mark that some people said making boys sit exams was just a front. Ed gouged two eye-holes in the snowman's face with a stick. He couldn't be bothered with schoolwork, but he didn't want to be written off as stupid either. He kicked at the hardened mud in a narrow empty flowerbed, and eventually found two stones that would do for eyes, of very different shapes, but roughly the same colour and size. He pressed them into the holes, then rammed the stick in by way of a nose. It looked stupid and sad, but he didn't care. He hadn't wanted to build a snowman in the first place. His mother had suggested it – all falsely bright and breezy, in the new way she had, like she was pretending to be a mother instead of actually being one. Asking her for a carrot for the nose would have triggered more brittle jolliness – exclamations, rummaging in the fridge. How long exactly? Peeled? Halved? The thought of it made him feel hollow inside.

It was getting dark now. His hooded top felt thin against the cold and his tummy was growling with hunger. Tea would soon be ready. When he came in from school Serena had been in the kitchen, stirring raw mince round a frying-pan. The smell of cooking as he crossed the threshold had been lovely, but Ed's stomach had clenched at the sight of the pink meat. He stared at the house now, not wanting to go back inside. In the drawing room the curtains were open and the lights on, revealing Maisie stretched out on the sofa with the TV remote control. Clem, no doubt, was still at her desk in her bedroom, beavering away at her homework. At a muffled crash from something a few gardens down, Ed jumped, his heart hammering at the thought of some monstrous assailant leaping at him in the dark. Straining to see in the dirty grey evening light, he could make out the top of the climbing frame in the garden next door and the outline of the small tree that bulged against their fence. Overhead a star had appeared, so low and bright that he thought for a moment it was an aeroplane. *Star light, star bright, first star I see tonight, I wish I were I wish I might have this wish I wish tonight . . .* But he couldn't think of a wish, beyond Arsenal winning the Premiership, which seemed shameful, and his stomach emitted another menacing growl. The mince would have become spaghetti Bolognese by now. There would be a pile of salad to go with it, a bowl of freshly grated Parmesan, as fine as pale sand, and some sticks of celery, which they would all dunk in the sugar bowl the moment Serena's back was turned. Tea as usual. And yet not as usual, because although things looked the same on the outside, on the inside they were totally different.

'Ed?'

'Oh, hi.' He looked up to see his aunt Cassie stepping out of the back door, placing her feet gingerly between the clumps of snow on the patio. She was wearing high heels and a long black coat with brown fur round the collar and cuffs.

'How are you?'

'Oh, fine.'

'Good.' Cassie hesitated, as stuck about what to say next as she had been with Maisie, who had answered the door, and with Serena, slopping pasta and sauce on to plates, still in a baggy T-shirt and jeans, as if she had forgotten their plan to go to the cinema. It had been Cassie's idea and she was rather proud of it. Elizabeth was due at any minute and Helen was meeting them there. They were going to see the new Meg Ryan film – a box-office hit romantic comedy – then going out for a bite afterwards. 'To get Serena out a bit,' she had explained to Charlie, on the phone, 'take her mind off things.' Her brother's response had been so feverishly enthusiastic, so solicitous on Serena's behalf, that it had made Cassie wonder tenderly what it must be like for such a close couple to endure something so terrible, how deeply their suffering would bind them. It had certainly made her feel closer to Dan. So much so that she had felt faintly guilty, as if she had used the tragedy in an improper way. She had shared all the details with him during his most recent visit to her flat – described the trauma of the funeral, how her tears had refused to stop – which had added a new intensity to their snatched two hours. When, eventually, they made love, it had felt extra special, as if they were each aware of how precious and fragile their stolen happiness was, how much in need of treasuring. Afterwards she had whispered, 'Imagine losing our child,' and he had kissed away the tears on her cheeks.

'Cool snowman.'

Ed scowled, partly because he knew his small leaning creation was anything but cool and partly at his aunt's choice of adjective. He hated grown-ups for being stuffy and staid, but cringed just as much when they attempted to use hip words. 'No, it's not, it sucks.'

Cassie, keeping to the path and away from the slush of snow on the grass, curled her toes inside her shoes, wishing she'd had the sense to wear her old suede boots instead. 'Bad luck about St George's, by the way. Kings Grove will be good, though. Mum says they do football.'

'Yeah, whatever.'

'She said you're to come inside for tea. I expect you're hungry, aren't you?'

He shrugged. 'Not really.'

Cassie gave up. 'Okay, then. I'll tell her you're on your way.' She turned back down the path and stepped over a plastic bucket, which was half full of brackish-looking water.

In the kitchen the twins were already sitting at the table, Maisie eagerly shovelling forkfuls of spaghetti into her mouth, while Clem, biting her lips in concentration, was cutting hers into a pile of slithering worms. Serena was leaning against the sink, arms folded, staring at the array of dirty pans and implements on the stove.

'Shall I deal with that lot?' Cassie, still in her coat, seized a couple of the saucepans and turned on the tap in the sink, careful to stand well back so as not to splash herself as Serena evidently had while preparing the meal.

'Oh, no.' Serena waved her hands vaguely. 'Charlie will do them.' She turned to her daughters and Ed – who had slid into his seat and begun eating, sniffing volubly and wiping the back of his hand across his nose between mouthfuls. 'You girls are in charge till Dad gets home, okay?'

Ed barely had time to groan before the front door slammed and Charlie appeared, in his old grey overcoat, his newspaper tucked under his arm. He had had a haircut that looked smart, but somehow brutal, exposing the trademark square Harrison head and the arrows of grey streaking his temples. There was a grey hair in one of his eyebrows too, Cassie observed. She kissed his cold cheek then tried not to watch as he moved round the room greeting his family. He tousled his daughters' hair and cuffed Ed with the newspaper, then slipped an arm round Serena, who dropped her head on to his shoulder briefly and murmured that she was going upstairs to change. Cassie draped her coat carefully over a spare chair, pushed up the sleeves of her shirt and began to wash up. 'You said you might be meeting Dad and Peter for lunch today. Was that okay?'

'Yes.' Charlie took off his coat and loosened his tie. 'It was fine, although with this new job work's fairly frantic at the moment so I didn't stay long. Peter was a bit distracted with this case he's working on – you know what he's like. Dad just seemed pleased to be out and about – they've been virtually snowed in for days by all accounts. He was going on to meet some of his old insurance fogies afterwards, which always makes him jolly, although God knows what anyone in insurance has got to be jolly about these days. Peter, as usual, told him he should consider pulling out of being a Name, and invest more in the stock market. Dad, as usual, wouldn't listen.'

Cassie waited for a moment to see if he was going to continue. As it happened, the stock market had been a little on her mind, too, thanks to a recent confession from Dan that, through the ill-timed advice of a friend, he had lost a lot in the boom and bust of one of the technology companies. He worried a lot about money, in spite of Cassie's repeated reassurances that if necessary she would live in a mud hut with him. She sighed, stealing a glance at her brother, who had fallen silent. He had been talking for the sake of it, she knew, delivering news about the business chat at lunch because the alternative was talking about Tina. Or, rather, the absence of Tina. The house, Cassie realised, was unbearably quiet. The three children were eating in virtual silence. Tina's high-chair, she noticed with a wrench, was pushed back against the wall out of the way of the table. She returned her attention to the bowl of suds in front of her, mouth dry. 'But, Charlie, how are you doing? Are you all right?'

'Oh, you know.' He managed a tight smile. 'It's difficult.'

'Of course.' Cassie tipped away the washing-up water and turned to face him, wishing there was something she could do or say, some consolation that would make a real difference. As the little sister she was used to her big brothers looking out for her, particularly Charlie, to whom she was closest and who had always cheered her out of difficult moods with his teasing and easy warmth. Looking at him now, so muted and drawn, she felt that nothing in what they had shared of their lives had equipped either of them for the circumstances in which they now found themselves.

'Dad and Peter . . . they mean to be supportive,' he continued, 'like you, and I . . . we appreciate it, Cass, we really do. Everybody has been unbelievably kind, writing letters and so on. It's incredible.' He slapped his hands on his thighs and stood up in a clear bid to dismiss the subject. 'But now, if you'll excuse me, I'm going running.'

'Running?' Cassie was so astonished – so relieved, too, at having something mundane to respond to – that she burst out laughing.

'Yeah, Dad's keeping fit,' growled his son disdainfully, running a finger round the rim of his plate to scrape up the last of the sauce.

'Every night,' added Clem, who had made a tidy pyramid of her chopped spaghetti and was teasing bits out with a fork prong.

'In this weather?' Cassie looked at her brother, still incredulous.

'Basically,' said Maisie, pushing her plate to one side and reaching for an apple from the fruit bowl, 'he's trying to lose weight, aren't you, Dad? Which is cool by me.'

'Thank you, darling, for your support.' Charlie shot her a grin, looking for one lovely moment quite like his old self. 'I have the backing of my entire family, as you can see. It probably won't last, but for now . . .' He was prevented from finishing the sentence by the doorbell and the subsequent appearance of Elizabeth, looking bulky and uncomfortable in a heavy overcoat. She waved at the children and kissed Charlie, talking all the while about the traffic jams she had endured and her concern at having had to park in a slot meant for permit holders. Charlie disappeared upstairs, while Cassie continued to clear up the kitchen, exchanging concerned looks with her sister who, still in her coat, hung awkwardly round the table, asking the children questions about school and what they'd eaten for tea.

When Serena emerged, resplendent in spite of everything in a long black velvet jacket and her chestnut hair scooped off her face with two big black combs, there were a few long and dreadful moments of silence before Elizabeth stumbled across the room to put her arms round her, too choked to speak. Serena, marvelling for by no means the first time that the nightmare of her bereavement required her to console others, patted her sister-in-law's broad back until she had recovered herself and said wasn't it time they were all going. Charlie, undignified and grim-faced in a pair of too-small jogging bottoms and some ancient grey plimsolls, stood on the pavement to wave them away then set off at a lumbering trot in the opposite direction.

Dan switched off his computer, took off his glasses and squeezed the bridge of his nose between finger and thumb. After an unusually quiet couple of weeks the surgery had been packed that afternoon, with such a long list of non-appointment late arrivals that they had run out of chairs in the waiting room. Going in search of a sandwich at lunch time, he had noticed a new damp mildness to the air the moment he had stepped outside. The hardened drifts of dirty snow, gathered in gutters and on street corners, had shrunk visibly during the morning. Cars swished by, spurting water from their wheels, tyres glistening. There seemed to be more of them than in recent days and more people too, scurrying about with bags and brief-cases, mobile phones pinned to their ears, as if the whole city was awakening after some enforced spell of hibernation.

While he was standing in the queue at the deli he had phoned Cassie to say that the week was looking tricky in terms of meeting up. As always, just the sound of her voice excited him, the girlish breathiness, the colour of her moods as readable in her tones as an open book. She had been full of trepidation about her approaching night out with her sister-in-law, so unsure, so eager for his advice and reassurance that, as he slipped his phone back into his pocket, Dan found himself resolving to sort things out with Sally that evening. There was no point in putting it off any longer. What he and Cassie felt for each other was simply too strong. Just that one short phone-call had summed it all up – her loving gentleness, her need of him, and his own trembling need of her, his desire to protect, cherish her for ever. Sally was never gentle or unsure about anything and certainly didn't seek his advice. Neither could the sound of her voice give him an erection. On the contrary, he found that he only really felt in the mood to make love to his wife when they folded their books away and slipped silently beneath the duvet in the dark, without the tetchy grind of conversation. And even then he often laboured to shut out images of Cassie (usually pornographic ones, flashing like delirium across his mind), which, rather than fuelling his libido, had the opposite effect. That he loved Cassie Harrison, Dan was in no doubt. What he remained less sure of was the timing of this new-found passion, whether he would have fallen for Cassie at any point along the time-line of his existence, or whether it related to more dubious, less edifying things like being forty, overworked and sharing a home with three exhausting small people and an adult who had long since seen through his charms to the less adorable and myriad human deficiencies that lay beneath. If he left Sally for Cassie would they, too, eventually reach a similar stalemate stage of disappointment and dissatisfaction? Was that what all marriages came to in the end? Or had he, at the unformed age of twenty-three, simply made the wrong choice of mate? In which case prolonging the agony for them both was pointless, Dan decided. He punched in the numbers of his lawyer friend and left a message for him to call back as soon as he could.

'Got anything nice planned for the evening, Dr Lambert?'

'Oh, no, not really, Meryl, unless you count bathtime with my three delinquents.' He made a funny face and the receptionist laughed. 'Then a few paragraphs of *Harry Potter* if I'm lucky.'

'Ah, bless.' Meryl, whose own children had reached the age where they locked the bathroom against intrusions and preferred computer manuals to fiction, sighed wistfully. 'I'll see you tomorrow, then. Mr Presbitt collected that prescription, by the way, and says now his wife's got the same thing. He made an appointment for tomorrow. Cheerio.'

Dan drove home slowly, rehearsing what he would say to Sally, for once not minding the turgidity of the rush-hour traffic. *Sal, we're getting nowhere. I know you feel as I do in your heart, so let's just sort out the mess and go our separate ways. It will be better for both of us in the long run . . .* The notion of telling her about Cassie was not, and never had been, on the agenda. Cassie had been superbly co-operative about the secrecy of the affair, seeing, as he did, that it would only exacerbate the inevitable bitterness of separation. *We've grown apart. It's time to recognise that properly and move on.* And, God, how he longed to do that. Move on. Start something new and good. A clean sheet. No baggage, no preconceptions and simmering resentments. No more having to be nice to his whining in-laws, no more of Sally's withering looks, her sulky silences, her recriminations about the hours he worked and the fact that they were stuck in London when the quality of family life would be so much better somewhere in the country. The grooves of their arguments, well furrowed during the course of the years, were exhausting and sickeningly predictable. Money would be difficult, of course. The children were currently at an excellent state primary but the plan had always been to move them into the private system later. His meagre investments had taken quite a knock in the telecoms crash and there was still a hefty mortgage on the house. In spite of Cassie's sweet reassurances about her income and inheritance prospects (which sounded pretty decent: he had seen pictures of Ashley House and heard enough about the Harrison clan to know she wasn't exaggerating), Dan felt very afraid whenever he thought about what he would have to pay out each month in a divorce settlement.

Having turned into his street, he slowed to a crawl in the search for somewhere to park. Like most of their neighbours they owned two cars and suffered the consequent maddening inconvenience of not being able to fit them all into the space available. The Espace, as usual, was right outside the front door, its 'Baby On Board' sticker taking up half of the back windscreen. Beyond it, as far as the eye could see, the street was solid with vehicles. After several minutes of cruising, Dan manoeuvred into a slot between a double yellow line and a skip in an adjoining street. Don't get cross, he told himself, dodging round the now seriously melting lumps of snow as he walked the hundred yards back to his own house. Be calm. Be reasonable. Firm but kind. *Get it over with.*

'Daddy! Daddy! Daddy! Polly took my train but I shared it with her and Mummy gave me an apple if I cleaned my teeth.'

'Did she now? And what are you doing still up?' Dan reached down and disengaged George, his four-year-old, who had attached himself with vice-like affection to his right leg, settling him on his hip instead. 'It's way past your bedtime, isn't it?'

'He had toothache – back molars. Remember they were bad for Polly too? I've just given him something.' Sally deposited the pile of laundry she had been carrying on the hall table and walked with outstretched arms towards her husband and son. 'Come on, you. Back to bed.' She kissed Dan's cheek lightly and eased George on to her own hip. At the bottom of the stairs she turned. 'Dan?'

'Yes?' There was an edge to her voice, a hint of subdued urgency.

'I've booked a babysitter. I thought we could eat out. We . . . I . . . There's something I need to talk to you about.'

'Right. Okay.' Dan's stomach convulsed, a curious mixture of excitement and presentiment. 'Me too . . . I mean, I want to talk too.'

'Polly's in the bath. Could you deal with her? Carol's due any minute.'

She set off up the stairs and he followed, watching the familiar curves of her bottom, bulging slightly in her too-tight jeans, and feeling treacherous at the sight of the sleepy face of his son peering down at him over her shoulder.

Helen had rushed home to change between work and going out to the cinema and found Rika, the au pair, in heated debate on the kitchen telephone, surrounded by the debris of half-eaten pizza and what looked like several earlier meals as well. From the sounds coming through the open door to the drawing room it was clear that Chloë, instead of being overseen through the trials of music practice and homework, was watching one of the early-evening soaps on television. On seeing her employer, Rika turned her back to concentrate more fully on her conversation. She was speaking in her native tongue, Helen noted grimly, which almost certainly meant it would be an expensive call.

'Chloë, darling, have you done your homework?' Helen had to raise her voice against both the guttural dialect going on behind her and the volume of the television, which was considerable.

'No, but I'm going to just after this.'

'Right. After this programme, then.' Helen inhaled and exhaled slowly, summoning the wherewithal for a show of toleration she did not feel. She wished she had gone straight to the cinema. She wished that Peter was at home to help her tackle Chloë, not to mention the increasingly insulting behaviour of their employee, but he had taken her night out as an excuse to have one of his own with an old friend from law school. Above all, she wished that her darling, rangy, pimply-faced son was not back in the exile of boarding-school, becoming a stranger again after the steady re-establishment of comfortable intimacy during their half-term skiing holiday. After much debate they had stayed on in Switzerland, flying home just a day early to be at Tina's funeral.

Astonishingly, almost wickedly, they had managed to have one of the best family holidays Helen could remember. Her period had dried up as quickly as it had appeared. The sun had shone solidly for the entire week and the slopes were kept fresh and powdery by a couple of timely overnight snowfalls. They had all had lessons during the mornings, then ski'd as a family in the afternoons, with even little Chloë keeping up marvellously well. In the evenings they had swum, eaten huge meals and collapsed into exhausted marathon sleeps in their respective rooms. It was as if there was some tacit understanding that they were all on borrowed time, that being abroad and therefore removed from the immediate body-blow of the tragedy to have hit the family, they had every right to make the most of it, to charge their batteries for the ordeal awaiting them at home.

And it had been an ordeal, from the unspeakable poignancy of the funeral to all the abrasive realities of everyday life that followed. Watching as her niece's tiny coffin was lowered into the deep soil, Serena and Charlie convulsed by grief, Helen had vowed never to be moody, cross or ungrateful about anything unimportant ever again. They had stepped back into their lives subdued and humbled. Yet all too soon the old pressures, work, Chloë's wilfulness, Peter's long hours, the volatility of her own moods – the warp and woof of reality – had reasserted themselves with depressing definition. Helen still thought of Tina daily (great swoops of sadness and compassion would assault her at the most unexpected moments: during meetings, sorting laundry, shaving her legs), but all the early ennobling effects of the tragedy had worn off as quickly as the honey-glow of her sun-tan.

She returned to the kitchen and began, amid much clashing of crockery, to clear the table, shooting pointed looks at Rika who, unabashed, continued to talk. The bin was too full to cope even with the hardened crusts of discarded pizza. Helen seized the bag, tied it with a clumsy knot and slung it over her shoulder, Father Christmas style, then marched – her anger ringing in the clack of her heels on the quarry-tiled floor – past her employee and out of the back door. Just as she arrived at the wheelie-bin, the bag split, spilling a messy cocktail of eggshells, yoghurt pots, coffee granules and a chicken carcass on to the pavement. 'Fuck, fuck and double fuck.'

'Always bloody happens, doesn't it? Last-straw department. Good for local foxes, though – they'll be round here like a shot, especially for that chicken.'

Helen, squatting awkwardly over the mess, trying to keep the tips of her smart shoes from getting smeared, looked up to see a woman with a pouchy face and a long ponytail grinning over her. 'Quite,' she replied tersely, picking out the yoghurt pots and flinging them into the bin.

'Hang on, don't move, I've got just the thing.' The woman, who was wearing a tartan tent of a dress and wellington boots, darted across the road and reappeared a moment later with a large spade. 'Used it to clear the drive of snow. Stand back a minute.' And before Helen could protest she was scooping the blade of the implement under the mess and depositing it in the bin. 'There, that's better, isn't it?'

'Thank you so much.'

'I'm Kay, by the way. Kay Sagan, like the French writer – no relation to my husband, or ex-husband, rather – although he is French. I live opposite and down a bit.' She gestured at the small row of 1940s terraced houses across the road, the least aesthetically pleasing section of the street, which had sprung into being thanks to a stray bomb during the Second World War. 'It's Mrs Harrison, isn't it?, I took a parcel for you once, but you probably don't remember.'

'Oh, yes,' murmured Helen, embarrassed, not remembering. Working the hours she did, she barely knew any of their neighbours, except by sight, and had never been enthused by the notion of improving the situation. Friendly neighbours, in Helen's eyes, introduced the unwelcome possibility of being sucked into tedious dinners, residents associations and campaigns for sleeping policemen. 'Thanks anyway.' She turned to go inside.

'They've changed the collection day, by the way.'

'I beg your pardon?'

'The council. The bin men are coming on a Tuesday now. And paper recycling has moved to Saturdays.'

'Right. Thanks.' Helen rubbed her hands, which were greasy with chicken and yoghurt.

'There's a new postman too, a dead ringer for George Clooney. *Gorgeous.*'

'Really. Well, nice to meet you . . . Kay . . . but I've got to go – I'm going out and I'm late as it is.'

'What are you doing, then? Anything nice?'

Desperate to be released from the conversation and wanting in some indefinable way to put the woman down, Helen said, 'Actually, not that nice, no. My baby niece was killed recently in a road accident and I am taking my sister-in-law out in a no doubt futile bid to try to cheer her up. What is more,' she continued, the release of her thoughts gathering a momentum that she was suddenly powerless to control, 'I'm having to leave my daughter with a girl who should be sacked for incompetence, but whom I can't afford to get rid of because my husband works even longer hours than I do and I simply haven't got time to go trawling round agencies for a replacement.' Helen glowered, expecting to see signs of dismay and retreat. During one of her recent aggressive diatribes at work her secretary – much to her horror – had burst into tears. But Kay took a step forward and touched Helen's arm. She was older than the high girlish ponytail had first led Helen to believe – early fifties at least. Her hair was thick and lustrous but grey. Her face, seen close to, was full and soft but distinctly weathered. Her eyes, painted on both upper and lower lids with sharp black lines that met in cat-like points at the sides, looked both quizzical and kind. 'You poor love, what a bugger.'

'Oh, it will be all right,' Helen stammered, appalled to find a lump in her throat.

'It's so bloody hard, isn't it, doing the unpleasant stuff? Like sacking that girl you employ, even though she's crap. I stayed married for years for similar reasons, to a complete bastard. But I couldn't bring myself to confront him because I couldn't face the nastiness. And then, when I finally did, it was so fucking simple. I say,' she grinned suddenly, 'why don't you give this girl her marching orders right this minute and I'll babysit for you? I mean it. I've got nothing on. I'd be more than happy to help. I've had three kids of my own – all grown-up now, of course – so I know what's what. You don't forget how to look after children. Like swimming and riding bikes – once it's there it's there for life.'

'Oh, goodness.' Helen found herself laughing. 'I don't think so, but thank you, Kay, thank you for offering.'

'Well, let me know if you ever change your mind. I work from home, but only in the mornings and I haven't got much on at the moment. Apart from that I've just got Toffee to worry about – that's my dog. I'm at number forty-two. Knock on my door any time and we can chat about the possibilities. Only if you want to. Apologies if I've seemed at all pushy. I do tend to sort of say whatever comes into my head. It's been lovely meeting you anyway. Must go.' She turned towards the street and gave a shrill summons to her dog. 'Toffee! Come on now, darling, time for dinner.' A small brown wiry creature with huge ears and short tail appeared from nowhere, sniffed briefly at Helen's ankles, then ran across the street in the direction of his home. 'Dinner – he knows that word all right.' Kay winked, adding in a whisper, her face softening, 'Your niece – so terrible, but it does get better. Loss leaves craters in us all, but they close over, like skin over a wound.'

Helen hurried back into the kitchen where she found herself telling

Rika – now off the phone and nibbling absently at a discarded pizza crust – that she thought it would better for all of them if she worked her four-week notice period and began to seek employment elsewhere. The girl offered no resistance. She nodded sullenly and said, 'Yes, I go at next month.' Almost, thought Helen later – as she jumped red lights and hooted at road-hogging lorries *en route* to Putney – as if she had been expecting it. Peter would be appalled, of course, but he had never been in the front line for dealing with the girl. He counselled conciliation, but remained very much back-stage in terms of implementing it. Helen thought of Kay, too, with her flashing black eyes and swishing steely hair, marvelling that she should find appealing someone so outspoken and wondering whether to distrust her extraordinary offer of help or give in to it.

The cinema, perhaps because its heating was still attuned to the freezing temperatures of the previous ten days, was very hot. They sat in the front row of the middle section, with Helen on one side of Serena and Cassie and Elizabeth on the other, as if they all sought in some obscure way to protect her. The sisters had succumbed to the temptation of confection: Cassie had opted for popcorn, while Elizabeth nursed a tub of strawberry ice-cream. They ate self-consciously, as aware as their companions that the gathering felt unnatural.

'I don't know how to *be*,' Cassie had wailed to Elizabeth, during a brief trip to the ladies', when Serena had volunteered to remain as look-out for Helen who was running late. 'To talk about it or not to talk about it. She looks so desolate, doesn't she? So wide-eyed and lost, as if she's not really here or doesn't want to be here or *something*. God, I feel so useless.' She checked her reflection in the mirror, and gave a desultory stab at her hair.

'Me too.' Elizabeth came to stand next to her younger sister, a reflex deep inside her twitching as it always did at the brutal contrast in their appearance: Cassie with her shining wheat-coloured mane and fine features, and she with her mousy crop and big bones. Only their eyes were the same, big and blue like their mother's. 'I guess we've just got to try to be ourselves, haven't we?

And when it comes to talking about Tina, just follow Serena's lead. But it has changed us all for ever, don't you think?' Elizabeth, enjoying a moment of big-sisterly protection, put an arm across Cassie's shoulders. 'It's certainly changed me and Colin,' she murmured, thinking of the new, eager kindness shown to her by her husband. 'Made us appreciate things more.' She sighed and dropped her arm, glad that she had not, after all, spilled the beans about the miseries of her marriage to Serena. She had been on the verge of doing so during their fateful day out four weeks before. In fact, it was only Serena's sudden concern about the whereabouts of Tina that had stopped her. But little about Elizabeth's home life was miserable any more. Since the accident, Colin had been amazing. All talk of the petty dissatisfactions at work had ceased virtually overnight. His concern for her seemed to know no bounds: he brought her cups of tea in the morning and whistled his way through household chores at the weekend. What had felt like the sinking ship of their relationship had somehow righted itself. That this extraordinary *volte-face* should have occurred as a result of the death of their dear little niece was something that Elizabeth found at once unsettling and deeply comforting. It meant good could come of bad, that no situation was completely barren in terms of the seeds it might sow. 'Colin and I are definitely . . . closer.' Elizabeth delivered the information guardedly. Her younger sister's tidily independent personal life had never encouraged her to release confidences about her own infinitely more volatile emotional state. With the Lucien failure already blotting her copybook, she was acutely aware of her position as the black sheep of the family when it came to relationships. Peter and Charlie's marriages were enviably solid, while the companionable five-decade alliance between her parents shone like a beacon to them all.

'God, Lizzy, I know exactly what you mean.' Cassie spun round, her eyes shining. She was aching to talk about Dan and the new hope, one day, not too far into the future, of having a family of her own. But, as ever, she found her primary loyalty remained with her lover and his vehement pleas for secrecy. 'I mean, it's put a whole new light on things for me too,' she concluded, more quietly, 'made me realise what's important, what really matters.' She turned on the tap and began to wash her hands, not trusting herself to say more.

The film, in spite of an unlikely plot and the cosy girl-next-door appeal of its main protagonist, felt harrowing. Every twist in the story – a plane crash, a car crash, a lovable urchin-faced child who went missing, a funeral – seemed cruelly designed to resonate with echoes of what the four women were feeling. Death, love, unhappiness – it was all there in bucketfuls. Helen, twisting the strap of her handbag round her fingers, not daring to look at Serena, wondered what had possessed her to agree to come. It was obvious that it would be beyond enjoyment for any of them. That she had chosen that evening to sack Rika didn't help matters. Anxiety about dealing with the consequences of her impetuosity kept making her pulse gallop, undermining any confidence she might otherwise have had in dealing with the wretchedness of her sister-in-law. The misery radiating out of Serena was palpable. Helen, sitting so close to her motionless figure in the dark, could almost smell it, the odour of hopelessness. What could she do or say to ease such a force? What could any of them?

Serena sat bolt upright throughout the film, staring at the images on the screen, oblivious to the storyline and the uncomfortable twitching of her companions. Their worries about her own discomfort were groundless. Nothing touched her any more – not the carnage wrought by suicide bombers, not the sagging misery of her family and certainly not the shenanigans of Meg Ryan, pretending to be an infertile widow. All her energy was focused on the pain inside her, which she nursed silently every second of every minute, as acutely aware of its writhing as she had been the kicks of each baby inside her womb.

Cassie had booked a table at a restaurant in Putney high street, a short walk from the cinema. She led the way there, talking to Serena all the time, brimful of determined chirpiness. Once inside there was the flurry of handing over coats and umbrellas before they were shown to their seats. As the architect of the evening she felt the burden of responsibility for making it go smoothly. She took charge of the ordering, asking about the chef's specials and for the wine list, in spite of beady looks from Helen who, as the eldest and most obviously assertive of the group, clearly thought such a duty should be hers. In the end the waiter said the house red was very good and they went for that. No one was hungry enough for a starter so they picked their way through the bread basket and various loose threads of conversation before the arrival of the main course. Helen then blurted out that she had asked Rika to work her notice, providing a huge source of fresh – and much-needed – conversational fodder. For three of them anyway.

Cassie, with no experience or expertise in such matters, found her attention wandering, first to her food, which was over-salted, and then to their fellow diners, of which there were many. At a near table two young men were discussing a football match. Beyond them, two smartly dressed elderly couples were chinking flutes of champagne. Behind them . . . Cassie froze, a forkful of cassoulet half-way to her mouth. At a table in the corner, with his back to her, was Dan, in the bottle green jacket that she liked, having dinner with his wife. His wife. Cassie stared, drinking in the details of Sally's appearance: the long dark sweep of hair, dark brows, a pale face, exactly like the photos he had shown her, but somehow different. Larger for one thing. And more real. Much more real.

'More wine, Cass?'

'What? Oh, yes – that is if you are . . .'

'I've asked for another bottle,' said Helen briskly, returning her attention to Serena, who thanks to alcohol and several blood-curdling evil-au pair anecdotes, was showing distinct signs of coming to life.

Cassie could not keep her eyes from the back of Dan's neck. He was rubbing it in that way he had when he was concerned about something. The conversation of her companions floated around her in snatches. '. . . turns out she had been hitting the child . . . the teachers were the first to notice . . . never work with children again . . .'

Sally was leaning across the table, both hands clenched round her coffee-cup, her face grave and intense. Cassie gripped her knees with all ten fingers, fighting an absurd urge to crash across the room and hurl herself between them. Part of her was jubilant: at seeing him, at the sheer outrageous coincidence of finding themselves in the same place at the same time. But a much bigger part of her felt utterly desolate. There he was, her lover, her man. Except he wasn't hers, he was Sally's. Close but untouchable. In his other world, just as she was in hers. And then, quite suddenly, Serena was sobbing into her hands and they were all exchanging anguished looks, reaching to touch her and flapping napkins like clucking hens. When Cassie next had time to glance across the room Dan's place had been taken by a black girl with braided hair and gold hoops in her ears.

'Sorry . . . sorry,' Serena gasped, in spite of unanimous protestations that she had nothing for which to apologise. 'I'm pissed so it all comes out . . . all the . . . all this . . .' She slapped her palm hard against her chest. 'God, I'd kill him, you know, the motorcyclist, if ever they catch him . . . I really would, I really would, I mean it.' She gulped air between words, as if having to prise each one out by force. 'He – took – my – baby – my lovely – darling . . . I don't think there can be anything so bad – a wife, a husband, a parent . . . No loss in the world could be so bad. I had a miscarriage, you know, between the twins and Ed, but that was nothing – nothing – compared to this . . .'

'I had a miscarriage once,' said Helen, in a small voice.

'There you go.' Serena waved her arm, sounding not so much sympathetic as vindicated. 'And Pamela, too, she had one – between Peter and Elizabeth. She told me at the funeral.'

'Did she?' Elizabeth raised her eyebrows at Cassie. 'I never knew that.'

Serena pulled out an old grey hankie of Charlie's and blew her nose. Her head throbbed and the inside of her mouth felt sticky with saliva. 'I probably shouldn't have said anything.' She was aware of her three companions looking at her expectantly. 'I think she was trying to make me feel better . . . It was quite a late one apparently.'

'How late?' prompted Cassie hoarsely, close to tears herself but only because of Dan having vanished without her even so much as catching his eye. 'Did she say?'

'Six months, I think,' muttered Serena, as the blackness of her own misery swelled around her, drowning concerns about discretion or anything else. 'They called her Miranda.'

'And why the hell has she never told us this?' Elizabeth looked with wide eyes across the table at her sister, searching for evidence that she wasn't the only one to feel put out.

'Oh, come on, in those days stuff like that just happened,' put in Helen briskly, glancing at her watch and waving her credit card at the waiter. 'That generation were much more stoical, weren't they? Got on with life and so on.'

'True, but I still think . . .'

'Don't say anything, okay?' said Serena faintly. 'I probably shouldn't have mentioned it.'

Cassie, a little calmer now, patted her hand. 'It's fine. Don't worry. I'm glad Mum told you. I really don't mind at all. It's no big deal.'

'You've got far more important things to worry about,' pointed out Helen, quietly.

Elizabeth, counting out pound coins for her share of the meal, murmured in agreement. But during the drive back to Guildford she found her thoughts returning again and again to this small personal disclosure about her mother. Pamela had always made out that the four of them popped out like peas from a pod, with no hint of difficulties either during the process or between. After the agony of her own labour with Roland (thirty hours of excruciating but ineffectual contractions followed by a Caesarian section), Pamela had remarked several times how odd it was that Elizabeth, with her wide, Harrison hips, should have struggled so hard. From her, as well as several female acquaintances at the time, there had even been a faint shadow (so faint that Elizabeth told herself many times she was imagining it) of criticism at her eldest daughter's failure to manage a natural birth. As if going under the surgeon's knife was some sort of cop-out. Elizabeth, remembering all this in the quiet of her car, could not help thinking that a tale or two about her mother's own gynaecological woes – albeit quite different ones – would have been rather comforting. To feel jealous of Serena was absurd – almost criminal, given what had happened. But for a few moments, between the Robin Hood roundabout and the Kingston underpass, Elizabeth let herself feel something akin to it. Memories of adolescent unhappiness, never far from the surface, stirred inside. Pamela, while irreproachable as a parent, had never talked to her intimately about anything. She managed life effortlessly and with charm, setting impossibly high standards in the process. Peter, the eldest, the male inheritor, had never been touched by such things, while Charlie and Cassie had the sort of easy-going personalities that just didn't seem fazed by it. It was always her, reflected Elizabeth bleakly, who felt clumsy and shut out, nurturing insecurities – even now at the age of forty-six – about falling short of expectations and letting the family down.

As she pulled into the drive she saw the light go out in their bedroom. She hurried upstairs, checked Roland briefly, then cleaned her teeth and slipped into bed. Colin asked her about the evening, but sleepily. When she got to the miscarriage story, he said, 'Well, well,' and turned on his side. Elizabeth turned with him, pressing her nose between his shoulder blades and nestling her legs against his. She rarely initiated their lovemaking, but that night she found herself wanting to. Not because she felt libidinous, but because she longed suddenly for the physical comfort – the graphic solidity – of sexual intimacy. She reached down and ran one finger gently from the back of his knee to the curve of his bottom, feeling the first stirrings of genuine desire. 'Colin?' She began to move the finger back down his leg only to feel his hand close round hers and remove it. He patted her arm and shifted away from her, murmuring goodnight. Soon he was snoring, so loudly that Elizabeth took refuge in the spare room. A few minutes later Roland, who had only been pretending to sleep, whispered farewell to his teddy and tiptoed along the landing to join her.

Stephen walked slowly, burrowing his chin into the roll of his polo-neck, his eyes on the ground. After the serene padded whiteness of the Sussex countryside that afternoon, the melting clumps of black snow lining the London streets looked particularly ugly. He had been nervous of returning to Ashley House, but also tremendously excited. Striding down the last few yards of the lane approaching the drive, the limbs of the tall trees overhead crusted with snow, he had felt as if he was in the central aisle of some vast natural cathedral. On the verges clumps of long grass were pushing through the snow, brilliant green straggles of hair against the white. The air was hushed and still, but when he stopped, bending down to attend to a shoelace, he realised that the silence was not silence at all but a bubbling whisper of melting snow. Somewhere to his left among a tangle of lush holly and rusty bracken he could hear the gurgle of a stream. Further on, the water became more visible, trickling into a ditch that opened up alongside the road. Ashley House appeared suddenly, as he rounded a bend in the lane, looking huge and firm against the chequered green and white of its surroundings, its chimney-stacks like the funnels of a ship, its vast soft-grey brick walls crawling handsomely with ivy. He had forgotten how big it was and yet how welcoming, managing in a way he couldn't define to combine all the grandeur of a stately home with the cosiness of a cottage. A plume of smoke was spiralling out of one of the chimneys, making pencil sketches against the white sky. The roofs of the main house and what he could see of the barns and outhouses were still plump with snow. A ginger cat was crouching on a section of the low stone wall next to the garage, its tail twitching as it watched a bird hopping across the roof.

Stephen paused, fearful suddenly of imposing his presence on something so perfect. Although it was only a couple of months since his initial visit, it felt far longer. He had been nervous then, but in nothing like the way he was now. Then it had only been his book that was at stake. Now it felt as if his entire life hung in the balance. The book mattered only in that it was his cover for being there. He had all sorts of questions planned, but all he really cared about was getting close to Cassie. In recent weeks progress on his manuscript had slowed from sluggish to virtually non-existent. His editor, understanding over one missed deadline for a glimpse of work-in-progress, was growing openly impatient. In recent phone-calls there had been unpleasant talk of non-negotiable publication dates and the financial implications of failure to deliver the goods.

Stephen, stalling as best he could, had felt more than ever that Cassie Harrison had somehow become his muse, that if he could make progress with her, the manuscript – its impossible sprawl and turgidity – would start to take shape.

There was a cast-iron boot-scraper next to the front door in the shape of a fox. As he waited for the door to be answered, Stephen tried it out with some curiosity, feeling the cold metal through his worn soles. And then, because the door remained unanswered, he began to whistle under his breath, staring so hard at the bush of yellow winter jasmine next to the bell-pull that yellow spots danced before his eyes. When he tugged on the bell a second time and still no one came, he began to think he was going mad. It was the day they had arranged and, approaching the door, he had distinctly heard the strains of piano-playing. Somewhere inside, Boots was in paroxysms of frenzied barking. Oh, God, the dog will have a heart-attack, he thought. The dog will die and it will be my fault.

He had been so relieved at Pamela's eventual appearance that it was a few seconds before he registered her peculiar dishevelment. Though her fingers fluttered to the loops of her bun, most of her hair had broken free of it and hung to her shoulders. The whites of her usually crystal blue eyes were visibly bloodshot and – worst of all, somehow – there was a blue smear of eyeshadow running from the corner of her left eyelid to her temple.

Stephen, having taken all this in, broke into a sweat of embar-rassment. 'Have I got the wrong day?'

'My dear Mr Smith – Stephen – no, of course not. Come in, come in. I'll make coffee – do go through – the kitchen – the drawing room. Make yourself at home – I'll be right with you.'

It had gone okay after that. Perfectly, in fact. Stephen had waited in the drawing room, which smelt of leather, and woodsmoke from a fire burning merrily in the hearth. Two large china dogs with painted faces sat on either side beneath a row of gleaming brass fire irons. Stephen took the poker and rummaged under the logs for the fun of it, then went to admire the photograph of Cassie on the table behind the sofa. At which point something curious and wonderful occurred, so wonderful that the warmth of it still glowed in Stephen's heart hours later as he paced the dark streets of London. A cream envelope had been lying behind the photo, addressed in neat loopy writing to John Harrison. The postcode was Pimlico and the letter, which Stephen, feeling like a spy, had eased out of the envelope, began, 'Darling Dad, I just wanted to write with a proper thank you for the latest advance on my inheritance! Seriously, you are very kind and I . . .' In two seconds the letter was back exactly as he had found it. All he had needed was the address at the top, the number and the street. It took no effort to commit them to memory, but he would have carved them with a knife on his own skin if it had been necessary. A few minutes later Pamela reappeared, her hair pinned back into place, her face smiling and glistening with a fresh dusting of powder. They had adjourned to the kitchen for coffee and home-baked honey and raisin flapjacks. Feverish with happiness at having secured Cassie's address so effortlessly, Stephen had eaten rave-nously, throwing out any old question he could think of relating to Eric and barely listening to any of Pamela's answers. When she had asked if he would like to visit the nursing-home he had said no, absolutely not, that thanks to her and John he already had a won-derful feel for the man and wanted only to commit it all to paper.

Pamela, watching her young guest wolf her flapjacks and wave his arms with enthusiasm, filling her big empty kitchen with his energy, felt remarkably composed. Composed and rescued. It was just what she had needed. A visit from an outsider, someone interested in but wholly disconnected from the family. Someone young and charming. On the doorstep she kissed him, even though she could see he wasn't expecting it. 'It's been a pleasure, Stephen. And I hope it helped.'

'Oh, yes,' Stephen had assured her, grinning like a madman. 'Enormously.' He had run nearly all the way back to Barham station, the address of Cassie's flat singing like a tune in his head.

And now . . . now he was visiting her. Having reached the corner of Cassie's street, Stephen stopped to breathe deeply, somewhat in awe of his own behaviour. A black cat with white paws sprinted across the road next to him, from left to right. Which was lucky, he told himself, edging forwards along the pavement, feeling like a climber groping across a cliff face. On reaching the bottom of the steps leading up to the entrance, he stopped again and stared longingly at the front door. Of course there was no question of ringing the bell, not that night anyway. It was already well past midnight and he needed a pretext. It was just a question of being patient, waiting for the opportunity, not losing heart. All his life he had given up on things, he reminded himself: his crap family, his university course, the job in Madrid where he had taken fright at the prospect of promotion, escaping to South America where he could be rootless and safe. And now his book on heroes . . . But he didn't want to think about that. Tonight he felt like a hero himself, a knight on a quest, a knight who would stop at nothing until he had attained his holy grail.

Stephen ran his eyes over the building, which was one in a line of tall red-brick Victorian blocks. He concentrated hard on the windows of the first floor where he knew she lived. They were dark, the curtains drawn, their white frames glowing gently in the dark. It was wonderful just to know she was inside, contained and safe.

Turning at last to go, Stephen recognised her black Volkswagen parked on the opposite side of the road and hurried over to it. Wanting to do something – to leave his mark – he traced a small heart in the thin film of frost covering the windscreen. Liking the effect, he drew another and then another, until the tip of his finger ached with cold and the entire windscreen was covered with dancing heart-shaped footsteps.

Exhausted from his sojourn in London, John slept in his armchair for an hour before dinner and then again during the ten o'clock news, using Boots as a footstool. When he woke during the weather forecast and saw that Pamela, too, was dozing, her head lolling, he had prodded her awake rather roughly, not liking to see her look so old. Upstairs he watched her, as he had many thousands of times, sit before the framed oval mirror of her dressing-table to attend to her face and hair. The dressing-table was one of the numerous handsome pieces of furniture that had belonged to his parents, made of soft golden cedarwood and inlaid round the edges with mother-of-pearl studs. His mother, too, had spent many hours in front of it, and his grandmother. The glass was faintly speckled with age but only near the top and bottom. Somewhere round the back he had taken a chip out of it with one of his front teeth during a game of chase with Eric. The tooth had disappeared into his gums, literally returned to its roots, then slowly grown out again as if nothing had ever been amiss.

'So, you had a good day, you say?'

Pamela smiled at his reflection in the glass. 'Yes . . . yes, I did. And you did too, didn't you? I'm so glad the boys were well.'

'Yes, they were fine. Charlie seems to be pulling through—' John broke off, suddenly remembering the marmalade, which was still in his briefcase. 'And Freddie Grimling sent his love,' he added quickly. 'He's having a hard time of it. His syndicates took a real bashing with the towers and Mary's arthritis is bad. They're thinking of moving down to Cornwall to be near her sister. George Crowell wasn't too good either, thinking of a hip replacement.'

'Oh dear, poor things.' Pamela, working in the last of her hand cream, paused before adding, 'Did you remember the marmalade?'

'Oh . . . yes, of course. Both very grateful.'

The blue eyes were open in an instant, sharp as knives. 'Oh, John, you forgot it, didn't you?'

Propped up in bed in his stripy pyjamas, his half-moon reading glasses balanced on the end of his nose, John squirmed among the pillows like a guilty child. 'I'm sorry, Pammy, I . . . It just slipped my mind.'

'Never mind.' She tied her hair loosely off her face with a velvet ribbon, her expression softening. 'It will be Easter soon. I'll give them all some then. It really doesn't matter.' She smiled again, wanting to show him that she spoke from the heart, too drained by the recent secret rollercoaster ride of her emotions to mind about such a small thing.

'Lucky you were in for that biographer fellow . . . Not like you to forget.'

'No, not like me.' Pamela sat on the edge of the bed and carefully swivelled sideways, easing both legs under the sheets. 'I don't think he noticed, and if he did he didn't seem to mind. He says he won't need to visit Eric, by the way, which is just as well. Oh, yes, and I think he might have a bit of a thing for Cassie. They did get on, didn't they, when he stayed that time? And I saw him looking at that photo in the drawing room . . . such a look.'

'A thing for Cassie . . . has he now? Well, charming he may be, but I think Cassie could do a lot better.'

'Oh, John, don't be so old-fashioned.'

'And you shouldn't be so romantic. Money matters, my dear, and unless I'm much mistaken that biographer fellow hasn't got very much of it.'

'I would like Cassie to fall in love, that's all,' murmured Pamela. 'I do admire the independence of our youngest. She's always been so good at knowing what she wanted – unlike Elizabeth – but it would be nice if she could meet the right man, regardless of his income,' she added, giving her husband a stern look.

John, who had spent a good portion of the day talking in various ways about money and feeling for the most part hugely reassured by it, gave an impatient stab at his glasses. 'Of course I'd like Cassie to fall in love – it's high time. But we don't want her making the sort of mistake Elizabeth did, do we? That Lucien fellow was a fortune-hunter if ever I saw one.'

'Was he? I'm not entirely sure you're right there. Anyway, I don't think Stephen Smith is a fortune-hunter.'

'Maybe not.' John reached for his book, opened it and closed it again. He was aware that this gentle bedtime banter was a good thing, that the icy unhappiness under which they had both, silently, been labouring since their granddaughter's death had at long last begun to disperse like the snow outside. If the visit from the writer had cheered Pamela then that was fine too. The man could visit a million times if that was the result. And in the end Cassie could marry whomsoever she chose, and whenever she wanted because, thanks to his financial good fortune, she would one day become a woman of considerable wealth. Even after the Inland Revenue had done its worst she, like Elizabeth and Charlie, still stood to inherit a good three hundred thousand pounds. This fact had struck John with fresh, reassuring force during the course of his lunch with his sons. We have been robbed of little Tina, he had thought, but we still have four wonderful children and their equally wonderful families. They were the future. And, thanks to family fortunes and his own hard work, they had a secure future to look forward to. They had a true inheritance, which was a rare thing these days. Such thoughts had warmed his heart as much as the port he had sipped in his club. Hearing his friends discuss financial losses, illness and plans for down-sizing moves to bungalows, John had basked in the resilience of his own happier circumstances. His liabilities as a Lloyds Member were spread over many more syndicates than theirs – reinsurance, marine, non-marine, he had a finger in every pie. Following the towers atrocity he had moved much more heavily into the American markets, capitalising on the premiums that had sky-rocketed as a result. The hit he had taken on the towers themselves had been minimal compared to that of his colleagues. 'My God, Pammy,' he burst out, slapping the counterpane so hard she jumped in surprise, 'we are so *lucky*, that's what I realised today. That vicar chap at Tina's funeral was absolutely right. Our family, contrary to most bloody families these days – fragmenting shambolic things – is strong. It's like a – a huge, indestructible . . . ocean liner, which will sail on long after you and I are gone.'

Pamela, hearing the emotion in his voice but too tired to respond to it, told him he was right but also a trifle sentimental and could they put the light out because she was sleepy. They turned towards the middle of the bed, kissed, and turned away – so that their backs were facing each other – to sleep. John, as he did so often these days, thought of death, daring it to frighten him. Which it did, though not quite as much as usual, partly because of the sentiments he had just expressed to his wife and partly because of Tina. The thought of his little granddaughter on the other side already was somehow of great solace.

Pamela, lying in the dark next to him, thought of Tina too, and then of the baby clothes, boxed in the attic just as her own unhappiness had been boxed inside her heart. She curled her knees up to her chest, as she had in childhood, glad she had done her weeping and got it over with; glad she had been brought back to her senses. She would throw out the contents of the suitcase at the very next opportunity, she decided, transfer them to a bag for the dustbin men to wheel away.

Dan lay with his hands behind his head staring up at the ceiling for most of the night. Sally, restless as always, turned many times with heaving sighs, once muttering something under her breath. He had seen Cassie in the restaurant, but only as they were leaving. His response had been to usher his wife hurriedly to the exit. Having the two women in his life in the same room made him feel more desperate, more aware that he was straddling two realities, in danger of crucifying himself with the effort of preventing them either bumping into each other or swerving even further apart. All hopes of resolving things that night were in tatters. The first hurdle had been George and Polly (as if they sensed his plans) choosing that evening, of all evenings, to be especially endearing, curling on his lap for stories and telling him tales of what they had got up to in school. Then his sleeping two-and-a-half-year-old, rotund in a new jumpsuit and pressing her muslin comforter to her peachy cheeks, had made him think of Cassie's niece. His children hadn't died, yet he was thinking of deserting them. Becoming a weekend dad. Parenting by proxy. Then Sally had sniped at him about something trivial and he had thought, Yes, I can leave after all, I need to leave this woman or I will go mad.

The second hurdle to his plans, however, had proved in-surmountable: in the restaurant, snapping her breadstick into smithereens, Sally had relayed the grisly news that an inconclusive smear test the month before had prompted a second test, which had in turn disclosed the existence of some dodgy cells. She had seen a specialist that morning who had told her they needed to do more tests. She hadn't told Dan before because she hadn't wanted to worry him, she said. But since the specialist – when she had pressed him – had admitted what Dan himself would know only too well, that a worst-case scenario could involve a hysterectomy, a course of chemotherapy and the removal of all her lymph nodes, she had felt it was time to tell him what was going on. She followed up these revelations with a plea for forgiveness about how difficult she had been in recent months: worries about her health hadn't helped and she was sorry.

Hearing her out, Dan had felt like a condemned man. Of course he felt compassion, concern, all those things, but he also felt trapped. A husband could not leave a sick – possibly very sick – wife, no matter how badly he and she were getting on. He just couldn't do it. It was too cruel, too . . . Dan hesitated to use the word even inside the privacy of his own head . . . immoral. Yet letting Cassie down, keeping her waiting, felt immoral too. He couldn't be without her, yet he couldn't have her. It was unspeakable. If he told Cassie he had to see Sally through a possibly serious illness she might give up on him and then he would die of misery. Cassie was the stardust in his life, the reason he sang in the shower and ran for buses, the reason he tolerated NHS bureaucracy and tetchy patients. She was his joy and he needed her.

Very very quietly, aware that he was breaking one of his own cardinal rules, Dan rolled over and reached for his mobile phone from his bedside table. 'Darling,' he typed, 'saw u 2nite. love u. plse be patient. r time will come i promise. D.' He then lay back in the dark in the same position, with his hands under his head, feeling pins and needles creeping up his forearms and into his palms, while tears squeezed their way out of the corners of his eyes and down his temples.

Chloë woke very early and lifted the corner of the curtain to look out of the window. She had had a dream about running away and thought, if the weather was nice, it might be an exciting thing to do. But in her dream she had had a big shaggy dog for company and had never been cold or hungry, whereas now outside looked quite empty and horrid with rain. So, although it would have been a good day to run away because she had a piano lesson and hadn't practised, as well as a spelling test of words she didn't know, she decided it probably wouldn't be much fun after all. Instead she got out of bed, put on her dressing-gown and some socks because her feet were icy, then went to check on the miniature cot where she kept the current favourite of her many dolls.

'Good morning, Tina, it's time to get up.' She picked up the doll and patted its back a couple of times then dressed it in a pink satinette party dress and matching pink shoes, which were annoying because they always fell off. The doll's real name was Jessica, but Chloë had rechristened her Tina after her baby cousin got killed by the motorbike, which her mother had said was an odd thing to do, but in Chloë's mind there had always been a whole string of names after Jessica (Florence Geraldine Wanda Tina Lucinda) so, as she tried to explain, all she had done was change the order a bit. She knew it was sad about her cousin and that she would miss helping her aunt Serena look after her sometimes, but everyone said Tina had gone to heaven, which couldn't be too bad. Chloë propped the doll against the window so she had something to look at, then went to the bathroom to pee, wiggling her toes because it felt so nice to get rid of the ache in her tummy.

As she came out of the bathroom she heard the beeps of the alarm being deactivated downstairs, which was interesting because it was still very early, and also very good since it meant she could watch television. (She wasn't allowed to turn off the alarm herself, except in an emergency, though neither of her parents had ever said what such an emergency would be. Theo was allowed to turn off the alarm but then her big brother was allowed everything, including staying up till after ten o'clock and having his own telephone.)

Chloë trotted downstairs, skated along the parquet floor in her socks and collided with Rika, who was standing, suitcase in hand, in the hall. Chloë had expected to see her father, who left early for work sometimes, and let out a squeal of surprise, prompting some frantic shushing from the au pair. 'Where are you going, Rika?'

'I am leaving this house, Chloë. Your mummy she say they don't want me any more.'

'Are you sure?' Chloë, who had been aware of nothing beyond the usual tensions the night before, eyed her with suspicion. She looked upset and all puffy round the eyes, just like half of the grown-ups at Tina's funeral. 'Where are you going?'

'Back to Izmir, to my home.'

Chloë let out a small gasp of envious awe. 'Are you running away?'

'I leave this here. So.' Rika set down her suitcase and plucked a letter from her pocket, which she propped against a pot plant on the hall table. She raked her hair, which was white blonde at the tips and a smudgy brown everywhere else, behind her ears, then kissed her charge on top of the head, opened the front door and disappeared out of it, stumbling under the heaviness of her baggage.

Chloë remained in the hall for several minutes, torn between her plan of watching cartoons and a sense that the departure of Rika needed reporting to higher authority. Who would meet her at the school gates now? And who would cook her tea? She wasn't particularly fond of Rika – the one before from Germany had been much nicer – but she was sort of used to her. And there were the biscuits she had baked from time to time, using half a tin of golden syrup, which she would miss terribly. She was saved from the decision by the appearance of her father, looking ruffled and grumpy in his pyjamas. 'Rika's gone but she left you this,' she said, feeling important. Instead of thanking her or seeming pleased, her father ripped open the letter and stomped back upstairs where Chloë heard his voice raised and then her mother's, and then both together. There were long words – *decision, thoughtlessness, consultation, audacity* – and other shorter, more worrying ones like *bloody* and *selfish*, with the gist, as far as Chloë could make out, being mostly to do with who would take the afternoon off to meet her from school. Then the bedroom door slammed and she couldn't hear any more. She went and poured the biggest bowl of Coco Pops she had ever had and took it to eat on the sofa watching television. She ate very carefully, only spilling the tiniest little bit on her nightie and the carpet, which she rubbed with a tissue until the dark stain was speckled with lots of tiny blobs of white.

Dear Clem,
  How are you? I am fine. It was my birthday yesterday and I got loads of money – twenty quid from Granny and Granddad,

twenty quid from Aunt Cassie, fifteen quid from Uncle Colin and
Aunt Elizabeth and some from your parents too . . .

(Theo was deliberately vague about Serena and Charlie's contribution since it had only been a tenner and he didn't want to make
his cousin feel bad. Everyone knew that, with Serena not working
and having so many children, their branch of the family had the
least ready cash. Although with Tina gone, they would presumably
have more, but he couldn't very well say that either.)

Mum and Dad sent me some CDs and a pair of trousers but my
proper present is going to be a microphone attachment for my
video camera. So I am really looking forward to the holidays.
Luckily Rika, our au pair, who was a real pain, has been FIRED.
Some new person who lives in the street is now looking after
Chloë till Mum gets back from work. Mum says Chloë is happy
because this person has a dog!

Theo, on the point of making a pejorative comment about little
sisters being a pain too, decided on reflection that this might be
rather tactless and began a new paragraph instead.

We are going to Ashley House as usual for Easter. I guess you lot
will be there too. Hope school isn't too bad. Mine is fine, apart
from games and corps (army training) which suck. If you could
find the time to write back that would be cool, though don't worry
if you can't. But I know you like writing because you keep that
diary, don't you?
   From Theo
   PS I'm going to carry on making my film of everybody at
Ashley House. Would you consider being my producer?

The postscript was something of an afterthought. Theo had every
intention of continuing with his documentary of the Harrison
family, but remained uncertain as to whether Clem's assistance
would be a help or a hindrance. It might be useful to have someone
to hold his new microphone, which, if he got the one he had picked
out from a catalogue, would be huge and need holding at just the

right angle and distance. But the real impulse for the suggestion was guilt about writing the letter, which had everything to do with being seen to have a female correspondent by his peers and very little to do with deepening his friendship with his cousin. It had been a toss-up between Maisie and Clem, the latter winning because she was so much less attractive and outgoing and therefore more likely (Theo had weighed up the matter very carefully) to be bothered to reply. And he wanted a reply very badly – just one – before the end of term, so that he could hold his head high among the swaggering majority of his year group who seemed perpetually to be talking about girlfriends, texting girlfriends or receiving letters in pink envelopes with things like SWALK scribbled across the flaps.

Dear Theo,

Sorry it's taken so long for me to reply but now that we're working on our GCSE courses we have so much more homework. I also had a piano exam (Grade V) and had to do lots of practice. It went okay, but Mum says I can give up whenever I want so it doesn't really matter.

YES!!! I would love to be your producer – thank you so much for asking. What do I have to do? I think we are going to be at Ashley House for quite a long time this holidays – to give Mum a break – and I was a bit worried about getting bored. So to be your producer would be just great. Maybe I could work on some scripts too. Think of questions to ask, etc. And what about Sid, are you going to include him? (I think you should, otherwise it's not the whole picture, is it?) Anyway, let me know.

I don't like games either. I only have to do netball but I'm quite slow and always drop the ball. Luckily I've been off games recently because last week I fainted. It was weird, actually, and really embarrassing too, because it just sort of happened and suddenly there I was on the ground with everybody staring down at me. Embarrassing or what? But still, it's cool being off games. Three days till we break up – HOORAY. See you very soon.

Love from Clem

APRIL

Sunlight was falling through the kitchen windows, casting a soft honeycomb of squares across the freshly washed pinky-grey stone floor. On the table a bunch of once primly budded tulips had thrown themselves open overnight, exposing the rich velvet of their petals and the trembling dusty black stalks at their hearts. Their stems curved languorously over the edge of the vase, their heads nodding at the butter glistening in its dish nearby and the porcelain tureen of a fruit bowl, so laden with apples, pears, tangerines, apricots and grapes that Chloë, invited by her grandmother to help herself, let her fingers run over first one then another in an agony of indecision. Their fruit bowl at home was half the size and usually contained apples patched with brown bruises and bananas with uninvitingly mottled skins. She settled finally on a large satin green apple, tugged it loose, then watched in dismay as a landslide of apricots and tangerines tumbled on to the table. Samson, who had been perched on the chair next to her pretending to wash his face but really eyeing the butter, took fright and leapt off the chair.

'Never mind,' trilled Pamela. 'I'll pop all that back. I'll give it a wash too – I forgot to do it before I put them in the bowl.' She swiftly rearranged the fruit, which she had bought along with a mountainous trolley of other supplies for the weekend, and ran the apple under the cold tap. After drying it carefully on a clean tea-towel she handed it back to her granddaughter. 'Don't let it spoil lunch, though, will you?' she said, speaking out of habit more than anything, thoroughly enjoying the feel of the spring sun on her back and the sight of her granddaughter, currently deprived of both front teeth, attempting to chisel a first bite with the side of her mouth. The tooth fairy had forgotten both times, she had been informed gravely, but then made up for it by leaving two two-pound coins. There had been several other interesting anecdotes during the course of the morning relating to departing au pairs, forgotten ballet kits and a dog called Toffee who chewed carpets, all of which had gone some considerable way to explaining the taut expression on Helen's face when she deposited her children on the doorstep of Ashley House before charging back to London. Life in Barnes was clearly in a state of upheaval, but all Helen had said was that she needed a day to interview girls from the agency and would return the following evening with Peter.

Charlie and Serena were also posting their offspring down ahead of the Easter weekend. John had already set off to Barham to meet the three of them off the train from Victoria. He and Serena wanted a little time to themselves, Charlie said, which was understandable, given what had happened. When the pair of them did arrive the utmost gentleness would be required, Pamela reminded herself, pressing open her cookery book at a recipe for chocolate mousse, which she knew by heart but liked to follow anyway. The pages were faintly sticky from the last time she had used it, and flecked with ancient specks of splattered egg and chocolate. She fetched eggs and a bar of Bournville from the larder and pulled out the largest of her mixing bowls, humming to herself, her mind half on cooking and half on the now imminent arrival of the family, scanning each one in her mind much as she scanned the familiar list of ingredients on the page in front of her.

Elizabeth, phoning to confirm her arrival with Roland the next day (Colin had some marking to catch up on and would join them in time for dinner), had sounded fraught. But Elizabeth often sounded fraught. Because she *struggled* so. She always had and always would. Even as a toddler she had seemed to find life so much harder than her brothers did, wailing tragically about things that the two boys could dismiss with a snivel or a laugh. And when Cassie had come along . . . Pamela, on the point of cracking the first of eight eggs, paused. Charlie had been closest in age but Elizabeth had shown the most signs of jealousy.

It all began so young, she reflected wistfully, pressing on with the eggs, expertly using just one hand, draining off the whites and dropping the orange-yellow yolks (each the size of a small fist and thick as treacle) into the mixing bowl. How they were now as adults was pretty much exactly as they had been during the days of nursery teas. Cassie knew what she wanted in life and Elizabeth didn't. Cassie made the most of herself, and Elizabeth for some reason . . . Pamela shook herself out of her reverie. She had promised herself not to do this. Not to dwell on things and get maudlin. The truth was that children, by and large (abuse and neglect apart), wrote the books of their personalities themselves and there was little parents or anyone else could do about it. As if to confirm this view Chloë charged back into the kitchen, complaining volubly, Samson dangling in her arms. Theo appeared behind her, crouching like a hunter, the lens of his video camera pressed to his eye.

'Theo's *following* me, Granny, and being *really* annoying.'

'I am not. I'm making a film of the family and you – worse luck – have to be in it.'

'Now, Theo . . .'

'Can I interview *you*, then, Gran?' He lowered the camera and stood upright, his face a picture of earnest supplication. 'Please?'

Pamela hesitated, wanting to defuse the argument between her grandchildren but not entirely happy about making herself available to the lens of Theo's camera either. She had never liked having her photo taken. In both of the developed versions of Sid's pictures from Christmas her eyes were closed, even though she had concentrated fiercely on not blinking. It had put her off seeing the portrait project through, though Mary Cavendish, who had recommended an artist, said she was sure it wouldn't matter. 'Well, I suppose so . . . if it won't take long.' Pamela eyed the camera uncertainly, doing her best to sound interested but understanding why Chloë should have found it so irksome. 'Shall I take off my apron?'

Theo lowered the camera and frowned, rubbing his free hand over the pimples on his chin. The apron was blue and white like a butcher's and had stains all over it. But then, when he thought about it, an apron summed up his grandmother and to keep it on might be rather appropriate. 'No, leaving it on is fine. And could you sit near those flowers? They look really nice – in that chair there, maybe with Samson on your lap . . .' It was such fun being in command and issuing instructions that Theo soon forgot about the time or that he was only fourteen years old. Before long Pamela was worrying about her half-finished mousse and Samson, reluctantly cooperative for a few minutes, leapt off her lap in disgust, doing a last-minute dart to avoid Chloë's ever-eager hands.

'I don't want to hear this, Martin. I've got the minister breathing down my neck and that's because the IMO are breathing down his. I know the meeting isn't until Tuesday but, as you might recall, the entire country breaks for a four-day weekend as of tomorrow, which means we need our ducks in a row by this afternoon. I've got a lunch, but will be back by two fifteen. The research has to be in a digestible form by then – if not in hard copy then at least on a disk. You've had two months, for God's sake, we simply can't build any more time into the schedule.' Charlie slammed down the phone. He could feel the adrenaline pulsing through his body, making him hot but also energised. In the past he had been too soft on people. It was one of the many reasons life in the Railway Directorate had become so intolerable; everyone always expected him to be lenient and understanding, to stretch deadlines and help in the prickly maze of internal politics and public accountability. Shipping, thank God, was proving a much less stressful posting – no hounding by the media helped enormously, but he still wasn't going to fall into the trap of letting down his defences and taking unnecessary flak.

Susan Drayling, who had been seeing to the secretarial needs of Charles Harrison since his arrival at his new post three months before, eyed him over the top of her spectacles, wondering what had happened to the gentle giant who had found time to ask her about her cats and who, if she was snowed under, had been known to tap out a letter or two himself, using one finger and saying hilarious things about his incompetence. These days, he barked as much as the rest of them and hassled her till she got all jittery and made silly mistakes. She knew about the terrible business of his little girl, of course. Everyone in the department did. He had taken a week off in compassionate leave and they'd all given him cards of condolence. And she knew about throwing oneself back into work during difficult times. She had done exactly the same thing when her father died; without the routine of work she would have fallen apart completely. So one made allowances. But, still, it was hard to see the kindness of such a man shrivel with unhappiness.

'Susan, could I have those letters sharpish? I've got to leave on time today.'

'I'll do my best.' Her fingers, busy with an e-mail, worked faster. 'Going anywhere nice? For the bank holiday?' she pressed, because there was no response.

'The usual thing. Down to my parents' place in Sussex. We've sent the children on ahead and are joining them tomorrow.'

'Lovely,' she murmured, encouraged that she had wheedled three sentences out of him. 'And I'll make sure I get those letters done.' She pressed *Send* for the e-mail and slotted her head-set into place with a sigh.

Cassie lit a cigarette even though she had told herself she wouldn't have one and looked impatiently at the door of the coffee-house, willing Dan's lean frame to step through it. She hated waiting for him. Yet it was what she seemed to do all the time: wait for the phone, wait for the chance to meet, wait for him to arrive – usually late and having to rush off again. Afterwards it sometimes felt hardly worth it, but then he would call and be so sweet and the prospect of another meeting would blossom like a flower and she would be all charged up again, planning what to wear and how to make the most of every second.

Outside the sun was shining, the first real kiss of heat that they had had in months. Cassie, strolling along Brompton Road because she was early, had dug out her sunglasses, dusty from lack of use, from the bottom of her handbag, feeling jaunty and full of hope. It was only on arriving at the coffee-house that her mood had turned. Several couples were sitting at tables outside and although there were two spare seats and it was where she, too, longed to sit, she knew that Dan would rule it out at once because no matter where they met he was paranoid about the risk of them being seen. So she had gone inside instead, where the air was stuffy and where her cigarette smoke clung to her instead of drifting off on a nice fresh breeze, and where her sunglasses served only to keep her hair off her face. The table wobbled too and one of the chairs had a nasty dark stain on the back.

'Darling, there you are. Sorry I'm late. Good table – well done. How are you, my love?' Dan kissed her quickly, glancing over his shoulder as he sat down.

'Not great, to be honest. I mean, the sun is shining and here we are stuck inside. I don't like to complain – I know the pressure you're under, really I do, but I think . . . ever since little Tina died I . . .' A lump the size of a golf ball was blocking her throat. 'God, sorry . . . I shouldn't.'

'Yes, you should.' Dan put his hand over hers, glaring at the waitress who had deposited their coffee and was staring at Cassie's trembling face with unabashed interest. 'Go on, darling, say what you feel. It's so important to share all our thoughts, to be honest with each other.'

'Oh, I do feel that, Dan,' she burst out eagerly, 'that honesty is one of the few things we really have between us.' She wiped her face hurriedly. She hated getting all weepy with him. She wasn't the weepy sort. She was a fortunate, successful, attractive woman who got on with things, like setting up her own business and actually making a pretty decent wage. In every other relationship in her life she had been the one in control, who had decided when it ended and why, seeing her own needs clearly. But with Dan all of that had gone to pot. With Dan she had discovered that it was impossible to be really in love with someone and remain wholly in control, because love was about losing control, handing over one's happiness to another person to use or abuse as they chose . . .

'You were saying?' he prompted, keeping his voice calm and confident when, inside, he was quaking because he knew exactly what she was going to say – the gist of it anyway – and because for the first time in the eleven months since they had met he was on the point of not being completely honest himself. He wanted to be. He really did. The rest of his life was thick with deceit; being straight with Cassie was like coming up for air. But now Sally was ill and he couldn't tell her for fear of it making her despair. Since the night in the restaurant he had thought of little else, sensing all the while that for Cassie, too, the episode had been some sort of turning point.

'Honesty. Okay, then. Here goes.' She looked at him, her dark blue eyes wide and trusting. 'I want more, Dan, and I want it now. I mentioned my niece because – because her dying like that has really given me a jolt about how bloody short life is. I can't wait for ever, I simply can't. Especially not if we . . .' Cassie had been going to mention starting a family, but couldn't quite bring herself to say it out loud, not with the waitress hovering and the neighbouring tables so near. 'I'm *so* fed up of keeping you in the shadows,' she whispered instead, still loudly enough for Dan to cast nervous looks to his right and left. 'I'm not a naturally dishonest person for one thing. I hate keeping you a secret. Like seeing you in that restaurant – I just wanted to grab you and introduce you to everyone, to make you a full and proper part of my *real* life. I want to show you off, Dan, get you to meet my parents, to see Ashley House. You would love it, I promise you. And they'd love you . . . I mean, they'd be sad, of course, that you had been married before, but they would understand when they saw how happy you make me and how completely wonderful we are together.' She had lit another cigarette and was waving it in the air as she talked.

'And I want all that too,' he whispered fiercely, 'so badly.'

'But?'

'But . . . I've spoken again to my lawyer and he says that at the moment financially . . .'

'I don't care about finances. I've told you, I'll live in a mud hut with you if necessary. But it won't be necessary. I've got my flat and enough money for us to live on. And I've told you already that when my parents die I'll be seriously well-off . . .'

In spite of the gravity of the circumstances Dan couldn't help chuckling. He loved how breezy and open she was about money, how she saw so easily beyond it, while he was so wretchedly tied to it – or at least to the lack of it.

'Is it money, Dan? Is it really? Or do you have other . . . doubts?

Please tell me.' She closed her lips tightly round the butt of her cigarette to stop them trembling.

It was the moment to tell her of the cells found on Sally's cervix, the moment to trust her with the truth, no matter how difficult. Dan felt that, yet he couldn't do it. He told her instead as much of the truth as he could, that he had no doubts, that he loved her more than he had ever loved anyone, that he wanted to share the rest of his life with her, that if she could only be patient for a little longer he would extricate himself from his family, that he needed just a few more months to get everything in order so that when he jumped ship it would be tidy and easy and as clean and painless as possible. Then he kissed her, not a stealthy, snatched, are-we-being-watched kind of kiss but a long sensuous, tender tongue-searching that made her skin tremble and the pit of her stomach contract with achy longing. As she watched him hurry out of the door a few minutes later, checking both ways before diving into the street, Cassie felt a surge of joyous certainty followed by a greater, suffocating wave of despair. He made her so happy and yet so sad. It was unbearable.

'Another coffee, madam?'

'No . . . yes . . . A single espresso, please.' It would make her late for Mrs Shorrold but she didn't care. A thought had occurred to her and she needed time to analyse it. A desperate, terrifying thought. But, then, her situation *was* desperate. She had been patient and passive for too long. She needed to take control. Dan wanted to move things on as much as she did, but he was struggling and needed her help. All her life Cassie had made a point of getting what she wanted. And she wanted this man. More than she had ever wanted anything in all her thirty-seven years. She reached for her briefcase, set it on her lap and clicked open the locks. Inside, under swatches and receipts and notes, there was a pad of paper, and an envelope too, just one, as if it was meant to be. As if her idea had been sitting there all the time, waiting for her to stumble upon it.

Dear Sally Lambert,
    My name is Cassandra Harrison. I have been having an affair with your husband for almost a year. I love him and he loves me.

*I know that you no longer make each other happy. Please let him
go. I am sorry you had to find out this way, but sometimes
honesty is all that's left.*

She thought long and hard about adding other things, like she knew
Dan was a wonderful father and she would never get in the way of
him seeing his children, how breaking up a family was the very last
thing she had ever meant to do, but refrained for fear of sounding
leeching and hollow. The letter, Cassie knew, was a bomb and no
amount of kind or explanatory sentiments could soften it. Then she
left for her appointment with Mrs Shorrold, tucking the envelope
into the side of her bag because she didn't have a stamp.

Helen had spent most of the drive back to London on her mobile
phone. At work, some perfectly straightforward business for one of
the companies she advised was going pear-shaped. Then her
mother had called to report that they were both bedridden with
flu and to complain – as she did from time to time – that they never
saw her or the children, which was true. In terms of visits Peter's
family took priority. They always had, and Helen had been perfectly aware that this would be the case when she married him. As
she was not close to her own parents and they spent half of their
lives dragging a caravan round Europe, this had never posed much
of a problem to either side. But now that her parents were frail and
travelling far less they were getting more demanding. Theo still
hadn't written a thank-you letter for his birthday present, her
mother said, and if they weren't going to see them at Easter could
they at least arrange – now, that very minute – a visit some time in
the summer. Helen had cringed at the prospect of persuading Peter
that the four of them should spend some of their precious free time
in her parents' higgledy-piggledy bungalow and said she needed to
consult her diary which, in spite of being true, had sounded harsh.
She would phone with some dates over the weekend, she had
promised, when she had spoken to Peter and checked what other
commitments were on the horizon. 'I know you're busy,' her
mother had replied, in a voice so whipped and clearly lacking in

comprehension that Helen had prolonged the conversation with enquiries about flu and the weather in a bid to appease her.

Accelerating and decelerating between speed cameras, Helen had finally made it back to Barnes in an hour and three-quarters, just ten minutes before the arrival time of her first interviewee. She teased her key into the lock, then rested her forehead briefly against the door overwhelmed suddenly with tiredness. She had been up late the night before, trying to get ahead on paperwork before the long weekend, then set the alarm for six so as to manage the round trip to Ashley House with the children. Peter had said she was mad – creating work for herself – and should put their two on a train with their cousins. They had argued about it, as they seemed to argue about most things these days. Helen had tried to explain that Chloë still needed watching like a hawk, when the simple truth was that she wanted both children out of the way much earlier than the train plan would have allowed to get on with the interviews. In the past, attempts to involve the children at such an early stage of an au pair-selection procedure had always backfired, partly because they invariably opted for different candidates and partly because Chloë tended to form immediate and entrenched preferences on the basis of arresting, irrelevant details, like the colour of a skirt or a hairstyle. Helen's rejection of a Dutch girl with a coiffure of pink stiff peaks in favour of Rika had caused a storm for weeks.

Helen picked up the post from the doormat and went into the kitchen, her heart sinking at the sight of the breakfast things still on the table. Theo had filled his bowl so full that a good portion of corn flakes had slopped over the sides, while Chloë had enjoyed a more than usually explosive encounter with the sugar bowl. White crystals were sprinkled not just across the table but on much of the floor too, as Helen discovered when she approached the mess with a cloth only to feel the disheartening crunch of granules underfoot. She had only just begun to clear it up when the bell rang. Cursing, she crunched her way into the hall and opened the door to a squat girl with ginger hair and a broad Scottish accent, with whom she could not imagine wanting to share her home or any aspect of family life. And so it continued for five long hours: girls of varying shapes and backgrounds, clutching fistfuls of sparkling references, proclaiming their commitment to childcare, their love of Barnes (and many other unlikely things) crossing the threshold and departing. Helen fired questions like an automaton, while inside far bigger ones burned in her mind. Why was she doing this? Why had she had children if only to farm them out to half-formed creatures who knew as much about motherhood as she did about karate? And why, above all, was she doing this when she had Kay? As she closed the door on the final and most hopeless appointment of the day, this last thought would not be argued away. It was, Helen realised now, at the heart of her incapacity to be inspired by alternatives. Kay was perfect. She was patient, motherly, accommodating, cheerful and flexible beyond most working mothers' wildest dreams. Chloë adored her and Toffee, and even Theo, for whom it mattered far less, had conceded that she was very funny and really good at cooking. (Helen had arrived home the other day to find the pair of them smacking their lips over some sort of fish pie. *Fish!* The very word was usually sufficient to make both children clutch their throats in a drama of retching.) Only Peter didn't like Kay. He said it was the dog. And it was true on his first visit that Toffee had attempted to sample a few of the long silk tassels fringing the edge of the Indian carpet, but he had received such a roaring castigation from his mistress upon discovery that now he didn't go near the sitting room without a look of anxious guilt on his foxy face.

No, it wasn't the dog, Helen mused, snapping the kettle switch down and dropping a tea-bag into a mug, it was Kay herself. Unconventional, outspoken, faintly shambolic, but for some reason hugely comforting. Taking over from her in the evenings towards the end of term, seeing her bustle round the kitchen in one of her vast colourful outfits, a purple scarf round her hair, arms in the sink and one beady eye on Chloë, sucking her pencil over some homework problem at the kitchen table, the little dog curled on a chair next to her, Helen had felt that a new and much-needed warmth had entered the house. A warmth neither she nor Peter could provide. And when Kay said it was time to be going and Chloë had been ushered upstairs to a bath, Helen often found herself deferring the other woman's departure with offers of tea or a glass of wine, which they drank at the kitchen table, chatting easily about the most improbable things. It turned out she was a freelance copy editor but could only work early in the mornings because, Kay claimed, by eleven o'clock the clever part of her brain shut up shop for the day. She had had an interesting and frequently traumatic life, the details of which she had no qualms about sharing with Helen, managing in the process to convey the impression of one who had learnt enough lessons never to be judgemental about the behaviour of others. As a result, Helen found herself confiding many things – partly out of the simple flattery of being confided in herself, and partly because she had never before met anyone with whom it felt so *safe* to share ideas. Peter, arriving tense and hungry from work during a couple of these sessions, had been embarrassingly unsecretive about his disapproval, virtually standing by the front door until Kay and Toffee had disappeared. She was a meddling neighbour with not enough to do, he said, and the sooner they got shot of her the better. She and Peter had never been so at odds over a person before and it worried Helen. Kay had picked up on Peter's attitude at once and been breezily accepting of it. 'I'm a woman's woman and he knows it.' She had laughed. 'Don't get me wrong, I like men – adore them, in fact, the darlings, wish I didn't sometimes – but the more I go through life the more I think women are the real Trojans of the world, fighting on all fronts, evolving in ten different directions at once, workers, wives, mothers, not to mention menstruation, childbirth and the menopause, while men for the most part toddle along wanting to play at being little boys and be babied long into their dotage.'

When the doorbell rang again Helen groaned. It was already half past three and she had many things still to cram into this enforced luxury of a day alone at home. In stockinged feet and clutching her half-drunk tea, she tiptoed her way round what remained of the sugar spillage and peered through the spyhole. 'You can tell me to go away – you really can. I was passing and thought I'd just pop in to see how it went.'

'Kay.' Helen swung open the door, beaming. 'Awful, thank you, truly awful. They all look so *young*, or am I just getting old? I was least sure about the first one but now think she might be the best . . . and to be going to all this bother when you . . .'

Kay held up her hand, first to stop Helen on a subject for which she had received many rambling apologies already, and second to remove her baseball cap, revealing a livid orange-red helmet of her normally grey hair. 'Don't say a thing. I misread the instructions and left it on for twice the time you're meant to. I think I could get to like it – one day.' She thrust her head round the edge of the hall mirror, then glanced away quickly again with a hoot of laughter. 'On the other hand, maybe not. As for you being old, I've never heard such bollocks.'

'The kettle's just boiled.'

'Tea would be nice, but . . . how would you feel about going out to find it?'

'Going out?'

'Richmond, I thought. So many heavenly shops – and some good tea-houses, come to that. There's one that does a particularly good ginger cheesecake.'

'I couldn't possibly, Kay, I've got – well, there's sugar all over the kitchen floor to start with.'

'I can deal with that while you change.'

'Change? But – but I—' Helen glanced down at her crisp white shirt and navy skirt, momentarily taken aback. 'But I simply can't, Kay, I've got so much to do – paperwork, laundry, packing for the weekend . . .'

'When did you last go shopping – and I mean *serious* shopping?'

Helen, weakening, had asked what exactly she meant by that, only to be told – in a voice that would brook no contradiction – that it involved going in pursuit of entirely unnecessary things, like kitten-heeled shoes, eye-shadow and lacy knickers. When Helen said she was only comfortable in flat soles, seldom wore makeup and bought her underwear in packs of five from a catalogue, Kay had retorted that it was high time she mended her ways and shooed her upstairs. A few minutes later they were on their way to

Richmond in Kay's Fiat because, as she pointed out, it was smaller and easier to park. Helen had swapped the skirt for some black trousers, and covered the white shirt with a green jumper, and felt like a schoolgirl being taken on an unexpected treat, both because it had come out of the blue and because she had so readily agreed to it. Kay might have been a woman's woman, but Helen certainly wasn't. She had always despised females who shopped and lunched and discussed handbag styles. It was a matter of considerable personal pride that her career had been forged on the back of her brains rather than her looks. Colleagues who used their feminine wiles to promote themselves or their arguments had always seemed to her to be colluding in some huge scam in which she wished to play no part. Yet here she was, aged forty-seven, playing truant from a stack of pressing phone-calls and urgent domestic matters in order to purchase lingerie. And wanting to do it. That was what was so awful. 'I've no idea why I let you talk me into this, I really haven't,' she murmured, looking out of the window. Kay had taken a route she would never have chosen, cutting through Roehampton and Richmond Park. The sun was low in the sky but very bright, illuminating the spring green of the trees and grass. A couple of deer, with speckled white spots on their gingery backs and antler sprigs sprouting next to their ears, looked up lazily as they passed, then sauntered across the road behind them towards a lay-by where several excited Japanese tourists were leaping out of a coach waving cameras. 'And I've no idea why you are doing this either. Kay?' She turned to look at her unlikely new friend, wondering suddenly how and why she had become so rapidly and deeply embroiled in her life.

Kay grinned. 'The self-employed are always seeking distractions and I'm no exception. And . . .' she hesitated '. . . I really do believe that in some curious way people appear as you need them, just as events take on patterns, that it's all about one's inner and outer lives being intimately connected for those prepared to recognise it. Synchronicity . . . or something.'

'Really? So I met you because I needed you?' Helen's voice rang with scepticism.

Kay made a face. 'Put like that it sounds stupid, doesn't it? And, anyway, it works both ways, so I must have needed you too, mustn't I? Which is certainly true in that copy-editing is a lonely business, and finding a new friend is always lovely, and Toffee adores Chloë . . . But to answer your question, no, you don't *need* anything, Helen, least of all me. You've got it all – the perfect life. You're just a little . . . sad at the moment. At least you were when you were putting the rubbish out that night all those weeks ago – and I happened to notice it.'

Helen was surprised as always by the extent of Kay's perception and her fearlessness in articulating it. 'Yes, I suppose I was.'

'Because of your niece.'

Helen sighed. 'Dear little Tina. Yes, that's true . . . although . . .'

'Yes?'

'Nothing, really . . . I was just going to say that, now I think about it, I had actually been a bit below par before Tina died – missing Theo and so on when I hadn't really expected to, and all sorts of other unconnected things like Chloë being difficult and working too hard and—'

'Nothing is unconnected,' Kay interrupted, sliding deftly into a car-parking space and tugging up the handbrake. 'Everything is connected. Absolutely everything.'

'Is it?' Helen glanced at her companion, impressed as always by her conviction.

'Everything,' Kay repeated, tipping out her purse in search of change for the meter. 'How is your sister-in-law, by the way? How is she coping?'

Helen frowned, casting her mind back to the gruelling evening at the cinema when she had last seen Serena. 'She's . . . fragile, up and down, but then we all are. I mean, nothing feels quite the same as it did. It's like the whole family has lost some sort of equilibrium. We're all meeting for Easter this weekend and, frankly, I'm rather dreading it. Ashley House is lovely and huge and we usually all just relax there and get spoilt by Peter's mother, who's the most fabulous cook, but this time I know it will be different . . . difficult.'

Kay, who had been listening intently, closed her purse with a quiet snap. 'A tragedy like that . . . it takes time . . . The ripples and repercussions will go on and on. In the meantime,' she added lightly, 'we've two hours before the shops close.'

'Look, Kay, I know you're trying to be kind, but I really don't need to buy anything, least of all kitten heels or lingerie. Peter would be appalled.'

Kay raised one eyebrow. 'Would he?'

'Yes,' replied Helen firmly, 'but it is his fiftieth soon – we're having quite a big do in the country at his parents' house. You could perhaps help me choose something for that.'

'Good. I saw some lovely eveningwear last week, strapless, low backs, just right for your slim figure. Look here,' she added, seeing Helen's expression, 'you're a gorgeous-looking woman in the prime of your life and the sooner you start recognising it the happier you will be. Before you know it you'll be like me, HRT-dependent and sharing pillow-talk with a dog. It's okay to *enjoy* yourself, Helen, it really is.'

Helen laughed uncertainly, and said she knew that perfectly well. Then she followed Kay into various shops and changing rooms, and purchased a blue silk evening dress with a back that plunged almost to the little V at the top of her bottom, and a pair of matching blue backless high-heeled shoes. At the last minute she let Kay add a minuscule pair of blue silk knickers to the pile as well, with tiny satin bows front and back and about an inch of blue lace to cover her rear end. 'I must be mad,' she muttered, scribbling her signature under the huge total on the credit-card slip, then tucked the receipt into her purse. 'I might just decide to bring them back,' she warned Kay, as they left the shop in search of a cup of tea, and added, a little desperately, 'I'm really not sure they're *me*.' Kay, who had treated herself to a huge turquoise bra for her ample chest and a volumi-nous silky black petticoat, merely smiled knowingly. 'But, then, what's "me", Helen, other than whom you choose to be?'

Peter removed his wig and mopped his brow with his handkerchief, then refolded it into a careful square and slotted it back into his breast pocket. The rape trial, after all sorts of delays, had finally come to an end. They had won but it had been a close call. The girl, so brassy and defiant about her story, had got close to alienating the jury. He had seen it in their expressions and warned her accordingly. 'Behave more like a victim,' he had wanted to say, but didn't because she had the sort of temperament that would probably have made her do precisely the opposite. Instead he said that she had to control her anger and win them round, that there were enough facts to speak for themselves and she should not let her emotions get in the way of them. Wary, her small, stony eyes narrowed permanently in resistance, she had more or less managed it. The jury, after a nerve-racking four hours, had found her assailant guilty. The judge had given him seven years and the girl had flung her arms round Peter like an exuberant child.

If only life had such obvious and satisfying conclusions, reflected Peter now, pulling a cigar out of a polished wooden box that he reserved for such occasions and leaning back in his leather chair to smoke it. Even when he lost a case there was a satisfying *shape* to the process, a sense, even in defeat, of closure. One could take a deep breath, dust one's palms together and move on. But with things on the home front at the moment there was only a feeling of relentless collision, messy unravelling, as if they were all lurching from one mini-crisis to the next without a lucid view as to where on earth they were heading. Helen, normally so on top of things, was all over the place. Without Rika the house was messy. The ironing, at which the girl had been indisputably magnificent, was sitting in piles on the stairs. For the time being his shirts were being done at the dry-cleaner's, which was better than nothing but still inconvenient because they needed collecting and Helen never seemed to have time. The Kay woman had offered to do it, but as far as Peter was concerned the less she did the better. There was something witchy about her, something he couldn't put his finger on and which worried him all the more for apparently being so appealing to his wife. She seemed to be there now whenever he got home, all side by side and cosy with Helen, as if the pair of them were hatching some invisible conspiracy. It made him feel shut out, threatened, undermined.

Peter drew deeply on his cigar, letting the thick sweetness of the smoke curl round his tongue and teeth before blowing it out in a wavering grey stream. The sooner they found a proper replacement for Rika the better. Remembering that Helen had taken the day off to interview candidates, Peter phoned home, drumming his fingers impatiently on his desk when there was no reply. He tried Helen's mobile but it was switched off. Wanting to share his victory with at least one member of his family, he phoned Charlie, only to be told that he was in a meeting. So he rang Ashley House instead, where he had an unsatisfactory conversation first with his mother, who was fussing and preoccupied about preparations for the arrival of the family for the weekend, and then with his father, who rambled first about the roof, which had sprung a few leaks, and then about the high returns to be had in the reinsurance market in which his syndicates had lately invested heavily. Peter, in no mood to reiterate his much-repeated mantra that the sooner his father resigned as a Lloyds Name the better, let him talk, all the while puffing heavily on his cigar and musing upon recent returns on his own investments, which, thanks to an excellent stockbroker, were considerable. He was about to sign off when there was a lot of rustling followed by the indignant voice of his daughter.

'Daddy, when are you and Mummy coming?'

'Tomorrow, darling.'

'Only Theo is being horrible.'

'Why? What's he doing?'

'His stupid camera. He won't turn it off even when I ask really nicely. And he keeps trying to film Samson so he's run away and won't come even though Granny has called him for his tea.'

'Oh dear. Well, I'm sure that Samson will come when he's hungry. And Theo's only practising because he wants to be a film director when he grows up.'

'Well, I think he's stupid.'

'Now, Chloë, that's quite enough. You be a good girl for Granny and I'll see you tomorrow.'

There was a long sigh, followed by the whisper, 'I want Mummy.'

'You'll see Mummy tomorrow too.'

Peter put the phone down and tapped the ash off his cigar. He hadn't eaten enough and the smoke was giving him a headache. He knew he should take the opportunity to have an early night but somehow he wasn't in the mood for Helen, especially not if she had the witch in tow, which he suspected she would. He phoned the old colleague with whom he had had dinner the month before, who happened to be both female and highly entertaining, and asked if she was free for a drink as he had an improbable victory under his belt and no one immediately available with whom he could celebrate it.

'Last-resort department, am I?' she quipped.

Peter laughed, relaxing already. 'I'm afraid you are, Hannah. I won't keep you long. I'm just not quite ready to face the domestic scene.'

'I know *exactly* what you mean,' she replied smoothly. 'And don't think it gets any better when they leave school. We've got *four* extras camping with us at the moment, all between the ages of nineteen and twenty-one. It's hell.'

'Foxton's wine bar in half an hour?'

'I'll be there.'

Serena had spent the afternoon doing . . . well, if she was honest with herself, doing nothing. Absolutely nothing. Fuck all. Sweet FA. The morning had been busy enough, cajoling the children into packing for the stay with their grandparents, making them a picnic for the journey, checking they had money, telephones, telephone numbers. She had been efficiency personified, issuing orders, herding them about the place like some kind of sergeant major, telling them to hurry when in fact it was she who was in a hurry, a hurry to be rid of them, to get out of Victoria station as fast as her legs could carry her. To be on her own. Don't think, she had told herself, waving them on to the platform, then hurtling back through the crowds, keeping her eyes averted from the café where Ed had made Tina cry and life had felt normal. Arriving at the double yellow where she had parked the car, she had groaned with relief both at having made it out of the station and at being on her own. Thank God, she thought, now I can do and be all that I need to do and be. With other people – whether her own children, or Charlie, or well-meaning friends – she felt constantly that she was holding herself in, keeping a lid on the tremendous, pushing pressure inside. And yet a moment later stabbing the key into the ignition, all the relief dissolved to a feeling of emptiness. A big nothing. But not nothing because it ached so.

The house was hollow and tidy. She folded laundry, patted cushions and made it tidier. She walked into the garden, picked up the plastic bucket over which Cassie had stepped four weeks before, and put it down again. She stared, arms akimbo, at the scruffy rectangle of grass, needing its first cut of the spring, at the rosebuds, out in such force that the flimsy branches of the bush trailed down to the path from the weight of the load, at the weeds tangled round the base of the shrubs. She was an impatient, over-hasty gardener, lacking the green-fingered skill of her mother-in-law yet keen enough on the results to have a go. The previous spring she had spent many happy hours in the garden with Tina, steering their ancient hand-mower round her daughter's darting crawls, pausing to pull sprigs of grass from her ever-hungry mouth and prise clumps of mud from between her chubby fingers. Tina had loved the bucket, banging it like a drum with a stick, or tipping it, heedless of rain water and dirt, on to her lap or her head. The bucket had only made sense because of Tina. In fact, Serena realised, pulling her cardigan more tightly around her, all objects – the roses, the sky, the house, a pair of socks, everything – only had value because of the human emotions connected to them. Without her daughter, their poky London garden was just a strip of grass, as desolate and devoid of meaning as a disused playground. Seeing it look so lush and sprightly in the spring sunshine only made Serena feel worse, the sheer resilience of all the buds and green sprigs appearing, to her tender heart, merely accusatory and insouciant. Nature might plough on, sprouting again after the assaults of winter, she reflected wretchedly, but she couldn't, she just couldn't.

Desperate for the consolation of action – no matter how pointless – Serena took her handbag and walked towards Wimbledon high street. She could buy bread and put it in the deep freeze. Or butter. No one could ever have too much butter. Mocked by the fresh brightness of the day, the sun beaming like a great smiley face in the sky, Serena walked with her eyes on the pavement, seeking something blank and ugly to match her mood. In the little supermarket she took a plastic-wrapped sliced loaf off the shelf, not bothering to check whether it was brown or white, thin- or thick-sliced, and then a pack of butter. The young Asian girl at the checkout smiled at her and she smiled back, thinking, If only you knew, if only you knew. My smile is a lie. I am a lie. I look normal but I am not. I am a sham of a person, a collapsed, hopeless, unfunctioning thing, going through the motions.

Out in the street, squinting at the sun, which was low in the sky now but still as bright as a penny, she saw a woman she recognised; not a great friend, but quite a good one. They had met at the antenatal clinic when she was pregnant with Tina and stayed in touch. She had a boy called Robbie who had been to mini-gym with Tina, and Tumbletots, and toddler swimming classes at the leisure centre. Tina had been to his first birthday party and given him a fat truck with detachable wheels. Serena looked at the woman, bracing herself, ready with the usual replies. 'Yes, okay, managing, thank you . . . other children fine . . .' But the questions never came. The woman, who was called Brenda, dropped her eyes and hurried off in the opposite direction, dragging her little son after her. It was understandable, Serena knew. Cowardly, but understandable. Oh, and so cruel. Serena dropped her little white plastic bag of shopping and fled down the street, turning down a side road she didn't know and then another and another, until she found herself outside a church, a big Victorian Gothic monstrosity, with dirty black walls and rusting wrought-iron gates. The door will be locked, she told herself, because of vandals and shorter working weeks for priests. But it was open.

Inside, the air was chilly and damp. Instead of pews there were rows of chairs with little wooden pockets on the back for hymn books and orange kneelers slotted between their legs. Serena wasn't religious. She had been confirmed mainly because she wanted to wear a pretty white dress and a real silver cross round her neck. Marrying in church had been grand and moving, but she would have been just as happy swapping rings with Charlie in a registry office. Attendance since then had comprised the Christmas family service at St Margaret's, but really just for the fun of singing carols and forcing the children to think of something beyond the frenzy of tearing off wrapping-paper. At her mother's funeral she had felt mostly relief – because the hideous suffering was over – but little compunction to analyse the possibility of the hereafter. Nor had the notion of a benign divinity shimmered at the funeral of her daughter. She had been both too focused on trying to control her own emotions and too wounded to seek solace from anyone, let alone a God in charge of some grand scheme that involved killing off toddlers. Efforts since then to imagine the reunion of these two lost loved ones in heaven had felt as pointless as a cynic trying to believe in a fairy tale. But now, she thought, now, she would give God a chance. Because she had stumbled upon a church. Because she could think of nowhere else to turn.

She sat on a chair near the front, next to the aisle and facing the altar. *Okay, God, if you're there come out now and do something. Show yourself. If you exist, help me.* She opened her eyes and looked about her, staring first at the waxy face of a madonna on a plinth next to her and then at Jesus pinned to a crucifix behind the altar, brown-red blood dripping from his hands and sides. His head was cast down and he looked gruesome and self-pitying. *Okay, I'll settle for a priest then; some charismatic, community-loving chap with understanding eyes and a kind voice who'll assure me my pain will pass, that he will pray for me even though I can't pray for myself.* Hearing a rustle, Serena looked about her, a brief wild hope pulsing in her heart. But nobody was there. She closed her eyes and let the tears, draining and inexhaustible, fall unchecked. Around her nothing moved, except for the flames of three thin white candles flickering on a rack near the door, stirred by the breeze that had followed her inside.

Charlie paused at the florist's outside the underground station. He wanted to buy something for Serena, but flowers made him think of death. They had been sent so many after Tina's accident, huge and beautiful bunches, all with sad little notes tucked inside. At the funeral, too, there had been hundreds of flowers both inside the church and at the graveside, many of them wreaths fashioned into the shape of hearts and teddy bears. He eyed a bucketful of red roses, their crimson velvet buds glossy in the last burst of evening sun. 'A quid off if you buy two bunches,' barked the man, jingling the change in his apron.

'No, thanks, I don't think so.' Charlie plunged into the entrance to the underground, his heart heavy.

Behind him he heard the florist quip, 'Ain't she worth it, then?' followed by a throaty cackle.

Serena was worth it, all right. She was worth everything. Which was why he would play it safe and buy chocolates instead, nothing posh – she didn't like fancy chocolates – but a good old Terry's Chocolate Orange, or maybe a bag of chocolate éclairs. She liked chocolate éclairs. Once, a long time ago, before hiding sweets from the children and worries about healthy eating, the pair of them would eat a whole bag at a sitting, dipping them in coffee until the hard outer coating began to melt, then licking the dribbles off each other's chin. Charlie, swaying torso to torso with his fellow commuters, clenched his jaw at the memory and stared hard at the newsprint of the *Evening Standard*. An ex-cabinet minister had written a biography claiming a string of affairs with eminent people. Telecom shares were climbing again. The Americans had arrested a suspected Taleban terrorist. And all Charlie could think was, So what? At work it was all right, he could shut things out. There was still so much to get to grips with: his briefcase was stuffed with reading matter – treatises on marine safety, piracy, terrorism, international environmental-protection laws, it would be months before he was properly up to speed. There was also a considerable amount of liaising with similar bodies overseas, some of which would necessitate travelling abroad. A trip to Paris was already scheduled for May, and in August the USA was hosting a conference at a Florida research institute as a preliminary round in negotiations for a new tighter international treaty on marine terrorism. One of the many challenges of the evening was to break this news to Serena. Charlie had never had to travel for work before and feared, given her fragile state, how Serena would react to the prospect. He was also planning, for the umpteenth time, to broach the subject of bereavement counselling. Unlike him she had so much time on her hands, time in which to get morose and think backwards instead of forwards. To talk to someone other than her usual gaggle of friends, many of them painfully surrounded by little ones of Tina's age, would surely be a help. Charlie wasn't over the loss himself, of course, not by a long way, but he was beginning to see that one day he would be. He still felt desolate, but was aware, too, of life moving on and a growing urge to allow himself to move with it.

Serena met him in the hall, porcelain-faced, a sparrow in his arms.

'If you get any thinner you'll fade away.'

'So will you.' She pulled back and patted his stomach, which, thanks to his running, had shrunk visibly in recent weeks.

'Hardly.' Charlie smiled, hoicking up his trousers. 'I bought you a little present. Close your eyes.'

'Oh, Charlie, I—'

'Close your eyes. It's nothing, really, something silly.' He placed the bag of éclairs in her outstretched hand. Serena opened her eyes, sighed, then burst into tears. 'Oh, darling, I didn't mean . . . oh, don't cry, Serena, please don't cry.' He put his arms round her, feeling a tight lump constrict his throat. 'Come on, now, a drink. We both need a drink. Then I'm going to cook us fried eggs, bacon, mushrooms, tomatoes, like I used to, remember? When you were pregnant with the twins and needed fry-ups at least twice a day. Do you remember, darling, do you remember?' He folded his arms round her head while she cried harder, trying between sobs to explain that there was virtually no food in the house because they were going away and certainly no bacon or tomatoes or mushrooms.

'Scrambled eggs, then.' Charlie put his arm across her back and steered her into the kitchen, taking the weight of her as he would an invalid. 'And,' he continued, easing her into a chair and beginning to hunt for a saucepan and wooden spoon, 'we're going to eat it in bed watching telly.'

'We'll make crumbs.'

'So bloody what?' He whistled as he worked, thinking, This is all it needs – the will to carry on, the desire to be cheerful, a determination to get life back on to an even keel. Serena was wrung out, so he would manage it for the pair of them. 'And the children, were they okay, getting the train and so on?'

'Fine.'

'And then what did you get up to?'

Serena dug her nail into one of the ingrained lines on the kitchen table. Next to it was a large faded pink stain where Tina, in a few unsupervised moments, had attempted to be creative with a red felt pen. 'Nothing.' The stain looked like a heart. Why had she never noticed that before?

'Nothing?'

'I . . . tidied the house. I went to the shops. I saw Brenda Howard, who pretended not to see me.'

'Oh, no, darling, did she? That's outrageous.'

Serena shrugged. 'I can understand it. And it's probably just as well. I mean, there's nothing anyone can say, is there? Nothing that we don't know already.'

'A bereavement counsellor might say something that would help,' he blurted.

'If I need a counsellor, Charlie, what about you?'

'Okay, I'll come too. If that's what it takes, I'll come too.' He swung round to face her, waving the wooden spoon. 'I'll do anything – anything you want, to help. I—'

'Oh, Charlie.' Serena got up from the chair and slipped her arms round his waist, pressing one cheek against his chest. There was shell in the egg, she noticed, a small pearly pink dagger at the heart of the yolk. 'I know you mean to be kind, but I don't need to see anyone. I know what I'm going through . . . denial, anger, acceptance. It's called grief and I'm in the thick of it. Someone else telling me I'm in the thick of it really won't make any difference.' She pulled back, dropping her arms to her sides. 'There's a bit of shell in the egg. Do you want me to fish it out?'

'No, I can manage,' he snapped, irritated suddenly by everything, her obstinacy, the eggshell, the unhappiness still filling their house like fog. 'You go upstairs and get into bed. I'll bring the food.'

They ate side by side with trays on their laps, watching – after much cursing and channel-hopping from Charlie – a programme about penguins. Penguins, the presenter explained, his glasses and orange kagoul speckled with rain, a backdrop of heaving grey sea behind him, take a mate for life, then set up house in huge colonies that operate with all the efficiency of a well-run commune, complete with crêches run by aunts, play-time sessions on the beach and a fair allocation of parental responsibilities. Behind him the birds, part of a vast colony on the Patagonian coast, blithely co-operated in a demonstration of this thesis, canoodling together under rocks, herding small charges into tidy groups and partaking in indulgent sliding and diving competitions into the sea. It was all improbably soothing. At least Charlie, sleepy with wine and food, thought so. Turning to Serena in the dark afterwards, he nuzzled his nose into the space between her neck and shoulder, venturing, after ten long weeks of not venturing anything, to slide his hand between her thighs.

'I went into a church today.'

'Did you?' he murmured. Her thighs were a vice, clamped together. 'Did it help?'

'No.'

'I know what would help me.' He moved his hand lower down her legs, stroking, seeking a way in between her knees.

'I think I might get a job.'

'A job. What sort of job?' Concentrating only on the conversation he was trying to have with her body, her words floated almost beyond his consciousness.

'I don't know – stacking shelves, working in a shop, anything.' She straightened her legs.

'Don't be silly.' He edged closer, pressing himself up against her back, trying to push a bend back into her legs with his knees.

'It would be something to do . . .'

He was aroused now and wanted her to feel it, to feel him.

'Charlie . . . I don't . . . I can't . . .'

'It would help, darling, surely, it would help . . . Wouldn't it help . . . just a little bit?' He moved his hand from her legs to her shoulder, trying gently to pull her on to her back. She resisted and then gave in suddenly, relaxing her limbs and rolling over with a little sigh. 'There . . . you see? There . . .' He eased himself inside her with a groan. She was warm and soft. As she always was. After so much pain, so much separateness, it was blissful, like coming home, like finding himself again, finding them and their closeness. Such closeness. Charlie groaned again from the pleasure of this alone. Then his head emptied and the rhythm of his desire asserted itself. He started pushing harder, deeper, the pleasure building, so sweet, so intense. And reassuring too, God how reassuring, to find it still there, this capacity to touch, to arouse, to connect. Charlie slipped one hand under her, tipping the angle of her hips to meet his. He was close now, he could feel it, like approaching a cliff top at full speed, ready to fling himself into the ecstasy of letting go . . .

'Charlie – my cap. I need to put in my cap.' Serena had stiffened and was pressing both hands hard against his shoulders, trying to push him out of her.

Not with him, he realised, not with him at all. 'Do you?' It took every ounce of his will-power to force the words out, to engage his brain. 'Why, my darling, why? What would be the harm if . . .?' He began to push again, the pulse of the desire building again, easily using the bulk of his body to overpower her. A baby, they would make a baby. To replace Tina, to make them whole again. To make things good again. And it felt so good, so *right*, so—

'Charlie!' It was a scream. His wife was screaming. 'For Christ's sake, Charlie!'

'What?' Charlie blinked. Sweat stung his eyes. He raised himself on his elbows looking down at her, seeing the flat moon of her face in the dark, her eyes wide hollows. 'What?' he rasped. He was hot, but she was cold he realised, unheated, undesiring. He could feel his own desire shrivelling inside her.

'How could you?' she whispered, turning away, as if the sight of him disgusted her.

'I only . . . I'm sorry . . . I . . .' Charlie pulled the duvet round him like a comforter. His body, still damp with sweat, was shivering and clammy. He could see the hard line of Serena's back on the other side of the bed, on the other side of the world. Accusing and unreachable. He had behaved badly, but he had meant well. Oh,

God, he had meant well. One day she might understand that. But what if she didn't? What if this distance between them, this curious separating sadness, never went away? What then? Never in his life had Charlie felt so alone, so full of suffering, so rejected. The knowledge that Serena, too, was suffering did not help. Instead, he found his thoughts straying with vengeful enthusiasm to the demands of his new post. Maybe time apart was what they needed. They had to get through the Easter weekend with his parents and then he would start firming up some dates for his trips. To find so much solace in the prospect of something connected to work was a new departure for Charlie and one that he embraced keenly. A few minutes later he slipped his hand between his own thighs and started, very carefully and quietly, to return himself to a state of arousal, knowing that sleep would evade him until he had released at least some of the tumultuous tension inside. Every time Serena stirred he froze. But he got there in the end, turning his face into his pillow and biting the linen as he came.

On Good Friday afternoon a grand party, comprising Pamela, Elizabeth, Cassie, Theo, Chloë, Ed and Clem, was despatched to visit Uncle Eric. They took with them a huge dark chocolate Easter egg that Pamela had ordered specially from a famous chocolatier in London. Roland was let off the duty because of a heavy cold that Elizabeth said she didn't want him giving to Eric, although it was quite clear to the assembled party, adults and children alike, that Roland was being protected rather than the other way round. Maisie, spying a chance to sneak into the village, had said she needed to do some work on a history project (they were doing Tudor monarchs and Clem, who had chosen Queen Elizabeth, already had twenty pages in her file, fat with illustrations she had downloaded off the Internet). She could help keep an eye on Roland too, Maisie said, innocent and wide-eyed, swinging her glossy ponytail, knowing that with her grandfather and Sid around, there was hardly any need.

Pamela had eyed her granddaughter a little sharply, a shiver of suspicion crossing her mind. Something wasn't right, but she couldn't put her finger on it and there were other things to worry about, like Sid and John conducting hair-raising examinations of the roof, scaling ladders like two excited Boy Scouts, pretending they could sort out the problem when it was perfectly obvious that outside help would have to be called in. Expensive outside help, which, of course, was why John was resisting it.

'We can all fit in the Range Rover, then, if Chloë doesn't mind sitting on someone's lap.'

Chloë believed herself way past the age where she should have to sit on anyone and her face burned; but then her grandmother said she could be in charge of the egg – now a huge shiny gold package – which made her feel a little better. It was still a squash. Ed, after some discussion, was allowed to take his football and just as they were leaving Theo raced back inside to fetch his camera. They sat in the back with Cassie and Clem, while Elizabeth took Chloë and the egg on her lap in the front, with all the women's handbags wedged by their feet.

Eric was parked in a wheelchair in the garden between a lavender bush and a wooden bench with a plaque on it, saying, 'In memory of Edna Greaves'. He had a green tartan rug across his knees and looked lopsided – as if, Clem decided, placing a wary kiss on his leathery cheek, he wanted to topple sideways and crawl into the shrubbery. He smelt of medicines and soap and looked so slack-mouthed and unresponding that she wondered how on earth her grandmother, briskly shifting the chair to face the bench and tucking the blanket more tightly round his stick legs, could chat to him so normally. The egg was presented with much aplomb, then unwrapped by Chloë. Everyone had some (Eric chewed the little pieces fed to him by Pamela with sudden and astonishing vigour, brown dribbles seeping from the corners of his mouth), but the enticing sugar chicks inside proved too sickly sweet even for Chloë, who put two into her mouth at once, and then spat them into the flowerbed. Theo, after the fuss of taking his camera, ignored it and began, inexpertly, to kick the football with Ed instead. Clem, watching them, decided boys were a pathetic and fickle breed. She had been quite excited about seeing Theo, what with their exchange of letters and the producer business, but when she had asked him about it that morning, he'd been very offhand, saying maybe later on in the weekend.

With the grown-ups taking up the bench, Clem found herself in charge of Chloë. She took her for a wander round the gardens where they encountered several other residents, in wheelchairs or tottering with sticks, until Chloë said she needed the loo and Clem had to keep guard while she squatted behind a tree. The sight of her cousin crouched with her pants round her ankles, chattering nonsense, made her think suddenly of her little sister and the red potty (on which she liked to sit, grinning importantly, with no idea of its purpose) now gathering dust in the cupboard next to the basin in the bathroom. So she told Chloë to hurry up, her voice sharp with sadness and then, because Chloë looked so dismayed, tried to make up for it by pointing out two fat squirrels quarrelling about something on a branch.

Clem could feel the sugar from the chocolate burning a hole in her stomach. She had only eaten it to be polite and because it was clear from her grandmother's beady glare that she was expected to. In fact, she only ate anything these days because she was expected to. Obligation rather than hunger. At school she asked for 'smalls', then spread the food around her plate. At home she waited until her mother's back was turned – which was often, these days – and scraped what she didn't want into the bin, deftly hiding it under something else (preferably something sludgy and safely untouchable) to reduce the likelihood of discovery and recrimination. Half the time it felt like a game, getting away with it and being one up on everybody else. But at other times, when she was forced to eat something she didn't want, like the chocolate, a huge rage would burst inside – a terror almost – at having to do something so against her will. It was like handing over the reins of her life to people who didn't care or understand. The chocolate episode had made her even crosser with Maisie for being let off the visit, cobbling together that cheap story about having to work and looking after Roland when it was obvious she had no intention of doing any such thing. Why couldn't the grown-ups see it? Why were they so bloody dumb? Maisie had had on her new skin-tight hipster jeans and enough makeup to start a beauty salon. It was perfectly plain to Clem that she was going to try to see Rosco again; as plain as the glint in her twin's eye that had alerted her to the first visit. Perched, agog, on the end of her bed in London a few days later, she had teased all the details out of her, torn in equal measure between admiration (Rosco – a truly *famous* pop star – had given her twin sister a *cigarette*) and trepidation on Maisie's behalf. This was dangerous, uncharted territory and she wasn't sure her sister was equipped to cope with it. Being told the secret was thrilling – made her feel less left out – but it had proved a burden too. A huge burden. So huge that sometimes, like that morning, Clem earnestly wished that Maisie hadn't told her so that she could have been as duped as the grown-ups and less weighed down with this weird mixture of being envious and worried at the same time.

'Clem, everything all right?'

'Yes, thanks, Aunt Elizabeth. I'm just taking Chloë inside to wash her hands.'

Elizabeth called, 'Good girl,' after her, then turned to her sister to remark that their niece was looking rather thin.

'They all are,' murmured Cassie. 'Look at Ed, he's a bean-pole. Even Charlie's in danger of getting svelte, although he is trying to, of course, with all that running . . . Poor loves, it must be so hard.'

'They grow so at that age,' put in Pamela, breaking off from telling Eric about Ashley House's leaking tiles and peering at her daughters over her spectacles. She had brought her new tapestry – a cover for a scatter cushion – and had been sewing fast and furiously, remarking on the magnificence of the natural light and holding the emerging patterns of fleur-de-lis and roses for her brother-in-law to admire. She felt energised and buoyant sitting in the spring sunshine with her girls, her grandchildren playing sweetly, the goose greased and ready in the pantry, Eric sucking sweets like a baby. The needles of silky gold and blue threads gleamed as she wove them deftly through the hessian. Her fingers, so stiff and inept at the piano on the day of Stephen's visit, felt powerful and full of mastery once more. So much so that she found herself able to look back at the day itself without a trace of fear. 'That biographer, Mr

Smith,' she said brightly, addressing Cassie, 'said he might visit
Eric, but when he called last month he had changed his mind.
Maybe we've seen the last of him. Until the book comes out, that is.
What do you think, Cassie? Have we seen the last of Stephen
Smith?' She beamed at her youngest, thinking how radiant she still
was, how in her prime and deserving of true love.

'Hm?' Cassie had her hand round the mobile phone in her pocket
even though it was switched off. Her letter to Dan's wife would
arrive the next day. Saturday. He would call then. It would all
happen: the explosion, the result. Messy but necessary. 'Maybe,'
she replied dreamily. 'Maybe.'

'You didn't meet him, did you, Lizzy?' continued Pamela. 'Such
a nice man. A book on Eric will be a nice addition to the study
shelves, won't it? Our very own Harrison hero, all of his exploits
recorded for posterity.' She patted Eric's shoulder, then slipped her
tapestry frame into the large much-patched floppy sewing-bag that
had belonged to her mother. 'I think we should love you and leave
you, Eric dear. Lizzy, could you help me with the wheelchair?
Cassie, perhaps you could round up the children.' Both women,
converted in an instant to obedient-daughter mode, leapt to their
feet and began to gather up their things.

'Does he . . . Did you tell him about Tina?' ventured Elizabeth,
gesturing at her uncle, whose head was bouncing slightly from the
motion of the wheelchair being propelled across the lawn.

Pamela pressed her finger to her lips, her blue eyes flashing with
some of the brilliance that had made her so striking as a young girl.
'Honestly, Elizabeth, I saw no need,' she whispered, 'absolutely no
need at all. Why cause pain unnecessarily? What the heart doesn't
know it can't grieve over, can it?'

'No, I suppose not.' Elizabeth gripped her allocated handle of the
wheelchair more firmly, wondering if her mother had meant to snub
her or whether, as Cassie would no doubt say, she was being over-
sensitive. 'Though personally I prefer to know things,' she ploughed
on, in her own mind laying the ground for the question she really
wanted to ask, which was about the stillbirth of her unknown sibling.
Colin thought she was silly to care but she couldn't help it. It was an

omission, a missing piece in the jigsaw of family history, not as grand, maybe, as Eric's soon-to-be-celebrated exploits on the battlefield, but hugely poignant none the less. A lost sibling, for heaven's sake, with her very own name. They would have been five not four. How could her mother not have told them? Elizabeth glanced sideways, tempted to let her curiosity explode out of her, but with the wheel-chair safely back in the television room, Pamela was busy with farewell rearrangements of Eric's legs and hair, which had been blown into tufts by the breeze. She would find the right moment, Elizabeth told herself, when they were alone and Pamela in a gentler, less organising mood, not clicking her fingers as she had been all day, getting them all to jump to her tune.

Clem could see at once from Maisie's glowering expression that the planned excursion into the village had met with disappointment. She was so relieved she almost hugged her. She was sitting at the kitchen table surrounded by notes, glue and pictures of castles and queens. Roland was opposite her, making great throaty sniffs and working on a picture – an astonishingly good one – of Boots. The dog was slumped on the floor next to them looking tired and mournful, his head resting on Theo's trainers, which Pamela had made him change out of for the visit to Eric. 'Blimey, that's good, Roll, didn't know you could draw like that. Have you seen this, Maisie? It's fantastic.'

'Yep, I have . . . really good.' Maisie began to pack up her things, ramming them into her satchel.

Chloë stood silently on the other side of Roland, torn between awe at the revelation of such a skill and jealousy because the sketch was so life-like and because it was of Boots, whom she considered more hers than anybody's (except her grandfather, who had only to make a tiny low whistle for the dog to come loping to his side). 'Wow,' she said eventually, her voice breathy, 'Roland, could you help me do one of Samson? Then Granny could put them in frames and hang them on the walls.'

'Which I would love to do,' interjected Pamela, coming into the kitchen and clapping her hands. 'But for now I need that table clearing and you lot out of the way. Jessica is outside. It might be nice if some of you went to play with her. She's staying with Sid for Easter. You could get the bikes out – you haven't done that for ages. There's a pump hanging on a hook in the garage if you need it.' The children dispersed, the twins fleeing upstairs, while Roland and Chloë trudged outside to find Sid's granddaughter.

'So you didn't see him?'

Maisie shook her head. 'But I'm going to try again, not this weekend, maybe, but when we're down next half-term for Uncle Peter's party. He was so cool, Clem, and really *nice* . . . You'll never tell, Clem, will you?' Maisie, who had been standing by the window, running her finger up and down the lead latticework that divided the glass into sixteen neat little rectangles, came to sit on her sister's bed.

Clem shifted to one side, making room for her. 'Of course not.'

'Promise?'

'Promise.' Clem found a loose thread in the candlewick counterpane and began picking at it furiously.

'Cross your heart and hope to . . .'

Their eyes met as they realised that the next word wasn't one that either could say.

Clem snapped the thread free and chewed one end of it. It tasted stale and salty. 'I said yes, didn't I?'

'Clem, is there anyone that *you* like at all?' Maisie stared hard at her sister, who had now pulled a chunk of hair across her face and was sucking the ends of it along with the loose thread. She was thinking of Jonny Cottrall, of course, but couldn't say so. Since reading Clem's diary she had felt bad about him, but not bad enough to stop their occasional furtive meetings in the alleyway between the gym and the science block.

'No, there isn't,' said Clem fiercely. 'Anyway, no one would like me because I never say the right thing and I've got a crap body.' She tugged at the sleeves of her black sweatshirt which, like all the current items of her wardrobe, were several sizes too large.

'Don't be silly,' Maisie muttered, but not terribly convincingly, because it had become apparent during the course of the year that in the muddled race to grow up she had somehow nosed ahead. She loved being fourteen, wearing a bra, keeping the boys at school on their toes, deciding how to split her modest allowance between new clothes and vouchers for her mobile phone – it was all so exciting. Clem saved most of her money – apart from investing lately in the occasional ugly tracksuit – and only used her phone in emergencies to call home. In fact, the only thing they really seemed to have in common, these days, was being sad about Tina. But there wasn't much more either of them could say on that subject and – for Maisie at least – it was impossible to be sad for every minute of every day. 'Sorry I jacked this afternoon, by the way,' she continued meekly, as a tide of guilt – about Jonny, being prettier, happier and everything else – washed over her.

' 'S all right.' Clem spat out her hair. 'It wasn't great, though,' she admitted. 'I had to look after Chloë and – I know it's mean to say it – Uncle Eric is kind of . . . *gross*.' She made a face and Maisie giggled.

'So is Roland. He kept licking his nose like this . . .' Maisie rolled on her back to demonstrate, sticking her tongue out and crossing her eyes in a vain attempt to touch her own nose until Clem was laughing, too, and they were both flopping hopelessly round the bed.

Cassie, hearing the mirth on the way down the corridor to her own bedroom, thought how wonderfully resilient children were to misfortune. She was thinking of Tina, of course, but in a trice her thoughts had raced to Dan's children and the belief that they, too, would quickly adapt to their now imminent new circumstances. Divorce wasn't nearly as bad as death. And in time they could come and visit, maybe even get to like her. She went into her bedroom and sat down in the little faded velvet Queen Anne armchair by the fireplace, with its dusty cave of a hearth, filled these days with a pot of dried flowers instead of coal. She tipped her head back and stared up at the familiar contours of the sagging beams as she took several long, slow, deep breaths. This time tomorrow it would be over. This time tomorrow the next and most wonderful phase of her life would begin. Inspired by the example of her parents' union, she had waited many years for the right man to come along. She had been patient. The circumstances weren't perfect, but few circumstances were. Down the corridor she could hear her nieces, still laughing. Cassie smiled, nervous but excited. The best was yet to come.

Pamela fed Chloë and Roland at six o'clock, it having been decided that the older children could stay up to eat with their parents. Chloë, sticking sausages into a frothy mountain of mashed potato, said it was unfair, but only as a token gesture. For one thing she was starving, and for another Roland was two years older than her, which made it seem more okay. They had also had a surprisingly interesting time with the redoubtable Jessica, first tunnelling through Sid's fresh tower of grass cuttings by the vegetable garden, then spying on Theo showing Clem how to work his camera. He had a big microphone, which Clem had to hold at different angles and which was pretty boring to watch until Jessica livened everything up by saying that maybe they were in love with each other. Roland said cousins weren't allowed to love each other, but it still made Chloë feel quite grown-up to think about it. Spying a little later on the grown-ups arriving in cars from London, she cast a sidelong glance at Roland, wondering if she might ever be in danger of loving *him*. But he looked so ugly, with bits of sleep in his eyes and a big red patch above his lips where he kept licking the drip from his nose, that she felt quite safe. Charlie and Serena were the first to arrive. Crouching behind a big bush with yellow flowers on it, the three children watched the car roll slowly down the drive. Roland pretended to fire shots using a big branch as a gun, while Jessica threw little stones under the path of the wheels. Their aunt and uncle, gratifyingly oblivious to these assaults, stared straight ahead, then sat in the car for what seemed like ages before getting out. Then Roland's dad arrived, bouncing in his big green car at a much faster speed and Roland put down his branch and said they really ought to go inside.

The goose was huge and perfect with dark crispy skin and textured succulent meat. Pamela placed the dish in front of John for carving, feeling the customary thrill of satisfaction at the sight of the family ranged round the handsome table, their faces and plates shining under the flickering light of the candelabra. They were more subdued than usual, of course. It was only natural. The last time they had all been assembled little Tina had still been with them. Such a shocking loss. Pamela felt her heart quicken. But they were recovering she reminded herself. All of them, in their different ways, were getting over it. Breathing more calmly, she settled into her seat and began to discuss the party with Peter, telling him about the quote from the marquee people and the list of B&Bs she had drawn up for guests wanting to stay the night. Helen joined in, talking about the invitations and saying Peter was thinking of making the dress code white tie and tails, because it was such a milestone of a birthday. Charlie, catching this, laughed loudly, saying thank God he'd lost a bit of weight because his set of whites was thirty years old. 'And probably demolished by moths – it's an age since I've worn them. When was it, Serena?'

'Summer ball. Hurlingham 1991 – with Jake and Patty Taylor,' Serena replied, without so much as a blink of hesitation. She speared a broad bean and popped it into her mouth, glad to have been offered the chance to say something so easy, something that made it look as if she was firing on all cylinders, when in fact there was only a splutter inside. The events of the previous night, Charlie, her gentle, lovely Charlie, pushing into her, not making love, but fucking her, injecting her with his desperation, were still raw. She had woken early and left him in bed while she occupied herself with mindless chores. Then he had gone running, not for his usual twenty minutes but for two hours, returning grey-faced, his tracksuit drenched. They had made the journey to Ashley House in silence, too much to be said to utter a word.

'Then you'll have to hire an outfit like the rest of us,' quipped Colin, smiling, but thinking how typical this conversation was of his wife's family and how utterly pretentious Peter was to insist on something so sartorially extravagant.

'Black tie would be easier,' ventured Elizabeth, detecting the edge in her husband's tone. Recently the kindness had been slipping again and she was desperate to get it back. 'What about you, Helen, what are you going to wear?' She looked a little wistfully at her sister-in-law, noting that there was something subtly different about her appearance: pretty pearl pendants dangled from her ear-lobes and her hair was falling into her eyes, without its usual angular lines.

'I bought something yesterday, actually.'

'Did you?' Peter looked in some astonishment at his wife. His drink with Hannah had turned into a couple of bottles and he had a headache. 'You never said.'

'Could I interrupt these proceedings . . .' John chinked his glass with a knife and stood up '. . . to say a few words?'

Silence fell at once. Serena dropped her gaze to her lap, her mouth dry. He would say something about Tina and she wasn't sure she could bear it. Yet she wanted him to so badly. Part of her wanted all of them to talk about Tina all the time, both to acknowledge her own pain and because talking about stupid things like what to wear at parties felt like betrayal, as if they'd all forgotten already and didn't care.

'Can I film you, Granddad?'

'Oh, honestly, Theo, not now.' Peter glared at his son who blushed violently.

'I think, maybe Daddy's right, Theo darling,' began Pamela, but John interrupted her, saying, why on earth not as it was an important family occasion but could he be quick about it. Theo caught Clem's eye and the pair of them rushed to fetch the camera and microphone, both exuberant, Theo because it would be a brilliant addition to his family documentary and Clem because it allowed her to leave her half-touched plate of food. Not eating was so much easier at home. At Ashley House meals were so much more of an event, with huge dishes of home-grown delicacies from the kitchen garden and Pamela in particular observing and commenting on everybody's capacity to do justice to them. After her grandfather had put three fat slabs of meat on her plate, Clem had watched with mounting horror as her father ladled three roast potatoes next to them, then held the plate out to her aunt Elizabeth (who always ate huge amounts), for mountainous helpings of carrots and broad beans. It had taken every ounce of willpower to eat one piece of meat, half a potato and three carrots. After that she focused on dissecting the beans, pressing the chewy outer skin with her fork till the little green hearts inside spurted free. These she had then herded one by one towards a growing pile of chopped meat and potato. Even so, standing as Theo instructed, with the microphone level and to one side of her grandfather, she was aware of her stomach, ugly and bulging against the waistband of her trousers.

John cleared his throat, his face sombre, his heart proud. He glanced at Theo and winked. 'Ready?'

His grandson nodded eagerly and pressed the button to record. He didn't have that much film left. He would finish off tomorrow, then have a grand viewing for all the family on Sunday. It had been Clem's idea and he had to confess it was rather a good one. They were going to set up rows of chairs in the TV room, like in a real cinema, and charge for entry.

'It is, as ever, wonderful to have you all with us. I can't tell you how much it means to Pamela and me, isn't that right, darling?'

Pamela nodded, wondering what he was going to say next and hoping it wouldn't be too sentimental because there was an air of uneasy expectancy round the table.

'I wanted to propose a toast, first to the family and, second, to . . . to absent friends.'

For a long moment no one spoke. Eventually it was Peter who led the way, booming, 'Absent friends,' and chinking glasses with Elizabeth, which promptly caused the rest of the family to follow suit. John took a heavy swig of wine, then continued with the announcement that because life was short and unpredictable he had decided to advance to each of his four children the sum of twenty thousand pounds. 'If I can work my way through a few complicated loop-holes, like not dying for a few more years, it will mean considerably less for the taxman when I'm gone.' Gasps of appreciation rippled round the table. Cassie leapt from her seat to kiss her father, followed closely by Elizabeth, then Peter and Charlie, who offered him warm handshakes.

'And now I believe we have a choice of lemon meringue pie or rhubarb crumble.'

There was a rush to clear the plates. Serena joined in, but mechanically, trying to feel glad about the money, but thinking only of the toast. *Absent friends.* Not even her name. He was like Charlie, they all were – so eager, so able, to be *normal* that she hated them. *Hated* them. In the flurry between courses Clem, meanwhile, managed to slip up to the bathroom on the top floor, where, with the aid of a toothbrush, she ejected the goose and vegetables into the lavatory. It felt horrible at the time, but fantastic afterwards.

After dinner the children were ushered up to bed, closely followed by Serena, Cassie and Helen, each for different reasons seeking the let-off of an early night. Elizabeth helped her mother wash the coffee-cups and saucers (the only survivors of a hand-painted set of crockery that had belonged to Edmund and Violet), while the men retreated with brandy to the drawing room.

'Mum?'

'Yes, Lizzy?' Elizabeth was washing and Pamela was drying, arranging the glass-thin treasures on a tray for storage in a special cupboard in the pantry.

'I hope you don't mind but Serena told me about your . . . about . . .'

'Miranda? Yes, I know. She warned me she had.' Pamela picked at a speck on the edge of one of the saucers, then rubbed hard with the cloth. 'I thought you might mention it.'

'I just . . . I was a bit surprised that you had never told us,' faltered Elizabeth, a little put out both at having her question anticipated and the breeziness of her mother's tone.

'That's because there was nothing to tell. It was a miscarriage, that's all. What would have been a little girl. Between you and Peter. Such a fuss is made about these things now, but really it's *very* common and in those days one was encouraged – quite rightly, in my view – simply to forget about it and get on. There.' She put the saucer down. 'Is this the last?'

'Six months.'

'I beg your pardon?'

'The . . . Miranda – Serena said she was six months old.'

'Twenty-eight weeks. There.' Pamela stood back to admire the cups and saucers. 'I am *so* fond of these.'

'Golly. These days that would be a stillbirth not a miscarriage. There'd be a death certificate, a funeral and everything.'

'Elizabeth.' Pamela's voice was sharp. 'Really, darling, do you have to be so morbid? I only told Serena because I thought it might in some small way make her feel less alone in her ordeal. What happened to me was far less traumatic in every conceivable way. Now, would you carry this tray for me? I'm feeling rather tired.'

Whereupon Elizabeth, still somewhat preoccupied by their conversation, missed the infamous step down into the pantry and fell forwards, pitching the stack of cups and saucers ahead of her. They flew, little white birds with handle wings, in one beautiful instant of silent symmetry before crashing against the hard tiles of the wall and floor.

'Oh, Elizabeth – so clumsy, oh, really.' Pamela was in tears. The men came running, their eyes glazed with brandy, their voices ringing with concern. 'Oh, really, of all things to break – Elizabeth, how could you?'

'It was an accident,' Elizabeth muttered, standing helplessly, close to tears too, while the men rushed round with brushes and dustpans. 'I'm sorry, Mum, it was an accident.'

'Of course it was,' interjected John smoothly, putting his arm round Pamela and steering her towards the door. 'Come on, now, bedtime. We're all tired.'

Colin followed them, while Peter and Charlie returned to the remains of their brandy and a meandering conversation that covered their father's unexpected gift, their sister's predilection for clumsiness, Peter's recent victory and the new challenges of Charlie's job. Of more emotional matters – grief, marital stresses – they made no mention. Peter, who had let off a little of his own steam to his friend Hannah on such subjects, felt little inclination to either unburden himself to his brother or press him on anything he didn't wish to discuss. Charlie, meanwhile, new to the agonies of shame and despair, preferred to keep their torturous intricacies to himself. The talk was consoling, though, for both of them.

Stretched out in his father's weathered leather armchair, the brandy having erased the last traces of his headache, Peter realised that a break at the family country retreat was just what he needed. While Charlie, watching his brother relax next to him, legs outstretched just as their father's would have been, features so similar in profile (the Roman nose, the eyes deep set, the widening bald patch, crisp grey hair curling against the collar of his shirt), had a vivid, reassuring sense of conventional time – birth, life, death – not mattering at all; of human lives spinning like planets round a sun, repeating patterns. Nothing ever ends, he thought, swaying slightly as he got to his feet. 'Night, then,' he said, 'Peter, son of John.'

'What's that supposed to mean?'

'You're so like him, it's almost spooky.'

'God help me.' Peter chuckled, flinging a friendly punch as Charlie passed his chair.

'No, you are,' persisted Charlie gravely, catching his brother's arm and holding it tight for a moment. 'One day, before too long, you'll be living here, you and Helen, and so it goes on . . . Life, it just goes on, doesn't it?'

'Yes, it does.' Peter sighed, a little wearily. 'Yes, it does. Go to bed, mate, you look bushed. Get a good night's sleep.'

'I'll do my best.' Charlie smiled bleakly, suddenly dreading the version of Serena he would find upstairs: still and unresponsive, dead to love, happiness, trust and the million other good things they had once shared.

> *Dear Mr Smith,*
>
> *I am sorry it has taken so long for me to respond to your letter, but I have not been well. I broke my hip in a fall a couple of months ago and have only just found my feet again. I am delighted that you are including a chapter in your book about Eric, but I don't really see how I could help. My memory is not what it was – full of small silly things that would almost certainly be of no use to you. One thing I will say is that Eric was always one to hide his light under a bushel, so that it is especially nice that someone is at last singing his praises for him. He did many*

brave things in the war but rarely talked about any of them. Even when he got invited for tea with the Queen he didn't tell any of us until it was over.

Yours sincerely,
Alicia Morrell

PS Spring cleaning this morning I did find the enclosed, which I thought might possibly be of interest to you. The photo I would like back, but the letters you might as well return to my brother so he can put them with all the other family archives at Ashley House. Our mother was a keen letter-writer – for years she wrote to all of us at least once a week – though I'm afraid the ink has faded rather with time.

Stephen pushed aside the debris of his late Saturday-morning breakfast and spread the letters across the table. They gave off a musty, faintly lavender smell and were all addressed in a thin spidery hand, so faded that it looked like pencil instead of ink. 'My dearest Eric, It is much colder today – the first real touch of winter in the air. The Virginia creeper shed all its leaves overnight – the barn looks quite naked without them . . . the wall for the kitchen garden continues apace . . . I trust you remain in good health . . . your devoted mother, Nancy.' Stephen skim-read the first and moved on to the second, sighing heavily with a lack of enthusiasm for what Eric's mother might have to say about her garden or anything else. Yet he did need a diversion, from both the dreaded moment of switching on his laptop and the increasingly uncontrollable urge to make one of his pilgrimages to Pimlico, where a pretext for ringing Cassie's bell continued to elude him. Last time he had left a red rose on the doorstep but, like the frost-writing on her windscreen, such gestures were beginning to feel inadequate. It was miserable and frustrating not to know if she had even noticed them (the rose might have been blown away in the wind, the sun might have melted the frost before she got to the car), not to know if they had *affected* her in any way at all. No, something much more direct was called for and soon. She liked him, Stephen reminded himself, thinking back wistfully to their game of Scrabble months and a lifetime before. All he needed was a bit of courage to take things to the next stage, to become a hero in action rather than one who sat dreaming at home.

Cassie spent Saturday morning trying to find quiet corners in the house and clutching her phone. But the call didn't come until Sunday, when the children were hunting for chocolate rabbits in the garden and she was in the bath. It was on its fifth ring before she unearthed it – the phone slipping in her wet hands – from her handbag, parked in case of just such an eventuality under the towel rail.

'My darling, do you forgive me?'

'No, he doesn't, and neither do I.' The number that had flashed on to the screen was Dan's, but the voice was Sally's. 'You are never to call or try to see him again. Never.'

'Is Dan there? Is he . . .?' Cassie made out the low murmur of Dan's voice in the background, and hesitated. 'Is he there?'

'He doesn't want to speak to you. Not now. Not ever.'

'Make him tell me himself,' she whispered. There was a pause and then Dan's voice was on the line. 'It's over,' he said, sounding like Dan but not like Dan because there was no warmth in his tone, no discernible emotion of any kind.

'There.' It was Sally again, spitting the word. 'Now leave us alone.' There was a click and then silence.

Gleeful shouts were coming from the garden. Dimly, through the misty window, Cassie could make out figures racing across the lawn. She pulled one towel round her and then another, the bathwater chilly on her skin. With feeble, shivering fingers she redialled, but there was no reply. And when she tried the main line all she got was Sally, explaining cheerfully that Dan, Sally, Harriet, Polly and George couldn't come to the phone but would reply promptly to any messages. The phone clattered to the floor. Cassie bent down to pick it up but found herself sinking to her knees instead. She crouched on the floor, pulling the towels over her head like a tent, muffling the steam from the bathroom and the cries of the children outside.

MAY

John stared longingly out of the study window. The clematis, winding its way round the pillars of the cloisters, was in full bloom, a riot of green and dusky violet. Behind it, the wooden bones of the pergola were dressed in equally colourful garb, the white roses and yellow laburnum hanging like the thickly clustered grapes of a ripe vine. He had spent the morning outside, working his way round the odd jobs that needed doing with more focus than usual because of Peter's party, now just two weeks away. Although in all likelihood the guests would see little beyond the canvas awnings of the marquee, Pamela was determined that not just the garden but the entire estate should be in prime condition. In the space of three hours John had nailed the loose slats of several perimeter fences, dug out the clogged part of the ditch near the garage and replaced the loose, dented handle of the garden-shed door. He had also done a tour round the barn conversion, which – since Alicia had declined her invitation – would serve as a guest-house for a couple of Helen and Peter's more honoured friends. All there was in perfect working order, apart from a lopsided trellis, heavy with pink floribunda roses, which he adjusted with his last nail, and the hinge on the main door, which needed oiling. He had then taken a circuitous route back to the house, through the field that was to serve as a car park. Thanks to a recent dry spell, the ground underfoot felt hard and relatively smooth, although the grass was already growing furiously. Knowing that the paperwork on his desk awaited him, John had taken rather longer over the inspection than was necessary, watching Boots lumber ineffectually after a baby rabbit and enjoying the view of the garden – the frothing blue wall of ceanothus, the rainbow reds and purples of the rhododendrons – before trudging in through the back door to his study.

It was hard to concentrate when he was yearning to be outside in the kaleidoscope jungle of early summer, and these days his mind couldn't cope with figures in quite the way it once had. Everything took longer to resolve, especially bad things, like the estimates for the roof. The cheapest quote was twenty-seven thousand pounds, but the firm wasn't free until the autumn. The other two were over thirty thousand – thirty thousand! – and could start more or less straight away. Except that was no good either because of the party. The last thing anybody wanted was skips blocking the drive and ugly scaffolding poles criss-crossing the walls, boxing in the beauty of the house like a badly wrapped parcel. Each bout of rain seemed to find new weak spots (Betty had discovered a large, muddy stain just that morning in Cassie's room, lurking in the corner behind the rolltop desk), but to the naked eye the slopes and plateaus of grey slate tiles still looked as sleek and smooth as a brushed hat.

With a sigh, John put the estimates to one side and turned his attention instead to the letter from his accountant, which had been in his keeping since before Easter and which related to his recent financial gifts to the children. In announcing the gifts at the Good Friday dinner John had been deliberately succinct and upbeat. With the Tina business still so raw, he had felt strongly that some good news was called for, a show of strength. And money, for all its limitations, could provide that. All the children had seemed genuinely – gratifyingly – touched, seeking him out during the course of the weekend to deliver extra heartfelt thanks. So it had been worth it, just for that. In truth, however, the situation was both more complicated and more daunting than John had indicated. Handing over so much cash might indeed reduce his tax liability, but only if he stayed alive for some years to come. John didn't regret the gifts, not for one moment, but was uncomfortably aware, alone in his study with only the ache in his back and the tick of his desk clock for company, that he was gambling with his own mortality. This, in essence, was what the accountant's letter was about. If he lived for seven years he would pay no tax at all. But if he died within that time a complicated sliding scale of tax payments would come into effect: one hundred per cent if he passed away within three years, eighty per cent if it happened within four, sixty per cent within five, forty per cent within six . . . John ran his finger down the paragraphs while his brain, maddeningly, kept losing the thread. Eighty per cent of what? The eighty thousand he had gifted? The forty per cent inheritance tax? What was eighty per cent of forty per cent anyway?

'Cup of tea?'

John grunted, starting slightly at the sight of his wife, hovering in the doorway with a mug and a plate of shortbread. She was wearing a lilac two-piece and a shade of lipstick that made him think of the floribunda roses outside.

'How's it going?' Pamela approached his desk warily, knowing from his demeanour – the set of his jaw and the furrows across his brow – that he was wrestling with the habitually thorny business of money. In spite of their wealth, paying bills always made him anxious and short-tempered. 'The roof isn't going to be cheap, is it?' she ventured, putting the mug on a coaster and balancing a piece of shortbread against it. 'But, then, it's got to be done . . . no point in patching bits here and there. Sid says that once the slate starts to go . . .'

'Yes, yes, I know. Thank you.' He nodded at the tea. 'The marquee people, they're invoicing Peter directly, aren't they?'

'Oh, yes,' she said, eager to lighten the gloom on his face. 'And the caterers and flower people – I've been liaising with Helen, it's all taken care of.'

Pamela backed out of the room, feeling like a child leaving a headmaster's study, which wasn't nice, but grateful as always that shuffling family finances did not fall into her domain. Modern relationships, she knew, were all about both parties having a hand in absolutely everything – money, childcare, DIY – but it had always been perfectly clear to her that having separate, defined roles to follow lay at the heart of her and John's marital harmony. He had always earned them a handsome living and fixed practical things (lightbulbs, shelves, fuses), while she had seen to more creative, nebulous matters like hurt feelings, children and preparing meals. Old-fashioned and sexist it might be, but it worked, Pamela mused, airbrushing John's surliness from her mind and retreating to the kitchen. Her elderflowers, crammed into an ancient stainless steel vat of a saucepan, were steaming gently, sending misty clouds into the kitchen rafters where they curled like smoke round the strings of dried flowers and garlic bulbs. Pamela lifted the pan off the heat to cool and pressed the flowers down with a wooden spoon, thinking as she did so of Cassie, who was a particular fan of her elderflower cordial, and with whom she had been trying and failing to make contact all week. A sudden work problem had called her away over the Easter weekend and Helen had complained recently that she hadn't yet sent a formal reply to their invitation to the party. Which was technically unnecessary – of course all the family would be there – but an oversight on Cassie's part none the less. It was only right to reply. Such things mattered, especially to Peter and Helen, who were great believers in doing things properly.

Cassie lay on her back, pressing the pillow against her face till her lungs burned and bright lights zigzagged behind her eyelids. She could feel her heart thumping, not so much broken as obstinately alive. It was nearly lunchtime but she was still in bed. Sleep evaded her at night now, which she used as an excuse not to get up, slamming the shriek of her alarm into silence and turning to face the wall. Her answering-machine was crammed with unreturned calls, her flat, once a cosy nest of welcome for her lover, was strewn with the debris of abandoned meals and unwashed clothes. That she had once sprung out of bed each morning, willing to race round shops and houses with fraying squares of fabric and a diary of appointments, seemed nothing short of miraculous; part of another life, belonging to a separate personality. Losing Dan felt like bereavement. Without him, her anchor, her hope, her happiness, Cassie could not think who she was or why life was worth living. In the weeks since Easter her existence had shrivelled to a monotone of suffering. And lonely suffering at that. For having confided in no one during the course of the affair, there was no one to whom she could now turn.

While she had been seeing Dan, Cassie had recognised but never questioned her utter dependence on him. She had been so sure of his love, and his promises, that there had been no need. The secrecy of the relationship had only been hard because of the exuberance she felt inside, the desire at times to burst with the joy of it. Yet now it sealed her isolation. In this respect – because she had lost something she could never share – it was actually worse than bereavement. At least with Tina (and Cassie thought of Tina a lot – almost as much as she thought of Dan) Charlie and Serena had each other and the children; they had the sympathy – the attempts at empathy – of family and friends. So that when Serena, during the screening of Theo's uncut film on Easter Sunday, had let out a howl at the sight of ten compelling, terrible, forgotten seconds of Tina waddling across the TV screen, clutching a doughnut, her face slathered in jam, all hands had rushed to her aid with cups of tea and shushes and tenderness. Theo, crimson with unhappy embarrassment, had needed almost as much reassuring as his aunt, while she, Cassie, had remained in the front row of Clem and Theo's makeshift cinema, the to-do going on around her, frozen in the silent world of her own misery. She had left soon afterwards, feigning an impromptu summons from the tyrannical Mrs Shorrold, prompting clucks of approval at her commitment to her career, which in turn caused her to feel so strangled by deceit that it was all she could do to steer a steady path down the drive. Once out of sight of her family, gathered and waving in front of the house like a troupe of actors on a stage, the children horsing around, the couples with their arms round each other, she had pulled on to the verge and wept until the windows misted and the steering-wheel was damp with snot and tears.

At one o'clock, summoning what felt like a superhuman effort of will, Cassie heaved herself out of bed and made some toast with a stale tail-end piece of bread, and black tea, because the milk was sour. Then she did what she had done at least thirty times a day for four weeks, which was to call Dan's mobile number, even though his consistent failure to reply almost certainly meant that he had got a new phone. She hadn't dared to call his home again and had only once tried the surgery where the receptionist had said he was busy and offered to take a message. 'No message,' Cassie had gasped, dropping the receiver, utterly humiliated by her longing and desperation.

'Cassandra, it's Mrs Shorrold speaking . . . just to say that I am very disappointed that you still have not found the time to call me back. I was considering recommending you to a friend over the road, who needs all sorts of help but, my dear, I really can't if . . .'

Cassie pressed the delete button. Her steady trickle of work, already stemmed by months of putting Dan before everything, had all but dried up. She hadn't checked her e-mails or website since mid-April. Thanks to the recent extraordinary generosity of her father, this posed no immediate financial problems. Her twenty thousand pounds was still sitting in her current account, much to the consternation of the bank, who kept ringing her up asking if she would like to transfer it somewhere it could gather interest.

The answering-machine beeped twice, then released the soft but firm voice of her mother: 'Darling, it's me, just phoning to say I hope you are all right and not working too hard. Oh, yes, and Peter and Helen are a bit put out that you haven't given an official reply to the party – silly, of course, but you know what they're like . . . and of course they do need to know exact numbers for catering. I was worried we'd all freeze eating in a tent – May can be bitter at night – but the marquee people have these marvellous heaters . . .'

Cassie turned off the machine and snapped her piece of toast in two, spraying the table with a dark sawdust of crumbs. Never once during the course of the year had there ever been any question of revealing the existence of Dan to her mother. *An affair with a married man? You foolish, foolish child* . . . There might be sympathy but it would be so tempered with disapproval that it would do no good at all. And her siblings too. *What did you expect?* they would say. *Married men never leave their wives. What did you expect? What the fuck did you expect?*

Cassie brought her fist down on the toast, missing it but catching the side of her hand painfully on the table. It hurt. God, it hurt. But that was good in a way. Distracting. Physical pain was distracting. Latching on to this thought, she got up from the table and walked slowly into the bathroom, her sore hand hanging limply at her side. Opening the little cupboard above the basin she searched, absently at first, but then with real, violent purpose, sweeping bottles and tubes off the shelves. She wanted her scissors, the sharp little scissors she used to trim her nails and sometimes, when it got too straggly, the tips of her fringe. When the cupboard was empty and the basin brimming with its contents, Cassie turned, with the trance-like calm of a sleepwalker, towards the bath. The scissors were there on the end, between her shampoo and a bleached pebble of old soap. She picked them up and spent a couple of moments working the little handles open and closed, studying their simple ingenuity. The metal looked so thin, so sharp, so basic. Could something so simple really do any serious harm?

Cassie sat down on the closed lid of the lavatory and pondered the question. In the end, she decided, life was about the smallest things: a phone-call, a smile . . . a little pair of sharp scissors. Despair, happiness – all the huge feelings – were balanced on the tiniest pinheads of possibility and coincidence. If she hadn't forgotten her prescription she wouldn't have found Dan. If she hadn't written the letter to Sally, she would still have him. Cassie opened the scissors as wide as they would go and ran the tip of her index finger along one of the narrow blades. Turning her left arm over, she examined the smooth whiteness of her forearm. The veins were barely visible; just fine blue spidery lines, shy little river deltas beneath the skin. Bad veins for drawing blood, a doctor once said, not dilated or big enough, too buried. Her hands, she noticed, were very steady.

The prospect of action – of resolution – was deeply calming. Taking a firm hold of the scissors with her right hand, she ran the sharp point of one blade across one of the bluest parts of her wrist, just below her watchstrap. When the first bubble of blood appeared she flinched, but only slightly. A ruby. A jewel. Easy. The second cut was harder. The pain of the first was taking hold, a cold, achy feeling, drumming up her arm like a heartbeat and the ruby of blood quickly smeared to a wet ugly mess that made it hard to see the effect of her handiwork. Which mattered a lot because she was in fact trying to carve the letter D. D on one side. L on the other. That was the plan. Not the greatest, most imaginative of plans, but a plan. Cassie seized a flannel from off the edge of the basin and began to mop away the worst of the blood. Underneath she saw that the flow was still a slow miniature trickle – nothing too bad at all – while the cut itself looked disappointingly tiny. She would have to try harder, be bolder. She wiped the blade on the flannel, then froze. Somewhere, somehow, the doorbell was ringing. Not the down-stairs outside doorbell, but upstairs. Her actual front door. Which meant whoever it was had a key to downstairs. Which meant . . . Cassie dropped the scissors and wrapped the flannel round her wrist, hiding the bulk of it under her dressing-gown sleeve. She flew to the door, weightless with relief, her mouth open to say his name, ready for the kiss of remorse, of reunion, of hope . . .

But it wasn't Dan, it was Stephen Smith. Stephen Smith with his crooked smile and shy eyes, blinking under his dark fringe. The door downstairs was open, he said, he hoped she didn't mind. He had something he wanted to show her, he hoped he hadn't caught her at a bad moment. A bad moment? A bad moment? The idea was such a ridiculous understatement of her circumstances that Cassie burst out laughing, pressing her hidden padded wrist to her stomach. Oh, no, she said, her voice quavering with hysteria, her mind crazed and beyond caring about anything. Oh, no, not a bad moment at all. He could show her anything he wanted. Would he like black tea and mouldy bread? She laughed again, a mad laugh, holding the door wide, beckoning with her good arm for him to enter the bombsite of her home.

Suffused with embarrassment and pleasure, Stephen thought momentarily of Pamela Harrison answering the door to him in a comparable state of unreadiness a couple of months before. He hesitated, but only for a second before stepping inside. There was no hiding the state she was in: her hair was lank, her face a blotchy yellow and pink, her pretty eyes bruised with distress, while the flat itself looked as if it had been ransacked by burglars – hungry burglars who had not only tipped out the contents of the cupboards but the fridge as well. Instead of minding, Stephen felt hugely encouraged. So she's not perfect, he thought. Behind the scenes she's a mess, like me. Thank God. Thank God because that means there is hope, after all. Heartened, he smiled. At which point Cassie, stepping forward to close the door, tripped on the edge of her dressing-gown and fell into his arms, all her wild laughter turning into heaving sobs. To have her in his arms, under any circumstances, caused Stephen such a piercing stab of elation that he almost burst into tears himself. She was sad and she needed him. It was unbelievable, fabulous. A fantastical dream come true. He stroked her tangled hair, smelling the salty mustiness of her body, murmuring anything that came into his head, while his groin hummed and his heart soared with gratitude at old Eric Harrison and the great-aunt's parcel of letters, which had given him a proper reason at last to come knocking at her door.

Charlie folded the taxi driver's receipt away in his wallet and stood looking up at the house for a few minutes before he pushed open the front gate. Every window was sealed and dark, even their bedroom, he noted, disappointment twisting inside that Serena had not found the wherewithal to wait up for him. At the front door he hesitated again, appalled at the dread in his heart. Paris had been spectacular. It was years since he had been there and he had forgotten the sheer charm of the place, the grimy classical buildings, the cafés spilling out across the pavements, the smell of fresh pastries mingling with the bitter-sweet tobacco of strong cigarettes. Their party had stayed in a hotel overlooking the Seine. He had got up both mornings to run along the river, dodging the artists arranging their wares for sale, feeling a spring in his step at the wall-to-wall blue overhead and the warmth of the sun. The meetings, which concerned tightening regulations on the transport of dangerous goods, had all taken place at the OECD, an extravagant but beautiful modern giant of a building with marble floors and towering sheets of glass. After a shaky start, Charlie had spoken cogently and well, inspired by the realisation that he was on top of his brief, that there was nothing anyone could throw at him for which he would feel ill-prepared. Between meetings they had eaten splendidly, particularly in the evening, when they ventured out of the hotel to be wined and dined by their hosts in small, exquisite restaurants that they would never have found themselves. He thought of Serena all the time, torn between wishing she was with him and relief that she was not.

Since Easter and the trauma of Tina's brief reincarnation on Theo's film, things between them had, if anything, got worse. On the surface Serena appeared to be coping better – she talked and cooked and said normal things. But at night she continued to shrink from his touch, curling into herself like an animal retreating into a shell. And although he knew he should be patient, Charlie had found himself beginning to resent the millstone of this relentless misery, hating the way it burdened and reduced them all. How could he recover with his wife so determined not to? How could any of them? For he saw it in the children too, the guilt on their faces when they laughed, the way they tiptoed round her, never arguing these days, unnaturally co-operative and mute. Clem spent all her spare time with her nose in her books while Maisie was always out, seeing films, shopping, sleeping over at friends' houses. Ed was usually glued to a screen, his fingers tapping keyboards or remote controls. Whenever Charlie tried to talk to Serena about it she snapped that their children were teenagers and what could he expect. Her lip would tremble and he would back off, guilty that he had the solace of work to escape to, prepared to accept anything if it meant avoiding more tears. He had never seen anyone cry so much. Sometimes he wondered where the tears came from, how on earth there could be such an inexhaustible supply of fluid in one head.

Charlie crept up the stairs, stepping round the creaky patch on the landing. Surprised to see a crack of light under Ed's bedroom door, he turned the handle and peered inside.

Ed was sitting at his desk, head bowed over an open textbook. He glanced anxiously over his shoulder. 'Oh, hi, Dad.'

'A bit late for that, isn't it?' Charlie went to kiss the ruffled top of his son's head, all the dread he had felt on the doorstep melting instantly to love.

'I guess, but I needed to get stuff off the Net and the computer jammed and now I've got to read this. Did you have a nice trip?'

'I did, thank you.' Charlie looked at the springy unbrushed mop of hair, wanting to kiss it again. 'Mum and I must take you lot to Paris one day – you're almost at an age where you might appreciate it.'

'What, museums and stuff?' He made a face.

Charlie smiled. 'Yes, museums and stuff. But also the best chips in the world.' He tapped the book. 'What's all this, then? Revision?'

Ed shook his head. 'We've got to do a project in geography. I've chosen hurricanes.'

'Hurricanes?'

Ed shrugged. 'I had to do something.'

'I should think they're quite interesting, aren't they?'

'They're okay.'

Hearing a creak, they both looked at the door to see Clem shivering in her nightie and yawning. 'Hello, Daddy.'

'Hello, my sweet. Come and give me a hug.' He sat down on Ed's narrow bed and held out his arms. Clem, pale with sleepiness, crawled on to his lap and curled up against him. 'That's it.' Charlie nuzzled her hair, which smelt dry and faintly lemony. 'It's like Piccadilly Circus up here,' he added happily, 'everyone awake when they should be asleep.'

'Mum's asleep,' murmured Clem, nestling more deeply against her father, loving the solidity of him, feeling that if she could only stay where she was nothing would ever worry her again.

'Is she? And what about that errant sister of yours?'

'Maisie's at Monica's.'

'Is she now? I thought sleep-overs were for weekends.'

'Mum said she could.' Clem burrowed deeper, so comfy she felt she might drift off to sleep.

'And what have you been up to while I've been gone?'

'She's been in trouble,' said Ed flatly, 'for not eating.'

'Have you?' Charlie tried to ease his daughter away from his chest, but she clung on like a baby marsupial, all hair, burying her nose in his shirt.

'Oh, shut up, Ed.'

'Have you?' repeated Charlie more gently, stroking his daughter's back, feeling with a pulse of alarm the protruding keyboard of her ribs.

'Well, now I'm eating lots,' retorted Clem, sitting up of her own accord. 'I was fat like Dad and now I'm not.' She jumped off his lap, and glared at her brother, then ran to the door.

'Well, thank you very much,' replied Charlie, pretending to be affronted in a bid to tease her off the offensive. In the space of just a few days both children seemed to have grown up; but Clem was definitely looking skinnier too, he decided, noting the lithe shadow of her once-padded figure through the flimsy material of the nightie and the new emergence of her cheekbones from the baby-roundness of her face. 'But it's important not to be silly with food, my love, you know that, don't you?'

Clem, now half hidden behind the door, rolled her huge blue eyes and looked reassuringly fed up with the whole subject. 'Of course,' she sneered, 'we've had lectures on it at school. I'm not *that* stupid. Anyway Mum has already been on at me and tonight I had *thirds*, didn't I, Ed?'

Ed, engrossed again in his hurricanes, nodded absently. 'Yeah, she stuffed herself . . . Dad, why does low pressure create strong winds and raise the sea level?'

'Does it? Blimey, Ed, I'm not sure I'm up to this right now.' Charlie picked up the textbook and began to thumb through it. 'Geography never was my strong point. History, Latin, maths – I'm your man, but . . . Hey, Ed, you look whacked. Does this have to be done by tomorrow?' Ed shook his head, yawning. 'Good. Well, I'll help you at the weekend, okay? Now, into bed with you.' When Ed was under the duvet, he bent over and kissed his forehead. 'Did Clem really have thirds at tea?'

'Yes, she really did,' Ed murmured, his eyes already closing.

Upstairs Clem, too, was virtually asleep. Charlie kissed her forehead as well, thinking as he did so of Tina and experiencing a rush of pain that made his throat swell and his eyes glaze. If Tina had looked like anyone it was Clem: she had had the same little turn-up to her nose, the same huge eyes and circular face. 'Now you look after yourself. Promise?'

'Promise,' Clem echoed, telling herself that this was what she was doing. Only she was doing it her way and not the way everyone else wanted. 'I love you, Daddy.'

'And I love you, little one.' Charlie used the bathroom on the landing and undressed in the corridor so as not to wake Serena. She was lying oddly, on her front with both arms up and half of one leg hanging over the edge of the bed, like a climber clinging to a rockface. Charlie looked at the leg for several moments, resisting the urge to reposition it. Or caress it. She had beautiful legs, long with neat bony knees and slim ankles. They were one of the first things he had noticed about her – her legs and her smile. Never in his life had he seen a more lovely smile: open, uncalculating, a smile that said, here I am and this is what I feel. There was no stealth in her, no hidden agenda. She had liked him from the start and made no secret of it. 'I want to make love with you,' she had said, on only their third meeting, 'I want to feel you inside me.' And when they had got their clothes off, hastily, messily, on the lumpy bed of his cramped bachelor flat, Charlie had found that watching her face gave him as much pleasure as touching her body: delight, tenderness, passion moved across her features like light, telling him better than words ever could the effect of his attentions. Previous girlfriends had been good lovers, good performers, but never before had he come across such genuine – such *innocent* – abandonment. But not any more, he reminded himself bitterly. Not any more. He lay on his back and stared at the ceiling, the dread seeping back into him. Serena was three inches away, yet he couldn't touch her. Losing Tina was bad enough, but to lose his wife as well was almost more than he could bear.

Objects, Colin mused, firing the hose at a clod of mud on the number-plate of their new red Ford Mondeo, were a lot simpler to love than people. The car, which had been bought with the aid of Elizabeth's hefty financial gift from her father, had already given him a huge amount of uncomplicated pleasure. Compared to their old fourth-hand green Volvo estate, it was a purring gem of a motor, reacting instantly – uncomplainingly – to the slightest touch of an instruction. Colin put the hose down and began to dry the bonnet, wiping away the smears until a dim, widened image of his own face shone back at him: deep-set grey eyes, a strong jaw, a good head of hair, peppered liberally, these days, but still impressively thick and healthy. Not bad at all for a fifty-six-year-old. Being a deputy head wasn't bad going either, he reminded himself, even if it was a shared post. All the prestigious schools had a posse of deputies, these days, even if Phyllis . . . Colin forced his thoughts to stop there and reverted to some more serious polishing of the bonnet. Objects were blissfully uncomplicated, he reminded himself fiercely. If treated well they gave and took nothing back. When they wore out or grew dull they could be replaced, unlike unruly children, or troubling staff, or problematic emotions . . .

'Colin, supper's ready.'

He looked up to see Elizabeth at one of the dining-room windows, positioned awkwardly to project her voice through the half-inch crack. Like all the windows at the front of the house it had special burglar-defence locks, fitted after a canny thief had broken in to help himself to the most prized items in the sideboard, including a set of ten silver napkin rings, emblazoned with the Harrison crest (left to Elizabeth by her grandmother), and several silver christening treasures (a Victorian cruet set with spindly legs and doll-sized spoons, a sugar bowl, a small jug and an intricately inlaid oval drinks tray with pretty curved handles), which, as luck would have it, Pamela had only recently entrusted to her daughter's care. The sense of having been violated was unpleasant, as was the fact that, although insured, such valuables were irreplaceable. Elizabeth, however, had seemed to place her mother's wrath above such considerations. So much so that she had begged Colin to break the news of the burglary to Pamela on her behalf.

The pair of them had a baffling relationship, which annoyed Colin more and more as the years went by. While claiming not to care what her mother thought about anything, Elizabeth seemed, even at forty-six, constantly to be seeking Pamela's approbation and bristling if it wasn't immediately forthcoming. Even the small revelation of Pamela's miscarriage was something she had managed to commandeer – in classic Elizabeth style – as a matter of personal affront. They had all had a *right* to know about such a thing, she had stormed, even after talking to Pamela herself about it over Easter. Colin, meanwhile, had struggled to see what the fuss was about. The past, as far as he was concerned, was the past, particularly when it related to the lives of other people.

What he also failed to understand was why, given the strains in the relationship, which he knew went way back to Elizabeth feeling miserable and misunderstood as a child, she should constantly be finding excuses to beetle across country to the family home. Colin's own enthusiasm for visiting Ashley House had waned considerably over the years. It was still exciting to be linked to the affluence of the place, to relish (if he was honest) the prospect of some portion of such wealth dropping into his lap one day, but he had discovered that such feelings were easier to savour at a distance. He had been looking forward to Easter, for instance, but the moment he got there all the old sensations of being excluded had exerted their stranglehold. Even during his father-in-law's generous announcements at dinner he couldn't help being acutely aware that John Harrison was making a gift to his children, that he, like Helen and Serena, only benefited as family hangers-on. At the time he had also been smarting from Peter's ridiculous pomposity about the party. He was damned if he was going to hire white tie and tails when he had a perfectly good black dinner jacket gathering dust in the cupboard. Elizabeth had agreed it was silly, but then devoted several conversations in subsequent weeks to get him to change his mind. To please Peter. To please her parents. Like her old family mattered more than her new one, which, in his heart, Colin suspected it still did.

'Colin? Did you hear me? Supper's ready.'

'Sorry. I'm coming right this second.' Colin turned off the outside tap and rolled the green coils of the hose into a neat circle. He shook the drips off the end, delaying for a few more moments the necessity of going inside, aware that he wasn't in quite the mood to assume the mantle of malleable pleasantness he had recently adopted to deal with the travails of domestic life.

Inside, Roland was sitting cross-legged and saucer-eyed about two feet from the television, while Elizabeth, her face pink from her exertions at the stove, was only just putting knives and forks on to the table. 'I thought you said it was ready,' Colin muttered, backing out of the kitchen. 'You'll ruin your eyes, sitting like that, you know, Roland.' He tapped his son's shoulder. 'Didn't you have some homework you were going to do this afternoon anyway? We agreed

I was going to check it through with you, didn't we? Find all those silly mistakes? All those *theirs* and *theres* . . . and so forth.' He bit the sentence short, prompted to do so by a steely look from Elizabeth, who had appeared in the doorway to say the food was on the table. That Roland, at the advanced age of nine, was still far more interested in drawing pictures than composing sentences didn't seem to bother her, but Colin was so worried he was seriously considering paying for some additional tuition outside school. But not tonight, he warned himself, rubbing his palms together and following her into the kitchen, not tonight. 'Mmm . . . curry. Smells lovely.' He rubbed his hands together even more vigorously, wishing irritation could be so easily soothed away. Since the traumas of February they had been getting on much better, which was good. What was not quite so good was the constant effort this seemed to require on his part and that a huge portion of the effort was inspired by guilt.

The day his niece had been hit by a motorbike had proved a turning point in more ways than one. Elizabeth thought it had made them closer. What she didn't know was that, wandering round Guildford's main shopping precinct that Saturday, Colin had bumped into his arch rival, Phyllis McGill. At her suggestion they had had a coffee. At his, they had prolonged the encounter to cover a sandwich lunch, followed by more coffee. During the course of this entirely unplanned, previously unimaginable social encounter, Colin had discovered several intriguing things: first, Phyllis's aggression at school stemmed from the fact that she was frightened (frightened!) of him; second, that he found this notion hugely stimulating; and third, that when examined close to, Phyllis McGill's green eyes had a sparkle that belied her spinster reputation within the staff room.

The curry was a lurid yellow, but tasted pleasant enough. Roland, as usual, had mince instead.

'It's from that new book,' said Elizabeth, eagerly scouring her husband's face for approval, 'the one Cassie gave me for Christmas – a bit hot for me, though. Phew.' She blew her cheeks out and reached for her water glass, experiencing a quick stab of envy for their son's simple little pile of brown meat. She'd never been a fan of

curry, going along with it in the early days because it was such a
favourite with Colin. At some indefinable point in their marriage, it
had become generally regarded as a passion they had in common.
And such myths, she had discovered, once woven, were almost
impossible to unravel. Hence Cassie's cookbook (one of a small
library of similar, well-intentioned gifts accumulated over the years,
several of them from Colin himself), not to mention innumerable
celebratory meals in Indian restaurants and an array of kitchen
spices of which any curry-devotee would have been proud. Wading
through her plate of food now, scalp prickling with heat, cheeks
burning, Elizabeth found herself pondering these facts and wondering suddenly if she had spent her entire life doing things to
please other people. And, if she had, whether this was a good or bad
thing. Unsettled but interested in the idea, Elizabeth would have
explored it further, had not Colin declared suddenly that the meal
was delicious and she was marvellous for cooking it. He got up to
pour them both some wine, then kissed her lips. And instead of
getting cross when Roland, finishing way ahead of them, asked to
get down, Colin said of course, but only after they'd had an arm
wrestle. Elizabeth watched, her heart full, as husband and son rolled
up their sleeves and locked palms, Roland puce with trying and
Colin pretending to be. It was a lovely sight and instantly made up
for everything – her own silly insecurities and all Colin's strictness
and impatience as a father. She could see that Roland felt the same:
his flushed cheeks and flashing dark eyes radiated happiness, even
when, after several minutes tussling, Colin pressed his little stick of
an arm flat down on the table, exposing the eczema that no amount
of prescription cream ever seemed to soothe away.

'You could have let him win.' She delivered the remark laughing,
once Roland was out of earshot, too pleased at their son's evident
delight in the game to care about its outcome.

But Colin's retort was sharp: 'He's old enough to know I'd be
faking so it wouldn't count, would it?'

'I suppose not,' she murmured, thinking that a little faking did no
harm at all.

'But I will wear white tie and tails to this bloody party, if you like,'

Colin blurted, his voice suddenly so warm that Elizabeth started. She was pleased, of course, to see him smiling again, but wondered at these new swings in his moods, where they came from and how she was supposed to anticipate them. 'I'll hire the damn things,' he continued, 'and I want you to buy a new dress – okay? Anything you want, never mind the cost. After all, we've got to spend that money of your father's on something, haven't we?'

'Oh, Colin . . .' Elizabeth left her place and went to put her arms round him. 'That's very sweet, but my old black thing will do fine. Besides, we have splashed out on the car and we did agree that every penny of the rest is for the school-fees fund, didn't we?'

'Yes, I guess we did.' Colin, returned his attention to his food, thinking as he had many times in the past how ridiculous it was to be scrimping and saving with his wife's inheritance so visibly on the horizon. He thought, too, but only fleetingly, how much simpler life would have been if February had seen the mowing down of his parents-in-law instead of his niece. Of course, in financial terms, it was grossly unfair (not to say, archaic) that Peter, being the eldest, would emerge from such an eventuality as the new owner of Ashley House. (Over the years Colin had privately protested this fact many times, infuriated by what he regarded as the brain-washed acquiescence of his wife.) Yet three hundred thousand was still three hundred thousand. Not to be sniffed at under any circumstances.

Consoled, as always, by the prospect, Colin set down his knife and fork and reached across the table to kiss Elizabeth again, so tenderly that he had forgiven himself by the end of it, not just for wanting (increasingly with the years) to be richer but for the small matter of Phyllis McGill as well. Nothing had happened and nothing would. Too much was at stake. In the intervening months there had been a certain, rather different tension between them, but otherwise it had been business as usual at school and he intended to make damned certain things stayed that way.

Two days after Stephen's visit to her flat Cassie did something she rarely did and phoned her eldest brother at work.

'Peter?'

'Cassie?'

'Sorry, are you busy?'

'Not at this precise moment. What a pleasant and unexpected surprise.'

'About your fiftieth . . . I'm sorry I haven't replied properly – Mum said you and Helen were cross.'

'Did she? Well, she got that wrong. We're not cross at all. I mean, we assumed you're coming. You are, aren't you?'

'Of course.'

'Excellent. Splendid. And how are you otherwise?' Peter continued, a little absently because he was in fact very busy indeed, acquainting himself with a complicated medical-malpractice brief and because he believed the purpose of his sister's call had been achieved. 'Working hard?'

'Er . . . yes,' Cassie lied, winding the telephone flex round her fingers and facing the new and disconcerting fact that no member of her family knew anything about her. Nothing that mattered anyway. She was the busy, independent little sister, the one with the bubbly personality who liked nice clothes and decorated people's houses. No one, least of all Peter with all his kind but brusque formality, wanted her to be otherwise. If she had confessed that she hadn't done any work for four weeks due to a state of paralysing misery brought on by the end of an intoxicating, sexually charged affair with a married father of three, he would have been both appalled and utterly lost as to how to respond. Such things were more easily said to strangers, she reflected bleakly, recalling with some shame how her once idle temptation to confide in the unwitting Stephen Smith had become a reality. Finding herself weeping in his arms on the morning of his appearance at her flat, she had told him everything, seeing him momentarily as a safe receptacle for her sad secrets precisely because he *didn't* know her. She had felt better afterwards, empty, but better, much as one did after being sick. 'There was something else I wanted to discuss . . .'

'Right-oh. Fire away.' The junior colleague helping Peter with the new case put his head round the door. Peter held up a hand indicating five minutes.

'The thing is, I think – that is, I'd prefer it if we actually met. Today, if possible.'

'Really? Today?' Peter, his full attention on her now, could not conceal his surprise. His mind scrolled with its usual efficiency through the possibilities behind such an unusual request: money, ill-health or some ludicrous birthday surprise. 'That might be tricky, Cass . . . But, of course,' he added hastily, hearing the intensity in her silence, 'of course we can meet if it's that important. You – er – can't give me any clues, I suppose? Terminal illness, murder – anything along those lines?' He had meant to be funny but she didn't laugh.

'Could you come to my flat after work? I'll be in all evening . . . and, Peter, if you wouldn't mind, don't tell Helen that you're seeing me, okay? You'll understand why after I've talked to you.'

'Bloody hell, Cass, are you okay? I mean, it's not a bloody illness, is it?'

'No, it isn't. Honestly, Peter, I'm fine. I'll explain everything tonight.'

Cassie put down the phone and surveyed the mayhem of her flat. With an impending visit from her brother – the most fastidiously tidy of all of them – she felt a new compunction to clean the place up. She hadn't cared a jot about Stephen Smith seeing the mess, but Peter was another matter. She began to empty ashtrays, gather up dirty mugs and takeaway boxes and to make a pile of clothes for the washing-machine, aware that she was attempting in the process to reassemble some superficial but important part of herself. Like the big pink sticking plaster on her left wrist. Covering the wounds and cracks; getting things acceptable on the outside. So that Peter wouldn't know anything was wrong. What she had to tell him related to the little bundle of letters Stephen had spilled on to her kitchen table, and was shocking enough, without her compounding matters by giving any inkling of her own fragile state.

She took the housework slowly, not wanting to rush herself, knowing that she needed delicate handling. Even the simplest things now required a superhuman effort; phoning her brother, tolerating the grating drone of the Hoover, scraping rock-solid baked beans off a plate – as she performed these tasks Cassie felt that she had to cling to the reality of them to prevent herself subsiding back into the mesmeric state of despairing calm that had propelled her to carve at her own flesh with a scissor blade two days before. The possibility of such behaviour remained, lurking at the back of her mind, a darkness that might swallow her if she relaxed her guard and gave it the slightest chance. Steering the Hoover between chair legs, under the sweep of her curtains, round tables and book shelves, she concentrated instead on the smooth swathes of clean carpet opening like tracks of mown grass in front of her and the fact that Stephen Smith, arriving to show her some letters of Eric's sent to him by Aunt Alicia, had unwittingly saved her life, both by ringing her doorbell and presenting her with the distraction of an entirely new and perplexing problem. She had watched absently at first, shaken both from her confessional and the secret throbbing of her sore arm, while Stephen pulled the letters out of envelopes and spread them on the table. They were all written on tissue-fine paper in a faint, spidery hand she hadn't recognised. All apart from one, which was of thicker paper and folded into a much smaller square than the rest and covered in her mother's unmistakable sloping handwriting. 'I thought you said they were all from my grandmother.'

'They are except this one.'

'I know. That's my mother's writing.'

Stephen, who had picked up the letter, dropped it again, catching his breath. 'Are you sure?'

'Of course,' Cassie murmured, not yet seeing the point and reaching for the letter herself. 'Is it to Eric too?'

'Cassie . . .' He put his hand on hers, but she pulled back, alarmed by the expression on his face, which looked fearful, yet intensely excited. 'I found it folded up in one of these others – it didn't say who it was from,' he explained, breathless now with anticipation and the general thrill of how unexpectedly well everything was going. She had let him hold her in his arms. She had poured out her heart to him. Some married bastard had rejected her. His timing simply couldn't have been more perfect. And now, on top of all that, there was this other astonishing thing to bind them. 'There's no name at the bottom, you see, I didn't know who it was from until just now when you . . .' but Cassie, absorbed in the letter, wasn't listening.

Ashley House, 4 April 1955

My dearest, sweetest, darling Eric,
Every moment of every minute of every hour, I think of you.
Going to sleep, waking up, even combing my hair, which always
reminds me of that very first time, when you stood behind me and
took the pins out one by one, smiling at me in the mirror and
stroking my neck. My sweetest heart, the joy you bring me is
simply beyond words. I never thought it possible to experience such
feelings. And so I want to say now – very quickly because it makes
me think of the end and I don't ever want to think of the end
between us – that whatever happens I will always treasure what we
have shared. It is utterly beyond regret. Never forget that, my love.
Always, your little bird

Cassie read it twice, torn in equal measure between a sense of trespass, curiosity and empathy. If she could have composed such phrases she would have done so for Dan. It was love, pure and simple, exactly the mad, raging, all-consuming passion on account of which she herself was suffering so bitterly. The recognition was so strong that, for a moment, she was almost thrilled. Then she remembered her own mother had written the note – to her uncle instead of her father. At which point it occurred to Cassie to inspect the date; she saw that it was three years into her parents' marriage. When Peter would have been two and Elizabeth a twinkle in her father's eye.

'But you wouldn't use this, would you, for your book, I mean?' she whispered, the implications of the discovery rippling through her mind.

Stephen, flush with a delicious sense of intimacy – of power – had replied, 'I don't know.' Which was why, after much agonising, Cassie had called Peter.

That Tuesday afternoon Clem took a detour on the way back from school. Her piano lesson had been cancelled, giving her an extra half-hour before she was expected home. Walking into the music block she had spied Jonny Cottrall through a half-open door, playing his saxophone in the school orchestra. He had seen her, too, and made a funny face, rolling his eyes at the music master, as if to say, I'd much rather be out there in the corridor with you. Which, in retrospect, had been an absurd assumption to make, Clem scolded herself, pausing to study some mannequins in a shop window and wondering what on earth she was going to wear for her uncle's big party. Maisie knew already, of course. Maisie always did. Clem was torn between wanting to show off her new skinny figure (only seven and a half stone on the scales that morning) and fear that she would receive a barrage of remarks on the subject from her family. Since Easter, when her lack of enthusiasm for her grandmother's cooking had alerted her mother to her secret campaign to lose weight, she had had to be much more surreptitious – with the consequence that the vomiting, initially a last-resort fall-back position, had become something of a habit. It was so much simpler to keep everybody happy by clearing her plate and then, in the quiet of the bathroom, with the tap running to hide the noise, eject the contents of her stomach down the lavatory. As she had said to her father, she knew all about eating disorders – she had read about people like Geri Halliwell, and they had done them in biology. She knew, too, that it was worries about such things that had prompted her mother to give her a telling-off after Easter. But Clem was equally clear in her own mind that the way she was behaving bore no relation to a disorder of any kind. Quite the opposite, in fact. First, without any shadow of a doubt, she had been overweight (Maisie, her *twin*, had been pounds lighter for years). Second, people with eating disorders were ill and out of control, whereas she, physically at least, had never felt better. For the first time in her life she was totally *in* control, particularly with the vomiting trick. She still didn't like doing it, but it was liberating. She could eat anything and then eradicate the consequences in seconds. She had got so proficient that she had only to touch the back of her throat with her finger for the familiar spasms to take hold.

Passing the Bay Tree coffee-house, she noticed Maisie and Monica sitting at a table near the window, puffing at cigarettes and fiddling importantly with their mobile phones. Clem put her head down to hurry by, but Maisie saw her and waved her inside. It was only twenty minutes since school had ended, but she had already put on makeup – eye-liner and lipstick – and pinned up her hair in a new arty way that got it to stick out in all sorts of clever spikes. 'Are you skiving off your piano lesson?'

'No, it was cancelled.' Clem sat down on a spare seat feeling, as she often did with her sister these days, especially when she was with Monica, thoroughly old-fashioned and not wanted. 'I was just window-shopping.'

'Right . . .' Maisie exchanged a look with Monica, a conspiratorial look, as if, Clem realised, her stomach twisting, they were wondering whether to tell her something.

'You shouldn't smoke – Mum'll smell it,' she muttered, hating herself but unable to resist making the comment. Their mother was so easily upset, these days – just this morning she had wept because the milkman got the order wrong – that Clem found herself doing everything she could to keep provocation to a minimum. It was typical of Maisie not to care. Typical and selfish. 'Look, I'd better go. I'll see you later.'

'No, hang on, Clem.' Maisie had ignored the smoking comment, which was unusual, and was looking truly animated. 'The most amazing thing has happened, hasn't it, Monica? *Amazing*.' Her friend nodded eagerly, her bunched curls swinging. Like a dog, Clem thought bitterly, like an obedient, dumb animal, jumping whenever Maisie gave the word. She looked daft with a cigarette too, all awkward and stiff-fingered, pouting her lips round the cork tip, as if deep down she was scared of it, unlike Maisie who somehow, Clem observed grudgingly, smoked like a bloody film-star, sleek silky grey streams slipping through her lips.

'What sort of amazing thing?' She put her satchel on her lap and leant on it with a theatrical sigh, determined not to gratify either of them with the remotest inkling of enthusiasm.

'She's only got a text message from Neil Rosco,' squeaked Monica, 'inviting her to a *party*.'

'Shut up, Monica – I was going to tell her.'

'You haven't, have you?' Clem looked at her sister in disbelief. 'But how did he get your number?'

'I gave it to him,' Maisie replied archly, 'that day I went there on my own. He asked me and I said it and he must have remembered it, which is pretty amazing in itself.'

'But you can't possibly go – Mum and Dad would never let you.'

Maisie grinned. 'That's the most beautiful bit. I *can* go because . . .' she paused, still choked with disbelief at her own good fortune '. . . because it's the same night as Uncle Peter's fiftieth. Don't you see?' she exclaimed fiercely, annoyed at Clem's blank stare, which wasn't at all the response she had hoped for. 'With all that going on no one will notice if I slip away for a couple of hours.'

'Oh, but, Maisie, you couldn't possibly—'

'Oh, yes, I could.' She stubbed out her cigarette and folded her arms, sticking out her jaw defiantly.

'Oh, fuck, there's my mum, I've got to go,' bleated Monica, ducking down and scrabbling for her schoolbag. 'I'll see you tomorrow.' The sisters watched her race out into the street, then turned to face each other again.

'You'll never get away with it,' whispered Clem. This was too much, she could feel it in her bones. Smoking and tarting up was one thing, but this was something else, something way off the map.

'Oh, yes, I will,' said Maisie slowly, leaning across the table so Clem had to look at her. The black eye-liner was in heavy wide lines across her upper and lower lids. It made her eyes, which were impressively large and green anyway, look like two vast orbs; fascinating but also horrible. 'Oh, yes, I will,' she repeated, 'if you help me.'

'Me? How on earth . . .?'

'By covering for me if anyone asks.'

Clem was already shaking her head. 'No way. Absolutely no way.'

Maisie pulled another cigarette out of her little pack of ten and sat back in her chair. 'Please, Clem.'

'No.'

Maisie sighed, struck a match, inhaled deeply and then said, her voice all husky with smoke, 'If you don't agree to help me, Clem, I'll tell Mum and Dad about the puking.'

Clem, who had been studying the strap on her satchel, froze, her mouth dry.

'I know your game, Clemmy, eating loads and throwing up afterwards. And I also know,' she continued, more gently, 'that you're trying to lose weight and you don't want anyone to stop you. It's just like a . . . short-cut, isn't it? Till you've got to the weight you want.'

'It is, Maisie, honestly, that's exactly what it is. I only do it sometimes.' Clem spoke breathlessly, desperate to explain and be understood, desperate, too, that her own secret be kept safe.

'You ought to try these, you know,' remarked Maisie, doing a little wave with her cigarette. 'They really stop you wanting to eat.'

'I don't *want* to eat . . .' began Clem. 'Anyway, I have tried and I hated it.' She smiled, feeling a little better. The party was two weeks away and Maisie might change her mind. In the meantime it was actually quite nice that her sister not only knew about her eating tricks but didn't think they were weird.

'Though you really don't need to lose any more weight, you know,' advised Maisie earnestly. 'Monica said just today that she'd give anything to have your figure, and I know for a fact that loads of boys fancy you.'

'Shut up.'

Maisie shrugged and gathered up her things. She didn't really know how to deal with her sister any more. She was so distant, so shy and reluctant to enjoy herself. The eldest by just thirty-three minutes, Maisie felt incomparably more advanced in every regard. If Clem wanted a good time she had to learn to look for it, she thought crossly. Like with Jonny Cottrall, for instance. Boys – men – had to be fought for, it was all part of the fun. Maisie recalled her brief meeting behind the gym with Jonny that lunchtime and felt a twinge of guilt, which she dismissed in the same instant. Clem had only herself to blame. What was the point in being keen on someone and running away every time they came into sight? If she behaved like that she didn't deserve Jonny or anyone else.

By the time Peter jumped into a taxi to keep his rendezvous with his little sister the sun was a low red disc in the sky. It sank steadily as they sped along the embankment, its blood-orange rays lending grandeur not just to the fine array of Thames bridges, strung like necklaces across the river, but also to the murky grey waters swirling beneath. It was Peter's favourite time of year; he loved the promise of summer inherent in the lengthening evenings and the accompanying sense that the best of the year was there for the taking. It was his favourite time of evening too, with the worst of the rush-hour past, another day's toil under his belt and the city illuminated and humming like a beehive. It was at such times that he was quite capable of sharing Helen's reservations about one day shifting the focus of their life to the country. London excited him; the traffic got him down, of course, and the rising crime rates, but all the best cities had an edge of chaos and danger. He loved working at the heart of one of the most excellent judiciaries in the world and had every intention of continuing until decrepitude or ill-health prevented him. Which would mean one day becoming a long-distance commuter like his father, Peter reflected, watching a lone oarsman on the water and experiencing some disquiet at the prospect of such a bind on his lifestyle.

But that scenario was years – possibly a decade – away, he reminded himself, and in the meantime he had rather more pressing things to worry about, the party for one thing, although that was mostly under control, thanks to Helen who was a wonderful organiser. Less satisfactory was the new presence of a carrot-headed teenager in the house, with a grating Scottish accent and the habit of filing her nails when he was trying to read the paper. She ironed scores of crinkles into the cuffs and collars of his shirts and had a terrible high-pitched laugh, which Chloë, unwittingly or otherwise (it was hard to be sure with Chloë) was beginning to imitate. Peter had a sneaking suspicion that Helen had hired the creature out of vengeance, but had so far resisted voicing such thoughts. Helen herself was briskly – stoutly – accepting of the foibles of their new employee, whose not entirely satisfactory first interview back in April had been followed by a much better second one, together with a clutch of fabulous references. In addition to which, Helen had worked so tirelessly on sorting out the party that Peter really didn't feel he had the right to complain about anything. She still saw Kay from time to time, he knew, but now much less visibly so again he had no grounds for making a fuss about it. She clearly relished the friendship and, as a result of it, had become noticeably less moody for which he was grateful. At the same time, however, Peter could not help feeling unsettled by the notion that his wife's happiness – once firmly connected to the palm of his own hand – now received so much of its inspiration from another quarter. That night, for instance, when he warned her he would be late home, she had sounded annoyingly pleased; in that case, she said, she might possibly leave Griselda babysitting and pop over the road for a drink. To bloody Kay, of course. Peter grimaced, then wrested his thoughts back to the more pressing matter of his little sister. It was money, he decided, pressing a twenty-pound note into the cabby's hand and pausing to survey the handsome red-bricked frontage of the flats where Cassie lived. Of course it was money. The twenty thousand had given her some notion of expanding her business – getting a set of offices, maybe – and she needed to borrow a bit more to see the thing through.

So convinced was Peter by his own arguments, that he was still pondering some minutes later how much he would be prepared to lend and on what terms when Cassie shoved a tumbler of whisky into his hand and announced that their mother had had an affair with their uncle. 'Don't be absurd, Cass, that's an outrageous thing to say.'

'I'm not being absurd. Read this. It was in a bunch of letters that Aunt Alicia sent to Stephen Smith, the chap who's writing about Eric. I'm convinced she had no idea it was there. Eric must have hidden it himself years ago.' She handed over the letter and folded her arms, watching intently as her brother absorbed the contents. 'It's her writing, isn't it?' she urged, a little excited in spite of herself.

'And look at the date. There's no question, is there, absolutely no question at all?'

'It would appear not.' Peter lowered the letter and took a swig of his drink. 'It would appear not indeed,' he repeated, looking again at the letter and shaking his head. 'Dad must never know,' he said hoarsely. 'Do you hear me, Cassie? Dad must never know.'

'Of course he mustn't.' She wrung her hands. They were sitting opposite each other in her little sitting room, converted back since her recent attentions into the tasteful, softly lit nest she had designed herself, with a lustrous blue carpet, a small cream-tiled fireplace, several tidy shelves of books and ornaments, and a suite of deep, comfortable chairs, each adorned with plump blue scatter cushions.

'And Mum too. I mean, she mustn't know that we know.'

Cassie nodded, thinking that this probably mattered a little less: Pamela would merely have to cope with the shame of being outed as an adulteress, while their father would have the carpet of his supposedly wonderful marriage pulled from beneath his feet, with all the accompanying ravages of betrayal and disillusionment. She herself was still deeply confused, torn between an angry sense of betrayal (who would have thought their mother, so perfectly wifely and wonderful, capable of such perfidy?) and a perverse relief at the revelation that, after all, Pamela was as flawed and foolhardy as the rest of the human race. Her own emotional predicament had made her more understanding, Cassie realised, seeing the unbridled horror on Peter's face and knowing instantly that, unlike her, he had no comparable experience that would allow him to be so forgiving.

'So we keep it to ourselves.' He drained his glass, scowling as his throat burned.

Cassie pressed her hands between her knees. 'Yes . . . Except that Stephen Smith hasn't ruled out using the information.'

'What?'

'That's why I called you. I mean, he hasn't exactly said he will – he only showed me the letter because he thought it was interesting that Uncle Eric, the soldier-loner, had had some great love and I – I'm afraid I recognised the writing,' she admitted, her voice shrinking with shame at the disclosure of this small but vital mishandling of events. 'I said it was Mum's before I knew what the letter was about.'

'Jesus Christ.' Peter ran his hand over his face. 'We could have done without that, Cassie, we really could.'

'I know,' she wailed, 'but I was . . .' Unable to finish the sentence without explaining her distracted state of mind at the time of Stephen's visit, she left it hanging and went to fetch the whisky bottle.

'So, how well do you know this fellow?' Armed with a fresh drink and knowing now the scale of the problem, Peter felt sharper and up to the job. From time to time he got the same sort of rush in a courtroom when some dreadful unforeseen skeleton had been hauled out of the cupboard during a cross-examination and he had to think on his feet. It was a question of knowing the issues. Knowledge was power. Once one knew all the facts – no matter how difficult – it was possible to make decisions.

'Not that well. I met him at Ashley House once and we had quite a laugh playing Scrabble, although . . .'

'Go on.'

'I think he likes me. A lot. You know how you can just tell?'

Peter, remembering a doe-eyed articled clerk who had developed a bit of an infatuation for him many years before, managed a wry smile. 'Yes, though I have to confess I'm somewhat out of practice in such matters.' He faltered, thinking suddenly of Hannah and wondering whether his assumption that they were nothing more than friends was wholly reciprocated. 'So you have some . . . er . . . influence, shall we say?' he continued, studying his sister and noting with some sadness that, while still an extremely pretty girl, she was, like all of them, beginning to look her age.

'I guess.' Cassie fought the urge to dig out her cigarettes and picked at a loose thread on the arm of her chair. She tugged a bit harder and instead of snapping it grew suddenly much longer, leaving a visible gap in the material. 'At least, I think I might be able to persuade him not to use the letter, make him see sense.'

'That's the girl.' Peter leant forward, rolling his glass between his palms. 'See what you can do. Otherwise things could get very complicated indeed.'

'Can one stop the publishing of a book?'

He shook his head gravely. 'Very difficult. And if we did questions would be asked on all fronts and the story would probably come out anyway. By far the best route would be to talk him out of it and it sounds like you're more than up to the job. If he gives any trouble you tell me at once, okay? You've got the letter itself, which is an excellent start – excellent. Make damn sure you hang on to it. In fact, hide it. Okay?'

Cassie nodded meekly, feeling as he kissed her goodbye like some sort of besieged heroine in a spy film. Except it wasn't a spy film, she reflected miserably, closing the door, her control slipping as it tended to when she was on her own. It was real life and it hurt. She poured herself a third large whisky and smoked several cigarettes, trying to watch television through a veil of tears, thinking all the while about Dan, wishing she had to be charming to him to keep her mother's secret instead of to some scruffy lost soul of a man with hungry eyes.

Peter's party was scheduled for 31 May the second Saturday of the children's half-term. On the Thursday morning a team of people arrived in a large white van and assembled a turreted castle of a marquee on the main lawn, cleverly linking one of its vast sides to the cloisters so that guests could move freely between house and tent without worrying about the weather or stiletto heels snagging in the grass. Which was just as well, since by Thursday evening thick grey sheets of rain were pouring from leaden skies. The deluge continued unabated throughout Friday and Saturday morning, until Pamela was worn out with scrubbing muddy animal prints from the hall and kitchen floors and John was in a state of barely controlled panic about a large patch of oozing mud running down the far side of the parking field. Just hours before the start of the party, with guests already settling into the converted barn and Helen rushing round the marquee tables with place cards, he and Sid rigged up an extra fence of orange tape in a bid to keep vehicles in the drier areas.

Upstairs, meanwhile, the bathrooms and bedrooms of Ashley House were buzzing with activity as the Harrison clan, all of whom had arrived during the course of the afternoon, prepared themselves for the evening. Pamela, seated at her dressing-table, carefully eased pins into the coiled plait of her hair. She had performed this task in front of the same mottled mirror, the mother-of-pearl studs twinkling at her from the dressing-table, so many thousands of times that it had taken on the ageless resonance of ritual: her speckled reflection, the feel of the wide metal pins in her fingers, the familiar contours of her scalp. Each occasion floated, a new gossamer thread of experience, on to the last, building layer upon layer over the years so that, sitting there now, she was all the things she had ever been – not just a seventy-three-year-old grandmother, but a timid young bride, a reckless and passionate lover, a bereaved mother and a joyful one. She was the sum of her parts, the picture produced by the myriad threads of thought and deed that constituted her life. Her earrings, button-sized opals ringed with diamonds, gleamed like miniature moons, as they had in the earlobes of her mother-in-law, to whom they had originally belonged. A matching pendant nestled in the soft fleshy crevice at the base of her neck, brilliant against the midnight blue velvet of her gown.

The worrying was over with, she told herself. On every front. The ache for little Tina was less insistent. The resurgence of grief over Miranda had passed. Elizabeth's curiosity had been deflected. The party, meticulously prepared for and poised now to start, marked a new beginning for all of them.

Downstairs the caterers had taken over the kitchen; girls and boys in black and white outfits were scurrying round the ground floor like ants, preparing trays of drinks and canapés, while two chefs were reheating huge saucepans, deploying both the Aga and a cadaverous hostess trolley they had brought with them. Samson and Boots, mournful and bemused, had been locked into the utility room, along with two large boxes of the best silver, which John – with his fastidious insurer's mind – had insisted be removed from temptation's reach.

John had been calmed by a weak whisky and her hand-me-down

bathwater, which was still piping hot and overlaid with meringue peaks of her camomile and lavender bath foam. It was a night to savour, Pamela reminded herself, dusting expertly at her face and neck with her powder puff and swivelling her head to check she had left no visible seams. A celebration of their son's half-century. Another grand milestone in the rich tapestry of family life.

A few yards down the corridor Elizabeth, decked out in a bath towel, cleared a porthole in the mist of the bathroom mirror. Pink-skinned and moist from the bath, she sighed with dismay at the heaviness of her face and the loosening flesh of her underarms, grateful for the good sense that had made her rely on the old black dress after all and not rush out to depress herself with impossibilities in cramped changing rooms. She had left Colin already kitted out in his hired suit, tugging at his shirt cuffs in the bedroom mirror, pleased, in spite of himself, at the flattering effect of the rich cream jacket and crisp wing collar. Roland, miserable in black-velvet knickerbockers, stiff shiny shoes and a bow-tie that tickled his chin, lolled on the bed behind his father, drawing sketches of the clouds that steamed like ships past the window. There was a dragon with smoking nostrils, a spindly claw of a hand and the head of a lady, in profile, with hair piled like a mountain on her head. He saved the lady till last, not really liking her because she reminded him of the woman he had seen talking to his father in a car outside Tesco's a few days before. He had been with a friend, whose mother had suddenly remembered ten things they needed for tea. His father hadn't seen him, which had disappointed Roland at the time, but then made him sort of glad because he didn't know the woman and couldn't think why his father would be out shopping with her. He and his mother did all the shopping and they only ever went to Sainsbury's. 'Good drawings,' remarked Colin, peering over his shoulder. 'Shame they're on the back of an envelope though. Not really worth keeping like that, are they? Far better to have used a proper piece of paper.'

Roland put his hand over the pictures, suddenly hating them and the scruffy envelope his mother had produced for him before going off for her bath.

'Don't you look smart, though?' continued Colin, tweaking his son's bow-tie back into a horizontal line. 'We'll be the smartest men there, won't we, you and me?'

Roland nodded, not believing this to be the case. He crumpled his drawings inside his fist, overtaken by a new and terrible fear that his mother might have forgotten to pack his plastic sheet – his magic plastic sheet, which meant, because he felt safe, Elizabeth had said, that he never had any accidents. Then his mother appeared in her dressing-gown, all smiles, her hair wet round her face. At almost the same minute the doorbell rang, causing a thunder of doors, voices and footsteps.

A few minutes later he was being herded down the stairs by his father, whom he then lost in a crowd of legs. A man gave him an orange juice, which he drank in one go, hovering by the door into the TV room as grown-ups trooped past him towards the big tent in the garden. Just as he was feeling at a complete loss he heard a hissed whisper and turned to find Chloë, sparkling like a fairy in a wide white dress, beckoning from a crack in the door to the utility room. 'Look, the poor things . . .' She indicated a mournful Boots and a sleepy Samson, draped like an abandoned fox stole across the top of the tumble dryer. They *need* us, Roland, they really do. They're *prisoners* and they're starving. I had some crisps but Boots has eaten them already.'

'I'll get some more, shall I?' he offered eagerly, pleased at having something proper to do at last, and charged off to fill the pockets of his voluminous knickerbockers with anything edible he could find.

Serena could feel the party gathering momentum, a tangible force, with her still and disconnected in the middle of it; like the eye at the centre of one of Ed's hurricanes, with the cylinder of everyone else's energy towering and whirling around her. The food had come and gone: the mounds of salmon mousse, carved slabs of pink beef, troughs of green salad, huge bowls of new potatoes, piled like steaming pebbles, had been queued for, half demolished and cleared away. With the coffee a vast white-chocolate pagoda of a cake had been produced, laden with piped cream greetings and trembling candles – fifty exactly (Ed, sitting next to her at the time, had counted them out loud) – wheeled into the marquee by two young waiters, straining visibly to keep it steady on the lumpy canvas floor. Serena had clapped along with everyone else, contributing to a sea of noise that then seemed to recede, like a wave pulling back from the shore, leaving her washed up and alone. As Peter blew out the candles and delivered his speech, she heard nothing, saw nothing but the flickering candles in the empty church and her own stuttering, isolating unhappiness. It was almost four months since Tina had died. And it was a Saturday too; another week's anniversary in the dogged, wearing process of continuing. Charlie, she knew, was giving up on her, going through the motions of concern but not quite believing in them any more. She knew, too, it was no coincidence that for the first time in their married life he was throwing himself into his work and squeezing in the business of being a father, rather than the other way round. He had raved about Paris and was already hyped up about a big trip to Florida for some conference or other, the details of which kept slipping from her grasp even though he had told her about them many times, yakking at her – as he did, these days – much as he would to a half-stranger. Because they had somehow forgotten how to talk. Because the alternative was silence.

Waiters were moving the tables for dancing. On a wooden stage at the far side of the marquee a disc jockey was plugging in electronic boxes and testing his microphone. Peter and Helen, standing among a throng of friends, looked relaxed and radiant. Peter effortlessly handsome in his formal evening wear, had his arm round Helen, who was wearing a becoming unHelen-like dress, which displayed the pearly bare slope of her back. As she talked she confidently tossed her new longer hair, which had allowed her natural waves to run riot, softening the fierce triangle of her face.

Serena was watching them enviously when Charlie, restless at her side for several minutes, suddenly introduced her to a passing couple, then promptly slipped away, leaving her to face all the pleasantries alone. *What do you do? How many children do you have?*

She did nothing, and she didn't know how many children she had because she still felt as if she had four – but to say she had only three because one had died was impossible. It was too much to throw at anyone, let alone a pair of well-intentioned strangers, in spangled evening costumes, expecting to have a thoroughly good time. And yet not telling them felt like lying: these days, her grief defined her, and not admitting to it left her feeling false and hollow. Consigned, therefore, to the loneliness of being unknown and unknowable, Serena hastily – rudely – excused herself and fell upon Cassie, who was twiddling an empty glass and looking, for Cassie, oddly ill at ease.

'Amazing party, isn't it?' Serena murmured, digging from somewhere deep inside her a comment appropriate to the circum-stances. She knew it *was* an amazing party, it was just that she couldn't feel it.

'Oh, yes,' agreed her sister-in-law, running a finger round the rim of her glass. 'Ashley House was made for things like this – celebrations and so on . . . though I suspect it must still be hard for you, what with . . . all that's happened.'

'Yes . . . that is, a bit. But life goes on, as they say.' Serena spoke sharply. She wanted – she yearned all the time for sympathy, but the moment it was offered she froze.

'They do say that, don't they?' Cassie's gaze flickered over her sister-in-law's shoulder, alighting briefly on her mother. She was standing among a group of elderly women by the entrance to the marquee, poised and immaculately elegant, her crown of silver hair ringed with a blue velvet band that matched the shimmering dark navy sweep of her gown. Peter was nearby, the centre of a large group of friends, laughing about something. He had behaved perfectly normally, as indeed had she. Yet there was a new tension between them, because of what they knew. Cassie stared till her brother, compelled by some sixth sense, turned and caught her eye. They exchanged a glance, knowing that when an opportunity presented itself they would have a proper talk. Then she returned her attention to Serena, who was muttering something about getting a job, some-thing to do with art or design, interior design, maybe, with her.

'With me?'

'It was only a thought – ridiculous probably.'

'Oh, no . . . That is, of course it's a possibility,' Cassie stammered, reminded of the lamentable state of her once-flourishing freelance employment. 'Though business is a little lean at the moment so . . .'

'I understand,' Serena murmured, the fizzle of courage that had prompted the enquiry gone. 'Just a mad idea.' She managed a smile, then sloped away, taking up a position well back from the now busy dance-floor, where she hoped she could watch without being seen.

Maisie was running down the muddy lane on the front tips of her high-heeled shoes, the folds of her long dress gathered in her arms, like some crazed princess in a fairy story. She had drunk two flutes of champagne and a glass of white wine and felt as if she was flying. A blessed and magic creature rushing – daring all – to meet her prince. 'I will get there when I can,' she had texted him back, with Monica squealing in excitement next to her. The phrase sang in her head now, over and over again, matching the rhythm of her skips and jumps round the puddles. It was much darker than she had expected and really rather spooky, although she could hear the throb of music from her uncle's party behind her and see the dim glow of the village ahead. On either side the towering trees, so solid and reassuring in daylight, were brooding, moving shadows with hissing leaves. She had never been so frightened in her life, or so elated. When she reached the Tarmacked section of road at the start of the village, she heard something behind her and stopped, her heart exploding. But nothing stirred in the darkness so she pressed on, running faster, past the almshouses and the pub and the post office, her satin evening bag banging like a little satchel across her chest.

'A dance, little sister?'

'Okay, big brother.' They moved to the centre of the dance-floor, dodging round two exuberant rock and rollers, and Colin, jigging with no exuberance at all opposite Elizabeth, who was swinging herself in circles with her eyes closed. Several of the children were dancing too, Roland doing shy hops round Chloë, while Theo and Ed were making bashful but much more rhythmic efforts near the edge of the dance-floor, as if they needed the security of knowing they could make a quick getaway, should the need arise.

'It's going well, isn't it?' Peter shouted over the music. 'I thought we'd over-ordered on the booze but at this rate we're barely going to have enough.'

'Lizzy's certainly had her fair share.' Cassie nodded in the direction of their sister, who now had both hands over her head and was swaying like a sapling in a gale.

Peter chuckled. 'It's good though, isn't it, to see her – to see everyone – letting go?' He performed a tentative twirl, pulling Cassie into his arms, then spinning her out again. Until his speech he had been pretty tense, partly with nerves and partly with a sort of dim anger at his mother for adding confusing feelings to an occasion that should have been blissfully simple. On seeing the familiar photo of his uncle on the sitting-room table, young and dashing in his military gear, dark eyes blazing, Peter had been tempted to smash his fist into it, inspired by a sort of vicarious outrage on his father's behalf. His poor father. As they greeted each other that afternoon Peter had found it hard to meet his gaze, fearing what his own expression might reveal. Men as steady and kind as his father were rare. His generosity to his brother, particularly in latter years, had known no bounds. It was unspeakable to think of how that same brother had betrayed him. Fifty or a hundred years ago, it made no difference. It was still a horrible crime. And as for his mother . . . Peter still found Pamela's treachery hard to comprehend. It was like a glimpse through a door into a much uglier world and an uglier person, separate from the gentle rock of a creature in whose steadfastness and integrity he had believed without question for fifty years.

'What's the news?' He bent down to croak into his sister's ear, hating the need to ask, hating above all the shadow being cast over his celebratory mood.

'All good,' Cassie whispered back, having to go on tiptoe even in her high heels to get her mouth close enough to his ear. 'I've spoken to Stephen. He has agreed not to use the letter – says it's not necessary to the purpose of the book.'

'Which it isn't.' Peter punched the air with his fist and performed a little jump of jubilation. 'Oh, well done, Cass, well done indeed. That's the best thing I've heard all week. Thank God for that.'

'Yes.' Cassie did her best to look as pleased, unequal to the task of explaining to her brother the discomfort she felt about her position. Stephen Smith had indeed promised to make no reference to Pamela in his chapter on their uncle, but had called her countless times since the supposed resolution of the matter. If she turned the phone off he left messages. He was concerned for her because of Dan, he said. He wanted to be a friend, a shoulder for her to cry on. Several times he had asked her out for a drink and each time she had – gently, politely – refused. It would have been hard enough without the business of the letter. But the letter made it harder still. Seldom mentioned in subsequent conversations, it hung over things; an invisible, Damoclean part of the deal. Be nice to me and your secret is safe. Reject me and it isn't. He had called again just that afternoon to say he hoped they all had a good time at the party and to ask again whether they could meet. And Cassie, worn down, wanting only the immediate peace of release, had said okay. They had settled on the following Friday and Cassie, the moment she put the phone down, regretted it. So fresh from a real love affair, where the ardour had been equally matched and spontaneous, these new unwanted attentions grated on her nerves like the scrape of metal on a blackboard. It seemed cruel beyond words that having been re-lieved of the burden of her own secret affair she should find herself weighed down by the far less rewarding task of protecting her mother's.

This time the big gates were open. At the end of the long drive Maisie could see several lights on in the ground floor of the house but only a couple of cars, which surprised her. She had imagined something more along the lines of the party she had just left, with scores of vehicles and glamorously dressed guests tripping around the place in high heels, clutching glasses and evening bags. The house appeared curiously silent, too. It had never occurred to her that a pop star would give a party without music blaring out all over the place. For the first time since she had embarked on her adventure Maisie thought seriously about turning back. She had focused so much on the thrilling challenge of slipping away and the ordeal of getting herself across the village that, presented now with the stark necessity of approaching the vast white portico of Rosco's house and pressing the bell, she felt suddenly not like a princess at all but a bumbling schoolgirl who'd bitten off rather more than she could chew.

She made her way slowly towards the door, then hovered on the steps, trying to see into the windows, hoping that Rosco might just appear as he had the last time, quite magically, with that glistening smile. Yet she felt exposed on the doorstep, almost as if she was being watched. Something rustling in the shrubbery to her left made her turn sharply. Behind her the drive stretched back towards the black jaws of the gates, now only dimly visible in the dark. It felt impossible to retreat down it. Simply impossible. She had come this far and would go on.

She rang the doorbell and waited for what felt like an age, until a woman in red satin trousers and an orange bikini top opened it. She had long black hair and staring eyes with pupils the size of saucers. Instead of looking surprised, or even asking Maisie who she was, she nodded over her shoulder, saying, 'We're out the back.' Maisie followed her across the marbled, dome-ceilinged hall, self-conscious in her long dress and pencil-thin heels, noting with dismay that, in spite of her efforts, droplets of mud were splashed liberally round the hem. They walked through the house, past several closed doors and into a sumptuous rainforest of a con-servatory, furnished with vast fan-backed straw chairs, glass tables and dozens of giant Oriental urns from which thick twists of greenery with fat leaves sprawled like rampant weeds, snaking up the walls and along the sloping white rafters of the ceiling. Beyond this, open to the skies but with a covered sunbathing area, was the large kidney-shaped swimming pool Maisie remembered from her first visit. On that occasion it had had a black tarpaulin pegged across it, covered with dirt and old leaves. Now the cover was off and the water, underlit on all sides, glimmered like a turquoise jewel. Thin veils of vapour were rising off its surface, so visibly that Maisie wondered, for a moment, if the water was too hot to use. But at that second a woman, naked apart from a tiny triangular gold thong, sauntered to the far edge and dived in.

'Maisie. Come and join us. Come here.' Rosco, lying like some Roman god at the centre of a small group of guests, all of them on sunbeds, lifted an arm and beckoned her over. The sunbeds were arranged round a towering silver mushroom of a heater, which explained why none of them was shivering with cold. 'This is Maisie, people, she's my new and very special friend. Come here, sweetheart, come right here.' He patted the end of his sunbed. Maisie approached uncertainly. This wasn't what she had imagined. They were all so much older than her and none of the women had tops on. And Rosco, in baggy Bermudas that revealed a flabby paunch of a tummy, didn't look nearly as handsome as she remembered from their meeting in February. He sounded different too, sort of sleepy, like he wasn't really in control of his sentences.

'I can't really stay,' she muttered, perching where he indicated and feeling daft. 'I'm supposed to be at another party, you see.'

'Wow – another party! Cool . . . Can we come?' They all laughed and Maisie blushed.

'I don't think that would be possible,' she faltered, going pinker still at the way this seemed to make them laugh even harder.

'Oh, don't listen to them, they're stoned,' drawled Rosco.

'Talking of which, Rosco sweetie, any chance of another line?'

'Not now, Carol, I'm busy.' He sat up and reached out to stroke Maisie's hair. 'Why don't you lie next to me, darling? Because you're my special friend – not like this lot of bloody spongers. You like me for myself, don't you, Maisie darling?'

The man on the sunbed nearest to his, who was wearing a skimpy, tightly packed pair of black Speedos, groaned and muttered, 'Give us a break, Ross,' then got up to join the woman in the pool. Instead of swimming she was standing in the shallow end, splashing the surface of the water with the palms of both hands, watching each eruption with the unblinking intensity of a child witnessing something for the first time.

'I'm so glad you came,' Rosco growled. He heaved himself on to one elbow and began to stroke Maisie's arm. 'Even if you can't stay long, it's great to see you and in such a pretty dress too . . . Christ, you look pretty. Hey, Tim, doesn't she look pretty?'

'As a picture,' grunted another man, who had his eyes closed and whom Maisie had assumed to be asleep. Rosco stopped stroking and tugged her arm instead, insistently enough for Maisie to find herself being pulled down alongside him until her head was in the crook of his shoulder while her legs dangled awkwardly over the edge of the sunbed. I'll go soon, she thought, feeling stiff and stupid, I'll simply say goodbye and go.

'And what's up in your life, Maisie? How's it all going?'

'Nothing really,' she murmured, doing her best to sound grown-up and breezy, but thinking with sudden, terrifying clarity of her life – her real life – Uncle Peter's party, the grind of GCSE course-work, the irritations of having a younger brother, the secret dieting of her twin sister, the zombie-like state of her mother. She remembered in the same instant that the initiation of this unlikely and extraordinary acquaintance had taken place on the day Tina died. A part of her longed to tell Rosco all this. Yet she knew that in doing so she would reveal herself to be a stressed-out fourteen-year-old instead of a sophisticated seventeen-year-old with a cool life. And uncomfortable as she was, with the curious salty smell of his chest pressing up her nostrils and her calves getting pins and needles, Maisie could not quite bring herself to do this. He was Neil Rosco, after all. With a diamond stud in his front tooth and three best-selling CDs and squillions of money and fans. Five more minutes, she told herself, five more minutes, then I'll explain that I've got to go.

Elizabeth knew she was drunk. As she had bent over Roland to tuck him into bed, rubbing the sheet so he could hear the reassuring crinkle of plastic underneath, she had felt so giddy suddenly that it had taken all her willpower not to crawl under the bedclothes with him and close her eyes. When she rejoined the party, she had danced wildly with a man she didn't know, then told Serena, who was lurking behind a garlanded pillar, that she was the bravest, most amazing woman she knew and that if Roland had been killed by a motorbike she would have wolfed a load of sleeping pills to join him as quickly as she could. Serena had murmured that no one knew how they would react to anything, then excused herself to go in search of her girls, whom no one had seen for a while.

Left to her own devices, Elizabeth tottered back on to the dance-floor, placed her handbag on the ground and began to do a little sword dance of a jig across and around it, feeling that she was in some way being true to herself in a manner that she seldom managed in everyday life. When Colin stepped into view, picked up her bag and suggested she sit down for a while, she told him to stop being so boring and leave her alone.

'You're making a fool of yourself,' he hissed, clutching the bag in a way that made her want to giggle.

'No, I'm not. I'm enjoying myself and you, as per usual, don't like it.'

'And what the hell is that supposed to mean?'

'Just that I've realised recently that all I ever do is try and keep other people happy and I'm fed up with it. And it doesn't work anyway, does it?' She turned sideways, wiggling her hips and clicking her fingers flamenco-style. 'I never really please anyone – except Roland, I suppose.' She frowned. 'But I know I annoy the hell out of you a lot of the time and I certainly annoy my mother.' She grinned, liberated by her own honesty, believing suddenly that she had the power to say – to be – anything she chose.

'Elizabeth, I think maybe it's time to think about turning in – the party's winding up anyway.'

'Oh, bollocks. You go to bed if you're tired.'

'Elizabeth, please.' Colin glanced around anxiously. There were only a few other couples on the dance-floor. Pamela and John, slow-dancing sedately to the music, which resembled none of the rhythms Elizabeth was attributing to it, were among them and looking a little concerned.

'You don't want a scene, do you, darling?' continued Elizabeth, both raising her voice and injecting a note of triumph into it. 'Lucien did, but not you. That's the trouble, nobody ever wants a scene, not you, and certainly not my parents over there. It's all got to be tickety-boo.' Liking the word, she repeated it several times, clicking her fingers to the rhythm of the syllables.

Pamela broke away from John and walked towards them, smiling. 'They're making more coffee – and hot chocolate. Maybe, Elizabeth darling . . .?'

'No, thanks. Not thirsty. You just want to shut me up as well. Naughty Elizabeth, mucking things up again. Clumsy Elizabeth, not being good enough at anything . . . Maybe the other one – the one who died – *Miranda* would have been less disappointing . . .'

Pamela let out a small gasp. 'Don't be silly, dear, you're tired.' She took a step backwards, looking round for John.

'Shut up, Elizabeth, for Christ's sake,' hissed Colin, beside himself with embarrassment.

And then suddenly her father was there, easing his hand under her elbow. 'Come on, Lizzy, time to sit this one out, I think.'

'Time to shut up, you mean,' she muttered, but unable to resist leaning on him a bit because she *was* very tired and because, for all his irritating fuddy-duddiness, her father had never been the enemy. In addition to which the floor and marquee were now spinning madly. She let him steer her away, but kept herself as proudly steady and upright as she could. Dimly, she knew that demon regrets were already sharpening their knives, waiting to pounce in the cold light of morning. Yet she was also aware that her state of inebriation had somehow brought her closer to the knowledge of a lost possibility – of being other than she was, of it not being her fault – and she wasn't ready to give up on it.

Everyone was in the pool now, apart from her and Rosco. Maisie had said, several times, that she had to go, but he had pleaded hard, making her sip his drink when she wouldn't accept one of her own and offering her puffs of his cigarette. 'At eleven,' she said, relaxing a bit because his drink was sweet and tasty, 'I really am going at eleven or my life won't be worth living.'

'And we wouldn't want that, my Maisie, would we?' As he spoke Rosco turned and rolled on top of her, so quickly that she had no chance to anticipate the movement. The next thing she knew his tongue was in her mouth, not at all like the gentle, curious probing of Jonny Cottrall or any of his modest string of predecessors but a huge swollen snake of a thing that sucked and swelled and made it hard to breathe. Maisie tried to wriggle out from under him but he was heavy and longer than her and suddenly not sleepy or gentle, but a great breathy, lumpen urgent creature, all mouth and muscle, suffocating her. He pinned her left arm above her head with one hand, then used the other to steer her right hand down to his crotch, grunting, 'Touch me, Maisie, touch me.' She tried to resist, but he had her hand by the wrist and easily thrust it between his legs. Then his entire bodyweight was back on top of her, entrapping her arm so that her fingers couldn't avoid feeling the vile rubbery stiffness of his erection. The sunbed was facing away from the pool. Squirming, Maisie managed to twist her neck sufficiently to see an upside-down snapshot of the other guests, lolling on the steps in the shallow end in a haze of cigarette smoke. One of the men was kissing the girl in the gold thong, his hand on her breast. The others sat on either side of them, looking bored and uninvolved. Maisie, who had been summoning all her might and courage to cry out, began to sob instead. There was no point, she realised. They wouldn't come to help her because they didn't care. She could feel his knee digging at her thighs now, wedging them apart, while the bulk of him ground painfully into her hips. 'Stop – please stop.' At last she freed her hand, but in a flash he had it pinned above her head with the other, and was grinning down at her, his face an inch from hers, all hot breath.

'You want it, you know you want it.'

'I don't, I don't,' Maisie croaked, feeling the fight go out of her. She had brought this turn of events upon herself, after all. She had come, shivering in her thin silk dress, to offer herself: a princess expecting a fairy tale, seeking something better and beyond a schoolboy hand inside her bra. Without envisaging the specifics of sex itself, Maisie had imagined that the attentions of a grown man – a famous man – would grant her entry into a more exotic, more romantic world: a place where she would shine and bask in the grown-up thrill of desiring and being desired. It had never occurred to her that such a world could turn out to be so brutish and alien. Rosco was pushing even harder now, grunting like a pig, trying to slide himself in under her pants. Her hips ached. And yet it was all her fault. So there was nothing to do but wait for it to be over, to hope that it didn't hurt too much. Maisie squeezed her eyes shut, promising herself she wouldn't open them again until it was over.

'Get off her. Get off her this minute, you – you pervert!' The voice began as a tremble, but grew louder and braver with each word.

Rosco froze and then, with a loud snort of surprise, rolled off Maisie and pulled up his swimming trunks. 'And who the fuck might you be?'

'I'm her sister – and you – you can – fuck off. Come on, Maisie.' Clem held out her hand. Maisie, dazed and shaken, unhitched her dress, which had got caught under the elastic of her underpants, clambered off the sunbed and took it.

'Bloody hell, I don't need this, I really don't.' The pop star scratched his head. 'You don't have to do what your little sister says, you know. Look, come back when you want, darling, okay?' He reached out an arm, but Maisie shrank away, clinging harder to Clem. Rosco shrugged. 'Up to you, of course.' He grinned, flashing the diamond, then sauntered over to the pool to join his friends. The two girls, still holding hands, dodged out of the maze of empty sunbeds and escaped round the side of the house. A minute later they were scampering down the drive, through the heavy gates and back up the dark lane.

JUNE

The morning after the party the sun rose in a cloudless sky. The slate-tile roof-slopes of Ashley House glistened like polished hide, belying the fragility of their condition. There seemed to be a special stillness to the air, a sense of suspension after the release of so much energy and noise the night before, like the calm after the storm. Samson, freed from captivity in the small hours, padded round the perimeters of the lawns, his paws making small tracks in the dew. Disturbed by the recent disruption to his routine and the continuing, dominating presence of the marquee, he checked and paced the boundaries of his territory carefully, his tiger-tail and whiskers twitching with suspicion.

In the house the silence was heavier still. Boots, envious of his companion roaming free outside, lay at full stretch with his nose at the gap along the bottom of the kitchen door, whining softly. Above him Roland's recently hung portrait showed him framed in a similar pose, his grizzled face resting on Theo's trainers. Above that, the hands of the old mahogany wall-clock ticked with metronome precision beween its big black Roman numerals, echoing in the emptiness like a heartbeat. Upstairs, several of the adults woke in the small hours with dry mouths and throbbing heads, only to fall back into deeper slumber. The first to stir properly were Roland and Chloë, who met on the landing and tiptoed downstairs to enjoy the usually forbidden indulgence of pre-breakfast television. Hearing Boots whimpering, they treated him to several fistfuls of Shreddies, eating plenty themselves in the process, then took him into the TV room where he sprawled on the carpet between them, bestowing grateful licks on their necks and faces.

In the largest of the guest bedrooms Peter and Helen dozed

fitfully in the creaky four-poster. The party had been an unqualified success, both as an event and as a vehicle for reuniting them with many old and treasured friends. Even more importantly, its mutual pleasure and momentum had reconnected them to a fresh sense of togetherness as a couple. After waving off the last of the cars at two in the morning, they had sat out on a bench in the cloisters, sipping wine, talking over the evening like excited teenagers. Through the arched walls in front of them the white folds of the empty marquee billowed gently in the night breeze like the ruffling wings of a great bird. Overhead the sky was black and thick with stars.

'Did I tell you that dress is fabulous?' Peter sidled along the bench and slipped his arm round Helen's icy shoulders. He longed suddenly, with this new closeness, to tell her about the shocking business of Eric and his mother. It was the perfect moment, but some fundamental safety-lock of common sense and caution prevented him. The smaller the circle of knowledge, the safer the secret. Peter tightened his grip on his wife's thin shoulders, determined to treasure her more, to be more grateful for the many facets of their own good fortune.

'I'm glad you like it.' Helen, tipsy and sleepy, let her head fall on to his shoulder. 'And look, you haven't seen these yet, have you?' She eased up the panels of her dress, revealing a glimpse of lacy stocking-tops and the tiny blue triangle of her new silk underpants.

'Bloody hell . . . I certainly haven't.' Peter, astonished and delighted in equal measure, couldn't resist trailing the backs of his fingers along her thigh. 'What's behind this lot, then? Trying to seduce your husband or someone else?'

Helen giggled. 'Definitely my husband. Kay helped me choose them.'

'Did she now?' Peter took his hand away.

Helen let the hem of her dress drop back to the ground. 'I know you don't like her, Peter, but I'm afraid I really do. She's so natural and uncompetitive. She's helped me see that life doesn't have to be a race to prove myself, that it's okay to be . . . well, to be *feminine* from time to time. Which might sound stupid but, you know, I think for years I've being trying not to let being female get in the way of things, trying to be as good as a man, trying, probably – if I'm really honest – to be as good as you.'

Peter groaned softly. 'That's absurd.'

'It's not, Peter.' Helen gazed out at the glittering tapestry of stars, framed by the archways in front of them like some huge bejewelled triptych. She was sobering up now, more aware of the sting of reality in her words. The last thing she wanted was to end this most wonderful of evenings on a sour note. Yet she was also burning to speak her mind, to share some of these vital, altered perceptions of herself and the world. Kay's understanding was no longer enough. She needed Peter's as well. 'But now I'm beginning to feel differently,' she persisted, 'to acknowledge that I *like* being a woman. Kay has played a part in that, I know, but I think it's also because my clock's ticking, with the menopause and so on . . .'

'The menopause?' Peter was bolt upright, forgetting his disdain in an instant. 'You're miles off all that, aren't you?'

Helen sighed. She was still coming to terms with this development herself. 'Well, no, unfortunately. Though it's taken me a while to realise it. I'm all over the place – heavy, irregular periods, mood-swings, it's perfectly obvious what's going on. I am almost forty-eight after all.'

'And why haven't you told me all this before?' Peter did his best to sound stern, although really he was fractionally relieved. It was awful to think of Helen already being on the brink of such a business (were they that old, already?), but it went a long way towards explaining why life on the home-front had been something of an ordeal in recent months, all fire-fighting and no fun. He turned to study his wife's profile, recognising a new forbearance in its familiar sharp lines. She's brave, he thought, and she's pouring her heart out to me, all ghostly and beautiful in the moonlight, like an eager girl. 'Why didn't you tell me?' he repeated softly.

'I'm telling you now.' Helen turned to face him, lacing her icy fingers in his. 'I'm taking these homeopathic pills that Kay recommended. I'm feeling so much better. Haven't I seemed better recently? Just a *little* bit easier to live with?'

'Come here, just bloody well come here.' Peter took hold of her hands. 'This feminine side of yours, are both of us allowed to explore it?' Without any warning, he scooped her into his arms and stood up.

'Put me down,' Helen squealed, caught completely off-guard. 'I'm too heavy. You'll hurt your back. Put me down.' But Peter didn't put her down, not until some minutes later when, having kicked the door of their bedroom shut with a back swing of his foot, he laid her gently on their bed. 'This menopause business, will it . . . does it have any effect on sex and so on?' As he spoke he was tugging at his socks, hopping comically round the room on one leg then the other.

'I might go off it a bit.'

'That would be bad news.' He stopped hopping, socks in hand, looking thoroughly dismayed.

'But no signs yet,' she whispered, beginning to unzip her dress.

'Well, thank God for that.' Peter stepped out of his underpants and flung them in celebratory and uncharacteristic fashion over one shoulder.

'And losing one's fertility does have its advantages—' She broke off to giggle at the flight of the underpants, which had ended on top of a lampshade. She eased herself out of the dress then began to peel off her silk pants until, catching Peter's eye, she changed her mind. They exchanged a look the like of which she had never known in their entire marriage: one that made her feel, just for a few seconds, like a glamorous heroine about to be ravished by the hero of her dreams. But, a moment later, when Peter, far too solid for a dream, crawled into her arms, Helen forgot everything but the warm reality of the man she had married, a pompous, at times selfish and irritating man, but one she loved none the less. They made love with a passion that felt fresh, undeterred by the creaking of the old bed, which on previous occasions had proved something of a restraint on their libidos. Afterwards they fell asleep holding hands, floating in post-coital euphoria, Helen feeling quite beyond the ravages of time and Peter delighting in the sensation that he had somehow reclaimed his wife for his own.

Elizabeth stretched one arm across to the other side of the bed, only to find it empty. The unoccupied expanse of sheet felt pleasantly cool, however, and after a couple of minutes she rolled into it, seeking relief from the pain in her body. Everything ached, her head, her neck, her arms, her legs, even her feet. For a few minutes Elizabeth indulged in the notion that this must therefore mean that she was not only hung-over but also extremely ill. It took her a little while to remember that she had spent several hours in high heels flinging her usually unexercised body in mad whirls round the dance-floor. The thought of it now made her hot with shame. Oh, God, and she had made Colin cross and been rude to her mother. Oh, God. Elizabeth turned on to her stomach, feeling like a beached whale, sick at the recollection of her foolhardiness, wishing it was all a bad dream. The woman who had danced had felt all that she longed to feel – young, inspired, independent, powerful. And yet she was none of those things and never would be. She was a sad, half-committed music teacher, who fussed about unimportant things and who maddened her hard-working, sensible husband.

At the thought of Colin Elizabeth opened her eyes. She had to find him and say sorry. She had to tell him that she knew she had embarrassed him and that it wouldn't happen again. And her mother . . . Oh, God. What had she been thinking to say such a thing? To be so unforgivably insensitive and stupid. To make a big deal of something so ancient and irrelevant. Colin, as usual, had been right: the past did not matter; she had got herself into a state about nothing. *Again*. Elizabeth levered herself upright, then waited for the throbbing in her head to subside before she got out of bed. She moved slowly, protecting her tender joints, not even bothering to clear the messy mop of her hair from her eyes. It felt right that she should feel bruised and ugly; remorseful sinners deserved no more. To have got so drunk, so out of control . . . Elizabeth squeezed her eyes shut, close to tears, wishing she could weep the images away. She would make up for it, of course – to Pamela, to Colin, her father, everyone. She had let them all down again. There was no one to blame but herself. Elizabeth dragged herself along the corridor to the nearest bathroom, noting with dismay that it was already past midday. She drank three toothmugs of water, swallowed two Panadol, then promptly threw the whole lot up. The retching was so bad that she had to kneel with her head virtually inside the lavatory bowl, holding back her hair with one hand and clinging on to the cistern for dear life with the other.

Clem, on an errand to fetch fresh tea-towels from the airing cupboard for her grandmother, heard the noise as she passed along the corridor and wondered who it was. She hovered outside the door, lost for a few moments in the reassuring fantasy that her own secret habit was shared by another member of the family. Then the lavatory flushed and she bolted for the back stairs, disappearing like a rabbit down a hole.

In the kitchen Pamela was frying twenty rashers of best back bacon and stirring a saucepan of scrambling eggs. Chilly when she had woken up, she had put on her blue twin set and a thick skirt and was now far too hot. Behind her, Serena was buttering toast and counting knives and forks, which Maisie and Clem were arranging round mats on the table. The twins, still in disgrace for their behaviour the night before (they had been discovered emerging round the side of the garage, reeking of cigarette smoke, their dresses splattered with mud) performed this duty in silence with their heads bowed. Pamela couldn't help feeling rather sorry for them. They were young and headstrong, after all, just at the age of wanting to push back boundaries and challenge rules. Especially Maisie. But she felt sorry for Serena, having to deal with it, just as she had once had to deal with Elizabeth. Just as she was still dealing with Elizabeth. Pamela flicked the bacon over. It was spitting badly, flecks of fat stinging her hands. She ought, she knew, to put her apron on, but she was already so hot that the thought of another layer of clothing was unbearable.

'Call the others, will you, girls? This is nearly ready.' She watched the twins dash gratefully from the room and ran a wooden spoon round the eggs, which were sticking to the pan. She had left them too long; the mass of lumpen yellow looked dry and overdone. Her ability to concentrate, usually so effortless in the kitchen, had deserted her. She was tired, of course, from the party. They all were. Serena, fiddling with spoons and napkins, was grey-faced. She had heard her shouting at the girls that morning, about smoking, about the dresses, and at Ed for having left his schoolbag in London. His Common Entrance for Kings Grove was three days away. He had to grow up, she had scolded, had to start taking responsibility for himself. Serena never shouted. And now Charlie was in the garden kicking a football with his son to make up for it, the change jangling in his pockets, his own face white and sweaty with fatigue and dehydration. The party had taken it out of them all – apart from Peter and Helen, who had appeared downstairs with sleepy but beaming faces at ten o'clock and decamped to the drawing-room sofa, where they were unwrapping the pile of gifts that had been left in the hall, exclaiming in delight and making lists of what had come from whom. Pamela scraped the egg on to a serving plate next to the bacon. In spite of her own fatigue and the bliss of sliding into bed, she had slept badly, her heart clogged with a nameless anxiety that she knew was connected to Elizabeth's drunken remark on the dance-floor. It was ridiculous, of course, and quite untrue. She loved all her children equally. Elizabeth, coming after the miscarriage, had been a particularly precious gift. And yet . . .

'Shall I take that?'

'Oh, John, darling, thank you.' Pamela handed him the plate of eggs and bacon. 'Hang on, you've a spot of shaving cream on your ear.' She dabbed it away tenderly, her heart swelling at the sight of the grooves of tiredness round his eyes and mouth. He hadn't heard what Elizabeth had said, which was good. And when she had asked him (seizing his last moment of lucidity as he turned out the light) if he thought she had been harder on Elizabeth than the others, he had murmured, possibly, but that was because Elizabeth had always been the hardest to deal with. Which had helped for a time. Until, alone in the dark, the demons had closed in.

Elizabeth ventured downstairs, blinking and sheepish, just after the plates had been cleared away. Theo and Ed, assigned to wash up by their grandmother, were standing side by side at the sink, tracking the progress of a woodlouse along the window-sill. Pamela was sitting on the kitchen sofa, stroking Samson, with Chloë on one side of her and Roland on the other. At her appearance they all chorused greetings, Roland adding, with a frown, 'You've slept for a long time, Mummy, but Daddy said not to wake you.'

'Did he? That was nice of him.' Elizabeth kissed the top of his head.

'And now he's gone home.'

'Has he?' Elizabeth looked to her mother for further explanation, her headache exploding with fresh vengeance at the thought of having to postpone her apologies to her husband.

'He said not to worry,' said Pamela smoothly, her palm sliding back and forth over the cat's soft head. 'Wanted to catch up on some marking, he said. Sid drove him to the station. There's coffee, darling, if you'd like some.' Her daughter, she couldn't help noting, looked terrible, which had the immediate effect of making her feel better. She lifted Samson off her lap and went to fetch the coffee-pot.

Half-way across the room Elizabeth awkwardly slipped an arm round her waist. 'Sorry,' she murmured, 'if I . . . last night.'

'Darling, don't be silly. We all had a lovely time, didn't we? There, now.' Pamela patted Elizabeth's back, aware of the children watching with some curiosity. 'And you boys better get a move on – it'll be tea-time before you know it.'

Theo, who was in charge of washing, plunged his hands back into the sink, grimacing with distaste at the slimy feel of congealed egg in the bottom of the saucepan. Ed flicked his tea-towel at his cousin's head, then neatly ducked out of the way as Theo attempted a return blow with the washing-up brush. Water and soap suds flew every-where. Ed let out a hoot of triumph, forgetting for a few lovely moments that school started the next day and that in precisely sixty-eight hours (he had counted) he would be locked in the school gym yet again with exam papers and the fog of panic in his brain. The whole of half-term had been ruined by the prospect. Even the nicest things, like swigging warm champagne from abandoned glasses with Theo the night before, or kicking a ball with his dad that morning, were hard to enjoy. It was like this huge shadow hanging over everything. Swamped again by the thought of it, he flicked his cloth, viciously this time, at Theo's neck, suddenly feeling that his boffin of a cousin deserved it.

Theo spun round from the sink, yelling in genuine pain and clutching his neck where a small red welt showed the efficacy of Ed's strike. 'You pig-face!' Baffled and enraged, he dug the washing-up brush into the younger boy's ribs. A moment later they were on the kitchen floor, pummelling each other.

'Children, children, stop this at once.' Pamela, horrified, shielded the coffee-pot as she tried to step round the furious bundle of flailing arms and legs. 'Really, Elizabeth, can't you . . .?' She cast a helpless look at her daughter, who was leaning against the wall looking equally horrified but doing nothing. They were saved by Peter, who strode into the kitchen and seized his son by the back of his shirt, lifting him to his feet. 'Theobald, what sort of behaviour do you call this?'

Theo, puffing with upset and indignation, his face crimson, hung his head, saying nothing. Ed, playing for time and sympathy, remained on the floor, groaning and clutching his chest.

'Apologise this instant,' bellowed Peter.

'But it was Ed's fault,' piped Chloë, leaping to the defence of her sibling. 'Wasn't it, Roland?' The latter shrank into the sofa, his own sense of justice dwarfed by both timidity and a desire to be loyal to Ed, who had said just that morning Roland could play with his gun whenever he wanted.

'I don't care whose fault it was,' Peter thundered. Chloë lowered her head, her bottom lip trembling. 'Theobald, apologise this minute, then go to your room until you have remastered the wherewithal to behave like a civilised human being.'

Theo muttered sorry and fled, still clutching his neck.

'You all right, Ed?' Peter helped him to his feet.

'Yup. I'm sorry too.'

'Good man. Now, no more nonsense, okay?' Tacit family rules dictated that telling off nephews and nieces simply wasn't on the cards. Ed was for Charlie or Serena to deal with.

'We're all tired,' murmured Pamela, handing Elizabeth her coffee and moving to the sink to finish the washing-up herself.

'I think I'm going to head home,' ventured Elizabeth, once the fracas had died down and she and her mother were alone.

'But you said you were staying till tea-time,' exclaimed Pamela, complaint creeping into her tone. 'I've got lots of cold meat and salad for lunch and all sorts of lovely cakes for tea . . .'

'I'm sorry, Mum. I know I said we'd stay the whole day, but I really think it would be best if we set off now. What with it being the end of half-term and everything, the traffic will be terrible and there's . . . so much to do,' she concluded lamely, unable to admit that all she really wanted was to scuttle home where she could nurse her hangover in peace and put things right with her husband. Colin might have told the family he had marking to do, but it was perfectly clear to Elizabeth that annoyance with her had driven him away. And right now, in her weakened state, her system brittle with pain and exhaustion, she wanted more than anything to get them back on the right track. Peace was what she wanted. Now and for ever. No more difficult thoughts, no more trying to assert herself, no more creating waves.

'Well, obviously, my dear, I can't stop you.' Pamela tipped out the dirty washing-up water and turned to her daughter, smiling in a continuing bid to conceal her true frame of mind. 'It's a shame, but if you need to go you need to go. I could make you some sandwiches for the journey if you like. That way I could use at least some of the food in the fridge.'

'Great . . . Thanks, that would be great.' Elizabeth tipped her head back against the sofa and closed her eyes.

'Good, I'll do that, then,' replied Pamela briskly, reaching for the breadknife and gripping the handle hard, thinking, This is Elizabeth, this is how she is and nothing will ever change.

'Theo and Ed had a big row.'

'I know, I heard.' Maisie plucked a tuft of grass from the lawn, then dropped it on top of a daisy. 'Stupid boys, always bloody fighting.'

'Uncle Peter lost it and sent Theo upstairs.' Clem, sitting beside her sister, rolled over on to her tummy, aware of her hipbones pressing into the soft grass. It was a good feeling, and the grass smelt good too, all mossy and full of rain; good enough to eat, like a delicious vegetable or fruit that no one had discovered yet. She put her face right into it and breathed deeply, enjoying the tickle of the little shoots, trimmed by Sid to a quarter of an inch for the party, on her nose and cheeks. She had that feeling she got when she hadn't eaten for a while, airy-headed but powerful. During breakfast she had sat next to Maisie and slid all three of her bacon rashers on to her sister's plate, then smeared the egg round her own until it looked convincingly sparse. Maisie had demolished the bacon without a word; neither did she bat an eyelid when Clem put half a piece of toast on to her lap. This was their new pact, not discussed or analysed, which had emerged wordlessly, effortlessly, from the events of the night before. Clem – and this was the real source of her new and completely lovely sense of power – had saved her twin sister. *From a fate worse than death*, a novel might have said. But it hadn't been a novel, it had been real life and she, Clem, would never, as long as she lived, forget the sight of her sister buried, wrestling, sobbing under the thrusting, half-naked man. A doll under a monster. It was the vilest, most terrifying thing she had ever seen. And terror had made her brave.

Sprinting back to Ashley House afterwards, with the puddles spurting up their ankles, it was she who had kept Maisie going, whispering that it would be all right, soothing her fears at what the grown-ups would say, assuring her that no one need ever know, that she would sort things out somehow. And she had, with a thunderbolt of a brainwave that had occurred to her just as they reached the bend in the lane. Maisie, of course, had cigarettes. A packet of ten Marlboro Lights. As they ran up the drive Clem, her voice breathless, had explained the plan, how they would be caught smoking and how it would put everyone off thinking anything else. And it had worked like a charm. She had played her part with aplomb, puffing hard even though the hateful smoke stung her eyes, and emitting a loud giggle so that Serena, hovering by the front gate, would peer round the garage and see them. It had been odd to act the part of Bad Girl deliberately: it had made Clem

recognise that rather than being more grown-up than her Maisie
had simply taken to playing a different role, being bad for the pair of
them, which, if she thought about it, sort of kept her off the hook.

'Are you okay?'

'Yup.'

'Sure? I mean, if you're worried that – that is, if he actually . . . He
didn't *do* anything, did he?'

Maisie shook her head fiercely, glancing over her shoulder to
check that no one was within earshot. Peter and Helen were sitting
with cups of coffee on one of the cloisters benches. Nearby Pamela
dozed in a deckchair, her tapestry untended on her lap. Chloë, bored
without Roland who had been dragged, amid much protesting, back
to Guildford, was playing a sort of hopscotch in and out of the side
entrance to the marquee. Maisie didn't know where their parents
were – asleep too, probably, worn out with telling them all off. Even
with so much else to worry about – and be grateful for – she had
burned with shame at the public castigation they had received on the
doorstep of the house, with guests milling around them and with
Ed and Theo, clearly pissed, smirking in the shrubbery.

'I mean,' continued Clem importantly, 'if you felt we should tell
someone . . .'

'No way. No bloody way.' Maisie pulled the head off a daisy and
began to pluck off its frill of petals.

Clem rolled on to her back, relieved. Any other response would
have involved huge trauma and unpleasantness, and jeopardised
the pact. Each had a secret, kept safe by the other. It was mutually
beneficial, perfect.

'But I do plan to get revenge.'

Clem sat up in alarm, chiding herself inwardly for imagining
Maisie would ever co-operate in keeping the situation simple. 'And
how on earth are you going to do that?'

Maisie frowned. 'Not sure yet . . . but I'm working on it. I'll
think of something. He practically – you know, you *saw*, for Christ's
sake – and I'm not going to let that go, I'm just not—'

'Oh, hi, Granddad,' Clem almost shrieked, aware that her sister
hadn't noticed John's approach.

'Hello, girls.' John had been shuffling ineffectually round the estate, attempting to take his mind off his hangover, and had stopped by his granddaughters, dabbing at the perspiration on his forehead with a handkerchief. In spite of his headache he was in excellent spirits, riding high on a general sense of triumph about the party. 'All shipshape, are we?'

'Yes, Granddad.'

'Butter wouldn't melt, I suppose,' he added, chuckling as he recalled Pamela's report on the recent misdemeanours of the twins and thinking how innocent the pair looked, sprawled in jeans and T-shirts on the grass, the scatter of freckles on their noses, their hair glossy in the afternoon sun. It didn't seem very long ago that he'd had one on each knee, thumbs in their mouths, rapt in front of a storybook. 'You mind how you go, eh, young scallywags?'

'Yes, Granddad,' they chimed, exchanging if-only-he-knew looks, but each in truth a little soothed by the timeless nonsense that could be counted on from his lips.

Charlie jogged slowly, the sweat in his eyes misting the arch of trees overhead to a green blur. His body felt uncomfortably separate from his skeleton, like a heavy, ill-fitting suit. The sun had dried most of what remained of the puddles, leaving shallow potholes in the road, which he avoided carefully, wary of losing his balance and twisting an ankle or worse. At forty-three one had to think of such things. At forty-three life got complicated in all manner of ways, he had discovered, particularly if one had been robbed of a child, and one's wife appeared to be sliding, inexorably, into a state of steely hostility and indifference. Increasingly he felt he loved the memory of Serena more than the reality of her. Watching her screech at the girls, eyes wild, voice close to hysteria, it had taken all his self-discipline not to leap to their defence. Of course they sneaked off for cigarettes. He had done the same at their age, down this very lane, ducking behind the trees with Peter at the sound of an approaching car. The girls were fourteen. Breaking rules went with the territory. And the trick, when dealing with it, was not to overreact, but to lay down the law gently, so they knew that somewhere beyond the reprimands you were on their side. That you would die with love for them, given half a chance. Serena knew all this too, of course. Once upon a time, a few months and an eternity before, Serena had been the master of such parental tactics, cajoling and loving, steering their offspring in the right direction much as a collie might guide its flock.

And then there was Ed. Charlie increased his pace, his heart aching at the thought of his son, visibly knotted with worry about Common Entrance, but now beyond the age where a hug or a quiet word could make him feel better. He shrank from physical contact, these days, unless it was taking place in the rough, easy context of kicking a ball. Charlie had wanted to defend him, too, when Serena let rip that morning. From what he had seen, Ed had worked hard. As well as revising he had put an awful lot into his hurricanes project, solemnly informing Charlie on the day after his return from Paris that although he would value his help he realised it would probably be better if he battled with the thing alone, since it was going to be considered alongside the marks he managed in the exams. Oh, God, the agony of being a child – and of parenthood: having to watch their trials and tribulations, unable to step in and make any of it one iota easier. There were simply no short-cuts, not for Ed, not for any of them.

Charlie ran as far as the entrance to the rather tasteless neo-classical pile on the far side of the village, then stopped for a breather. He leant on the wall next to the gates to stretch his calf muscles, remembering that Maisie had got quite excited about the owner of the place, some pop star or other but he couldn't dredge up the name. Modern music was a mystery to him – all noise and no tune. But, then, his parents had said the same about Genesis and the Rolling Stones, he reminded himself, comforted by this small reminder that the patterns of life repeated themselves, generation after generation, that everything changed and yet stayed the same. Just as Serena, although changed, was the same, reflected Charlie, his thoughts returning, as they so often did, to the damnable, alienating unhappiness of his wife and what to do about it. So far he had discouraged her mutterings about getting a job, but maybe that *was* the right way to go, he mused now. It would get her out of the house at least, offer some distraction. He was still tussling with the idea when the strident toot of a car horn sounded over his left shoulder. The gates next to him opened and a hefty four-wheel-drive vehicle nosed its way between them. Charlie was all set to nod in greeting when the driver, a surly-faced, scruffy young man with a stud in his front tooth, leant out of the window. 'This is private property – can't you read the sign?' he barked, then accelerated noisily into the empty road.

As he loped back in the direction of Ashley House, Charlie's spirits lifted at the sight of his younger sister dawdling along the lane with her back to him, fiddling with her mobile phone. Dearest Cass, life went on for her at least, unshackled by all the troubles of parenthood and partnership, ploughing her own sweet furrow. Although as Charlie watched his sister, something in the intentness of her expression, fixed upon the phone, while her fingers raced with impressive dexterity across its tiny keypad, gave him pause for thought. She had, now he thought about it, been a little subdued the night before, looking gorgeous as ever in yellow satin, but not quite joining in. She had also taken on the highly uncharacteristic role of being the first of the family to go to bed. Maybe her life was more complicated than he supposed. Charlie called her name and made a last effort of a sprint to catch up with her. Maybe, for the first time in her life, some male was giving her a hard time.

'Phew.' He bent over, leaning on his knees to catch his breath. 'Who are you on the phone to, then, on this fine sunny morning? Wrapping some new victim round your little finger, no doubt, a substitute for . . .' He clicked his fingers. 'What was the last one called?'

'Richard,' said Cassie flatly, the habit of protecting Dan snapping like a reflex, independent of the ocean of feelings swelling round him.

'So, go on, then, who is he?' Charlie persisted cheerfully, standing now with his hands on his hips, glad of any distraction from the conveyor-belt of his own thoughts.

Cassie hesitated, aware that her brother was looking for entertainment rather than enlightenment. She had turned to Peter for help in the crisis over Stephen Smith and the letter because she knew he would offer cool, clear analysis as to what she should do. But cool, clear analysis had done nothing to make her feel consoled, or less lonely. Peter now believed that the problem had been solved, that they could dust off their hands and move on. But the problem wasn't solved because Stephen was still there, refusing to be forgotten. Charlie's appearance had coincided with yet another message, a text this time: 'Hope the party was good. Looking forward to seeing you on Friday.' A harmless few words. Nothing too insistent or sinister. Yet Cassie felt pressed, on all sides.

'There is sort of someone, actually. One of those he's-keener-on-me-than-vice-versa situations,' she explained lightly, switching off the phone and dropping it back into her bag.

'I might have guessed.' Charlie rubbed his hands, looking pleased. 'Typical Cass.' They fell into step beside each other, walking in companionable silence for a few minutes. 'Though it will happen one day, you know,' he added, with vehemence, 'the proverbial thunderbolt, just when you're least expecting it. Someone will sweep you off your feet and before you know it you'll be choosing colours for a nursery instead of a drawing room.'

'Shut up.' Cassie gave a playful thump to his arm while inside she ached with recognition, seeing again the grey morning at the surgery, her hair dirty, her face pasty, the forgotten prescription and Dan charging down the street after her and into her life with the force of a tornado. Unforeseeable, unprecedented, unimaginable, unignorable. Oh, God, she missed him so much. She missed the feelings he had allowed in her – of uninhibited loving and being loved. In the weeks since her reckless, clumsy attempt to resolve matters, with its catastrophic consequences, her longing had, if anything, got worse. She had lost the love of her life, it was as simple – and complicated – as that. The scar on her wrist had faded, but the pain in her heart was still raw.

'In fact,' continued Charlie, deep in his own train of thought, his voice tremulous, 'I bloody well hope it does happen – and soon – not just because I'd like my lovely little sister to discover the joys of true love but because it's just what this family needs. A bit of a new start.

New little ones . . . a future . . .' He broke off, covering his face with one hand, caught off-guard by the rush of his own emotions.

'Oh, Charlie.' Cassie looped her arm through her brother's and squeezed hard. Instinctively, they both slowed their pace, aware that the conversation needed to find a satisfactory close before they got back to the house. They were half-way down the drive, with the front lawn sloping away to their right and the orchard of silver birches on their left. Ahead Ashley House already filled the skyline, basking like some huge sleek animal in the sun, its walls thick with ivy and purple clusters of wisteria, its windows winking like knowing eyes. 'Do you know,' Cassie confessed, squinting at the familiar sight, 'I always struggle to imagine Peter and Helen living here? I mean, I'm perfectly happy about all the family arrangements – I really am – but when I try to picture it I just can't. It would suit you and Serena far more. Helen and Peter are such *townies*. They worry about things like cat hairs on cushions and mud on boots, whereas you . . .'

'Whereas we're a complete shambles,' Charlie finished for her, throwing back his head and roaring with laughter.

'I didn't mean . . .'

'I don't care what you meant.' He hugged her hard, then changed tack, asking if there was any way she could find a small role for Serena with her work.

'Oh dear. She's already asked me.'

'Has she?' Charlie couldn't conceal his astonishment, or his pleasure. Serena taking such a step was encouragingly significant. It meant that somewhere inside she was trying. It meant, too, more importantly, that they were at least – albeit unwittingly – on the same wavelength about something.

'Yes, last night, at the party.'

'And what did you say?'

Cassie looked at her feet, recoiling at his eagerness. She was wearing strappy white sandals with far too much heel for a country walk. The red varnish on her big toe was already chipped, revealing an ugly zigzag of nail. 'I'm afraid I said it's really not possible at the moment. Business isn't great, it really isn't.'

'But I thought you were rushed off your feet with customers?'

'Sometimes I am, but it's gone sort of quiet.' Cassie squirmed, inwardly despairing at the myriad half-truths about her life. 'Besides,' she gabbled, 'working with members of the family isn't exactly recommended, is it? I mean, it's a bit like selling a used car to a friend – business and pleasure, one shouldn't mix them . . .' she faltered, quavering under Charlie's determined expression.

'It's not remotely like that, no. Serena's bloody good, you know – really artistic. She's got a fantastic eye and she's good with people – and numbers come to that, if all you want is a bit of help with the accounting. And if it's money, I assure you she won't be expecting a huge wage. In fact,' he concluded eagerly, 'if it's about money *I*'ll pay.'

'Don't be ridiculous, Charlie.' They had come to a standstill a few yards from the front gate. Next to them the silver birches rustled softly, like an impatient audience.

'I'm not, Cass. We . . . Serena is pretty desperate, to be honest. She needs *something*, some reason to get out of bed in the morning, get out of the house. I can't tell you how much you would be helping her. Helping us. I mean it about the money, Cass, I'll pay, I really will.' He took hold of her shoulders, forcing her to look him in the eye. 'Will you at least think about it?'

'Of course I will.' Cassie managed a bleak smile, wishing it were possible to confess that she had virtually no work to share and that employing her sister-in-law would both advertise this and force her to do something about it. The truth was she had got rather used to floating round in a bubble of indolent despair, dipping into her father's gift to pay bills. Part of her wanted to keep things that way, to be free to brood over Dan, to continue to wallow in self-pity. In addition to which, Serena would need careful handling and, given the private mess of her own emotions, Cassie wasn't sure she was up to it. 'Of course I will,' she repeated, patting Charlie's chest, where a huge dark patch was spreading from the exertions of his run. 'I'll call you next week, okay? Let you know what I come up with.'

'You're a brick, Cass.'

'I haven't promised.'

'No, but you're still a brick. Now, you go on in. I'm going to do a bit of stretching or I won't be able to walk this afternoon.' He trotted over to the nearest of the silver birches where he seized one of the branches and embarked on some comical twists and bends that, in spite of everything, made Cassie laugh.

The sandwiches, neat, bulging parcels of chicken and home-made coleslaw, wrapped in tin-foil and with the crusts cut off, were very good. Eating them as she drove, Elizabeth felt a customary stab of exasperated affection for her mother. Nothing was ever badly done, not even a makeshift last-minute picnic. There were two without coleslaw for Roland, as well as a carton of low-sugar blackcurrant squash and a bag of Monster Munch. For afters there were two crisp, waxy-skinned Granny Smiths and a couple of Flakes, which Elizabeth meant to avoid but to which she succumbed when Roland unwrapped his. She wolfed hers down, as she had her sandwiches, aware that eating was dulling the edge of her headache. By the time they reached the Hog's Back just outside Guildford, she was feeling as if she could recall a state of physical normality even if it was not quite within her grasp.

'Do be careful, Roland, you're spilling chocolate everywhere. It's a new car, remember?'

'I hate it,' retorted her son sulkily, his mouth stuffed with Monster Munch and Flake, an interesting combination.

'Don't be silly.'

'I do. It makes you and Daddy cross. In the old car it didn't matter.'

'Trying not to make a mess always matters,' countered Elizabeth primly, feeling, as she often did with such necessary but petty reprimands, that she was reading from a script written by someone else. Someone who knew the Right Way to be a mother, a teacher, an adult. Without such a script her wicked true self might have been tempted to urge her uncertain, over-cautious child to make as much mess as possible because a Flake was a delicious little tree-trunk of chocolate designed specifically to explode on contact with teeth and that was as much fun as dabbing up all the little shards of chocolate afterwards, feeling them melt to nothing the moment they touched your tongue. But she couldn't say that, of course. It would be irresponsible. More to the point, Colin had only just cleaned the car, inside and out, using a snouted little upholstery Hoover he had bought especially for the purpose. Prompted by this last thought, Elizabeth reached into her son's lap and removed the empty sweet and food wrappers.

'I hadn't finished,' Roland protested untruthfully, seeking revenge for having been dragged away from his cousins. It had been the best visit to his grandparents that he could remember. Because of the party he had been allowed to stay up later than he ever had in his life before. He had loved his and Chloë's picnic breakfast in front of the telly; and when Chloë went all funny because of the fight in the kitchen Ed had come to his rescue by inviting him to join in with a quick spying game in the bushes. They had got really close to their grandfather, sitting all pink-faced and sweaty on a log in one of the fields, then crawled on their tummies along one side of the biggest flowerbed, surfacing to find Chloë and Theo's mum and dad standing by the sundial and kissing. Not in a normal way but with their lips glued together for ages, like they were eating each other. Ed had to stuff his fist into his mouth to stop himself laughing, which made Roland want to laugh, too, so badly that he had wet his pants a little bit. And then his mother had called that it was time to go and they had to scrabble back the way they had come. 'Can I play on your phone?' he asked now, seeking distraction from the contrasting boredom of his current circumstances.

'No, the battery's almost dead and, besides, we're nearly home. Look, we're just going past the turning to your school.'

Roland looked, gloom swamping his heart. Some ten minutes later they turned into their own road and pulled up outside the house.

'Help Mummy with the bags, there's a good boy.'

'Why can't Dad help?'

'He will, just as soon as we get inside. Ring the bell if you like so he knows we're here.' Elizabeth clicked open the boot and grappled with the luggage, reaching first for Colin's evening gear which, like hers, was laid flat across the top of everything, protected by trailing sheets of see-through plastic.

'Daddy's not answering.'

'Well, come and help me, then.' Elizabeth staggered to the front door, groping in her handbag for her keys. As she got there the door swung open and Colin appeared, smiling broadly. 'Hello, darling. You're back early. Look who dropped by.' He turned as he spoke, revealing the presence of Phyllis McGill.

'Oh, hello there . . . Goodness . . .' Elizabeth found it hard to conceal her surprise. Phyllis thrust out her hand, then withdrew it because Elizabeth was too laden to respond.

'School politics,' said Phyllis, rolling her eyes. She was dressed in her usual hippie style, in a long purple dress, with pendulous purple earrings and several silver bangles jangling round each wrist. 'We had a talk.'

'Really?' Elizabeth glanced at Colin, seeking some evidence of annoyance that the last Sunday of half-term should have been so rudely disturbed. 'Is something going on? Is it something serious?'

A pause followed, broken by Colin with a brittle laugh. 'Oh, no, nothing serious – just this new directive from the head about how to handle the inspectors.'

'But I thought they weren't coming until the autumn,' murmured Elizabeth, her arms aching too much now to care about school inspectors or being polite. She squeezed past them to get rid of her load. She slung Colin's evening gear over the banisters and put down the bags. 'I'm dying for a cup of tea. Would you like one, Phyllis?' She delivered the invitation in as lukewarm a manner as she could, wanting to show Colin that she knew his patience would already have been tested sorely and that she was only going through the motions of civility.

'I've had one, thanks. I was just going.'

'Okay, fine. Good to see you.' Feeling released from further duty, Elizabeth gave Phyllis a little wave and went into the kitchen to put the kettle on. Roland followed her, saying he was hungry. Elizabeth, humming as she ran the tap, said he couldn't possibly be because he'd only just had a picnic lunch.

Roland, feeling more bereft than ever without Boots to stroke and no one to play with, began to whimper. Elizabeth realised he was as tired as she was, put her arms round him and said he could choose two biscuits and eat them watching television. It was only as the front door slammed, as she was reaching for a clean mug from the cupboard, that she realised Phyllis had not had a cup of tea. The dishwasher was empty (Elizabeth had emptied it herself before they left for the party) and the shelf where they kept mugs was full. And the kettle, now she thought about it, had been both empty and stone-cold.

'Well, she certainly got the message,' she observed, when Colin returned from the hall.

'Who? What message?'

'Phyllis, realising she wasn't exactly welcome. Mind you, what did she expect? Coming by like that on a Sunday – talk about not having a life. Poor you having to deal with it. Full marks for not giving her tea.' Colin was standing with his back to her, facing the stove. She went to put her arms round him. 'Sorry I went a bit overboard last night. Forgive me?'

'Of course,' he muttered, 'it was nothing. Don't worry about it.' Behind them the kettle boiled. 'I'd love a brew.'

'I'll do it.' Elizabeth dropped her arms from his waist and went to fetch the teapot and a second mug. Colin settled with the papers at the kitchen table. She gave him his tea and took hers through to the drawing room where Roland was curled in a ball on the sofa. 'All right?'

'Why did Daddy's friend come?'

'Which friend was that?' Elizabeth closed her eyes, as a sudden sleepiness washed over her.

'The lady just now. Daddy was with her at Tesco's. I saw them when I went to Jack's.'

Elizabeth opened her eyes, very slowly. 'Did you? When was that?'

'When I went to Jack's,' repeated Roland, impatiently. 'His mum took us shopping – for *ages*, so we hardly had any time to play. Can I have another biscuit?'

'Go on, then.'

Elizabeth watched him trot back into the kitchen and then stared at her tea. It was nothing, of course. Some simple explanation. No point in saying anything. No point in rocking the boat. She drained her mug, swallowing a few loose tea leaves, then studied the little sludge of black remains in the bottom. Somewhere they had a strainer but she seldom bothered to use it. If tea leaves told the future, hers, she decided, looked pretty murky. She set the mug on a coaster and went upstairs to unpack, taking all the bags and clothes from the hall with her. Phyllis McGill at Tesco's with Colin. It didn't make sense. Roland had to have been mistaken. She was on the point of hanging Colin's white tie and tails suit in the wardrobe when she realised they needed to be returned to the hire shop and took them into the spare room instead out of harm's way. The bed was a little messy, the duvet all dimpled and the counterpane at an odd angle, barely covering the pillows. Elizabeth hung Colin's evening wear over the back of a chair and set about straightening it, wondering vaguely when Roland had had the time to sneak in for a forbidden romp. She had changed the sheets on Friday and left the room in pristine condition. She was sure of it.

She would have forgotten the matter in an instant . . . had she not felt something under her shoe. Something hard and round. A bracelet. A bangle. Half under the bed. A silver bangle, with a small purple stone in the middle. She picked it up and sat on the edge of the bed, turning it round and round in her hands, groping, even as the truth dawned on her, for a version of events that would explain it all away. But there was too much – Tesco's, rushing home early, a cold kettle, a rumpled bed, a bangle – there was simply too much. The purple stone blurred before Elizabeth's eyes. In the spare room, alone with this new knowledge, she felt utterly marooned, not just in her home but in life. When she looked back, the jigsaw of clues, dropped like a trail of litter through the preceding months, was sickening in its obviousness. And how easy she had made it for Colin, scrabbling for approval and affection, interpreting his paucity of warmth as a sign of her own failings. How well – how pathetically well – she had played the role of the duped wife. Elizabeth's self-disgust was so strong that for a moment she almost retched at the physical taste of it, rising like bile at the back of her throat. Of course Colin didn't love her: she was unlovable; dull, worthless and unlovable. Of course Phyllis McGill, even with her loud voice and sanctimonious ideals, was a better bet. She wore purple and had a throaty laugh. She was feisty, successful, more attractive in every way.

Elizabeth lay back on the bed and pulled the counterpane right up over her face like a shroud. Under the warm darkness of its protection she felt calmer. It was a relief in a way to have the truth – shelved, sidelined, excused for so long – exposed. Her husband did not love her. He did not respect her. There it was. Out at last, as solid and irrefutable as stone. The only really bad thing was that irrefutable truths needed to be acted upon. Elizabeth's gradual recognition of this made her quail almost more than any other aspect of her predicament. For there was no hiding now, no protecting shield of ignorance. A reaction was required. Something bold. She moaned softly, pulling the counterpane into an even tighter cocoon around herself, wishing the flimsy fabric had some power to keep the world at bay.

On the Friday afternoon after Peter's party Stephen patted his completed manuscript into a tidy pile and left his flat to go shopping. Cassie had agreed, after some cajoling, to come round at six o'clock. He knew exactly what he wanted to buy (champagne, flowers, smoked salmon, wholemeal bread and a lemon) but with the state of his finances it wasn't going to be easy. For the last couple of months he had been living off a diet of sliced plastic bread, cheese and baked beans, with the occasional bottle of plonk thrown in as a treat. His overdraft was massive and even paying the minimum on his credit cards was getting hard. He had kept his bank quiet with reassurances that a hefty cheque from his publishers was just round the corner. Which, as of today, Stephen reflected excitedly, it really was. On delivery of the manuscript he would get three thousand pounds, which, while not exactly hefty, would at least clear his debts. Six months later, when the book got published, he would receive another cheque for a similar amount. All he had to do in the meantime was find a part-time job – writing freelance articles maybe, or possibly offering private English lessons to foreign students.

Stephen whistled as he walked, fiddling with the loose change in his shorts pocket and wondering which credit card to try in the supermarket. Having recently suffered the ignominy of having a card rejected (in the off-licence the week before, trying to buy crisps and two measly cans of beer), he had no desire to repeat the exercise. But he didn't want to hold back either. Cassie deserved the best – absolutely the best – and he wanted to give it to her. In addition to which, Stephen reminded himself, his hand hovering between the cheaper tail-pieces and the beautifully packaged tawny-pink slabs of Scottish salmon ('Organically cured'), he was celebrating. He had worked like a fiend for weeks, ever since he had called at Cassie's flat with her great-aunt's letters, impelled by a new and indescribably joyous hope. Such a simple thing, hope, but so all-embracingly powerful and impossible to manufacture. 'I've found a muse,' he had confessed to his editor at their last meeting, patting his briefcase, even though it contained nothing but a newspaper and a Mars Bar. 'There's no stopping me now.'

'That's good to know, Stephen, because we're scheduling your book for the coming spring. March, probably. If it's not going to be ready it would be far better if you told us now.' The editor twiddled a pencil. 'A muse, you say, that's interesting. Though I've always assumed such things to be the territory of poets rather than biographers.'

'I've been writing a bit of poetry too, as it happens,' Stephen had blurted, 'nothing too polished yet, though I was thinking that maybe, one day, I might put together a collection.'

'Really?' The editor had raised one of his thick dark eyebrows in a show of decidedly muted interest. 'Not something we do a lot of, I'm afraid. Not much money in it either, of course.'

'Of course.' Rebuffed, Stephen, had returned the conversation to his unsung war heroes, cursing his weakness in even mentioning the poems, which were all about Cassie and love and therefore very private. He might show them to Cassie one day, though, he decided now, pushing his trolley, which contained a lemon and a pack of organic smoked salmon, in the direction of the drinks aisle. There were several brands of champagne, ranging from Own Label (£12.99) to a vintage Moët et Chandon (£39.99). Stephen deliberated for a good ten minutes, wondering whether to forget the flowers in favour of the more expensive bottle, but in the end getting both the Moët and a bunch of red carnations from the stalls by the entrance. What the hell? he told himself, whisking out his Visa card for the cashier and saying a brief prayer as she slid it through her machine.

Half an hour later he was safely at home with his purchases, fussing round the flat like an old woman, adjusting pictures and ornaments, wanting everything to be perfect. He opened all the windows, too, wishing the day wasn't quite so hot and thinking longingly of the ceiling fans he had had in his apartment in Quito. He had spent many a humid night lying on his back with his hands under his head staring up at their big, mesmerising blades, soothed as much by their soft whir as the kiss of cool air across his naked body. With such accoutrements his cramped flat in Hackney might have feigned some glamour, a little romance, even. Instead of looking like the hot shoebox it was, filled now (thanks to the open windows) with the drone of traffic and the stench of car fumes.

With two hours to go Stephen showered and changed into clean jeans and a fresh T-shirt. He shaved carefully, checked his nostrils and ears for rogue hairs and his teeth for flecks of food. He cut up the lemon, spread the bread with butter and slabs of salmon, then wedged the whole lot into the fridge on top of the champagne. The flowers, which he had been planning to present to her, looked so wilted that he propped them in a bowl of water, then decided to arrange them in a vase. Since he only possessed one and it was very small, the result was far from satisfactory.

When the doorbell rang his heart stopped, then pumped furiously, sending tremors down his arms and legs. He rubbed the clamminess from his hands, wished there was time to change into another fresher T-shirt, and raced down the stairs to the door. The buzzer release sometimes didn't work and he had no intention of risking it now. And suddenly there she was, all sunny-haired and smiling, framed in the dingy doorway in a sleeveless pink cotton dress and strappy white shoes.

'Great,' he said, beaming so broadly he could hardly get the word out. He would have kissed her, but she thrust out her hand, cool against his hot palm.

'We could go out,' she said.

'Oh, no . . . I've got in a bit of stuff. And I wanted to show you the manuscript,' Stephen stammered, appalled at such an early potential derailing of his plans. Stuffy shoebox that it was, he still felt a burning need to introduce Cassie to his home. Not just so that she could begin to know him better, but because he wanted to see her in his space, to imprint the reality of her – so long confined to his mind – upon his everyday existence.

Cassie followed him up the stairs with a heavy heart. After the heat of the June sunshine the stairwell, with its whitewashed brick walls and concrete floor, felt so chilled that she shivered in her thin dress and was almost pleased when they stepped into the green-house warmth of the flat. A moment later, however, with the door closed behind them, her unease returned. It was quite the smallest living space she had ever seen. It made her own flat look like a mansion. The kitchen was merely a corner of the sitting room, its one counter within reach of the sofa. A TV was wedged on one side of a gas fire and a desk on the other, but at an awkward jutting angle because it didn't quite fit the slot. There was no obvious surface for eating off, other than a knee-high tray-sized table in front of the sofa, on which, Cassie noticed, her gloom thickening, had been set a bottle of champagne and two wine glasses. A half-open door beside the sofa revealed a cupboard of a bedroom, swamped by a double bed, and a narrow chest of drawers. Shirts and trousers hung along the dado rail, dangling among a hotchpotch of pictures and ethnic hangings. The walls of the kitchen and sitting area were just as crowded, with several loaded bookshelves, framed prints and a couple of large canvases depicting cave-painting-style beasts in a panoply of colours. The effect, for Cassie at least, was to make an already tight space feel tighter. Instinctively she edged towards the largest of the open windows, fanning herself with the palm of her hand. 'Quite a view you've got up here.'

Stephen made a face, wondering if she remembered he wasn't good with heights. 'I hate this flat, especially in this heat.'

'It is *baking*, isn't it?' Cassie agreed, relaxing a little. 'I always want to moan and then I think this might be our only glimpse of summer so I should be grateful.'

'I thought this might cool us down. It's been in the fridge.' Stephen seized the champagne, hoping she'd noticed the label and thinking how much better it would have looked in an ice bucket, with a starched napkin draped over the edge. The bottle, moist with condensation, slipped in his hands. 'There's some food too – smoked salmon. I hope that's okay?'

'Oh, yes. Lovely.' Pained by the sight of him struggling with the cork, aware that he was trying, with every sinew, to impress her, Cassie turned her attention to the desk. 'Is this it?' She tapped the manuscript.

His face lit up. 'That's it. Finished this morning. All ready to go. Due for publication in March. Have a look, if you like. Your uncle is the third chapter—' Stephen broke off, his face contorted with the effort of twisting at the cork, which popped free a moment later, with sudden and squeaky violence, splashing his T-shirt and the carpet with liberal quantities of champagne. He swore silently, shaking the drips off his hands, then filled the two glasses carefully, not wanting to lose another drop. 'There we are.' He handed her the fullest and stood, grinning and very close, to watch her sip it.

'Hmm . . . super,' Cassie murmured, responding to the pressure of his hopeful gaze. 'Only eight months or so to go, then. How exciting.' She set down her glass and began to thumb through the loose pages, trying to look casual, but anxious to see that he had kept his word, that her mother's secret was safe.

'Take it to the sofa. Make yourself comfortable,' Stephen urged, drinking his own glass in one go, thrilled at the sight of her, in his sitting room, sipping her drink, reading his words. 'I'll just fetch the food. There's lemon as well, but I wasn't sure if you'd want some so I've just cut it up.'

'Whatever,' Cassie muttered, beginning to skim-read the chapter on Eric. A few moments later Stephen sat down next to her with the plate of bread and smoked salmon and lemon wedges on his lap. While she read he watched, taking in the details of her appearance, loving everything, from the creases of concentration in her forehead to the faint freckles on her arms and the smooth curve of her calf muscles. He had never seen so much of her bare skin before and it made his head quite fuzzy with excitement.

'I didn't mention the . . . you know, your mother's letter and so on.'

'Thank you.' Cassie put the manuscript down and smiled at him properly for the first time. 'It would cause so much pain. Unnecessary pain, not just to my mother but the whole family.'

'And I'd hate that,' he blurted. 'I love your family. I never had anything like that, you see. I never got on with my parents. I couldn't wait to leave home. My father was a bully.'

'Oh dear, I'm so sorry.' He had turned to face her and was resting one arm along the back of the sofa. His brown eyes were fixed upon her face, burning with the trust of one believing himself to be in the company of a soul-mate.

'Untidiness, clumsiness, bad homework, not-so-bad homework – just my existence was enough to provoke him into a rage. He hit me with his belt usually. It had a metal buckle that hurt like hell.'

'But surely your mother . . .'

'Took my part? And get hit herself?' Stephen laughed. 'It was better when my elder sister was around – he never laid a finger on her. When she left home things got really bad. I took off soon afterwards.'

'How utterly terrible.'

'It's all right. I mean, I'm all right. I just wanted to tell you. I hope you don't mind?'

Cassie shook her head, unsure whether she minded or not. Such unhappy revelations were on one level deeply – inevitably – engaging. And yet there was an inherent intimacy in them too,

of which she remained wary. He held out the plate and she took one
of the laden pieces of bread, to be kind, and because it occurred to
her that when the plate was empty it would be all right to go. He was
sitting so close that she could smell the muskiness of his skin and see
her own reflection in his pupils, which were black-brown and huge.

'I've not told many people about all that.'

'Haven't you?' Cassie turned her attention to her food, chewing
vigorously, hoping that if she ignored the tension – thickening like
the afternoon heat between them – it might somehow dissolve.

In contrast, Stephen was floating on the euphoria of confession,
dazzled by the conviction that what he had dreamed of for so many
months was all coming true. She was here. She was close. She was
his.

'Maybe you should have told a few more people,' Cassie
ventured. 'Talking is good . . .'

'Oh, yes, I know that. You taught me that. I can't tell you how
much it meant when I came round that time and you poured your
heart out . . .' She began to protest, but he wasn't listening now.
'Cassie, I'm sorry if this shocks you but I have to say that ever since I
first saw you, that evening at your parents' house, it's been like – like
I had been waiting my whole life to meet you. I wanted to show you
that letter your mother wrote, not just because of your uncle but
because . . . because of how I feel about you. *Every moment of every
minute of every hour I think of you.* I think it is one of the most
beautiful letters I've ever read . . . the sentiments it expresses – the
love, so real, so raw.'

The words, rehearsed so many times, had come out all mangled,
but with Cassie looking dumbstruck rather than appalled, Stephen
could no longer contain the urge to touch her. While he talked he
had been watching her neck, wondering what it would be like to
slide his tongue into the tiny hollow at her throat and along the
ridges of her collar-bone. He imagined her tipping her head back,
her lips parting to release a little sigh of pleasure. He would cup the
crown of her head in the palm of his hand, hold her steady for their
first kiss – the gentlest of kisses, so she wouldn't take fright,
wouldn't realise that his passion was volcanic and terrifying even

to him, who had lived with it now, smouldering and frustrated, for months and months.

Cassie started to say something about the letter, about love, but Stephen was concentrating on moving his hand, the one draped carelessly over the back of the sofa, towards the rippling curtain of hair concealing the nape of her neck. The moment he touched her her entire body stiffened, as if she had been stabbed or electrocuted or seen some nightmare vision in his buffalo picture above the gas fire. The next moment she was on her feet, clasping her empty glass. 'I'm sorry, Stephen, I just can't—'

'Of course, you're not ready yet – after that bastard. I understand, I can wait. I'm sorry, I shouldn't have rushed you.'

'No, you *don't* understand.' Peter had said keep the man sweet, but Peter had no idea what he was asking of her. She couldn't do it any more, she simply couldn't. 'I'm sorry you . . . have feelings for me.' She glanced from his stricken face to the manuscript and back again, taking heart at the wad of completed pages. It was written now, after all, without one damaging word. 'And I think you are a good – a truly *excellent* writer . . . but,' she continued, more firmly, reaching for her handbag and gripping it under both arms, 'I'm afraid I just can't have you saying Dan's a bastard because – because the fact is I still love him. And I always will.' To have stated the central truth of her life – even to the hapless Stephen Smith – felt so wonderful, so liberating, that she repeated it: 'I always will.'

'Just friends, then,' he said hoarsely, not moving.

'Just friends,' Cassie echoed, working her way round the furniture towards the door.

Stephen remained on the sofa until the clack of her heels had died away down the stairs. Then he stood up, seized his overcrowded vase of wonky carnations and hurled it with all his might at the closed door. Water, red petals and shards of glass exploded up the wall and across the carpet. Stephen watched motionless, not even blinking, seeing only the scattered fragments of his dreams.

'I think rowing is boring and stupid,' declared Chloë, yanking on Toffee's lead to see if the dog could be persuaded to do something more entertaining than sit panting on the grass. Being in charge of the animal for a week hadn't been half as great as she had expected. Toffee wasn't nearly as much fun without Kay, not chasing anything – not even his tail, which Kay could make him do for hours.

'That seems to be your opinion of most things at the moment, young lady,' replied Peter, exchanging a look with Helen, then returning his gaze to the river where four boats, each containing four boys, were bobbing around waiting for the signal to start.

'But Toffee agrees with me. Look at him. He's so bored he's *dying*.'

'He's not bored,' Helen corrected her, 'he's hot, like all of us. And this is the first team your brother has ever been in and I think you should stop complaining and be proud instead.'

'You and Daddy didn't come to my rounders match.'

'No, we didn't,' conceded Helen, marvelling at her daughter's unnerving ability to strike at the heart of any matter on which she herself felt vulnerable. 'Unfortunately we both had to work that day, but it's your sports day soon and we're coming to that.'

'I'm only in one smelly race.'

'Nonetheless we shall be there and cheer you all the way to the finishing line, just as we're cheering Theo. And, anyway, I thought Miss Harris said you would be in three races—'

'No, I am NOT,' Chloë shouted. 'And I don't CARE anyway, I don't CARE.'

'Stop it, Chloë, this minute, or I'll go and tell Granny right now not to buy you that ice-cream.'

'I don't want ice-cream,' sobbed her daughter. 'There's only vanilla and I wanted strawberry and—'

'I want never gets,' retorted Helen, using a phrase she had hated as a child, and gazing over the heads of the other onlookers for any sign of her parents, who had disappeared many minutes before on a mission to locate both lavatories and the ice-cream van they had passed while trying to find somewhere to park. Clearly uncomfortable in the heat, her father, purple-faced under an ancient floppy cricket hat, and her mother, sheltering beneath a moth-eaten straw boater, had leapt at the chance of tottering off in the direction of shade. Helen had invited them at the last minute, inspired to do so by

Pamela and John announcing that they couldn't come after all because of the unfolding crisis concerning Elizabeth. Colin, it transpired, had been having an affair with his fellow deputy head. Instead of sorting it out, Elizabeth had bolted back to Ashley House with Roland and a suitcase of clothes. At least, that was how Peter had relayed the news to her, coming off the phone to his parents mid-week, his eyes rolling with despair at this new turn in the hopelessly shambolic life of his sister. Of course it was dreadful of Colin – despicable, in fact – but any other woman (and this was a view clearly shared by Peter's parents) would surely have stuck around a bit longer to try to sort something out. Mistakes were made in marriages, Peter had thundered, but they didn't necessarily have to be fatal. When Helen phoned Pamela the next day, she had gathered that they were being as supportive as they could of Elizabeth, but remained concerned that the situation should not be allowed to spiral beyond retrievability, and that Roland had been plucked out of school mid-term without any understanding of what was going on.

'Poor Elizabeth,' Helen had ventured.

'Yes, indeed,' her mother-in-law countered, 'poor indeed – and we all feel for her – but nothing has ever been solved in this life by running away, has it? And poor Roland doesn't know if it's Christmas or Easter. Luckily, little Jessica is coming to stay with Sid this weekend, so at least he'll have someone to play with. But the fact remains that sooner or later Elizabeth has got to return to Guildford to face the music. Colin has phoned many times but she won't even speak to him.'

Remembering the conversation now, Helen felt a fresh stab of sympathy for her hapless sister-in-law. She had never warmed to Colin and had noticed how Elizabeth flapped around him during their visits to Ashley House, perpetually anxious about his mental well-being, clearly believing it to be a matter for which she should take full responsibility. The effect of having her anxious attentions rewarded by betrayal was something Helen could hardly bring herself to contemplate. Yet there was also something of the victim in Elizabeth, lumbering and fretting through life, which qualified any sympathy one might feel for her. Almost as if she brought things upon herself, as if she *expected* things to go wrong and thereby, subtly, connived in her own misfortune.

The race still wasn't under way and the sun was growing more ferocious by the minute. Helen could feel it searing into her neck and shoulders, soldering her sleeveless shirt to her bare skin. She wasn't good in heat. No matter how much sun-protection she used or extra fluid she drank, it made her listless and cross. It didn't help that she had been fighting a bad headache all week, one that had proved impervious to analgesics and to the wonderful stock of homeopathic alternatives Kay had given her. Kay herself was on a week's holiday in France, and Helen missed her. Chloë, meanwhile, with a child's razor sense of the vulnerable, had chosen the last few days to be even more difficult than usual, in spite of the treat of having Toffee lodging on the kitchen floor.

'A bit more of this, I think, Chloë. Look, I'm having some too.' She squeezed a generous blob of suncream on to her fingertips and massaged it into her arms and face. 'Your turn now.'

'No.'

'Chloë, don't be silly. You'll get burnt and sore.' Helen checked quickly that nothing was happening on the river and approached her daughter with the tube. 'Just a little, on the back of your neck and legs.'

'No,' Chloë shrieked, hitting out with her arms. Helen struggled with her, smearing cream on bits of leg, but misdirecting most of it on to her daughter's clothes and Toffee, who was springing round them, barking to join in the new game. They were saved by the arrival of grandparents and ice-cream, which in spite of being half melted and vanilla-flavoured brought both co-operation and peace. It was only as Helen was rubbing the last of the sunblock into Chloë's nose that a roar of applause from the riverbank alerted her to the fact that she had missed the race. Theo's boat had won. She stood up just in time to see Peter charging along the towpath to congratulate him, sunglasses bouncing on his nose.

Perched on a rock holding a string baited with a beef scrap from his sandwich, Ed could not remember when he had last been so happy.

It was hot. It was the weekend. His exams were over. Everything was cool, including – and especially – his father, who had turfed them all out of the house into the car with the announcement that they were going to spend the afternoon at the seaside. The journey had been a pain, the beach was made up of pebbles that were agony to walk on (the girls had made a real fuss hobbling into the sea), the water was icy and there was almost certainly not one fish daft enough to close its mouth round a scrap of soggy beef, but to Ed none of this mattered. Watching his string being tugged by the little waves, a tiny part of him hoping (in spite of everything) that it would suddenly go taut with some huge Moby Dick of a catch, he felt as if the world had righted itself. Almost as if the summer holidays had started, bringing that delicious buzzy feeling they always brought, as if a ton of good and wonderful things were just round the corner.

'Ed's cheerful.'

'Yes.'

'And the girls, they're happy too – and getting on so well at the moment, it's brilliant.'

'Yes, everyone's cheerful. Except me, right?' Serena threw another pebble into a small pile she had been building next to the picnic blanket. 'Sorry I didn't swim – I just couldn't face it.'

'That's okay,' murmured Charlie, who had been disappointed at his wife's refusal to join in the expedition (a long one because the tide was out) to the water's edge. She needn't have shrieked with glee – or pain – or even swum. But she should have come. To show willing. To show that she was prepared at least to *try*. Then they would all have known that she wanted to join in even if a part of her still couldn't. Instead, she had sat huddled in towels watching them with the hair blowing across her face, her bones like marble, her big blue eyes filled with distance. 'Clem is still far too thin.'

'I know.' They turned to look at the twins, lying side by side on their tummies with magazines on a patch of scrubby grass between the beach and the car park, having complained that any sort of comfortable sitting was impossible on the stones. 'Don't look at me like that.'

'Like what?'

Serena threw another stone. 'Like it's all my fault.'

'Of course it's not your fault,' began Charlie, exasperated.

'I've talked to her, several times, and she is eating more – much more. I've spoken to the school and they say she is definitely going to lunch every day. Short of force-feeding her I really don't see what else I can do . . .'

'Serena, I'm not blaming you. I'm just saying I'm still worried.' Charlie rolled over on to his side, wincing as a sharp stone cut into his hip. 'Darling . . .' He laid a hand on her forearm, pressing his fingers into her cold skin. 'I want to take care of what we have left, that's all.'

He had meant only to be kind, to express how much he wanted both of them still to treasure their family – beaten up and damaged as it was – but Serena sprang to her feet. 'I don't need that, okay? As if we didn't take care of what we had before – I really don't need it.' Her hands were in fists and her hair stuck across her mouth. 'And by the way, did you say something to Cassie? About working with her? Did you? Because at first she said no and then, all of a sudden, she phones up and says yes, as if something – or someone – had made her change her mind. Did you?'

Charlie squinted at the sea, which was now edging inshore, eating up the rock pools and muddy flats. It looked choppy and grey as it always seemed to in England, no matter how blue the sky. Two seagulls were playing tag overhead, swooping and hovering, their blinking black eyes alert for scraps of picnic. 'Does it matter if I did?'

'Yes, it does. It matters very much.' Serena was standing between their towels looking down at him, her hands on her hips. Her feet, pink from the sun, looked uneven and uncomfortable on the pebbles. 'I don't want charity, Charlie.'

'You don't want help, you mean,' he muttered, rolling away from her, inexplicably moved by the sight of her sore feet.

'What did you say?'

'Help,' he snapped. 'I said you didn't want help. Which is quite a different thing.' He turned back to find that she was walking away

from him, arms out to balance herself as she picked her way towards
the sea. 'Serena,' he shouted, but his voice was lost in the wind and
she didn't turn.

'They're not getting on, are they?'

'Who?' murmured Clem, though she knew perfectly well.

'Mum and Dad. They were arguing and now Mum's stormed
off.'

'So? Married people always argue.' Clem kept her eyes on her
magazine. The pages were flapping in the wind like a trapped bird.
She had been so hot at home and then in the car, but the moment
they had arrived at the beach there was such a strong breeze that she
had felt all goose-pimply and totally not in the mood to swim. She
had gone in to please her father, who was trying to be jolly for all of
them, and because Maisie, in spite of having her period, had been
typically determined that it shouldn't hold her back. Watching her
sister plunge into the waves, Clem had felt a mixture of admiration
at her bravery and relief that her own boldness had only to
encompass inuring herself to the numbing grip of the sea. Though
she had been the first to start menstruating, it was months now since
she had seen any sign of her own blood. She knew this should
probably be a cause for concern. Yet it was hard to mind, hard to
miss the deep aches in the pit of her stomach and the horrible warm
rush between her legs.

'Do you think they'll get divorced? Like Aunt Elizabeth and
Uncle Colin.'

'Don't be stupid. And, anyway, Aunt Elizabeth's not getting
divorced – not necessarily. A trial separation, Dad said. A cooling-
off period.'

'That's what people always say, just so it doesn't sound so bad.
And then, after a bit, they get divorced anyway. Aunt Elizabeth's
already done it once, hasn't she? I wonder if it's easier the second
time.' Maisie frowned, turning the pages of her own magazine,
which was full of stories of on-off liaisons between famous people. 'I
mean, maybe it doesn't feel such a big deal the next time.'

'I think it must feel even worse – getting everything wrong *again*.'

'I guess.' The two girls read on for a few more minutes, silent apart from the smack of their chewing-gum. 'Poor Roland, though,' added Maisie. 'Can't be much fun for him. And he was sort of getting better too, wasn't he? Not nearly such a drip. Even Ed thought so—' She stopped mid-sentence and thumped her sister across the back.

'Ow.'

'Oh, my God. OH – MY – GOD. Look . . . just look at this.' She sat up and thrust her magazine in front of Clem. 'Look at him, the minging bastard . . . LOOK.'

'I'm trying to – get off – I can't see.' Clem elbowed her sister's arm out of the way to reveal a large colour picture of a smiling, well-groomed Neil Rosco:

ROCK STAR SPEAKS OUT
AGAINST DRUGS

> Chart-topper and heart-stopper Neil Rosco this week opened a new wing in the Kyle Young Offenders institution in south-east London where he spoke inspirationally about the dangers of substance abuse. 'I know what it's like to come from a tough background,' the star said, 'and how drugs can seem to offer a quick-fix escape. If I hadn't had my music I could well have ended up in a place like this. But there are other ways out,' he told the youngsters, 'like just getting a decent job and trying to be a decent person. No one needs drugs to be cool.' After a tour of the premises Rosco signed autographs and then sang the title song from his new album *Dead Geraniums*, before returning to his penthouse home on the Chelsea Embankment.

Maisie slapped the page in disgust. 'What a fucking hypocrite.'

'Oh, Dad'll hear.'

'I don't care. It makes me sick, acting like he's such a great do-gooder, when he probably takes drugs all the time. They were all on something at that party, their eyes were staring, just like they said in that drugs lecture at school, and one of those women asked for another line – of cocaine, obviously – and he said not now—'

'Oh, so what?' snapped her sister. 'It's over, Maisie, just forget it. The guy's a fraud and his music's crap and he'll probably kill himself with an overdose or something anyway one day. Who cares?' Clem sounded much more dismissive than she felt. It always alarmed her when the Rosco business came up, partly because Maisie got so feverishly agitated and partly because, instead of dissipating with time, her own fears about the incident had some-how ballooned. It was both confusing and odd to feel afraid of something that was over – particularly something so horrible. Maisie was safe – she had saved her. And yet every time Clem thought about it now – the surreal scene with the steam rising off the turquoise water, the night sky, the sunbeds and Rosco's hairy backside pumping, crushing her sister – she felt giddy with new terrors. Her own bravery no longer offered any reassurance. It had just been a fluke, nothing that could be relied upon. Nor did the fact that they had coped with and accommodated the episode on their own. As each day passed it felt as if the ordeal wasn't over and that it involved her just as much as her sister.

Maisie was now thumbing back through the magazine, chewing furiously on her gum. 'Who wrote this thing anyway? Because I am going to write to him.'

'Who?'

'The journalist, that's who.'

'Don't be silly.'

'I'm not. I'm going to write to him and tell him what Rosco is really like. Look here's the name. L. J. Cartwright.'

'Maisie, you can't do that,' whispered Clem, tugging feebly at the magazine. 'It wouldn't do any good.'

'Oh, yes, it would.' Maisie clasped the pages protectively to her chest. 'It would make me feel better. Are you going to help or not? You're good with words – better than me.'

'Of course I'll help,' murmured Clem. They were sitting up now, side by side. Their father had left his towel and joined Ed on the big rock next to the breakwater. They had given up fiddling with his lunatic string of a fishing-rod and were spinning stones into the sea, making them hop along the steely surface of the water. A few yards further on their mother was still picking her way across the beach, pausing every so often to stare at the horizon, scanning it from side to side as if it contained something she had forgotten or lost. 'But I think a phone-call might be better – it would be more anonymous, less likely to get us into any sort of trouble.'

'Clem, you're a genius. That's exactly right. We'll phone the magazine, get the journalist's number, then call him and – and just tell him what we know.'

Which wasn't very much, thought Clem, but did not say so because Maisie was looking so elated. Though what, after all, would be the harm? she consoled herself. It seemed highly doubtful that this L. J. Cartwright would want – or be able – to use anything they had to say, particularly if they refused to give their names and had only suspicions to offer instead of hard facts. Just going through the motions might make Maisie feel she had got the revenge she was after. It might also, Clem decided, pondering these possibilities, go some way towards helping her to lay the episode to rest. 'Not now, though,' she said hurriedly, frightened that Maisie might race at that very moment for her mobile phone. 'We should do it from a phone-box. Oh, but look, Dad's coming over.'

Charlie was indeed lumbering towards them, with Ed in rather more nimble pursuit behind. 'Ice-creams,' he called, smiling and waving a ten-pound note. 'What are your orders, girls?'

'You better bloody have one,' hissed Maisie, smiling and waving back.

'Of course,' retorted Clem, getting to her feet and quickly wrapping her towel round as much as she could of herself. She knew they all thought she was thin. She knew, too, that her costume hung in little loose wrinkles while Maisie's was stretched tight across her hips and the now quite sizeable mounds of her breasts. What was also true – but impossible to explain – was that whereas Maisie somehow looked okay, Clem knew full well that she didn't.

Her hips were so wide and ungainly, while her thighs, half hidden under the towel, were huge white planks that she would happily have trimmed with scissors if she could. 'I'll have a ninety-nine, please, Dad,' she announced, spotting in the same instant a painted arrow on the edge of the dunes saying, 'Toilets'. It was a splintered, rickety sign, but at the sight of it Clem felt a rush of something like love. She was in control, after all. She could eat the ice-cream without fear. And when she sprinted across the dunes afterwards, in the direction indicated by the arrow, Maisie would say nothing, first because she understood and also because of how co-operative Clem was being about the journalist. 'With two Flakes, if that's okay?'

'It certainly is, sweetheart,' agreed Charlie happily. 'And we'll get the same for Mum, shall we?' They all turned to look at Serena, a speck now beyond the next breakwater, her towel billowing like a cloak in the onshore breeze. 'She'll feel left out otherwise, won't she?'

'Right,' the children chorused, forced by the determination in his voice to collude in this happy half-truth, wanting to protect him as much as themselves.

JULY

Elizabeth sat on a bench near the cathedral to eat her croissant, which was thick and greasy and splurging with spinach and cheese. Tourists and foreign students swarmed on all sides of her, posing for pictures in front of the cathedral's solid square walls and the rather more easily photographed poultry cross, which sat in the middle of the pedestrianised cobblestones a few yards to her left. These landmarks were at the intersection of Chichester's four main streets – called, in recognition of this, North, South, East and West Street. She was at the geographical and emotional heart of the city; the central point of the compass. Elizabeth pondered the wooden signpost advertising this fact, and wondered that she could be at such a focal point on the planet and yet feel so lost herself.

She ate slowly, savouring the heavy pastry, feeling a dim comfort at the way it filled her stomach. She had walked past the bakery several times, resisting the smells, telling herself that the last thing she needed was a mid-morning snack, but then thinking, Why not? Why the hell not? Given her current circumstances, battling with her weight seemed futile. She could swell to the size of a small cottage and it wouldn't matter. Roland would still love her; and Colin, whose dry little quips on the subject had sometimes inspired bouts of intense calorie-deprivation, was no longer someone she had to worry about. It was perhaps for similar reasons that, before entering the bakery, she had gone into a shoeshop and bought a pair of yellow trainers with two-inch-thick heels. They did not look very elegant, particularly with the wide green cotton skirt she was wearing, but they had air-holes and felt springy and comfortable, even in the heat.

Having finished the croissant, Elizabeth picked the flakes of pastry off her shirt-front, delaying to the last second her return to the hot car and the thirty-minute drive back to Ashley House. She hated being there – partly because it was a limbo, decision-delaying existence, but mostly because it made her ashamed. Yet again, she had lived *down* to expectation. A grown woman with a son, she had been able to think of no more inspired solution to her marital crisis than to scuttle back to the family home like a beaten dog. Tiptoeing round Colin at five o'clock in the morning three weeks before, almost choking with terror as she cajoled Roland, sleepy and bemused, out of his pyjamas, there hadn't seemed a huge range of alternative options. A hotel would have felt desolate, temporary, not to mention being expensive. Finding a house to rent would take time. Of her few local friends there were none she knew well enough either to confide in or to ask for the loan of a spare bedroom. Which left Ashley House as the only possible refuge; the lesser of all evils.

Her parents were ashamed of her too. They hadn't said anything, of course, not outright. On the surface there had been nothing but kindness – tuts of understanding, fresh sheets on the beds, cups of tea and sympathy – but as the days slipped by (where had the three weeks gone?) Elizabeth sensed, increasingly, the heaving sea of disappointment behind the displays of support. While her father coped by making tactical withdrawals from conversations and rooms at every opportunity, her mother's impatience with the situation had begun to sound like the tick of an invisible clock, pulsing in every word she uttered, every meal she cooked, every suggestion she made about Roland, Resolution and Compromise. To Pamela the circumstances were simple: Colin had strayed and needed forgiving. She knew, because Elizabeth had told her, that he had said sorry, both to her face and in a long rambling letter that had dropped on to the doormat of Ashley House shortly after her arrival. They were bigger than what had happened, he said, and would survive. Elizabeth, however, did not feel bigger than what had happened, she felt very small, so small that if she went back to Guildford she knew she would be swallowed by the force of everyone's willpower but her own.

It had taken every ounce of courage to walk out. When she had confronted him, Colin had had the grace to be honest and penitent, but also aggressive. It was just one of those things that happened, he said. It was over already and meant nothing. When Elizabeth suggested he might consider moving out he had laughed in disbelief, telling her she was overreacting and that every marriage in the world had to take a few knocks along the way. He loved her and was sorry. He knew that, deep in her heart, she still loved him too. He was glad she had found out. He had been going to end it anyway. He wanted to make amends, to take care of her, to give Roland the childhood he deserved. By the end of this and many subsequent conversations Elizabeth had felt as if she was being the unreasonable one, that it was *her* lack of commitment that was jeopardising the stability of the marriage and – worst of all – the well-being of their son. Trapped thus by her conscience, it had been several days into the ordeal when, making a cup of tea one sleepless night, she had seen the car keys on the hook behind the kettle and realised suddenly that escape, in purely physical terms, was possible. It was like a door sliding open, a glimpse of a pathway out of the maze, but one, she knew, that would slide shut the moment the morning arrived, bringing with it the sanity of ordinary life, its easy routines – breakfast, work, school, tidying, cooking – and Colin overpowering her with his penitence, using it to make her own doubts feel treacherous. He was still doing it now, bombarding Ashley House with phone-calls and messages, trying in every way to persuade her of her unreasonableness in not agreeing to return. And maybe she was being unreasonable, Elizabeth reflected bleakly, brushing the last of the crumbs off her green skirt and heading reluctantly towards the car park. Clearly her mother thought so. Just that morning, after Roland had dashed off to find Jessica and John had shuffled outside to monitor (as he did each day) the progress on the roof, she had turned to Elizabeth with a look of exasperation. 'You should at least talk to him.'

Elizabeth, stacking breakfast things, had shaken her head.

'How can you sort this mess out if you won't even talk?'

'He . . . muddles me . . . muddles what I feel.'

'And there's Roland.'

'I *know* there's Roland, Mother, believe me, I know that.'

'I'm only saying—'

'I realise it's difficult having me here.' At that instant, as she stacked the dishwasher in the way her mother liked it, with the cups at least two inches apart instead of slotted cheek to handle as she did with her own machine, Elizabeth had conceived the idea of going to Chichester. Anything to get away. Time and space to think. Plans kept skidding into her brain and out again. What to do about her job (the head, presented with a vague story about a family crisis, was assuming she would return in September); what to do about Roland, running wild every weekend with the dreadful Jessica; what to do, in fact, about her life.

'It's not that, darling,' purred her mother at once, 'you can stay as long as you like, you know that. Your father and I would never dream of turning you out. It's just that . . . well, marriages need working at sometimes.'

'Thanks, Mum, I know that too.' In the process of shutting the dishwasher, Elizabeth, had momentarily closed her eyes. As ever, she was aware that her mother's soothing tone belied the steeliness of her true opinions: namely, that her elder daughter was weak, gave up on things, made bad choices, bad decisions. If such criticisms had been dealt out directly Elizabeth was sure she could have defended herself against them. But with Pamela any negative feelings – anger, reprobation, disapproval – were always couched in kindness, dressed up, *disguised*, so there was nothing to strike back at except air and a smile. 'I have to go out,' she had said, spinning the dial of the dishwasher, 'to Chichester . . . to get some things. Do you need anything?'

There was a little intake of breath before Pamela answered, as if she was swallowing the exasperation. 'That's a kind thought . . . Cream – double cream for strawberries. The more Sid and I pick them the faster they seem to ripen. And Roland does love them so, doesn't he?'

'Oh, yes . . . yes, he does.'

Remembering the conversation now, Elizabeth slapped the

steering-wheel. After all that, she had forgotten the cream. The one thing she was charged to buy and she had forgotten it. And now there was no time left on her parking ticket. And no change in her purse to purchase another. Which meant she'd have to chance her luck at one of the village stores *en route* home, where they'd probably have clotted or single or long-life or sour or none at all. The problem bulged uncontrollably in Elizabeth's mind, merging with all her other worries until it seemed as tumultuous as leaving Colin and the guilt she felt about the upheaval for their son. It would be easier to go back to Guildford, she decided miserably, to play the bruised wife, let Colin resume control. The unhappiness of such a prospect was at least familiar; a far less daunting proposition than this new and terrifying course on which she had set herself, where she continued to disappoint everyone and was paralysed into inaction by the weight of choice and responsibility. She simply wasn't brave or strong enough to see it through. She might have broken away but she had no long-term vision of how to make herself or Roland happy. It could only result in more failure, yet worse on every front because she would be facing it alone.

When Roland heard Jessica shouting for him he didn't move. He was lying on his tummy with his head sticking out of the flaps of the tent his grandfather had put up on the lawn in front of the cloisters. A butterfly was perched on a blade of grass about two inches from his nose. Its wings were a brilliant orange engraved with tiny intricate patterns of blue, black and white, each one identical, as if they had been pressed together to make a mirror image of the design. He had made paintings like that at school, but they had smudged when he pressed the paper down, whereas these wings were as clear as anything, like they'd been drawn with the tiniest tip of a felt pen, and sort of shiny and dusty at the same time. He wanted very badly to touch the colours, to see if they felt as soft as they looked, but feared his own clumsiness. As it was, the butterfly was trembling, as if it was afraid and might fly away at any moment. If he shouted back at Jessica he was sure it would.

'There you are,' exclaimed Jessica crossly, jumping out of the cloisters and skipping towards him with an impatient toss of her bushy hair.

'Hang on.' Roland held up his hand, but it was too late: the butterfly had taken off and was already a black speck in the sky.

'What's this?' Jessica twanged one of the guy-ropes.

'A tent, stupid. It was my Great-uncle Eric's when he went on his expeditions. Granddad says I can sleep in it tonight if I want.'

Jessica's eyes widened. 'Blimey, won't you be scared?'

'Nope,' said Roland, even though he knew he would be terrified. Fortunately his grandfather had delivered the suggestion with so many conditions attached – about the weather, being good and securing the agreement of his mother and grandmother – that he was pretty sure it wouldn't happen anyway. 'Come in, if you like. We could play a game.'

'What sort of game?' Jessica lifted the flap to peer inside, her voice breathy with new respect for her companion, whom she had always regarded as a fall-back solution to total boredom rather than a real friend. Her secret favourite of the Harrison gang was Ed because he wasn't remotely stuck-up like the rest of them could be and because he could do forty kick-ups with a football. But Ed wasn't coming till later in the summer, Sid had said, so she had to make do with what came along in the meantime.

Roland shrugged. He was still cross about the butterfly and not at all sure he wanted to share the tent with Jessica. When he couldn't find her after breakfast, he had felt a bit lonely until his grandfather unrolled the canvas and started banging pegs into the grass with a big wooden hammer. Roland had helped, his heart swelling with excitement as the saggy heap grew into a tight-roofed little house, complete with plastic windows and a zip for sealing the entrance. The moment it was finished he burrowed inside, not minding the heat or the weird, stuffy mackintosh smell. It was a TV room of his own, somewhere safe but also tremendously exciting. After a while he went to fetch his drawing things and stacked them neatly in one corner, next to the bottle of water his grandmother had given him. He had to drink it all by lunch, she said, or he'd get one of his headaches because it was so hot. Roland didn't like water much so he'd only had a sip or two. He hadn't had a headache for ages. His tummy hurt a bit but that was because he was hungry. He was quite often hungry at the moment, even though he had seconds at practically every meal. His grandmother had said just that morning that if he kept it up he'd grow to be as tall as his grandfather, which was an impossible but rather thrilling idea, since his grandfather seemed like a towering mountain, so towering that Roland had twice seen him bang his forehead on the low beam in the kitchen. He had said rude words each time, like he had in the Easter holidays trying to fix the hinge on the music-room door. Then Roland had felt afraid, but now he didn't mind so much. Grown-ups, he realised, weren't nearly so in charge as they pretended to be. Not even his parents, who, after two days and nights of terrible arguing, were *taking a break*. Roland knew that behind his mother's brief explanation lurked all sorts of unseen terrors; being allowed to miss school – not to mention their leaving home when it was dark and with his dad still asleep – made it impossible to think otherwise. But he also knew that it was lovely to wake in the night with only the hoot of an owl or the faint rumble of his grandfather's snoring to listen out for instead of harsh voices, the slam of a door and his mother's muffled sobbing. The shadow of adult unhappiness was still there, but at least this time Roland knew – thanks to overheard comments and occasional oblique references from Elizabeth – that it had nothing to do with his crying or bed-wetting or bouncing on the spare bed or getting his spellings wrong. It was because of his father's friend. The woman in the long purple dress. It was all to do with her. And if this meant that his father didn't love his mother enough then that wasn't very nice, but yet sort of okay because Roland felt more than up to the job of compensating for it. Loving his mother was something he found easy, the easiest thing in the world. He could do it non-stop, for ever, without even trying. Just as he knew she loved him, no matter how much she snapped or smouldered or sobbed. He knew it like he knew his own name.

'We could play showing each other our *things*.'

'I don't think I want to play that.' Roland blushed furiously, all curiosity at the notion quashed by alarm at the sly look on Jessica's pixie face. She could be fun to play with, he knew that now, but he knew also that she didn't *feel* things in the same way he did. She never said quite what he expected and was always laughing without him fully understanding why.

Jessica had her hands in her pockets and was flapping the legs of her voluminous pink shorts. 'No one would see in here.'

'I think it sounds a stupid game.'

'Well, what ideas have you got then, scaredy-cat?'

'I'm not scared I just think it's stupid. I know –' Roland seized his pad '– I'll draw you, if you like. I was going to draw a butterfly but it flew away.'

'Draw me?' Jessica looked uncertain.

'You'd have to sit very still.'

'That's *easy*.' She folded her arms and pouted. 'See? I'm not moving, am I?'

'It's so hot, let's go outside.'

They were scrambling out of the tent when Elizabeth appeared. Roland ran and put his arms round her waist, closing his eyes while she stroked the back of his head where it felt nice and tickly.

'Hello, my darling, are you having a lovely time?'

Looking down, he saw her new trainers. 'Those are nice shoes.'

'Do you like them?' Elizabeth shuffled her feet, pleased in spite of herself.

'Are you going to draw me or what?' They both turned to look at Jessica who was busy practising poses between the scaffolding poles now skirting the house.

Roland let go of his mother, grinning. 'I'm going to do a picture of Jessica.'

'That's a good idea . . . Darling . . . I was thinking we – we could go home soon, if you like.'

Roland looked up at her blinking furiously. 'I don't want to go home.'

'Don't you?' Elizabeth whispered hopefully, appalled at her own desperation.

'I like it here. Let's stay, Mummy.' Roland turned and raced towards the cloisters, the pages of his drawing pad flapping under his arm.

'Okay, we'll stay a bit longer, then,' she called after him, her voice hoarse, then trudged back to the front door, the bag containing a pot of long-life cream banging against her leg.

Cassie didn't realise how hot it was until she ventured out to gather all the unfiled papers strewn around in the boot of her car. As she crossed the street the Tarmac felt soft and warm under the thin soles of her sandals. The air was as dry as sandpaper and smelt faintly stale, as if all the odours of city life, normally dispersed by brisk breezes and showers, were suspended within it. Cassie liked the heat, but this was getting to be too much. It hadn't rained for weeks. In the little park opposite the grass was withered and brown, the flowerbeds like cracked pavements. The car was so hot that when she touched its metal surface with her knuckles as she turned the key she winced.

The papers, left unattended for so long, were smeared and curling at the edges, and somehow thicker too, so that it took several minutes to marshal them into a manageable pile. Cassie shied away from filing at the best of times, but in recent months things had got out of control, with the back seat of the car acting as the prime repository for all the invoices, quotes and correspondence that wouldn't fit into her briefcase. She would probably have left things that way, too, if it hadn't been for Serena, due that morning for a trial run at being some sort of secretarial assistant. Charlie's plea in June had been followed by a sweet, beseeching letter: 'I know it's a tall order, Cass, but Serena is too proud to ask you again herself and I am so worried about her being on her own all day every day . . .' Cassie had phoned Serena on the spot, beating all her sister-in-law's protestations into an agreement that she would come over to do a couple of sessions of phoning and filing during the last week of the summer term. Upbeat during the conversation, she had put down the receiver with a feeling of gloom.

Charlie's irrepressible concern for the welfare of his wife, while admirable, only made her more aware than ever of the gaping hole in her own personal life. She would have given anything to experience such a mutually supportive partnership, even – she decided bitterly – one highlighted, as Charlie and Serena's had been, by tragedy. Her life seemed so empty in comparison. With neither her mother's ugly secret nor Stephen Smith to worry about (he hadn't phoned since the toe-curling awkwardness of their last meeting), there was nothing to focus on but Dan. Or, rather, the lack of him. Cassie knew there wasn't supposed to be just one Mr Perfect on the planet, that circumstance and mind-set meant that hundreds of possible partners lurked in the shadows of every human life, but sifting, as she often did, through mementoes and memories of their time together, remembering his tenderness and his promises, she could feel neither conviction nor consolation in the thesis. He was the man for her and she had lost him, not to something inarguable and easy like death but to a parallel life just across the river with a woman he did not love. Such thoughts still plagued her all the time, although they were no longer over-shadowed by leanings towards self-annihilation. She might sniff Dan's aftershave, still on the top shelf of her bathroom cabinet, like a starving beast, but her hand never hovered with malign intent over the scissors. Occasionally she studied the small silvery scars on her left wrist, but felt no temptation, even in her darkest moments, to reopen them. This was good, she knew. Progress of some kind. Even if it did not stem from acceptance or any noble burying of her desires.

'Cassie?'

'Serena.'

'I'm early, I'm sorry.'

'Don't be, that's fine. No problem.' Cassie, clutching the papers to her chest, slammed the car door and kissed her sister-in-law, inwardly marvelling that one who had suffered so much could still look so good. She wore no makeup and was dressed entirely in white – a long loose shirt hanging almost to the knees of baggy thin-cotton trousers, with very worn-looking beige espadrilles on her feet. There was a new, chiselled gauntness to her face, but this only served to highlight her wide sandy-lashed eyes and the fullness of her mouth. Her chestnut hair straggled attractively from three simple white combs, the strands curling round the pearl studs in her ears. 'How are you?'

'Fine.' Serena folded her arms, then quickly unfolded them again. 'Can I help with anything?'

'Oh, no, it's quite all right.' As Cassie delivered this assurance three or four pieces of paper broke free of the bundle and floated to the pavement. Both women bent down at once to gather them up, elbows clashing, eyes too close for comfort. Serena was quicker.

'Oh, look,' she exclaimed, reaching for the fourth and last sheet, which had caught under the wheel, 'someone's written your name.'

'What?'

'In the bit of dry mud here.' She pointed to a spot on the car just above the mud guard. 'Obviously with a stick or something. It's very clear.'

Cassie crouched next to her. 'Oh, yes, so they have.' She stood up again, her heart racing with a mad, wild thought. 'Shall we go inside? I feel as if I'm being gently boiled out here.'

'But what a funny thing to do – I mean, who would do that?' Serena hurried to catch up with Cassie, who was already crossing the road.

'God knows – one of the children, I expect.' As Cassie offered the explanation she realised, her spirits nose-diving, that this was almost certainly true. The wild thought – that Dan had been trying to make contact – fizzled and died.

'Which children?'

Cassie sighed. 'At Ashley House. I was there last weekend. Roland was too because of . . .'

'Yes, I know – the business with Elizabeth and Colin. Terrible.' Serena spoke with genuine feeling. The downturn in Charlie's elder sister's life had touched her deeply, the first thing in many months to do so. She added, in a murmur, 'When sorrows come, they come not single spies but in battalions.'

'Sorry?'

'Nothing . . . just a . . . Nothing. So, you think it was Roland?'

'And that little grandchild of Sid's, Jessica. They're inseparable at the moment, which is rather sweet if you think about it and just as well too – Roland would be so bored down there otherwise. He's such a sad little chap in many ways, don't you think? Goodness knows how he'll cope if Elizabeth doesn't patch things up with . . .' Cassie left the sentence hanging, patched-up marriages being a subject on which she had decidedly conflicting opinions. She hated whatever patching up Dan was managing with Sally and yet if her mother hadn't stayed with her father she wouldn't even exist. 'Here we are, anyway.' She pushed open the door of her flat and led the way inside, dropping the papers on to the hall table as she went. 'Now, what can I get you? Tea, coffee, orange juice?' She turned to see Serena standing stiffly in the middle of the sitting room, both hands clutching the shoulder-strap of her bag.

'Look, Cassie, can we get one thing straight? I know I'm here because Charlie—' Cassie tried to interrupt but she held up both hands, shaking her glossy hair and all the combs restraining it vigorously. 'This is my dearest husband's idea of therapy, which is very sweet but also ridiculous. It's important you know that I know that. It will save a lot of time and play-acting. I'm here to shut him up. You've allowed me to be here to shut him up. I'll gladly reshuffle your files, answer the phone and put the kettle on, but I've also brought a book to read.' She patted a bulge in her shoulder-bag. 'And I categorically refuse to accept a single penny in payment. Is that understood?'

'But I—'

'Is it understood, Cassie? Because if it isn't I'm walking out now and then we'll both have Charlie on our backs all over again.'

'But I can't have you working for nothing, I simply can't.' Cassie wrung her hands.

'Well, I won't work, then, I'll read,' retorted Serena, pulling a fat novel out of her bag and throwing herself into a chair. 'Please, don't make an issue out of this. We both know we're playing a game and it will be so much easier if we establish the rules up-front. The children break up next week, anyway, and by September Charlie will have got a new bee in his bonnet.'

'He only wants to—'

'To help. I know.' Serena sighed. 'I know he does, silly sod. He wants me to get *better*, like I'm ill or something. He thinks that one day things will go back to the way they were. A normal family, three children, not four, but otherwise *fine*.' Serena paused, close to tears suddenly, furious with herself for still having so little control and for having mentioned the one subject she had vowed to avoid. Cassie watched her sister-in-law in silence, noting the whites of her nails as she gripped the book and feeling helpless. She thought in the same instant, *At least Dan is alive*, which she knew was selfish, but consoling none the less. 'He's right about one thing,' continued Serena, with forced cheerfulness, 'it *is* nice to be out of the house. In one's own home it's simply impossible to ignore all the things that need doing, don't you find? Washing, ironing, tidying, it all sits there, doesn't it? Crying out for attention.'

'And what if I really do need help?' exclaimed Cassie. 'What then?'

'Then I will give it. Free of charge. Just ask.' And with that she slapped open her novel at the first page and began, pointedly, to read.

'Hold my hand to cross the road.'

'Only if Theo does.'

'Theo is older, he doesn't need to.'

'I don't need to.'

'Yes, Chloë, you do.' Helen seized her daughter's hand and stepped off the kerb, nodding gratitude at the taxi that slowed to let them pass. Chloë resisted, her hot little fingers sliding around inside her mother's. 'Chloë, honestly, come *on*.' Having made it safely to the other side, Helen rounded on her daughter. 'I will not have you behaving like this, do you understand? I will not have it. This is a busy street. Crossing roads is dangerous. Think of little Tina, for heaven's sake—' Helen broke off even before Chloë burst into tears. She had gone too far, of course. She was a terrible mother. As if to verify this, Theo had divorced himself from the scene, turning the uncannily Peter-like expression of steely resignation with which he had endured the morning's retail torture towards a display in a shop window.

Chloë, meanwhile, was weeping and thumping ineffectually at her mother's legs. 'I don't care about anything, I don't care about Tina.'

'Chloë darling, I'm sorry, I shouldn't have said that. Mummy is cross and hot. We're all cross and hot.' Helen bent down and managed, in spite of four shopping-bags and Chloë's not in-considerable weight, to lever her daughter on to her right hip. 'I know shopping is boring, but we've only a couple more things to get – shorts for Theo and a swimming costume for you. Remember? You wanted a pink one, like your friend Isobel, didn't you?' Shoppers in skimpy summer gear, their expressions inscrutable behind sunglasses, were streaming by on all sides, bulldozing unhelpfully into Helen's shoulders and laden bags. Chloë, squirm-ing, was oblivious to everything but her own misery. 'Maybe we could get new armbands too, so you can swim to the middle of the lake this summer with the big boys. How about that? Just a few more days and Mummy will have a whole week off work instead of just one day and we'll all be on holiday at Granny's having a lovely time.'

Helen knew she didn't sound convincing. She didn't feel con-vinced of anything except that she was at the end of her tether. It seemed incredible that shopping in the sales with the children on such a hot day was a plan she had actually conceived herself. A precious day off and she had voluntarily turned it into a nightmare. Chloë had her knees clamped round her waist but was still flinging her upper body from side to side. If she carried on Helen knew she would either overbalance or drop her. The dull headache with which she seemed to awaken most mornings now had worsened that day to a dizzying nausea. The heatwave didn't help, of course, but she was beginning to see that she couldn't continue to blame the weather for everything. Something sinister was at work in her system, she was sure of it. Kay had been murmuring about the virtues of HRT, but Helen was nursing the darker fear that instead of the natural inconvenience of the menopause she might be grappling with something infinitely less benign, like a brain tumour. The wife of a colleague at work had died of one just the year before: three months of bad headaches, followed by four weeks from diagnosis to death. Peter poohed-poohed such terrors when she voiced them, but he, too, was worried. So much so that, ranting about her prevarications on the matter, he had that very morning phoned the doctor on her behalf and arranged an appointment for the following week. 'Why you haven't done it yourself, I do not know,' he had growled. Helen had been unable to muster a response. Now, however, with Chloë's jigging knees pinching her hips and rivulets of sweat streaming from her armpits, she knew that the plain answer was that she was afraid. Perhaps because she was forty-seven, perhaps because of Tina, but death – disaster of every kind – felt so much closer these days, so much more *possible*. Acknowledging this fear in the packed swelter of the West End, Helen abandoned all hope of appeasing her daughter and burst into tears. Not the invisible, soundless tears so easily disguised during a sad film, or the ones she'd hidden behind a veil at the funeral of her niece, but huge, loud, hot, angry explosions, impossible to conceal from Chloë or anyone else.

Chloë stopped wriggling. 'Mummy, you're crying.'

'Yes,' sobbed Helen, 'silly Mummy.' She tried to keep her face averted, but Chloë, intrigued and concerned in equal measure, cupped both her hands round her jaw and swivelled her gaze to meet hers. 'Are you *really* sad, Mummy?'

'Just a bit.'

'And I've been naughty. Sorry, Mummy. Don't be so sad. Chloë loves you.'

'And Mummy loves Chloë,' Helen wailed, 'she loves her so much and she's so useless.'

Chloë looked appalled. 'You're not useless, you're lovely.'

'Mum?' Theo, recognising that, no matter how shaming, the situation warranted some direct intervention, had shuffled to her side. 'Are you okay?'

'Oh, yes, absolutely.' Helen was still crying but sort of half laughing too. Chloë was hugging her so hard that it hurt. Her shoulders ached from carrying her and her handbag and all the shopping, but she didn't mind. For those moments she felt as if she would never mind anything again. She had spent thirteen years believing that a truly good mother had at all times to remain in charge of situations and emotions, praising, scolding, organising, setting boundaries, that only by doing this could she present herself as a reliable source of wisdom and trust. It was nothing short of a revelation therefore to find that betraying all of these tenets – breaking down like a distraught teenager – had induced the most wonderful, ground-breakingly intimate exchange with her daughter that she had ever known. She had the sense to grasp that it wouldn't last, that probably that day – that very hour – Chloë would metamorphose back into a prickly, difficult seven-year-old requiring a firm parental hand and the patience of Job. But she also knew that something monumental had happened. Love – always there, but so often muffled by a million other things – had risen out of the crisis, and wrapped them in its arms. It would sink away again, of course, back into the invisibility prescribed by the mundane, but the joy – the exquisite relief – of having its presence reaffirmed, made Helen, in those few minutes on that stifling, head-pounding day, feel immortal.

'And now to John Lewis. Shorts and a pink bathing costume.' She set Chloë carefully down on the pavement. 'If I carry you a moment longer my arms will drop off. The shop will be lovely and cold, like a fridge. And after we've done the shopping we'll go to the café and have sticky buns instead of a proper lunch. Okay?'

Both children nodded and turned to follow her down the street. After a few yards Chloë trotted to catch up properly and then, without a word or look, took hold of Helen's hand.

Maisie settled down at the meeting point she had agreed with Clem just outside the school gates. She sat on her satchel with her sleeves rolled to her shoulders and her skirt hoicked up round her thighs to maximise the exposure of her bare skin to the sun. She was having a sort of unacknowledged sun-tan race with Monica, which, according to their watchstrap-mark comparisons that lunch-break, she was now winning by some considerable way. Monica had tried to be gracious about it, but she wasn't very good at being gracious and had soon resorted to bragging about the villa in Portugal where her family was due to spend three weeks of the summer holiday. Maisie, who knew that the only holiday destination on her own family's horizon was Ashley House where the lake was freezing even when the sun shone, had hurriedly changed the subject. She didn't feel nearly as keen on Monica these days. Everything between them had become a sort of competition. And she had been a real pain about the Rosco business, digging around for details, her eyes all narrowed and disbelieving, as if Maisie's refusal to go into exactly what had happened was an indication that Maisie was lying and hadn't met him at all.

Maisie didn't want to tell Monica what had happened. It would make it more real for one thing, instead of safely boxed away. For another she hated the thought of Monica's beady curiosity, her wide-eyed horror, her recognition – painful enough to Maisie – that she had brought the entire near-calamity upon herself. Clem knew and that was enough. Clem didn't judge and, most important of all, could be trusted.

'Sorry I'm late.' Clem hurried towards her sister, her satchel jigging on her back. 'I had a grade-five theory lesson and it ran over. I don't understand a word and we've got loads of practice papers for the holidays.' She looked for a moment as if she might burst into tears, but Maisie had the suspicion that it was because of anxiety at what they were about to do rather than anything connected to the theory of music. Clem was good at music, like she was good at most things.

'Take them to Ashley House,' she suggested, clambering to her feet and rolling down her sleeves, 'and get Aunt Elizabeth to help you.'

'Hey, that's not a bad idea.' Clem grinned.

'Ready?'

'I guess.' The grin faded.

'By the way,' ventured Maisie, as they set off down the street, 'you're getting quite thin, you know. I mean,' she rushed on, sensing her sister tense, 'I know it's what you wanted and that's great, but I think maybe you could sort of steady off now.'

'Steady off?' Clem trailed the back of her hand along a stretch of garden fencing.

Maisie frowned, searching in vain for a kind way of saying what she meant. 'All the puking, Clem, it's got to stop.'

'I don't always do it.'

'You do it a lot, though.'

'That's not always, then, is it?' She turned to her twin and stuck out her tongue.

'Mum and Dad are getting really worried – I heard them arguing about it.'

Clem shrugged. 'They're always arguing. And, anyway, I thought we had a deal.'

Maisie sighed. 'Yes, we do. And thank you for agreeing to do this, by the way,' she added, fearing that Clem might decide to punish her by backing out. 'I'll do all the talking, but I need you there for – for—'

'Moral support?'

'That's it. Moral support. Exactly.' Maisie slung one arm across Clem's shoulders to give her a half-hug of appreciation. As she did so she couldn't help noticing how hard she felt, how *bony*. It wasn't right. She knew it wasn't right. Everyone knew. Behind her back at school people were remarking on it. Today someone had referred to Clem as the Stick Insect. The remark, coming on a day when all sorts of things had gone wrong, had upset Maisie enormously. *Stick insect.* It was a horrible thing to say and came from a horrible girl too, a big-mouth with nothing good to offer about anyone. Maisie, fresh from being told by Jonny Cottrall that he didn't want to meet her any more – not for snogging, anyway – had leapt to her sister's defence and then been told off for talking by a teacher. The worst thing about the remark, she decided now, watching Clem stride a little ahead of her, was that it was so true. She was the thinnest girl in the year and yet she still didn't *believe* she looked good in anything. Even Maisie's most heart-felt encouragements about her appearance were dismissed out of hand. Yet telling her she was overdoing things never worked either. They were getting on so much better, these days, but each time Maisie broached that particular subject Clem clammed up and turned hostile.

'There it is.' Clem slowed her pace and groaned as the phone-box, jointly and carefully selected for being discreetly positioned but *en route* home, came into view. 'What are you going to say exactly?'

'God knows . . . Come *on.*' Maisie raced ahead into the phone-box, which was unoccupied, and pulled out her purse and cigarettes.

'You are absolutely *not* smoking in here,' wailed Clem, wedging herself in next to her. 'We'll reek and Mum will go mad.'

'I'll just hold one, then. It'll make me feel better.'

Clem giggled. 'You are so sad, do you know that?'

'Yes.' Maisie began to giggle too, mostly with nerves, and had to suck in her cheeks to compose herself. 'You do the money, okay?' Clem nodded, unzipped her purse-belt and scooped out a clutch of pound coins she had been accumulating specially. The more Maisie had gone on about the plan of phoning the journalist, the more her own apprehensions had increased. They risked exposing some foolhardy behaviour of their own, and for what? Mr Cartwright almost certainly had far bigger fish to fry. He would want evidence and dates and names, all of which they would be unable to provide. The whole exercise was doomed and pointless. And yet Clem had allowed all her common-sense arguments to be whittled into acquiescence. Maisie wanted to do it so badly. Even if it came to nothing, it would make her feel better, she said. Heaps better. And since Clem, even as a mere spectator, still felt sick at the recollection of the events of that night, she could only imagine how the memories made Maisie feel. They were twins, after all. They looked out for each other, felt things for each other, now more than ever. Of course she would help Maisie in any way she could. Clem reminded herself of these sentiments as, on her sister's instruction, she fed the first coin into the slot in the machine. She then watched with wide eyes as Maisie unfolded the torn segment of paper, which had lived in the bottom of her purse since their trip to the beach, and dialled the number of the magazine.

'Could I speak to Mr L. J. Cartwright please?' She made a face at Clem and drew an imaginary puff on her cigarette. 'Isn't he? Oh dear . . .'

'Home number,' hissed Clem, 'or mobile.' They had got this far and she wasn't going to give up now.

But Maisie, putting on the voice Serena used for dealing with unwanted tradesmen and incompetent sales staff, needed no assistance: 'I realise that, but I assure you Mr Cartwright would be extremely disappointed if you did not give me his number. It is *most* important that I speak to him this afternoon. I have vital information relating to some research he is carrying out. Tomorrow will be too late. It is *extremely* confidential.' In a matter of minutes Maisie was gesturing for a pen and scribbling a string of numbers on the lid of her cigarette packet. 'Home *and* mobile,' she shrieked, slamming the phone down and dropping her unlit cigarette in her exuberance. 'Which shall I . . .?' she began, before glancing over Clem's shoulder through the smeary glass and wailing, 'Oh, no, there's Ed.'

Emerging from a newsagent with a Snickers Bar and a football magazine, Ed was surprised to spy his sisters bursting out of a phone-box on the opposite side of the road. They both had mobiles, for one thing, even though Clem never used hers. And they were laughing and breathless, like – like they'd just done a prank call or something. He hurried across the street, calling their names. As he approached, however, he could tell they didn't really want him. They stopped laughing straight away and started asking him boring things about school and when he was going to get his results even though they knew jolly well that they were supposed to have arrived in the post that morning. People often remarked that it must be interesting to have twin sisters, but it wasn't at all. At best it was no big deal. At worst it was downright annoying, especially when they were getting on, as they had been for the past few weeks. Secret looks and closed doors. Ed had found himself almost longing for the next argument, when the pair of them would come in pursuit of his allegiance, treating him like an equal instead of an outsider to some exclusive girls' club. It had been so bad recently that he'd found

himself missing Tina in an entirely new way. Not because her dying
still made him feel guilty (which it had for a while) or because it had
mucked his mum up and made his dad all weird and serious, but
because of *her*, Tina herself. He told himself it was daft, a twelve-
year-old boy missing a one-year-old girl, even if she was his sister.
You couldn't really *know* a one-year-old, after all. But lately he had
started thinking how nice it would have been to have her there to
tickle and make faces at, recalling fondly all the noises she made
when she wanted his attention, the general distraction of her
company. He even missed all the things he had hated, like being
asked to hold her when he was busy, to entertain her when she was
bored, to do his special flying aeroplane trick with the last dollops of
her food – a skill he had many times regretted discovering since it
had so often delayed his own departure from the kitchen table. But
now, with Maisie and Clem so thick, school so dull (with the exams
done it seemed increasingly pointless going in at all) and his results
to worry about, Ed felt the gap in the family more keenly than ever.
It had made him wonder properly what it must be like for his
mother with the whole day to fill and no nappies to change or
mashed meals to prepare. It had made him understand why his
father had punched the air when she'd said she'd agreed to help
Aunt Cassie after all. Although everything had felt its usual dodgy
self at breakfast, it had made a nice change to have his mum dressed
and pretty at the table, instead of slumped in bed in her dressing-
gown, eyes closed pretending to be asleep when she wasn't.

'What were you doing in the phone-box?'

'Nothing, okay? Nothing.'

Clem recognised that being so hostile would only fuel Ed's
curiosity and nudged Maisie hard, adding, far more gently, that
they'd had to tell Monica something and Maisie's battery was flat.

'Yeah, right.' Ed stuffed the last third of his now melting Snickers
bar into his mouth. He didn't believe them and he felt left out,
but he didn't want to weaken his position by revealing that. They
walked the rest of the way home in silence and then waited, all three
bad-tempered in the belting heat of the covered porch, while Maisie
rummaged in her satchel for the house keys.

They had been inside for a good thirty seconds before Ed saw the letter lying on the floor between the skirting-board and the door-mat. It was a thick white envelope, addressed to him. He knew at once what it was, as did the girls, who exchanged looks and caught their breath, murmuring about waiting until their mother got in before opening it. 'If they've sent it to you, it must be good news,' announced Maisie, peering over his shoulder, torn between offering the right advice and a burning curiosity to know what was inside. Ed took the envelope up to his bedroom and closed the door. If he'd failed Kings Grove, he'd kill himself. But that would finish off his mother, he reflected bleakly, resolving that in the event of such bad news he would have to confine himself to packing his bags and leaving home. For a few moments he fantasised about presenting himself on the doorstep of the Arsenal Football Academy, boot-bag in hand, his pocket-money savings bulging in his back pocket. But then the reality of the thick white envelope got the better of him and he ripped his finger under the gummed seal of the flap.

> *Dear Edward,*
>
> *I am writing to inform you that the standard you achieved in your recent Common Entrance paper was sufficient for us to decide to offer you one of our three Prestwick Scholarships, which we award to boys of exceptional potential and ability. We shall of course notify your parents and headmaster . . .*

Ed read the letter once, then slowly laid it on the bed next to him. If someone had forewarned him of its contents he would have expected to find himself leaping round the room, shouting jubilation to his sisters and the rest of the world. He would do that, probably very soon. But for now, for these still, quiet, precious moments, the jubilation – the sheer relief – assailed him in a quite different way. He walked to the window – his legs like jelly – and looked down on the scrubby rectangle of the garden and the small metal goal against which he practised his penalties, its frame lopsided and dented from all the batterings of his near-misses. This is happiness, he thought. This is being happy. He thought of how pleased his parents would be and tears pricked his eyes. And then, just as suddenly, the tears had gone and his heart felt like an erupting bomb. 'Maisie! Clem!' He seized the letter off the bed and ran down the stairs, taking the steps three at a time and skidding on the mat in the hall.

The train was like a furnace, its small, high, rectangular windows open as far as they would go, mere vents for the warm air outside. Stephen shifted uncomfortably, aware of his jeans sticking to the back of his thighs and the prickle of heat on his stomach and arms. In South America he had got used to functioning in a humid swelter, but after almost a year in England his stamina for high temperatures had shrunk back to its original level. Looking out of the window as the train rolled through the industrial hinterland of the urban sprawl where he had spent his childhood, Stephen felt as if he had reverted to his former self in ways that went far deeper than heat-tolerance. He had been a sweating, pale-skinned boy and he was a sweating, pale-skinned man, a cauldron of disappointments, now returning to the place and memories he had spent two decades trying to leave behind. *So we beat on, boats against the current, borne back ceaselessly into the past.* He had always liked Scott Fitzgerald, particularly *The Great Gatsby*, finding solace in the glittering prose and the fact that wealthy, privileged lives could be as integrally ugly as those shackled by the more obvious limitations of poverty and abuse.

The train doors slid open with a hiss, a dark mouth opening on the past. Standing in a cluster with others preparing to disembark, Stephen found it hard to move. He did not know why he had come, other than because there was nothing else left to do. What he had imagined to be a new phase of his life looked now as if it had never started. The energy that had empowered him to write his book, so intertwined with the energy of his love for a relative of one of the protagonists, felt as distant as a dream. He had fallen, he realised now, not just for Cassie but for the whole sprawling, robust branching tree that was the Harrison clan, so blessed with all the things his own origins lacked – identity, pride, history, wealth, roots.

His decision to give up on it, accept that he would remain an outsider, the biographer of a tiny portion of it, had grown no easier to live with in the weeks since Cassie's disastrous visit to his flat. He had left the shards of the broken vase for days, stepping round them, needing to see the pieces of his dreams to prevent them re-forming in his mind. She did not love him. She loved someone else. The honesty of her rejection still turned like a knife in his heart. He had always known that love and hate were supposed to be either side of the same blade but had never before experienced it. He ached for what he could not have and in that aching felt a resentful loathing for the object of his desires. He had been a child with his nose pressed up against a shop window. Nothing more. It was time to move on. Again. The book was finished, a chapter in his life had closed.

Thanks to the delivery of the manuscript, he had a little money. He had made a start on the long-postponed project of a novel. His editor, on hearing the plan, had been almost encouraging – certainly more so than he had been at the idea of poetry. Stephen had started writing feverishly the moment their conversation ended, only to find himself on a fruitless quest to articulate his own misery. Storylines and characters shimmered out of reach. Swamped by hopelessness, his efforts were clumsy and undisciplined, spewing on to the screen like vomit. Other, nobler creatures might fashion and edify their suffering into art, but Stephen had had to accept, after four torturous weeks, that he could not. Instead he had slowly – unwillingly – hatched the plan of heading north.

It was years since he had been home. He knew that his sister, who had settled long ago in New Zealand, sent cards occasionally, a few scrawled sentences, but he had made no contact with his parents since he had left for Spain in his early twenties. Their issue of sorry little Christmas and birthday cards had dried up at some long-forgotten point during his time in the southern hemisphere. At the time he hadn't cared. That they had given up, too, made him feel both less guilty and more free of the grim eighteen years that had passed for an upbringing. And he was only going back now because . . . because . . . Stephen paused to get his bearings. The city centre was packed with people and full of buildings where he remembered gaps. The bus stops had changed too – numbers in different colours indicating routes he no longer recognised. He found the right one eventually, then cowered in a back seat, irrationally terrified that he would meet someone he knew.

The bus lumbered round a new one-way system, then took to the more familiar route through the suburbs. Stephen cowered less and looked out of the window more, torn between embracing and hating the familiarity of the streets – more traffic-lights and zebra crossings, more housing estates and different shop fronts, but essentially the same. He might not even ring the bell, he told himself, pausing at the end of his road, absorbing every forgotten detail of the physical terrain of his childhood: the low walls running along the front gardens, the two lines of different-coloured front doors, the stone lions on the doorstep outside number fifty-two, the heaving paving stones where the roots of a couple of healthy trees were still bursting out of the ground. It was peculiar to see again the geography of the street, to feel it merging with the emotional terrain, borne for two decades inside his head. He would just look at the door, he decided, tugging the peak of his baseball cap more firmly over his eyes and beginning slowly to walk. There was no need to do more. Maybe it would have changed colour. Maybe his parents had moved away or died. Maybe there was nothing to face after all. Maybe that was all he needed to know. But as he stood outside the little wrought-iron gate and the cracked stone path leading to the door, still brown, Stephen saw the curtains twitch in the front room and the blurred face of his mother – wider, saggier, white-haired but unmistakable – appeared at the window. There was perhaps a second or two when he could have run away. He wanted to very badly. Adrenaline flooded his system as it would that of an animal confronting mortal danger. His limbs felt both light and leaden. The curtain twitched again and his mother raised her hand. Stephen remained on the pavement, staring at the brown door, waiting for it to open.

'Theo, supper's ready, can you come down now, please?'

'Coming, Dad.' Theo carried on polishing the lens of his camera for several minutes, then set it carefully next to the rest of his equipment and his box of miniature film cassettes. He had been having a grand sort-out, inspired by several weeks' absence from his room and all the beloved objects it contained. At first, surprisingly, it had been something of a let-down to come home for the summer holidays. He had been looking forward to it so much, only to find himself thoroughly irritated by his little sister and the fact that everything was so exactly the *same*. Like he had changed and his family hadn't. There had been an initial fuss, his mother all misty-eyed, his father quizzing him about teachers and the end-of-year exams and Chloë showing him pirouettes and muddy paintings, but then they had all sunk back into being their usual predictable selves. After the buzz of life in his boarding-house and the thrill of winning both the history prize and his junior rowing colours, it had all seemed empty and thoroughly dull. On the shopping trip with his mother two days before he had felt that he might literally die of boredom – not to mention embarrassment at Chloë's tantrum and the cringe-worthy display of emotion that had ensued. The thought of it still made him shudder, as did the recollection of his mother's subsequent exuberance in the department store, waving ten pairs of horrible shorts at him, joking in a loud voice with the sales assistant about sizes and styles. But for some reason once they got home things had begun – and continued – to feel much more all right. Chloë had gone for a sleepover with a friend and his parents let him sit up with them eating takeaway pizza and watching a 15-rated sci-fi with quite a lot of sex and the most brilliant computer graphics. They were having a takeaway that night, too, from the Thai place in the high street – they'd each been allowed to choose their favourite dish and were going to eat it sitting at the wooden table in the garden. His father had organised it all. Which was unusual, and connected, Theo knew, to the fact that his mother had another of her headaches; a bad turn of events but also good because it made his father, usually pretty brusque and businesslike, all sort of caring and concerned in a way Theo had never seen before. That day, for example, he had insisted on cooking a Sunday brunch, which was unheard-of and also quite amusing because he couldn't cook. Burnt bacon and fried eggs frilled with scaly brown had been served with much aplomb on cold toast. He had then led the way in the clearing up, putting on a silly apron and barking orders at him and Chloë to load the dishwasher properly and put things away in the right places. Theo hadn't enjoyed it particularly but it had introduced him to a new, interesting side of his father as well as to the notion that maybe things at home weren't quite so fuddy-duddy and unchanged after all.

'Theo, what the hell are you up to?'

'Coming, Dad.' Theo closed the lid of his cassette box and put it back into the bottom drawer of his toy cupboard. Of the used tapes there was nothing of which he was yet particularly proud. His grand interviews of all the family at Ashley House already made him blush they were so amateurish. In any case the whole project had been tainted irretrievably by the cock-up over Tina. He had realised, seconds before his cousin waddled on to the screen, doughnut in hand, what was about to happen, but instead of flinging himself at the 'off' button, he had remained as if spellbound in some terrible dream while the scene unfolded around him, with everybody gasping and his aunt Serena bursting into tears. Any serious film-maker was only as good as his editing, and Theo regarded the whole episode as a huge personal failure. He should have airbrushed his cousin from the footage, not to mention a hundred other clumsy bits. Even without the cock-up the end result had been desperately below his expectations. And yet Theo rejected the thought of eradicating it completely – re-using the tape for something better – the moment it entered his head. He gave the box a fond pat as he closed the cupboard door. It was part of his archive now, a crucial building block in whatever he would eventually become and achieve.

Downstairs he found his family dishing food from tin-foil containers on to their plates. Chloë was already nibbling chicken off a wooden stick. She only ate chicken and rice when they had a Thai, but in impressive quantities.

'Mum's refusing to help me out with any of this beer. Would you like some, Theo?'

Helen, tapping her temple to indicate the fragile state of her head, raised her eyebrows at his father but offered no objection. Theo nodded eagerly.

'And me,' piped Chloë, her mouth bulging with chicken.

'Not you, sweetie,' Helen murmured, 'but your orange is nearly the same colour, isn't it?'

Chloë paused. 'Nearly,' she conceded, dislodging a last piece of skewered chicken with her teeth, then laying the wooden stick next to her plate. She would collect them, she decided, and use them to build something or maybe paint them so they looked like the pick-up-sticks game she had got in her stocking at Christmas.

The four of them busied themselves with eating, exchanging occasional comments about the food, school and plans for the holidays. Chloë broke up on Tuesday. Helen was seeing the doctor on Thursday. Griselda, their Scottish nanny, was setting off on her own holiday on Friday. The following two weeks Theo and Chloë would spend at Ashley House, with Helen there for both and Peter joining them for the second. As Peter and Helen now explained to the children, they had decided to postpone a more exotic summer holiday until the autumn half-term, or possibly Christmas.

'But we go to Granny's at Christmas,' Chloë reminded them, concerned at the notion of a change to a routine she treasured and Father Christmas's ability to locate her bed in some hotel room on the other side of the world.

'Maybe we'll do both, or maybe we'll just do something a little different this year.' Peter smiled fondly at his daughter's grave expression. 'Whatever happens, you'll have a lovely time, I promise you. We'll go somewhere with fantastic beaches, like St Lucia, which is a little island in the Caribbean or—'

'Oh, Peter, could we?' Without thinking, Helen seized his wrist. 'Could we really?' She converted the grip into a little pat, fearful that he would see into her mind and recognise the appeal – suddenly so crystal clear – of not having to go to Ashley House for Christmas. She loved his family, of course she did. She loved all the rituals too, their way of doing things – the grand meals and all the mayhem of nephews and nieces and piling into cars for visits to Uncle Eric and services at St Margaret's. But for that moment at least, with her head humming and the exhaustion of enduring a heatwave without air-conditioning or swimming-pools or any of the other luxurious props with which she normally associated such soaring temperatures, she loved much more the idea of their being alone and far away. 'I just think it might be nice to be just the four of us for once,' she added, as she stacked the plates. 'Like the skiing . . . that was lovely, wasn't it? Apart from—'

'You've been silent, Theo,' cut in Peter. 'What are your views on the subject?' He turned to his son. He didn't want a Tina conversation. Not for himself and certainly not for Helen, who was quite fragile enough without finding something extra to be upset about. He was desperately worried about her. Never one to make a fuss, she was, he could tell, doing her best to carry on as normal, going to work and keeping order at home. But there were dark shadows under her eyes and deep lines round her mouth that belied the pain which had taken residence inside her head. It was odd to worry about her, and in many respects he resented the way it clouded his concentration at work and pricked his conscience about things like the time at which he got home and whether he could justify a game of squash or a drink *en route*. Just that Friday he had refused a late-in-the day offer to meet Hannah, although when her voice tensed at his explanation he had been thoroughly pleased he had. Clearly she didn't like him giving precedence to his wife, which meant the suspicion that had tripped across his mind at Cassie's had been well founded and he shouldn't see her again, even if his own intentions remained innocent. A yet more drastic sign of the extent to which his wife's state of health was preying on Peter's mind was that he had even found himself encouraging a get-together with the dreaded Kay, who'd hardly crossed their threshold since she had returned from France. Wary as he was of the woman, Peter guessed that in this limbo time before consulting a doctor, Kay might be able to offer just the sort of soothing reassurances that Helen needed. Instead of leaping at the idea, as he had expected, Helen had merely muttered that her friend was snowed under with a pile of editing work and not in a position to see anyone.

Theo took a few moments to answer his father's question. He ran one finger round the rim of his beer glass, wondering what his parents would think if he told them about the amount of secret drinking that went on at school. To worry about Christmas when they were still only in July felt pointless. He loved Ashley House but had also felt on recent visits that he was growing out of it. 'The Caribbean would be cool. Would we eat roast turkey on the beach like they do in Australia?'

'Would Father Christmas still come?' blurted Chloë, looking up from her pile of sticks, her trim bob of black hair swinging, her blue-black eyes wide with concern.

Peter and Helen exchanged looks and laughed. 'Of course. He's magic, remember? He goes everywhere.'

'He'd be hot, though, wouldn't he, in his big red coat?'

All three members of the family were still pondering how to respond to this most reasonable observation when the doorbell sounded. A few moments later Peter, disgruntled in spite of himself, was ushering Kay through their glass-domed conservatory and out on to the patio. She was wearing a black tent of a dress and a chunky amber necklace. Her hair, which hung loose, was topped by a curious skullcap of grey where the regrowth of natural colour was pushing into the red. She looked hot and wheezed audibly as she moved round the table issuing greetings. 'I'm so sorry to barge in like this on a Sunday evening – Lord, you haven't had pudding yet, have you?' she added, winking at Chloë.

'Where's Toffee?'

'He's at home asleep, lying on his tummy with all four legs splayed out, and his tongue hanging out too. He hates it when it's hot.'

'We were going to have ice-cream. Would you like some? And a glass of wine, perhaps?'

'Thank you, Helen, but, no, I really just popped in because—' Kay broke off, clearly troubled. 'I need to talk to you.' She looked at Peter. 'Both of you . . . that is, if you had a minute or two.'

'Er . . . of course. Take a seat and perhaps the children could . . .' Peter looked to Helen for inspiration, which she supplied at once by

suggesting that they could have their pudding on their laps in front
of the television. Theo and Chloë, needing no further encouragement, fled from the table, and a moment later Helen heard them
arguing about which channel to watch. The age-gap, once relatively
manageable over such things, had recently become hopelessly
unbridgeable. It wouldn't be long, she knew, before one of them
was back, whining about the other.

'What is it, Kay? You look upset.' Her friend had wedged her
sizeable frame on to the section of bench vacated by Theo and was
fanning her face with one hand while rummaging in her holdall of a
handbag with the other. Helen poured her a glass of water and
pushed it across the table, apprehension stirring. Her headache was
galloping and Peter, she could tell, was annoyed at the intrusion.
Yet Kay had been a comfort to her on so many occasions that it
would have been churlish to be anything other than welcoming.

'Oh dear, I don't know where to start.' She sipped the water, then
pulled out a thick file of papers from the side compartment of her
bag. 'It's all to do with this. It's a manuscript I've been editing –
portraits of war heroes, unsung war heroes . . .'

'Goodness.' Helen turned to Peter. 'You don't suppose it could
be the thing that man went to see your parents about, could it? That
was going to be called *Unsung Heroes*, wasn't it? The one with the
chapter on Uncle Eric? What was he called, the biographer? It was
something simple.'

'Stephen Smith,' said Peter, clamping his mouth round the
syllables.

'That's it,' put in Kay, 'that's the name exactly. Stephen Smith.
And there's a chapter on Eric – Eric Harrison.'

'But how extraordinary. Peter? Don't you think that's extraordinary?' He was looking so unresponsive that Helen felt the
need to prod him.

'Most extraordinary.'

Now throughly enthused, Helen returned her attention to Kay.
'Talk about a coincidence. Is it any good?'

'Yes . . . that is, it's quite well written.' Kay drank more water,
casting, as she did so, a somewhat anxious glance at Peter, who was

staring stony-faced at the manuscript and tapping one finger on the table, very evenly, like a pulse.

Although she didn't know it, it was what he always did when he was thinking furiously, weighing up options of defence and attack. For Peter feared he knew what Kay was about to say. At the same time, he was aware that he might not – that their neighbour might have called on them merely to share the exhilaration of a small coincidence. Hope with regard to this latter scenario kept him silent.

'The chapter on your uncle – quite a man, wasn't he?'

'Isn't,' growled Peter.

'I beg your pardon?'

'You should have said *isn't*. Eric is still alive.'

'Oh, heavens – oh, Lord.' Kay pressed a hand to her chest, gripping the chunky segments of her necklace. 'Of course – I'm so sorry.'

Helen felt the need to make up for what she regarded as unnecessary hostility from her other half and reached eagerly for the manuscript. 'I'd love to have a look—' She was prevented both from completing the sentence and fulfilling the intention it expressed by Kay, who rooted the folder to the table with a firm slap of her hand. 'There's an Appendix, I thought you ought to know, a whole page of extra notes relating to – oh dear, I hope I'm doing the right thing here – relating to—'

'An affair. Between Eric and my mother.' Peter wanted to be the one to speak the dreadful truth.

'What?' Helen let out a laugh of disbelief, looking from one to the other.

Kay looked merely relieved. 'So you *did* know. Well, thank goodness for that. I just wasn't sure and having something like that coming out suddenly in a book would be the most dreadful shock for any family, wouldn't it?'

'Well, *I* didn't know.' Helen, still shaking her head in wonderment, hardened her gaze at her husband. 'Darling, why didn't you—'

Peter thumped his fist on the table and stood up. 'Bloody Cassie! I should have known I couldn't rely on her.'

'Cassie? What on earth has Cassie . . .' Helen looked helplessly at Kay, who shrugged. She would have repeated the question had not Peter, now pacing up and down the patio, his hands rammed into the pockets of his shorts, looked so distracted. 'These extra notes don't include a letter, do they, by any chance?'

'No, but there's a reference to one, if I remember correctly.' Kay rummaged in the folder. 'Why not have a look at what it says yourselves? I brought it so you could, although it's probably unethical or something. But it is about a member of your family, isn't it, which must make it okay? Here we are, it's this bit.' She tapped a page of close writing and handed it to Peter.

At which point Chloë came running through the conservatory to announce that Theo wouldn't let her watch *Nickelodeon* and they both wanted more ice-cream. While Helen sorted out the problem – by shooing Chloë upstairs to bed – Peter read what Stephen Smith had added to the manuscript he had shown Cassie, then handed it back to Kay to take home. On the doorstep she paused, clutching her handbag under both arms.

'I'm sorry, Peter, I really am, if this is going to cause upset.'

He laughed sharply. 'Upset? You could put it like that, yes.' He looked over Kay's shoulder at a swarm of gnats hovering at head height by the front gate. 'We'll just have to see what we can do.'

'In my experience,' she ventured, 'truth invariably finds a way of coming out in the end.'

'Really? In mine it doesn't. Not necessarily.' He spoke brusquely, still seething inwardly both at the naïve trust he had placed in his sister and at Stephen Smith's meddling into deeply private affairs. The gnats were drifting closer, a little grey cloud. He swiped at one with his hand, catching nothing but air. 'What happens next – to the manuscript, I mean? What's the routine after you've done your editing?'

'I send it back to the publishers. They make a proof copy, which is checked again for errors. A jacket gets designed and then—'

'And how long does all that take?'

'A few months. I think it's due for publication early next year – February or March.'

'Right. Good. Thank you.' Peter began to close the door, then paused to add, 'It was good of you to come round, Kay, I'm most grateful. And Helen, she . . . You're a good friend to her and I'm grateful for that too.' He scowled. 'Even if I'm not very good at demonstrating it.'

Kay smiled. 'Thank you, Peter, that's very sweet.' She leapt on to the step and kissed his cheek, then trotted out of the gate and across the road, the wide hem of her black dress swirling round her ankles.

Helen came down the stairs as he closed the door. 'Why didn't you tell me?'

'I should have.' He put his arms round her and sighed. 'I should have. I thought the fewer who knew the better.'

'Cassie knows, does she?'

Peter nodded. 'Cassie got on well with the man – thought she'd talked him out of using the information. The bastard clearly decided to go ahead anyway. So now, I fear, the time has come to tell the others – Elizabeth and Charlie. We need to get together and decide what to do. A family consultation. But not just yet. First, I need a little more time to think, to work out a strategy, consider all the options.'

'Pamela and Eric,' murmured Helen, 'unbelievable. I wonder if your father knew?'

'Of course he didn't. Your own brother – you couldn't forgive that in a hurry, could you? But if we don't do something he's going to find out soon enough, isn't he? Christ, what a mess, what a bloody mess.'

The heat lingered even in the wide high-ceilinged ground-floor rooms of Ashley House. Pamela, unable to share her daughter and husband's professed enthusiasm for an early night, had stayed downstairs after supper, first with her eyelids drooping in front of the ten o'clock news and then, with slightly more vigour, writing letters in John's study. She was exhausted, but knew she would not sleep until the stuffiness, which gathered each day like an invisible cloud in the upstairs rooms, had eased. The spell of hot weather, at first such a joy, was wearing her out, slowing her down and wringing the life from her bones. In spite of Sid's noble attempts with the hose, the garden, too, was withering: the lawns were yellowy and sparse like thinning hair, the beds lumpen and cracked, while the vines of clematis running round the arches of the cloisters, usually in their second bloom by now, had, as if in some sort of consensual suicide, metamorphosed into a tangle of twiggy shrivelled brown. John kept saying it was great weather for the roof. Which, of course, it was. The workmen, shinning up and down the ladders and scaffolding, shirtless and with burnt chestnut torsos, were clearly enjoying themselves, commenting each day that they'd never had a job so blessed by the elements. Pamela, however, found it hard to feel blessed by them or anything else. Ashley House, its roof a balding pate where the old tiles had been stripped away, its walls caged by metal poles, looked to her both trapped and suddenly fragile. Every time she saw it, when she looked up from cutting flowers, or from sewing in the shade of the apple tree guarding the furthest end of the pergola, one eye on Roland sketching or practising handstands, she felt profoundly disturbed, as if something much more than the state of the roof was at stake. The presence and predicament of Elizabeth, Pamela knew, lay at the heart of this new unease. Everything about her elder daughter jarred on her nerves, from her stubborness over the unmended state of her marriage to the ridiculous heavy yellow canvas shoes she had acquired in Chichester. How typical: the wrong cream and some silly shoes. At the time, she had been so maddened that she had to leave the room to prevent some expression of her fury exploding out of her. Trying to explain to John how she felt did no good at all. He simply blamed the household's general tetchiness on the weather and said that – like their daughter's marital troubles – it would all blow over with time. On the day of the cream incident Pamela had retreated to the TV room for some peace, only to find herself assailed by the sound of Elizabeth playing the piano. The strains, drifting through the wall and down the hall, were faint but clear. It was a sonata Pamela recognised from her grade-eight days. A Beethoven sonata with a tricky third movement. Elizabeth played it with flair but badly, a combination of lack of practice and lack of application. Trying to sew, her fingers sliding on the needle and sticking on the threads, Pamela had closed her eyes at the familiar but painful recognition of wasted potential. She had eventually given up on her tapestry and mused upon the unremitting difficulty of loving someone who set no store by her talents, who dabbled and bungled, getting by with the least rather than the most of what she had to offer.

That evening, sitting over her letters, freshly irked by a series of recent incidents – stepping over Elizabeth's pile of washing on the landing, glimpsing the bombsite of her bedroom (even little Roland was tidier), finding that three of her best silver spoons had been put through the dishwasher – Pamela remembered again the messy piano-playing and shuddered. Domesticity, music, marriage, it was all the same. Elizabeth had no true discipline, no inner steel, no *guts*. What Colin had done was nothing – *nothing* – a mere fling. Why could Elizabeth not see that and forgive it? Something good and positive would result. Just as it had when – when–– Pamela gripped her fountain pen, trying to focus on the line of congratulation she was writing to Ed. She was going to put in a ten-pound note when she'd finished. His scholarship was wonderful news, just the sort of boost Charlie and Serena needed; something for the future, to which they could look forward and be proud. Pamela tried hard to keep her thoughts there, but they shot out of control, as they seemed to have been doing all year, locking on – like some missile programmed to a single target – to her own private marital crisis almost half a century before.

Eric hadn't been a fling. He had been the grand passion of her life. Her worst crime and her greatest love. Giving him up had been the hardest and noblest thing she had ever done. With John not knowing, there had been no luxury of forgiveness either, only guilt and longing. Years of it. In a perverse way Eric's stroke had come as a blessing, because it put him, finally, out of reach and gave her a legitimate reason to nurture him openly, to stroke his thick hair and kiss his eyes. Reward after deprivation. Made after the miscarriage of Miranda, Pamela had never doubted the rightness of her decision, never once wavered from it. In many ways she recognised it as the cornerstone on which she had built her life, as solid and irrefutable as the foundations of Ashley House. But now her beloved home looked like a shipwreck and Elizabeth – wretched Elizabeth – had churned up all the old feelings again, making the secret burn like acid in her heart, making the past feel not like 'another country', as it had once famously been termed, but a living component of the present. Just as losing darling Tina had. Christ, what a year it had been. One ordeal after another. Forgetting the ten-pound note, Pamela sealed her letter to Ed, and dropped her head into her hands.

A few moments later when the phone rang she reached for it slowly and stiffly, wiping the dampness from her palms.

'Mrs Harrison?'

'Yes.'

'It's Mrs Cordman from Merrybell nursing-home. There is no immediate cause for concern, but I thought you ought to know that Mr Harrison has suffered another mild stroke. He's resting comfortably now. We just thought you ought to know. We will phone again if the position changes.'

'Right. Thank you, Mrs Cordman. I'll tell my husband at once. He's comfortable, you say?'

'Oh, yes. No cause for alarm.'

Pamela had to shake John awake to tell him. She repeated verbatim what Mrs Cordman had said. John sighed heavily. 'I guess this is the beginning of the end,' he murmured, and she did not contradict him.

Told by his father that he could name the treat of his choice, Ed had opted for a day at Thorpe Park with his best friend. Lying late in bed on the first day of the summer holidays contemplating the prospect, he wondered if anybody in the world could possibly be as happy. Ever since he'd heard about the scholarship he had felt as if he was floating on air. Suddenly everybody was pleased with him. On the last day of term even the grumpiest teachers had given him warm adult handshakes and wished him well. At home the girls had been unusually deferential, while his father, after some manic hugging and a ridiculously generous settlement of his pocket-money debt, grinned idiotically every time he caught his eye. His mother, too, had been pleased, but in the new, subdued manner she had towards everything, as if she could feel all the right stuff but not quite show it. She had pressed his face between her palms and stared at him for several seconds, so intensely, that Ed, terrified she was going to cry, had found an excuse to wriggle free.

Moved by pangs of hunger to get out of bed, Ed bounded downstairs and gathered up the newspapers and post from the doormat. He glanced at the sports pages, then saw there was a letter for him from his grandmother. Scenting the possibility of cash, he tore at the flap only to find a notelet covered in daffodils, saying, 'Edward, darling, you clever boy. How proud we all are of you.' He was momentarily humbled, until he spotted an extra note on the opposite side of the card – 'Thought the enclosed might come in handy' – whereupon he shook the envelope furiously and checked the hall floor.

'What are you doing?' asked Clem, appearing all pale-faced and tousled at the top of the stairs.

'Granny sent me a card and forgot to put the money in.'

'Bad luck.' She giggled and floated on past him to the kitchen where she smeared milk and a sprinkling of sugar round a spoon and bowl and squashed a couple of Frosties into the bottom. Then, checking that Ed hadn't followed her, she took two crispbreads from the cheese-biscuit tin and nibbled each one slowly, rolling the sticky crumbs round her mouth before swallowing.

Serena appeared just as she finished. 'Have you had breakfast?'

'Hm, just finished. I had Frosties. Look.' She held up the bowl. For good measure she picked up one of the now soggy crumbs and placed it on her tongue.

'I'm making a picnic, what would you like in your sandwich?' Serena reached into the bread bin and began lining up slices of bread for buttering. A distant part of her sensed that she was being lied to, that her daughter, with her big knuckles and bony knees, visible where the hem of her nightie ended, was playing some sort of elaborate game. She sensed it but could not muster the strength to act on it. She felt drained even by the thought of having to make sandwiches. With Ed's friend, due any minute, they would need six rounds at least. She did not want to go to Thorpe Park. Upstairs Charlie was pulling on shorts and loafers, exclaiming – as if it was some new phenomenon – on the brilliance of the weather and, as usual these days, making up for her lack of enthusiasm by exuding extra quantities of his own. Its force made her shrink inside and want to run into some cool dark corner where it would be okay never to smile – never to have to *be* anything again. Recently, since she had agreed to help Cassie, he had left her – or, at least, her feelings – more alone. While this was precisely what she had hoped for, it had had the baffling effect of leaving her feeling even more wretched and adrift. 'Cheese and ham?'

'Sounds great.' Clem opened the newspaper and began to read, noting as she did so that the hairs on her forearms had got thicker and longer, like an animal's. She stroked them absently, humming to herself.

Serena caught sight of the novel she had started at Cassie's, sitting next to the breadboard, a mindless sex-and-shopping romp, full of improbable characters doing improbable things, and slipped it into her handbag.

'Whatever are you taking that for?' boomed Charlie, appearing from nowhere, sunglasses in one hand and Ed's empty notelet in the other.

'I might not go on the rides,' murmured Serena, not looking up from the butter, so soft that it was sinking into the bread like oil.

'Don't be ridiculous. Of course you're going on the rides. We're all going on the rides, aren't we, Clemmy?'

Clem grinned. 'Yes, Dad.'

'There, you see. You won't need this.' Charlie reached into the bag for the book, knowing he was being brutal but thinking that if he acted with enough light-heartedness and aplomb he might get away with it. His hopes were short-lived. Serena snatched the book from him. 'Leave it, Charlie, just leave it, okay? I'm coming, aren't I?'

Yes, he wanted to cry, you're coming, but you're not really going to be there, which is worse than not coming at all, because your absence would at least preclude the bitterness of disappointment. 'Fine. Naughty Charlie.' He slapped his hand, trying for Clem's benefit to make the incident look like a joke. 'Look at this.' He waved the notelet. 'My poor mother is clearly going senile. A card for Ed and she forgets to put in the cash. What do you think? Should we tell her or just pay him ourselves?' He dropped the card next to the butter dish. 'What do you reckon? Alert the old bat to the fact that she's losing her marbles or cover up for her? Tricky one, isn't it?' At which point Ed glided into the kitchen on his skateboard, one of the many normally forbidden practices he had lately been getting away with, and deftly seized a slice of buttered bread as he passed his mother.

Serena swung round, ready to fling out a reprimand, but couldn't see the point: Ed, looking impish, was already three bites into his catch. There were plenty more slices in the bag, and half a pack's worth of melting butter. Instead she pointed at her handbag with her chin, telling Charlie that she had a spare tenner in her purse. She looked nonchalant, but her blue eyes burned, daring him even to think of trying again to remove the novel. 'I suspect your mother is feeling the strain of having Elizabeth,' she murmured. 'They've spent years not getting on and not admitting it.'

'Really?' Charlie, pleased to get a voluntary remark on any subject, but also a little surprised, picked out her purse and extracted a ten-pound note. 'Do you really think so?'

Serena merely shrugged and returned to the picnic. Charlie, feeling that a door had opened and closed before he could get his foot in it, strolled over to Clem and kissed the top of her head. 'Had any breakfast yet, Mouse?'

'Yes. Mum already asked me.'

'Good girl. I'll use your bowl, then, shall I?'

'That's Ed's.'

'Whatever.' Charlie shook out the business section of the paper and began studying the share prices, soothed by the factual definition of the numbers, so unlike the invisible gusts of emotion swirling round his home.

Upstairs Maisie, unaware that Clem had already woken up, put her head round her sister's door. She had a top she wanted to give her, a lilac one with shoulder straps and a little red satin rose stitched to the front. It was only just too small for Maisie and she liked it a lot. The decision to offer it to her twin had not been arrived at lightly. In spite of the heatwave Clem was still dressing in baggy tracksuits as if she wanted to hide her hard-won slimline figure instead of showing it off. Still hostile to any direct approaches on the subject, the lilac-top plan was Maisie's new tack to induce her daft sister, so capable of being pretty, to open her eyes and recognise that if she dieted any more she really would be a stick insect. The previous week Monica had celebrated the loss of a measly couple of pounds by buying a hipster mini-skirt, merrily parading her hefty thighs and the still considerable flab of her tummy as if she were Kate Moss in her prime. Which was typical and pretty dumb, but not nearly as dumb as having a great body and covering it up with ugly, shapeless clothes.

'Clem?' Seeing the bed was empty, Maisie was about to withdraw when she caught sight of her sister's diary lying open but face down on the shelf next to her bed. She stepped towards it and hesitated. The only other time she had been presented with – and taken – such an opportunity had been on an exceptional, dreadful day when it felt like there were no rules about anything. Things were different now, better. Clem didn't deserve such a betrayal of trust. Through all the business of phoning the journalist, Mr Cartwright, she had been as solid as a rock.

When they finally got through on his mobile (the day after Ed had interrupted them) it had been a bit of an anticlimax. Unprepared to disclose any details beyond that she had met Neil Rosco at his mansion in Barham and he was not the clean-cut teen-idol he appeared to be, Maisie had been painfully aware of the flimsiness of her information. The journalist, however, had been kind enough not to make her feel she was wasting his time. He said he respected the anonymity of all his sources, asked her how old she was, how she knew Barham and said he'd bear it all in mind. So it hadn't changed anything, not obviously. Maisie had put down the phone feeling rather let down, and Clem had seemed to understand, going on for ages about how brave it had been just to make contact and how the important thing was to have done *something*, no matter the invisibility of the result.

It was like she just *knew* what was going on in Maisie's mind. Knew it and accepted it. Which was how things should be: they were twins, after all, and had spent most of their fourteen years being incredibly close. The only trouble was that Maisie felt, increasingly, as if there were great swathes of Clem that she didn't know or understand at all. The hateful dieting was one thing, but there was also Jonny Cottrall, whom she clearly liked but went out of her way to avoid, and the piano, which she said she hated but practised like a fiend for at least an hour every day.

So all she wanted, Maisie decided now, eyeing the diary, was simply a little assistance, a leg-up towards understanding what the hell was going on in her sister's mind. Convinced by the irrefutable virtue of this argument, she tiptoed out on to the landing and leant over the banisters. Downstairs she could hear the radio on in the kitchen and the rumble of Ed's skateboard wheels in the hall. Satisfied that she had a couple of minutes at least, she sprinted back into Clem's bedroom and threw herself on to the bed to begin reading. Having given little concrete thought to her expectations – moans about school, maybe, or Monica, whom Clem loathed, or Ed's dreadful swollen head, which was getting them both down – Maisie was so unprepared for what she found that she gasped out loud. There was no juicy titbits about her or Monica or Ed or anyone else. In fact, there was nothing, just huge empty spaces under each date . . . but not empty, because printed in the middle of each one, in tiny, skeletal writing, was a weight, recorded in pounds and ounces. Clem's weight, Maisie realised, feeling sick with terror as she flicked through the pages. There were weeks of it, sad, stark entries, some so small she had to press her nose to the page to read them. As if Clem was afraid of her own writing. As if she was literally shrinking into the emptiness of each page. *7st 12lb. 7st 5oz. 6st 13lb. 6st 12lb. 6st 10lb 3oz. 6st 7lb* . . .

'What are you doing?'

Maisie looked up to see Clem, ghostly and trembling, in the doorway. Not knowing what to say, she looked down at the diary, open at that morning's entry – *6st 6lb 3oz* – and back up at her sister.

'How dare you? How *dare* you?' Clem was on her in an instant, scrabbling and spitting like a wild cat. Maisie fought back, trying to keep the diary out of reach, half crying, half trying to shout some sense into her. 'It's not right, Clem, it's not right.'

Clem, who had sharp nails, clawed at her sister's arms and hands. 'You bitch, you utter bitch, give it back.'

Serious injury was only prevented by the arrival of an astonished Charlie. 'What the hell is going on?'

They pulled apart at once, sullen and snivelling. Clem was the first to speak, saying in a small voice, 'She was reading my diary.'

'Maisie? Is that true?'

Maisie nodded, not looking up. She could feel Clem's gaze on the top of her head. She could feel the terror in it, the pleading. She could feel her own terror too, both at what she had discovered and at the knowledge of what revealing it would lead to. Panic from her parents for one thing. A bollocking for another; with their pact broken Clem would tell them everything. But worse than all this was the thought of how heartbroken and angry Clem would be, how alienated and unremittingly hostile. Maisie would lose her love and, for the moment, that was more than she could bear.

'What possessed you to do such a thing?' Charlie sounded – and felt – more helpless than angry. He wasn't in the mood for this. It was supposed to be Ed's treat day and already it was going hopelessly wrong. 'Apologise at once, do you hear? And if you don't you – you . . .' He faltered, not wanting to come up with the only punishment that sprang to mind, but unable to think of an alternative '. . . you can stay at home today.'

Maisie burst into tears. 'I don't want to come on Ed's stupid treat anyway. I don't want anything. I hate everyone.'

'Just say sorry,' Charlie repeated, begging now, so wanting the day to right itself.

'Sorry.' Maisie shrieked the word, tossed Clem's diary on to the floor and ran from the room.

The pub was thick with the smell of beer, smoke and sweat. Two men at the bar, with bloated bellies and shaved heads, had taken their shirts off and were having a noisy debate, stabbing the air round each other's faces with their cigarettes. The barmaid, make-up and hair-do wilting in the muggy heat, kept a wary eye on them while her hands worked the pumps and her mouth flashed smiles for other customers. Stephen watched her for a bit but glanced away quickly when she tried to catch his eye. He had come to this place to lose himself in the humming of other people's lives. He wanted to be as undetectable as a grain of sand on a beach, beholden to no one and nothing, not even the glance of a stranger. Unable suddenly to face the prospect of returning to his flat, he had spent the past few nights at a dingy hotel near King's Cross, venturing out only for food and alcohol. Each evening he had found a different haunt, huge and crowded and impersonal. It was a cliché, of course, to try to use drink as a method of accessing oblivion. As he ploughed steadily through pints of beer and whisky chasers, Stephen was bitterly aware of this and disdainful at his own lack of imagination. Of most immediate concern, however, was that, for him at least, the process wasn't working. No matter how drunk he got, all the things he sought to forget – the vengeful cruelty of his amended manuscript, the unrequited, unassuageable pain of loving Cassie, the wounds of his childhood – remained, heaving and monstrous and unresolved.

His trip up north had offered no solutions beyond that there was nothing to solve. His parents, shrunken versions of how he remembered them, had greeted him with muted surprise, hand-shakes and cups of tea. There were no revelations, no emotional explanations, no emotion at all, in fact. They asked him about his travels, much as any stranger might, with one eye on the clock and another on the television, which had flickered at low volume in the corner of the sitting room throughout his visit. When he said he had written a book, they murmured interest but looked distant and dumbfounded. They read newspapers and magazines, he remembered, not books. Clare had been ill, they said, with breast cancer, but was recovering well. Mrs Dawkins across the road had died of a heart-attack. Had he seen the England–Germany match? Would he be staying in London long? If it hadn't been for his father's belt buckle, the same belt buckle, glittering under the lower buttons of his shirt, Stephen might even have convinced himself that he had got the wrong house, the wrong set of parents. Whatever version of the past they carried in their hearts was sealed for ever, he realised, certainly from him and quite probably from each other. They were old people riled by the weather, edging from one day to the next via meals and the news headlines, their eyes on the ground. They weren't a threat any more but they weren't an answer either. 'Call again soon,' they said, when he left, but they closed the door even before he got to the gate, leaving him to make his way alone to the bus stop.

'All alone, ducky?'

'Yes, and happy that way, thank you.'

The woman, who was in her fifties with brittle bleached hair and red lips, cackled. 'No one's happy that way and anyone who says otherwise is pretending.'

Stephen drained the last of his beer, picked up his bag and left.

AUGUST

John pulled back his bedroom curtains and peered through the lattice of scaffolding at the seamless blue sweep of sky. There had been no rain since the party and the countryside was a mass of sapped yellow and brown. With a hosepipe ban now in force, even the colours of the garden were fading to a pastel version of their usual August brilliance. Only the copse, sprouting on its mysterious subterranean tributary, looked truly green. John squinted to make out the silver of the lake at its heart, glistening like shards of glass between the tree-trunks. Although the nineties had produced a couple of record-breaking summers, the heatwave had made him think more than anything of the distant merging dream of his childhood, when he and Eric had whiled away seemingly endless hot days running wild around the estate, homemade spears and daggers tucked into their shorts, along with other more serious tools, illicitly borrowed from their father's work-shed to build tree-houses and boats and precarious diving-boards. Having the house full again of grandchildren, camping in the garden and trooping to and from the copse in bathing costumes with towels slung over their shoulders, had sharpened such images, making him feel at once heartened and deeply nostalgic.

John left the window and stooped to check his appearance in the dressing-table mirror, running his hand over his cheek for missed bristles and smoothing the stiff, sparse sides of his hair. He was going to visit Eric and wanted to look smart. Pamela had offered to accompany him, but he had resisted for once, knowing that he would, as ever, use her marvellous coping as a shield behind which he could himself remain safe and disengaged. The exact purpose of the visit was something John had not yet analysed, beyond a dim sense that with Eric's recent stroke and the doors of his own life closing, a certain shaping to the process was called for: proper farewells, a tying-off of loose ends. He had continued to make good preparations financially (he had replied to his accountant, understood fully the complexities of avoiding inheritance tax and was planning to make further gifts to all four children the following year), and felt that the trickier geography of emotions could no longer be ignored either. It was time to play his part properly, to make his own sense of this last act in their lives.

Satisfied with his face, he began to search for his hat, a battered Panama to which he was devoted and which Eric had given him on his return from his travels many years before. Overhead he could hear the men at work already, whistling and chatting between muffled thumps and bangs. It wouldn't be long now. The patches of new tiles grew each day, spreading like treacle over the dips, curves and slopes of the roof. Having cursed the expense and inconvenience, John was aware that he had grown rather attached to the project. The men were good sorts and seeing the effects of their labours gave him a vicarious sense of achievement, perking up days that might otherwise have seemed indolent and unsatisfactory. He couldn't find the hat so went downstairs to look in the cloakroom, where Boots, slumped on the cool of the linoleum, greeted him with a hopeful thump of the tail. 'Not now, old fella, it's no dogs allowed.' The hat wasn't on any of the pegs either. Muttering under his breath, irritation mounting, he turned to see Serena and Elizabeth, with sunglasses and handbags, clearly preparing to go out too.

'Pamela said you were going to visit Eric and might be able to give us a lift.'

'Did she, now? And where are you two off to, then?'

'I just want to go to St Margaret's,' replied Serena, dropping her eyes, clearly not wanting to be pressed on the matter.

'Well, of course—'

'And I'm catching a train to London. The lunch with Peter, remember?'

'Ah, yes, the lunch, of course.' John frowned. The subject had come up during dinner the night before. At Peter's instigation his four children, without spouses or hangers-on, were having a get-together in London. On the face of it it was an entirely normal thing to do. But somehow, for a reason John couldn't quite put his finger on, it was also a little odd. It had even crossed his mind that it might be something to do with the plan for their inheritance, that perhaps, somehow, somewhere, a little dissatisfaction had crept into the works. 'Well, my dears, I am entirely at your disposal the moment I find my hat . . .'

'Do you mean this?' Helen popped her head round the door, waving the Panama. 'I'm so sorry, John, Chloë had it – some sort of dressing-up game – none the worse for wear, I promise. Are you two off, then?' She delivered the enquiry with breezy nonchalance. In truth she had been a little put out at Peter's insistence that the crisis meeting about the book should be for siblings only. Neither was she entirely happy that she was to be in sole charge of six children for the duration of the morning. To reveal resentment on either score would have been unacceptable, though. Pamela's indiscretion and how to handle it was a purely family affair, as Peter had said many times. And Serena's sudden announcement that she wished to spend time at the church was hardly a matter with which one could take issue. Six months on, Helen still found her sister-in-law's grief both frightening and unapproachable, as if she had pegged an invisible electric fence around herself, which hummed and prickled when anyone got too close. Although they never had been great confidantes, she missed the old Serena dreadfully.

Of more immediate concern was that the children, as usual, were clamouring to go swimming, which meant she, too, would have to make the trek to the lake to keep an eye on things. As the only grown-up, it would be a lonely – not to mention stressful – vigil. Although Jessica could not swim, she flung herself like a lemming into the deepest, weediest eddies. In addition to which there would be all the usual races, ducking games and competitions to see who could stay under the longest, when they all lolled in the water like floating corpses. Helen had ventured in just once that week, only to find that the lake's iciness made her still tender head throb like an engine. Sunbathing had much the same effect. The doctor, disconcertingly mystified, had given her a thorough check-up and taken some blood for tests. Peter, still resident in London until the weekend, was diligently checking the post each morning for anything resembling a set of results, although the doctor, a sombre young man with pouches under his eyes, had promised that if anything remotely sinister presented itself he would call her on her mobile. No news, as Peter kept saying, was therefore good news, but Helen had packed her phone for the swimming session anyway, tucking it into the largest of Pamela's many wicker baskets, along with the picnic, tubes of sunblock, bottles of water and a copy of *Homes and Gardens*.

'You look good in that, Dad.' Elizabeth stepped forward and tweaked the brim of John's hat. 'Quite the man about town.'

John smiled. He knew Pamela found the continuing presence of their elder daughter irksome, but he had got rather used to having her around. True, she was messy and disorganised and almost certainly not facing up to things, but it had been nice to have the extra company and to hear her strumming away on the piano and reading stories to help Roland sleep. Most gratifying of all was how Roland was coming out of his shell – he was so much more chatty and, with his sandy suntan, quite unrecognisable from the pale, red-nosed child who had arrived the month before, with purple shadows under his eyes and a brooding look that didn't seem right on any nine-year-old. It was dreadful, of course, the whole sorry business, but John maintained the view that, rather than running away, Elizabeth was taking a much-needed extended break; that, come September, she would return refreshed and reinvigorated to her responsibilities in Guildford.

'Shall we go, ladies?' He held out both elbows for Serena and Elizabeth to take and led them out to the car, feeling suddenly young and chipper and more than up to the always daunting business of a visit to the nursing-home.

Lucien Cartwright, peering round the gateposts of Ashley House at the very moment that John, Serena and Elizabeth were climbing into the Range Rover, leapt back in surprise. In Barham to nose around the Rosco story, he had ambled down the lane out of sheer curiosity, lost in a bubble of the past, never once imagining that his ex-wife would be in the vicinity as well. He had spent the last eighteen years trying to forget the Harrisons, putting behind him not just the pain of happy memories but also the youthful, lazy creature who had squandered them. Twenty-three had been a ridiculous age to get married, although at the time he had felt so old. Elizabeth, older but not much wiser, had been desperate to exchange vows, mostly out of love but also, as Lucien came to realise, because she was seeking some sort of escape from the pressures and oppressions of her family. Coming from a cheerful extended set-up full of step-parents and half-siblings, Lucien had found it baffling. Elizabeth had talent, money (loads in prospect), but seemed incapable of enjoying either. Yet, as he recalled now, stepping out from behind a wide tree after John's Range Rover had rumbled past, they had had some good times: a camping holiday on a rainy Brittany coast, listening to jazz in the basement club round the corner from their flat, making love in the afternoons in the bed with the lopsided headboard, pizza remains and beer bottles strewn among the sheets. Elizabeth had let go then, all right. At other times she had been like a woman in two halves, each one straining against the other. As an indulgent, unsorted and aimless whole, Lucien had had neither the patience nor the capacity to understand. At that stage life had seemed to him to be simply for the taking, a heaped tray of delectable food from which one could pick or scoff as one chose. Elizabeth was either at his side being equally indulgent, or standing over him with tears on her face and a wagging finger. What had begun as love of his *laissez-faire* attitudes had soured to suspicion, and finally distrust.

Lucien returned to the gatepost and peered round it up the drive. Elizabeth, in the glimpse he had had of her, had looked fuller-figured, with longer, more straggly hair – older, of course, but somehow *softer* too, as if some integral part of her had relaxed or matured, or maybe just given in. He had liked the scruffy hair, streaked naturally with grey, and also the long floral skirt she had been wearing, reaching almost to the rim of improbable, electric yellow shoes. The other woman, whom he recognised as Charlie's extremely pretty girlfriend of two decades before, had been the more obviously beautiful of the two, but his eyes had been drawn to Elizabeth, springing into the car in her thick-soled shoes, her good mood still as readable, after so many years, as an open book.

With the Range Rover safely out of earshot Lucien, ducking, though there was nothing to duck behind, scurried past the little orchard of silver birches towards the wall that ran along the front garden and peered gingerly over the top. He had surprised himself already, coming this far and staying so long. Intrigued though he had been to receive a phone-call from what was clearly some young relative of Elizabeth's (the girl had disclosed, reluctantly, that she had family living at Ashley House), Lucien had only meant to visit Barham to see if he could sniff out a story behind her hazy allegations. Rumours had been flying round about Neil Rosco for months – coke, prostitutes, usual sort of thing – but without a sting operation (and Lucien didn't approve of those) it was difficult to make anything stick. He had parked at the Rising Sun, had a ham sandwich and a half-pint and asked a few questions. Then he had walked to the gates of Rosco's country retreat for a nose-around, peering through the bars, aware that he was probably wasting his time. Afterwards he had meant to return to his car and drive home, but found himself instead sauntering on through the village towards Ashley House, partly out of curiosity and partly because it was nice to be in the Sussex countryside, surveying the hot dusty colours through his Oakleys while his mind took an indulgent meander down Memory Lane.

Seeing Elizabeth was like being grabbed by the scruff of the neck. And the old man too, so much more stooped and frail but wearing the same hat, for Christ's sake, as if it was yesterday and not eighteen years ago that Lucien had last laid eyes on him. The sight had made him hungry for more. Was the girl who had made the phone-call here too? he wondered, peering now with more confidence over the wall, his eyes scanning the familiar, impressive tapestry of his ex-mother-in-law's garden, with all its bulging beds and clever, unexpected contours, where plants were trained to be wild and colours spilled into each other like paints on canvas. Absorbed for a few moments by this lovely, unpeopled scene, Lucien failed to notice the small boy sitting with his back to the wall directly under his nose. When the child looked up and said, 'Who are you?' he almost jumped out of his skin. Quite as shocking as the realisation that he had been observed was the fact – instantly and unequivocally plain to Lucien – that he had been addressed by Elizabeth's son. The boy had darker hair, but the set and deep blue of his eyes, the steep neat nose and the ever-so-slightly jutting chin were unmistakable.

'I,' said Lucien, recovering himself and easing off his sunglasses, 'am a secret. Can you keep a secret?'

Torn between maternal warnings on the subject of talking to strangers and bursting curiosity, Roland frowned. The man was tall and very thin, with interesting green eyes that looked like they laughed a lot. Having retreated to the wall for a sulk (now that the other cousins – and particularly Ed – were around, Jessica was ignoring him) he was in the mood for a diversion. 'I think I can, but I don't like them much,' he added, his face clouding at the recollection of his father's secret friendship with the woman in the purple dress and all the upset it had caused his mother.

'Oh, and why is that?' Lucien leant further over the wall. He, too, was enjoying the diversion. This was Elizabeth's son; it was impossible not to be intrigued. After his marriage he had moved to a long partnership with a woman too obsessed with her career to consider a family. It had become a bone of contention in the end, one of many that had led to a parting of the ways. Now he was with a much younger girl, who talked so much about getting married and making babies that he found himself constantly digging out excuses to pull the other way. Life, he mused, smiling at the boy, who had an endearing pixie mouth but the familiar worried expression of his mother, was a funny old business.

Roland hesitated again, aware that a full explanation of his fears would be both inappropriate and impossible. 'My mum and I are staying here with my granny and granddad and all my cousins and

Aunty Serena and Aunty Helen. All the daddies are coming at the weekend. Except mine. He lives in Guildford. Mummy and I are living here now, except she's gone to London but she's coming back later today . . .' Roland stopped abruptly, losing confidence.

Reeling slightly from the unexpected delivery of so much fascinating information, Lucien could see that it was time to take his leave. The child was looking more anxious and the last thing he wanted was to frighten him.

'You're a great little chap, do you know that? And I have so enjoyed meeting you.' He offered his hand over the wall, which Roland took, looking solemn but also pleased. 'My name's Lucien, what's yours?'

'Roland Patrick Ashley Jessop.'

'Okay, Roland Patrick Ashley Jessop, I've got to go now, but I want to give you something. Once, a long time ago, your mother was a very good friend of mine. Look . . .' Lucien dug into his back pocket for his wallet and pulled out the little wad of photos he kept under his press pass. At the bottom of the wad, under nephews, nieces, siblings and parents, there was a dog-eared picture of him and Elizabeth, heads squashed together, pulling funny faces into the tiny window of a photo booth. Roland peered at it, then exclaimed, 'That's you and Mum. You look weird.'

Lucien laughed. 'I'm afraid so. We boys all had long hair then. Your mother's was much shorter though, wasn't it, compared to now? While I've got practically none at all.' He laughed again, running his hand over his hair, which he liked to keep, these days, to a number-four on the scalping machine. 'Like we've swapped styles—' He broke off, kicking himself for talking so carelessly and making his young companion look worried all over again. 'Anyway, the fact is, we're old friends from way back before you were born and sometimes it's best to leave things that way. If your mum wants to, that's fine. But just in case, I'm going to write my number on the back of this picture and give it to you to give to her. Okay? Will you do that for me?'

'So you're not a secret, then?'

'Not to you or your mum, but don't tell anybody else.'

'I see,' replied Roland, though he didn't really see at all. The man put his sunglasses back on, reached over the wall to pat his head, then strode away down the drive. Roland stood alone for several minutes, listening to the man whistling long after he had disappeared from sight. It was a tuneful whistle, very bouncy, high and loud. It made him feel glad, until he glanced again at the little photo in his hands and his heart crowded with fresh uncertainty. It was odd to see his mother looking so like a girl. It was like staring at someone else, someone he didn't know. They were making silly faces but their cheeks were touching. Something about it made Roland afraid. And all the secrecy business, that made him afraid too. With the man there it had seemed all right, but standing alone by the wall, the whistling quite gone, Roland wasn't so sure. Should he tell his mother or would it make her cross? Would she say, 'Roland, I'm disappointed in you, talking to a stranger'? But he wasn't a stranger, he was a friend. But if he was a friend, why hadn't Roland met him or heard about him or seen other bigger photos of him? For a moment he toyed with the idea of screwing the photo up into a tiny ball and hurling it over the wall. But then his aunt Helen called that it was time to go swimming and he tucked it hurriedly into his shorts, then set off at top speed for the house, slicing the air with his hands as Ed had said you should do if you wanted to run really fast.

Serena didn't go into the church but made her way round to the graveyard at the back. The area near the building was flat, with well-ordered plots, crosses and slabs, but beyond that it sloped in a more higgledy-piggledy arrangement of mounds and gravestones, many pitching at odd angles out of the grass like unruly teeth. Serena picked her way among them, pausing every so often to study the mossy inscriptions, feeling superior and dismissive at the great ages recorded under the names. *Ethel Rhys 92 years. Bernard Merris 89 years. Florence Dewhurst 88 years.* The notion of mourning such ancients was almost laughable. Even a fresher stone headed, *Grace Peeble, aged 7 years*, brought only a flutter of compassion. Seven whole years! Compared with the measly seventeen months she had

had Tina, it was a lifetime. Seven years of memories and joys and photographs and ballet certificates and little playmates and conversations and hugs and breathy kisses . . . The mere thought of it made Serena giddy with envy. She had gone through her own memory bank so many times that it felt lifeless and picked clean. There was nothing left to be gleaned, nothing new – not a single moment, not a single smell that she had not remembered a million times, squeezing it harder and harder for drops of recollected happiness. Even the wobbly few seconds of footage screened by Theo on Easter Sunday had been something to which she had returned, countless times, in her head. Seeing Tina like that, so alive, so busy, in a brief hitherto unknown snapshot of her short life, had been truly dreadful but also magical, as if, for a few moments, she had come back to life. And afterwards Serena had felt she had been given something new to treasure, a fresh image on which to feed the bottomless hunger of her sorrow. But the others had not seen that. They had seen only tears, which meant unhappiness, and their own blinding helplessness.

There were six Harrison graves in all, set out like giant table mats along the hedge separating one side of the graveyard from a field of rape, an ocean of brilliant yellow so vivid that, after a minute or two, Serena found her eyes seeking solace in the gentle brown and violet of the South Downs, breasting the horizon like breaking waves. She had brought an apple and sat next to one of the graves to eat it, keeping as much of herself in the shade of the hedge as she could. Having the deceased clan of her husband's family around her was somehow soothing, as if they were all seated together at a table, gathered, apart from the munching of her apple, in companionable silence. On the odd occasions she had gone up to the graveyard in Cheshire she did not feel this. For one thing the church was much newer and the graveyard larger and more ordered, laid out among wide gravel paths like some ornamental garden. Her mother, who had been cremated, had a small cross near the car park. Tina was next to her, the plot marked by a little stone angel carrying a book engraved with the date of her death and the words, 'Our Guiding Light'. Serena, visiting with high hopes of consolation, only ever left the place in a state of acute anguish. As she sat now, on the lumpy piece of grass by the hedge, legs stretched alongside the handsome black marble slabs commemorating the lives of her husband's ancestors, idling chewing through the core and pips of her apple, it occurred to her that this would have been a much cosier spot in which to bury their daughter. More sensible too. They were always visiting Ashley House and, since her mother's death, very rarely went north.

During the dark days of preparing for the funeral Charlie, in shock himself and tiptoeing on eggshells round her grief, had never once openly contradicted her suggestion of Tina's burial place, though she had sensed his doubts. Sensed them and ignored them. Engulfed by her own needs and what felt like burning instinct, she had stuck to what felt right at the time. But now . . . Serena, flicked the apple stem into the hedge and plucked a juicy blade of grass to chew instead. Now, she could think of nothing more comforting, nothing more natural, than having Tina tucked up among Edmund, Violet, Albert, Nancy and the rest of them, in the lee of the old privet hedge, with the primrose-coloured sea in the field next door and the big old hills ranged behind, watching like great custodians over it all.

Peter got to the restaurant early, wanting to make sure they had a good table and also to impose his authority on the occasion. With Elizabeth's train journey in mind, he had chosen a moderately priced Italian in Ebury Street, just a hundred yards' walk from Victoria station. He followed the waiter to the back of the restaurant and felt, for the first time, truly nervous when he saw the four empty place settings, glasses and cutlery shining, napkins plump and expectant. Both Charlie and Elizabeth had quite enough to deal with as it was. It hadn't helped that when he phoned to suggest the lunch they had both been excited at the prospect, Elizabeth openly exultant at the chance to get away from Ashley House, and Charlie saying the four of them should have such get-togethers more often. Peter had felt obliged to prepare his brother in some way and explained that, beyond the obvious pleasure of seeing each other, he required a serious decision from all three of them on a delicate subject. At which point Charlie, having probed for more and got nowhere, had become quite cross, even implying at one point that Peter was getting a kick out of being mysterious, tweaking the strings of his siblings like some grand puppeteer. Which couldn't be more wrong, reflected Peter grimly, ordering himself a Scotch and musing upon what a tricky bastard Truth could be, both inside a courtroom and in the equally problematic arena of everyday life.

Cassie arrived first, which was a relief. She ordered a glass of water, which she sipped meekly, apologising, as she had many times already over the phone, for having so misread the situation. 'I thought he liked me enough not to use the information,' she explained. 'I was wrong.'

His anger with her long since vented, Peter patted her arm. 'The man's a head case. It's just a question of handling it right. We've got a few months till publication and I've got a plan. You'll see. Now, look at the menu and cheer up. Ah, here's Charlie – and Elizabeth. Good.' He stood up to wave them over, shook his younger brother firmly by the hand and kissed Elizabeth on both cheeks. 'What about this, then, the four of us? You're right, Charlie, we should do it more often. How are things? How's Serena doing? Working with Cassie now, I gather, which is splendid.'

Cassie, who had joined in the greetings, quickly returned her attention to the menu, willing Charlie not to quiz her on the subject of his wife's employment. Serena had come twice, answered two phone-calls, sorted out Mrs Shorrold's file and read her book. On the second occasion she had brought a bottle of lemon barley water and consumed a good half of it during the course of her stay, along with a tin-foil package of sandwiches and a Greek yoghurt. She read while she ate, curled up in an armchair with the book propped on her lap, as if she had no more connection to Cassie or her surroundings than a commuter awaiting a train.

'And how are you, Lizzy?' continued Peter, in full avuncular mode now, pulling out the chair for his sister and signalling to the waiters for more menus and drinks. 'How are you bearing up? Tough times, I guess.'

Elizabeth sat down, shook out her napkin and looked round the table at her siblings' expectant faces. 'I'm fine. No, really,' she added, as they all continued to stare at her, 'I'm not too bad at all. But in case you're all wondering, I'm not going back to Colin. I've decided.' She pressed her hair behind her ears, pleased at the sound of her own certainty. The decision, such as it was, had evolved during the morning, as she stared through the train window at the baked browns and greens of the Home Counties. It had presented itself suddenly as something very simple. Usually it felt complicated – and impossible. Her emotions swung like a pendulum, yet this time she was going to hang on. With both hands. Just getting it out into the open now – expressing it, giving it shape – was an enormous help. As was the sight of her brothers and sister digesting the notion, as if it were fact rather than wishful thinking.

'What will you do?' murmured Cassie.

'Don't know yet.' Elizabeth picked up a menu and began to study it. 'I can't stay at Ashley House for the rest of my life. I'd go mad. And so would Mum.' She made a face. 'Her and Dad, they're like two prehistoric rocks glued together. She simply can't understand that it's not like that for everyone. She can't forgive me for getting it so wrong – *twice*.' This unfortunate truth wrought a moment of silence that Elizabeth filled. 'If we're doing starters I'll have the stuffed mushrooms – heaped with garlic, no doubt, which Colin hates, but that doesn't matter now, does it? Peter? Are we doing starters?'

'Whatever . . . whatever.' Having already exchanged several anguished glances with Cassie, Peter stared, unseeing, at the options on the card in front of him.

'Artichoke salad and veal for me, I think.' Charlie slapped his menu shut and turned to his elder sister. 'It goes without saying, Lizzy, that anything I – Serena and I – can do, you have only to ask. Okay?' He squeezed her arm. 'Promise you'll ask?'

Elizabeth nodded gratefully, for a moment not trusting herself to speak. Then she said, 'Just . . . well, just having you lot . . . all of us here . . . helps you know . . . makes me feel less alone.'

'Of course you're not alone,' Cassie burst out, thinking suddenly that it was quite wrong, unnecessary and wrong, for her and Peter to be involving the other two in all the mess over Stephen's book. She shot a pleading glance at him, willing him to read her mind. But Peter had had enough of all the high emotions whizzing round the table and the intolerable suspense of suppressing what had to be said. Once the waiter had been despatched with their orders, he launched, succinctly and fluently, as he did so often before judges and juries, into the painful business of the day. Cassie, twisting her napkin in her lap, watched the faces of the other two as he talked, reading the shadows of astonishment, disbelief and pain that had characterised her own reaction to the news.

'Fucking hell,' said Charlie, when Peter had finished. 'Uncle Eric! Fucking hell.' He took a swig of his wine, and then another. 'Mother and Uncle Eric – it's unbelievable. Christ, does Dad know, do you think?'

Peter shook his head. 'It seems unlikely.'

'Maybe,' said Elizabeth, in a small voice, 'maybe he did know and forgave her.' Inside she could feel the pendulum swinging back again, no longer hard and cool and graspable but a bar of soap slipping from her fingers. Would it be wrong, after all, to give up on Colin? Her parents hadn't given up on each other and they had had forty subsequent happy years. Then she thought of what Pamela had actually done and a huge rage swelled inside her. Her mother, her fucking mother, having an affair, no better than Colin, no better than anyone, it was outrageous, unbelievable. All that self-righteousness, all that judging, all that debilitating perfection based not on virtue but betrayal. And of the worst kind, too. Her husband's brother. Christ. She thought the word and then said it out loud, almost shouted it: 'Christ.'

'Steady on,' growled Peter, glancing at the other tables and the waiter approaching with their plates of food.

'It was a long time ago,' ventured Cassie, adding, as a wave of desperation about Dan rolled over her, 'and it must have been hard . . . if she really loved Eric . . . to give him up. You should have seen that letter . . .'

'Didn't you bring it?'

'No, I—'

'I asked you to bring it.'

'I'm sorry, Peter, I forgot. It's quite safe, in my bottom drawer.'

'Hard?' snapped Elizabeth. 'I'll tell you what's hard. Hard is having a mother who parades her moral virtues like a set of fucking medals, making sure you fail in every attempt to emulate them. Hard is a mother who thinks you're an emotional failure. Hard is a mother who turns out to be a total hypocrite.'

'Lizzy, stop it.' It was Charlie who cut in. 'I can see – we can all see – that, given your current circumstances, this must be particularly difficult, especially if Mum, as you say, has been giving you something of a hard time.' He paused, thinking of what Serena had said about the relationship between his elder sister and his mother, and how perceptive she always was, particularly about Elizabeth. 'But,' he continued gently, 'as Cass says, it *was* a long time ago and she did do the right thing and managed to have a great marriage and just wants the same for you.'

'Yeah, I guess,' Elizabeth conceded. 'And don't get me wrong, I am grateful to her and Dad for all that they've done – Roland has been so happy . . .' She placed her knife and fork together, took a deep breath and folded her arms. 'Sorry, everybody. I guess I'm not really very fine after all.'

'Yes, you are.' Peter spoke firmly, pushing away his own plate, wanting to get things back under control. 'And all this mess is going to be fine too. Because . . .' he cleared his throat and patted his lips with his napkin '. . . I have decided that the best thing to do, since appealing to this wretched man's better nature has failed, is to appeal to his worse nature instead.' He hesitated, quailing at what he was about to suggest, aware that it fundamentally contravened the ethics to which he had devoted a lifetime of unwavering personal and professional support. 'With the view that desperate situations call for desperate remedies, what I propose is that we offer Mr Smith money – quite a lot of money. From what Cassie says he's completely broke. We offer it as, shall we say, a *reward* for editing his book so as to preclude causing our family any unnecessary grief? The thing comes out in the spring. It's hardly likely to win the Booker or make the bestseller list. By the time – if ever – he changes his mind it'll be out of print. Or Mum and Dad will be dead. Or both.'

'Bribe him, you mean?' Elizabeth laughed, incredulous.

'Call it that if you like.' Having given the matter a huge amount of thought, he was not about to change his mind. 'And I would like to be the one to foot the bill – both for today and for the business of writing a cheque to Stephen Smith.'

'That's daft. We should all contribute,' put in Charlie, scowling because he was unhappy about the proposition but unable to think of an alternative. Peter was right: their parents probably only had a decade at most left to them; it was intolerable to think of their last years being blighted by the distant past when all that had followed had been so redeeming and good.

'I don't want contributions from anyone. I am responsible for the conception of this plan and I will be the one to carry it out. Please, don't cross me on this, Charlie, or you two.' He looked at his sisters. 'It is not a matter on which I will be persuaded.'

'How much will you give him?' whispered Cassie, as appalled as the others but also hopeful. Her visit to Stephen's humble flat, the thick, cheap glasses and tawdry furnishings, was still vivid. Money, though crude, would surely do the trick.

'I was thinking of ten.'

'Ten thousand pounds?' the other three echoed, incredulous.

Peter nodded. 'It has to be significant or it won't work. Probably double what his publishers have given him. He's a rat. He'll scuttle back down his hole. I'm going to sort it, okay? I wanted you lot to know, but not to worry. And it really need not go any further. Helen knows, obviously, because it was her friend who – thank God – alerted us to what the bastard was playing at. But, Charlie, there's really no need to tell Serena. The tighter we keep this thing, the safer it will be.'

Charlie frowned, making no promises, because he told Serena everything and because he felt that to be a matter on which he, not Peter, should decide. A little later the four said their farewells in the street, then parted to return, slowly, to their respective lives, each a little heavier of heart, each a little afraid.

Pamela cut the crusts off the bread and arranged the slices round the largest of her pudding basins, then tipped in the cooked fruit and sugar and pressed it all down with the back of a spoon. For a summer pudding the fruit mixture had to be tightly packed or its beautiful crimson juices didn't soak into the bread enough, leaving dry, unsightly patches of white. If they were compressed too tightly they were reduced to a mushy pulp and that didn't do either. Apart from the cellar the kitchen was easily the coolest room in the house, especially with the back door open, as it was now, allowing what paltry breeze there was to drift in across the stone-tiled floor, lifting the corners of the curtains and the tea-towels hanging along the front rail of the Aga. With John at the nursing-home, Helen and the children at the lake with a picnic, Elizabeth in London and Serena still in the village, the house was quiet. Blissfully quiet. Pamela had not realised how much she was in need of silence until the last of the doughty Jessica's high-pitched screeches had died away and the swimming party had disappeared over the brow of the hill towards the copse. Now all was still, apart from the buzz of the fat bluebottle bashing itself against one of the kitchen windows and the occasional drone of an aeroplane following the well-worn trail of the Gatwick flypath. The workmen had stopped, as usual, for an early lunch. They were off to find sandwiches, the foreman said, which meant they were going to the Rising Sun for some beer and a pork pie or two. With the end of the job now well within their sights – and on schedule too – such indulgences had crept into their routine. The day before only two men had come instead of four and by half past three they had disappeared. Going home, they said, though John, watching the dusty white van disappear down the drive, had remarked that they were probably off to make a start on the next job.

Pamela pressed a plate on top of the summer pudding, in a final bid to encourage the juices out of the fruit, then placed it carefully on the bottom shelf of the fridge. With so many people in the house

the fridge was packed with food and it had taken some rearrange-
ment to create sufficient space. Having crouched right down to do
the job, she stood up too quickly and found dancing pencil points of
light flecking her field of vision. She held on to the fridge to steady
herself, feeling suddenly unbearably hot and frail. It was lovely, of
course, having all the family again, but also quite a strain. Catering,
laundry, tidying – it was a lot to keep on top of, especially without
Betty who was away visiting a sick brother in Penge. She should, she
knew, take the opportunity of an empty house to rest, to take some
time out, as Helen had called it when she had caught Pamela
cleaning silver in the dining room the night before, a hankie tied
round her nose and mouth because of the smell, and rows of
gleaming Harrison treasures laid out on the table before her.

Time out. Pamela wasn't sure what the phrase would mean for
her, other than sifting through recipe books on the sofa or sliding
her needle and thread through her latest growing thatch of silky
flowers. But it was too hot for sewing now, and sitting on the sofa
would only make her feel guilty. There was simply too much to do,
not just in the kitchen but around the rest of the house as well.
Pamela tried not to mind the clutter – mess, with so many, was
natural, she knew – but with the house empty it was somehow
harder to ignore, particularly in the downstairs rooms where
abandoned shoes and single grubby socks seemed to be everywhere, along with strewn packs of cards, half-started board games
and empty sweet wrappers. The utility room was piled high with
unwashed laundry and she could feel grit under her shoes on the
kitchen floor. When the phone rang Pamela, standing with one pink
sandal, a blue sock and a half-sucked boiled sweet she had found on
a window-sill behind a curtain in the hall, answered it with some
reluctance.

'It's Colin. I'm so sorry to trouble you . . .'

'Colin, my dear, no trouble, of course.' Pamela sank into a hall
chair, her voice softening in an instant. As she had said many times
to John, she had no intention of taking sides over the thorny
business of their daughter's marriage, but every time she heard
Colin's voice on the telephone, so thin and lost, she found it

impossible not to feel compassion for his predicament. Elizabeth, if she was punishing him, had already – in her opinion – gone way too far.

'I was wondering, Elizabeth isn't . . . available, is she?'

'No . . . she's not here. She's in London with Peter, Charlie and Cassie – some sort of get-together Peter has organised.'

'Really?'

In revealing this, Pamela had meant only to offer reassurance that, on this occasion at least, Elizabeth was not standing next to her, signalling that she had no desire to take the phone.

Colin though, picturing Elizabeth pouring her woes out to her siblings, talking about the situation – about *him* – felt a surge of fresh unease. Since the start of the holidays the reality of his new circumstances had hit home. Waking alone each morning, with nothing to attend to but his own needs, life felt considerably emptier, but also freer in a way that was undeniably pleasant. He didn't miss Elizabeth's presence so much as feel riled by her absence. That she thought she could just walk out on everything, snap shut their life like a suitcase, was outrageous. Regardless of what remained of his affection for her, something in Colin felt honour-bound to fight such an attitude, just to show her that a joint existence, no matter how unsatisfactory, could not simply be thrown away like that, as if it were of no more intrinsic value than a used tissue. And there was Roland, of course, whom Colin missed and who – he had no doubt – needed him. With all his babyish insecurities he was more in need of a father than most boys. Colin shuddered whenever he thought of the detrimental effect the separation must be having, with only his mother's haywire emotions and indulgent ways for guidance and no opportunity for his own firm, infinitely more authoritative hand to balance things out.

'Could I have a word with Roland, then?'

'I'm afraid he's swimming at the lake with all his cousins.'

'I see. Never mind,' said Colin, minding very much, feeling yet again that the Harrisons were ranged against him, bent upon denying him not only his rights as a parent and husband but also what had once seemed the most secure of prospects. While

Elizabeth might be able to sail on towards the promise of a hefty inheritance, taking half his worldly goods with her, a divorce would leave him considerably poorer. For one thing he would have to sell the house, and he liked the house a lot, with its glistening black mock-Tudor timbers and spacious rooms. He had spent a considerable amount of his life working towards being able to afford such a property and it seemed unfair that he should have to surrender it now. A marriage was entered into jointly and, in his view, should be terminated with the consent of both parties. He wasn't a saint. He was a man who had strayed. He had admitted his sin and said sorry. What more was he supposed to do? 'Would you say I called?'

'Of course, Colin, of course. I could get Roland to call you back, if you like.'

Colin was on the point of replying when, looking out of the window, he saw Phyllis walking up the path to the front door. Her hair was loose and she was wearing a long turquoise cotton dress and gold flip-flops. 'Don't worry, Pamela, I – I'm going out. It might be easier if I called back. Tell Elizabeth that we need to talk, that I do desperately want to work things out.'

'I know you do, Colin, believe me, I know.' Pamela put the phone down and stared gloomily at the sock and sandal in her lap. At a loss as to what to do with the sweet, stuck firmly now between two fingers, she popped it into her mouth. It had a gluey bubblegum taste that was almost nice. She licked her fingers, and noticed the morning's post, which someone, irritatingly, had picked up off the doormat and left by the telephone. It was all junk mail, apart from a large brown envelope addressed to her in writing she didn't recognise. Inside, there were sketches of the family portrait she had commissioned so many months before, now nearing completion, the accompanying note said. It went on to explain that the sketches were just to give her an idea and that she was welcome to a proper viewing any time. Based on the photo Sid had taken at Christmas, the drawings showed them all striking the poses that Peter had helped to choreograph on and around the sitting-room sofa. For a moment Pamela felt excited. It would make such a good eightieth-birthday present for John, well worth the hefty three thousand pounds the artist was going to charge. But then, staring at the pencilled faces, Pamela realised with dismay that the picture was already wrong, already history. Theo looked so round-faced, as did Clem, quite unlike their new, skinny, adolescent selves. And then there was Colin, stiff but proud, his arms crossed in the back row, still quite the son-in-law instead of a lost voice on the phone. Most poignant of all, however, was the sight of Tina, dear little Tina, captured wonderfully by the artist as a chunky-limbed cherub, sitting sweetly in her mother's arms, her eyes wild and inquisitive, one wispy strand of hair floating across her cheek. Pamela gasped and pressed the blue sock to her mouth to stifle the sound. How precious that time had been and how little they had known it. Six months, and the world – as if in one half-turn of a kaleidoscope – had changed irrevocably.

As the front door opened Pamela just had time to shove the drawing back into its envelope. She looked up to see Serena, bedraggled from her walk back from the church.

Serena dropped her handbag to the floor and leant back against the door with a sigh. 'Hi, there. God, it's hot, isn't it?' She prised her sandals off each foot with the toes of the other and raked her hair off her face with her fingers. 'Relentless, isn't it? Though it was quite cool at the church,' she murmured, half to herself, remembering the kiss of the breeze on her cheeks as she had sat in the lee of the hedge and the echo of something like peace that had briefly stirred her heart. Then she peered at her mother-in-law, who was still sitting, motionless, in the chair by the phone. 'Pamela? Are you all right?'

'Fine, dear. Like you, a little weary with this heat.' Pamela stood up, tucking the envelope under her arm. The commission, however advanced it was, would have to be cancelled. It seemed now that a sort of smugness had prompted it, a desire to show off, to revel in, the glorious, sprawling solidity of the family. When, in fact, nothing was solid, or could ever be made so by a few brushstrokes of paint. She would pay the full fee, if necessary, write it off as a well-intentioned scheme that had gone wrong. There were all sorts of other things she could give John for his birthday: a new pipe-stand, for instance, or a boot-scraper for the back door, or a pair of calfskin slippers to replace the dreadful tartan ones he insisted on wearing with the backs down, exposing the yellowing scaly skin of his heels. 'Did you enjoy your walk?'

'My walk? Yes, thanks, it was good . . . I . . . Pamela, this may sound an odd question to ask, but do you know anything about moving graves?'

'I beg your pardon?' Pamela, her mind still on slippers, blinked in puzzlement.

'Graves. Changing where someone has been buried.'

'Heavens . . . No, I can't say I do, except that I expect it's rather difficult. Why? Are you . . .'

'Nothing. I just wondered, that's all. It's nothing, honestly.' Serena retrieved her sandals, looped the straps over one finger and headed for the stairs. 'I'm going to change and join the others at the lake for a swim. Give Helen a breather.'

'Okay, dear.' Pamela, still clutching the envelope, stood watching as her daughter-in-law made her way up the stairs. She took each step very slowly and kept her head bowed, as if studying the progress of her own bare feet, as if it was a matter of huge importance which few inches they chose to occupy of the carpet. Then the phone rang again. This time it was John, sounding distant and suspicious as he always did on his mobile, explaining that the staff at the nursing-home had said he was welcome to stay for a spot of lunch and he thought he might because . . . Here he faltered, then concluded, 'Because it's not something I've done before.'

'How nice, of course, how nice,' Pamela murmured, concerned both for the trout fillets she had defrosted for their lunch and the faintly unsettling notion of Eric, silent and chair-ridden, somehow showing preference at this late stage for a human being other than her. 'I'll see you when I see you,' she added lightly, shifting the position of the envelope under her arm. She had been gripping it so hard that the edge was cutting into her skin. 'And you can have your trout as a starter tonight.'

'What?'

'Nothing. It doesn't matter. I got some trout out of the freezer for our lunch, but you can have yours tonight.'

'Trout, yummy,' he said sweetly, sensing that she was put out and wanting to make up for it.

'Give Eric my love, won't you?'

'Of course.'

John put his phone back into his pocket and returned to the tray of lunch that the pretty Irish nurse with green cat-eyes had kindly brought up for him. Baked potato with cream cheese, cold salmon and a tomato salad sprinkled with fresh chives. No wonder the place cost a fortune. Eric had already been fed his own plate of food, and had his mouth patted dry like a baby. He was sitting now, spruce and only slightly lopsided in the chair next to his bed, his stick legs covered, in spite of the heat, with a green tartan rug. The stroke had induced no visible deterioration in his appearance. John, squeezing both papery hands in greeting, had even wondered whether his compulsion to make the visit had not perhaps been a touch self-indulgent and melodramatic. Nothing had changed after all. The clammy medicine-smell of the room was the same. And Eric, mute but unbowed, was as he had been for nearly three decades.

'How are we? Not too bad, I'm told, not too bad at all.' Even after so many years John found his brother's lack of response hard and was soon longing for Pamela to cluck and tuck and soothe them through the gaps with her soft commentary. Without her, he felt brash and inept. Thoroughly useless, in fact. He'd stay ten minutes and go, he had told himself, sitting on the windowseat and sipping the coffee brought by the little Irish nurse; there was no urgency, after all, and – now that he was actually here – he had no clear sense of what needed saying. But in that ten minutes John had studied the slack, inscrutable expression on his brother's face and had seen that something had changed, after all. After so many tenacious, obstinate years, some force within was letting go, slipping back, much as a drowning person clinging to a hand chooses at last to release it. Time, John realised, was truly running out. So he had started to talk, with staccato awkwardness at first, but then more slowly, finding that if he looked out of the window, addressing himself to Eric's presence, rather than to the disconcertingly vacant, gawping body behind him, it wasn't so hard. The things that spilled out of him were trivial: the progress on the roof; the volatility of the insurance market, soaring premiums and subsiding profits; the car needing a service; the parched state of the country-side; the children all meeting in London for a jolly.

It was only when his own lunch plate was mopped clean – with a tasty crust of brown bread – that John ventured into the other, trickier territory, feeling his way with each sentence, fighting the debilitating doubt as to whether he was being heard. 'You gave me Ashley House, Eric, and I want you to know that I will always, to my own dying day, be grateful for that. The house links us to the past and the future and I love it so.' As he talked, John remembered again the full shocking circumstances of his brother's decision all those years before. The handing over of a birthright was nothing short of extraordinary. As a second son John had learnt to live without expectation. He had even tried, for many weeks, to talk Eric out of it, fearful of repercussions and regret. But Eric had been adamant, expounding not only the conflicting needs of his own, infinitely more itinerant personality, but also the theory that houses such as theirs had *natural* inheritors. His younger brother was the only man for the job, he had insisted, with his wife, his growing family and predisposition to put down roots instead of gazing, as Eric did endlessly, at the possibility of distant horizons. Affected by the crusading zeal of such arguments, John had allowed himself to be persuaded. Even so, it was years before he appreciated the full extent of Eric's gift, understood that Pamela, with her capacity for nurturing love of him and their offspring, was an integral part of it, that without her at his side he would have been as ill-equipped as his elder brother to assume the mantle of ownership.

'You chose a harder route, old man,' continued John now, 'in so many ways, a much harder route, allowing me, somehow, to be the lucky one and I don't know why. And that bothers me. Why did I become the lucky one when we started out so equally? Or, rather, not so very equally, given how I worshipped you. Do you remember that, Eric? Do you remember how I followed you round, like a puppy? All those games. Do you remember the games, Eric? And now the children, the grandchildren, are playing the same games – little ruffians running wild. They've been at the lake all week and we've got your tent up, and yesterday I dug out the little calor-gas heater so they could make their own campsite tea. Baked beans, I think it was, with sausages and a loaf of bread. I can't tell you what memories it brings back, Eric, to watch them, this new generation of youngsters, their lives echoing ours and none of them realising it. I've tried to explain, but they don't listen or care much, of course. Neither did we at their age. I can't tell you how it makes me feel. On the one hand so happy and on the other so damnably sad because it seems like yesterday that it was our turn to have all that, to be at the beginning of life instead of . . .' John wrested his gaze from the window and went to stand over the chair, pinning Eric's empty eyes to his. 'Do you suffer in there, old man? Do you suffer? My back aches most of the time, these days. In the morning I'm as stiff as an old tree and I lose things and forget things and Pammy too – she's all over the shop – and the truth is . . . the truth is, Eric, it's . . . I'm scared as hell . . . scared as hell.' John thrust his hands into his pockets and returned to the window. 'We've had a bastard of a year,' he continued huskily, scanning the gardens and thinking of his little granddaughter and the new troubles confronting Elizabeth. On the path directly below a tiny bird of a woman was edging her way along with a walking frame, bent almost double in concentration upon the potential treachery of the gravel under her feet. In the middle of the lawn next to her a weeping willow shimmered in the midday sun, a resplendent fountain of lime and yellowy green. 'Whereas you,' continued John, turning back to face his brother, 'have had not much of anything to worry about, have you? In fact . . .' John laughed, quietly at first and then so loudly that the Irish nurse, hovering outside the door with knuckle poised, drew back in some astonishment. 'In fact, maybe, after all these years, you're the bloody lucky one, after all. You, with just this window on to the world, a window that, for all we know, you may not even be able to look through. Your pleasures may have been limited over the years, old boy, but, by God, so has your pain. So has your pain.'

When the nurse entered John was standing with his hands clasped, jaw resolute, staring out of the window with the air of one who has completed the purpose of his visit. 'Mr Harrison?'

'Fabulous lunch. Just fabulous. Thank you so much, my dear.' John picked up his hat and patted it into place on his head. 'He gave me this, you know,' he said, tugging the brim. 'My brother gave me this hat, many moons ago.'

'Did he? It's very fine.'

'Isn't it just?' John stepped towards the chair, put a hand on each of Eric's shoulders and kissed the top of his head. 'Thank you, Nurse, for looking after him. He's been happy here. I feel it in my bones that he has been truly happy.'

At the lake the children were organising a race – a complicated process since, in order to be remotely fair, it required different starting points to accommodate their differing abilities. Maisie and Theo, in joint and sometimes conflicting charge of the operation, were lining the others up, beginning with Jessica who, much to Helen's relief, was commanded to the waist-high shallows, where she could perform her idiosyncratic doggy-paddle flops without too much endangerment to her life or anyone else's. Chloë, in her armbands, was also assigned to the shallow side, but a little further back than Jessica, which, judging from the broad grin on her face, was a matter of some considerable relief. Roland, too, was looking happy, since Maisie had overruled Theo's suggestion that he should stand behind Chloë and directed him instead to a rock at the beginning of the deep bit, from where he could launch into his top speed non-breathing crawl secure in the knowledge that the muddy bottom was within a couple of feet of his toes. After a few last-minute quibbles, Ed, Theo and Maisie, who were all powerful swimmers, picked their way round to the big rock at the widest point of the lake where they were to dive in unison from a spot several yards behind their less able siblings and cousins. In the meantime Clem, who had done no more than paddle all morning, declining even to remove the thick towelling bathrobe (an old dressing-gown of John's consigned to the large trunk of Ashley House swimming things), had volunteered to be referee. With this intention she had taken up a central position on the furthest side of the lake from where she had torn out a huge feathery frond of bracken to use as a starting flag.

Helen, propped against a tree in the shade, watched the proceedings through the blue haze of her sunglasses, admiring the mutual co-operation but fearing that it would be short-lived. Jessica would lose and protest volubly, as would Chloë, while Ed and Theo, if beaten either by each other or by Maisie, would almost certainly lapse into deep sulks. Judging from Maisie's demeanour, as lissom and glistening in her black one-piece as a seal, her hair bunched in a tight wet ponytail, her pretty features flexed in fierce determination, the boys had a lot to be worried about. Only Roland, Helen suspected, puffing his chest out and rubbing his knobbly ribs in excited preparation to jump, would remain truly happy regardless of the race's outcome. The transformation in her younger nephew was extraordinary: tanned and fuller-faced to look at, bordering on cheeky to talk to, everything about him refuted the traditional view that marital separation was supposed to stress a child. If anyone appeared stressed it was Clem, huddled on the rock like an old man in the dressing-gown, looking almost – unbelievably – *cold*, when Helen herself, in the protective shade of her tree, was so hot she hardly knew where to put herself. It was evident to Helen that the extraordinary shivering state of her niece related to her having grown painfully thin; yet she had certainly eaten well enough, tucking into their picnic of crisps and sandwiches and sausage rolls with as much gusto as her cousins. Maybe she was in love, Helen decided, remembering her own first all-consuming passion for a young sports master at the age of fourteen, which when she had discovered he was far more interested in his own sex, had metamorphosed into a crusading zeal to convert him. Helen smiled and closed her eyes, feeling rather sleepy. The race had been held up by Ed's announcement – greeted with a round of groans – that he needed to pee. So there was no need to watch just yet, she told herself, no need to do anything but be very still and quiet. Her headache had receded to a distant, manageable place at the back of her skull, where it lay coiled like a sleeping snake. The other children had been left standing, poised in their positions like comical water statues, waiting for Ed to emerge from the bushes. Helen sighed, floating so blissfully in the weightless dark behind her closed eyes that when the bleeping tune of her mobile sounded from the basket next to her, her first instinct was to ignore it. Then she thought, Oh, God, the doctor! and lunged into the basket with both hands, groping through apple cores and half-eaten sandwiches to get to it in time.

'Mrs Harrison? It's Dr Fuller.'

'I knew it would be, I just knew . . .' Helen pressed her back hard against the tree-trunk behind her, seeking its solidity and the reassuring cool of the rough bark through the hot thin cotton of her shirt. Across the lake she saw Ed beating his way out of the bracken with both arms, as if fighting off a swarm of assailants. He was shouting something, but Helen, enclosed now in the silence of her own fear, heard nothing. 'Yes, Dr Fuller, Helen Harrison speaking.'

'It's good news, Mrs Harrison.'

'Is it?' Helen pressed her hand to her chest and looked up at the sky, visible in asymmetric slices of blue through the mesh of branches overhead. There is a God, she thought, there is a God.

'You're not ill, Mrs Harrison, not in any way. You're pregnant.'

Serena, clad only in her bathing costume with a towel slung, shawl-like, across her shoulders, walked with deliberate slowness, enjoying the shady cool of the copse and the springy dryness of the mossy path beneath her feet. Every so often the patches of brambles and already ripening blackberry bushes on either side were so overgrown that she had to turn sideways to pass through without snagging her skin on a thorn. Before coming out (and having checked that Pamela was safely ensconced in the kitchen), she had called Directory Enquiries for the number of the vicar at the church in Cheshire. A small action on the face of it, but it had felt enormous. It was the first thing Serena had truly *felt* like doing in months. It had reminded her that such simple processes were the basis on which she had once lived her life: wanting to do things, then carrying them out. Instead of being some dumb, reactive thing, going through the motions, saying the words of a part expected by other people. After securing the number she had folded the piece of paper into a tight fat rectangle and placed it in an inner pocket of her purse. The logic of her thinking was that to move a dead body there was no better place to start than with the person in charge of the graveyard in which that body was buried. St Margaret's, too, would have to be consulted, but she wanted Charlie to take care of that. Charlie, dear Charlie. Serena pulled the towel more tightly across her shoulders. She couldn't wait to tell him. It was too important for the phone, so she had decided to hang on until he joined them all at the weekend for a week's holiday before jetting off for his conference in Florida.

Absorbed in her thoughts, Serena was only a few yards from the point where the path burst through to the clearing that housed the lake when she became aware that the muted noises filtering through the trees represented a commotion beyond the usual high spirits of a communal swim. The lake itself, a bulging oblong of browny green fringed by boulders and tall reeds, was unoccupied, as was the flat sandbank to her left that was commonly used for sunbathing and picnicking. A blanket and basket set back a little under the shade of two grand old oaks looked similarly abandoned. What noises there were emanated from the jungle of bracken on the far side of the lake, in the thickest part of the copse where, at this time of year, the path was too overgrown to follow. Looking in that direction, Serena could make out bobbing heads and the occasional flash of a bare limb, as if the entire party was beating around in search of something. A ball, perhaps, she decided, squinting across the water, or maybe a pair of goggles, flung in petulance or as an ill-judged prank.

'Hey,' she called, waving an arm, 'what's going on?'

Chloë was the first to emerge and waved back, both arms at once, high over her head. 'Aunty Serena, Aunty Serena.' Her voice sounded shrill and upset.

'Chloë, what's happened?' Serena took off her sandals and began to pick her way round the edge of the lake, which was hard because there was no proper bank and in some places the mud was so deep that it oozed up to her shins. 'Where's Mummy?'

'She's here. We're all here. She's crying and Boots is here too but he's – he's—' Chloë broke off, convulsing with tears. 'Boots is *dying*,' she wailed. At which point, Serena hurled her towel and shoes into the bushes and plunged into the water. For a moment the iciness took her breath away, but she was an excellent swimmer and in a few fast, powerful strokes was heaving herself out on to the other side. 'What is it, sweetie? Is Boots sick?' She tried to hug Chloë, who squirmed out of reach of her slippery cold arms and pointed into the bracken. 'He's in there. Ed found him, all walking funny, and we got Mummy to look but she doesn't know what to do and she's . . . crying.'

'Oh dear, oh dear. Let me see.' Serena let go of her niece and strode into the tangle of bushes, ignoring the stabs of sharp stones and twigs on the soles of her feet and doing a sort of breaststroke to get herself through the mass of fronds, all well above head height. She broke through eventually to a flattened section where the children were clustered round Helen and the stricken dog, whom Helen had by the collar. She was trying, ineffectually, to persuade him to walk in the direction of the overgrown path. When they saw Serena the children all turned at once, shouting simultaneous and unintelligible explanations.

'Shush everybody. Helen? What's happened to him?'

'I don't know,' sobbed Helen, releasing Boots's collar as the dog let out a whimpering snarl. 'I'm just so hopeless with animals. He's obviously hurt but he won't let us lift him and he won't walk and—'

'Theo.' Serena turned to her eldest nephew. 'Run back to the house and tell Granny to call the vet. Stand back a minute, Helen, let me have a look.' She knelt by Boots and gently stroked his head, noticing as she did so that there was a large swelling on his neck, and two small but clearly visible puncture marks in the middle of it. 'It's an adder,' she shouted after Theo, who was already crashing away through the bracken. 'Tell Granny he's been bitten by an adder.'

'If we try to lift him he growls,' sobbed Helen, standing back now, wanting to hug Serena for being so cool and knowledgeable. An adder bite, of course, why hadn't she thought of it? But all she could think about was the baby. A baby! Another child, growing inside her, a terrible mistake of a child. She was almost forty-eight. It had been a big enough decision to have Chloë at forty, but this – this was impossible. She wasn't one of those super-mothers who could manage such things. A baby would shrivel her body, suck the colour from her hair, sap the last of her already faltering energy. Peter would agree. In fact, Peter was going to be appalled. She had been crying even as she dropped the phone, even before the children were hollering at her about the wretched Boots, whom Ed had found staggering around the undergrowth moaning, his back legs collapsing to the ground.

'Ed, fetch the biggest of the towels,' commanded Serena. 'We'll see if we can wrap and carry him back in that. Maisie – Clem – is there anything either of you can find to put some water in? It might help, if he's thirsty, or just to cool the wound. Quickly, children. There's not much time.'

'What can I do, Aunty Serena?' whispered Roland, coming to stand next to her with Jessica.

'You, my sweetheart,' said Serena, crouching next to him and looking into his big solemn dark-lashed eyes, 'you and Jessica can help by packing up the picnic and suncreams and things and putting them all in the basket ready for going back to the house. Okay?'

Some ten minutes later, a curious procession, with Ed, Theo, Helen and Serena in the middle carrying the bulky bundle of Boots in a towel, like hunters returning with a kill, wound its way back through the woods and across the fields to Ashley House. After struggling hard, Boots went very still and remained so even after they had laid him gently on the cool floor of the cloisters and unwrapped the towel. When the vet arrived, followed closely by John, it was clear that he was dead.

By the time Charlie joined his family, catching an early-afternoon train on Friday, a small wooden cross had been erected in the middle of the orchard of silver birches where Boots had been laid to rest. John had chosen the spot, to the left of the drive at the front of the house, because it was where Boots had spent many months during his latter years, mostly asleep, but with an ear cocked both for the rustlings of unobtainable wildlife in the grass around him and for any signs of arrivals and departures from the house.

Sid had dug the grave, sweating profusely at the effort of ramming the blade of his spade against the concrete earth, so hard in places that if he hadn't been aware of John watching from the study window behind a cloud of pipe smoke, he might have been tempted to give up. He could feel the man's pain, knew what the dog had meant to him, both as a companion and as a link to an era now gone. He'd been the same when Scot, beloved Yorkshire terrier of his dear Ruthie, had passed away: it had been like losing Ruthie all over again, losing a last little part of her. So he had laboured on, watched intermittently by various grandchildren, until the soil grew dark and moist and he could shovel it out with ease.

For the burial itself they all assembled round the plot, the little girls solemn-faced with posies of wild flowers and everyone whispering amens to Pamela's softly spoken prayers. John, jaw clenched, had concluded the proceedings by throwing in the frayed, much loved blanket off the old dog's bed followed by a fistful of earth. He then nodded at Sid to commence the business of covering the body.

During the course of the week, Charlie had been given detailed accounts of all aspects of the proceedings by various members of his family and felt as if he had lived through the drama himself. Serena, clearly the saviour of the hour in spite of its unhappy outcome, had at times sounded almost unnaturally energised by it.

Helen had fallen apart completely, she said, and still didn't seem to have recovered. John, too, fresh from a long visit to his brother, had been shaken to find them all on the cloisters with poor Boots dead at their feet. He had said all the right things, then and many times subsequently, about the dog having had a happy life and a good innings, but always in a clipped, strained way that suggested he was far from accepting such consolations himself. He was smoking so many pipes that Pamela, normally mutely accepting of the habit, had let slip a few remonstrations about how it was making him cough and setting a bad example to the children. What Serena never mentioned to Charlie – because there was no need – was that, after Tina, coping with a dead dog was nothing. Peanuts, in fact. She, more than Pamela, had helped the children organise the funeral and taken drinks out to Sid while he hacked out the grave in the keen afternoon sun. I can do this, she had thought, I can be strong for this. And it was precisely this strength that Charlie had detected in her breathy excitement over the phone and which gave a definite bounce to his step as he pushed open Ashley House's heavy front door and shouted his arrival to anyone within earshot who cared to take notice of it.

'Hello, Charlie, we're in here.' Charlie traced the greeting to the music room where he found Clem and Elizabeth sitting at the little rosewood table in the window poring over music-theory practice papers.

'Daddy.' Clem pushed back her chair and ran at her father, who squeezed her hard, resisting the urge to remark on her gauntness, which had hit him like a hammer-blow the moment he had laid eyes on her. She was, unbelievably, thinner. Not having seen her for a week, he was sure of it. Living day to day one lost perspective on such things. Next to his sister, whose now unrestrained curves pushed out merrily in all directions from a tight white T-shirt and wide Bermuda shorts, she was all bones and eyes.

'What are you two up to, then?'

'Grade five theory.' Clem made a pouting face, looking, for one happy minute, quite like her old self. 'I suck.'

Elizabeth laughed loudly. 'She doesn't suck . . . well maybe at spotting the difference between appoggiaturas and acciaccaturas but . . .'

'Appo-whats?'

'They're horrid little notes you have to play before a main note,' explained Clem, sitting back at the table with a sigh. 'I get them muddled.'

'I'm not surprised, they sound vile.' Charlie crossed to the piano and played chopsticks very badly and very fast, standing all the while with his foot on the pedal, flooding the sound. Seeing Clem still so skinny after a week of his mother's cooking was a blow, but apart from that he felt full of hope. There was a week's holiday to look forward to – with a wife who seemed, at last, to be recovering some of her *joie de vivre* – and then, after the August bank holiday weekend, he was off to Florida for four days of discussions on a new international marine treaty, being hosted by his counterparts in America. There was a hefty agenda, but the institute and hotel where they were to be based, on the edge of the Keys, was reputedly one of Florida's finest: swimming-pools and golf courses galore. Not that Charlie was a golfer, but he liked the thought of them – all those shimmering greens and undulating fairways – and he could admire them while he ran round the edge. 'Where's everyone else, then? Where's Mum?'

'Yours or mine?' quipped Clem, rubbing out a bunch of little notes she had just written on a stave.

'Both.'

'They're in the raspberry canes, I think, picking for supper. The other children are at the lake with Helen. Clem didn't want to go, did you, Clem?'

'Nope.' She spoke firmly, not looking up from her work.

'Too bad about old Boots.'

'Yes, it was awful, Daddy,' agreed Clem gravely, looking up at him now, her big eyes flooding with tears.

'Awful,' echoed Elizabeth, recalling not the family's mourning for the pet on her return from London, but her own tumultuous state of mind. After the extraordinary revelations over lunch, seeing her mother had produced many difficult and conflicting feelings, ranging from anger to understanding. Pamela was maddening, perfectionist, critical, but also in the end, Elizabeth realised, rather noble. How she had conducted herself proved that a bad affair did not preclude a good marriage. The thought, once there, would not go away. It pushed the pendulum inside her head back again, where it lodged, obstinate and unignorable. A break had undoubtedly done her good. It was wrong to deprive Roland of the company of his natural father. With Colin penitent she could start the relationship again more on her own terms: be herself; be less afraid. When Pamela informed her that Colin had called that morning, she had phoned him back to announce, in a quavering voice, that she had decided to give their marriage another go after all. A trial reunion. 'To follow the trial separation,' Colin had quipped, sounding relieved but not remotely penitent.

'I want it to be different,' Elizabeth said. 'Not like before.'

'No, of course not. Quite different. Better. When will you come home?'

Elizabeth had hesitated, loath, in spite of this new resolution, to surrender her freedom so soon. 'Well . . . everyone's here next week, and the weekend after that Mum wants us all here for Dad's birthday dinner, so I think I'll stay till then . . . Come back on the first Monday in September . . . if that's okay?'

'Absolutely. Unless you'd like me to join you at any stage?'

There was so much reluctance in his voice that it had been easy for Elizabeth to dismiss the suggestion, which held far less appeal anyway than she knew it should, and to steer the conversation into smoother waters, like how to get hold of the head to confirm that she would be resuming her duties and when Roland would be returning to school.

Charlie found his mother and wife, as Elizabeth had said, picking raspberries. Or, rather, Serena was picking raspberries while Pamela sat, one full basket on her knees, on a tree stump in the shade at one end of the cages. She got up to greet Charlie, saying Serena was being marvellous and she didn't know what she would do without her, then tactfully excused herself to wander back up to the house. Charlie slipped under the green netting and pulled his wife into his arms, so fiercely that several of the berries on her own already mountainous basket, tumbled to the ground. 'I don't know what I'd do without you either,' he murmured, kissing her mouth and tasting fruit. Aroused, he pressed a little harder, wanting her to feel how much he missed the physical intimacy they had once taken for granted but which, for so many months now, had been absent.

'Me neither.' Serena spoke fondly enough but pulled away and began to search for the lost berries in the tufts of grass at their feet.

Rebuffed, Charlie put his hands in his pockets, while the now familiar sensation of physical deprivation, a deep ache, swelled and hardened inside. Maybe nothing had changed, after all, he reflected bleakly. All week he had been saving the astonishing news about his mother and his uncle, looking forward to his wife's cool intuitive wisdom to help him make sense of it. Yet now, looking down at the top of Serena's head while she scrabbled for raspberries instead of returning his embrace, the desire to tell her anything disappeared. 'All well?' he said instead.

'Oh, yes . . . very well.' Still crouching, she looked up at him. 'Charlie, I've been wanting to tell you . . . I've had such an idea . . . such a wonderful idea . . . couldn't say it on the phone.' Her voice trembled but her face – eyes brilliant, cheeks pink – shone so brightly that Charlie, his own fragile hopes blazing again, crouched down next to her and seized her hands. 'What, my darling, what?'

'Tina . . . I want to move her . . . here . . . to St Margaret's. I've spoken to the vicar and the diocesan registry and we need to apply for something called a Faculty, which is a court order from the consistory court, and also a licence, which you get from the Home Office; and then, of course, there's the local environmental health people and the funeral directors who would organise the move—'

'Whoa there – hang on a minute.' Charlie dropped her hands and stood up. 'Move Tina? You want to *move* her?'

'Yes.' Serena set down the basket and stood up, crossing her arms. 'It will be hard because she was buried on consecrated ground and apparently—'

'And you've decided this, have you?'

'It would be so much better,' Serena persisted, hearing the edge in his voice but deciding to ignore it. If he didn't understand this, he was incapable of understanding anything. 'We're here so much, it would be lovely to have her—'

'You have *decided* this, have you? Without consulting me.'

'I am consulting you. Now.'

'Well, it doesn't feel much like a consultation, I can tell you.'

'Oh, Charlie, please understand—'

'No, you understand. I lost her too. Our darling daughter. Our precious Tina. We laid her to rest *together*. Next to your mother. As *you* wanted. Forgive me if I do not immediately leap to the notion of digging up and carting her little body across the country because of some new whim of yours, which you have seized and acted upon without deigning to refer to me first.' Charlie turned and fought his way out of the cage, tugging at the green netting as it caught at his shoes and elbows. Serena watched, furious and helpless, until he was striding away, past the rows of wigwammed runner beans towards the gate in the privet hedge and into the garden.

In spite of the heat Stephen decided to wear a beanie for his meeting with the brother. The big brother. Big wanker brother. He didn't want to meet him. He didn't want to have anything to do with any of the Harrisons ever again. But the guy had rung so many times and been – even Stephen had to admit – very charming, with chat of mutual interest and excellent propositions, that he had eventually given in, seduced as much by curiosity as anything else. With the hot wool of the beanie, grey with black stripes, pulled down to his ears, he felt somehow safer. Uglier, but safer. The brother would no doubt be in City-gent gear – pinstripes, matching-shirt-and-handkerchief, suede brogues and a silk tie. Stephen knew what Peter's face would look like because of the photos he had seen at Ashley House: a fuller, younger version of the father, with short, crisp grey hair, deep-set eyes, a long Roman nose and a square jaw. A face full of pride and self-assertion, with lines of age rather than doubt. A man in the prime of life, sure of his place in the world. Contemplating the meeting, Stephen had at first been tempted, in some small way, to compete. Back in his flat after his futile spell in

July of failing to blot out the world with the anonymity of benders and bedsits, he had spent some time that morning surveying the smarter items of his disparate wardrobe, ranged round the dado rail in his bedroom. Then he had thought, What the fuck? and pulled on his baggy khaki shorts, a faded brown T-shirt and a pair of old leather sandals, bought several years before at a roadside market in Quito for the equivalent of fifty pence.

Peter had insisted they meet on Westminster Bridge, of all places. He would have a *Financial Times* under his arm, he said, as if they were two characters meeting in a spy novel, exchanging passwords and information on dead-letter drops. Stephen was to arrive in the middle of the bridge at three o'clock exactly, he instructed; he would be waiting for him, leaning on the railings of the east side, looking towards the London Eye. Stephen, who had never liked being told what to do by anyone, set off for the bus stop deliberately late: a little tardiness would make Peter squirm, destroy just a touch of that grand, affluent cool. But the moment he got to the bridge itself and saw not only Peter but Cassie, unmistakable with her curly halo of hair and long pale-skinned limbs, waiting in the middle of it, he broke into a trot, fearful that they would give up and hail a cab before he reached them.

Cassie saw Stephen first and nudged her brother. He hadn't wanted her to come, but she had insisted, having seen the shaming crudity of Peter's plan and hoping, somehow, to soften it by her presence. Peter would be all businesslike and unfeeling, while she might be able to explain things better, make Stephen see that as well as protecting themselves, they hoped to help him. Genuinely help him. Or so Cassie told herself. For the closer the day came the more uncomfortable she had felt about it. A bribe was a bribe. Demeaning. It would also – no matter what Peter said – open them up to more bribes in the future, make them vulnerable, when what they really sought was impregnability. By the time Stephen's jogging figure came into view on the bridge, she had, with increasing jitteriness, suggested many times that they give up and go home. Seeing him proved even more terrible than waiting for him. In his woolly hat and baggy clothes he looked so scruffy and boy-like that

Cassie's heart tore at the thought of what they were about to do. 'Peter . . .' she began, but her brother had broken away from the railing and was already walking towards their adversary with his hand extended.

Composed as he appeared, Peter was, in fact, a jumble of nerves. This was as close to the wind as he had ever sailed, as desperate, probably, as he had ever been. It didn't help that from the moment he had mentioned it, Helen had been openly sceptical and incredulous – yet when pressed she could offer no alternative beyond a suggestion that the truth be allowed to come out. Which, in Peter's view, was unacceptable. Protecting one's loved ones took many forms. In this case, it involved risk and the possibility of dreadful backfiring. But he was prepared to see it through for the sake of the family, for the sake of his parents' happiness, which, surely, had only a few more years to run. The demise of Boots earlier that week was a reminder, if any of them needed it, that his father, about to enter his ninth decade, was already on borrowed time. All too soon he would be dead too and the truth could weasel its way to the surface, wreak whatever havoc it wanted and be damned.

'Mr Smith? I'm Peter Harrison. I believe you already know my sister.'

'Hello, Stephen,' said Cassie, in a small voice, goosebumps of shame tiptoeing up her bare arms. 'How are you?'

'Great, thanks, just great.' Stephen thrust his hands into his pockets and looked at his sandals. He could feel where the leather had worn under the pressure of his soles and toes, creating perfect indentations for them to rest in. 'I can't think why you wanted to see me,' he added, with less confidence, wishing she didn't look quite so fresh and delicate, in a silky blue sleeveless dress, which, though full, did nothing to hide the slim neat contours of her figure.

'Shall we walk?' cut in Peter. 'There's a place on the south side near the wheel – I thought we might have a coffee there.'

'Bit hot for coffee, isn't it?' said Stephen, feeling the force of Peter's determination to control the proceedings and instinctively resisting it.

'A cold drink, then. Quite right, far too hot for coffee.' Peter began to walk, glancing behind to check Cassie and Stephen were following. Next to them the London Eye turned slowly, like a huge, stranded waterwheel. Beneath it the river fluttered, silvery white in the glare of the afternoon sun. After so many rainless weeks the mudflats on either side were plainly visible, punctured in places by rusting objects and beached driftwood.

'What's all this about, then?' ventured Stephen, falling into step alongside Cassie, managing, in spite of the awkwardness of the occasion and the roller coaster of his emotions during the preceding months, to enjoy being next to her with the sun on their heads and the arched pavement of the bridge stretching ahead. He had hated her many times in his heart, but now that she was within sight once more the love flooded back in, as simple and overpowering as a tidal wave against a sandbag.

'It's about the book,' replied Cassie. 'Your book. Peter will tell you.' Not wanting to reveal more, she increased her stride until the three were walking abreast. They continued in silence, each locked in the tangle of their own thoughts.

Peter waited until their drinks had arrived, an iced tea for him and Sprite for the others, then launched, glib and fluent, into the matter of his financial proposition. Cassie watched, sickened, as Stephen's expression moved from one of simple enquiry to embarrassment – at the revelation of their knowledge of his addition to the manuscript – to pure shock. Peter, oblivious, or perhaps merely disregarding, ploughed on.

'I'd like to call it a simple business proposition, one that is mutually beneficial, alleviating the possibility of unnecessary anxiety on our side and financial discomfort on yours. The sum I mentioned is considerable and—'

'The sum you mentioned,' interrupted Stephen, squeezing his empty can until it collapsed under his grip, 'is degrading.'

'I see,' murmured Peter, patting his breast pocket where he had stowed his cheque book and fountain pen, his mind racing over the ramifications of raising his offer and by how much. It wasn't a question of what he could afford – for many years, money had been no object to anything in his life – but of the far more important issue of not appearing weak. The man looked harmless enough, but clearly had no qualms about playing hardball. 'I might be able to add another five—'

Stephen shook his head, looking from Cassie's pale downcast face to Peter's. 'You don't get it, do you?' He stood up suddenly, knocking over his chair and just catching it in time. 'Here.' He pulled a five-pound note out of his back pocket. 'That's for the drinks. You could have just asked me, you know. You could have just asked me. I don't want your stinking money. I'll change what I've written if it matters so much to you. I admit I wanted – for a time – I wanted to hurt you, you bloody Harrisons with your grand façade of a family, so *rooted*, so fucking sure of yourselves. I don't – have never had – anything like that and part of me did want to knock it down. I admit that. But another part just wanted to tell the truth, to tell the story of your uncle as it really was. Your mother loving him was a part of that. And however despicable you think me, I understand love, I really do. Love matters. And if your family is half as strong as you like to believe then it would survive, whatever truths crawl out of the woodwork, courtesy of me or anyone else. I'll give the version you want. But I'll give it freely, and not as part of some sordid deal.' He pushed the chair into the table. 'I'm sorry for the pain I've caused you, I really am. I may have behaved badly but I would do anything not to hurt you . . . anything.' As he said these words he looked hard at Cassie, then turned and left the café, charging at the door with his shoulder in his eagerness to get out.

'Well,' began Peter, laughing in disbelief, 'do you think he means it?'

'Of course he means it,' gasped Cassie, close to tears. 'He's right . . . It was degrading. We should have just asked him, explained what it meant to us. Our family secret is safe, Peter, but right this minute I can't feel too good about it, I really can't.' She fumbled in her bag for a tissue and blew her nose. 'We expected the worst of him and it was wrong . . . It's wrong to expect the worst of anyone.'

Unable to share her dismay, Peter waved Stephen's five-pound note at the waitress. 'Come on, now. All's well that ends well. What a business. Thank God it's over. Do you think we really can trust him?'

'Oh, yes,' she murmured, 'I think so.'

'Excellent.' Peter rubbed his hands together. 'Now, I'm driving to Ashley House for the weekend. Why don't you come too?'

'No, thanks.'

'Go on. We can celebrate.'

But Cassie, who did not feel there was much to celebrate, resisted all her brother's efforts at persuasion. Outside the café she found herself scanning the streets for Stephen, thinking that somehow he had behaved more honourably than any of them and cursing herself for having misjudged him so badly.

Perched in the apple tree at the end of the pergola Theo, with some difficulty, was keeping his camera trained on Samson, who was sitting on a branch next to him, tail twitching at the sight of a blackbird pecking on the lawn below. After what he perceived as the failure of the structured-interview approach, Theo had decided to experiment with a more spontaneous method of filming, catching objects and scenes of activity unawares. Clem, somewhat conveniently – since this new approach didn't require her services – seemed to have lost interest in being his producer, although he had hinted that he still wouldn't mind the odd letter. He was thinking more about this than about Samson when he caught sight of his mother scurrying across the grass in the direction of his hideout. Instead of turning his camera on her, or announcing his presence, something about her – the way she glanced anxiously over her shoulder at the house – prompted Theo to draw back into the leaves. Rather to his horror, she came right under the tree and leant against it. She was so close he could see the glints of grey in her hair and the small mole on the side of her cheek. She was breathing heavily, her chest rising and falling under her shirt. It felt somehow deceitful to be watching her, but the longer Theo remained invisible the more impossible it felt to call out. He didn't even dare switch off his camera for fear that the click would make her look up into the branches. Samson, thankfully, had settled down on his own branch, his tail trailing like a vine, his eyes closed as if bored at the notion of chasing blackbirds or anything else. Below them Helen reached into the pocket of her skirt and pulled out her mobile phone.

Theo peered down in mounting horror, certain that he was witnessing something illicit and dreadful. A lover, perhaps. Oh, God, his mother had a lover. Oh, shit, oh, fuck, oh, fucking shit. She looked so furtive, so perturbed, he could think of nothing else. When Helen, speaking clearly, addressed herself to Kay, he almost groaned aloud in relief. His comfort, however, was short-lived. Close as he was, it was impossible not to hear every word; impossible, therefore, not to glean that his mother was consulting her friend because she had accidentally become pregnant and didn't know what to do about it. Soon she was crying. Theo clung to a branch with his free hand, the camera trembling in the other. If he could have blocked his ears he would. Adult distress held no allure for him. Neither, for that matter, did the unappealing notion of his parents having sex. It was gross. Unthinkable. Almost as unthinkable as the idea of his mother, grey hairs peeking through the brown, webs of wrinkles round her eyes, the skin on her thighs visibly loose in her staid navy blue bathing costume, having a baby. Christ, no wonder she was crying. Although, Theo realised, peeking again through the branches, whatever Kay was saying was clearly helping. The crying had stopped. There was even a laugh or two. 'Yes,' Helen was saying, wiping her nose on the back of her arm in a way that, had he or Chloë done it, would have caused the most disgusted parental reprimand, 'it must have happened the night of Peter's fiftieth – we got . . . carried away . . . With the menopause and so on I thought I was safe.'

This was simply too much detail and Theo's cheeks burned.

'I want it and I don't want it,' continued Helen, sounding choked again, 'and I'm so scared to tell Peter because he will be *so* appalled and take the decision away from me before I've decided what *I* think and yet, of course, the longer I leave it the harder a termination will be both physically and emotionally—'

At which point Theo fell out of the tree, landing heavily on the arm holding the camera. Samson, alarmed at the vibrating of the branch on which he had been resting, landed neatly beside him, then sauntered off across the lawn, tail high, its white tiger-tip pointing like a pencil at the sky.

'Theo! Darling! Heavens – Kay, I've got to go . . . Darling, are you all right? Oh, my poor boy.' Helen slipped her phone back into her pocket and knelt beside her son who was making dry racking noises at the back of his throat and clutching his arm. 'What on earth were you doing?'

'Filming Samson,' he gasped, looking down at his arm, which ached badly but looked all right. 'I was just filming Samson and then you came and I didn't dare say and then—'

'Can you move your fingers?'

Tentatively, then vigorously, Theo wiggled his fingers.

'Well, I don't think you can have broken it – I don't know why not, falling like that. The camera's broken, though, I'm afraid.'

When he saw the lens lying in the grass, Theo began to cry. Helen, murmuring soothingly about getting it fixed, about nothing mattering but him being all right, put her arms round him. Theo wept on, feeling four instead of fourteen, a small, secret part of him relishing this half-forgotten ritual of receiving physical comfort from his mother. In spite of the highly traumatic circumstances, Helen relished it too, feeling, as she had with Chloë that day in Oxford Street, that the bond between her and her lanky man-child, however seldom expressed, would remain unbreakable.

'I suppose you heard everything,' she murmured, rocking him, 'all the things I said to Kay.'

Theo nodded, gulping.

'I'm going to talk to Dad when he gets here this evening and we'll work out what to do together. In a way I'd like another baby, but I'm pretty old and also I'm not sure I've been too fantastic in the mum department.'

'You have,' sobbed Theo, hugging her harder.

'The good thing is, I'd been feeling so lousy I'd thought I was ill – really ill – so in a way it's a huge relief. I'm so sorry you heard like that, darling, it must be quite a shock for you too.'

'I think you should have it,' blurted Theo, sitting up and drying his eyes with the palms of his hands. The arm felt tingly but not too bad. 'The baby. Chloë would love it, wouldn't she?' He grinned at Helen, who rolled her eyes, unable to resist smiling back. 'Yes, I suppose she would.'

'And I'd probably *quite* like it, when it got a bit older.'

'And Dad?'

'Well, he likes us all right, doesn't he? Me and Chloë. So I guess he'd probably like another one.'

'Dad doesn't like things he hasn't planned, though,' said Helen quietly, adoring her son's simple logic, but experiencing a fresh current of fear at the thought of Peter's reaction.

That night, while the rest of her family assembled among the glinting silver and crystal of Ashley House's dining room for a grand feast of smoked salmon, roast beef and fresh raspberries, Cassie took her mother's letter to her uncle from its hiding-place in her bottom drawer and burned it. She held it over a plate and lit one corner with a match, watching the paper curl and the ashes float down into a dusty pile. Love mattered. Stephen had said so, and he was right. But love was about choices too. For whatever reasons, her mother had chosen to stay with her father. And her own heart still burned for Dan, not as often, maybe, but still with an intensity that made her afraid; afraid that she would never get over it, but stagger on as an emotional cripple, with every future happiness a shadow of the one she had known.

Serena had more or less taken charge of the evening meal, while Pamela floated in the background, too wrung out by the heat for any of her usual pride about handing over the reins of her kitchen. Keeping busy was a cure for all sorts of things, she told herself, watching from her favourite vantage-point in the corner of the kitchen sofa and musing on the happy fact that this daughter-in-law had never needed much instruction about anything. Unlike Helen, who never quite remembered which wine glasses or tablecloth to use; or Elizabeth, for that matter, who insisted on chopping vegetables as thin as two-pence pieces instead of into bite-sized chunks, and Cassie who required intricate guidance on any domestic chore, no matter how small. Serena outshone them all. She knew instinctively just how things should be done. Pamela's exclamation to Charlie on the subject that afternoon had come from the heart. With so many mouths to feed, the awful business of Boots, and Elizabeth and Helen being, in their separate ways, quite *hors de combat* (Helen with a migraine and Elizabeth with patching up her marriage) the week would have been quite unmanageable without Serena's cool commanding hand on the wheel.

It was nine o'clock now and they were between courses. Serena had stacked the dishwasher, put the vegetable dishes to soak in the sink and retrieved a towering bowl of raspberries from the larder. Outside the air temperature had dropped, but inside the heat still hung and smothered like a lingering fever. The weathermen were talking of a break towards the end of the week, thunderstorms in September. The children, gathered round the TV earlier in the evening, had groaned in unison at the prospect of rain, but Pamela had felt a burst of hope, as if they had all been given notice of the chance to breathe freely again and return to normality.

'This is off, I think.' Serena had taken an open carton of cream out of the fridge and was sniffing it. 'Curdled like the milk this morning. Do we have any more?'

'I think so. Try the bottom shelf at the back, behind the sausages and bacon. Can't have raspberries without cream, can we?'

'Here we are.' Serena dropped with enviable agility to her knees and delved into the lower recesses of the fridge. 'Smells fine, this one. Do you want to take it and I'll bring the raspberries?'

Their entry into the dining room was greeted with oohs and aahs of appreciation.

Charlie joined in, watching not the crystal bowl of fruit but Serena as she placed it on a central mat, then returned to her seat. He had been too hot and angry to enjoy the meal. The beef had felt like leather between his teeth, the vegetables tasteless. No amount of chewing seemed to make any mouthful easier to swallow. Each time he recalled their conversation that afternoon he felt freshly enraged. One didn't have to be particularly religious to find the thought of unearthing a buried child repellent. But it was more than this that Charlie brooded over. It was the selfishness of how she had pursued the idea. Serena's grief, right from the start, he realised, had been utterly selfish, quite without reference to his feelings or anyone else's. As if she alone *owned* the right to be sad, staking it out as her special territory where no one else could intrude. Her decision, without a murmur to him, that digging up their daughter was the right thing to do was all part and parcel of that. And he was fed up with it. Truly fed up. Just as he was fed up with her porcelain emotions. What kind of a marriage was it when the husband couldn't say anything for fear of upsetting his wife, when he couldn't even make love to her? It was a fucking nightmare, that was what it was, decided Charlie, pressing his knife and fork together over his half-eaten dinner and thinking, with unbalanced and sudden longing, of his approaching few days in the impersonal, soothing comfort of an air-conditioned Florida hotel.

'Dad, any chance of a dessert wine from the cellar?' boomed Peter who, thanks to the Stephen Smith development, was still in the mood for celebrating. 'To go with these delicious raspberries.' At a nod from John he left the room to see what he could find. Once in the cellar he took his time, aware that while his own spirits might be soaring, all was not well with the rest of the family. The children were cheerful enough, their faces shining and freckled from time in the sun, their conversation pitted with unintelligible references to in-jokes and joshing as to who had done what to whom; Serena, too, seemed a little happier, which was a turn-up for the books, but Elizabeth and Charlie (even after he had broken the good news about Stephen Smith) were both twitchy as hell, while his parents, no doubt because of the heat and the old dog dying, seemed depressingly drained and subdued. Most disappointing of all, however, was Helen. Naïvely, perhaps, Peter had hoped that a week's holiday in the country would take the edge off whatever illness she was suffering from and her anxiety as to the still pending diagnosis. No news, as he kept telling her, was good news. A brain tumour would have had Dr Fuller on the phone in an instant and pulling out all the stops. Yet ever since his arrival from London she had seemed more anxious than ever, saying her head still ached but refusing to take anything, not even the new analgesics he had bought specially in his lunch-hour, recommended by a colleague who had revealed himself as a slave to migraine.

Peter returned to the dining room with a bottle of Sauternes. All of the adults accepted some, apart from Helen who – much to his dismay – promptly excused herself from the table. In pursuit of an early night, she said, casting him a departing glance that was hard to read. Something between reprimand and supplication. Feeling thoroughly thwarted, but also by now quite concerned, he had just one glass of the Sauternes when he would have liked two, and followed her upstairs.

He found her lying on the bed in the dark, still fully dressed. He eased off his shoes, then went to lie next to her, putting his arm across the back of her pillow. 'I think we should call Fuller – it's outrageous that he still hasn't responded, if only to put our minds at rest.'

'Peter, he has responded. On Monday. While I was at the lake with the children. When Boots got bitten. Dr Fuller called me then.' Helen stared at the ceiling rose overhead. Her eyes were accustomed to the dark, and its intricate white circle of carved plasterwork was clearly visible, as was the beaded glass lampshade hanging from its centre. When the light was on the beads cast expanding circular shadows out from the rose, like ripples across still water.

'He has?' Peter hoisted himself on to his elbow and looked at her. 'Why the hell didn't you tell me?'

'Because,' continued Helen, steadily, 'I needed to collect my thoughts.'

Instead of speaking, Peter buried his face in his hands, succumbing in those first few moments of shock to a private miserable rage at this worst of all body-blows fate was now dealing him. Helen sat up and prised his hands from his face. 'No, it's not what you think – it's not so bad as that . . . It's . . . Peter, I'm expecting a baby. The headaches are hormone surges or something. I didn't feel great with the other two, did I?'

'You're pregnant?' Peter's voice trembled, whether from relief or shock, he hardly knew himself. 'How can you be? It's not possible. I mean, what about the – I thought you said you were in the middle of the menopause. Weren't you? Aren't you?'

Helen explained what she thought had happened, while Peter rolled away from her, head in his hands once again. 'Jesus Christ, I don't believe this, I just don't believe it.'

'I knew you wouldn't be pleased.' Helen lay down and crossed her arms.

'Of course I'm pleased you're not sick, darling – of course I am,' he assured her hastily, reaching out to pat her folded hands. 'But it's hardly what you'd call good news, now, is it? I mean, we almost decided not to have Chloë, and you'd be the first to admit what a struggle it's been for you – work and motherhood and so on. A *third* child would be even harder. It would also change everything, make the future so much more complicated—' He broke off, adding a little too eagerly, 'You must be – what? Thirteen weeks gone? I mean that's still . . . fairly early days, isn't it?'

'Probably still early enough to have a termination, if that's what you mean.' Helen levered herself into a sitting position and folded her arms back across her chest. 'But I'm not sure I could have one. I know it's supposed to be a joint decision and everything and I know it's what you would ideally want, but I'm the one who would have to go through with it and right now I'm just not sure. A part of me wonders, you see . . .' She paused, marshalling the thoughts that had been raging inside her since her call to Kay and Theo's fall. '. . . whether this baby could be my chance – our chance – to get it *more* right, to find the balance that I haven't so far between enjoying work and enjoying being a mother. Things have been happening to me this year, Peter, difficult but good things. I've tried to explain some of them to you, not very well probably. But the fact is, in spite of all our clashes I'm feeling much closer to Chloë – and Theo too. It's helped me realise that, although I will always need work and so on, ultimately what matters most in the world are our children. Being a family. I want more of that. This could be my chance to have it, to *enjoy* it properly, to—'

'It's that woman, isn't it? She's talked you into this, hasn't she? All her lah-di-dah about getting in touch with feminine feelings, which is all very well until one considers the nitty-gritty of what life is *really* about—'

'And what is life really about?' interjected Helen quietly.

'Practical things, day-to-day stuff – money for starters, work, sleepless nights, not to mention health. Forgive me for being bleak, Helen, but at your age the chances of something being wrong with a baby are pretty high, aren't they? How would we cope with that, eh? A handicapped child, or brain-damaged or something . . . Oh, no, oh, Helen, don't cry, I'm sorry, don't cry. I know I'm being a brute, but this is so important we can't just sail into it with our eyes closed. We've got to think it through, see all sides and come to the right decision.'

'I want to have the baby,' Helen wailed, so loudly that Peter, fearing some other member of the family might be passing along the corridor outside, was tempted to cover her mouth with his hand.

'Shush, Helen, please. We'll think about it, okay? We won't make a decision now. We don't need to make a decision now. Okay? We'll just sit on it for a bit, let it sink in, see the right doctors, talk through the options.' He held her to his chest and stroked her hair, murmuring, 'I'm sorry to seem unkind, darling, you're going through a lot, I know that, but I'm here now to go through it *with* you . . . We'll sort this out together. Okay? Together.'

'Theo knows,' said Helen, her voice thick and high. 'He over-heard me talking to Kay. He thinks I should have it.'

'Oh, does he? Great, that's absolutely great,' muttered Peter, resorting to sarcasm because his head was throbbing and for that moment he had no other cards left to play.

SEPTEMBER

By the first of September the weather in the north of the country had broken, releasing slanting rods of rain that bounced off the hardened earth like a storm of glass arrows. Further south the skies over London and the Home Counties were ranged with billowing clouds, as dark and thick as belched fumes of industrial smoke. The compressing dampness of the heat seemed to suck the oxygen and energy from the air, making each breath feel as if it was being drawn through the stifling mask of a wet flannel. Charlie, buckling his seat-belt in preparation for his flight across the Atlantic, sighed with relief under the funnels of icy air-conditioning and the saccharine smiles of the stewardesses.

Serena, who was refreshing herself under the feeble sprinkle of their *en-suite* shower having sent the children to the Wimbledon Odeon for the afternoon, groaned in recollection of Charlie's departure and the unsatisfactory manner of their parting. They were like a pair of unbalanced scales – one up, the other down. It was almost as if he had been waiting for her to start to feel better so that he could take the mantle of misery upon himself. Throughout their week in Sussex he had refused to discuss Tina or anything else. He had run, swum, bowled cricket balls – generally played the role of good father – but had treated her as if she was invisible. Since they had returned to London he had left for the office before she was awake and got back when she was on the point of going to bed. When the taxi had arrived to take him to the airport he had been packed and ready for hours, suitcase and laptop parked – with unprecedented clinical efficiency – by the coatstand in the hall. As if he could not wait to be gone. As if he could no longer stand the sight of her. As he had stepped outside, Serena, miscalculating badly, had tried a last shot on the Tina front. She had been quiet on the matter for days and was desperate to move it along, desperate for him to recognise the importance and ingenuity of the plan. Charlie had glowered at her, his face shining with the perspiration of despair rather than heat. 'Something's got to change,' he hissed. 'Something's got to change or I can't go on.' Taken aback, Serena had still been rallying her thoughts for a reply as he pulled the taxi door shut. She tapped the window, wanting to say something – anything to make the farewell better – but all he did was raise his hand in a single emotionless valedictory wave, such as a chauffeured dignitary might bestow on an ogling stranger.

Pamela, palms round a cup of tea she did not want – it had seemed a tolerable way to fill the dead time between three and half past as she mustered a second wind to get on with preparations for John's birthday weekend – stared at the leaden canopy of cloud pressing down upon the garden. Any time now, she thought, any time now and it will be over. The storm will break and we shall all be released.

John, drinking an equally unwanted cup of tea and chugging on a pipe within the fortress of his favourite armchair, reached absently with one foot for Boots and found only air.

At Helen's offices the air-conditioning had broken. With the windows open her papers kept lifting off the desk, as if bent upon escaping the filing cabinet or her stapler. Exposed thus to the street, she could detect with the new super-olfactory powers bestowed on her by her pregnancy the stale, faintly metallic odour of hardened dog faeces on the pavements outside, mingling with the pungent spices used by the chef in the Indian restaurant across the road. In recent days the aching in her head had shifted to her belly. It was too early for the baby to move but she could already imagine its shadowy shufflings somewhere deep within her abdomen; the first stirrings of a life, which, despite all Peter's solid, logical arguments, she felt increasingly powerless to resist. The consultant they had seen together on Monday, rushing to Harley Street in their lunch-hour, had been equally cool and rational. It was still relatively early days. A termination was possible, perfectly understandable for a woman a couple of years short of fifty with a busy career and two older children to care for. Except that it didn't feel possible to Helen. Not just because she could sense the bud of her child, flowering inside her, but because, as she had tried to explain to her husband, it felt like a third and final chance (a God-given chance, despite her agnosticism) to do it right: to embrace instead of fearing motherhood. To cherish the upheaval of love. To go with the flow instead of trying to resist and manage it. No decision had to be made yet, the doctor had said. But soon it would. Probably during the course of the approaching weekend. Ashley House. Again. John's eightieth this time. Pamela had cracked her whip and, as usual, the entire family was running to do her bidding. As if they hadn't spent enough time there already, marching to the Harrison tune through most of the summer, neglecting the rhythm of their own family lives in the process. Helen was dreading it, just as she was dreading the inevitable showdown with Peter when she broke the news that, no matter how much common sense he spouted, nothing would stop her having the child. Spina bifida, Downs syndrome, autism, premature labour – she would take the lot. She would take the fucking lot.

Stephen, too, standing at the bus stop near his flat, felt the mushrooming weight of humidity in the air. He was wearing new cheap plastic flip-flops, which rubbed uncomfortably between his big and second toes. His old leather sandals had broken, one vital strap shredding to nothing as he had strode back across Westminster Bridge two weeks before, still choking with indignation at Peter's arrogant, belittling offer of money to buy his silence. He had taken them off and dropped them into a bin, finding perverse comfort in the gritty warmth of the ground beneath his bare feet.

On getting home he had phoned his editor at once to say that he did not want the added passages about Eric Harrison's love affair with his sister-in-law included, making no reference to what had happened other than to say that he had decided he had no desire to run the risk of causing pain to the family. The editor had made a joke about being glad there would be no danger of anyone suing them and left it at that. Stephen had put down the phone feeling deflated but also clear-headed. Dreadful as the afternoon had been, he was aware that it marked a turning-point. Rejecting Peter's insulting proposal – not for one moment tempted by it – had given a tiny boost to his floundering self-esteem. He might be a hopeless case, but he wasn't that hopeless. He had a toehold at least on some sort of rocky moral highground – more than Peter Harrison anyway, with his bulging cheque book and greed to cover the truth. He had seen at once, from the look of shame on her face and the way she picked at the tab of her Sprite can, that Cassie did not share that greed. She had been as uncomfortable as he was, just as appalled at the level to which they had sunk.

The rush of love he had felt at the sight of her, while painful, had also been reassuring. Amid all the ups and downs of his emotions, it had risen like a phoenix from the ashes of that afternoon as something beautiful and certain, something that transcended the cruel inconvenience of non-reciprocation or hurt to his pride. All that was now accepted. What remained was the simplicity of his passion and within that his even simpler desire for the happiness of Cassie Harrison above his own. In time he would move on, find a steady job, marry someone, maybe even have children, consigning to memory what he had felt for Cassie; a jewel in his heart. In the meantime she was unhappy, Stephen knew, not just because of the shame of being party to a bribe but because the love of *her* life had rejected her. The doctor. Daniel Lambert. A GP in Putney. Bound by duty to a wife he did not love and three young children whom he did love, fiercely.

When Cassie had poured out these and all the other details during the course of his impromptu visit to her flat back in May Stephen had taken pleasure in consoling her, imagining naïvely that her need of a confidant could somehow, with time and tenderness, be transmuted into love. Knowing that this was now impossible, Stephen had begun, with the title of his manuscript, *Unsung Heroes*, staring up at him from the proof copy next to the phone on his desk, to hatch another plan; a way forward that would, without warfare or mortal courage, make him something of an unsung hero himself.

At the bus stop that Friday, however, his toes sore, he could feel all such brave resolve in danger of melting like the treacly black Tarmac on the road. If a bus didn't come in five minutes . . . in ten minutes . . . He pulled off his sunglasses and tried to clean them on his T-shirt, only making the smears worse. They were old and scratched anyway, like a worn record, like his life. He lost patience and set off on foot, leaving the disgruntled bus-queue behind him, his flip-flops slapping noisily against his heels.

Dan was closing down his computer when Meryl, the receptionist, popped her head round his door to say that one more person was asking to see him. 'He's not registered but says it's urgent,' she explained nervously, not at all sure she had handled the situation correctly. The man looked scruffy and hot, with great damp patches under his arms and across the front and back of his T-shirt. He had entered the surgery barefooted, then slipped on a pair of blue flip-flops while he was talking to her. His toes and heels, she noticed, were thick with dirt, as if he had spent all day wandering the streets carrying the flip-flops instead of wearing them. Alone behind the desk Meryl had done her best to remember the security procedure for violent or drug-crazed patients. There was a red button somewhere under the counter, but she couldn't remember where. But, then, it would be too awful to press it for someone who was perhaps slightly eccentric but making an innocent enquiry. And something about Stephen was profoundly innocent, she decided, looking into his big brown pupils for signs of dilation but seeing instead an intensity of determination that was disarming but not remotely hostile. His voice, too, was pleasingly gentle; not at all the voice of someone desperate for their next fix, with a knife or something worse tucked inside his pocket. He knew Dr Lambert's name as well and said, very sweetly, that he wasn't a regular patient and had no appointment but was prepared to wait for as long as was necessary.

Exhausted from a busy day, Dan followed Meryl out into the waiting room. Stephen was seated by the magazine stand, flicking absently through an ancient dog-eared copy of *Hello!*, drawing cheap comfort from the supposedly heartfelt public professions of love by celebrity couples who had subsequently gone their separate ways. His own love needed no limelight for its validation. Nor would any other face in the world ever make his heart beat quite as fast. Giving Cassie up, as he was about to do, was not inconsistent with loving her. It was just very, very sad.

Taken aback by the hippie-scruffiness of this would-be patient, Dan launched at once into standard explanations about the practice's registration procedures and the fact that the surgery was now officially closed. 'It's not about me,' said Stephen quietly, putting down the magazine, 'it's about Cassie. Cassie Harrison.'

Dan's expression changed, encompassing in a few seconds everything from terror to surprise. 'You'd better come in,' he muttered, nodding reassurance at Meryl as he turned to lead the way into his consulting room. 'Do sit down.' He pointed at the chair next to his desk but Stephen was too busy studying the object of his own love's passion to respond, trying to see whatever Cassie saw in what appeared to him to be Daniel Lambert's rather indifferent features; sandy-grey hair, a narrow, already quite lined face, wide thin lips, hooded grey eyes – there was nothing obviously special or compelling. 'I've not much to say.' He remained standing behind the chair, childishly, irrelevantly, pleased to note that he was taller than his rival by several inches. 'I'm a . . . friend of Cassie's. I have come simply to tell you that she still misses you terribly and to say that if you truly . . . love . . .' Stephen struggled with the word, a part of him wanting to resist, at this crucial moment of his sacrifice, the necessity of allowing this somewhat haggard doctor to share any of the territory occupied by his own emotions. 'If you truly love her and need to be with her as much as she needs to be with you then you should get back in touch. It would make Cassie very happy. We only have one life, Dr Lambert, and should make the most of it.'

'Well . . . I . . .'

'And just one more thing. If you do choose to go back to Cassie, please promise me that you will never breathe one word of this meeting.'

'I'm not sure that . . .'

'Do you promise?'

'Yes, if you insist, but . . .'

'Thank you.' Stephen left the room before Dan could say anything else.

Outside the gun-metal skies glowered, close now to bursting point. Close to bursting himself, Stephen walked as fast as his horrible footwear would allow, sustained by the inimitable consolation of having acted well. His heart was swollen with pain but there was virtue there too now, and truckloads of the kind of self-esteem that can only blossom from courage.

The storm broke on Saturday afternoon. The purple blanket of cloud that had smothered the southern half of the country for days began to heave like an inverted sea, releasing rain, zigzags of neon lightning and gun-shot cracks of thunder. Samson, who had been spread across two children's laps on the sofa in the TV room enduring caresses to his head, tummy and tail, leapt to the carpet and ran for somewhere less exposed to hide. The picture on the television flickered and fuzzed as the aerial, freshly secured by the workmen a few weeks before, swayed in the buffeting wind. Rain clattered on the cloisters' roof like deafening applause, prompting Maisie, who was sprawled on the rug in front of the television, to press the volume button on the remote control till it was almost at maximum. The film they were watching, a Disney tale of separated parents being united by the efforts of their children, was ending. There was an air of subdued gloom in the room, born of the knowledge that their glorious summer was over, with nothing to look forward to but school and shortening days.

Roland had followed the story of the film with especial concentration, his innards churning in confusion. He knew now that they were staying for his grandfather's birthday, then going home. Back to their own small house with its heavy silences. Back to school. Back to his father, which made him glad in a way but also afraid. Upstairs, his mother was already packing, ferrying clothes from the airing cupboard to their open suitcases, talking brightly about things she thought he'd like to hear: Art Club, his own cosy bed, seeing Dad. Roland had done his best to be pleased, but still felt as if he might cry at any moment for the silliest reason.

'Biscuits, anyone?' Pamela had come in with a heaped plate of homemade cookies, fat with honey and oatmeal, and beamed as her six grandchildren clustered round her like eager puppies.

Clem, not so eager, took hers last, then sat cross-legged on the floor next to Maisie where she sucked five crumbs off one edge and let them melt on her tongue. Alone among the children she was looking forward to getting back properly to the routine of home. Their few days in London that week had reminded her how much easier it was to control what she ate in the relaxed bosom of her own family rather than under the beady eye of her catering-obsessed grandmother. During the course of the summer holiday she had taken to exercising, feverish with heat and the fear of detection, once Maisie was asleep. Sit-ups, leg-lifts, press-ups, bicycles – each time she forced herself to do more repetitions, as the sweat poured off her and the blissful but maddeningly transient sensation of being in control, for those moments at least, took its soothing hold. Her grandfather's dinner – pâté to start, roast duck, a three-tiered pavlova on which she had helped spread the snowy peaks of whipped cream – loomed now, huge and horrible: a terrifying obstacle course that would tax her powers of self-discipline and stealth to the limit. Two ducks were already stuffed and ready for the oven, pinky-brown and fatty, with onions and herbs sprouting out of their cracks and orifices. The very thought of them made Clem's stomach clench. It was getting harder to make herself sick after each meal – she didn't want the food in her stomach in the first place. But there were the exercises, she consoled herself now, and the laxatives – another recent acquisition in her increasingly formidable arsenal in the never-ending war against the dial on the bathroom scales. She could double her usual dose, she decided, liquidise whatever remained in her stomach before its hateful calories could circulate round her bloodstream.

'Hey, look,' squealed Ed, his mouth bulging with biscuit as he pointed at the television, 'it's that guy you're so keen on, Maisie, Neil the-crappiest-singer-that-ever-lived Rosco.'

'You shouldn't swear, Ed,' scolded Chloë archly, looking round for their grandmother, who had retreated to the kitchen with an empty plate. The children all returned their attention to the TV screen, which promptly split into several bands of black and white as the aerial performed another ducking dive at a particularly ferocious blow from the wind raging outside. A few moments later the bands had dissolved and re-formed to reveal a bedraggled Rosco being led from his home by police officers, arms crossed in front of his face in a vain attempt to mask his identity from the waiting cameras: 'Teenage pop idol Neil Rosco was today taken in for questioning by police investigating allegations of drug abuse and the accessing of illegal child-pornography websites on the Internet. Police searched the star's riverside penthouse in Battersea, emerging several hours later with boxes of disks, videos and a personal computer. Speaking through his lawyers Neil Rosco said he was innocent of all charges and would work ceaselessly to clear his name.'

'A right pervert, in other words,' remarked Ed, licking his fingers.

'But innocent until proven guilty,' declared Theo, grandly, feeling that with both parents in the legal profession he was duty-bound to make the point. Neither of them noticed the twins, staring in mute astonishment at the television, each silently wondering what part, if any, they might have played in the rock star's disgrace.

'I'd really gone off him anyway,' said Maisie at length, stealing a glance at her sister, hoping for some support. 'There's something really *creepy* about him, don't you agree, Clem?'

'Uh? Oh, yeah, a real creep.' Clem's attention had already shifted from the news to the chunks of uneaten biscuit by her knees. She couldn't care about Rosco or Maisie or anything. All that mattered was disposing of the biscuit without detection. With a sudden swoop of longing she thought of Boots, whose fat pink tongue would have Hoovered up the evidence in seconds.

Maisie, drawing unconsciously on years of mental alignment with her twin, saw in the same instant not only the abandoned wedges of biscuit but Clem's obsessional preoccupation with them. She saw, too, as if for the first time, the hollows in her sister's cheeks, the brittle thinness of the wrists sticking out of the arms of her unseasonably heavy and voluminous sweatshirt. Maybe something about the news report helped – a sense, simply, of closure to the worst chapter of her own short life – but in those few moments Maisie realised that her love for her sister had to surpass her fear of alienating her. Clem was starving herself to death. Suddenly the burden of that knowledge was too much for Maisie to bear alone. Something had to be done. Someone had to be told. Even though it meant betraying Clem. Even though it meant her sister might never love her again. Even though it meant her own sordid escapade would almost certainly be publicised in revenge.

With the suitcases half full Elizabeth remembered a last load of washing still hanging on the line outside. It would be sodden by now, more so than when she had pulled it out of the machine. She ran at such a pelt along the landing that she bumped into Maisie coming the other way. They bounced off each other, apologising. Or, at least, Elizabeth apologised. Her niece, who seemed breathless and distraught, said she was looking for Serena and had Elizabeth seen her.

'She's in the dining room, I think, laying up for dinner. Is something the matter?'

'No, nothing.' Maisie sped back the way she had come, both hands clutched round her stomach, as if, Elizabeth couldn't help thinking, she was concealing something under her T-shirt. Dismissing the thought, she hurried on down the staircase and made her way to the utility room, which offered the nearest exit to the small cordoned-off area where Pamela kept her washing-line, strung between a sturdy wooden post and a cherry tree. She flung open the door, and leapt back in shock at the torrent of water teeming from the skies, so thickly that although it was still only early evening it looked like the middle of the night. It was pouring off the roofs, too, of the main house, the cloisters and the garden sheds, splashing in fountains out of the gutters. 'Bloody hell.'

'A cracker, isn't it?' agreed her father, appearing behind her *en route* to the cellars to pick out some of his finest wines to accompany the evening meal and already a little perked up by his first gin and tonic. 'Thank God we had the roof done, that's all I can say. Not going out, are you?'

'Just for some washing I'd forgotten – for packing.'

'Ah, yes. Packing.' John eyed his daughter fondly. It was just the outcome he had anticipated: a cool-off followed by reunion. Everyone stronger and better as a result. 'Well, I for one will miss you – and little Roland, of course.'

'Oh, Dad, I'll miss you too.' Elizabeth put her arms round her father's neck and hugged him hard so he wouldn't see her tears.

Never good at heavy displays of emotion, John patted her back, much as he had once patted Boots and his predecessors. 'Glad we could help. There's always a home for you here.'

'Thank you,' Elizabeth whispered, wiping her nose surreptitiously as she pulled away and reached for an anorak. 'Back in two ticks.' In fact, it took rather longer. The washing-line, dancing crazily in the storm, fought all her efforts to control it. Then, having unpegged the clothes, Elizabeth found herself wanting to stay a little longer, relishing the pummelling of the rain on her hood and the dramatic floodlighting of the countryside as the storm tossed over the South Downs. There was such energy, such drama. It made her feel small and inadequate in comparison. Tomorrow she was returning to her husband. To the momentous decision of a fresh start. But it didn't feel momentous. It felt remote and impersonal, like something that had been decided and would be enacted by someone else.

Back inside the utility room, she opened the door of the tumble-dryer and fed in the wet clothes. As she did so, she felt something hard in the pocket of a pair of Roland's shorts. She investigated and found a stone, almost perfectly round, coral-coloured, and smiled,

thinking of the assortment of other such mementoes that had
gathered on his bedroom window-sill during the summer and
which he had insisted on packing to take home: feathers, odd-
shaped sticks, half an empty thrush egg, a flint – nothing was ever
too ordinary to be beyond his interest. But there was something else
too, Elizabeth realised. She set down the stone and put her hand
back into the pocket. Something papery and damp. Hurrying now
– she still had so much to do before dinner – Elizabeth turned the
pocket inside out and gave it a good shake. A photograph slipped
out of the lining and floated to the ground. It landed face upwards,
presenting Elizabeth with a faded but recognisable image of herself
cheek to cheek with her first husband.

'What on earth . . .?' Unable to believe her eyes, she picked it up
by one corner. Studying it, she reached out, closed the dryer door
and set the timer for an hour. How could Roland have a picture of
Lucien? It didn't make sense. She didn't even have one: after the
split she had destroyed or given away everything, right down to the
last stray notepad and guitar string. Where could Roland have
found it?

Elizabeth squinted at the picture, remembering as if it was
yesterday the mad exuberance of the rainy afternoon on which
it had been taken. They had run into the supermarket to buy steak
and wine and jumped into the photo booth on a whim, her hair all
wet and spiky and Lucien's sticking in rat-tails to his neck. She
could remember the moist coldness of his cheek on hers, the
leathery smell of his tatty jacket. The only possible explanation
for her son to have it was that he had chanced upon it at Ashley
House in a bottom drawer somewhere, or during one of his forages
in the attic. Struggling to convince herself, Elizabeth turned the
photo over and saw a telephone number written on the back, the
figures faint but clear, written in Lucien's distinctly extravagant
style. Elizabeth had a head for numbers. She could still have recited,
if called upon to do so, the telephone numbers of every flat she had
lived in, every school she had worked at. She knew, too, effortlessly,
the number of her father's mobile phone, Cassie's place in Pimlico,
Peter's chambers. As she stared at the figures before her, Elizabeth

was struck by their lack of familiarity. More puzzling still, it was a mobile number. During the distant days of her first marriage, mobiles hadn't existed. What was a new number doing on such an old picture? And, most importantly, what was it doing in Roland's pocket? The obvious thing, of course, was to ask Roland.

Elizabeth left the utility room with this intention, but on finding her son bedded among floor cushions and cousins in the TV room, she decided to leave it until a quiet moment presented itself. Instead she returned, in a state of some agitation, to her half-filled suitcases, which gave her a hollow feeling, reminiscent of Sunday nights as a teenager, packing to return to school.

'How's it going?'

Elizabeth looked up to see Serena's head round the door. 'Oh, fine, thanks – at least, not too bad.'

'You're being very brave, you know. Going back is brave.'

'Do you think so?' Elizabeth smiled tightly.

'You are brave,' repeated Serena solemnly, stepping into the room. 'In fact, I've been meaning for weeks – months, actually – to thank you for your courage that day . . . our day in London when . . .' She paused. 'When Tina got killed. You were amazing, Elizabeth – calm, phoning everybody. I want to thank you for that, I should have done so before. It must have been terrible for you.'

'Oh, Serena, I did nothing – *nothing*.' Elizabeth had nursed a dim guilt about her ineptitude that day. She hurried across the room and clamped her arms round her sister-in-law, pulling her to her motherly chest. 'In fact, I've often thought that if we hadn't met for lunch, or if I hadn't been so wrapped up in talking to you . . .'

Serena pressed her fingers to Elizabeth's mouth to prevent her continuing. Self-blame, she knew now, was just a way of trying to make sense of the incomprehensible. It led nowhere. 'It happened,' she said simply. 'It was the most terrible thing and it happened. And you were wonderful.' She stepped back, studying Elizabeth's sad face through tear-filled but calm eyes. 'Now I must let you get on. And Pamela needs me downstairs.' Prompted by her sister-in-law's still stricken expression, she added, 'You and Colin, I'm sure it will work out if it was meant to.'

'Do you believe that? Really?' Elizabeth, who had returned to her suitcases, clasped a shirt to her chest, rumpling all Betty's careful work at the ironing-board. 'Things work out if they're meant to,' she murmured, repeating the phrase like some new mantra for survival. 'Thanks, Serena. Oh, by the way,' she added, suddenly remembering, 'did Maisie find you?'

'No. When?'

'Just now. Ten minutes ago. She was looking for you. I'm afraid I said you were in the dining room.'

'I was, but then I came up here to call Charlie. He said his mobile would work over there but I can't get through.'

'Maisie . . . she . . . It looked sort of urgent.'

'Did it?' Preoccupied with the sudden horrible thought that Charlie might be deliberately screening her calls, Serena made a face. 'I'd better track her down, then. Give me a shout if I can do anything, won't you?'

Elizabeth smiled and nodded. Then, once the door was closed, she dug the little photograph out of her bag and stared at it for a long time. The sight of Lucien, after so many years, had shaken her, not just because it was a sore reminder of past mistakes but because the image, creased and sodden as it was, offered a glimpse of a past, happier self. She reached for her phone and began to dial the number on the back of the photo, but stopped half-way through and called Colin instead. It was several rings before he answered.

'Hello, it's me.'

'Hi. How's it going?'

'Okay. How are you?'

'Fine.'

'You sound . . . muffled.'

'Do I? There, is that better?' Half buried in bedclothes, with Phyllis in a state of post-coital luxuriance next to him, Colin levered himself upright and shifted nearer the phone. The idea had been to say goodbye. Phyllis respected that he had to try to make his marriage work, for the sake of Roland if nothing else. They had begun sombre-faced – Phyllis almost tearful – promising themselves one drink, one kiss, one embrace until, three drinks later, they were tearing frenziedly at each other's clothes and clambering up the stairs.

'A bit better. I'm packing.'

'That's good.'

'Colin, you do want me back, don't you?'

'Absolutely. Of course.'

'And do you think we can be all right?'

'Of course I do. A bit more . . . give and take, maybe . . .'

'What was that?'

'What was what?' Colin shot back, with an impressive innocence given that his lover had chosen that moment to place her tongue inside his left ear.

'I don't know. Nothing. I'll see you tomorrow evening, then, as planned.'

'As planned. Yup.' Still trying manfully to ignore the attentions of his companion, Colin added, 'I'm looking forward to seeing you, I really am.'

'Me too.'

For several seconds after the call Elizabeth stared at the phone, wondering at her unease. He hadn't been passionately reassuring but, then, neither had she. So she had no right to blame him for that. But there had been something else too, something in his tone that she couldn't put her finger on but which she knew was wrong. It was like he didn't *care*, like he was going through the motions. She had at least been fearful, tentative, which, while not exactly positive emotions, certainly came from a true and trembling heart. How could she trust that trembling heart to a man who didn't care?

Running bath water which they would take it in turn to use, the Ashley House boiler being in its usual over-stretched state, Peter and Helen were floating in their own bubble of suspended tension a few yards down the corridor. Helen climbed into the bath first, resting her palms on her stomach as she sank into the foam. Peter stood at the basin, shaving, then flossing his teeth.

'I'm already bigger.'

'No, you're not – at least, not that I can see.' He peered at the white bubbles half covering his wife, seeing nothing but his own determination for the conversation not to veer out of control, forcing demands he was not yet prepared to concede. He had told Helen many times already that they should make no attempt to address a decision until his father's eightieth-birthday festivities were over. She was angling to talk about the pregnancy all the time, picking away at it like a fingernail on a scab. He knew she was into the fourth month now, but a day or two more, surely, would make no difference. It would also give him a little more precious time to continue the torturous process of assembling his own thoughts.

Since Helen had broken the news Peter had done nothing but go over the arguments inside his own head. He knew he hadn't handled that first conversation well, and when they next broached the subject properly he wanted to be fully prepared. Not unkind, not sarcastic, but as tender and convinced as the loving husband he knew himself to be. He didn't want a third child for the same reasons he didn't want to get Chloë a dog: the added work, the commitment, being tied down again just at the point where their freedom as a couple was about to open up. They were fortunate in that money, even for a private education, would be no problem, but the most robust financial state could not make up for the fact that by the time this still theoretical third child went to university Peter would be almost seventy. It was unthinkable. In addition to which, there remained the issue of a late baby's health; Peter had taken the precaution of reading up on the subject and found the statistics terrifying. As if all these reservations weren't enough there also hung, like a large shadow over a small picture, the broader question of how they envisaged their future. *Where* they envisaged their future. Helen wanted, rightly, to continue working. If, in the next few years, Ashley House – through increasingly imaginable circumstances – were to become theirs, Peter couldn't see the feasibility of them both spending four hours a day commuting and leaving a little one at home. It wouldn't be right. Which meant committing themselves, for another decade at least, to staying in London. Which, confusingly, had its attractions but also conflicted with every vision of the future he had ever held.

'Your turn.' Helen stood, brushed the thickest suds off her body, then stepped out on to the bath mat. Overcome suddenly by the pink, pearly beauty of his wife, her body – though he had denied it – indeed riper and fuller with her condition, Peter reached for a towel and wrapped it and his arms round her. 'I'm sorry if I'm appearing hard-hearted in all this. I don't mean to be. I know how tough it must be for you, Helen, I really do.'

Helen rested her cheek on his shoulder and cried quietly for a few moments, as she had taken to doing with increasing frequency in recent days. 'I so want to feel pleased,' she whispered, 'and I can't, and I hate it that I can't.'

'Tomorrow.' Peter rubbed her back through the towel. 'We'll have a good talk about it tomorrow, I promise. Let's get tonight over with first. Dad's going to be opening his presents soon, he'll want us all there.'

'I know.' Helen pulled back and wiped her eyes on the towel. 'Chloë's made him something, did she show you? A stuffed animal from one of those kits she got for her birthday. Big stitches with the filling hanging out. A cross between a kangaroo and a giraffe. She wouldn't let me help her – but that's our Chloë, isn't it?' she added, her eyes shining with pride and the new tenderness that had been unravelling in her all year and lay at the heart of her desire to nurture their accidental baby rather than terminate its existence.

'Her mother's daughter in many ways,' murmured Peter fondly, kissing the top of Helen's head. He started in alarm as a vicious blast of wind rattled the bathroom window. 'That's quite a storm going on out there.' He went to check that the bolt was secure. 'And there's a hurricane brewing in the Caribbean by all accounts – Hurricane Louis, they're calling it – just starting to spin itself into a frenzy.'

Like me, thought Helen, but didn't say so, because she knew Peter needed her to be calm and she was determined to manage it, for a little longer anyway.

The entire family gathered in the drawing room for the opening of presents. John took prime position in the middle of the sofa, with

Pamela on one side and Chloë, breathless with excitement about her own misshapen, heavily Sellotaped gift, on the other. The remaining grown-ups occupied the armchairs while the children arranged themselves in various positions on the carpet. Serena, burdened now with what Maisie had revealed about her sister's true state of mind, evidenced by the dreadful, stark entries of the diary, sat as close to Clem as she could, her eyes glued to the pinched, starving face of her daughter. She had known it, of course, but not *seen* it. She hadn't been able to see it. Hadn't wanted to see it. Maisie had told her everything: the throwing up, the pills, the late-night exercises in the dark, the countless stealthy ways of hiding food. Afterwards they had put the diary back, Maisie returning the key to the slot under the skirting-board that Clem thought was known to her alone. Fearing recrimination, guilty at her own collusion and her disloyalty, Maisie had required a lot of reassurance.

Lying on her bed with her daughter in her arms, Serena had stressed that she was not angry, merely relieved to know the full ugly extent of the truth. She had been grateful that Maisie could not see her own terrible guilt, or know the other relief she felt at finding she was still needed. Somewhere in the aftermath of her grief over Tina, it was that sense of her children's need – her own self-belief as a mother – with which Serena had lost touch. Deprived of Tina, and her small round-the-clock demands, she had disconnected herself from the nurturing still required of her by the others. And by Charlie, too.

Oh, Charlie. Serena, surrounded by the family, felt her own need of her husband like the ache of a wound that, after the numbness of shock, wakes to pain. She would try to call him again after dinner, she decided, tell him what had happened, seek his comfort and wisdom before she decided what to do. Clem, their child, was sick, and they would sort it out together.

Maisie sat as far away from Clem as she could. Unable even to look at her, fearing that her puffy eyes would betray her, she focused instead on her grandfather's sweet, maddeningly slow exploration of his gifts. A pair of slippers, a pen, a bottle of port, some handkerchiefs, a floppy, badly stitched animal from Chloë – all were reverently unsheathed from their wrappings, all greeted with equal exclamations of pleasure and surprise. Given her own state of mind, it seemed right to Maisie that a storm should be prowling round this cosy scene, making the curtains tremble and sending explosions of dust down the chimney into the empty fireplace. Her mother had been kind, promising not to confront Clem until the time was right, murmuring again and again that Maisie had done the right thing. Maisie knew this. Just as she knew she would have to endure the consequences. Clem would go to some horrible hospital. Her parents, upon disclosure of her own reckless behaviour during her uncle's party, would be beside themselves with anger and disappointment, particularly when they grasped that it was protection of her own shame that had caused her to keep silent about Clem for so long. Thinking of it was like waiting to be executed; except, reflected Maisie bleakly, a prisoner on Death Row at least had the prospect of oblivion to look forward to instead of weeks of punishment and emotional exile.

'Do you girls want a drink?' Peter glanced at Serena, who said why not, if they wanted one. 'Theo's got a bottle of beer. Would you two like one?' Both twins shook their heads, Clem because a safe calorie-less glass of water was all she would allow herself and Maisie because she felt too miserable to indulge in anything. 'No?' Peter raised his eyebrows in surprise. 'Lizzy, are you on wine or sherry?'

'Gin, thanks,' replied his sister, waving her empty glass. 'Don't worry, I'll get it.' She began to get up but Peter seized the tumbler and pressed her back into her seat.

'One gin coming up.'

'Thanks. Quite strong, if you don't mind.' Peter gave his sister a look but said nothing. Everybody knew the strain she was under, but had no doubt that she had made the right decision. If the revelation of their mother's temporary fall from grace was what had prompted the change of heart about her marriage then, as far as Peter could see, that was one solid positive to have come out of an otherwise thoroughly negative set of circumstances. Making a go of a relationship was hard work – Christ, if he hadn't known that before, he knew it now. Then he remembered Helen rising, Venus-like, from the bath suds, and felt a rush of love for her, coupled with gratitude that they were grappling with an unscheduled pregnancy rather than the potentially fatal damage of infidelity. He trusted Helen absolutely on that front, just as she trusted him. Even the crossed wires with Hannah earlier in the year had made him feel bad, when nothing had happened and he had scotched the friend-ship the moment it felt like it might. 'What about everyone else?'

'I'd like wine, please,' said Cassie, giving Peter's shirt a little tug as he passed her chair. She hadn't slept well all week and was so tired that if it weren't for the hubbub of her nephews and nieces she might have fallen asleep. Samson was curled up in her lap with his head on his paws, his gingery ears twitching occasionally at exuberant exclamations from the children and the rip of wrapping-paper.

'And I'll have another sherry I think, Peter, my love,' said Pamela, feeling pleasantly reckless as she handed her eldest son her glass. Elizabeth was leaving the next morning and she couldn't help being glad, for her daughter's sake, of course, but also for her own. She and John would have the house to themselves again, all their quiet routines, all that lovely peace, nothing to grate on their nerves. Also, the calfskin slippers were a perfect fit, and a perfect colour too; John had been so effusive about them that she believed for once he was being honest instead of kind. His birthday dinner was keeping hot in the bottom of the Aga and ready to go. The evening, under preparation for many days, was sailing smoothly, a ship in a calm wide sea that needed little further guidance from her at its helm. She would eat and drink a little too much and sleep soundly – more soundly than she had in weeks, with the smothering humidity gone at last and the comforting drumming of the rain. The summer, although good in many ways, had been arduous. The thought of autumn, with its warm colours and crisp breezes, was, as always, infinitely soothing; such a joyous, vital breathing space before Christmas and New Year when the whole merry-go-round of the family year would start again.

Peter disappeared in the direction of the dining room, returning a few minutes later with a tray of drinks, which he handed round the room. 'Here's to you, Dad. Happy birthday.' He raised his glass and they all followed suit, while John, sitting with his presents piled around him, Chloë's giraffe taking pride of place on his knee, beamed with pleasure and pride.

They were finishing dessert – the pavlova a ruin – when the nursing-home rang. Peter, who was sitting nearest the door, took the call and came back grave-faced to report that Eric had had another stroke and the doctors needed to talk to John. The conversation – which had been zigzagging vigorously on all sides, encompassing Jessica-jokes at the children's end of the table (Ed performing a seated version of his admirer's attempts at front crawl) and a rather less hilarious discussion of the country's traffic-congestion problems among the adults – came to an abrupt halt. John, tight-faced, hurried out of the room. 'It doesn't sound good, I'm afraid,' murmured Peter, resuming his position next to Pamela and patting her hand. 'Not good at all.'

'Oh dear.' Pamela pressed her napkin to her lips, inwardly trembling as she studied the thin lipstick print of her mouth on the white linen. 'Oh dear, tonight of all nights.'

'Is Uncle Eric dying?' asked Chloë, prompting a beady stare from her mother.

'Well, we're all dying, aren't we?' interjected Theo, trying to be helpful. 'From the moment we're born—'

'Thank you, Theo . . .' began Peter, admiring the observation but fearful of the pale faces of the women ranged round the table. Without Colin or Charlie the occasion had felt oddly lopsided and much harder work than usual. He had missed his brother especially. Charlie's natural high spirits were so infectious and it would have lifted things to have him around. Helen had been understandably quiet, while Cassie had spent most of the evening yawning. Elizabeth had drunk so much that Peter seriously doubted her capacity to remain upright without the support of her chair. The news about Eric was the last thing they had all needed. The last bloody thing.

'I think Theo is right,' announced Elizabeth, her voice unnaturally high and careful. 'We are all, as he says, dying. From cradle to grave. The human condition . . . and so on . . .' She waved her hand, knocking her wine glass and catching it by the stem just in time.

'More pudding, anyone?' Pamela stood up so abruptly that she had one of her dizzy spells and had to hold on to the edge of the table. She wished now that she hadn't had the extra sherry. She wished, too, that John hadn't opened the fourth bottle of wine. From what she had seen, Elizabeth had drunk most of it. She recalled her elder daughter's behaviour at Peter's fiftieth, and glanced uneasily across the table noting the distinctly glazed look in Elizabeth's normally alert blue eyes. There was an unnatural crimson flush to her cheeks too, which made her look younger but also rather wild. As she registered these details, Pamela experienced a fresh surge of anger that Elizabeth should still present herself as a cause for concern when Pamela had so much on her plate already, with her perfect evening in tatters and her heart pounding because of the news about Eric.

John walked briskly into the dining room, jangling car keys, no trace of his birthday mood remaining. 'I'm going over there. No, Pammy,' he continued quickly, knowing what she was about to say, 'I'll go alone, I think. If you don't mind.'

'But, Dad, you shouldn't drive, should you?' interjected Peter, as tactfully as he could. 'Maybe we could call a taxi.'

'That would take too long. I'll be fine.'

'I could drive you,' volunteered Helen. 'I've hardly drunk anything. Really, John, I'd like to. I'll just drop you there – it will be no bother. Then, when you're ready to leave, you could call a taxi home.'

Peter shot his wife a look of gratitude. 'Dad, it makes sense.'

'Thank you, Helen, that might be better.' John crossed the room and kissed Pamela. 'No need for you to come, my love. They say he's almost certainly got a few more days. I just want to see him tonight. I'll take my phone. I'll call Alicia on the way there – she should know the situation.' He turned to the rest of the room, surveying the silent faces of the children, in awe at this new turn of events, and the sombre expressions of the adults. 'Sorry, everybody. Not what any of us expected.'

Peter followed them out to the door, helping to dig out umbrellas and mackintoshes *en route*. As the security light flicked on, illuminating their huddled figures in the drive, he shouted, 'Drive carefully,' but his words were tossed away on the wind. 'Hang on, I'll come too,' he called, much more loudly this time. Helen, hearing, waved at him to hurry. A few moments later, having charged back into the dining room and informed Cassie, on her way up to bed, and the others of the change of plan, he ran, coatless, to the car and clambered into the back, dripping like a dog after a swim. 'We'll take you straight there, Dad.' He touched his father's shoulder, his heart constricting at the proud poise of the familiar wide grey head with its wrinkled neck, resolutely facing the frenzied sweep of the windscreen wipers. One day he would be rushing to Charlie's bedside, or Charlie to his. One day, in some unimaginable way, it would be their turn. Peter shifted along the seat until he was behind Helen, who was stiff with concentration as she negotiated the dark, wet lane. Leaning forward, he reached round the side of her seat and placed his hand in her lap. She squeezed his cold fingers in her warm ones, then returned her hand to the wheel. Peter sat back and reached for his seat-belt, but not until he had slid his hand gently across the small swell of her belly, thinking properly, for the first time, of the minuscule foetus resident inside, clinging like a barnacle to a stone.

Serena had taken command in the dining room, marshalling the children to clear the table and go up to bed, insisting that Pamela and Elizabeth remain where they were while she washed up and made some coffee. They both acquiesced meekly, Elizabeth refilling her wine glass and Pamela absently steering a stray piece of meringue round her mat with a finger. Serena closed the door on them and wondered that Eric's turn for the worse should have induced such desolation. Of course it was shocking, and the timing terrible, but as she watched the jet of the hot-water tap in the kitchen she had the feeling that there was something else going on, something beyond Elizabeth's anxiety about returning to Guildford and the inevitable sadness that the most ancient member of the family should be losing his fight for life. She puzzled over it, but with some impatience. Her heart was brimming with concern for Clem; everything else paled into insignificance. She wanted, more than anything, to talk to Charlie. Before pulling on the rubber gloves she tried his mobile again, but there was still no reply. Seeking distraction, she switched on the radio and began to scrub her way through saucepans and the countless silver and ceramic treasures too precious to be subjected to the dishwasher. It was nearly ten o'clock. She would clear the kitchen, make coffee, then check on the children. She would hug Clem tightly, but not say anything, not yet. Not until she had spoken to Charlie.

'More wine, Mum?'

'No, thank you, dear . . . and I think maybe you . . . That is, you've got a big day tomorrow.'

Elizabeth sucked in her cheeks in a show of sarcastic surprise. 'I have, haven't I? Big, big day. Back to the unfaithful husband, eh? Back to my unfaithful spouse to make a go of my marriage. That's what they say, isn't it? To make a *go* of things, patch it up, get the picture nice and pretty on the outside, like one of your clever tapestries. Tell me, Mum, has it ever occurred to you that Colin is not good enough for me? No one has really thought that, have they? It's all been the other way round, that *I* am the one who is somehow not up to the mark.'

'Don't be silly,' Pamela murmured, eyeing her daughter's flushed face with mounting unease as she prepared to leave the table.

'Hey, where are you going?' Elizabeth seized her arm. 'Where are you going? I want – I *need* – to talk to you.'

Pamela stared at her arm, shocked at the tight grip of Elizabeth's fingers. 'I was going to give Serena a hand. Could you let go, dear?' She spoke shakily, folding her napkin until she had created a neat crisp square. With the crimson imprint of her mouth hidden in its folds, it looked almost as good as new. 'Serena could do with a hand.'

'Serena can manage. I can't. I need to talk to you, Mum.'

'You're worried, dear, of course you are, about tomorrow . . . and Colin. As to whether he's good enough for you, it's really not a question—'

'Yes, I'm worried about tomorrow and Colin,' cut in Elizabeth impatiently, slurring her words but feeling fluent inside her head where it mattered most. The pieces had been falling into place for weeks, months, years, only she hadn't known it until now, until the sudden imminence of Eric's death. Eric, her uncle, her mother's lover. She had been born around that time, after the miscarriage. She of all four children had never truly felt loved. She was the misfit, the one who never felt secure, never felt quite *right*. 'But I'm worried most of all about . . . Eric.'

'Eric? Really?' For a moment Pamela's unease dissolved. 'Well, we're all sad, of course, but—'

'The thing is, Mum,' Elizabeth was sitting bolt upright now, hands clenched in her lap, 'the thing is, if Eric is actually my father I'd prefer to know about it before he dies.'

'Eric? What are you talking about? What, in God's name, are you talking about, you stupid, stupid girl?'

'Stupid, right.' Elizabeth nodded furiously, tears streaming down her face. 'That's what you've always thought of me. Well, I'm not so stupid that I don't recognise that I've been treated differently – harshly – all my life by *you*. You don't love me like you do the others, you just don't, and since I now know that you were in love – that you had an affair with Eric it seems perfectly logical to me—'

'How dare you – how *dare* you talk to me like this?' said Pamela, in a strangled voice.

'How dare I speak the truth, you mean,' sobbed Elizabeth.

'The truth,' rasped Pamela, 'you know nothing of the truth.' She tried to reach for the folded napkin but her hands were jumping. Her old, liver-spotted hands. She felt in that moment both overwhelming longing and envy for her husband's brother, slipping away from his moorings, slipping away without her there even to hold his hand, leaving all the dreadful difficulty of living behind.

'Well, did you or didn't you have an affair with Eric?' persisted Elizabeth, not prepared, now they were at the nub of things, to let go. 'Is he my real father?'

Pamela looked at the door, needing to see that it was still closed, that they were the only ones sharing the horrible reality of the conversation. A conversation she had dreaded, protected, evaded for nearly fifty years, sometimes imagining having to endure it with her husband, but never with her elder daughter. The door was closed, which meant they were safe, but there was nowhere to hide either. It was, Pamela realised, as the flutter in her hands receded, one of those moments of truth. One of those rare, unavoidable moments that spun lives in different directions. Like the one with Eric among the silver birches in the dark forty-seven years before. When she told him that, with the miscarriage of their child, she would stay in her marriage. That she would stay with John, see her life through in another way. It had taken just a few seconds to end their dream. Two whole years of hope, gone in an instant.

'You are not Eric's child, Elizabeth. The baby I lost was Eric's. If I have treated you harshly I'm sorry. I never meant to. I found you . . . harder than the others. I think maybe . . . oh, my God.' Pamela swallowed and summoned the wherewithal to voice what had always been unvoiceable: 'Maybe, in part, because you weren't Miranda. You came so soon after. Maybe I couldn't forgive you that. I did my best. I am sorry. I did my best.'

For several minutes neither of them spoke. Drunk as she was, Elizabeth knew that her mother had spoken from the heart. The ring of truth in her words was unmistakable. And it all made sense. So much sense. 'So,' she whispered, conjuring a blurred image of Colin, awaiting her return under the shiny beams of their home, 'you stayed with Dad even though you didn't love him.'

Pamela folded her arms across her chest, so tightly she could feel each quick beat of her heart. 'Oh, no,' she said softly, 'not at all. I loved your father. I have always loved him. But there are different kinds of love. Eric was wild and difficult, a free spirit . . . different in every conceivable way. I don't think we would have been happy. He never wanted to settle or be responsible or . . . any of those things. What happened was for the best. At one point, we were going to run away together, then I lost Miranda and changed my mind, realised it was hopeless. Eric handed over the rights to Ashley House and went abroad. It was hard in many, many ways, but it was the right thing to do. I, for one, have never regretted it. Not once, Elizabeth. Not once.'

Elizabeth looked at her mother's face, seeing the strength in the soft, powdered lines and the steely blue of her eyes. For a few moments the sense of her own separate, younger self merged with a picture of how her mother must have been, passionate and torn, making momentous decisions on her own. An extraordinary wave of empathy spread through her, uninvited and so physical that she shivered involuntarily. 'How much of this does Dad know?'

'Only that Eric decided to hand over his birthright and leave England.' There was a certain pride in Pamela's voice. 'There was no need – no justification – to tell him more. The hurt it would have caused . . .' She closed her eyes. 'I couldn't do it to him. It would have been unthinkable . . . but how . . .?' She blinked, as if waking from a vivid dream. 'How on earth did you know . . . about my . . . about Eric?'

Elizabeth shifted uncomfortably in her chair. The alcohol was bringing her down now, from insouciant fluency to a much less comfortable engagement with reality. Peter would go mad. He had gone to such lengths to manage the situation, to protect the truth. When he had related how Stephen had backed down during the meeting with Cassie, he had been jubilant. And now, without permission or even consultation, she had found some cheap Dutch courage and blown it all. Elizabeth, staring at her mat, its wintry Brueghel scene flecked with dots of dried gravy, thought grimly of all this, yet could summon no remorse. Prising out the truth might not have offered any solutions, but sitting next to her mother now, with a hangover already mushrooming at the base of her skull, she was aware of the possibility of a new sort of peace with the world and herself. The sort of peace that comes with understanding. All her life a deep part of her had been battling against something –

invisible demons, an incomprehensible sense of having been wronged. She had been fighting in the dark. Now it was as if a light had been switched on. The demons were still there – would, to some degree, always be there – but they had been exposed and could therefore, perhaps, be comprehended. Forgiven, even. It was impossible to regret that. Impossible too, Elizabeth saw suddenly, to go back to Colin, whom she did not and could never love again. 'Eric's biographer,' she said slowly, chiselling at the congealed gravy with her fingernail. 'Stephen Smith. He found out. There was a letter that you had written to Eric hidden inside a bundle of correspondence Alicia sent him. He was going to put it in his book. He told Cassie, who told Peter, who told me and Charlie. But then Peter and Cassie talked Stephen out of it. So you're safe.'

'Safe?' The word came out on a half-laugh. 'I'm not safe. I never have been. Not from anything – not from what I did, not from all those feelings. I thought I was for a while, but this year, when little Tina died, it all seemed to come back at me . . . The grief . . . it has been indescribable.' Pamela pressed her fingers to her mouth to hide the tremble in her lips. 'It was a double blow, you see, losing Miranda and then, of course . . . losing – giving up – Eric. And I had no one to talk to, except your father, who deserved only kindness.' She continued to talk through her fingers, patting her mouth as if she would have stemmed the flow of her words if she could. 'And now it turns out that I've hurt you so very badly . . . I never meant to, Lizzy. I did my best.' She repeated the phrase, shaking her head, struggling still with the dark, hitherto unacknowledged fact of her failing as a mother and the causes behind it. 'I tried so hard to be fair. I only ever wanted the best for you. All your talent, I loved it so and yet . . .' She shook her head again, causing her already dishevelled bun to slip half an inch further down the back of her head.

'I didn't love my talent, did I?' Elizabeth answered for her. 'Maybe,' she said gently, 'because it's hard to love anything if you don't feel loved yourself.'

'But I did – I do – love you,' Pamela cried. 'All five of you, I loved all five.'

'It's okay, Mum, I know that. I know it. And I was a pain of a child and I'm sorry for that. So much makes sense now and I love that. I love it that it makes sense.' Elizabeth leant across the space separating their chairs and placed one arm across Pamela's back. She could feel the resistance in the sharp points of her mother's shoulder-blades, the years of suppression. 'I'm *so* glad you've talked to me,' she whispered, recognising that Pamela was close to tears and feeling like a good cry herself, 'so very glad. We won't tell Dad about Eric, Mum, none of us will, ever, I promise. I'm so sorry if I've upset you, but I needed to get the picture straight. For *me*. Which might be selfish but . . .' Elizabeth dropped her forehead on to Pamela's shoulder with a groan. 'I can't tell you how cross Peter's going to be. He's been so desperate to protect you from all this book business and now I've mucked everything up.'

Elizabeth felt her mother's shoulder stiffen and lifted her head. Pamela's pupils were dark holes in the blue of her eyes. 'But he needn't know,' she said softly, her gaze boring into her daughter's. 'None of them need know. This whole talk we've had, we could keep it to ourselves. Couldn't we?'

It was a plea from the heart. Elizabeth breathed in and out very slowly. 'Yes, we could,' she said. 'Of course we could.' She stood up and pushed her chair into the table. 'Mum, there's something else . . . I won't be going back to Guildford tomorrow. If Dad agrees I'll move into the barn, pay you a proper rent until I've found somewhere of my own.' She waited, both hands gripping the back of the chair in reflexive preparation to defend herself against the inevitable volley of admonitions about hasty decisions, giving things another go, thinking again, thinking of Roland. She gripped the chair harder. She would not be swayed this time, not by anyone, not by anything. She didn't open her eyes again until she felt Pamela's hand close round hers.

'Move into the barn if you like, darling,' she said, 'but we won't need rent.'

Approaching the dining-room door with a tray of coffee things, Serena heard raised voices and turned back for the TV room. She reflected, with some despair, on the persistently prickly relationship between Elizabeth and her mother-in-law, grateful that the situation between her and her own mother had been so straightforward. By the time the cancer had won its grisly battle, there had been nothing left unsaid, no gratitude or love unexpressed. And Tina too, she mused, setting down the tray and switching on the television, had known – if she knew nothing else in the bewitching baby-chaos of her mind – that she was loved. It was a comforting thought and Serena relished it as the steam of her coffee warmed her face and she settled down, mobile at her side, in the deep leather sofa facing the television.

She had left Charlie three messages now. She had apologised for forcing the business of moving Tina's grave so uncompromisingly upon him. She had said, even, that she would be all right if they decided not to do it, that the essence of so momentous a decision was, she saw now, meaningless without his desire for the same thing. She had said, finally, that something else big had happened and she needed to talk to him. She had kissed all their three children goodnight and said she loved them. She had reassured Ed, who was nervous about starting at Kings Grove, tried to stroke the sadness from Maisie's drained, sleepy face, then hugged Clem with all her might, feeling the thinness of her frame as if for the first time, wishing she could press some of her own motherly vigour into it, feed it, literally, with love.

The late news was just starting. 'Hurricane Louis, having gathered pace on its journey through the Caribbean, causing widespread damage to the scores of island tourist resorts in its path, this afternoon reached the Gulf of Mexico, where it turned eastwards and began to batter the Keys and southern coast of Florida. The National Hurricane Center in Miami reports that it is now the biggest storm system to hit the United States since Hurricane Andrew, with wind speeds of up to ninety-five miles an hour and waves over fifteen metres high. Initial reports indicate that eleven lives have already been lost although the final toll is expected to be much higher. The President has declared the state a national disaster zone and emergency services are already working round the clock to provide shelter for those who have lost their homes and livelihoods.'

The face of the newsreader was replaced by images of roofless houses, cars upside-down in trees and waves the size of tower blocks plunging into the coast. A rain-drenched reporter, yelling into his microphone against the din going on around him, added that an American Airways plane carrying thirty-six passengers was missing and that several ships in the area were also unaccounted for.

Serena stared at the screen, then at the phone next to her, then back at the screen. The anchorman had moved on to a different story. Three Islam extremists had been arrested in North London. Outside, their own little British storm was dying down: the rain was pattering instead of thundering on the cloisters roof; the wind, subsiding like an animal tiring of a game, was no longer pawing at the window-panes. But not in Florida. In Florida the worst hurricane in fifteen years was tearing buildings from their foundations, spinning vehicles, trees and people. Eleven lives lost already. Emergency services at full stretch. A disaster area. Serena crept closer to the television, wishing she could press rewind to hear it all again, wishing she had paid more attention to Charlie's curt delivery of the details of where he would be. They were negotiating some new international marine treaty. She knew that much. Somewhere near Miami, or was it in Miami? She couldn't even remember the name of the hotel. When he had said his mobile would work she hadn't thought it mattered particularly. But it mattered all right. It had always mattered. She should have listened. Just as she should have treasured their farewell instead of letting the treadmill of her own selfish preoccupations get in the way.

'Mum?'

'Darling?' Serena swung round to see Ed standing in the doorway in only his pyjama bottoms, one leg at his ankles, the other hoicked above the knee. His tummy was brown and his chest was peeling where it had burned a week before.

'I can't sleep.' He yawned and stretched, revealing the satiny white underside of his arms.

'Ed, darling, you know about hurricanes, don't you? You did that lovely project.'

'Yeah. Why?' Ed eyed the television, puzzled both at the question and the searching expression on his mother's face. He had entered the room expecting to be sent back upstairs. His main concern had been how to elicit permission to raid the fridge before he did so. He couldn't sleep because he was still thinking about his new school but also because he was starving. He was always starving, these days, no matter how much he crammed in at meals. 'Why, Mum?' He looked at the TV again. Two distraught parents were putting in a plea for a missing child.

'It's just that there's one going on now, quite near where Dad is, and I don't know anything about them.'

'Near Dad?'

'Yes. I'm sure he's fine, but I just want to know about them.' Serena, fearful of an imminent recap of the headlines and the effect that the sight of Florida's flattened palm trees might have on her son, switched off the television.

Ed scratched his head. 'Well . . . I remember that they can be up to six miles high and that one of the reasons they twist is because the earth is rotating and,' he continued, gathering confidence as the details of the project came back to him and from his mother's rapt attention, 'they start because warm sea heats the air above it and that rises really quickly and creates a centre of low pressure which drags in all these trade winds, and that makes everything spiral upwards more and it releases heat and rain and stuff. Oh, yes, and the amount of energy released is the equivalent of three hundred and sixty billion kilowatt hours a day, which would be six months' supply of electrical energy for the whole of the USA. They can travel up to four hundred miles a day but usually die out after about three thousand. They are bad but also important to the earth's atmosphere because they transfer heat and energy between the equator and the poles . . . Mum, is Dad right in the middle of this thing, then?'

Serena crossed the room and ruffled his already tousled hair. 'I don't honestly know, darling, but he is in Florida and that's where a bit of the hurricane is at the moment. It just makes me feel better to know a few . . . facts. Thank you. What a clever love you are.' She smiled and pressed her fears into abeyance, for the sake of Ed who was looking worried. After so many months of being at the mercy of her own emotions, it was good to find that she could master them; good to know she could be strong again, even if it was only on the outside. 'Clever and, I suspect, a little hungry?'

'Starving,' admitted Ed ruefully.

'Come on, then. Let's get you some cereal or something.'

They stepped into the corridor just as Elizabeth and Pamela emerged from the dining room. 'Have a bowl of Shreddies, Ed,' she instructed, and pushed him on ahead. Then she turned to the other two, and without paying much attention to their somewhat shell-shocked state, burst out with the news about the hurricane and her concern for Charlie. In the same instant the front door opened. Helen and Peter tumbled into the house with dripping umbrellas, anxious about the weather across the Atlantic. They had heard a bulletin on the car radio, explained Peter, helping Helen off with her coat, then leading the way into the TV room in search of more news.

Ten minutes later, with Ed back in bed, Peter had found CNN on Sky and they were all huddled in front of it, nursing mugs of coffee and murmuring in horror at the images of rain-lashed marinas and gutted buildings.

'You've tried ringing, have you?' asked Peter, for the third time, having managed to restrain his incredulity at Serena not knowing the name or location of Charlie's hotel to a glance at his wife. They were sitting on the sofa with Pamela, shoulder to shoulder, holding hands. The night, with the breaking of the weather, Eric's stroke and the ferocity of an originally mild Atlantic-bound hurricane, felt endless in its capacity for shock. Peter squeezed his wife's hand and could not think when he had last felt so protective of her, so at the mercy of forces beyond their control.

'I'm sure he's all right,' said Elizabeth, which all of them had said at intervals, when the atmosphere of concern grew too tight to bear. 'A government meeting like that – there would have been reports by now if their hotel had been hit . . . all those big cheeses, someone would have said something.' Although her head throbbed and her

lips were still stained faintly crimson from all the red wine she had
drunk at dinner, she was sober now. More sober, indeed, than she
had ever felt in her life. Her decision about Colin shimmered at the
back of her mind, already as irrevocable as if she had acted upon it
and far more manageable than the thought of something dreadful
happening to Charlie. From time to time she glanced at Pamela,
needing to reassure herself that their conversation had not been a
dream, that she had found the understanding she had been seeking
incoherently all her life. She thought of Eric too, glad that he was,
after all, just an uncle; and of her father, wronged but protected,
going through goodness knows what at his brother's bedside. What
a night. Terrible but amazing, as terrible things often were. Deep in
her heart, Elizabeth was sure that Charlie was all right. Not just
because, statistically, it was improbable that he wouldn't be, but
because of Tina. Tragedy like that didn't strike twice. Not in one
year. Not in one family.

  Pamela said little, other than to dismiss someone's suggestion
that Cassie be woken to join in the vigil. 'Let her sleep,' she had
commanded, in a tone that silenced the idea at once. It felt like the
least she could do, to protect her youngest from unnecessary pain.
Just as she had protected John, just as she had tried to protect all
of them in various ways over the years. Not always succeeding, of
course. Particularly with Elizabeth: clumsy, suffering, struggling
Elizabeth, born, Pamela saw so clearly now, when she herself was
still in mourning both as a mother and a lover, nowhere near ready
to deal with anything beyond the neediness of her own heart. It was
astonishing that this unsavoury truth, exiled for so long from her
consciousness, should have brought Elizabeth so much relief. Yet
Pamela had seen the instantaneous effect of it in her daughter's
face, as she picked away at her mat – like a light spreading, a shadow
lifting. Even now, gazing at the footage of devastation on the TV
screen, presumably contemplating the possible demise of her own
dear brother, Elizabeth looked somehow radiant. As if nothing
could harm her again. For Pamela the sight was a tiny pinprick
of consolation in an otherwise dark night. To her, the threat of
losing Charlie seemed only too real. Death, unforgiven but

accommodated – at huge personal cost – five decades before, seemed to have been reasserting itself all year as a malevolent, omnipresent force: Tina, Eric, Boots, and now Charlie – everything loved was there to be taken away. Particularly from wretches like her, who had dared to imagine that secrecy would preclude punishment, that the layer of years could ever truly bury the past. Talking to Elizabeth had brought it all back; not just the anguish of her loss but, buried deeper still, the ugliness of her adulterous deceit – making love with Eric and then, when she had realised she was pregnant, seducing her husband, teasing like a whore for sex, not because she wanted it but so that the identity of the foetus in her womb could never be called into question. Forced again to confront the graphic details of her treachery, it seemed to Pamela only right that Eric should be at death's door, that Charlie should be drowned or crushed or hurled into the sky. Because she deserved it. Because chaos reigned and all her battles against it had been for nothing.

It wasn't until Serena, exhausted by her own desperation, flung her mobile on to the carpet instead of clutching it to her heart, that it rang. They all watched it, spellbound, apart from Serena who dropped her face into her hands and burst into tears. 'It might not be him,' she sobbed.

'Of course it's him.' Peter picked up the phone and thrust it under her nose. 'Who else would call this number in the middle of the bloody night?'

Serena took the phone with trembling fingers, as if expecting it at any moment to explode in her face. 'Charlie?' she whispered, turning her face from the others in a futile bid for privacy. 'Oh, Charlie . . . oh, darling, it *is* you.' There were exclamations of relief all round. Serena, smiling now, turned to face them with a thumbs-up sign. 'So you're fine, are you? Well, we were a tad worried, yes . . .' She rolled her eyes at her audience and then took herself and the phone off in search of a place where all the things she had to say could not be overheard.

John, watching his taxi disappear up the dank darkness of the lane, knew nothing of the jubilation going on in his TV room. Alone in the rain, falling now in a thick drizzle, he studied the familiar contours of his home, the lights in the downstairs rooms shining like the welcoming smile of an old friend. He had talked to Eric that night of Ashley House, describing the views towards the copse and the Downs, the dusky white roses rampaging up and down the legs of the pergola, the polished brass of the sundial. He wasn't great with adjectives, not like Pamela or Peter, but he had wanted to give Eric one last flavour of the still pulsing heart of the family home. *Their* family home, even though he had been the one to live in it.

And now Eric was dead. Mrs Cordman, who had phoned during dinner had warned that he would not last the night. John had reported otherwise to Pamela and the children but had felt only a small qualm about lying. Death, he knew, from having watched his father strain stubbornly for every last breath, was neither serene nor beautiful. When he entered the room, Eric had a trickle of yellow vomit at the corner of his mouth and the glaze of what looked disturbingly like panic in his usually lifeless eyes. Even without such details (the little Irish nurse quickly dabbed his mouth clean) the sight of the wasted body was harrowing enough. Mentally prepared as he was, John had flinched at the visible deterioration since his last visit: the birdcage frame under the bedclothes, the thighs as thin as wrists, the contours of the skull painfully clear through the papery skin of his once handsome face, as if the life was literally being sucked out of it. He had wanted, he told himself, to spare Pamela – to spare all of them – such a sight. But most of all he had felt a keen selfish desire to say this last farewell alone, to make it brother to brother, ending their acquaintance as they had begun it, before the complications of fate and fortune had got in the way.

It was a while before John felt ready to go inside. Standing in the drive, with the rain seeping over the edges of his coat collar and down his neck, he felt both freed and burdened by the new, absolute, absence of his brother. He felt, too, a mounting trepidation at how Pamela would react. Her devotion to Eric, he knew, had been unwavering, as had Eric's to her.

As John watched the house it seemed to heave and breathe as the water slid off its walls and dripped from its gutters. With Eric gone, the path to his own death had opened up, stripped and stark. One day soon only Ashley House would remain, the thread through the years, connecting the generations with the solidity of its stone walls and the whisper of old conversations floating under its high beams. And thank God for that, John reflected, wresting consolation from what might have been a desolate thought and forcing himself, still stiff from his vigil in a hard chair at Eric's bedside, to move towards the front door. The old metal handle creaked as it always did before it granted him access to the hall. Peter appeared first. 'Dad?'

John shook his head, unable for a moment to speak.

'Oh, no . . . I'm sorry, Dad. And on your birthday too. Christ, how awful.' Peter touched John's arm, shy, even in such dire circumstances, of offering anything more intimate than their customary handshake. 'I'll get you a Scotch, shall I? Expect you could do with one. The others are in the drawing room. Mum, Lizzy, Helen, Serena – we're all still up—' Peter broke off, instinct warning him that it wasn't the moment to mention the false alarm of Charlie and the hurricane. 'I'll get that whisky.'

John walked towards the drawing room and stopped in the doorway, momentarily daunted by the sight of them all chatting quietly and looking so comfortable. Pamela, sitting on the near end of the sofa, saw him first. 'John, darling . . .'

'I'm sorry, Pammy, the end was nearer than they thought. He's gone. I'm sorry.' He went quickly to stand behind her, placing his hands on her shoulders, unable to bear the glimmer of recrimination in her eyes. She would need to forgive him, he knew, for having gone through the ordeal alone.

'Poor you, Dad, and poor Eric. But Charlie's all right,' added Elizabeth hurriedly, wanting to give her mother time to recover and feeling they all needed a reminder of their recent good fortune.

'Charlie?' John looked from one to the other. 'Why shouldn't Charlie be all right?'

Suddenly they were all talking at once, telling him about the twist in the path of the hurricane and their fears. How, just when they were getting desperate, Charlie had phoned to say that, apart from the inconvenience of the conference being evacuated north to Tampa, all members of the international delegation were fine.

'He's absolutely fine,' echoed Serena, still exultant with relief and the sheer joy of hearing Charlie's gravelly voice saying he loved her and would always love her, that together they would sort out Clem and everything else. 'I thought I'd lost you,' he had murmured, 'my darling Serena, I thought I'd lost you.' And she had said that he had for a while because she had lost herself.

'So that's good, isn't it?' said Pamela softly, patting one of the hands on her shoulder, inwardly fighting with the parallel reactions of having lost Eric but been granted the safety of her son. There was a balance to it, a pattern she recognised but was yet too numb to find consoling. Her beloved Eric, gone at last, after all those years, all that pain of loving him. The pain didn't stop, of course – it never had – but there was some peace in that his side of the story had found an ending. While her side had yet to complete its unravelling, she reflected bleakly, and glanced anxiously at Elizabeth. Her daughter returned her gaze but with a new, heartening composure. The secret had leaked, but not spilled entirely, Pamela reminded herself. She had fought hard for that and would continue to do so. For her own sake, but mainly for John's. She squeezed her husband's hand harder, saying with her fingers what words could not.

John took his whisky from Peter and drank deeply but unsteadily. 'Hurricane Louis, eh? The last I heard it was burning itself out in the Gulf of Mexico.'

'It was,' said Peter, sipping the much smaller Scotch he had poured for himself. 'It picked up today and turned on Florida. Got nasty. For a time we were worried as hell.' He put his glass back up to his lips, then dropped it again as another thought occurred to him. 'Talk about a dramatic exit.' He shook his head. 'Eric, I mean, going on your birthday and with the worst hurricane in two decades raging across the globe.' He drained his glass.

Shortly afterwards they all made their way up to bed. All, that is, except John, who told Pamela he needed some time on his own, then took his glass and the whisky bottle into his study and closed the door. He needed time on his own, all right, not just to mourn his brother, as she supposed, but to consider the potentially far grimmer blow of Hurricane Louis. Overcome, understandably, with concern for Charlie, it hadn't occurred to any of them – not even Peter – that a hurricane of such immense proportions posed a threat of another kind; a financial threat of a magnitude that John, nursing his drink in the old leather chair in his study, could hardly bring himself to contemplate. None of them knew by how much he had lately allowed his liability across the Atlantic to grow, drawn by the irresistibility of all those generous, post-9/11 premiums. A hurricane was one of those rare natural disasters that could affect the entire spread of his syndicates – marine, non-marine, aviation, windstorm and, worst of all, reinsurance. He could be hit twice on every claim. In which case the cost would be astronomical. Possibly even bankrupting. As the whisky seared his throat John did his best to keep his rational self in gear. Worst-case scenarios rarely materialised. There was no need to worry yet, not until the claims started to come in. He poured himself another tot and sipped steadily. But the whisky burned like acid in his throat and stomach. What Peter had said kept coming back to him, until John could not separate Eric's death from the hurricane, until it seemed, in his befuddled state, that the conjunction of the two constituted some final epic act of ironic revenge. Eric had appeared, in life, to give him everything. But in death he had somehow whisked the security of Ashley House – of the future – from under his nose.

Upstairs Peter rolled on to his side to find Helen already half asleep, facing away from him. 'I need you,' he whispered, slipping one arm under her hip and the other across the upper side of her waist. He pulled her into the curve of his body, placing one hand protectively over the small mound of her belly, letting it linger there tenderly as he had wanted to do in the car. 'This baby of ours . . . I've been thinking, maybe – just maybe – we should have it after all.' For a moment she did not speak, but he could feel her wake up, feel her coming to life in his arms.

'Because Eric has died?' she said at length, her voice a whisper in the dark.

'I guess that might have something to do with it. Life is short, isn't it? And precious. Very precious.' He nuzzled her neck with his nose. 'It would change everything, you know that, don't you? Tie us down, exhaust us. We would be ancient parents.'

'I know.' She sighed.

'What does Kay say?'

'Kay?' Helen tensed slightly. In spite of Peter's recent efforts, she knew something in him would always struggle to feel warm towards her friend. 'Oh, you know Kay, she doesn't think anything happens by accident.'

'Well, maybe she's right. Maybe we were *meant* to have another baby.'

'Oh, Peter, do you think so?' Helen twisted out of his arms and rolled over to face him. 'It would be so lovely if you really thought that.'

He grimaced. 'I'm trying . . . but it would change so much, not just in an everyday sense but fundamentally. I mean . . .' Peter cleared his throat, approaching, in his own mind, the heart of the matter. 'Take this place, for instance.'

'Ashley House?'

'Yes. Ashley House. Things are changing here too, aren't they? And so bloody fast. Nothing's quite the same.'

'No, nothing's the same,' echoed Helen, whose own state of mind had been changing colours, changing shape all year.

'Dad's eighty, for Christ's sake,' continued Peter, 'and Mum . . . well, she forgets things now and clearly finds just running the house something of a struggle, especially with all of us down here. Lately it's felt somehow as if the whole set-up is at breaking-point. Like tonight, what with Eric and that bloody hurricane – I got this terrible feeling that everything might fall apart at any moment.' He pulled his head back, trying to make out Helen's expression. 'What I mean,' he pressed on, 'is that we might be called upon to move here rather sooner than we think. Next year, even, or the year after. If Mum and Dad can't manage they might ask us to take it over before they die. Which should be fine. It's what I've always known would happen, in some form or other. Except . . .' he faltered '. . . except that what you said, about the family mattering more than anything, is right, just as I was right to say that all the nuts and bolts of how that family holds together – money, health, all the practicalities – they matter too. And the fact is that with a new baby and two careers in London, not to mention Chloë being too young and thoroughly opposed to the idea of boarding-school, I just can't see us living here,' Peter concluded, despair in his voice. 'I just can't see it working.'

Helen was not sure what he was saying, or what response he was looking for. 'So . . .' she paused '. . . what can you see?'

'I don't know,' he whispered, 'I just don't know. I've thought it all through from every angle, and all I'm certain of is that the pattern of the future depends on what we decide about this.' He stroked her stomach again, through her nightie, with the back of his hand. 'Which is why we've got to get it right. At this precise moment, with all that's happened tonight, I feel we should go ahead, but I know that, come tomorrow or the next day, I'll be as full of doubt as ever.'

'But, then, that's what making a choice is all about, isn't it?' she said softly, kissing the ruff of grey hairs that poked out of his pyjama top. 'You choose in spite of doubts, then deal with the consequences.'

Peter sighed. 'Yes, indeed. The consequences. Like, for example, deciding not to move down here when the time to do so presents itself. But the truth is, that wouldn't be such a problem for you, would it? Because you . . . you've never been mad on the idea of taking this place over, have you?'

It was a long time before Helen replied. A time during which she weighed up the myriad choices of how to reply. Peter had an unwavering instinct for the truth; it was one of the many things she respected about him. What he had said was true, and as each year passed she had grown less and less mad at the prospect, as the enormity of such an undertaking became ever more real. They hadn't clashed on the subject for months, but it had been hovering in the background, an unavoidable obstacle that would have to be negotiated or climbed when the time presented itself. 'Not really,' she whispered, shy herself of this terrible truth, fearful that it would harden the wonderful gentleness of her husband's new mood and send him spinning back to the standard smouldering defence of the Harrison scheme of things and his place in it.

Peter remained silent, which Helen might have found worrying were it not for the feel of his fingers, still gently caressing her tummy. When he did speak, it was on another subject entirely and so many minutes later that it was too much of an effort even to open her eyes.

'Mum looked pretty cut-up, I thought.'

'Yes, I suppose she did.'

'I wonder what she really feels about Eric dying, whether a part of her still loved him.'

Helen shrugged, too exhausted to imagine what her mother-in-law felt about anything, or even to care about it very much. She fell asleep with Peter's hand still pressed to her belly, relaxed by the simple liberation of having spoken the truth and the comforting sense that, although nothing was yet decided, resolution was within their grasp.

OCTOBER

On the morning of the first Thursday in October Cassie woke to see a rainbow arching across her bedroom window, which was bare because she was redecorating. The curtains were in a neat pile next to the skirting-board. Several smears of sample colours were daubed round the walls. The rainbow's stripe was as brilliantly clear and solid as a stick of rock, and seemed to spring from the still unopened paint pot perched on the window-sill, curving with mathematical precision up to the top step of the ladder leaning against the wall on the near side.

She stretched luxuriously, then reached out to switch off her alarm clock. The rainbow felt like a sign, as if she needed it, that things were getting better. Even during the prematurely wintry wind and drizzle that had set in after Uncle Eric's death, as if in deliberate counterbalance to the vehement heat of August, Cassie had been aware that she was in the thick of emotional recovery. Huge swathes of time now passed without her thinking about Dan. When she did think of him it was more as a memory than as an existing, torturous emotion. The pain and longing were still there, but now had to be sought out instead of shadowing her every waking moment. Being busy had helped this process, as had the innately flattering fact that new work had come her way without her scouting for it. London, it seemed, was full of people waking up after the lull of summer to the knowledge that they hadn't blown all their money on holidays and that a little redecorating could do wonders to lift the gloomy spirits induced by a damp autumn. Things had got so frantic that Cassie had tried to persuade Serena to come back and work for her in earnest, preferably without a novel in her handbag.

'I need you,' she had pleaded, imagining she was being helpful as well as truthful, adding, a little slyly, 'and it would make Charlie happy, wouldn't it?'

Rather to her surprise Serena had laughed. 'Thank God I don't have to worry about that any more. Other worries, yes – heaps in fact – but not that.'

'Sorry? I don't follow.'

'You know, Cass, the frightening thing about losing the plot is that the one losing it never realises.'

'No . . . of course . . .' Cassie had murmured, still uncertain what her sister-in-law was referring to and wondering which tack to try next. 'I could pay quite well . . .'

'Oh, crumbs – thank you, Cass, but no. Working for you at the moment is out of the question. I *am* sorry,' Serena added, sounding energised rather than regretful, 'but there's rather a lot going on at home, what with one thing and another.'

'Oh, God, Clem – of course. How is she?' blurted Cassie, appalled at herself for not having enquired earlier about this new drama going on in her brother's household.

'Oh, not so bad, thank you. She's on what they call a treatment plan and seeing this wonderful psychologist every Friday and an equally wonderful psychiatrist once a month. I never knew the difference between the two till now, but one does all the therapy side of things while the other focuses on diagnosis and gauges how it's going. And it's not just Clem who's being counselled up to her eyeballs, poor love. Early on – much to Ed's disgust, though the girls and Charlie were fine about it – we had a couple of family sessions too, and I'm now seeing a bereavement counsellor which I should have done yonks ago—' Serena broke off from her flow. Then she added softly, 'It all goes back to Tina, of course. Everything goes back to Tina.'

'To Tina, of course,' Cassie had echoed, humbled by the comparable triviality of her own needs and wondering – as they all had at different times since the revelation of Clem's condition – what more she could have done to prevent her niece getting into such a state. The poor darling had shrunk to a skeletal six stone –

before their very eyes – and none of them had done anything except exchange the occasional muted remark and offer second helpings of roast potatoes.

'It's a relief in a way,' continued Serena, talking with all her old openness, 'I mean, having a problem recognised at least means you can start to deal with it. Life, to be frank, had got really ghastly. I was all over the place, yelling at everybody or ignoring them, not facing up to anything. If it had carried on Clem would have starved herself to death by now and Charlie and I would be living under separate roofs.'

'Really? You mean you and Charlie . . .' Cassie tailed off at the notion that the mutual grief of such a close couple could have been so divisive. 'Because of Tina?'

Serena sighed. 'Yes. Of course. What else? Our ways of suffering were so different . . . We couldn't help each other. We were drifting apart. But not any more,' she added firmly. 'Not any more. There are no miracle cures, of course, on any front. Clem certainly has her ups and her downs – but at least we're *functioning* again as a family. Maisie's being difficult, which is always a good sign, and Ed's cock-a-hoop because he's been made football captain for his year. And Charlie and I have started having sex again, which can't be bad, can it?'

'No,' Cassie had agreed, laughing because Serena was. Her sister-in-law had been subdued for so many months she had forgotten how emotionally fearless she could be, how she could offer up the most intimate information with such uncalculating and endearing candour. 'That's great.' She laughed again, at the same time experiencing a small tug of regret at her own tiny world and the recollection of how she had hoped – quite recently – to expand it to encompass all the things Serena was talking about. Cassie's life was full, but only of things connected to herself. She worked, she ate, she slept. If any spare moments presented themselves they were now allocated to the insular and somewhat pedestrian challenge of redecorating her flat.

Lying in bed that bright October morning, recalling this conversation and her reaction to it, it occurred to Cassie that what she missed quite as much as Dan was being in love, the adrenaline of desire, the focus on someone other than herself, the magical transformation of the simplest mundanities that love allowed. Next to her the rainbow was fading, shrinking into the blue canvas of the sky. For a few moments an ephemeral shadow of colour shimmered, a faint imprint of the once glorious arc, and then, suddenly, it was gone. Cassie felt irrationally bereft. For a while longer she stared through the window, part of her still hunting for some signature of colour among the sea of blue. Finding none, her good mood ebbed away. A moment later her eyes were pricking with tears. Instead of giving in to them, aware that the abyss she worked so hard to avoid was yawning, Cassie threw back the bedclothes and went in brisk search of breakfast. These days, her fridge and bread-bin were kept properly stocked, one of several encouraging signs that she regarded herself once again as an independent, coping individual, who deserved proper nurturing by herself if no one else. Soon she was sipping freshly filtered coffee and spilling croissant crumbs across her daily newspaper. When the phone rang, she answered it absently, her mouth still half full, her attention focused mostly on a heartrending story of a surrogate mother who had handed over a baby, then changed her mind.

'Cassie, it's me.'

He didn't need to say more. Cassie had waited months to hear those very words. At the sound of his voice, so sorely missed, she gasped. It was a spontaneous, electric moment of pure joy, all the more wonderful for arriving when Cassie had almost convinced herself of its impossibility.

'I need to see you. Tell me I can see you.'

'Oh, Dan.'

'I need you. Tell me you need me too.'

'Of course . . . of course I do. Oh, Dan, it's been so awful.'

'My darling, I'm so sorry. It's been awful for me too. Unbearable. I've tried to be without you, I've tried and I can't do it any more. Nothing makes any sense without you. Cassie, my darling, just hearing your voice . . . Christ, it's good to hear your voice.'

'And yours,' she whispered, while another voice, steely and

commanding, bellowed somewhere inside her head that she was mad and reckless and foolish and inviting back all the agonies she had spent months taming out of being. But this is love, she bellowed back silently, shivering in spite of the sun streaming in through the kitchen window. This is love and I cannot give up on it. This is how every human longs to feel. This is the emotion striven for and described and defended across centuries, not just by poets and knights, but by every single human on the planet.

'When can I see you?'

'I don't know, Dan, I—'

'Today? Can I see you today?'

Cassie's gaze shifted from the newspaper to her diary, open at the week's list of commitments and appointments, so solid that barely a patch of white showed through the tidy lines of her handwriting. 'It's hard—'

'Because you don't want to see me—'

'No,' she interrupted fiercely, 'not that, not that at all.'

'Lunch-time tomorrow, then – our usual place?'

'Oh, Dan.'

'Please say yes, my darling. Just say yes.'

'Yes,' Cassie murmured, as she succumbed to the old swelling feeling of need and the familiar not-so-difficult business of carving time out of her schedule to fit in with his. 'Yes, of course,' she added more firmly, as the need blossomed obstinately into hope. He had tried to live without her and couldn't. Love had triumphed. It would be messy but they would find a way through. Her mother might have been able to give up on the one true love of her life – if that was what Eric had been – but she, Cassie, wasn't like that. Here was a second chance and she had every right to seize it with both hands.

Sitting on the train to London that Thursday morning, Pamela gazed out contentedly as the bright autumn sun illuminated the burnished coppers and golds of the countryside. From time to time she nudged John to point out a particularly vivid display, hoping to puncture his mood with these small revelations, which were so dear to her. He looked where she pointed, grunting dutifully, but Pamela could see that the brooding darkness, which had closed round him after Eric's death, remained as impenetrable as ever. At the funeral he had stood at the graveside long after the rest of the small gathering had hurried off to seek shelter from the rain. Concrete-faced under the black cloud of his umbrella, motionless, barely blinking as the rain lashed against his sombre expression and dark clothes, he had looked to Pamela like some tragic latterday Ozymandias, a statue of a man left to face the elements alone. The umbrella was eventually exchanged for a cup of tea, but the black cloud hung on, so obvious to Pamela that she flinched at the sight of him struggling with the social niceties of the wake and then, later, of seeing Alicia safely back on to a train to Wiltshire. As the days passed she waited for the cloud to go away. When it didn't she tried tempting him out of it with little treats and kindnesses: she ran him baths, found his reading glasses before he realised he had lost them, produced unexpected snacks of all his favourite things – potted shrimps, Gentleman's Relish on slivers of toast, shelled quail's eggs perched next to miniature mountains of crushed black pepper – she even asked Betty to save the Hoovering until he was on one of his daily excursions round the estate, knowing how the grinding noise jarred his nerves. None of these measures lifted his spirits, but still Pamela did not give up. She saw the cloud both as a challenge and a fresh chance of atonement.

The memories of her buried sin had reached their apex on the dreadful, extraordinary night of the storm. The incredible conversation with Elizabeth. Eric's death. After almost fifty silent years she had spoken the unspeakable and felt not worse but better. Elizabeth was nesting happily in the barn now, keeping herself to herself, giving private piano lessons on an old upright between strolls up and down the lane to deliver Roland to and from Barham village school. Limited by its catchment area and a lack of concern about league tables, the school had few budding Einsteins. Roland, for the first time in his ten years, was at the top of his class. Peering through the hall window in the afternoons as the two entered the drive, then turned down the path to the barn, Pamela could see how her once frail grandson glowed, how he bounced on his toes, how he seemed to have grown not just a couple of inches but several feet. The sight filled her with grandmotherly contentment and another, infinitely more complicated kind of happiness on behalf of her daughter, alone but finding her feet at last, at the age of forty-seven. Pamela found it hard to explain the entwining of this happiness with Eric's passing, beyond the fact that alongside her grief at the sight of Sid, John, Peter and Charlie bearing the coffin into the church, she had experienced the most wonderful and unforeseeable sense of release. Brutal as it was, death had offered closure, she had discovered, and opened her throat to sing in a way she hadn't for years: 'Onward, Christian soldiers, marching as to war'. She pushed the notes through the lump in her throat. It was a clean slate, a chance to be better, to try again. That John, with his black mood, seemed bent on making this harder was fitting. Of course it was hard. Good things often were or they were of little worth.

That morning she had given him his favourite breakfast of poached egg and bacon, then cajoled him into letting her accompany him to London. She needed to make a start on her Christmas shopping, she had claimed, which was true; she had been reluctant to watch him trudge out of the front door so ashen-faced and alone. He had put up quite a fight: he was seeing business acquaintances all morning and for lunch, he said. Christmas was months away and she would do just as well trawling the shops in Chichester. Only when Pamela had produced the trump card – via a hasty phone-call to Serena – of her own lunch date in Wimbledon, had he given in, albeit with gruff warnings that he could make no firm commitment as to which train he would be catching home.

Roland tipped back his chair and squinted at his Roman soldier, who was still far from the magnificently muscled and imperious figure etched in his imagination. One leg was fatter than the other and his shield looked flat and flimsy. Sighing impatiently, he rubbed out the offending leg and weaponry, sharpened his pencil and tried again. He liked the Romans. They were brave and strong and good at things. Not just fighting either, but building and looking after people. His particular Roman was called Hadrian. Behind him he had sketched in a few turrets of the famous wall, copying from the poster the teacher had pinned next to the blackboard. He was saving the writing, which he hated, till last, although he knew already what he was going to say, all about the wall and how the soldiers took it in turns to guard it and live in it and how some of them married local ladies and had families and started farms. When he contemplated how the finished page would look – the beautiful picture, his best handwriting – Roland burned with excitement. It would be perfect. So perfect he had decided it might be one of the things he took to show his father when he went to stay at half-term.

He was also going to take some of his new music: there was one piece in particular that he could already play quite well. He wasn't doing grades any more. When he told his new teacher how afraid his first two exams had made him, how he had mucked up and only scraped just enough marks, she had said, as if it was the simplest, most obvious thing in the world, that he never needed to take another music exam in his life if he didn't want to. She had then produced a fat new shiny orange book full of tunes with funny titles like 'Boogie Woogie' and 'Mad Cat Jazz'. They had funny rhythms, too, which Roland found he could get the hang of quite well if he just listened to the sounds and stopped trying to make the printed notes add up like impossible sums. When, after considerable urging, he had played some of them on the Ashley House grand piano the previous weekend his grandmother had gone all watery-eyed and said he took after his mother, which had made Roland feel strange (how could a boy take after a woman?) but also rather pleased. His grandfather had clapped a little but carried on looking grumpy, as he always seemed to, these days, as if he had simply got too ancient to enjoy himself.

The bell rang when Roland was still on the leg. But it was a good leg now, the same size as the other and with a convincing knee. 'Time to stop,' said the teacher, peering over his shoulder with a smile. 'That *is* coming along, isn't it?'

Roland smiled back. 'I'd like to stay and finish it now, please.'

'And miss break?' The teacher, who had a big friendly face with two chins, laughed. 'It will still be here tomorrow, you know.'

Roland frowned. He wanted to finish his picture – so badly it was like an ache inside – but then he thought of the playground, which he could see through the window was already filling with children, its black Tarmac gleaming in the sun. He had a friend called Polly whom he usually met by the swings. His break snack was always fruit or a cereal bar, but Polly got crisps. Today, Roland remembered, she had promised to try to bring an extra bag for him. Ketchup flavour. His mouth watered. He looked longingly at Hadrian, seeing exactly how the shield should be, how intricately patterned, held up as if the great Roman was ready to defend himself against the world. 'Can I take it home, Miss? I'm going to show it to my dad soon, you see, and . . .'

The teacher's face softened. They knew, of course, of the situation at home. Sadly, there were many such situations among the class, some horribly divisive and unsettling for the children. Although Roland had presented no obvious cause for worry, there was an uncertainty and a solitariness about him that she knew they would have to keep an eye on.

'What a good idea. Your dad will be very proud, I'm sure. Now, pack up your things, there's a good boy, and go and make the most of this sunshine.' She clapped her hands to make him move faster, prompted by the thought of the coffee and biscuits awaiting her in the staff room.

A few hours later when he came out of the school gates, Roland saw his mother standing across the road talking to Polly's mother and Polly's little sister, Tessa, who was all rosy-cheeked and still in a pushchair like Tina had been. He had told Polly about his baby cousin dying, making it sound as dramatic as he could to impress her, then feeling bad because her eyes had gone pink and after not saying anything for a long time she had admitted that she hated Tessa but still wouldn't like her to *die*.

'Hello, darling.' Elizabeth, momentarily forgetting Roland's recent instructions about not hugging him in public, put out her arms, then slapped them quickly to her sides. 'Hello, you.' She ruffled his hair and kissed his forehead. 'We were just talking about getting Polly over for tea. Would you like that?'

'Cool,' said Roland, tracing a circle on the pavement with his toe. 'I've brought my soldier home to work on – the crayons we've got are much better than the school ones.'

Elizabeth and Polly's mother exchanged looks. 'I think that's a yes,' murmured Elizabeth, grinning. 'I'll call you tonight.' Then she turned to Roland and suggested that, as the sun was shining, they should go home via the village shop and treat themselves to an ice-cream. After a crisp start to the day the afternoon had turned unbelievably warm. By the end of her walk to school Elizabeth had tied her new pink sweatshirt round the hips of her equally new denim skirt and yanked the sleeves of her T-shirt up over her shoulders. She was also wearing new shoes, blue ones with comfy flat soles and pretty bows across the top. These additions to her wardrobe had been possible thanks to Colin's first cheque, haggled for through several draining conversations during the course of the previous few weeks.

Colin's reaction to her change of heart on their marriage had been an icy rage, focused primarily on her selfishness and lack of rationality. If he had been gentle, or pleading, or truly penitent, Elizabeth might – even at such a late stage – have caved in. But Colin, she now saw clearly, had little concept of gentleness or, indeed, of any emotion that did not involve asserting his own demands. He was a bully, to whom she had formed an attachment at a time in her life when she had had little confidence in her own abilities, when she had been only too willing to abdicate personal control to someone else. Someone older. Someone forthright and brimming with self-conviction, no matter how ungenerous. Armed with such hindsight, Elizabeth's own self-belief had grown stronger under verbal attacks that would once have left her quaking. With the result that during their most recent conversation, Colin, protesting bafflement and injury, had promised not only to send a cheque but also to enlist a firm of lawyers to act on his behalf. Elizabeth, drawing on what was left of her father's gift, was already paying some lawyers of her own and working out meticulous lists of her spending and income. A permanent settlement, in her view, couldn't come too soon. In spite of her parents' protests, she was insisting on paying them rent. Modest though the sum was, it was still proving difficult to make ends meet on the meagre income generated by a few hours' teaching the piano. The sweatshirt, skirt and shoes had all come from a sale; the rest of Colin's money had been gobbled up in gear for Roland, who was growing in all directions by the minute.

When they were back at the top of the lane, choc ices still only half eaten, Roland relaxed and merry, Elizabeth slowed her pace and turned to him. 'Darling, there's something I've been meaning to ask you – a silly little thing . . .'

'Is it about my feelings?' he volunteered cheerfully, catching a shard of sliding chocolate with his tongue, knowing in spite of Elizabeth's endeavours to disguise it that they were entering 'grown-up' territory, which, ever since the permanent separation from his father, had constituted long chats on how he felt about virtually everything under the sun.

Elizabeth laughed a little sadly, wondering briefly whether her relentless candour of recent weeks had protected her son's innocence or destroyed it. 'No, not your feelings, not this time.' She watched Roland attempt a leap over a long thin puddle and land well short, splashing mud up the backs of his legs. Once upon a time, she thought, gathering courage to continue her enquiry, he wouldn't even have tried such a jump. He would have been afraid of failing or getting dirty. 'It's just about a photo . . . a little photo I found in your shorts – oh, ages ago now.' A few paces ahead of her Roland stopped, then continued walking without looking back. 'I just wondered how you got hold of it. Roland? Please answer me. I'm not cross or anything, I just want to know.'

Roland spun round, swiping the back of his hand across the vanilla smears on his cheeks and upper lip. He had done his best to forget about the man and the photo, even though one of the many difficult things he had learnt in recent weeks was that forgetting about something didn't necessarily make it go away. Standing now in the lane, with the sun dancing in yellow specks round his feet, his stomach pleasantly full of sugar, and his lovely Hadrian tucked safely inside his satchel, the last thing he wanted was to be told off. But his mother's eyes glittered expectantly and his heart quailed at the daunting task of trying to lie.

'The man in the photo gave it to me. He came to Ashley House one day. He said he was my friend. He said I could tell you, but I decided not to.'

'Oh!' exclaimed Elizabeth, so clearly more astonished than angry that Roland galloped on with a thorough account of his morning's encounter with Lucien, even mentioning how loudly he had whistled as he walked away.

'He came here?' said Elizabeth stupidly. 'Whatever for?'

'To see *me*, silly. And you, I suppose,' Roland conceded, already bored with the subject and baffled at how grown-ups could switch from being scary one minute to downright thick the next. 'What's for tea? I'm starving.'

'Fish fingers, potato waffles and peas,' murmured Elizabeth, still marvelling at all she had heard and wondering what, if anything, to do about it.

Pamela got to Wimbledon much later than she had intended, with aching feet and several bulging shopping-bags. Serena greeted her with a warm embrace and a finger pressed to her lips. She explained in hushed tones that Maisie was asleep upstairs. 'She's not really ill,' she whispered, unlooping the bags off her mother-in-law's arms and leading the way into the kitchen, 'but thinks she is, which is more or less the same thing, isn't it? Actually it was good for Clem to be able to play the role of healthy one for a change, trotting off to school and seeing her sister laid up with a thermometer in her mouth.'

'Dear Clem, how is she?' asked Pamela, unable to contain a sigh of relief as she flopped into a kitchen chair while Serena scurried around with knives, forks and glasses. There was a lovely smell from the oven, which turned out to be a fish pie, perfectly cooked with crusted peaks of mashed potato covering a creamy concoction of soft cod, hard-boiled eggs, capers and nutmeg. Through the window to her left the recently mown narrow strip of grass shimmered in stripes of light and dark green, like the lanes of a long swimming-pool. On the path a huge quantity of leaves had been raked into a tidy pile next to what Pamela could see, with her expert eye, was a freshly and expertly trimmed Old Blush China rose, which had probably bloomed hard all summer and would, after such attentions, almost certainly be in flower again for Christmas.

'Clem is doing all right,' replied Serena firmly, dishing out spoonfuls of the pie as she talked and adding enticing clusters of petit pois and steamed French beans next to each portion. 'The weight is going on slowly – but the main thing is not to pressure her, to make her feel that she's doing it all for herself. The doctors have been fantastic – eating disorders are so horribly common, these days, and they've got all sorts of clever ways of treating them. She sees her psychologist tomorrow – that's always a difficult day – but then she settles down again. We've got this thing called a treatment plan, all about what she should eat, what she's aiming for, the point being it's *her* plan not ours. She's not being sick any more – at least, I'm pretty sure she isn't – although,' she added, with traces of the desperation she felt at her daughter's plight slipping into her tone, 'I do hear her exercising late at night sometimes when she thinks we're all asleep.'

'My dear, how terrible . . .'

'Oh, no, honestly.' Serena looked squarely across the table, wanting her mother-in-law to know that she had no need of pity, not any more. The desperation, like the sadness, was a constant companion, but one whose acquaintance could now be endured because she shared it with Charlie. When she had first told him – just before he boarded his return flight from Tampa – the full version of events with regard to Clem, her actual weight, the pitiful diary entries, the vomiting, the laxatives, he had offered ten sensible manly responses, then wept like a child. When they had fallen into each other's arms at the airport he had wept again, as had she. They had stood in the middle of the airport concourse, travellers, shoppers, loaded trolleys, petulant children streaming on all sides, clinging to each other like distraught lovers. Their tears were not just for their sick daughter but for each other, for Tina and the alienation of their grief, for the scare of the hurricane and the whole fragile business of being alive. 'It's tricky at times,' admitted Serena, still wanting to melt some of the compassion from her mother-in-law's gaze, 'but not terrible. I'm getting help too now, from a bereavement counsellor. So it's not as if Clem is the only one having her head examined.' She paused, momentarily overcome by how far things had gone, how in the space of just a few months the world of her lovely blossoming family had been turned upside-down and shaken to its core. 'The hardest thing is admitting one needs help, but at least, these days, the help is there, unlike when you . . .' Serena stopped abruptly. With Charlie having told her only recently about the extraordinary business of Pamela's affair with Eric, she had meant to leave the whole subject of her mother-in-law's past well alone. Although the more Serena had thought about it, the less extraordinary the affair seemed. Her father-in-law, though sweet, was a little dour and dull. That Pamela should have been attracted to his wild-spirited war hero of an elder brother was just one of those unfortunate but thoroughly understandable things. Looking across the table now at Pamela, primly loading peas on to her fork, Serena was aware that this new knowledge of her mother-in-law's past misdemeanours only made her like her more. It was comforting to find that no one was exempt from the business of being human: that life, with all its joys and disappointments, was complicated all the time for everyone. 'I just meant . . . when you suffered your loss . . . Miranda – how hard it must have been . . .'

'As I have said, Serena dear,' countered Pamela easily, 'that was *years* ago. Things were different then. We had our ways of coping.'

'Yes, I'm sure you did,' agreed Serena gently, 'and, of course, coping without Tina is what is going on now, for all of us. It all goes back to Tina,' she murmured, struck afresh by the truth of the sentiment.

Pamela slid her knife and fork into a tidy pairing across her empty plate. She wondered, but only fleetingly, if Serena – thanks to Charlie – knew about Eric. It didn't matter, she knew, since it was hardly a subject to which her daughter-in-law would feel able to refer. No, all Serena was interested in, Pamela decided now, was Miranda, but she didn't want – and didn't have – to talk about that either. She didn't need to. She had coped, Pamela reminded herself, not at first, maybe, but certainly now, with the unwitting help of Elizabeth and the unexpected release of Eric's death. There was peace in her heart now, there really was. 'John's not well, though,' she said, the words slipping out on the slipstream of her thoughts.

'Oh dear. What sort of not well?'

'Eric's passing . . . he's taken it hard. I think maybe he feels, somehow, that he'll be next. He worries about money too, I think – whether he'll live long enough to outwit the taxman.'

'Oh dear.' Serena made a face. 'But he's in great shape for his age . . . loads of years left in him. Aunt Alicia, on the other hand, now she did look frail, I thought, leaning so hard on her stick after all that business with her hip. Oh dear, but that's probably not much consolation, is it?'

Pamela smiled. 'Not really, no. Although Alicia, in spite of what she's been through this year, was actually in very good spirits. Paul has invited her to Australia for Christmas and she's determined to go.'

'Good for her,' declared Serena. She cleared the plates and went in search of the fruit salad she had prepared for dessert.

Maisie, who had been eavesdropping from behind the door into the dining room, turned and tiptoed back upstairs to bed, placing her bare feet carefully round the squeaky patch at the top of the landing. She had felt ill that morning, terrible, in fact, but mainly, as her mother knew, from lack of sleep. They had met in the small hours on the landing, as Maisie was making her third or fourth trip to the bathroom for a drink of water. Her mother, with her new look-every-problem-in-the-face boldness, had asked what the matter was. Maisie had started to say, 'Nothing', then burst into tears. Curled up five minutes later on the sitting-room sofa with a mug of Ovaltine and Serena's arm round her shaking shoulders, she had poured out her woes, beginning with Clem's shunning of all her attempts at affection and then wending her way, tearfully, bitterly, to a full rendition of the events both during and subsequent to the night of her uncle's party. 'We agreed to keep each other's secret,' she sobbed, 'it was like this huge promise we made to each other, but then I broke it by showing you Clem's diary, which I thought would make her go and tell you everything anyway, but instead of that she's just being horrible – she hardly talks to me, she won't walk home from school with me, it's like I don't exist and I hate it so much that I'd have preferred her to tell you all about stupid Rosco, I really would.'

Serena had fetched a box of tissues and stroked Maisie's hair where it sprang from the top of her forehead, remembering as if it was yesterday the same line of little curls she had stroked as a shell-shocked but deliriously happy mother of twin baby girls. Friends had been delighted but sympathetic. Twins! Double the worry, double the work. And then with Ed, too. Three children under the age of three. Poor Serena! But she hadn't felt 'poor': she had felt blessed, enriched beyond her wildest dreams. And now the girls were little women, and Ed, with his gel-spiked hair and sinewy muscled legs, a little man, all as beset with foibles and hang-ups and precarious hopes as any adult, as vulnerable to life's pitfalls as the palm trees she had seen snapping in the Florida winds. 'My darling, my poor, precious darling. What a thing to go through alone. What a horrible thing. You should have told me—' Serena broke off at the realisation of how impossible this must have seemed, not just because she could recall clearly her own anxious teenage secrets – a horrible first kiss with a drunken friend of her father, being caught cheating in her mock maths O level, two pregnancy scares in the sixth form, none of which she would have dreamed of confiding to her own parents – but also because she saw how unapproachable her zombie-like state of grief must have made her seem. To her family, to the whole world. 'It sounds as if Clem was wonderful.'

'Oh, she was,' agreed Maisie fiercely, 'she really was. And then she helped me too, calling the journalist, and it must have done some good because now Rosco's been arrested.'

'Has he?' Serena stared in astonishment at her daughter.

Maisie sniffed. 'I don't know if we had anything to do with it. I don't care, really. It made me feel better anyhow, like I'd sort of done *something* to get my own back.'

'You certainly did,' murmured her mother, her expression shifting from astonishment to undisguised admiration. 'And who was he, this journalist, if you don't mind my asking?'

Maisie blew her nose loudly several times. She felt empty but also sort of fantastic, as if nothing could ever really worry her again. 'Mr Cartwright. Mr L. J. Cartwright.'

'Was he now? Blimey.' Serena felt a shiver creep up her spine. It might be chance, of course – similar name, same profession, L stood for lots of names – but it was something of a weird coincidence, one that made her feel as if the world was very small and densely interconnected in a way that was preordained but unknowable. Then another thought occurred to her, a horrible one, which would not go away. 'Darling Maisie, are you sure that . . . I mean, might it be wise for you to have a . . . test?'

Maisie turned to look at her mother, her face puffy, her nose scarlet. 'What sort of test?'

'Oh, darling . . .' Serena plucked at the used tissues scattered across her lap. 'A pregnancy test or . . . AIDS.' She whispered the word, fearful both of its ghoulish implications and Maisie's reaction, which, much to her relief, was one of exasperation.

'Mum,' she groaned, 'nothing *happened*. I promise, okay? It wasn't like that. I don't need a *test*, I really, really don't.'

'Okay.' Serena smiled with relief. 'Good. And I will talk to Clem, but you must understand, darling, she's being difficult with all of us, it's not just you. She's going through an awful lot – we can only imagine the half of it. We've all just got to try and *be* there for her, show her we love her . . . and she does love you, you know, of course she does. It's herself she's not too keen on. She's got to learn to like herself again and that can be very hard.'

Maisie had gone back to bed and sunk into an exhausted sleep, only to wake – thanks to the Ovaltine – with an aching bladder a couple of hours later. When the household stirred to the buzz of alarm clocks, she didn't move, telling Ed, who scoffed at her slothdom from the doorway of her bedroom, that she felt too ill to get up. Serena, peering over his shoulder, had colluded without a murmur, shooing her son downstairs and instructing Maisie to go back to sleep.

It had been nice to lie there and hear all the familiar rushing going on around her, feet pounding on the stairs, the faint scrape of spoons in cereal bowls (Clem would have her usual single Weetabix and a special strawberry milk drink, which Ed would swig only to get ticked off for doing so). Then the kitchen noises had stopped and she had heard her father, late as usual, shouting if anyone had seen his glasses. After that there was lots of key-jangling and the slamming of doors. A lovely silence had followed, during which Maisie had turned her face to a cool uncharted stretch of pillow and thought blissfully of being able to feel normal again, with only Monica's fawning to worry about and whether *ut* took the sub-junctive and what to wear to Jonny Cottrall's sixteenth birthday party.

Maisie hadn't woken until her grandmother arrived for lunch. Initially drawn downstairs by the smell of the fish pie, when she heard the serious tenor of the conversation going on in the kitchen, she had made a last-minute decision to listen in on it, partly because she was fifteen and curious, but mainly because of a sudden knee-weakening apprehension that Serena would feel the urge to tell Pamela everything about her. It was just that sort of conversation – Clem, Tina, and some terrible thing that had happened to her grandmother that she couldn't quite fathom. During each lull Maisie braced herself to hear her mother say, 'And another thing . . . You'll never believe what Maisie told me last night . . .' But the words never came and, as Maisie scurried along the landing and back upstairs to bed, she had the heartwarming feeling that Serena never would tell anyone either, that there was something about the whole episode that she would want to guard as closely as Maisie did.

Clem dawdled outside the school gates, wondering idly if Maisie had already set off home before remembering that she had spent the day sick in bed. If her sister had been around Clem would have avoided her, but knowing there was no possibility of her company made her feel perversely sad. She knew, somewhere inside her head, that in alerting their parents to her weight loss, Maisie had been trying to do the right thing; but this knowledge was still like a distant fact and not something Clem truly felt. What she *felt* was that her twin had blown the whistle on a covert but perfectly legitimate way of being, resulting in an at times almost unbearable sensation of entrapment. The doctors, her family, the beady-eyed teachers following her progress with her lunch tray at school were like an army of vigilant inspectors, all preventing her living as she wanted to live. As she had a *right* to live. They said she had an eating disorder, but that was because they didn't understand. They were judging her against how she *had* been, as if that was the norm, when in fact she had been thoroughly overweight. A girl in her class called Tamsin had weighed under seven stone for months and months and nobody had carted her off to a doctor. Clem was co-operating with the hateful *treatment plan* because not doing so would mean being hospitalised. It was as simple as that. But she didn't have to co-operate with Maisie, Clem reminded herself, glancing down the street and wondering if she had time – if she trotted fast enough – to go the long way home, which would allow some shedding of the hateful calories she had been forced to acquire during the day. For a moment she felt quite exultant at the prospect. Then she remembered that failing her weight target would only tighten the already strangling noose that had been placed round her life and her courage dissolved. It was pointless, she reflected miserably. She crossed the road to take the usual route home, fresh anger at her sister burning like acid in her heart.

'Hey! Clem – wait a minute.'

Clem turned to see Jonny Cottrall, clutching his battered guitar case in one hand and sax in the other, striding across the road towards her. A car, approaching at speed, tooted and swerved.

'Fucker,' yelled Jonny cheerfully, and galloped to Clem's side. 'Hi, how are you?'

'Okay, thanks.' Clem looked at the ground, horribly aware of her unwashed hair and makeup-less face. She didn't try to go near cool people like Jonny any more. In fact, she didn't try to go near anyone very much, except a new girl called Anna Mason who was spotty and shy and safely unpopular.

'Did you get it, then?'

'Get what?'

'The invitation, dumb-cluck, to my party. You'd better bloody come.'

Clem raised her eyes, emboldened enough to forget, temporarily, her greasy fringe and bare eyes. 'Why?'

'Because I bloody like you, that's why.' He sounded furious but blushed so violently that Clem had to make a conscious effort not to burst out laughing. Repressed, the merriment rippled inside her, rejoicing not in his embarrassment *per se* but in the sudden sense of kinship with his pink face. As one who felt awkward and uncertain most minutes of most days, it gave her the sensation of being just the tiniest bit less alone.

'Well, I might, I suppose,' she conceded stiffly, without any trace of the empathy she felt inside. 'If I'm not busy.'

A moment later he was bounding back across the road in response to the hooting of another car, this time containing his mother. Clem hurried on down the road, turning over the exchange in her mind and rehearsing how she could explain such a sudden climb-down to Maisie, whose alacrity in accepting her own invitation to Jonny's party had been one of the main reasons Clem had so far not responded.

At home she found her grandmother on the doorstep, hugging her mother goodbye. A taxi waited in the street with its engine running and the driver holding open the door.

'Clem, darling, how lovely to see you.'

'Hello, Granny.' Clem kissed Pamela's powdery cheek, feeling shy of her grandmother's surreptitious – but obvious – appraisal of her looks. Thinner or fatter, that was what they all wanted to know. It made her feel like a specimen in a jar, a butterfly pinned to a board with a needle.

'Here's ten pounds, dear, to treat yourself to something nice. I was going to leave it with your mother, but seeing as you're here . . . and now I really must go. Take care, darling.'

Serena, Clem and Maisie, who had appeared at the last minute still in her nightshirt, stood on the step to wave the taxi off.

'Did she give you a tenner too?' asked Maisie, once they were back inside.

'Yup.' Clem waved the note, already heading for the stairs, not looking at her. 'By the way,' she added, not turning round, 'I've changed my mind about Jonny Cottrall's party. I think I might go after all, *if* that's okay by you.'

'Of course,' began Maisie, exchanging a look with her mother. 'In fact, I'm really . . . pleased,' she finished, but Clem was already rounding the bend in the stairs.

Once inside the sanctity of her bedroom Clem found herself reaching for her diary, her heart swelling with angry sadness at the sight of all the entries recording her weight loss. The pages of recent weeks were blank. Writing down her torturous accumulation of ounces held little appeal, but Maisie having shown the diary to their mother had been an act of violation from which Clem had found it hard to recover. She would throw it away, she decided suddenly, and rammed the little leather book into the wastepaper basket next to her bed. Then she turned her back on it, folding her arms tightly and gripping both sides of her ribcage with her fingers. For a few seconds she remained like that, clenching herself in the small tight circle of her arms. As she sat there, however, all coiled and knotted, the afternoon's encounter with Jonny tiptoed into her mind. Her fingertips tingled. She wanted to write about it. But why? What was the point? She gripped her ribcage harder but the tingling wouldn't go away. Angrily, she plunged her hands into the wastepaper basket and pulled the diary on to her lap.

Jonny thinks-he's-so-cool Cottrall has BEGGED me to go to his stupid party. Think I might go, but only to annoy Maisie to whom I am now nothing but an embarrassment. Well, she can fuck right off. In fact everyone can FUCK OFF.

Clem locked the diary and slipped it under her pillow, then looked round for a new place to hide the key, eventually settling on one of the tiny drawers in her dressing-table. It was a pretty obvious place, but then, she decided, ramming the drawer shut, if Maisie was treacherous enough to read what she'd written this time she'd hurt no one but herself in the process.

That evening, while Clem slowly spooned tomato soup into her mouth, studiously not watched by her family, and Pamela spent her return journey staring again at the panoply of autumn colours streaming past the train window, and John brooded over pages of figures in the reading room of his club, a glass of whisky perched on the leather arm of his chair, Peter and Charlie met a few miles across town at Peter's club for their second game of squash of the year. Without Peter's insistence the encounter would not have taken place. Charlie, busy at work and with all that was going on at home, had felt a mounting reluctance at the prospect. At five o'clock, after an excited call from Serena (she had made it half crouched, like a thief, on her mobile, behind the mountain of leaves they had raked off the lawn) to say that Clem had changed her mind about the Cottrall boy's party, Charlie, thrilled at such a sign of progress in their reclusive daughter, had phoned his brother to cancel the arrangement.

'You can't not come, I won't hear of it,' barked Peter, himself snowed under by a fresh set of medical testimonials and the absence of his key junior barrister, who had succumbed, uncharacteristically, to a bout of flu. 'I need a run-around for one thing and for another there's something I want to discuss. A couple of things, actually.'

'What sort of things?' enquired Charlie wearily. He sometimes forgot how, once his elder brother got an idea into his head, it was a task of Herculean proportions to dislodge it. It was maddening, but also, Charlie reminded himself, one of his indubitable strengths. Only Peter, for example, could have had the tenacity to tackle the awful business with the biographer head on and scotch what would otherwise have been an extremely distressing set of circumstances.

Mollified by the recollection of this unhappy episode and Peter's brave leadership in dealing with it, Charlie backed down. 'Are these things important, then?'

'Very,' replied Peter, gravely. So gravely, in fact, that recalling the conversation as he hurried up the steps of Green Park tube station Charlie found his thoughts returning again to the dreaded Stephen Smith, wondering if a new ugly twist to the tale had presented itself. His concerns were not allayed by the visible tension in his brother's face. Peter asked tenderly after the family, particularly Clem, then refused to discuss anything else until they had played their game. Most astonishing of all, instead of charging round the court in a relentless pursuit of victory, he then proceeded, for the first time in the forty-four-year history of their relationship, to concede defeat with barely any over-exertion – or even swearing – at all.

'What the hell is up with you?' Charlie burst out, once they were back in the changing rooms, towelling themselves after a shower. 'Are you ill or something?'

'I don't feel too hot, actually,' Peter admitted, stroking his throat, which felt somewhat sandpapery. 'I think I might be getting a touch of flu. It's been going round chambers.'

'That's too bad.' Fastening his watchstrap, Charlie eyed his brother carefully. 'Might have guessed there was *some* good reason for my being granted the unprecedented satisfaction of two wins on the trot. I knew it couldn't have anything to do with *my* abilities.'

'Oh, but it did,' countered Peter, deliberately not acknowledging Charlie's teasing tone and patting him on the back. 'You're so much fitter, these days. It really shows.'

Charlie zipped up his sports bag, shaking his head in amused disbelief. 'So much humility, so much generosity of spirit, I warn you, Peter, I could get used to this.' He slung the bag over his shoulder and turned to his brother, grinning. 'Am I at least allowed to get the drinks?'

'Oh, I think I can let you do that.' Peter grinned back at him, while his heart performed a double-flip at the thought of what he had to say and how Charlie would react.

They sat at a table in the furthest corner from the bar, where a group of rowdy young bankers were finishing a long lunch. In spite of considerable joshing from his younger brother, Peter insisted, as he had on the last occasion they had met for squash, on having a pint of orange squash instead of beer.

'Helen's off alcohol,' he explained, as Charlie set their drinks down, 'and I'm supporting her.'

'That's above and beyond the call of duty, isn't it?' Charlie tugged open a pack of peanuts with his teeth, spilling them on to the table. 'I mean, surely, if Helen—'

'She's pregnant,' declared Peter abruptly, picking up his drink and setting it down again. 'She's pregnant,' he repeated, looking properly at Charlie who was opening and closing his mouth like a fish. 'It wasn't planned but we're pleased,' he added, because Charlie still hadn't spoken and he thought he might as well answer the obvious questions before they were asked. It took Peter a few moments to realise that his brother's fish-mouth muteness stemmed not from any lack of enthusiasm but because the news had moved him deeply. 'Hey, mate, steady on. Christ, of course.' He groaned, thinking of Tina. 'I should have known . . .'

'I'm not upset, you great berk,' gasped Charlie, slinging an arm across the table and seizing Peter by the shoulder. 'I'm just delighted, bloody delighted – for you and Helen, for the family, for everyone. It's what we all need, a baby in the family. I said as much to Cassie a couple of months ago when I thought for one misguided minute she was keeping a Mr Right up her sleeve. It never occurred to me . . . I mean, I thought you and Helen were past that stage.'

'We were,' admitted Peter ruefully, 'but . . . er . . . fate stepped in and we changed our minds.'

'And I for one couldn't be happier.' Charlie sighed contentedly, wiping his eyes with the backs of his hands. 'You sneaky old things,' he added, with a chuckle. 'How many weeks is she?'

Peter pretended to work on a calculation that he knew perfectly well. Charlie and Serena, he remembered, had been disarmingly frank about their drunken, haphazard conception of Tina, nearly

three years before. 'It's over four months now,' he said at length,
unwilling – unable – to be so candid himself, but noting as he
recalled the magical night of his fiftieth the irrelevant but interesting
fact that both his and his brother's accidental conceptions had
occurred under the slate roofs of the family home. 'Helen wanted to
wait until we were absolutely sure everything was all right . . . the
results of the amnio and so on. She's had quite a time of it – got these
terrible headaches at first – but she's fine now, apart from being
tired, of course.'

'And will she go straight back to work this time, do you think?'

'Oh, no, she'll take a decent bit of leave. And when she does go
back she's determined to ease up a bit, maybe even cut down to a
four-day week – get the balance right, which she didn't really
manage before.' Peter paused, steeling himself for his next bit of
news, feeling suddenly unequal to the task of delivering it. 'Do you
know? I think I will have a drink, after all. Don't tell Helen, will
you?'

Charlie laughed. 'Wouldn't dream of it.' He leant back in his
chair and watched happily as his brother fought his way through the
drunken rabble at the bar.

Peter ordered a double whisky for himself and another pint for
Charlie. He took a sip the moment the bartender set down the glass,
closing his eyes to summon the certainty resident somewhere in his
heart. He knew that what he was about to say, once uttered, could
never be unsaid. Ever since the tumultuous weekend in Sussex he
had thought of little else. Apart from the baby, of course, he thought
about the baby all the time. It was a girl, they had discovered. They
even had a name: Genevieve. According to a little book of Helen's
it meant *womankind*, which for some reason had pleased Helen
enormously, although Peter couldn't have cared less. He just liked
the name, its Frenchness, its three soft syllables. Out late the night
before, he had said it aloud several times, feeling a glorious
excitement at the prospect of becoming a father again, an excitement purely to do with getting to know a new child, rather than the
more egotistical pride that had characterised his anticipation of
their first two. In no hurry to find a taxi, he had cut down to the

Embankment, then strolled to the middle of Albert Bridge, which glittered like a giant cats' cradle across the dark waters of the Thames. Leaning his elbows on the cold metal of the balustrade, he had let his thoughts drift from the prospect of a second daughter to the new map of the future that had been triggered by her conception, a future crafted by the living needs of his own family rather than designs preconceived by his parents. I am ready, he had told himself, tipping his head so that the wind blowing off the water below buffeted the expanding hairless circle in the middle of his crown. It is right and I am ready to do it. For Helen. For me. For our family. His eyes streamed and his ears were pink with cold, but he had felt more alive, more hopeful, than he had in years.

Which wasn't to say that his decision didn't also fill him with fear. As he was walking back from the bar he tripped on a ridge in the carpet, almost losing his balance. Beer slopped over his hand, splashing the starched cuffs of his shirt.

'Hey, are you all right?' Charlie got up and seized both drinks, fresh concern clouding his heart. Something wasn't right. He could feel it. Peter was all over the place, stumbling like an old man. 'If you're going down with flu maybe you should . . .'

'It's Ashley House,' blurted Peter, his voice choking at the enormity of what he was about to do. 'I don't want it. Ever. I want you to have it, you and Serena. It's right for you. It's never been right for me and Helen. Helen's never really wanted to live there and lately I've begun to recognise that I would probably be happier staying in London and, with another child on the way, it makes even more sense. We love where we are and neither of us wants to give up work and—' He stopped, arrested by the sight of Charlie looking not so much pleased as aghast.

'Just stop there, will you?' Charlie raised both palms, as if to ward off any more unwelcome sentiments. 'You don't know what you're saying.'

'Oh, believe me, Charlie, I do. These thoughts . . . they've been building inside me for weeks, months. I know it's right.' Peter thumped his chest. 'Here, I know it's right in here. Ashley House was *made* for you and Serena. You're the right ones to take it on – and besides . . .'

'Yes?' Charlie whispered, looking between his legs at the ground, which seemed to be heaving.

'Our lives are about our families, right?' He swigged his whisky, watching Charlie, who nodded, too stunned now to speak. 'And what I've realised is that at some point one exchanges the priorities of one's first, *original* family for one's second. By that I mean the needs of Helen, Theo, Chloë and, God willing, our new little one have to take precedence. If I was an only child or something it would be different, but there's you – and Serena – so perfectly suited to running the place. It's been staring me in the face for years only I didn't – I couldn't see it.'

'Look, Peter, I appreciate what you're trying to do, okay? But—'

'There's no *but*.' Peter drained his glass, set it down carefully and smiled at his brother. A warm, open, certain smile. 'Uncle Eric did it. For reasons that, I suspect, were not too dissimilar. Whatever really went on between him and Mum, he was always the loner while Dad was the family man. I think he felt, like me, the *rightness* of Dad being the one to inherit,' he mused, liking the parallels the more he thought about them.

'Or he was trying to get away from his affair,' muttered Charlie, darkly.

Peter shrugged, undeterred. 'I guess we'll never know. What I *do* know is that I want to carry on working and living in London for as much of the future as I can contemplate, and that Ashley House should be yours. Yours and Serena's . . . I expect you'll have another child anyway one day,' he muttered, avoiding his brother's eye.

Charlie ignored the remark, even though the thought of Serena and the children and a new baby one day running round the airy rooms of the family home thrilled him beyond measure. He tried a new tack. 'And Dad? What has he got to say to all this?'

'Ah. Yes. Dad. I've yet to tackle him.' Peter frowned. Telling his father was the aspect of his decision he dreaded most. It was impossible to know how he would take it. He had such set ideas about things. Although sometimes, when Peter imagined the conversation and all the echoes of what had taken place fifty years before, he couldn't foresee any difficulties. He had already prepared his arguments, the most important being that this new plan would do nothing to jeopardise the key priority of keeping Ashley House in the bosom of the Harrison family. 'But I have every intention of doing so soon.' He made a face, wanting Charlie to know that it was a matter about which he felt some trepidation in spite of his firm words. 'I thought I'd wait until we're all down there next month for the usual Guy Fawkes bonanza. You can bet Sid's already working on his bonfire – the highlight of his year.' Both brothers laughed, conjuring images of Sid's towering creations over the years, some of them the size of small houses.

'What if I don't agree?' asked Charlie quietly, a few minutes later, as they were pulling on their coats. 'Or Serena? What if . . .'

Peter fixed his grey eyes on his brother. 'Is that really likely?'

Charlie thrust his hands into his trouser pockets, feeling for the comforting solidity of his loose change and the ridge of fresh stitches where Serena had recently darned a hole. 'Probably not,' he admitted, 'but I must talk to her, of course.'

'Of course.' They were in the street now, threading their way back towards Green Park tube. 'She is marvellous, your wife,' Peter added, 'how she helps Mum these days – no fuss – whereas Lizzy and Cass, and Helen, frankly, are quite hopeless, and after all that you two have been through . . .' Peter swallowed a lump that was swelling at the base of his throat. His emotions were so near the surface, these days, as if Genevieve, unborn and unknown, already had him by the heart. Just the thought of her made the death of his niece, months ago though it now was, seem freshly – vividly – insupportable. 'I wanted to say, by the way,' he continued gruffly, 'when Tina died, we should have come back from Switzerland.'

'But you did come back,' said Charlie, surprised.

'No. I mean we should have come back at once. To be there. To go through it with you. We should have. I see that now.'

'That's a kind thing to say, Peter. Thank you.'

The two brothers walked on in silence, until Peter, responding to a tug of elder-brother responsibility to conclude with a pragmatic overview of the situation, pointed out that his proposed realignment of their inheritance prospects was almost certainly premature. 'Dad could go on for years yet and even when he's gone I can't quite see Mum leaping at the chance to exchange Ashley House for an old people's home.'

'Maybe Serena and I could move in with her,' blurted Charlie, then slapped his hand to his mouth, embarrassed at this evidence of how his thoughts were racing. Such a seismic shift to his horizons and already he was accommodating it, envisaging how to make it work. 'Early days, though, as you say.' He smiled sheepishly.

Two taxis hove into view. The brothers clasped hands and exchanged hasty valedictory pleasantries, then got into them, each a little unnerved but also excited at how their worlds were changing.

The next day the sun shone again. Having sprung out of bed with uncharacteristic alacrity, Cassie found herself singing in the shower – love songs, one after the other, really badly. The reedy notes ricocheted unconvincingly off the steamy tiled walls of her small bathroom, but inside she felt like some exotic diva, velvet-voiced and beautiful. Afterwards, still humming, she towel-dried her hair with extra vigour, knowing that that way the curls would be just a little tighter and more alluring. Examining her face in the mirror, she pouted, as if to blow herself a kiss, and brushed her lids with the bluest of her eyeshadows. Her eyes glittered, sapphire jewels, shining as she had never thought to see them shine again.

A little later she was bouncing over sleeping policemen, shooting amber lights and rattling through phone-calls, her mobile pressed between her shoulder and her ear so as to leave both hands free for the steering-wheel. She had two appointments, one with a batty widow in Hans Crescent and another with a newly-wed Sloane Ranger in Markham Square. After that she had to call in at Osborne and Little and the Designers Guild to order various materials and stock up on new swatches. Then . . . then . . . As the moment of her reunion with Dan approached Cassie felt less and less able to contemplate it. The anticipation, the joy were simply too huge. Dan. After all these months. Her darling, darling Dan.

The morning dragged. The widow wanted to chat, mainly about her ailments – a mysterious pain in her knees, the palpitations of her heart. Did Cassie believe in acupuncture? she wanted to know. Oh, yes, Cassie said, her own heart racing, prepared to believe in anything that would ease her passage through the morning. Acupuncture – marvellous. And reiki and reflexology. Yes, and mustard would look lovely in the sitting room. The Sloane Ranger was easier, focusing solely on the question of décor and more than willing to let Cassie make choices for her.

By the time Cassie got to the shops she was running late. Both places were unusually busy. As she looked round the displays of shimmering printed silks and cottons, the rich brocades and velvets, she felt too overwhelmed by her own brimming emotions to make any sensible choices. After picking samples at random, then joining the tail end of the long queue for service, it all seemed so pointless – so trivial – that she abandoned her basket and fled into the street.

Arriving at the restaurant a little early, she hurried into the ladies' to run a comb through her tangled curls and check her face for imperfections. By the time she emerged Dan, as if conjured out of some magical puff of smoke, was seated at their favourite table in the corner by the window. He looked so *solid*, so exactly as she remembered him – the long, slim nose, the frown-lines along his forehead, the kink of hair on his crown – that it felt suddenly as if moments, not months had passed since they had seen each other. He had a menu open in front of him, but was staring, clearly lost in thought, at the single pink carnation occupying the vase in the middle of the table. Breaking all the old rules of caution and discretion, Cassie called his name, heedless of the swivelling heads of other diners. He looked up at once, then got to his feet, as if in preparation to bound towards her, before he remembered himself and clenched his hands instead. Cassie stumbled to the table, feeling as if they were the only two people in the room, the only two on the planet. Nobody and nothing else mattered. She dropped her bags and flung her arms round him, burying her face in his neck. For a few instants he squeezed her with equal fervour, then gently prised her arms off and cast anxious glances over her shoulder.

'You look wonderful.'

'So do you.' She sat down opposite him, her heart bursting with joy at the sight of the loving tenderness in his eyes.

'I've been so wretched without you.'

'Me too,' she whispered. 'When Sally phoned I . . . it was so awful . . . hideous . . .' She was overcome at the recollection of what still ranked as the worst moment of her life. 'I thought I was going to die,' she whispered, as the memory of her desolation swept through her, almost real again.

Dan took both her hands in his. 'Cassie, my love, I am so sorry. So sorry. To this day I don't know how Sally found out. She said someone had told her, but who? Who would do a thing like that?'

Cassie went still. She had assumed Sally would show him her letter. Her daft, rash, hateful letter. 'Who indeed?' she echoed.

'She knew your name, how long we had been seeing each other . . . everything. And when she confronted me I just broke down. It's hard to lie to someone you've known for twenty years.' He shook his head, and added, despairingly, 'Especially if that someone is ill.'

'Ill?' Cassie pulled her hands free in surprise, forgetting the awkward secret of her letter.

'I *should* have told you, I know I should, but the fact is Sally was – is – very ill. She has cancer.'

'What sort of cancer?'

'Cervical. She only told me in March – that night we were in the same restaurant as you, she told me then.'

'Oh, my goodness,' murmured Cassie, a reflex of genuine compassion clashing head-on with rather less edifying thoughts. Her lover's wife was going to die! God had intervened, because they were *meant* to be together. They would have to wait for a decent interval, of course, but then, without the ugly stigmas or traumas of divorce, they would be together properly.

Dan was still talking, absorbed once again by the horror of his own predicament. 'It just made it so impossible. I mean, I couldn't just walk out on her.'

'Of course you couldn't.' Cassie reached again for his hand, affection swelling as she realised she couldn't possibly have loved someone who *would* have been prepared to leave his sick wife. 'And now?' she whispered. A waiter, pad and pencil poised, hovered at the table and disappeared again.

Dan looked at their hands, still clasped together next to the carnation in the middle of the table. 'She's had a hysterectomy and her lymph glands were removed as an added precaution. She's started a course of chemotherapy. After that they'll do radio-therapy. So . . .' There was apology in his voice and eyes. 'I've got to see her through, Cass, for a bit longer anyway. The main thing is they got it early and she's going to be fine.'

'That is the main thing, of course,' murmured Cassie dutifully, pressing away the other treacherous thoughts.

'But I have been so miserable without you, my darling. It's been like living a half-life, you've no idea.'

'Yes, yes, I have.' She smiled sadly. 'I have every idea.'

'I love you,' he said simply, recalling and dismissing the image of the tall, scruffy young man who had called at his surgery. 'I got back in touch because that love won't go away.'

'And I love you, Dan.' Cassie leant forward, expecting, hoping for a kiss. Instead Dan steered his mouth to her ear and suggested, in a breathy voice, that they forget lunch altogether and take a taxi back to her flat.

Cassie hesitated, but only for a moment. The thought of once more being touched by him, after so many months of deprivation, was irresistible. As soon as they were in the safe privacy of the taxi he let down his guard, covering her face and neck with kisses, stroking her arms and the small of her back where her shirt rode up over the waistband of her skirt. Cassie relaxed, sighing at the familiar pleasure of his caresses. Somewhere inside she knew that they should have stayed in the restaurant and talked more. So much had happened that he didn't know about, that she wanted – yearned – to share. He needed updating on her thoughts too, her increasing awareness that at thirty-eight time was starting to run out, if their precariously planned life together was to include a child. In that regard, fleeing to her flat for sex would solve absolutely nothing. But the smell of Dan's warm skin flooded her senses, stirring a hunger that was too strong for common sense. There would be time for talking, she told herself, on the phone, or when they next met. In the meantime she was happy just to be in his arms, to feel the simple reassurance of his physical desire.

That afternoon Stephen took a break from his writing for a stroll in Victoria Park. A jogger had been killed there the previous week, jumped by an as yet unidentified assailant, who had raped her and then strangled her to death with his bare hands. Seeing the paths and grass bathed in autumn sunshine, filled by parents with push-chairs and people flying kites or kicking balls, it was hard to believe the place could have played host to such depravity. What madness of lust or hatred could prompt such behaviour? Stephen wondered, shivering as he walked past the orange tape and signs appealing for witnesses. The only extreme emotion he knew about, he reflected wryly, was love. The madness of love. For, looking back over the weeks of sleepless nights, the delusional conviction that the ex-tremity of his ardour would be enough to ignite reciprocal feelings in Cassie, the clutching at straws as if they were weighty indicators – a game of Scrabble, a smile, a throwaway remark – Stephen recognised now that he had been suffering from a genuine form of insanity. Rudderless, pitching on storms of insecurity and ancient unresolved unhappiness, he had truly believed that Cassie Harrison offered the only direction his life could take. His north, his south, his east, his west, as Auden had so beautifully put it.

He had been reading a lot of poetry since his visit to Cassie's doctor friend. And writing it again – rather more objectively now and on all sorts of subjects. It helped, Stephen found, not only to vent his emotions but to create a sense of order in what he now accepted as an intriguing but disordered world. To the same end he had also started work on a thriller featuring an Irish detective called Jack Connolly, who drank too much but had a nose for a criminal.

Begun purely as an intellectual exercise, Stephen had been pleased enough with the results to share three chapters with his agent. So enthusiastic had been the response that, these days, Stephen was setting his alarm clock and writing eight hundred words before he allowed himself lunch. Structured thus, time had begun to motor instead of crawl, revealing the life-saving truth that survival as well as art could be managed effectively with the application of a little routine, with the gripping of the small realities of existence rather than grasping after its impossibilities. Greatly steadied by the process, Stephen had even ventured back up north to visit his parents, this time without the burden of expectation – or apprehension. He had stayed for lunch, an overcooked roast with soggy vegetables, and talked about football results and the weather. His parents, he saw now, were old people with shrivelled horizons and selective memories. They didn't know that their idea of parenting had fucked him up and they didn't want to know. So what? He'd returned to London feeling separate from them. Safe and separate. That night he'd eaten out in the Indian round the corner and asked one of the waitresses if she'd like to meet up on her night off. They had gone to the cinema and held hands in the dark, and Stephen had thought, I can do this, I can be normal and happy and sane. When Cassie entered his mind he made himself remember the doctor's chiselled face and wished her well in her own separate pursuit of love. Truly caring for someone meant wanting their happiness more than one's own. He knew that now and it had brought a sort of calm.

He spotted a little pink teddy bear lying on the grassy verge of the path, dropped or hurled by a toddler, and stooped to pick it up. He brushed off flecks of dirt and dried leaves, then propped it up, tenderly, on the back of a bench, in conspicuous view of the path. A few yards on he turned to check that it was still there, hoping with a rush of sentimentality that its young owner would reclaim it. The thought of the little bear never finding its way home, could have – if he had let it – made him weep. His feelings did rush at him, these days, from unexpected angles and with inappropriate vehemence. He stood still for a few moments, waiting for this new surge of emotion to pass, much as one might wait for a shower of rain to fall before venturing outside. He could use the bear in a poem, he decided, starting to walk on. Something poignant. A tacky pink bear, loved beyond reason. He turned on his heel and strode back in the direction he had come, not looking at the toy any more – not needing it. The lines were already forming in his mind, begging for release on to the crisp whiteness of a fresh page in his notebook.

St Peter's School

Dear Mum and Dad,

I hope you are well. I am fine apart from having rather a lot of work. Sometimes I wish I hadn't been put forward to do French and maths GCSE early, though I suppose it gets them out of the way. Also I am not enjoying rugby very much. I have bought some shoulder pads and put them on the school bill – hope that's OK.

It is the house drama competition this term and we are doing a one-act play called The Gunners, set in the Second World War. I think it will be quite good although the sixth-former directing it – George Rogers – is USELESS. I am helping behind the scenes which is OK so long as they don't ask me to do too much painting etc. As you know, I'm not much good with a paintbrush. I was wondering if there was anything of Uncle Eric's we could use for props. Do you think Granny and Granddad would mind?

That's about all my news for now. I am looking forward to half-term already. Tell Granddad to do double the amount of fireworks this year!

Love from Theo

PS Tell Chloë – because she might be interested – that a boy in the year above me got bitten by a dog in the summer while he was on holiday in Kenya and they thought he might have RABIES. He had to have some huge injections but is OK now.

PPS Also tell Chloë NOT to go in my room while I am away. PLEASE.

Theo put the cap on to his fountain pen, then took it off again, wondering whether to add another PS expressing specific concern for his mother's health. Both he and Chloë had been told not to advertise the business of the baby yet – because of things still being able to go wrong. His sister had squeaked in dismay, while Theo, secretly, had felt a certain relief. It was, of course, exciting that they were to acquire another sibling. All the encouragement he had given his mother after his fall from the tree at the end of the summer had come from the heart. But the prospect of sharing the news with his schoolmates was quite another matter, since it meant – inadvertently – addressing the notion of his parents having sex. Of course, every member of year ten knew he had not arrived in the world by a process of immaculate conception and yet . . . and yet . . . Theo sucked his pen-top, trying and failing to equate the stirrings triggered, these days, by the mere thought (let alone any glimpse) of a nude woman with any comparable impulses shared by his parents. It was impossible. Gross, in fact. In the end he did add another postscript, but only to say, 'Write soon!' Clem hadn't written for a while and any letter – even one from his parents – was better than none at all.

Helen, reading her son's letter over a leisurely breakfast the following Saturday, laughed out loud then handed it across to Peter. They were eating in the conservatory although it was a little late in the year to be doing so. Her legs, protected only by the folds of her dressing-gown, were goosebumped with cold. It would take a long bath to warm her up properly, steaming with scented oils and foam. At the thought Helen let out a little sigh of pleasure. She wasn't ready to retreat upstairs just yet, though: it was too nice just sitting there, watching Peter's face as he read the letter and the dust motes dancing in the sunbeams next to him. Through the door into the kitchen she could see the now familiar plump figure of Griselda, their nanny, in pursuit of a new diet, carefully peeling fruit and chopping it into a bowl of yoghurt, her tongue curling round her lower lip in concentration. She still ironed badly and smoked the occasional cigarette in her bedroom, but there was a pleasing quietness about her – an instinct for withdrawing at appropriate times – that made her presence in the house very easy. She was also fabulous at the piano, which had done wonders for Chloë's recalcitrance towards her own music practice.

'A good letter, isn't it?'

'Very good.' Peter tucked the single page back into its somewhat crumpled envelope and smiled at his wife. 'You look cold.'

'I am. I shall have a bath in a minute.'

'I've got to do some work today, I'm afraid.'

'Poor you. I'm taking Chloë into Richmond. She needs some new ballet shoes. Kay's coming too,' Helen added, quickly enough to betray the habitual reflex of wariness about her friend. 'If you're working we might grab lunch there, a pizza or something.'

'Sounds good.' Peter folded the newspaper, which he had opened next to his plate, and prepared to retreat to his study.

'Peter?'

'Yes?' He paused in the doorway, the paper under his arm.

'About – about what you said to Charlie.' Helen shifted position, tucking her dressing-gown more tightly round her freezing thighs. She was slowly getting bigger now: she could feel it everywhere, as if her whole body was swelling protectively round her child. 'The Ashley House thing . . . You can always change your mind.'

'No.' He looked at her gratefully, but also a little sadly. 'No, I can't. And I don't want to. It was *waiting* to be done and I've done it.'

'Not just for me, though?' she whispered, glimpsing the strain of his decision and knowing that she would prefer the burden of her own unhappiness to being responsible for his.

Peter sighed. He had no regrets, not deep down, but a part of him was still in the process of letting go and it wasn't easy. 'Not just for you, no. For me, too. For all of us. I'm going to talk to Dad about it at half-term. It will all be fine, you'll see.' He walked back to the table and tapped her fondly on the head with his newspaper. 'Now get into that bath. You're blue.'

As Helen got to her feet Chloë skipped into the room dressed only in a tutu. 'Look, Mum, a handstand.' She performed a little leapfrog on to her arms, waggled her legs in the air for perhaps half a second, then collapsed amid dramatic panting on to the floor.

'Hm. Very good, but I shouldn't practise in here, the floor's too hard. You'll hurt yourself.'

'No, it's not,' shouted Chloë, lurching back on to her hands for a second attempt.

'Yes, it is, and you need to get dressed.'

'I *am* dressed.' Chloë, puce from her exertions and feeling they hadn't received quite the praise they deserved, sat upright and folded her arms.

'You're not going out in that.'

'Why not?'

'You'll be too cold.'

'Shan't.'

'Oh, Chloë, don't start.' Helen had stacked the breakfast plates and stepped round her daughter *en route* to the dishwasher. 'If you want new ballet shoes, you dress sensibly. It's as simple as that.'

She busied herself in the kitchen, thinking all the while that it wasn't as simple as that at all because Chloë catching pneumonia in a tutu was a more attractive prospect than Chloë sulking all afternoon from the torture of being forced to wear sensible clothes. On first being told about the imminence of a new sibling her daughter had been as excited as Helen could remember seeing her. 'If we're going to have a baby I don't want a dog,' she had shrieked, much to the amusement of the rest of them. For a few days her behaviour had been so transformed that Helen had begun to believe it might be permanent. She wanted to pat Helen's stomach, to press her ear to it, to be told time and time again that she would be required to help with everything, from bathing and feeding to nappy-changing and pushing the pram in the park. 'It won't last,' Kay had warned, and she was right. Impatient with her playmates' lack of sustained interest in the subject (Chloë had announced the pregnancy to the class in spite of being told not to) and the *slowness* of the process (five months felt to her at eight like an eternity) Chloë had gradually slipped back into her old ways – sunshine one minute, storms the next. Above all, she must hold firm, Helen warned herself now, going back into the conservatory where Chloë was lying on her stomach sobbing pitifully, her tutu springing like flower petals from her hips. 'Chloë . . .'

'I – won't – be – cold. I won't, I won't, I won't.'

'Okay, but you're wearing a coat,' Helen snapped. She stepped back over her daughter and out into the hall. Trudging upstairs to run her bath, the small new weight of her baby pressing inside, all the old doubts about her capacity to *enjoy* being a mother crowded back in on her. Instead of savouring her bath, she splashed in and out of it, desperate to get out of the house and spill her woes to Kay, who, though they saw each other less often these days, remained a beacon of compassion and reassurance.

'I was mad to keep this baby, mad to let Peter give up on Ashley House, mad to think to anything would ever *change*,' she wailed, as they strolled along the river after their pizza lunch.

Kay, who had recently discovered that something less desirable than a foetus was growing in her own womb, put a motherly arm round Helen's shoulders. 'Everything has already changed. You feel like this now, but you won't later on – by this evening, probably. The truth of one's emotions moves around. You're doing the right thing, every instinct in your body tells you so. Which doesn't mean it's not difficult. Like Peter with this house business – it *feels* right, which isn't to say it's not the most enormous sacrifice. In fact, just for the record, I think your husband is being bloody marvellous.'

'He is, isn't he?' Helen smiled, then broke off to exclaim at the antics of her daughter, who had abandoned her anorak and was performing pirouettes along the riverbank. 'Look at her, she's impossible – and right on the edge near those swans. They'll attack, won't they? Don't swans attack?'

Kay laughed. 'Only if they feel threatened and they look quite happy to me. As does Chloë. I'm sorry I didn't bring Toffee to entertain her but, as you know, he's not at his best in shops and restaurants.' She paused, then added, 'Chloë, believe me, will always be fine. Difficult, but fine. You can only do your best, you know, Helen, you should be satisfied with that.'

'Thanks, Kay. As ever, I don't know where I'd be without you.'

'You'd be precisely where you are now,' said Kay firmly, leading the way to a bench and sitting down. She had recently had a haircut, reducing the strands of scarlet to dramatic fiery tips. She wrapped a strand absently round one finger. Helen would, of course, want to know that she was ill. But the fact remained that Kay didn't want to tell her. It had been hard enough telling her own children. Besides, there was no need. She was going away anyway. She let a few moments pass before saying as much out loud.

'Going away? Where for heaven's sake?'

'France. My ex has died and – somewhat astonishingly – left me a house. It's in the south, just outside Montpellier. One of my daughters has settled not far away in Cap d'Agde. I, too, need a change, Helen,' she added quietly. 'Time to move on.' She folded her hands in her lap, while her gaze shifted to the swans who were gliding downstream. 'I can afford to retire now,' she added, by way of further explanation, omitting the other immense consideration, which was a desire to go through the indignities of her illness, which was terminal, in private.

'Oh, Kay, I'm pleased for you, of course, if it's what you want but . . .' Helen's gaze followed her friend's, tracking the elegant bobbing of the birds, moving effortlessly towards the bend in the river. 'I shall bloody well miss you, though. I mean, this year you've seen me through so much, I can't imagine how . . .'

'You, too, will be fine,' said Kay quietly, patting her hand and then, somewhat abruptly, getting up from the bench.

'Well, can we come and stay?' Helen asked, almost indignant.

'Of course you may.' Kay glanced at her, a shadow of wistfulness passing across her round, cheery face. 'But I don't think you will.'

'We'll see about that, shall we?' retorted Helen, going to pick up Chloë's coat and shouting to her daughter that they were going home.

During the journey back to Barnes they spoke little, Kay because there was nothing more she wanted to say and Helen because she was torn between upset and a sort of outrage. Friendships didn't just end because of geography, did they? But there was something so very final about the way Kay had handled the delivery of her news, as if she was withdrawing already, as if she had decided that their brief but curiously intense acquaintance was at the beginning of its end. She remembered in the same instant what Kay had said early on, about people appearing as they were needed, about patterns and synchronicity. Maybe they would visit her in France. But Kay was right: it would be hard, with a newborn and work and Peter almost certainly – understandably – not wanting to go.

'When are you off, then?' she asked, as casually as she could, as they were getting out of the car.

'Next week.'

'Next week? God, that's so soon.'

'I've rented the house to a young family – a barrister, actually, though she doesn't work. They seem very nice. Better still, their rent will provide me with an income.'

'Great.' Helen felt desperately awkward, as if she was trying to hold on to something that hadn't really existed. 'Well, anyway, we'll see you, obviously, before you go.'

'Oh, yes. I'll pop in and say a proper goodbye,' Kay assured her, then turned and hurried across the street, her flame-tipped hair bouncing on her shoulders.

As the house came in sight Elizabeth slowed her pace. It was odd to come to Guildford by train, to arrive on foot in her own street instead of by car, as if she were a mere visitor. Which she was now, she reminded herself, pausing to absorb that the drive was empty and the house therefore unoccupied. She had her keys, but would it be right to use them? Maybe it would get things off on the wrong foot if Colin returned to find her scouring bookshelves and CD collections. They were supposed to be meeting to talk through various difficulties the lawyers were having, but she had brought an empty suitcase to collect a few things. A larger scale division of possessions was something to be organised for the future, they had agreed, with, in Elizabeth's case, a self-hire van and the strong arms of a friend, or possibly one of her brothers.

She walked up to the front gate and stopped, staring ahead at the white stucco walls, the black beams and window frames, trying to summon some recollection of how she had felt arriving at this same spot with Colin and the estate agent who had shown them round. Roland, she remembered, had been in a carrier on her back, squirming and snuffling with a bad cold. She had been more concerned with quietening him than appraising the merits of the house. Colin had taken charge, exclaiming in satisfaction at the spacious built-in units, the luxury of four bedrooms, the size of the garage. Out in the garden she had set Roland on the grass where he had crawled happily for a few minutes, offering her a much-needed breather from the relentless business of motherly consolation. To one side of the scrubby lawn there was a single small tree, a John Downey apple, as Pamela had subsequently informed them on the first of her infrequent visits. Roland had made his way towards it, then levered himself upright, lunging happily at the clusters of white blossom and looking for a few minutes so idyllically content that Elizabeth had decided, irrationally, that the house was meant for them. Anything that could make her distressed, whingeing child happy could make her happy too. Then Roland had tried to stuff the blossom into his little scarlet mouth and she had had to prise him away, shattering the moment but not her conviction in its significance.

Elizabeth checked her watch, then tried the key. There was still five minutes to go until the time they had agreed. Next door she saw the curtain twitch and her neighbour's head bob out of sight. She shuddered, thinking with longing of the barn where there was nothing to watch over her but the homely rooftops of Ashley House and the jigsaw of green and brown countryside sloping towards the Downs, as soft and velvet in the October sunshine as new carpet.

Once inside the hall the sheer familiarity of her surroundings – the carriage clock on the table, the scuffmarks on the skirting-board by the stairs, the brown stain on the floor by the sitting-room door – was somehow shocking. This is my home, she thought, I didn't have to leave it. It took a few minutes for this idea to dissolve, minutes in which Elizabeth silently toured each room, absorbing the fact that in spite of the myriad traces of her former occupancy, the house had, during the course of her absence, become an alien place. Nothing had been moved or rearranged – the picture of the poppy field, the fridge magnets, the position of the kettle, the limescale stain under the dripping tap – all was just as she had left it. And yet everything was different. Different and empty. Because, mused Elizabeth, picking up an ornamental jug and putting it down again, she no longer felt any emotional connection to the place. The signposts of her old life were all still there, but they had lost their power over her and therefore their meaning. But there was something else too, Elizabeth noticed, something that had contributed to her instant and overpowering sense of estrangement. The *smell*. The entire place *smelt* different. Alien. Just like other people's houses sometimes did when one opened the door to be greeted by that unfathomable olfactory cocktail of general living, evident to all but its perpetrators. Elizabeth was so struck by the observation that she began to explore each room with new purpose, sniffing the air like a dog. Upstairs, maybe because of its hotel orderliness, the scent seemed, if anything, stronger, especially in the main bedroom and bathroom. She was standing in the doorway to the *en suite*, staring at the plump creaseless duvet covering the bed and the gleaming basin taps, still pondering the matter, when she heard the slam of the front door.

'I'm up here,' she called at once, feeling like a burglar.

'Are you? I see.' She could hear the indignation in his voice and in the thump of his footsteps on the stairs.

'Sorry, I was early.' She started towards him as he appeared in the bedroom doorway and then stopped, at a loss as to how they should greet each other. Colin, too, looked lost. And somewhat anxious, she realised, studying his expression as his eyes glanced from her face to the room and back again. Almost as if he thought she might have taken something, stolen a march on the grim business of dividing their possessions. 'I haven't—'

'Downstairs. Last night I made a start with some boxes – I'll show you now.' He turned to go and Elizabeth was on the point of following when it dawned on her – some sixth sense, connected, she thought, looking back on the moment later, to all the feelings that had assailed her since entering the house – that he wanted to get her out of the room. That he didn't *like* her being in the bedroom.

'You're still seeing her, aren't you?' she said quietly, not moving. 'You've been seeing her all along, haven't you?'

'I don't know what you're talking about. Now, do you want to look at this stuff or not?'

'It doesn't matter, it really doesn't. It makes no difference. I would just like to know.'

Colin leant against the doorway, folding his arms and sighing in an exaggerated show of weariness, as if being forced to deal with something tiresome and trivial. 'Seeing who exactly?'

'Oh, Colin,' Elizabeth whispered, giddy with the power of not caring – of being beyond his capacity to hurt her. 'The truth matters. Though you may choose not to tell it to me, it *matters* and I know it anyway.'

He rolled his eyes. 'Are you going to talk nonsense all morning?' Nonchalant and sneering as he intended the remark to be, there was a tremor in his voice as he said it. A tremor that Elizabeth heard and Colin knew she had heard. Unacknowledged, the veracity of Elizabeth's accusation therefore reverberated round the room like the clang of a bell. So deafeningly that Elizabeth felt no need to pursue the matter, settling instead for the implicit power it gave her as they embarked on the labour of negotiation. By the end of the morning he had agreed to everything their lawyers had been arguing about, including raising her monthly allowance from three hundred pounds to four and putting the house on the market before Christmas instead of waiting until the spring.

Having settled herself on the train for the journey home Elizabeth called Ashley House to check that Roland was all right, then retrieved the little screwed-up photograph of her and Lucien from the bottom of her handbag. She spread out the creases with the tips of her fingers, and studied the numbers written on the back. The temptation to call remained strong, but she distrusted it. It was too easy, too pat, to remember the good things and filter out the bad. Nothing could have altered what had happened. They had married for love and then, through their own weaknesses and insecurities, lost touch with it. To imagine one could do anything to rewrite such a script was both foolhardy and delusional. Elizabeth screwed the photo into a little ball, dropped it into the bin behind her seat and put it from her mind. She was what her history had made her. She understood that now, accepted it. Much as her mistakes had damaged her, they had also made her stronger, and she needed no cavorting with the past to prove it.

John was sitting on a log in the orchard, when he heard the crunch of the wheels in the drive. A few minutes later the mingled greetings of Roland's piping treble and the mellower voices of his wife and daughter drifted towards him through the trees, compounding the ache in his heart. They sounded happy. The encounter with Colin must have gone well. Or maybe it was the simple pleasure of family reunion that lent the birdsong merriment to their voices. John slapped the heavy tree-trunk on which he was sitting. It had fallen during the night of the storm, much as his fortunes had fallen during the same few hours. He pressed both palms against the gnarled ridges of bark on either side of him, while the palpitations – never far away, these days – galloped back and forth across his chest. The picture wasn't complete yet, but claims were already winging their way across the Atlantic and John feared the worst. So much so that he could not bring himself to share his fears, not with his old colleagues, not with his children, and certainly not with Pamela, whose own spirits seemed recently to have gathered fresh momentum. He could hear her calling for him now, her voice reedy with enthusiastic affection. John dropped his head into his hands, not moving.

'Mr Harrison?'

'Ah, Sid.' The gardener was standing right next to him, his weathered face fixed as always in an expression of polite amiability.

'I've made a start on the bonfire – thought I better as there's only a week to go.'

'A week – heaven! So there is.' John managed a twitchy smile.

'Put it in the lower field as usual. Coming along nicely, though I say it myself. All that stuff from the storm helped no end.'

'Excellent, Sid, excellent.'

'Would you like to see it, Mr Harrison?'

'Not now, Sid, maybe tomorrow.'

His employee paused, pushing the peak of his tweed cap up his forehead, then promptly tugging it down again. 'That tree . . .' He pointed at the trunk John was sitting on. 'I was thinking it was about time I chopped it for firewood – fill the shed for the winter.'

John looked down at the wood under his thighs, experiencing a rush of irrational reluctance at the thought of Sid's axe splintering it. 'I don't . . . Not just yet, Sid . . . I . . . Not yet.'

'Right you are, Mr Harrison. You let me know when you want it done.' The old gardener's expression did not change, though a trace of gentleness had crept into his gravelly voice. 'I'll see you on Monday, then.' He set off at his usual lumbering pace for the house, then turned after a few yards to add, 'I thought I'd make it a real big 'un this year – the grandchildren love it so, don't they?'

John nodded because he couldn't speak. The thought of his grandchildren – of his children – was almost too poignant to bear. They were the future and he had failed them. When he thought of all Peter and Charlie's jointly held reservations about his staying in Lloyds, how they had counselled him over the years to pull out and invest more in the stock market, he felt physically sick. On the basis of current forecasts from his syndicates, the final settlements would leave him with no liquid assets at all. Which meant . . . which meant . . . John closed his eyes, trying to imagine breaking the news that after his death Ashley House would have to be sold; to produce enough funds to cover inheritance tax and to ensure that all four of his children received something.

When he opened his eyes again the sun had edged behind a chimney-stack, casting the orchard in shadow. John shivered, feeling the presence of winter in the air. Normally it was a time of year he savoured: the shortening days and colder weather induced cosy images of roaring log fires and the tiptoeing approach of Christmas. Now, looking ahead, he could see nothing but the darkness and shame of his own failure. Stiffly, groaning, he levered himself up from the log and made his way round the perimeter fences, noting bleakly all the odd jobs that needed his attention. He didn't have the heart for them, these days. It seemed pointless, given that the estate was as good as lost anyway.

When he turned at last for the house, John glimpsed Sid's towering pagoda of branches and wood in the lower field. He stood staring for several minutes, admiring its size and masterly solidity, but feeling no joy at the prospect of his family gathering for the ritual of setting light to it. At the kitchen table a little later, the tenderness with which Pamela set down his cup of tea only made him want to weep. She was gushing with news of Colin's new acquiescence, her eyes pleading with him to share some of their daughter's gladness and relief. John nodded to it all, sipping his tea, aware of the shortfall in his responses but powerless to amend them. He was on the point of sloping off to his study when Roland plunged in through the back door, dragging a huge straw-stuffed guy behind him.

'Look, Granddad. Look what Granny and I made today.' He propped the guy against the table, proudly patting the lopsided head and causing a small explosion of straw and sawdust on to the kitchen floor. 'We used some of your old clothes and a pillowcase for the head. I did the face myself,' he added proudly, standing back to admire the felt-pen features, which included thunderous eyebrows and a forest of a moustache. 'Sid's going to put him right on top so everyone can see him burn.'

'Marvellous,' John murmured, forcing a smile of congratulation, while inside he felt a dreadful ghoulish affinity to the misshapen creature, trussed in his own clothes, ready to face his public execution and shame. 'Marvellous,' he said again, flinching under Pamela's distressed and enquiring gaze and fumbling in his pocket for a couple of commendatory pound coins.

NOVEMBER

The music was so loud that Clem, taking a breather in the room next to the disco, could still feel the floorboards vibrating beneath her feet. She had danced a lot, first with Sally Mason and then on her own, closing her eyes to shut out any curious stares and letting her body do what it wanted with the rhythms. She had almost not come, partly out of a last-minute stubbornness at complying with Jonny's insistence that she should, and partly at the sight of Maisie, preening herself with makeup brushes and hair-rollers hours before it was time to leave. I can't compete, she had thought, then seized on the brainstorming notion that she didn't have to. Maisie could stagger round in high heels if she wanted, her lips glossy and hair twirling out of her artfully criss-crossed sticks and pins, but all Clem wanted, she saw suddenly, was to feel *comfortable*, in terms of how she looked and her general state of mind. Scanning the contents of her own wardrobe, she decided that for her there would be nothing worse – nothing more potentially humiliating – than looking as if she had tried too hard with her appearance. Maisie might be able to pull it off, but Maisie actively sought the spotlight of appreciation whereas Clem, while longing to attend the party, longed in equal measure not to present herself in a manner that was too *visible*. With this intention, ignoring quizzical looks from her twin, she waited until it was almost time to leave before she had a quick shower, dabbed on a little makeup and slipped into her green combats and a black T-shirt.

And she felt fine, Clem decided now, retreating to a corner with an orange juice, wondering how she could ever have concerned herself about being too conspicuous in such a packed environment. Jonny appeared to have invited the entire school, irrespective of whose company he sought in and out of the playground. The party was being held in a small cricket pavilion, comprising three rooms and a porch overlooking the playing-field to which it was attached. The doors to the porch had been wedged open but it was so bitterly cold that few guests were venturing outside. Her thirst quenched and feeling suddenly in need of fresh air, no matter how icy, Clem put down her glass and elbowed her way out through the crowd. The porch was empty and she walked the length of it a couple of times, then sat down on the steps leading to the grass.

'Are you avoiding me or something?'

Jonny was standing on the top step behind her. He, too, was in dark green trousers, much wider and lower on the hip than hers, and a skin-tight white T-shirt that showed off the impressive musculature of his arms and torso. His face wasn't that attractive, though, Clem decided: his eyes were sunken and haunted-looking, and his lips too full, almost like a girl's. She swivelled back to face the grassy darkness ahead of her and shrugged her shoulders. 'Don't be silly.'

'Do you want a dance?'

Clem's heart performed a small involuntary skip. She liked dancing – loved it, in fact. But the thought of strutting her stuff in front of Jonny, with everyone watching, passing remarks behind their hands, was too much. 'No, thanks.' She returned her gaze to the dark playing-field, wondering when he would give up on her and go back inside.

Jonny, who wasn't one to give up on anything until he was ready to, skipped down the pavilion steps and came to stand in front of her. 'Can I show you something, then?'

'What?' Clem narrowed her eyes suspiciously.

'Something great. Come on.' He marched back up the steps and round to a side door, nodding at her to follow, which she did, keeping her arms folded to indicate reluctance. The door led into a small changing room, empty apart from a few stray articles of clothing hanging on pegs, and a stack of cardboard boxes. 'Extra drink,' he explained, pointing at the boxes. He reached behind them and pulled out a guitar. 'What do you think?' He held it out to her, his brown eyes glittering, his bony face and curiously soft mouth crumpling with delight. 'It's my birthday present from Mum and Dad. It cost a fortune. A beauty or what?'

'Yeah, it looks nice.' Clem unfolded her arms to stroke the wood, which was a rich yellowy brown and inlaid with circular patterns of pearly diamond shapes. 'Wow. Really nice.'

'I'm starting up a band . . . been working on some songs.'

'Really?' Clem observed that he had put the guitar down on the bench and was moving towards her. She hurriedly folded her arms again.

'We need a singer. Can you sing?'

Clem, forgetting all her awkwardness, hooted with laughter.

'Someone told me you could sing,' protested Jonny, 'that you had a good voice . . .'

'Oh, blimey,' Clem gasped, still laughing. 'I suppose if you count aural tests for my piano exams . . .' She was consumed once more with giggles at the notion of her, with her shy soprano, being invited to contribute to a rock band.

'Will you at least give it a go?' Jonny persisted, now too busy planning how to engineer the mechanics of a first kiss to share her amusement. He had liked Maisie but she was so *obvious*, but this twin of hers, with her huge wary eyes and angular body, was much more interesting, not just as a challenge, but as someone he wanted to get to know, with kissing, certainly, but other things too. She was supposed to be ill, he knew, wanting to starve herself, but that only made her more intriguing. And she had a bloody good voice, he had heard it himself that very night, dancing near her when she was swaying to the music all on her own, singing along with the tune, her face all closed and trembling. It trembled now as he touched her, holding each hollow cheek steady between his palms as he lowered his lips on to hers. It seemed to take for ever to get there. She flinched but only momentarily, not withdrawing even after he had relaxed his grip on her face. Then she opened her mouth, shyly and not very wide; but enough for him to taste the sweet softness inside and know that he wanted more.

It felt funny to be back in Guildford, holding his father's hand for the walk to the shops; like coming home, but not coming home because he was there without his mother and because Roland had never once walked to the shops with just his father. He had forgotten how big his father's hand was, smooth and warm inside, like a glove. But the steps he took were big too and Roland had to trot to keep up, which made the zip of his anorak jab annoyingly against his chin. It was getting too tight and had blue zigzags across the back, which he hated. When his mother had zipped him into it that morning for the journey, saying it was cold and he was to be a good boy and keep his coat done up whenever he was outside, he had asked if he could have a new one – preferably a huge black one with a big white tick across the back, like Ryan from his class at school. She had rolled her eyes, not saying yes but not saying no either. Which meant there was hope, Roland decided now, tugging at his father's arm with the aim of slowing him down.

Colin glanced at his son. 'All right?' When Roland nodded he strode on as if they had a train to catch, instead of six chicken nuggets and a small portion of fries. Today's treat was McDonald's and then a video. His dad had chosen it before he arrived – *Free Willy 2* – and parked it on top of the TV ready for watching after tea. The next day, if the weather was fine, they were going to Chessington. If not they would go to the cinema. Then it would be Monday and his mum would come to fetch him in her new secondhand Ford Fiesta and they would drive back to his grandparents'.

With his legs aching and the McDonald's sign still nowhere in sight, Roland found himself fixing on the end to his three-day visit with sudden longing. He was pleased to see his father, of course, but not as pleased as he suspected he *should* be. Everything felt so strange with just the two of them and although his dad kept asking how he was and what he was doing, Roland felt reluctant to profess too much contentment, for fear of implying that he hadn't been happy before, when mostly he had. Given the choice, he would prefer his mum and dad to live together. Yet waking in his bed in the alcove in the barn, with school seeming not too bad and his mum humming as she moved around the little kitchen, and games in the Ashley House grounds with Polly to look forward to, Roland was happy too. Just as he was happy now, being with his dad. It was weird. Like belonging in two worlds but only being able to have one at a time, both okay but miles different from the one he had known before. Later, dipping nuggets into his little plastic punnet of ketchup, chatting about Hadrian and the Romans, such confusions slipped easily to the back of his mind.

Colin, however, eyeing his small son over an unpleasantly boiling and watery cup of tea, saw the untroubled chirpiness – that peculiar live-in-the-moment innocence of childhood – and envied it. He knew no such peace. The sight of Elizabeth unloading Roland and a bulging overnight case from her car, chatting breezily about pick-up times and trying new routes to avoid the traffic, had stirred him deeply. Her independence, her sheer I'm-okay separateness, was more galling than he could possibly have imagined. And the tears in Roland's eyes as she drove away – that had been hard too. He knew he loved his son, but he had been unsure suddenly whether Roland truly loved him in return. When they had lived under the same roof as a family, such a question had never seemed at issue; but ushering his son inside the house that morning, trying not to watch as he blinked away his tears, Colin had felt for the first time as if he had to work to win Roland's affection, as if he had to *earn* it instead of believing it – as he had in the past – some sort of God-given right. Hence McDonald's, which he hated. Hence the video, of which he disapproved. Hence Chessington, which in half-term week would be hellishly overcrowded.

'Is there more ketchup?'

'Do you really need more?' Colin cast a gloomy look at the long queues for all the tills at the food counter. 'You have had *two* pots of the stuff already.'

'But I've got my chips left. I need more for my chips.' Roland, having detected the anger in his father's tone and unaware that it was connected to things of greater significance than tomato sauce, felt his lower lip tremble.

'Now don't get upset – it's hardly something to get upset about, is it?' Colin's voice was harsh with panic, not just at this reminder of his son's sensitivity but at the sudden fear that the new part-time relationship on which they were embarking would always be too fragile to allow proper, strict parenting. Roland would cry and he would give in. Out of guilt. Out of fear of not being loved. It was intolerable.

'I want . . . I need . . . Please . . . may . . . I . . . have . . . more ketchup . . . *please*,' Roland repeated the word, the 'magic' word, as his mother liked to call it. Thinking of her made him want to cry even more. With his mother, things like wanting more ketchup were so simple you didn't notice them. They certainly didn't make her angry.

'Okay, okay . . . There, now.' Colin, aware suddenly of enquiring glances from two women at a neighbouring table, had softened his tone. He reached across the hateful little polystyrene picnic and ruffled Roland's mop of dark hair, noting with distaste how long it was, all messy and curly like a girl's. 'I'll get some more, okay? But next time let's remember to ask for three pots instead of two and then we won't have any of this bother, will we? It's called thinking ahead, Roland, and as you get older you'll have to learn to do a bit more of it.' He shot a sort of who-would-have-them look at the women and strode to the head of the shortest queue to see if he could slip his meagre request between the orders of new customers.

Colin found the evening no easier, not because Roland cried or misbehaved but because he was so docile and acquiescent, so desperately keen to please. No TV until the video, Colin commanded, expecting resistance. Roland, who had lost some of his passion for television since he and his mother had moved into the barn, nodded meekly and asked if he could play the piano instead. He had memorised something specially, he said. He pushed up his sleeves as he took up his position on the piano stool and closed his eyes until he could hear the sounds inside his head. 'Ready and waiting,' said Colin reaching surreptitiously for the newspaper. But when Roland began to play he found his gaze drawn at once from the headlines to his son's racing fingers, thumping and twirling with a mastery that even Colin, tone deaf as he was, recognised as exceptional.

'That was amazing. Play it again, if you like.'

'Nah, don't really want to.' Roland slipped off the stool and tipped a box of his old model cars out on to the carpet.

'That piece, what's it called?'

' "Mad Cat Jazz".'

'Is it, now? Well, you were good. Very good indeed. You must have practised very hard.'

Roland looked up from his little pile of cars, puzzling. 'I just like playing it.'

'Right. And would you like to watch that video now?'

'Yes, please.' He leapt to his feet and threw himself on to the sofa. Colin managing not to mention either the abandoned cars, strewn round the armchairs and under the coffee table, or that furniture was not for jumping on, slotted the video into the machine and retreated back to the sofa. There were other things he wanted – needed – to do, like fixing himself a drink and phoning Phyllis, but it seemed right that he should sit with Roland for part of the film anyway. Then, just as he was thinking of sneaking into the kitchen, Roland, fighting yawns, edged towards him and tunnelled his head under his arm, so snugly that Colin found he didn't want to move after all. When Phyllis herself phoned, much later on, Colin was sitting at the end of Roland's bed watching him as he slept, his beloved Teddy and Beaky, a tatty duck stitched clumsily back together many times over the years by Elizabeth, tucked firmly under each arm. He looked so sweet, so peaceful, so fragile.

'I thought you were going to call *me*,' complained Phyllis, when he finally arrived at the phone.

'I said I would when I could and it's not been . . . easy.'

'Oh dear, is he being a handful?' she said soothingly, eager both to grant her lover an excuse for his unprecedented, most unwelcome curtness and to present herself as an ally in the face of any separation difficulties he had still to overcome.

'A handful? Not at all, no.'

'Oh.'

'Look, Phyllis, I'm a little tired,' Colin explained hastily, too caught up in the poignancy of his own confusion to summon the effort to respond properly to the hurt in her tone. He didn't want to gang up with this woman against the foibles of his son, he realised, not that night – not ever, probably. And, anyway, Roland had been far from a handful. Apart from the little show of petulance in McDonald's he had been easy and affectionate. So affectionate, indeed, that by the time Colin had given him a piggy-back up to bed, feeling the grip of his wiry legs and arms round his waist and neck, he had felt quite wretched with affection himself. It was different without Elizabeth. Worse, because it was much harder work – relentless and threaded with guilt – but better too. Closer. If Elizabeth had been there Roland would have curled up next to her, and Colin wouldn't have questioned it. He might even have enjoyed some private critical musings on the subject of Disney videos and motherly physical indulgence, pouring a second drink while Elizabeth tucked Teddy and Beaky under the duvet, drew the curtains and picked the discarded socks off the floor. He would have sat happily alone on the sofa while Elizabeth, not him, perched on the little bed upstairs, stroking Roland's wide forehead and fielding sleepy unanswerable questions about whales. How long did they live? How deep could they dive? How fast could they swim? But now Colin had done those things because, without Elizabeth, he *had* to. Because their new circumstances called for it. Some fighting, obstinate part of him felt resentment still. Yet the day had brought joy, too, unexpectedly, in the simple pleasures of its entanglement, its *closeness*.

Sitting beside his sleeping son, Colin had, for the first time, felt both the complicated weight of this joy and the inherent sadness of glimpsing something good only after it could never be properly retrieved. The shrill ring of the phone had been jarring beyond words. As had the hard-done-by edge to his lover's voice. I have lost so much, he wanted to say, but couldn't because it would only have made her uncomprehending and jealous. Instead, he kept the burden of his revelations to himself – the glimpse of love, the handcuffs of part-time parenthood within which that love would now have to be explored – and spoke gruffly instead. He could feel Phyllis bristle at his coldness. It would take a lot to reassure her.

And this is how it will be, he thought, putting down the phone. This is how it will be.

'Look.' Pamela held up six inches of yellow knitting, tugging the border so that it hung in a tidy rectangle from the needle. 'The front will be harder – a blue bunny every three inches, I don't know how I shall manage.' She smiled, knowing she would manage very well.

John, who had gone to the fireplace to stoke the fire, turned and nodded. Without his glasses both the knitting and his wife's face were hazy smudges; an unframed yellow blur next to a paler, cream one. He returned to the fire, but it was a few seconds before he could even focus properly on that. It had no need of stoking, he saw now. The logs Sid had chopped from the fallen tree were so thick they took an age to burn; and air was circulating nicely too, the flames leaping out of a healthy molten carpet of orangy red. No stoking. No log. His journey from the armchair, across the yards of faded cornflower Axminster, had been for nothing.

'It's going to be a layette for Helen and Peter's baby.' Pamela clutched her knitting to her chest as the joy of expectant grand-motherhood swelled inside. 'For the baby,' she repeated, a little sharply, annoyed that not even this most astonishing news – delivered so matter-of-factly by Peter on the phone just a few days before – could inject a little *joie de vivre* into her husband's increasingly stooped and slackened mien. Seeing him now, shifting from one foot to the other on the hearth-rug, staring at some spot on the wall as if he wished he could vanish through it, Pamela felt the stab of annoyance mushroom into something deeper. After weeks of trying to cheer him she was feeling the strain. Undoubtedly it had been a tough year for all of them, there was no denying that, losing Tina and then Eric, yet their blessings were still so numerous – especially now, with this extraordinary news of the baby. Pamela shot her husband a wary glance, thinking, as she had started to do, that his prolonged state of misery smacked of self-indulgence. I will tell him so, she decided, and began again to knit fast, her fingers expertly looping and threading the fine yellow wool. I will declare my impatience.

'John, darling . . .' She faltered, quailing as ever at the prospect of stirring up any unpleasantness. 'John . . .' She fixed her eyes on her sliding needles, though she could knit just as well without looking. 'I hope you don't mind my saying, but I can't help wishing you could seem more . . . pleased. About the baby. In fact,' she continued, gathering courage, 'I think it's quite *wrong* of you not to be more pleased. It puts a dampener on the rest of us . . . on *me*. The children will be here the day after tomorrow – they're bound to notice how low-spirited you are. For *their* sakes, I think you should try to pull yourself together a bit. On top of which there's still so much to do, all those boxes of fireworks to sort out, not to mention the pumpkins, which Sid has put in the garage. It's such a chore, I know, but they look so lovely with candles in and I'll be able to use some of the flesh to make a pumpkin pie. I'll use that marvellous recipe of Dorothy's but . . .' Pamela faltered again, aware that she was losing her way, thanks to a distracting image of John the previous year, whistling jauntily as he carved the tops off ten pumpkins, scooped their stringy flesh into a huge pudding basin, then sliced his penknife through their plump orange carcasses to make masterfully ghoulish expressions. Jagged teeth and gaping eyes. When Pamela inserted and lit the candles, the pair of them had laughed like gleeful schoolchildren at their handiwork. Happiness comes in unexpected moments, she thought now, as the image dissolved like a dream. She realised in the same instant that, after five decades, her own capacity for happiness had become inextricably entwined with her husband's. She could rejoice in nothing with him so glum. Her joy simply wouldn't take flight without his alongside. Maddened, but also a little inspired, Pamela glanced up from her knitting to find the stubborn hunch of her husband's back still set against her, as articulate as a grimace. 'Eric would have hated his death affecting you in this way, you know,' she scolded. 'It's the very *last* thing he would have wanted.'

'And you would know what Eric would have wanted, wouldn't you, my dear?' He jerked round, gripping the mantelpiece to steady himself, then launched himself away from it, glowering at her as he strode out of the room.

Pamela's heart stopped, then started again at twice its normal speed. 'I only meant—' she began, but he was already gone. A moment later the front door slammed. Pamela lowered her knitting on to her lap. She was half-way through a row. Two stitches had slipped off the needle and begun to unravel, creating an unsightly hole in the dense, even pattern below. He knows, she thought. Maybe Elizabeth had said something. Maybe – worse still – he had known all along and his punishment had been not to tell her, to let her stew for fifty years in the juice of her own guilt. With the death of Eric, and his own mortality suddenly so unignorable, it had begun, after all this time, to eat away at him, to seep like poison from an untended wound. His black mood was because he wanted, finally, to have it out, to clear the air before they were both in their graves. Pamela sat motionless, her thoughts spinning and meshing like the little yellow jumper in her lap. It was all so obvious – obvious and inevitable. She had been right not to feel safe. How had she ever imagined one could be safe from the consequences of one's own sin? A revelatory conversation with her daughter, her own guilt and desire for atonement, they were all nothing when it came to the relentless surfacing of the truth. Pamela looked at the open door, then looked away again, dreading the prospect of John, his accusations marshalled, storming back through it. The room was very still. A few more minutes passed and then, slowly, she picked up her knitting and retrieved the stitches, painstakingly looping them back on to the safety of the needle.

Outside, John paused on the doorstep, then headed for the front gate and left towards the garage. He had been vicious, he knew, cruel, even. Yet he had wanted to hurt her. Her serenity, sitting there with her clicking needles, trying to smooth the surface of things as she always did, as if her life were so perfect, sickened him. How dare she chide him for not being more glad? As if gladness was something one could summon with the snap of a finger, regardless of shame, failure and weakness.

It was cold inside the garage. The Range Rover was a black bulk in the darkness, a sleeping metal beast. John edged round it, fumbling along the wall for the light switch. Alone in the icy dark he felt suddenly afraid, certain of nothing but his own unhappiness. And death. One could be certain of that above all things. Everything else – the house, the car, the cold stone under his fingertips – seemed ephemeral in comparison. Illusions of security.

How laughable to have worried about tax liability and backache. How laughable to fear the only thing that offered release. On finding the switch at last, he flicked on the light, screwing up his eyes against the sudden glare. The brightly decorated boxes of fireworks, stacked along the wall to his right, glimmered accusingly. This time last year he had already drawn up a map of how to arrange them, a numbered map indicating the order in which they were to be lit: catherine wheels, shooting stars, Chinese fountains, small rockets, big rockets and a couple of giant ones for the end. Now he felt only dread at the approaching festivities. With all the family there it would be the obvious time to break his news. He would have to wait till they were all assembled, at the end of dinner, when the children had gone to bed. He would stand up, chink his glass and clear his throat. Their eyes would be expectant, hopeful of good news, even, like the last time, when he had made his announcements about the gifts of cash. You'll have to launch into it quickly, John warned himself now, leaning against the car and running his hand over his brow, which was damp with perspiration in spite of the cold. Cut to the chase. Cut to the quick. State the bald facts: I have failed. As a father. As a man. As a husband. I thought I had everything, but I had nothing. Nothing now and nothing for the future. It was all an illusion. John groped for the handle and tried to open the car door. It was locked. Of course. Damn fool. The keys. He needed the keys. He thrust his hands blindly into his pockets and let out a lunatic cry of triumph as his fingers alighted upon the familiar metal circle of his key-ring. Soon he was easing himself into the front passenger seat and leaning across to switch on the engine. The CD player sprang into life. A compilation of classics. Elgar. *The Enigma Variations*. Yes, that would do. That would do nicely. He wound down the windows and closed his eyes. *Death will release me*. He recited the phrase in his mind, thinking of Eric and breathing as slowly and deeply as he could.

Pamela finished one row, then another, and another. The clock on the mantelpiece ticked in time with her heart, it seemed. Unbearable in the silence. As if she was the only person on the planet left alive.

Waiting for something to happen was no good, she decided at last. Alone or not, one couldn't just wait to see how life turned out. One had to take control, pick up the stitches, sort out the mess as best one could. Wearily, her hands trembling, she stowed her knitting in the beloved old sewing-bag that had been her mother's and levered herself out of her chair. She would find John, confront whatever had to be confronted, honour him with the truth. She slipped on her overcoat and opened the front door, then stood still for a few seconds, smelling the faint scent of cut grass in the damp air. The last cut of the year, Sid had said, sipping his mug of tea on the back-door step that morning, turning his leathery face to the grey sky. Ready for the celebrations. The Harrison fireworks. He had handed back his empty mug, cackling happily.

Oh, there would be fireworks, all right, reflected Pamela grimly, glittering ugly ones, eruptions of truth, sprinkling burning shards over their heads and hearts. She stepped uncertainly on to the front lawn, trying to imagine how it would feel to have her perfidy exposed, how alien the world would seem without the warmth of her husband's love. Not that there had been much warmth lately, she reminded herself, trying to shake some courage into her heart and noticing the faint glimmer of the garage light. For a moment her spirits soared. He was in the garage, sorting fireworks and pumpkins. Everything was all right. Everything normal. She began to cross the lawn, only registering the hum of the car engine as she reached the gate. And music. There was music. Something searing and dramatic. Half-way across the drive she started to run, awkwardly because her skirt was knee-length and tight and her stockinged feet slid in her slippers. She opened the garage door and paused for a moment, the implications of the scene before her – the running engine, the open windows, John sitting with his eyes closed – taking time, in spite of her presentiments, to dawn fully. Then she was screaming and skidding in her slippers to the passenger door. 'You stupid man – stupid. Nothing is worth this – nothing.' She fumbled for the ignition and turned off the engine, then started to slap his face.

John, who had only had the engine running for a few minutes and was far from dead, opened his eyes at once. 'I've lost everything,' he said, blinking at her hand, poised to deliver another strike across his cheek. 'Eric gave me everything and I lost it.'

'Nonsense. Get out – get out of there.' She tugged on his arm, ineffectually, since her own limbs were limp with shock.

'You don't understand, Pammy.' He began to sob, his chin flopping on to his chest. 'I should have told you, I've known for so long, but – the shame of it – I couldn't.'

'The shame?' She let the arm, so heavy and unresponsive to her efforts, fall from her hands. 'The shame is mine.' She glanced sideways and noticed a bag propped against the wall next to the crate of pumpkins. The big sturdy paper bag with plastic handles into which, months before, she had stuffed the baby clothes from the suitcase in the attic. Miranda's clothes. The bin men had never taken them. John must have retrieved them, perhaps to use as evidence against her. Perhaps to torture himself. Whatever the case, it verified Pamela's worst fears. He knew it all. 'The shame is mine,' she repeated.

But John, swamped in his own despair, marshalling the words to articulate the reasons behind it, did not hear her. 'I have lost almost two million pounds,' he said dully, lifting his chin and looking at her, eyes bleary from despair and lack of sleep. 'The claims on the hurricane . . . There will be no money for the children, no money to cover inheritance tax. They will have to sell . . . to sell Ashley House. I didn't know how to tell you. I don't know how I'm going to tell them. Pam, I'm so sorry.'

Pamela stared at him, numb with shock and the most despicable relief. 'Is that all?' she whispered, the words sliding out of her.

'All?' he croaked. 'Isn't that enough?'

'Oh, John, oh, you silly, silly man.' She leant further into the car, trying to put her arms round his slumped frame. 'It's only money,' she whispered. 'Money doesn't matter as much as – as much as love.'

'Oh, but it does matter,' he groaned, burying his head in her chest, 'money matters so very much. Without it the family is lost. Eric knew that – knew he couldn't cope with it – which was why he entrusted everything to me, not just the house but the whole responsibility of securing the future of our family. Christ,' he laughed bitterly, 'he even gave you up . . .'

Pamela froze, her arms still round his waist, her chin resting on his collarbone. Here it comes, she thought, here it comes, after all.

'You know how he loved you, don't you?' he said.

'Yes.' She had been holding her breath. Now Pamela parted her lips and let the air out, slowly and soundlessly. 'Yes, I knew that.'

'Throwing himself across the globe like that, it was partly to keep himself away from you.' John groaned, tipping his head to rest on hers. 'I have always known that. Known it and been grateful for it. Just as I was grateful you resisted his manifold charms and stuck with me.'

Pamela clung to him, her face still half buried in his collarbone. Was this a declaration of knowledge or ignorance? To be so unsure, at such a moment, in the midst of such calamity, was intolerable – like hanging on to the edge of a precipice with one ripping fingernail. 'You know how fond I was of him,' she muttered into his shirt, easing out the sentence like a probe on a string, not knowing if it would prove a lifeline or a noose for her own neck.

'Oh, yes.' John made a noise in his throat, something between a chuckle and a sob. 'And I'll admit it made me jealous sometimes, still makes me jealous . . . You were so good with him and I was so bad. When he died,' he blurted, the other secret, festering part of his unhappiness spilling out of him, 'the night of that damned hurricane, I lied to you about what the nurses said. I knew Eric was going to die but I lied. I wanted to be there by myself, to have his death to myself. How shameful is that?' He felt her tremble and, not knowing it was from relief, buried his face in her hair. 'I'm so sorry, darling, for everything . . . Please forgive me.'

'There's nothing to forgive,' Pamela whispered. 'He was your brother, your own blood. Of course you wanted to be with him at the end. I understand why you lied. Some lies are necessary.'

'Oh, Pammy, how can you be so kind, so understanding? The money . . . There's enough for us to live on, but the children . . . I've failed them. When we're gone they will be left with so little.'

'They'll sort it out.' Pamela spoke almost briskly, raising her

head, daring to look at him at last. 'The house – what to do after
we're gone – they'll sort it out in their own way. We can only do our
best, John. We can't control what happens next. Like the hurricane
– it just happened, didn't it? Robbing us in one way, but not
harming Charlie who was there in the thick of it. And I know what I
would rather, given that choice again – if it was a choice . . .' Pamela
left the sentence hanging, overcome in equal measure by a sense of
life's impenetrable mysteries and an ache in her shoulders from
leaning for so long at such an awkward angle. 'Let's go inside,' she
urged gently. 'I'm so cold and so stiff, and we can talk everything
over so much better with a cup of tea.' She helped him ease himself
out of the car and they walked back to the house together, arms
linked, their bodies leaning inwards, as if each would fall without
the other's support.

The next morning, while her parents, worn out by the previous
night's dramas, slept late, backs turned but touching, Cassie opened
her newly hung bedroom curtains to see Stephen Smith standing on
the pavement next to her car. Her first instinct was to leap backwards,
jerking the curtains shut. But then, when several minutes passed
with no ring on the doorbell, curiosity got the better of her and she
ventured back to the window. She parted the curtains gingerly and
peered down into the street. He was leaning on her car, arms folded,
as if he owned the damn thing. The cheek of it was too much.

'Hey!' She yanked open the window, struggling because her
recent exuberance with gloss paint had glued the frame to its fitting.
'Hey! What do you think you're doing?'

'Hi.' He looked up and smiled. 'How are you?'

'Fine, thank you very much,' she retorted, astonished and faintly
disturbed – given the past traumas of their acquaintance – at how
casual he seemed, how *relaxed*. He looked different too, sporting a
new, much shorter haircut, crisp grey jeans, fancy-looking trainers
and a black jumper – all in all, such a far cry from the scruffy,
anguished creature who had pressed himself upon her in the
summer and fled in disgust at Peter's seedy proposition that Cassie
found herself somewhat lost for words.

'Don't worry, I'm not stalking you or anything,' he declared, grinning at an old lady with a scuttling dachshund, who shot him a nervous glance before tottering after her pet. 'I really was just passing. Thought I'd stop and see how you were.'

'By hanging round the street?'

'Sorry. It must look odd, I know. Only I thought presenting myself at your door might make you more nervous than you clearly are already . . .'

'I am *not* nervous.'

'. . . which, given how I once behaved, would be perfectly understandable, so I thought I'd just wait out here for a bit and see if you emerged, have a quick chat and then go.'

'We have nothing to *chat* about,' she retorted, recalling that in the end, in terms of his behaviour, he hadn't done too badly at all.

'Your car needs a wash, by the way, we could talk about that.'

'Well, don't lean on it, then.'

'I've just come from my publishers. I've got a couple of proofs of the book. I'm rather pleased with it.'

'Good. I'm pleased you're pleased and now . . .' She reached up to pull the window down.

'So you are okay, are you?' Stephen called up. 'I really did just want to know that. Honestly. You and your doctor, I hope it's working out. You certainly *look* well.' He squinted up at the window, relieved to see that it still framed her rather pink face surrounded by the morning dishevelment of unbrushed hair.

Cassie peered back out. 'My doctor?'

'Daniel Lambert. You told me all about him, remember?'

'So I did,' she murmured, somewhat put out both at his mentioning Daniel and at his assumption that they were back together.

'Look, I'm sorry, it's none of my business, I know.' Stephen pushed himself off the car. 'I'm glad you're okay. It was just a whim, honest. Don't hold it against me.' He shot her a parting grin and began to walk away, then shouted as an afterthought, 'Tell your parents I'll send them a copy of the hardback. It's due out in March – I might even sign it.'

'Hang on . . .' The sight of him strolling away, looking so

unperturbed, so *harmless*, made Cassie fear suddenly that she had been unnecessarily rude. It made her think, too, of how he had stridden away from her and Peter out of the café, so painfully crumpled and offended. 'Hang on.' She raised her voice to repeat the plea but he didn't turn. She watched until he had disappeared round the corner, then pulled on some jeans and a jumper and raced down the stairs. She arrived in the neighbouring street a couple of minutes later to find him astride a large blue motorbike strapping a helmet under his chin.

'Hello again. To what do I owe this honour?'

'I'm sorry – I thought maybe I had seemed rude. I don't like rudeness in any form.' She made a face. 'Can we shake hands or something?'

He laughed. 'Sure.' He took off one of his black leather gloves and gripped her fingers, then released them. 'And since you're here,' he rummaged in a small luggage box behind his seat, 'take this. First proof, full of typos, and of course that won't be the cover, but you'll get the gist.'

'Thanks.' Cassie took the book and folded her arms across it. 'Seeing as you asked,' she added, following an urge to set the record straight, 'that doctor, Daniel Lambert, I did start seeing him again but now I'm not. It would never have worked out. Married men.' She rolled her eyes. 'All the bloody same.'

'Right.' Somehow, in spite of this information, Stephen got the bike going, glad of the camouflage of the thick gloves for his trembling hands. This was what he had promised he would do, he reminded himself, and he was going to stick to it. He had a good life, these days, not just because of the advance on his thriller, but because of the girl from the Indian restaurant and a new flat with decent-sized rooms. Cassie was part of the nightmare of before, when he had been out of control on every front. Doctor or no doctor, he wasn't going to break his vow to himself and balls everything up. Not now, not ever. He was revving the engine loudly when suddenly it cut out.

'Oh dear.' Cassie pressed her hand to her lips to conceal her amusement. 'Maybe cars are best after all, even unwashed ones.'

'Yeah, well . . . The mud on yours is thick enough to carve messages in,' he muttered, fiddling with the key.

Somewhere, deep inside Cassie's consciousness, a penny dropped. 'Oh, my God, it wasn't you, was it? My name – in the mud by the wheel. Was it you?'

Stephen blushed so heavily he was glad of his helmet. 'Guilty as charged.' The words, so light, seemed to stick in his mouth. He remembered in a flash all the other things he had done – the secret vigils, the flower on the doorstep, the dancing hearts on her icy windscreen – and blushed again. 'Look, I'm sorry. I had a bad patch, sort of lost myself for a bit. I'm sorry you, er, got caught up in it.' The engine flared at last, much more healthily this time, drowning the tail-end of his sentence. ' 'Bye, then,' he shouted. Ride away, he told himself, ride away, but she was trying to say something now, pressing her mouth close to his helmet.

'Will – your – publishers – have – a – launch – party – for – the – book?'

'Maybe.' He nodded. 'Next year.'

'Invite me,' she said, or at least that was what he thought she said, although it was hard to be sure through the clamour of the motor-bike and the shouting inside his head: *You shouldn't have come, nothing has changed, you shouldn't have come, nothing has changed.*

Frowning as the bike sped away, Cassie was musing on precisely the opposite notion. Everything changed, she decided, strolling back to her flat to pack for the weekend with her family. Everything always changed, because the world and people were in constant flux, bouncing off each other and situations like atoms in the quantum-theory business she had struggled with so badly as a schoolgirl. Every incident, every action, every thought triggered myriad consequences. Like Tina dying and Stephen finding her mother's love-letter and Dan's wife getting sick. Each event was a stone in a pond, the impact rippling endlessly into countless lives, creating consequences in countless ways. Nothing happened in isolation. Nothing stayed the same. Like her feelings for Dan. She had simplified deliberately in her explanation to Stephen; it hadn't been easy to give him up, in spite of her growing recognition of his indecisive, deeply married state. She still missed him, or at least she missed the hope of happiness with which she had always associated him. But after a couple of encounters, intense and passionate and wonderful though they had been, something inside her – some instinct for self-preservation, perhaps – had clicked into place. She deserved, she needed, more than half-hopes and a half-life of clandestine meetings and hazy promises. It's over, she had told him, a few weeks after they had got back together. I don't want to do this any more. Live your life with Sally and let me go. He had begged her to change her mind, but then, confronted perhaps by the limitations of his own position, his inability still to offer the full commitment she had always sought, accepted defeat. They hadn't spoken since and the silence felt permanent. Instigated on this occasion by her own strength of mind, this second separation had proved much easier to cope with. The flames of love, if unfanned for long enough, could subside, Cassie had discovered. Emotions, too, changed with time and altered circumstance.

Like Stephen Smith, she mused, going over their meeting as she threw toiletries and clothing into a bag. The events of the year had certainly changed him – for the better, it seemed. Maybe rejecting Peter's offer (even more unbelievably crass and desperate in retrospect than it had seemed at the time) had been the making of him. Whatever the cause, Stephen was a more mature, composed version of the creature who had tremblingly dispensed champagne and stammered out his feelings on that stifling day in June. And more attractive too, Cassie admitted, frowning at the uncomfortable and uncharitable fact that the man should seem appealing only after his desperation for her affection had run its course.

'Life's a bugger,' she declared, directing the remark cheerfully to her new lime green Osborne and Little wallpaper and picking up the proof copy of Stephen's book, which was lying next to her bag. 'But an interesting bugger none the less,' she murmured, riffling slowly, and then with some urgency, through the pages. Just to be absolutely sure, she told herself, skim-reading the chapter on Eric and sighing with satisfaction to find that Stephen had not let them down with another last-minute change of heart. As she was closing the book her eye was caught by a blank page at the front – blank, that is, apart from '*for C*'. The dedication page. Cassie stared at it for a few seconds, then snapped the book shut, chiding herself for the arrogance of her own speculations. He was over her and she was glad of it, she reminded herself, and dropped the proof into her bag to show her parents.

The house, large as it was, seemed to shrink with the arrival of the family. Within an hour of their habitually awkward reappraisals of each other, the children had settled into a variety of entertainments, Theo instructing Clem on the new attachments to his recently mended camera in the drawing room, Maisie playing Chopsticks in the music room with Ed, Roland and Chloë chasing around every room on the ground floor with Roland's new chocolate Labrador puppy yelping ecstatically at their heels. Instead of minding the noise, as she had during the course of their recent visits, Pamela, shifting a rucksack as she passed the TV room, where Charlie and Peter were watching some sporting fixture, found it soothing. The house had come alive again, its walls and floorboards vibrating with the energy of its young occupants. For all its spaciousness, oak-beamed charm and spectacular views, a home had no pulse beyond that generated by its family, she reflected sadly, wondering how on earth they were all going to react when John broke his terrible news.

Since the traumatic episode in the garage the pair of them had thought and talked of little else. With virtually all his liquid assets drained by pay-outs from his syndicates, the children would have to sell Ashley House to pay the inheritance tax levied on its value. After which they'd still end up with a hefty three hundred thousand or so each – a fortune by any standards – but the house, their beloved Ashley House, would be gone. To another, alien family. Or, worse still, to a property developer, who would bulldoze everything to exploit the beauty of the views and make his own fortune. Pamela strained her ears for any sounds of movement upstairs where John was having an afternoon nap. In the last couple of days he had slept a lot, much like an invalid in convalescence. Second only to his preoccupation with the long-term effects of his financial losses was his penitence for what he had put her through, for the selfish desperation that had prompted him to close the garage door and turn on the car engine. Never again, he promised, and Pamela believed him. Ministering to his needs, however, noting the new disturbing gauntness of his face against the pillow, she could not help being reminded of Eric during his final months. Yet when he was awake and they were talking there was more ebullience to him than she had seen in weeks, simply, he said, from having shared the extent of his woes instead of letting them fester in the solitary prison of his mind. That morning he had woken her in the small hours, gripping her arm to say, 'It might come good yet, if the next three years are profitable . . . It might not be so bad.' Knowing he was half asleep, needing reassurance before he dared lose himself to the oblivion of proper rest, Pamela had stroked his head until his eyes closed, then stayed awake for hours herself, racking her brains for some other, more concrete solution to their problems.

Alicia hadn't ended up with much money and what she did have would, quite rightly, go to Paul. Pamela felt it would be wrong even to consult her sister-in-law about their problems, since she was leaving that week for her Christmas visit to Australia, succumbing to twenty-four hours on a plane in spite of her hip and extensively expressed terrors of deep-vein thrombosis. Armed with packets of aspirin and support stockings, she was planning to spend most of the flight pacing up and down the aisle – beating the air stewards with her stick, no doubt, John had joked when Pamela told him, chuckling for the first time in ages. A card, Pamela thought now, putting her head round the door of the TV room and catching Peter's eye. A card to wish Alicia well for her journey. Such small things mattered, they always did, no matter the other, bigger dramas circling overhead. 'Peter, darling, could you go up and see Dad? He said to wake him when you arrived. He wants a word, just the two of you.' She gave Charlie, already pulling himself out of his seat, a fierce look.

'Is he ill?' demanded her younger son suspiciously.

'No, certainly not.' Pamela did her best to sound incredulous. 'He takes naps, these days. At eighty it's hardly surprising. He'll be down soon. He just wants a word with Peter first.'

'Good luck,' murmured Charlie, catching his brother's eye as he left the room, acutely aware of Peter's own agenda and wanting to communicate his support.

Pamela retreated to the kitchen to find Elizabeth making a pot of tea and Serena up to her elbows in flour, rolling out pastry for the pumpkin pie. Helen, who had had a scare with a bit of blood earlier in the week, had been instructed to remain on the sofa where Cassie, perched on one arm, was entertaining her with the story of the biographer turning up out of the blue on his motorbike with a proof copy of *Unsung Heroes* and talk of a launch party. 'We could all go,' she was saying excitedly, 'like a sort of final tribute to Uncle Eric.'

'It'll be very limited numbers I expect, dear,' Pamela warned, wary now of Stephen Smith and his book, although a hurried check of Cassie's copy had already confirmed that it contained no disclosures she should fear. John would be delighted with it, she knew, although an irrational part of her remained nervous at the thought of him taking his turn to thumb through the pages on his brother, as if the untold part she had played in the story might yet leap out at him from between the lines. That the children themselves all knew most of that story now was oddly comforting, as was their tactful silence on the subject. Protecting their father, of course, Pamela reminded herself, catching an arch look from Cassie, although from what, exactly, she was increasingly uncertain. John, it was now clear, had known the broad truth of the situation all along. Who had loved whom. Who had chosen whom. He had known and accepted it, lived happily with it. And given that, Pamela realised, the details behind those big truths were almost irrelevant. 'Peter,' she exclaimed, jolted from her thoughts by the sight of her eldest hovering in the kitchen doorway.

'I thought maybe Dad would like some tea.' He looked so uncertain that Pamela wondered if he could possibly have some instinctive foreknowledge of the bleak news awaiting him upstairs.

'That's a good idea,' she agreed, recovering herself. She handed Serena a clean knife with which to trim the pastry. 'Elizabeth, would you pour another cup?'

Peter remained in the doorway while the tea was prepared, his gaze fixed on Serena's steady hand slicing strips of pastry off the pie. Around her plates of food lay ready for the cook-out that night: homemade sausages and burgers, chicken drumsticks, slabs of marinating steak and bagfuls of round and oblong buns. Sid had already set up a trestle table and a makeshift barbecue of bricks in the corner of the lower field. The bonfire would be lit and they would cook and eat in the warmth of its glow, marvelling at the sparks and starry sky until John wiped the grease from his hands and, with a lighted spill, set off, to complete the evening's magic with the spectacle of the noise and exploding colours of the fireworks, a celebratory ritual that his own father had performed before him and that Peter had expected, one day, to carry out himself. But not now, he reminded himself, not now. He glanced at Helen, aware of her attention, the comforting knowledge of their shared apprehension. If he was venturing upstairs to his father then it could mean only one thing. As he left with the tea he shot her a quick smile, wanting to show her that he was all right about it, that there would be no wavering from the course upon which they had agreed. Although it had been undeniably hard, sweeping into the drive that afternoon, seeing the massive grey beauty of the house with its large, friendly windows and frothing ivied walls. The extent of what he had elected to give up had hit Peter then, with such winding force, that he had reached for Helen's hand to steady himself.

'Let me do something,' Helen cried, after Peter was gone, seeking activity to mask her nerves. She had wanted to talk to Serena about the new twist in their future, but Peter had pointed out that until his parents had been consulted such discussions would be insensitively premature. Seeing the house for the first time since their decision to surrender it had made him sad, Helen knew, but for her it had been the other way round: relieved of the burden of knowing that she would one day be responsible for the place, she had found herself instantly fonder of it. I'll never have to worry again, she had thought, sitting in the drive in the shadow of its long stony front. I can always be here as a guest, passing through, enjoying the best bits, then retreating to our other life without a care.

'You can help control that dog if you like,' laughed Elizabeth, as

Chloë, Roland and the puppy bounded into the kitchen, then clambered on to the sofa in a panting heap.

'He's so sweet,' crooned Chloë, giggling as the puppy put his paws on to her lap and began delivering hungry licks to her chin.

'He's a little devil,' said Pamela, whose initial sceptical reaction to Elizabeth's ability to cope with him had mellowed considerably. The puppy was a dear thing and a fast learner. More importantly, John's face lit up every time he caught sight of it, tugging Roland round the garden or sitting at the back door having slipped out of the barn. 'Off the sofa. Off!' She pushed the dog back on to the floor where he flopped with surprising obedience, his little barrel-body pumping with exhaustion.

'You shouldn't have called him Little Boots,' declared Chloë. 'It's a silly name because he isn't Boots's *child*, is he? Not like this baby is going to be *ours*.' She gave a proprietorial pat to Helen's stomach, wanting both to underline the superiority of her good fortune and to quell the tremors of envy she felt about her cousin's pet. The dog would always be there to play with, her mother had consoled her a little earlier, which meant she could enjoy him without having to do any of the boring or yukky things like walking and scooping up his mess. Chloë could see the sense of this but struggled still to *feel* it – although when the puppy had done a wee on the drawing-room carpet it had been fun to watch Roland all mad with worry, rushing secretly for a cloth, while she had laughed so much she'd had to have a wee herself. 'We thought of *hundreds* of names for our baby,' she continued, not looking at Roland, whom she knew was proud of his daft choice for the dog, 'Fleur, Rachel, Lily, Harriet . . .'

'Only girls' names?' put in Cassie, moving from the arm on to the sofa itself and bending down to pat the puppy.

'That's because—' Chloë stopped, going bright pink and glancing frantically at her mother.

'It's a girl,' said Helen quietly, after a pause. 'It was *supposed* to be a secret.' She pretended to look crossly at her daughter. 'For a bit longer anyway. We're calling her Genevieve.'

'A girl . . . Genevieve . . . How lovely.' Serena, who was modelling a set of decorative pastry leaves, gave a heavy sigh. A long slow moment followed, a moment so full of thoughts, on all their parts, about Tina that no one knew what to say. Serena understood what she had done – the injection of sadness into something so happy – and felt wretched, then resigned. I can't help it, she thought, offering them a sad smile. I can't help it. My past is their past. I can't change how this feels, how they feel. The silence clung on, until Chloë, entranced by the fat leaves of dough slipping so expertly from her aunt's slim fingers, wriggled off the sofa and ran to the table. 'Can I eat some, Aunty Serena? Please?' She picked up a scrap of pastry and squeezed it longingly.

Serena laughed, and relaxed at once. 'It won't taste very nice, my sweet, but by all means try. Better still, can you make me a little flower? To go in the middle of all these boring leaves?'

'And we'd like you, Serena, and you, Elizabeth, to be her god-mothers,' blurted Helen, prompted to make the announcement, which she and Peter had planned together, by the sight of Serena, so mended and brave and kind, and Elizabeth, all pink-faced from the steam of the kettle. 'No offence to you, Cassie, of course . . .'

'Absolutely none taken,' replied Cassie lightly, only the speed with which she patted Little Boots indicating otherwise. I'm just not the maternal kind, she thought, stroking the soft chocolate hair feverishly. I'm just not. I might die an old maid.

'You're my godmother, aren't you?' Roland reminded her softly.

'Oh, darling, I am, aren't I?' Cassie hugged him hard. 'Although I'm not very good at remembering, am I? I tell you what, though, I'm going to be the best from now on, you just wait and see. And if I'm not, I want you to tell me, okay?'

Roland nodded, but thought that this was an impossible demand, and wondered why his aunt should look so upset in making it. Grown-ups, as he and Polly had agreed many times, were com-plicated.

Discussions of names and godmotherly duties were in full flow when the telephone rang. Charlie was passing through the hall and got to it first. He arrived in the kitchen to announce, his face dead-pan, that Lucien Cartwright was on the phone wanting to speak to Elizabeth.

'Lucien?' Elizabeth froze, tea-towel slung over one shoulder, mug of tea in hand, with all eyes upon her.

'Is that . . .?' began Roland.

'Yes, darling, it is. Thanks, Charlie.' Elizabeth set down her mug and hurried from the room, the tea-towel flapping on her shoulder.

'Oh, my,' said Pamela, raising her eyes to the ceiling, then hurriedly lowering them again at the thought of Peter and John going through goodness knows what in the bedroom upstairs. How far had they got? she wondered. Where was it all going to end?

'Weird,' remarked Ed, returning from his post at the music-room door and placing a foot on the back of his sister, sprawled invitingly on the floor.

'Get off.' Maisie hit the leg. 'What's weird?'

'Aunt Elizabeth's old husband calling her up, Lucien Cartwright, she's on the phone to him now. Come and listen, if you don't believe me.'

'Lucien Cartwright? But he's a journalist, isn't he?'

Ed shrugged, his foot held threateningly over his sister again. 'Is he?'

Maisie clambered to her feet, staring at her brother with a mixture of curiosity and disbelief. They all knew, of course, that their aunt had been married before. It was ancient knowledge, so ancient it was never asked about or discussed. Even to want to know the man's name had never occurred to Maisie before. 'How the hell did you know Aunt Elizabeth was married to someone called Lucien Cartwright?'

'I heard Mum and Dad talking about it,' Ed crowed, delighted to have surprised her. 'And now he's phoned her up. She's in the hall, red as a beetroot. And I also know that Uncle Peter was having some heavy chat with Granddad upstairs and has just come down and asked Dad, Granny and Aunt Cassie to join them. And Aunt Elizabeth, too, if she ever gets off the phone. *Something* is going on, I tell you, something big.'

'Where's Clem?'

'With Theo, I think. They were going up to the attic to look for army stuff for his school play.' Ed, distracted by a swell of emptiness in the pit of his stomach, looked at his watch and groaned. 'At this rate we're *never* going to eat.'

'Come on.' Maisie crept to the door and peered round it like a spy. Her aunt had put down the phone and was walking – or, rather, drifting – upstairs, her eyes all staring like a sleepwalker's. 'Let's go up to the attic and find the others – quick, before Mum asks us to do something in the kitchen.' They waited until Elizabeth had floated out of sight, then scampered up the stairs after her.

Elizabeth hesitated at the door of her parents' bedroom, wondering whether she should knock before going in. As children they had always knocked, fearful of intruding on some unthinkable act of intimacy. But that could hardly be the case these days, she reflected wryly, with her father looking every inch his eighty years and her mother creeping round him like a withered Florence Nightingale, tray of tea or soup at the ready. He was ill, she was sure of it, sure too that that was what this curious summons was about. She raised her knuckles to rap on the wood, then lowered her hand, tempted to flee back down the stairs. Life was good and she was in no mood for bad news. The conversation with Lucien was still ringing inside her head . . .

'It's me, Lucien.'

'I know it's you.'

'The Ashley House fireworks weekend, is it? I remember it well.'

'Some things never change.'

'I met your son.'

'I know you did, he told me.'

'I was in Barham . . . I even saw you getting into the car with Serena and your father.'

She had laughed, incredulous. 'So you came here to spy on us?'

It was his turn to laugh. 'Not quite. I was there on business. It is, as they say, a long story. I might tell you one day . . . over a drink, maybe?'

'Why?' Elizabeth had gasped, baffled at his determination to collide their lives together, after so much time apart. 'Why?' she repeated.

Lucien sighed. 'I don't honestly know, Lizzy, except that I saw you that day, without having planned it, and I just thought . . . well, I just thought, I wish I still knew that woman. And the next thing I know I'm chatting to your son – God, he looks *so* like you – and he was all serious and suspicious but so polite—' He broke off, then added, with some desperation, 'If we met I could explain everything so much better.'

'How do you know I'm *free* to meet you?'

Lucien chuckled. 'Your boy told me quite a lot.'

'Did he now?' Elizabeth steeled herself to say what had to be said. She had forgotten what a nice voice Lucien had, his easy charm. 'I don't want to meet you,' she said, 'because there is no point. I'm fine now, very good in fact. I'm on my own. I'm happy. I have absolutely no desire to go *back* to anything—'

'Christ, neither have I,' he interrupted, laughing easily. 'Who would want to go back? No, thanks. We were crap, to put it mildly. But what about meeting with a view to going *forwards*? What about that, eh? Or with a view to . . . nothing. Just to meet. See where we are, see *who* we are now. Where's the harm in that?'

To which, because Charlie was signalling over the banisters for her to join the gathering upstairs, Elizabeth had said that she wasn't sure and maybe and if he gave her his number again she would think about it. Maybe. Yes, in other words, thought Elizabeth now, closing her palm round the cool brass of the door handle. Yes, because I am better – different – and because his voice had sounded so warm and familiar and because, as Lucien had said, where, after all, would be the harm? With which thought she blinked herself back to the present, patted her jeans pocket, where the number was safely stowed, and opened the bedroom door.

Given the size of Ashley House, it was, on the face of it, an odd place for the family to assemble. Like a deathbed scene, Cassie decided, but not like one at all because her father was dressed in green cords and a brown jumper and standing by the window, and

Charlie was the one lounging on the main bit of the bed. Her mother was perched on the edge of her bedroom chair, nervously fingering her bun, while she and Elizabeth sat side by side on the *chaise-longue* next to the dressing-table. Peter had planted himself in the middle of them all on the dressing-table stool, a king on a small throne, leaning forward in a very unkingly way, with his legs apart and his elbows resting on his knees.

'Would someone mind telling me what's going on?' demanded Elizabeth, to whom courage came more easily these days.

'Dad?' Peter swivelled on the stool to look at his father.

John, who had been studying the dusky violet outlines of the garden and fields, turned his head slowly.

He's dying, thought Cassie suddenly, biting her lower lip as she watched the slow turn of his head, seeing not the soft tufts of grey hair, but the curvature of the skull beneath. He's dying and we're all to be told about it. Even Mum. She glanced across the room, noting the look of rapt concern on Pamela's face, as blank and terrified as the rest of them. Only Peter, his chin now resting on the tips of his fingers, his eyes moving quickly from face to face, looked remotely composed, though it was the concrete composure of someone holding something in rather than having let it out. Her father was clearing his throat. Cassie, aware of Elizabeth's hand resting close to hers on the soft blue velvet of the *chaise-longue*, shifted her arm until their fingers were touching. Elizabeth responded at once, slipping her hand over Cassie's and squeezing hard. She had big hands for a woman, muscled from all her years of piano-playing, and Cassie felt better for their protection. I hope she treads carefully with Lucien, she thought suddenly. I hope he doesn't hurt her.

John, having wrested his eyes from the view, tugged at his cuffs, cleared his throat again, and found that there was nothing left to do but speak. 'I thought I had one thing to tell you all, but it seems . . .' he hesitated, looking from Peter to Charlie '. . . it seems that I have two. The situation, as situations often are, is more complicated than I had envisaged. Complicated and better.' He cleared his throat once more. 'I asked Peter up here to inform him, as the eldest and prime inheritor . . .' He paused to cough yet again, though the bubble in his throat, fuelled as it was by emotion, still refused to clear. '. . . to tell him that, courtesy of the recent hurricane in Florida, I have lost an enormous sum of money, so enormous that apart from this house I will have nothing to bequeath to you all. Which means that to pay its own inheritance tax Ashley House will almost certainly have to be sold.' He waited, letting these words sink in, his heart swelling with shame at their muted gasps and crestfallen faces. 'That tax paid, you would each receive about three hundred thousand pounds.' John hesitated. 'But Ashley House would be lost to the family for ever. The second thing I have to tell you is that upon receipt of this appalling news Peter informed me this afternoon that he had already decided that Charlie and Serena should be the ones to live here after your mother's and my death, and that so fixed is he upon this as the *right* course for the future that he will, if necessary, use his own funds, which are more considerable than I could possibly have imagined, to settle the tax bill, should that need arise.' John was compelled to stop by the tears now rolling freely down his cheeks.

'Oh, John.' Pamela, looking as small and fragile as a little girl, crept to his side and slipped her arms round his waist. Charlie had sat up and was clutching a pillow to his chest. 'Peter . . . no . . . not with all this . . . I couldn't, it wouldn't be right.'

'I have made a lot of money,' said Peter simply, casting his eyes round the room. 'Helen and I do not want to live here. Ashley House is at the core of this family. I am prepared to do anything – *anything* . . .' He repeated the word very slowly, giving equal emphasis to its three syllables. '. . . to keep it that way.' He felt giddy – elated – by the implications of his words. The spark of generosity, or whatever it was, that had been ignited by the decision over Helen's pregnancy – the decision to go with the flow of the needs of his own family – had become a raging fire. It was liberating, he had discovered, to have such power at his fingertips, to be in a position to save them all. 'Charlie and Serena *should* live here, I have never been more certain of anything. Although,' he added, smiling, 'I hope we'll all be able to visit from time to time . . .'

'Visit?' exploded Charlie, flinging the pillow across the bed. 'You can fucking live here too – all of you. We could divide the place up – give everyone their own patch. It could be a second home for all of us.'

Peter laughed quietly. 'Now, I'm not sure that would work, old bean. Four families sharing one house, however big, sounds like a recipe for disaster.'

'I wouldn't need more than I've got already,' said Elizabeth, in a small voice. She had been kneading Cassie's hand in hers, but dropped it now to run her fingers back through the straggly mane of her hair, as if she needed a clearer view of Charlie, to whom the statement was addressed.

'Of course . . . of course, Lizzy. You could stay in the barn as long as you wanted—' Charlie broke off and suddenly they were all looking at Cassie.

Slowly, very carefully, she folded her hands into a tidy parcel in her lap. There was a lot to take in and it didn't seem the moment for complaint. 'Ashley House matters more than anything,' she said quietly, aware of five sets of pleading eyes; aware, too, of the huge adjustment this would mean to her own future. She would never have described herself as grasping: she had easily dismissed all Dan's early concerns on such matters. But the fact of her inheritance had always been there: a buffer between her and possible hardship, more solid than practically any other expectation in her life. 'It would be wrong to sell this house,' she added, trying in her heart not to be selfish, to see the big picture. Hadn't she said herself that Charlie and Serena would be ideally suited to take over Ashley House? Yet all she could think now was that Elizabeth, with the barn, would be all right, Charlie, getting Ashley House, would certainly be all right, and Peter, with all his millions, would be all right. While she, the youngest, would get nothing, except a room for the weekends.

'Cass, a quarter of this house would be yours,' Charlie urged, as if reading her mind. 'You could come and go whenever you wanted. It would be *yours*. Serena and I would just be . . .' he groped for the right word, and alighted upon it with triumph '. . . custodians.'

'And then?' asked Cassie, doing her best to sound curious and innocent, so that while they might guess at her selfish reservations they would never know the extent of them. 'What about the next generation? Would it go to your three or to all seven – eight,' she corrected herself, remembering Helen's pregnancy, 'grand-children?'

'That will be for Charlie and Serena to decide,' answered Peter firmly, glancing at his brother.

'Well, what about a sort of trust thing?' Cassie ventured next, her voice still steeled with objective interest. 'So that we're all co-owners.'

Peter shook his head. 'Not possible, I'm afraid. No beneficiaries of such a trust could live here without paying rent, set by the taxman according to the market rate. For such a scheme to work we would have to install an outsider, which would rather ruin the point, wouldn't it?'

'Yes, yes, it would,' murmured Cassie, glancing at her parents, aware of the indecency of the conversation: they were talking as if the pair of them had already died.

'I'm sorry, Cassie,' growled John, who had been watching his youngest anxiously. She was his sweetest, his baby: the thought of leaving her nothing was intolerable. 'All of you . . . I'm so sorry.' Keeping Pamela tucked tightly into the crook of his arm, he reached with his free hand into his trouser pocket for a handkerchief and dabbed his forehead and eyes.

Pamela was too heartened, too proud, for tears. She stared instead at Peter, her firstborn, thinking what a package of surprises each child was, half-way through their lives and still with personalities as deep as conjurors' hats. She had meant it when she reassured John that their children would sort out the future for themselves, but never, in her wildest imaginings, could she have predicted the solution they were offering. Peter, the most unbending and ambitious of her offspring, in many ways the most blinkered, was being so selfless, so *visionary*. It was wonderful; almost miraculous, in fact.

'Dad, don't be sorry,' Cassie begged, every selfish concern dissolving at the sight of his sad, crinkled face and dabbing handkerchief. 'I don't want you to die – I don't want any of you to die,' she wailed, looking round the room, then dropping her head into her hands and bursting into tears.

In the kitchen the two sisters-in-law were busying themselves counting plates and pricking sausages, acutely aware of the ticking wall-clock and the tension prowling round them. Both were, in different ways, poorly equipped for the sudden joint exile in which they found themselves. Used as they were to each other's company, there was no history of natural intimacy for them to fall back on and both felt the lack of it.

Helen, watching Serena glide round the kitchen, her hair falling into her face as she so effortlessly attended to the preparation of the meal, thought how for years she had underestimated her sister-in-law's strengths, writing her off as unambitious and domestic, not seeing the extent of the qualities behind such characteristics. Armed with her own meticulously organised, career-oriented life, she had, she saw now, always felt faintly superior. A part of her longed to confess to this and also to explain that there was no sense of superiority whatsoever in her and Peter's decision to hand over the reins of Ashley House, just – on her part at least – the most monumental gratitude. Aware of Peter's warning about premature discussions, however, Helen said none of these things, confining herself instead to remarks on the fatness of the sausages and silent musings upon the remarkable converging and diverging of fortunes that had shaped the previous twelve months: so much lost, so much gained. Robbed as they had been of dear little Tina, Charlie and Serena would be the ones to acquire Ashley House; whereas she and Peter, on the face of it, had lost a house and gained a child. Synchronicity, symmetry: it was all there if only one looked hard enough. Helen sighed, thinking as she so often did, of Kay, from whom she had heard not a word since her departure for France.

Serena, immersed in mental battles of her own and misinterpreting her sister-in-law's sigh, decided it was time to make an attempt at clearing the air. 'About your baby, Helen . . . Genevieve . . . I want you to know that I am *so* happy for you and Peter, and more touched than I can possibly say to be chosen as her godmother. It was just the kindest thing to ask me. The last baby in a family is so special too, different somehow – spoilt rotten for one thing.' She beamed, her eyes shining with tears. 'As godmother, will you let me spoil her?'

'Of course,' whispered Helen, 'of course. I realise,' she added, her voice faltering, 'how hard it must be for you . . . That us expecting a girl must make you think of Tina.'

Serena, grinding pepper and salt over a pile of hamburgers, looked up, her eyes still sparkling. 'Oh, but, Helen, you mustn't mind that. Everything makes me think of Tina. Everything, all the time. That's how it is. You just learn to live with it and, with time, the living gets easier.'

'Oh, Serena . . .' Helen felt so much compassion she thought she might burst. Instead, throwing caution and Peter's warnings to the the wind, she blurted, 'I think it's lovely that Peter wants you and Charlie to live here, just lovely. I wouldn't want it any other way.'

'Really?' Serena put down the salt-cellar and wiped her hands on her dress. 'Oh, Helen, what a wonderful thing to say. Thank you so much. I've been bursting to talk about it but Charlie said not to until Peter had spoken to John and Pamela.'

Helen burst out laughing. 'Me, too. Peter told me not to breathe a word.'

They giggled, all the ghostly tension gone. 'Hey, I tell you what, how about a drink?' Serena, smiling wickedly, pointed at one of Peter's precious bottles of Brunello di Montalchino, already un-corked for dinner. 'Oh, heavens, you probably don't feel like it, do you?'

'I was off alcohol for a bit, but not any more. In fact, right now it feels *very* high on my list of needs.'

'Will Peter mind, do you think?'

'Possibly.' They both laughed. Then Helen took two glasses off one of the trays Serena had laid ready for transporting down to the field and held them out to her. 'Let's go for it. Mind you,' she glanced upwards with a frown, 'I don't suppose we're the only ones gasping for a drink. Haven't they been *ages*?'

'Ages,' agreed Serena solemnly, pouring out the wine. 'Here's to

Genevieve.' She raised her glass. 'Your darling little girl and my godchild.'

'And here's to Ashley House,' said Helen. 'To you and Charlie and Maisie and Clem and Ed being happy here.'

They chinked glasses, then hugged each other, spilling a little wine in the process.

The puppy wandering in after a rolling session with Chloë and Roland in the TV room, lapped at one of the little red puddles before sniffing in disappointment and retreating to the sofa where, rather to his surprise, no hand nudged him back on to the floor.

Sid had set the pumpkin lanterns round the barbecue and the trestle table of food, although with the roaring glow of the bonfire there was hardly any need for more light. A brisk wind tore at the grand flames of the fire, making them spark and billow like sails in a storm. Protected by their pumpkin cases, the little candles danced madly, lending an eerie orange flicker to their hollowed eyes and cadaverous mouths. Padded in coats and hats against the November cold, the children munched their hamburgers and hotdogs, mesmerised by the colours of the blaze and its fierce blasts of heat. Behind them the adults, bundled even more heavily against the night chill, sipped their wine, the men manning the barbecue while the women spooned out salad and passed bread and potatoes, breaking off to upbraid any child who stepped too close to the fire.

'The sparklers – we've forgotten the sparklers!' cried Pamela. 'Children, would one of you run in and fetch them? I got giant ones this year – they're in a box on the hall table.'

'I'll go,' said Clem at once, pushing the tail-end of her burger into her mouth. 'I'll go, Granny.' She set off at a run across the field.

Maisie watched till she got to the garden gate, then took off after her. Arriving at the front door a few minutes later, she was greeted by Little Boots, wagging his tail so hard that his entire sausage of a body swung with it, but there was no sign of Clem. The packet of sparklers, Maisie saw at once, was exactly where her grandmother had said it would be, on the hall table next to the telephone. 'Clem?' Maisie stood still, straining her ears for any sound. 'Clem?' she called, more urgently, walking along the hall and peering into the rooms.

She was stopped in her tracks by the sound of a flushing toilet and her sister emerging from the downstairs lavatory next to the kitchen. 'Clem?'

Clem read the look on her sister's face and said quickly – crossly, 'I wanted to pee, okay?'

'Sorry . . . sorry, Clem. Just for a moment I thought . . .'

'I know what you thought. It's okay, I just had a fucking pee,' mumbled her sister, seeing no need to mention that other possibilities had crossed her mind, as they always did. The desire for physical emptiness was still there, beckoning, tempting, like a dark figure with a crooked finger at the back of her mind. She resisted it, that was all. And sometimes, these days, between meals, like when she'd been having a laugh with Theo that afternoon, or later, when they were all scrambling round the attic looking for Uncle Eric's army gear, she even forgot it was there.

'Sorry, Clem,' repeated Maisie miserably, 'it's only because . . .'

'You care, I know. Everybody cares.' Thinking of Jonny, who also cared but in a completely different and totally exhilarating way, Clem grinned.

'What?' exclaimed Maisie, smiling herself at her sister's altered expression. 'What?'

'You might as well know, I suppose . . . Jonny Cottrall. I'm going out with him. It started at his party and, well . . . he's just great . . . great at kissing anyway.' Clem peered out impishly from under the thicket of her fringe.

'Clem – bloody hell!' Maisie shrieked, so loudly that Samson, venturing out from the drawing room, his green eyes alert for any sign of his new enemy, ran back in the direction he had come from. Little Boots, spotting him, took off in pursuit.

'Don't tell Mum and Dad, okay? Promise you won't tell.'

'I promise,' Maisie agreed solemnly, promising also, deep in her heart, never to let her sister know that she, too, had once enjoyed Jonny Cottrall's kisses. Jonny, she was sure, wouldn't have mentioned it. And quite right too. Hurtful disclosures never did anyone any good. 'Amazing about Lucien Cartwright, isn't it?' she exclaimed instead, wanting in part to change the subject but also to have a proper talk about Ed's revelation of this stunning coincidence. The twins had been with their cousins all afternoon and hadn't had a moment to discuss the matter properly.

'Isn't it?' agreed Clem excitedly, picking up the box of sparklers and leading the way back outside. 'Do you think he knew who we were when we phoned?'

'I suppose he might have guessed,' conceded Maisie, with a frown, having puzzled over exactly the same question herself. 'I asked Mum about it and she says she knew pretty much straight away who our journalist was but thought it best not to say anything. She also said,' Maisie added gleefully, 'that in her view Lucien was the love of Aunt Elizabeth's life and now that he's called she'd put money on them getting back together.'

'In which case we'll be able to ask him all about it ourselves one day, won't we?''

'Not bloody likely.' Maisie seized her sister's arm. They had reached the gate to the field. Ahead of them the blaze of the bonfire was once again in full view, the silhouettes of the family moving like shadow puppets across its spitting yellow face. 'It's bad enough Mum knowing about that horrible night. I don't ever want to talk about it with anyone else ever again.'

'I was only joking,' Clem reassured her, a little surprised at the note of desperation in her sister's voice. It made her wonder if anybody ever really got over anything; whether life didn't just gather bad things in its wake, and all one had to do was learn to put up with them, as she, for ever it seemed, would have to put up with the desire not to eat. 'Now, come on, Granddad will be starting the fireworks.' She took Maisie's hand and they ran back down the field, stumbling among the molehills and grass tussocks.

When they were a few yards short of the party Theo came to greet them. 'You took your time.' He grabbed the sparklers from Clem's hand and ran back to the fire.

Maisie looked at her sister in astonishment. 'What's up with him?'

Clem shrugged, equally unsure why she was suddenly out of favour with their cousin, who had left the attic before the rest of them and been decidedly frosty ever since. 'You know Theo, moody as hell.'

'And, by the way, do you have a clue what the grown-ups were all huddling about this afternoon? Talk about moody, they all trooped in like they were going to a funeral and next thing they're all smiles and hugs. Ed said something weird was going on and he was right. I asked Mum about that, too, and she just said it was business about the future and not to worry. She looked bloody happy, though, and so did Dad, so I guess it must be good. Some *future* good . . . What do you think?'

Clem, unable to maintain interest in any future beyond seeing Jonny on Monday morning, gave a dismissive groan. At which point Chloë and Roland trotted up, gleefully sky-writing shapes with their lit sparklers, and shrieking for the twins to watch.

'Firework time,' announced their grandfather, as they rejoined the group. 'Now, all of you stay here. Girls,' he said, addressing the twins, 'were Samson and the puppy safely inside?'

Clem and Maisie looked at each other and nodded.

'Here we go, then. I don't think any of you will be disappointed,' John added, with a chuckle, and set off, spill in hand, to light the fuses Sid had helped him plant across the field.

Depends what you mean by being disappointed, mused Theo, watching his grandfather's receding figure with a disgust that astonished even as it consumed him. After leaving the others in the attic he had spent several minutes crouched outside his grandparents' bedroom door, his uncle's army boots and helmet clutched in one hand. He hadn't heard it all, but he had heard enough. His uncle and aunt were to have Ashley House, he had heard that all right – and his aunt Cassie crying, everyone consoling her, and his own father, saying loudly that the children weren't to be told. Not yet. Not until they were older. The first rocket bombed into the sky, then exploded in shards of silver that sprayed downwards, disappearing before they touched the ground. Over my dead body, thought Theo, noticing Ed approach and moving away. Ashley

House should go to his father, and then to him. That was how it was *supposed* to be. The thought of one of his twin cousins, or Ed – daft Ed with his football and silly jokes – getting the place one day made him feel sick.

Behind Theo the grown-ups had clustered into a group to watch the display. Peter had a fierce grip on Helen's right hand, while the other rested lightly on his mother's shoulder. Next to him Charlie and Serena had their arms round each other's waists, mute still with a sense of good fortune that they had thought never to know again. I don't need to move Tina here, thought Serena suddenly. She's here anyway, in our hearts.

Beside her Elizabeth, chin tipped to the sky, watched the bursts of colour in a daze, her mind fixed upon the new conundrum of Lucien and what to do about him.

Cassie stood a few feet from her, a little apart from the group and feeling somewhat apart herself. They had comforted her, saying that no one was going to die just yet, that with the insurance market one never knew, that things might still come right, that it was important for her to be happy with the arrangements, that there was still plenty of time, and who knew what the future would bring? Who knew indeed? reflected Cassie now. Of course Ashley House mattered more than anything, of course it did. And if Charlie and Serena ended up living there, she knew they would make her feel welcome whenever she chose to come and stay. It was just the thought of being alone, she decided, shivering in spite of her thick coat. With no partner, the prospect of money simply mattered a little more, that was all. But she would get used to it. One got used to anything with time. The family came first, it always had. The way they had rallied round the various crises of the year proved that. Suddenly she remembered the mysterious 'C' on the dedication of Stephen Smith's book, and frowned. She would ask him, she decided – gatecrash the launch party if necessary and ask him outright. Though small, the diversion of this thought lifted Cassie's spirits immeasurably. It would be interesting to find out. Interesting, too, if she was honest, to see Stephen again. 'Lovely,' she exclaimed, as three catherine wheels, pinned along a line of fence posts, fizzed into action, ejecting smithereens of blue and gold.

'You look cold,' scolded Elizabeth, tugging on her sleeve. 'Come here.'

'Careful with Lucien, Lizzy,' she whispered, side-stepping obediently to her sister's side. 'Call him, but be careful.'

Her sister gave her an arch look. 'Thank you, Cassie. I'll bear that in mind.'

Pamela, feeling Peter's hand on her shoulder, seeing the grand-children's transfixed, upturned faces, and her daughters huddling together while Charlie and Serena clung to each other like young lovers, wished that the moment would never end. The bonfire was subsiding now, the bag of baby clothes she had tucked into its centre nothing but burning ash. The relief was like a taste in her mouth, sweet and satisfying. If only I had known, she thought; if only I had known that good can come of bad, that it's how we react to things that matters, not the things themselves.

John, working his way back up through the field, crouched stiffly to light the last rocket, then paused. Ahead of him the bonfire still twisted and curled, a triangle of violent oranges and yellows. After the first lighting he had stood back between his sons to watch the drama of the flames licking up the steep sides and engulfing the guy. 'He's falling,' Roland had shouted, tragedy in his shrill voice, as his straw creation keeled to one side, then sank, suddenly and rapidly, into the waves of fire.

'He's gone,' someone shouted.

'Gone,' John echoed, straining through the screen of smoke and his own tear-filled eyes, to discern any last glimpses of his old pinstriped trousers. It could have been me, he thought, it could have been me. Eric might have been an unsung hero, but so were Pamela and Peter, and the whole damn lot of them. The accep-tance, the sheer generosity of his family's response to his dreadful news, still took his breath away. After years of priding himself on his own strengths, openly relishing the roles of protector, guide and patriarch, the one holding the family together, it had been humbling beyond words to realise, as he had during his shameful episode in the garage, and that afternoon, that his strength existed only by virtue of his family, that without their love he was nothing.

'It's coming,' he shouted now, touching the spill to the fuse and stepping back. 'It's coming,' he repeated, although with the wind and the crackle of the bonfire there was no way any of them would hear. He needed to shout for himself, to release the emotions welling inside. He had lost a fortune, a grandchild, a brother, a beloved dog; the ache in his back was infernal. He was eighty and would die, but not just yet, not now. Now he was alive and loved and full of hope. At the sight of the flame racing down the fuse of the last and biggest rocket, his heart thudded just as it had when he was a schoolboy, with Eric at his side and their father barking at them to stand back. 'Eric,' he shouted, bidding a last, proper farewell to his brother as, with a hiss of air, the rocket took off, scudding upwards with a great whine. It travelled higher than any of the others, seemed to disappear into silence, then erupted in a deafening volley of gunshots.

Inside the house, Samson and Little Boots crept under the piano, united in mute terror.

Outside, vast flowers of colour mingled for a moment with the stars themselves, then cascaded downwards, over the fields, the barn and Ashley House, illuminating its great grey presence, its white-framed windows alert as watching eyes. John, admiring the spectacle, felt his heart constrict. Would the house prove a unifying force or a separating one, he wondered suddenly. A burden or a blessing?

Then the cries of congratulation from his family reached him. He forgot his fears and moved towards them, the stump of the spill still smoking in his hand.'